D1626731

# THE
# DEATH
## OF
# CHAOS

# L. E. Modesitt, Jr.

# THE
# DEATH
# OF
# CHAOS

ORBIT

An *Orbit* Book

First published in the United States by Tor Books in 1995
First published in Great Britain by Orbit in 1996

Copyright © 1995 by L.E. Modesitt, Jr.

The moral right of the author has been asserted.

Colour endpaper map by Laszlo Kubinyi
Interior maps by Ellisa Mitchell

A CIP catalogue record for this book
is available from the British Library.

ISBN 1 85723 369 7

Typeset in Century Old Style by
Palimpsest Book Production Limited,
Polmont, Stirlingshire
Printed and bound in Great Britain by
Hartnolls Ltd., Bodmin, Cornwall

Orbit
A Division of
Little, Brown and Company (UK)
Brettenham House
Lancaster Place
London WC2E 7EN

*For my parents, again,*
*with more understanding,*
*and for Carol Ann*

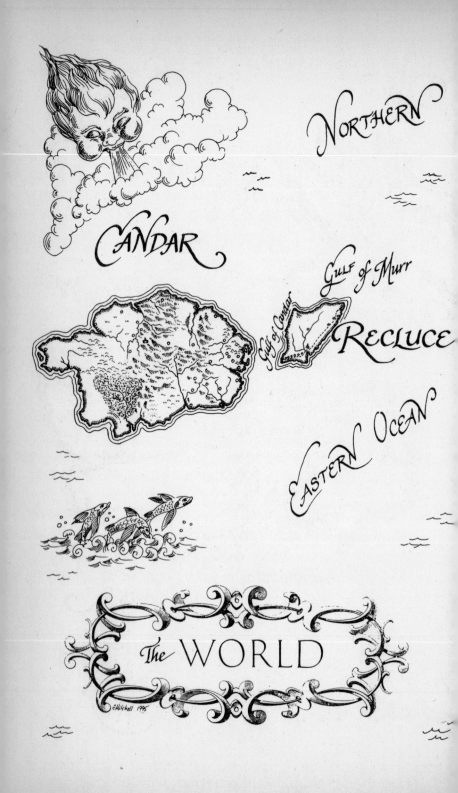

NORTHERN

CANDAR

Gulf of Murr

Gulf of Candar

RECLUCE

EASTERN OCEAN

The WORLD

E.Mitchell 1995

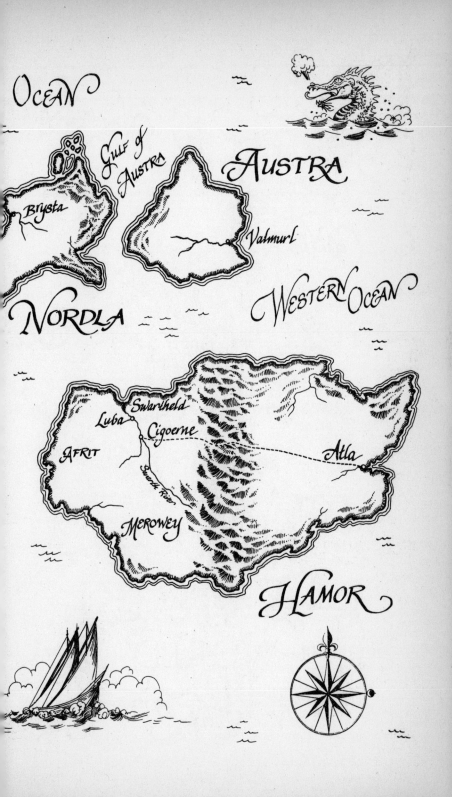

# I.

---

# FINDING
# CHAOS

# I

I'd just applied the thinnest coat possible of a satin finish on the black oak wardrobe for the autarch of Kyphros – Kasee – when I felt the presence of horses, and their riders. Krystal was not with them, and I didn't like the idea of the Finest tramping up to the shop without my consort, but as subcommander of the autarch's forces, Krystal's schedule wasn't exactly predictable.

I finished the section of the wardrobe I had been working on before I met the troopers outside the stable. The stable hadn't been my idea, but Krystal's, and she had paid for most of it, especially the part that doubled as a bunkhouse for her personal guard. Funny things like that happen to the consort of the second-highest-ranking military officer in Kyphros, not that either of us had planned where we would end up when we – and Tamra and a few others – had been thrown out of Recluce years earlier because we hadn't been 'ordered' enough for the black Brotherhood – or my father.

'Greetings, Order-master!' In the green leathers of the autarch's Finest, Yelena sat easily on the brown gelding.

I'd known Yelena from my first days in Kyphrien, when I'd been fortunate to best the white chaos-master Antonin and rescue Tamra. Yelena had been my escort part of the way on that troubled trip, but she still called me order-master and threatened to lash any member of the Finest who even hinted at any familiarity. If she weren't so serious about it, it might have been funny, but I understood her reasoning, and couldn't say it was wrong. People had this idea that I was a great wizard because I'd managed to get rid of three white wizards. One of them had actually plagued not only Kyphros, but all of the continent of Candar.

'Greetings, Leader Yelena.'

She wrinkled her nose. 'What's that smell?'

'It's a satin-finish varnish – except it's got a touch of some other things that make it more like —'

'Enough, enough . . .' The broad-shouldered squad leader grinned as she dismounted. 'Until I met you, I always thought woodworkers were small little men who hid in their shops, toiling endless days in the dark until they produced something like magic.'

'You have the endless-days part correct, and I'm not that big.'

She shook her head. So I am a bit taller than the average Kyphran, who tend to be shorter and darker than people from the north or from the island continent of Recluce. That didn't make me that big a person.

'Where is Krystal?'

'The subcommander is meeting with the autarch, and will be here shortly.'

'So, why are you here?' I looked down at the varnish-stained cloth in my hand. 'I've got to get back to the wardrobe, or I'll have the demon's own time getting the finish to match.'

'Commander Ferrel wanted to make sure that no one disturbed the subcommander.'

That didn't make much sense. If Ferrel didn't want Krystal disturbed, why weren't the guards with her?

'How many for dinner, Master Lerris?' Rissa was still barefoot and wore trousers that looked more like shorts. I'd given up on correcting her, but I had noticed that she only used the term 'master' when others were present. Rissa had grown up not far from the burned-out buildings I'd received from the autarch and rebuilt, but Yelena had rescued Rissa from bandits who killed Rissa's consort and daughter not long after we moved in. Rissa hadn't spoken at first, but my uncle Justen – the only true gray wizard in Candar, or perhaps anywhere – had been convinced that being around Krystal and me would heal her. Besides, at the time, Justen had had his hands full in rebuilding Tamra's abilities and confidence after her near disastrous encounter with Antonin when the white wizard Sephya had taken over Tamra's body.

So . . . I'd done what I could for Rissa, and so had Krystal, and it had gotten to be nice to have someone else do the cooking and cleaning. That way, I could concentrate on setting up my workshop and getting customers. Krystal was a good cook, not that she ever had any time for it, being the chief military trainer and administrator of Kyphros. I still was a bit amazed, when I thought about it, that Kyphros, like ancient Westwind, was run basically by women. Unlike Westwind, they didn't run out men or tromp all over them. It just happened that in Kyphros, most of the people with the ability to govern seemed to be women. That was fine with me, since I never had any inclinations along those lines.

'He's off somewhere, again,' snorted Rissa. 'Master Lerris . . . dinner? How many?'

'How would I know?' I turned to Yelena. 'How many do you have?'

Yelena frowned gently. 'We ate before we left, and they have their rations.'

'Would you join us? And why aren't you with the subcommander?' Was Krystal being sent off somewhere else again?

'Not tonight. The subcommander told me to tell you that the wizard Justen and his apprentice would be arriving with her.'

I took a deep breath. As usual, things were getting complicated. Krystal had been out for the past eight-day, doing something with the local levies around Ruzor, and I'd hoped to have some time with her. Now the whole world was arriving. Yelena, who usually joined us, even if her troops didn't, wasn't going to, and that meant something worse was about to happen.

Yelena smiled gently, understanding my thoughts.

'Five, so far. And make sure we have some ale for Justen.'

Rissa shook her head and padded back into the house.

'I've got —'

'—to get back to your finish. I am sure I wouldn't wish to spoil a piece meant for the autarch.'

'How did you know?'

She shrugged, turned, and motioned to Weldein and Freyda and two others I didn't know. Weldein grinned at me, and I gave him an exaggerated shrug.

As I turned back to the shop, I wondered, not for the first time, how anything could be kept a secret in Kyphros. Inside, I took a fresh cloth and dipped it into the finish and began to rub it into the wood. 'Rub' is really the wrong term, because there's almost no pressure involved. The finish I had cooked up was thin and took a long time to dry. I needed to apply several coats, but the eventual result was a hard, but almost invisible coat – without magic – and that was what I'd wanted with the wardrobe, because the doors generally took a beating.

The inlaid design glistened and seemed to stand out from the dark wood. Inlay work was, for me, the hardest part. Not the grooving or the channels in the base wood – that was a matter of patience and care – but the creation of the inlay pieces themselves. The grain has to add to the design and not just appear as though it had been stuck there any old way. I also tended to make my inlays a shade deeper, but that meant ensuring that the base wood was fractionally thicker to avoid sacrificing strength.

The design was a variation on the autarch's flag – an olive branch crossed with a blade – golden oak set in the base, black oak on the panel above the doors. That was it – nothing else to mar the smooth finish of the piece. That sort of work is tricky, because any flaw is instantly noticed. Errors in more elaborate inlays often aren't seen.

I was probably extra sensitive to flaws in woodworking, and in wood, because one little flaw when I was working as an apprentice for my uncle Sardit had gotten me exiled from Recluce, carted across the Eastern Ocean and dumped in Candar to discover the 'truth' of order, with only a staff, except it was a special staff, bound in order and black iron. Because I was a potential order-master, one of the so-called blackstaffers, no one had told me much, and I had gotten into more and more trouble. I'd been chased out of Freetown, chased out of Hrisbarg, and generally on the run across Eastern Candar until I ran into Justen. Then, I'd thought he was just a gray wizard, and I was glad to be his apprentice. It took me more than a year to find out he was my uncle – and well over two centuries old. So I'd ridden with Justen, almost gotten possessed by one of the white wizards bound centuries earlier in the ruins of Frven. Justen saved me there, and then had taught me how to heal sheep, and a few other things. Nothing went quite as planned. I'd rescued and healed a street slut in Jellico. That hadn't been such a good idea, because all unlicensed healing there was forbidden, and I'd had to leave Justen and, once again, ride for my life, heading west across Candar.

Eventually, I'd gotten through the Easthorns – through storms and snows in those towering mountains – and made my way to Fenard – the capital of Gallos. I actually found a place with a woodworker, old Destrin, and got back to working wood. There I lasted about a year before I did something else stupid – I infused some chairs we made with extra order. The extra order reacted with the chaos in the Prefect's officers, and some were burned. That meant I had to leave Gallos, but not until I'd found a suitable match for Destrin's daughter Deirdre.

At that point, Gallos and Kyphros were fighting an ugly war, fomented and fueled by Antonin, one of the nastier white wizards I'd ever had the displeasure of running across. I'd found out that Krystal had joined the forces of the autarch of Kyphros. So I went to Kyphrien, the capital of Kyphros, to see if I could help, although my skills were certainly weak compared to those of Antonin.

After rescuing some of Commander Ferrel's Finest and disposing of one white wizard, I reached Kyphrien. I found Krystal had worked her way up to the number two position in the Finest, and that I'd missed being with her – except I'd been too stupid to see that. Of course, it wasn't that simple. Nothing is. So, I'd had to go seek out Antonin. He and his white colleague Sephya had enslaved Tamra, who had been exiled from Recluce with me. Sephya had started to take over Tamra's body – that's how the body-switchers prolong their lives – and both of them tried to tempt me. Because after two years of refusing good adult advice, I'd finally gotten around to reading *The Basis of Order*, I had this half-finished idea that I could stand up to Antonin. I did, sort of. In the end, he died because, after I'd figured out that I had to break my own staff because part of my soul and abilities were locked in it, I'd managed to separate him from the forces of chaos. His castle came apart, and Tamra and I had barely made it out. Tamra lost half her mind, and I'd rebuilt it – with Justen screaming from half a country away that I couldn't, but I did anyway. Then I got a reward for the success of surviving my stupidity and was smart enough to tell Krystal I loved her. After that, I built the house and shop and tried to get back to woodwork and avoid unnecessary wizardry.

And all of it happened just because I hadn't applied the glue clamps right to a tabletop in my uncle's workshop in Recluce.

I shook my head because Justen and Tamra were arriving, and reminiscing wasn't going to finish the wardrobe. I actually got the finish on before three more horses clinked into the yard. I shrugged, set the cloths aside, and hurried out into the cool fall breeze. When winter nears in Candar, the air carries an acrid tang, not quite musty, not quite bitter – something to do with the graying of the leaves.

My dark-haired and black-eyed subcommander got a hug first, then a kiss, almost as soon as her boots hit the ground. Tamra and Justen were still mounted – Justen, as always, on Rosefoot.

'You did miss me.' Krystal grinned.

'I always miss you.' I hugged her again.

'Don't seem so pleased, Krystal,' said Tamra.

'I am pleased. Someday you'll understand.' Krystal gave me another hug, and a long, lingering kiss, and I didn't even mind where the hilt of her sword jabbed into my guts.

'Disgusting . . .' Tamra swung off her horse. She wore her usual dark grays, with a scarf to set off her red hair. The scarf was blue this time, matching her ice-blue eyes.

Justen slipped off Rosefoot with an ease borne of long practice and looked at his apprentice. 'We can stable all three horses, Tamra.'

'Give him hell, Krystal,' said Tamra as she took the reins of Krystal's chestnut.

In her own way, Krystal was, and we were both enjoying it, but we eventually went inside, where Krystal slipped off for a moment to wash up while I washed in the kitchen and then joined the others at the table.

Rissa had set a loaf of fresh bread on the table along with olive butter and some redberry preserves she'd gotten from somewhere. I missed the pearapples of the north, but Kyphros was really too warm to grow them.

Tamra reached for the bread. The redhead was always hungry, but stayed as slim as a rail. 'One good thing about visiting you, Lerris – good food. You're getting fat and sloppy, though.'

'Hardly. My trousers are looser.'

'Rissa must be letting them out.'

'I do believe I saw you with a needle the other day,' offered Justen, looking at Tamra.

Tamra flushed. Rissa giggled. Justen raised an eyebrow at Tamra, his still-unruly apprentice. I had learned a lot as Justen's apprentice, and could have learned more if I hadn't been forced to leave him because I hadn't paid any attention and healed that street slut in plain sight in Jellico. That had gotten all the Viscount's troops after me. I'd been lucky to survive and would have done better if I'd listened to Justen more, but Justen was like all the wizards who dealt with order. Besides telling me to read *The Basis of Order*, he didn't volunteer much. Tamra didn't seem to be doing much better than I had, and, as with me, Justen still wasn't saying much.

By all rights Justen should have been a doddering old fool, since he had been born over two centuries earlier, according to what I'd eventually figured out. He never admitted anything, except that he did happen to be my uncle and that he too had left Recluce. That also explained why my father – who was even older than Justen – had been extraordinarily evasive about our family history, and just about everything else. That lack of knowledge had gotten me, and a lot of other young exiles from Recluce – poor dangergelders – into a bunch of trouble. A lot of them died, and I almost did on more than one occasion. Ignorance is deadly, especially when it's not apparent.

Justen just looked middle-aged, with brown hair that occasionally streaked with silver-gray if he had been working hard in dealing with order – or various disasters – like when he finally bottled up the demons of Frven. Then again, in retrospect, I didn't feel that bad about that, even if I had nearly killed him, since he was the one who created that mess – he and my father. Of course, neither one had bothered to tell me. That's what dealing with order-masters is like. They never reveal much because they believe it doesn't mean anything if it isn't hard-earned. That's also why most ordermasters or chaos-masters don't live that long.

While we ate the bread and waited for Krystal – my consort and subcommander – while she washed up, Tamra, Justen, Rissa, and I sat around the table. Like a lot in the house, it was a reject, something that hadn't quite worked out the way I'd intended. The table was octagonal, with an inlaid pattern. The reason it was a reject wasn't that it was bad, but that it had been commissioned by Reger. He had been a produce factor in Ruzor, until he fell out of an olive tree and broke his neck. How he could have broken his neck with a fall of only about six cubits was beyond me, but he'd had too much wine and was arguing with his brother. Anyway, it's hard to collect a commission when the person who commissioned it is dead. So we had a table that was far too elegant for the main room of a woodworker's home.

Krystal had told me it was fate, and that I should have at least one good piece of my own. 'Would you trust an armorer who had only misshapen blades on his walls? A mason who lived in a house with crooked walls?' she had asked, and there was certainly some logic in that.

I tried the bread, but, conscious of Tamra's gibe, not the olive butter or the preserves.

'Have you reread *The Basis of Order* recently?' asked Justen, who ignored food unless he really needed it.

'No,' I admitted.

'It might be worth it.' He turned to Rissa, sitting on a stool at the side of the table closest to the cooler. 'Is there any more of that dark ale?'

Rissa slid off the stool with the grace that all the Kyphrans seemed to have, for which I envied them, and set the pitcher before Justen. 'Hurlot says that his is the best. So does Ryntar. This comes from Gesil's casks, and he spends more time brewing and less in the market.'

'Good.'

'I still don't see how you can drink that,' mused Tamra.

'Neither does my brother. Or he didn't.' Justen looked at me. 'About *The Basis of Order* . . .'

'I've been busy. There's the wardrobe for the autarch, and I had to do the dining set for —'

'Lerris . . . you don't have any competition. You could spend a little time studying.'

'What for? I'm a woodworker.'

'You're also considered one of the most powerful wizards in Kyphros, even when you're just pretending that you're only a poor woodworker.'

Krystal slipped into the seat next to me, wearing just the green leather trousers and a plain shirt. She'd left off the short jacket with all the gold braid. 'I'm sorry. Kasee kept me. We have a problem – another one.' Krystal looked toward Rissa. 'Some of Justen's ale would be good.'

'Justen's ale, yet?' asked Tamra under her breath.

I ignored her.

Rissa brought Krystal a mug and poured ale from the pitcher.

Krystal took a long, and very deep, swallow before continuing. 'The new Duke of Hydlen has occupied the brimstone springs in the Lower Easthorns.'

'Brimstone?' asked Rissa.

'That's for powder. You mix it with nitre and charcoal,' Tamra explained.

'Explosive powder isn't that useful,' I ventured. 'Any chaos wizard—'

'That may be the problem.' Krystal sighed and turned to Justen. 'You've heard of Gerlis, haven't you?'

Justen pulled at his chin. 'Yes. He's a body-changer. He's also probably the most powerful white wizard in Candar now.'

'He's the court wizard to the new Duke – that bastard named Berfir,' explained Krystal.

Dukes changed often in Candar, almost as often as the powerful white wizards changed bodies.

'Where did he come from?' asked Tamra.

'Berfir's the head of the Yeannota clan. His family has owned the range-lands between Telsen and Asula for ages. We don't know much more, except he raised an army, made some agreements with the merchants on taxes, and ... poof ... one day Duke Sterna died and named Berfir his heir. Very neat.'

'You think Gerlis had something to do with it?' Tamra poured herself more redberry.

'Who can tell? If he didn't, he's certainly taken advantage of the situation.'

Rissa got up and stirred whatever was in the big stewpot and the noodles that had been simmering in the other pot. The odor of onions and lamb drifted across the table, and I licked my lips.

'What does this all have to do with the brimstone springs?'

Krystal shrugged. 'We don't know yet, but Kasee thinks that it bears watching, and that means sending a detachment to do the watching.'

'When do you leave?' I asked.

'I don't. Ferrel says that it's her turn to take a trip. She's been stuck in Kyphrien running the Finest for years, and it's up to me to see how it feels. She's tired of everyone second-guessing her. Besides' – Krystal grinned and looked at me – 'she says I've been neglecting you, and neglecting order-masters isn't a good idea.'

I liked Ferrel even more, assuming she'd said that, or Krystal for thinking of me. Then, I'd always liked Ferrel – ever since she'd returned my knife at that first dinner I'd had with the autarch. I'd left my knife with the captives I'd freed in order to charge the first white wizard with a staff. That had been a very dumb thing to do, even if it had worked. Anyway, when I'd first come to Kyphros, Ferrel had confirmed my rescue efforts by returning the knife. 'What does Kasee – I mean the autarch – think?'

'Her Mightiness the autarch agrees that the experience of standing in for Ferrel will do me good.'

'Experience rarely does anyone good,' grumped Justen. 'It just does them in.'

'How about some real food?' Tamra looked toward the stove.

'It's almost ready,' said Rissa.

I got up and began to pass out plates, brown crockery things I'd purchased in Kyphrien with the last of the stipend the autarch had bestowed on me for ridding Kyphros – and Candar – of some unwanted white wizards. I had spent most of those coins on building the house and workshop, and in getting tools. Good tools are expensive, and I still didn't have everything I really needed.

Justen was the only nonwhite wizard I knew who really made a decent living from wizardry, and he traveled across most of Candar to do it.

Because I was technically master of the house, although Krystal was certainly far more important, Rissa set everything in front of me, and I got to ladle out the stew and noodles while Rissa set out two big long loaves of steaming dark bread. I made sure Tamra got enough stew and noodles to choke her.

For a time, no one spoke, and the only sound was of eating. Tamra slurped even more than some of the junior guards in the Finest, hardly lady-like, but Tamra had never wanted to be a lady anyway.

I caught Justen's eye, and my uncle shook his head, but I wondered if he were shaking it more at my judgment than Tamra's manners. Krystal ate with the quiet efficiency I had noted the first time I met her, and I reached under the table and squeezed her knee.

'Tell Ferrel to be careful,' cautioned Justen.

'Ferrel is very careful. You don't survive to be guard commander if you're not.'

I squeezed Krystal's leg just above the knee again, glad that she would not be doing the scout mission. White wizards were always dangerous.

'You need to eat more, Master Wizard,' said Rissa, gesturing at Justen. 'The birds, they eat more than you. So do the ants.'

'It's not good to overdo anything,' said Justen with a laugh.

'Then don't overdo the starvation,' answered Rissa.

Even Tamra grinned, and Justen did eat a few more bites of stew and noodles before he spoke again. 'How did the autarch find out about the springs?'

'Travelers. The spring is on the main east road to Sunta. The Hydlenese troops closed the road, and there were some very unhappy travelers.'

Travelers made sense. The water route, going down the Phroan River from Kyphrien through central Kyphros to Felsa, then down the metaled river road to Ruzor, the only real port in Kyphros, and taking a coaster to one of the ports in Hydlen, was just as fast and a lot easier, if longer. It was also much costlier; so some travelers preferred the mountain way, but few traders.

'You think the Duke meant for Kasee to find out?' asked Krystal.

'How long had the Hydlenese held the spring before you found out?' asked my uncle the gray wizard.

Krystal nodded. 'I'll mention that to Ferrel.'

'Is there any more of that dark ale?' asked Justen.

Rissa handed him the pitcher, and he half filled his mug.

'Benefits of being a gray wizard.'

'White wizards don't get those benefits,' I countered.

'When you get a little older, you'll get gray, too, Lerris. I guarantee that.'

I hoped I didn't get either gray or into terrible puns.

After more talk about everything from the unseasonable rain – rain more than once every two eight-days was unseasonable in Kyphros, even in winter – to the autarch's decision to try to open the old wizards' road through northern Kyphros, Krystal yawned. 'I'm sorry, but . . . it has been a long day.'

'Shoo . . .' said Rissa.

We shooed, leaving Tamra and Justen sitting at the table, talking about the Balance between order and chaos. I understood the Balance well enough, having played into Antonin's hand myself by creating too much order in Fenard. But once you understand that order and chaos *must* balance, one way or another, there's not that much else to be said. You try to live by it, although I wasn't about to give up crafting the most orderly woodwork I could. I wasn't about to put extra order into my pieces, though. That was the sort of mistake I didn't want to repeat.

Krystal smiled softly at me when I shut the door.

'You . . .'

'I was tired . . . I was tired of people talking.'

Still marveling that I had not seen her warmth when first I had met her, I opened my arms.

Later, much later, when Krystal lay asleep beside me, her face as open and as innocent as a child's, I watched her for a long time, knowing, somehow, that the latest wizard business would drag us all into it.

Outside, I could hear the faint clinking of whoever was on guard. Sometimes, I still shook my head at it all – the very idea of a woodworker's shop and home being guarded by the autarch's troops, because his consort was so important.

I kissed Krystal on the cheek. She murmured sleepily and squeezed my hand. I finally rolled over, snuggling up beside her again.

# II

## Nylan, Recluce

The black stone exterior of the hillside building frames a series of windows overlooking either the harbor of Nylan, the Gulf of Candar, or the great Eastern Ocean. On only the north side are there no windows. The windows – both those that slide open and the larger central expanses of glass that do not – are framed in black oak fitted so closely that the lines of the mitred corners are invisible. Behind the south-facing second-story window with the optimal view of both the harbor and the breakwater is the main council chamber of the Brotherhood.

In the late afternoon, whitecaps crown the two-cubit-high waves off the southern tip of the isle continent of Recluce. The same cool fall wind that raises the whitecaps blows through the narrow western windows of the chamber and out the equally narrow eastern ones. The three councilors sit behind the antique curved table that faces the now-empty chairs reserved for those meeting with the Council.

'Maris, do you have any sense of what is coming?' The broad-shouldered mage in black looks at the bearded man.

The thin-faced woman lifts a goblet and sips the green juice. Her eyes gaze blankly out the wide window in the center of the southern wall, but she says nothing.

'You seem to think I'm blind because I'm a trader. We see things. We just see them differently,' offers Maris, the fingers of one hand brushing his square beard. 'That's one of the reasons why the Council has a trader, and not just —'

'Heldra represents the people, and you—' Talryn begins slowly.

'Spare me the fancy words, Talryn.' Maris sighs. 'Heldra is a mage who is also a marine leader. She represents arms, and the people with the coins to buy them. She also likes to play marine leader in her spare time. I also represent coins, the traders with coins, and I detest playing with blades. You represent the order-masters of the Brotherhood, who have few coins, but the black iron warships and the power of wizardry. Arms, coins, and power, that's what we represent, and you've got two votes in real terms because no one can make the Brotherhood do anything. But you need our coins, and I need your visions.' Maris pauses and sips from his goblet. 'I can see that there will be problems in Candar, but exactly where? I can also see that we're back to the problem of chaos focuses again. Chaos focuses disrupt things in Candar, and that disrupts trade – every time. But when? And in what market?'

'It doesn't seem to hamper the Hamorian traders,' observes Heldra.

'They deal in mass-produced, low-cost goods, and that's what people buy in troubled times. We deal in quality goods, and those are what people don't buy when there's trouble.'

'Maybe you traders should take the words from the Hamorians' scrolls.'

'Heldra, you can't be that stupid ...' Maris fails to keep the exasperation from his voice. 'The only true commodity we could produce and export is iron, and you and Talryn have —'

'Enough,' rumbles Talryn. 'You were speaking about the problem of chaos focuses.' His eyes flicker toward the water beyond the harbor where the Gulf and the Eastern Ocean run together. His fingers twist around the stem of his goblet. 'We don't have a problem with chaos focuses right now. The last one was Antonin, and young Lerris took care of him. Rather neatly, I might add.'

'Too neatly.' Heldra's sharp green eyes swing from Talryn to Maris and back to Talryn. She purses her lips. 'He cannot have been as ignorant as he seemed when he left here. No one could have been that ignorant, not with Gunnar as his father.'

'He was,' insists Talryn. 'You didn't teach him. I did.'

'You said we don't have a problem with chaos focuses now. That would indicate that we might before long.' Maris fingers his beard again.

'All that chaos that Lerris released has to go somewhere.' Talryn's fingers leave the stem of the goblet.

'Have you talked to the Institute?' pursues Heldra.

'Gunnar, you mean? He may be a weather mage, but he's not a real part of the Brotherhood,' points out Talryn. 'The Institute – Gunnar, anyway – hasn't exactly been an ally of the Council, even if he hasn't ever actively opposed the Council. If I asked, all he'd do is quote the Balance. Besides, his son is part of the problem – his son and his brother.'

'That's what I mean. Gunnar's the one who pushed his son into early dangergeld. Why?'

'Heldra . . .' Maris offers an exasperated sigh.

'He sent his son into dangergeld long before we detected his power. The boy didn't really even know why he was going, for darkness' sake.' Talryn clears his throat. 'And Gunnar told us that Lerris could be a danger to Recluce if he didn't undertake dangergeld early. That doesn't exactly sound like favoritism, even from the head of the Institute.'

'Yet, barely two years after Lerris completed dangergeld training, he took on and defeated a white master who was also a chaos focus? We didn't train him as an order-master. So who did?' Heldra sets down the goblet. 'The whole thing is still hard to believe.'

'You're both forgetting one thing,' suggests Maris. 'Who did young Lerris just happen to run into within an eight-day of arriving in Candar?'

'Justen.' Heldra nods. 'It was no accident.'

'Maybe not,' responds Maris,' but you haven't answered my question. Are we going to have problems with another chaos focus? How soon? It might be nice for us traders to know where we could run into trouble – before it happens.'

'Trade, always trade,' mutters Heldra.

'Trade pays the bills, and supports the trio, not to mention the Council and a lot of the Brotherhood's expenses.'

'Trade is important,' interjects Talryn, 'and we're still likely to have a problem with the next chaos focus. I personally think it's going to be Gerlis, but I can't tell you when. Not yet, anyway.' Talryn pours greenberry into his empty goblet and takes a sip. 'The amount of chaos seems to be growing in Hydlen, and we don't know any other whites there. There's something happening in Sligo, too.'

'Wonderful.' Maris coughs. 'We have young Lerris in Kyphros,

Gerlis in Hydlen, Justen going wherever he wants, and now you tell me that there's going to be more trouble in Sligo. But you can't tell me when.'

'The trouble in Sligo is your humble would-be hermit,' Talryn points out to Heldra.

'Is that the smith who wanted to be a scholar and teach the world?' asks Maris. 'Sammel?'

Talryn nods. 'There are some volumes missing from the hidden shelves. Old volumes, some attributed to Dorrin.'

'You were all so worried about Lerris.' Maris frowns. 'He seems to keep to himself. If this Sammel has all that old knowledge . . .'

'So Sammel has old knowledge? Who outside of Recluce – or Justen – has the ability to apply it? That's exactly why I worry about Justen.' Heldra shrugs. 'He was an engineer, and gray wizardry is the sort of bastardization that could destroy us all. Where chaos is concerned, nothing is certain. We didn't know Lerris would become an order focus, either. Who's to say he might not follow Justen?'

'We have time if that should occur.' Talryn sips his greenberry. 'Gerlis is a more imminent problem. Especially with Colaris pushing to reclaim the Ohyde Valley.'

'Ohyde hasn't been part of Freetown for hundreds of years.' Maris snorts.

'They haven't forgotten, and Colaris is using the issue to stir people up.'

'Just send one of the trio,' suggests Heldra.

'Just in case.' Maris nods. 'Have the *Llyse* pay a port call in Renklaar.'

'As you wish,' Talryn answers.

'What about Lerris? Or Gunnar?' asks Heldra.

'Right now, there's nothing to be done. Do you want to take on Gunnar?' Talryn looks at Heldra. 'Or those he's gathered at the Institute?'

'No, thank you. Let sleeping dragons lie.'

'You've been talking to Cassius again. We've never had dragons on our world. He admits they didn't exist on his, either.'

'Gunnar's still a sleeping dragon.'

'What about Justen?' asks Maris.

'Justen doesn't usually confront chaos focuses; he somehow works around them.' Talryn takes a deep breath. 'That might be why he's survived so long. Somehow, he can anticipate what will happen.'

'You seem to be hinting . . .'

'I think young Lerris is going to get sucked into dealing with one chaos focus after another. Justen is a gray wizard. We all know that.'

'Lerris can't keep surviving chaos focuses,' observes Maris. 'Each one will get stronger.'

'That's going to be a real problem,' adds Heldra. 'We'll be right back in the mess that existed in the time of Fairhaven, and we don't want that. Even Gunnar wouldn't like that.'

'No.'

'No.'

The three look to the whitecapped surface of the Eastern Ocean beyond the harbor.

# III

While Krystal was filling in for Ferrel, and while Ferrel was investigating the brimstone spring, I was working on the first chair of the set of eight for Hensil – the olive trader who owned groves from Kyphrien to Dasir. Like everyone lately, he wanted something 'original.' He'd liked a sketch of a square-backed armchair where the upper joined corners were more like arcs than right angles. The design took four dowellike shaft-spokes around a long diamond brace with his initial in the center. I couldn't turn the shaft-spokes all the way down because the middles had to be grooved. So I worked on one of them.

I was worried about the chair. The spokes still didn't feel right. I hadn't been sure of the proportions. That happens the first time on a new design, and I'd rough-cut them too big. My frugal side told me not to waste the wood, but that meant a lot of work. Planing cherry is hard work, even after turning it down as much as possible.

I'd gotten one almost rough-finished, and it was time to start on the rest of the set. The grooved spokes were the hardest. What I needed to do first was steam and bend the backs, since the longer and more gently I worked the wood, the stronger they'd be. While they were setting, I could go back to the time-consuming work of the spokes and the diamond backplate with the inlaid initial *H*.

As usual, nothing worked quite as I planned. I didn't have enough clamps to do more than two backs at a time, and the glue I'd made had gotten too thick.

While I was mumbling to myself about that, a single horse galloped into the yard. That was bad. Krystal never rode alone, not anymore, and no one galloped unless it was a trooper in a hurry. Although the last eight-day had been uneventful, that could change at any moment, especially when I had actually been seeing Krystal more than occasionally.

I ran out. 'What's wrong?'

'Nothing, Order-master, ser . . . nothing.' Weldein drew back in his saddle, brushing his long and lank blond hair back off his forehead. He did not wear either his cap or battle helm. 'Leader Yelena sent me to fetch you. The subcommander and the autarch want to see you immediately.'

'Just a moment.' I went back into the shop, cleaned and racked the saws I'd been using, and put away the clamps. I studied the chairs and the desk in the corner for a moment, then nodded before heading out to the washroom and the shower. I did take a few moments to shave, both for comfort and appearance. A little stubble wasn't bad, but more than that just made my face look dirty, and it itched if I sweated at all.

I dressed in my best, my good browns that were decidedly modest for an audience with the autarch, and I wondered how Deirdre and Bostric were making out. Memories, and the good browns, were all I really had of Deirdre, old Destrin's lovely daughter. It wouldn't have worked, but I did wish her and Bostric the best. Someday, he'd even be a decent woodworker. After changing, I went out to the stable, saddled Gairloch, and walked him out into the yard.

'You wizards and your ponies, and your bridles that are not bridles,' said Weldein, still waiting patiently.

'We can't spare the time to ride those monsters you use.' Besides, Gairloch answered easily to gentle pressure on the hackamore.

Weldein laughed, and we turned onto the highway back to Kyphrien.

'Where am I supposed to meet Krystal?'

'In her quarters. Then you'll go to see the autarch.'

The autarch didn't really have a palace, more like a walled residence that adjoined the guard complex housing the Finest, who were the mounted troops that formed the core of the autarch's forces. There was a much smaller crack infantry, but generally they only served as the autarch's personal guard when she actually led forces into battle. Most ground troops were drawn from the outliers, and they were locally recruited and housed in barracks all around Kyphros. That lack of a large central military force had almost been the autarch's undoing in the recent war with the Prefect of Gallos.

I guided Gairloch through the open gates behind Weldein and toward the front stable. The ostler outside the guard area looked stolidly at me, but said nothing, only nodded. I couldn't blame him . . . not too much. After stabling Gairloch in the end stall with the lower headroom, I walked outside, and Weldein saluted me before turning his mount toward the guard stables.

'Good day, Order-master.'

'Good day to you, Weldein.'

'And to you, ser.' He tipped the cap he had put on just before we entered the autarch's walls.

I walked across the paved courtyard and entered the main building, where Bidek looked away as I passed. Herreld was the guard outside Krystal's door, and he rapped on it, but didn't let me in. He never did, not without Krystal's command, and I'd never pressed it.

'Yes . . . good! You're here.' She motioned, and I stepped past Herreld.

Once the door was closed, and I saw that no one else was in the conference room, I gave her a hug, but didn't get as far as a kiss.

'I love you, too, but we don't have much time before we meet with Kasee.' Her eyes had deep circles under them, and she pursed her lips after speaking.

'What's the problem?'

'Ferrel's dead. At least, we think she is.'

'That wizard of the new Duke's?'

'Something like that. I'll tell you what we know when we get to Kasee's study.'

That was serious. I'd never been invited to the autarch's private study. Krystal did give in and kissed me warmly, if quickly, after she pulled on the vest-jacket with all the braid proclaiming her the subcommander. She straightened her blade, the same one I had bought for her in Recluce when we were still training for the dangergeld, back when I thought she giggled too much, and when she probably wished I'd grow up. She had stopped giggling, mostly, but I felt I still had some growing up to do, even if I was considered an adult with a profession – or two of them.

We walked down one flight of stairs and turned right – toward the wing with the autarch's quarters, offices, dining rooms, who knew what else. Even as a walled residence, and not a palace, the place smelled important – scented lamp oil, wood polishes, a spray of lemon incense, and, underlying it all, the distant odor of polished metal and working leather.

The whole setup was much less grandiose than, say, the palace of the Prefect of Gallos, with its fountains and columns, and carpets. The modesty impressed me. There were two guards outside the study door, the no-nonsense kind that look able to cut you apart and not raise a sweat. Krystal and I could have taken them, but, then, she could have done it single-handedly.

The autarch, who insisted I call her Kasee, even if I didn't always think of her on a name basis, sat behind a wide table heaped with parchment, scrolls, and even a set of ledgers. She did not stand up when we entered.

The table wasn't that good despite all the ornamentation, and I could see where the grain hadn't been quite aligned right in the inlays, and that the larger spooling on the front legs was too much larger and visually unbalanced the piece, so much that it seemed to tilt forward.

I bowed.

'Order-master.' She gave me a respectful nod in return. 'I wish I were glad to see you, Lerris. I have this feeling that I'll always see you either before or after some disaster.' Her black hair – shot with silver-gray – was not neat, as at functions, but unruly, and she had a black smudge above one eyebrow. The green eyes met mine for a moment, not quite twinkling.

'I hope not . . .' I still didn't feel right not putting a title in, and my words trailed off.

'That's the problem facing wizards and rulers. No one really wants us around, and all their troubles are our fault.' She brushed a strand of silver-gray hair back off her forehead before continuing. 'Krystal has told you about Ferrel?'

'Only that you believe she is dead. We came immediately, and Krystal didn't have time to tell me everything.'

'There isn't much else. There were two survivors, lucky laggards.'

'How many did you lose?'

'Two squads.' Krystal rubbed her forehead. 'That's just as we're finally getting back up to strength. You can't train good troops overnight.'

'Do you know how?'

Krystal and Kasee exchanged glances. Finally, Krystal spoke. 'No. The two troopers who escaped said the Hydlenese troops – or the wizard – used some sort of firebolts. They were waiting for Ferrel.'

'Did Ferrel just march down the road toward the spring?'

'No. She took a side road, not much better than a trail, according to the troopers. They were a good twenty kays from the spring when they were ambushed. The whole thing doesn't make any sense. Why would Berfir start something now? He's got his hands full with Duke Colaris. Colaris is talking about reclaiming the Ohyde Valley.'

Kasee took a deep breath, and I looked at her.

'Freetown and Hydlen have been fighting over the valley and the control of Renklaar for as long as there's been history. Hydlen's held it since before the fall of Fairhaven,' the autarch explained, 'but no one seems to forget. They have long memories.'

'And long knives,' added Krystal.

'So that's why he needs the brimstone spring? Is he going to try to use cannon against Colaris?' I speculated.

'It could be, but he would be gambling that Colaris couldn't round up a white wizard,' mused Krystal.

'Given Colaris's reputation, that's not much of a gamble. All of the dukes of Freetown have been rather brutal, and frugal, and Colaris is cast in the same mold,' said Kasee. 'But Berfir is very practical, from all reports, and he could hang onto the spring, string us out, and finally give it back after he got a lot of brimstone. Why deliberately start another border conflict?'

'It doesn't make sense. Not from what we know,' ventured Krystal.

'I wonder if there were any vulcrows around.'

'Is there anything to that?' asked Kasee. 'You think this is tied up with another white wizard?'

'I don't know, but Antonin used one to spy on me. And, remember, Antonin really didn't care who won between you and the Prefect. He only wanted to increase his powers, just like all white wizards.'

'How did anyone ever overcome them?' asked Kasee dryly.

'I think it took about a thousand years and enough power to melt Frven,' I answered.

'We don't have that much time or power.' Krystal pursed her lips.

'Has anyone seen Justen?' I asked. 'He should know something.'

'I talked to Tamra this morning,' Krystal said. 'He left two days ago.'

'Rather convenient,' observed the autarch.

'She didn't go with him?'

'According to Tamra, Justen told her that she was now perfectly able to take care of herself for a while and he needed a holiday. He was headed west, but he didn't say where he was going.'

Both women looked at me.

I sighed. 'I guess I'd better take a trip.'

'I'm not commanding,' Kasee began. 'One requests from order-masters – politely. Very politely.'

I wasn't certain that the half-lucky disposal of a mere three white wizards merited so much deference. Still, I had to smile. 'You can't afford to lose your subcommander.'

'Commander,' interposed Kasee.

'And neither can I.'

'Lerris . . .' began Krystal.

I shrugged. 'I'll pack up some tools and wander into Hydlen. I'll be an apprentice, looking for a situation. I still look young enough for that.'

'I appreciate that offer, Lerris. You don't have to undertake this.'

'I have an interest.' I looked at Krystal. 'A strong interest.' Then I looked back at the autarch. 'This is going to take time. I don't intend to march over the pass directly. Don't you have to do something? I mean, soon?'

Kasee looked at me with the hint of a smile. 'What? I can send more troops and have them slaughtered. If Berfir invades Kyphros, I'll get plenty of warning, and it's easier to fight in our desert hills than in the mountains. Acting too soon can only cost us. There's only Jikoya there, and the town's worth less than the troops I could lose. I might need the troops, and their commander, for when they're more useful.'

Krystal nodded.

I didn't quite swallow. The idea that troops were more important than a town – that I hadn't thought about.

'Anything else you might need, Lerris?' asked the autarch.

I forced a grin. 'It would help . . . if I could obtain some . . . donations for . . . travel expenses.'

'You've gotten hopelessly mercenary,' Kasee said dryly.

'It's much less expensive than losing troops because you don't know what's going on,' I pointed out. 'You just said that.'

Kasee did smile, briefly.

'How would you go?' asked Krystal.

'The land route. A poor apprentice wouldn't arrive the easy way.'

'You never have taken the easy route.' Krystal rubbed her forehead. I appreciated the worry, but I stood a better chance than she did, what with wizardry and firebolts apparently flying around.

'Thank you, my dear subcommander.'

'What about an escort partway?' asked Kasee. 'It would speed up the first part of your trip, wouldn't it?'

The message was clear enough, and I bowed to the need for deliberate haste. 'It wouldn't hurt to have a few troopers, at least until I get to the Lower Easthorns. As Krystal can tell you, I'm hopeless with most weapons.'

Krystal snorted. 'He can only hold off or disable two or three at a time with that staff of his. That's how he translates "hopeless."'

'Are you on my side or this Gerlis's?' I asked.

Kasee smiled.

'How soon?' I glanced from one woman to the other. 'Yesterday? I can't do that. How about tomorrow?'

'Tomorrow . . .' mused the autarch. 'There are reasons that tomorrow might be a little . . . precipitous.'

'The day after?' I just wanted to get on with it, a tendency that had a way of getting me in trouble, and Kasee had indicated the need for haste.

'That would be better, for everyone.' The autarch gave Krystal a broad smile, and my consort actually flushed. So did I. Then the autarch stood and nodded at Krystal, and she nodded back. I gave the autarch a half-bow.

As we left the study, I asked, 'Do you know where Tamra is?'

'She was in the small guest quarters off the Second's barracks. Do you think she knows where Justen is?'

'She might.'

Krystal shook her head. 'Justen isn't about to be found.'

'Probably not. He seems to vanish whenever I'm headed into trouble.'

'Do you really think so?' Krystal rubbed her forehead again.

'Sometimes . . . still, he didn't get that ancient by walking into trouble.' I reached out and squeezed her shoulder, offering her both reassurance and a bit of order.

'Thank you.'

Although the autarch's residence wasn't a fortress, it was designed for defense, with thick walls, small windows, and shadows everywhere, even at midday. We walked down the long corridor toward the gate to the guard building.

The two soldiers on duty nodded as we passed, and before long we reached Krystal's quarters, and the always-present Herreld, who opened the door for us. He didn't smile, but he no longer frowned when I showed up.

Once the door was shut, I did manage another hug, and a kiss.

Krystal disengaged herself. 'I don't know how you enjoy that with a blade half between us.'

I just leered.

'You're terrible.' Her eyes twinkled, and she turned and dropped the bar in place. Then she unfastened the sword belt, and kicked off her boots with two rapid thuds.

I grinned, but I didn't finish the grin because Krystal had both arms around me. Somehow, I did manage to get my boots off.

Later, as we lay entwined in the green quilt, I stroked her forehead. 'You won't be coming home tonight, will you?'

'No. We have to meet with Mureas and Liessa. How did you know?'

'I have my ways, lusty wench.' I hugged her tightly, enjoying the feel of her satin skin against mine, and the perfume of her short hair against my cheek. All we could do was use the times we had together, and with Krystal's promotion and the troubles ahead, I knew those times were about to become a lot less frequent.

Outside, the bell chimed four times, and the quick sounds of booted feet below the balcony told of the changing of the guard.

Finally, Krystal sighed, turned, and squeezed me for a long while, then released me.

'You have to get to your meeting? What sort of meeting?'

'It has to do with the new commander.'

'That's you. Kasee said so.'

'That's what Kasee wants. And probably Liessa. Mureas wants her nephew Torrman —'

'Isn't he the one whose hand you took off?' I nibbled on her ear.

'If I don't get up, I never will.' Krystal gave me another hug and kiss, and swung away. 'That was an accident. He threw sand in my face. I only meant to disarm him.' She began to pull on her uniform, and I reluctantly began to dress. 'Mureas will make Kasee pay some price.'

'She won't make Torrman the subcommander?'

'Kasee's indebted, but she won't cut her own throat, not even if Mureas threatened to quit as Finance Minister. Besides, Mureas won't. She likes the power and position, but she'll make it hard, politely, on Kasee.'

'I don't like her.'

'No one does, but she's good with the coins, and she knows what works with them.'

Like who to tax and how much, I had gathered. I stepped up behind Krystal and put my arms around her, kissing her neck, and holding her in a most familiar manner. She leaned back for a moment, then took a deep breath. I gave her a last light kiss on the neck and let go.

'I need to find my boots.' Krystal stood up and looked toward the other room.

'You left them in the conference room.'

'You left yours there, too,' she pointed out.

What could I say? I didn't, but she didn't open the outer door until we were both presentable. Herreld remained as impassive as ever as we went down the corridor and down the stairs, hand in hand.

At the bottom, Krystal let go of my hand. 'Tomorrow night . . . I hope.'

So did I.

I couldn't find Tamra, but I left her a note, then reclaimed Gairloch and headed back to the house and shop.

# IV

# West of Arastia, Hydlen [Candar]

The man in the muddy leathers, wearing a hand-and-a-half sword across his shoulders, and carrying a coil of rope in his left hand, rides up to the dirt-spattered white tent in the middle of the camp. In front of the tent is a red banner with a crown emblazoned across the middle.

'Gerlis! Gerlis!'

The white wizard stands up from behind the portable table. 'Yes, ser?'

'What were you thinking?' The big man marches into the tent, his boots spraying mud across the carpet.

'About what?' Gerlis knots his eyebrows, looking down at the mud the other has brought in.

Berfir throws the scroll on the table, right across the crockery, ignoring the grease it picks up from the uneaten mutton. 'That! Here I am, trying to build up enough forces in the north to keep Colaris from invading us, and here you are, using the rockets on the Kyphrans and trying to start another war I don't need. The rockets cost dearly enough . . .'

'The hermit charged you very little at all, I recall.'

'Getting the information was the easy part. The coins for the smiths and the chemists were what cost.'

'They don't work as well as chaos fire.'

'But I don't need a wizard for them. That was why you were here. The idea was for you to keep that hothead Cennon out of trouble, not help him get into it. You were just supposed to hold the spring, not have Cennon invade Kyphros. I thought that all of the rockets were coming north. That's where I need them. That bastard Colaris could put an army on the Hydolar or Renklaar roads anytime. He's raising levies, and he's buying more mercenaries.'

'You already have a great many of the rockets, and it does take some time to transport them.' Gerlis bowed, his clean-shaven face thin under the dark hair carefully combed to affect a widow's peak. 'Colaris's troops are camped barely beyond Freetown, in any case.'

'Stop picking nits with me! You were supposed to restrain Cennon, not encourage him. You were supposed to send the rockets to Hydlen.' Berfir draws the heavy sword, and the worked steel tip centers less than a span from Gerlis's trim stomach. 'If you won't help me, what use are you?'

'You did retain me for my judgment, Your Grace. After Cennon's decision, I thought some of the rockets should remain here. I did have half of those remaining dispatched.' Gerlis steps back and bows. 'You may have passed them on your way here.'

'Stop changing the subject.' Berfir sighs and lowers the big sword.

'Cennon seemed to think the attack a rather good idea, ser. In your interests, you know.'

'And you let him? You need a healer!' The sword flips back up, almost to Gerlis's chin. 'You know as well as I do that those Kyphrans were only scouting. Scouts aren't invaders, and they were on their side of the border. The autarch isn't interested in conquest. She wasn't even trying to get the spring back yet. You know it, and I know it. The longer things dragged out the better. So why did you tell Cennon to attack them?'

'It wasn't quite that way, ser. Cennon saw them as a threat.'

'Why didn't you stop him?'

'A wizard overruling a field commander?' asks Gerlis reasonably. 'Especially the eldest son of —'

'Idiots!' Berfir sighs deeply. 'Am I surrounded by idiots? How can I hold Hydlen together when I am indebted to idiots like that? I didn't even want to be Duke – not that much, anyway, but Sterna would have given Colaris all the fields on the north side of the Ohyde River, almost the whole Ohyde Valley, and then where would we have been? With Colaris at our front door, and with the best land . . . and now, if I don't fight, all the farmers will claim that because I'm a Yeannotan, I betrayed them. And you give me a fight I don't want and don't need.'

'Duke Sterna, the angels bless him, only wanted peace.'

'You don't get peace by giving things away, not to bastards like Colaris. And calling on the angels certainly doesn't become you, Gerlis.' Berfir laughs harshly and resheathes the sword.

'Perhaps you could use another enemy,' suggests the white wizard.

'Another enemy? I need another enemy? Everyone thinks I'm an upstart. The Temple priests say I'm in league with the demons of light because you're my wizard, and I need to get into a war with Kyphros? When I'm already trying to avoid one with Freetown? One that will break out in open war in eight-days, if not sooner.'

'Well . . .' mused Gerlis. 'If Kyphros attacks you, and you drive off the autarch, everyone will forget your origin. They might also forgive you for the casualties that will mount in the conflict with Colaris.'

'But the autarch won't attack.'

'She already did, according to Cennon. You might as well use it as best you can. For several purposes.'

Berfir pauses and scratches his unruly salt-and-pepper beard. 'I see what you mean . . . I think. But what do I do now? I can't back down to the autarch now. That would give Colaris even greater reason to attack. And if I don't back down to her, I'll have to shift troops here. That would encourage Colaris to quick-march those troops down the road to Hydolar within an eight-day. Demons! What a mess! Why do I owe so much to Cennon's clan?'

'Well . . . Cennon has proved his worth, and he and his troops have earned the right to meet the enemy first.'

'I presume that means the real attackers? What if the autarch merely ignores the attack, or sends a more secretive group of scouts?' Berfir looks toward the closed flap of the tent as the fall breeze shakes the white cloth.

'She probably will. But Cennon and his troops will fight valiantly for Hydlen in any case, and after a sufficiently bloody stand-off, you and the autarch will reach a mutually beneficial agreement, which you will tout as a display of your heroic leadership . . . and that will free you to fight off the real invader.'

'And how does that work when we still will have the autarch's brimstone spring.'

'We'll give back the land.'

Berfir reaches for the sword, then stops and lowers his arm. 'What? The whole point —'

'I've just about traced the underground springs, and I can shift them so that they come up farther downstream on your side of the border.'

'Then why did we take the spring, for light's sake?'

'Because I couldn't figure it out unless we held it.' Gerlis lowers his voice. 'So what we need to do is to make Cennon a hero – one who died valiantly in the cause of Hydlen. You will shed copious tears in

telling his dear father, and award some title to his infant son. And
the next would-be Cennon might think twice before —'

'Did they teach you such deviltry somewhere, or did it spring from
the depths of the earth?'

'I do appreciate the compliment, ser.'

Berfir shakes his head again, and walks across the muddy ground,
swinging himself into the saddle of the big stallion.

Gerlis smiles, a toothy grin that reveals large white teeth and reddish
gums. His eyes flicker across the odd-shaped carts and the crimson
banner with the gold dagger that signifies Cennon's force, the banner
that will soon pass to Cennon's heir.

Then his eyes return to the ducal banner, and he nods slowly.

# V

With the sound of horses, I set down the chisel and stepped out into
the yard. The sky was clear blue-green, and a chill breeze blew out of
the north.

The open-topped carriage, drawn by matched chestnuts, stopped
precisely opposite the door. On the driver's seat sat a driver and a
guard with both a blade and a cocked crossbow. Both wore gray
leathers and gray shirts, but the driver wore brown boots and the
guard wore black.

The single occupant opened the half door herself and vaulted onto
the packed clay of the yard.

'Master Lerris?' She might have reached to my shoulder. Her eyes
were a gray even stonier than her hair, and, under the green silk shirt,
the brushed gray leather trousers and vest, she seemed whipcord-thin.
Her high boots – gray leather – did match her outfit. For all the
trappings of wealth, I did not recognize her. The faintest hint of roses
flowed from around her.

'The same.' I bowed. 'How might I help you?'

'By inviting me into your shop.'

I bowed again and gestured toward the open door. 'My pleasure.'

'From what I've heard of your lady, your pleasure is bound to be
only visual.' Her laugh was easy and practiced as she stepped into
the work-room.

'Nice design.' She pointed at the first of Hensil's chairs. 'How far
along is that?'

'It's not quite rough-finished.'

She studied the tools, the partly completed desk in the corner, and the spoked shafts I had been working on. 'Do you have any finished work I might see?'

'An inlaid table in the house,' I offered.

'Then let us go view this masterpiece.'

I led the way, conscious that the guard with the crossbow followed us both with his eyes as we walked back out and into the house. The crossbow wasn't exactly trained on me, but I knew it would have taken but an instant.

I could have had a door between the kitchen and the shop, but that idea hadn't felt right, and I really wanted some separation. Besides, it kept the sawdust from drifting into the house.

When she saw the table, she looked – just looked. Finally, she nodded. 'You are as good as they say. Why is this here?'

'The man who commissioned it fell out of a tree just before it was finished. He broke his neck and died. My consort insisted I keep it.'

'Wise woman. You should keep listening to her.'

'I try.'

She looked up from the table. 'I would like to commission a desk.'

I had to spread my hands. 'I need to know more. What style? A table desk, or a pedestal desk? Do you want drawers?' I paused. 'I can show you some sketches of general types of desks.'

'I know what I want.'

I waited.

'Something like your table, except even less elaborate. The lines should be almost straight, very clean. Only an inlaid border on a top with beveled edges, but with drawers in the pedestals on both sides – and false backs to the top drawers on each side.'

'No special carvings or designs?'

'Would you suggest any?'

'I could put just a single initial – inlaid – somewhere not terribly obvious.'

'Why would you go to the trouble of inlaying an initial and not making it obvious?' Her smile was amused, as if she knew the answer.

'To show, tastefully, that it was a special piece.'

She nodded again. 'How much would such a piece cost? Done to the same standards as the table?'

'Do you want a matching desk chair?'

'Yes.'

'Fifty golds. Forty for the desk and ten for the chair.'

'How much of a deposit?' she asked.

'Nothing.'

'You are so rich that you need no deposit?'

'No, madame.' I bowed again. 'If I take your deposit, then I must accept your advice, because you already own the work, or part of it. I would prefer to do the best I can. If it does not suit you, you are under no obligation.'

'So idealistic, Master Lerris. And so young.' She laughed, but it was not an unkind laugh.

'Practical, madame. If you did not like the work, with your wealth, you could easily reclaim your deposit. And,' I added, 'I have found I can sell whatever I can make.'

'I like you, young fellow. But please do not call me madame. My name is Antona.' She waited.

'I beg your indulgence, Lady Antona, but I am relatively new to Kyphrien and have not had the pleasure of knowing of you.'

'I'm sure you will hear sooner or later. Don't believe everything you hear. Only half of it is true. I will not tell you which half.' She turned toward the door, then paused. 'When could I expect this piece to be completed?'

I frowned. 'Normally, for something like that, about a season.' I held up a hand. 'It doesn't take that long in workmanship, but if you want it to weather well and not have the wood split later, I need to let parts of the joints and any curving set for a while. Also, I have already been obligated to . . . spend some time I had not planned on, so this might take a bit longer. If that bothers you . . .'

'No. As you pointed out, I have not paid you yet. It's a fair bargain.' Antona stepped back from the table after taking another look at the inlay work. 'The grain angles are very delicate.' She paused. 'Would you mind if I paid you a visit to see how things are going in some several eight-days?'

'Not at all.' I held the door for her and waited in the yard while she climbed into the carriage.

Then I went back to the shop and drew up a rough plan for the desk, sketching out what I had in mind, while those details we had discussed were still fresh. I also wrote down the price – higher than I thought necessary, but I had learned that everything seemed to take longer and cost more. I wasn't in the business just for artistry. I was learning that I did have to buy, not only wood, but such things as food, feed for Gairloch and the old mare, and more than I would have liked for the mounts of Krystal's guards, although Krystal paid for most of their feed and some of the food. She would have paid more, but I didn't feel right about asking her.

After completing my quick rough plan, I put both the sketch and the estimates in the folder for commissions – thin, but growing – and went back to working on Hensil's chairs.

I'd gotten the one rough-finished, and had the backs of the next two done. That left five more. The grooved spokes were still the hardest. After I finished bending the backs of the next two with my too-few clamps and they were setting, I could go back to the time-consuming work of the spokes and the diamond backplates with the inlaid initial *H*.

As usual, I didn't get as far along as I would have liked, since I was working on the fourth chair back when I looked up at a faint sound.

'So? What did you want?' Tamra stood in the doorway to the shop. 'It couldn't have been that important, or you would have tracked me down. I was only out in the market.'

'How was I to know?' I set aside the clamps, wiping my forehead on my upper arm, only half-annoyed that she'd shielded her approach to catch me unawares. I was more worried about the chairs. Doing the backs was, like everything, going to take longer than I had planned.

'You could have looked – with your order senses.'

'Would you like something to drink?' I unfastened the leather apron and hung it on the peg, then wiped off the clamp with a cloth to make sure it was perfectly dry. Glue on the clamp surface would set rough and ruin the wood. Good and clean tools are a woodworker's livelihood.

'Of course.'

We walked past the rail where her roan was tied and into the house. She sat at the table while I got out the redberry. Rissa had taken the cart and the black mare to Kyphrien to market.

'Do you know where Justen is?' I poured two mugs and set one in front of Tamra, then sat down across the table from her.

'No. I already told Krystal that. You wanted to see me for that?' Tamra flipped the end of the green scarf back over her shoulder.

'Partly. I was wondering where he had gone, and how long before he'd be back.'

She shrugged, then swallowed about half the redberry in her mug.

'Why would he go off without telling anyone?' I got up and retrieved the pitcher of redberry, refilling Tamra's mug and setting the pitcher on the table where she could reach it.

'Lerris, you are still so . . . obtuse!' snapped Tamra.

I wasn't the one who had been dense enough to get enslaved by a white wizard, but I was obtuse? 'So where is he?'

'He didn't tell me, but just because he's been around for a while doesn't mean he's not a man. You, with all your leering at Krystal, should certainly understand that.'

'Justen?' Somehow, the thought of my uncle Justen with a woman was disconcerting. 'Justen?'

'You're impossible! Haven't you ever looked at Justen, really looked at him? With your order senses?'

'No. That's not something that exactly crossed my mind.'

Tamra sighed. 'How you ever bested Antonin —'

'Lucky for you I did.'

'Lucky is right. Lucky.' She took a deep breath. 'If you look at him with your order senses, if it ever crosses what passes for your mind, you can see an order tie – it looks like it stretches forever.'

'He's linked somehow to someone?'

'That's what I'm trying to tell you.'

I frowned. 'The secrecy would make sense. He's probably got enemies . . .'

'Of course it would.' Tamra looked toward the pantry. 'Do you have anything to eat?'

'There's some cheese in the cooler.'

'I'll get it.' She rummaged through the cooler – running water from the stream runs around the sides of the thing, a design that dates back to Dorrin, but I'd never seen one in Candar, so I had to have Ginstal, one of the local smiths, make it up specially for me. 'You've only got the yellow stuff?'

'We finished the white the other night, and I haven't broken the wheel in the cellar yet.'

Despite the complaints, Tamra hacked off two healthy wedges and broke off a large chunk from the bread in the breadbox. I sipped the rest of my redberry while she sat down and ate.

'You going to eat, Lerris?'

'I had some cheese before you came.'

'Late breakfast?'

'Lunch.'

She winced.' . . . barely past mid-morning . . .' she mumbled with her mouth full. 'When did you get up?'

'Early. I always do when Krystal's not here. Then I can stop whatever I'm doing when she comes in.'

'What happens when she's off somewhere?' Tamra refilled her mug.

'I get a lot of work done. I've gotten a lot of work done lately.'

'That's woodwork. What about real work?'

I frowned.

'You've gotten slow and sloppy.' Tamra flipped a strand of short red hair off her shoulder and looked at my chest.

'I have not. Not sloppy, anyway.'

She prodded my stomach. 'Not sloppy . . . but slow, I'd still bet.'

'You just want an excuse to show your prowess.'

'Naturally.' She grinned. 'You've been insufferable in your humbleness. Just the humble woodworker whose consort is the important one. Your humbleness is almost arrogance. Bah!'

I could use the exercise, and a break from planing the damned chair spokes. 'All right. A short sparring session, but not for blood.'

'So get out that old staff.' Tamra drained the last of her mug and wiped her mouth.

'It's new. The old one got broken, remember?'

'I don't remember, thank the darkness. Let's get on with it. I'm supposed to work with the trainees later.'

'You like getting pummeled?'

'They have to hit me first. Or don't you remember?'

'That was a while ago, and it only happened once.' Once had been enough. Back in Recluce, the first time I'd sparred with Tamra she'd beaten me black and blue, and knocked me out – with a padded staff yet. I'd gotten a lot better since then, but I wasn't that enthused about sparring with her.

After rinsing the mugs and setting them in the rack, I led her out, stopping by the shop to reclaim my new staff.

We squared off in the center of the yard. A light breeze blew out of the west, bringing the acrid scent of graying leaves and a hint of chill all the way from the Westhorns.

'I hope you're better with it than with the old one.'

'We'll see.'

'So we will.' Tamra circled left.

I turned with her, but kept my feet balanced, knowing she was quicker.

*Flickkk* . . . Her staff flashed, but I slid it off to the right.

*Thwack!* No finesse there, as that slight form shifted her weight to focus it all on the staff. My fingers were numb from the blow to my staff, and I backed up, trying to flex them while not letting go of the staff itself.

*Thwackkk! Thwack!*

Sweat was already popping out on my forehead, and Tamra

looked cold, almost dispassionate, like some ancient Westwind guard must have.

I feinted, then dropped, and came up under her guard. She parried but not before I cracked her on the thigh, not hard. I couldn't do that, not in sparring.

'Think you're good?' She grunted, and her staff turned into a blur.

At that point, I had to surrender to my own sense of order and let my body respond.

The whole thing became a blur. I got in some blows, and she got in some. I got in more, but hers were harder. She didn't have the restraints I did, which is why she got in trouble with Antonin, but why it took more work for me to hold her off with the staff.

'All right!' I finally puffed, backing up, and sweating like a roasted hog. 'You're doing this every day. I only do it occasionally.'

She put down her staff, looking only a bit warmer than before we started. Her red hair was slightly disarrayed. 'When do you leave?'

'Leave?'

'About half the Finest know you're headed somewhere, and Ferrel hasn't come back, and Krystal's taken over the Finest. And you're asking about Justen.' Tamra snorted. 'It doesn't take much in the way of brains.'

'Soon.' I bowed to the inevitable. 'Since you know so much, what else can you tell me?'

Tamra brushed her hair back off her forehead. 'I can't tell you that much. I can tell you that if Justen were here, he'd be telling you to take your book – *The Basis of Order*. Read it. You won't survive forever on dumb luck and your staff work, even if it is getting better.'

'Thank you.' I bowed, and my ribs ached, reminding me that I wouldn't survive long at all on staff work by itself. 'You're also improving.'

'I've been practicing against the Finest. You have to get faster when you're working against blades. Krystal's a good instructor. Has she been working with you?'

'Only a little.'

'It shows. You ought to do it more often.'

'When?'

Tamra gave me a quick smile. 'I know how you two spend your free time.'

'There hasn't been that much.'

Her smile got wider, and I wanted to crack her, but I walked across the yard and set the staff in the rack inside the shop door.

In the end, after Tamra rode off, pleased with herself, I did have to go back to the chairs. With the break, the work seemed easier, and I even got the fifth chair back bent and clamped in place, and went back to the demon-damned grooved spokes that I had begun to wish I'd never designed. Elaboration, even of a good design, can be a definite pain, and I just didn't have the experience of Uncle Sardit or Perlot. That hurt, because I spent more time on some things than was definitely wise.

The clinking of the harness and the faint creaking of the cart wheels told me when Rissa returned.

She looked in on me. 'How many for dinner?'

'I'd guess on six or seven. Three of us, and three or four guards.' I shrugged.

'You . . . Never do I know who is coming for dinner.'

'Neither do I, and it's at least partly my house.'

'Fantesa, she says she could never cook in such a place. Are there three or fifteen?' Rissa put both her hands on her narrow hips. 'Or in the morning, I think I will feed three, and ten hungry people sit down in the evening. Or it is the other way around.' She lifted her shoulders. 'In the market, they all look at me and laugh. And Brene, she cackles like her chickens. We should have chickens.'

'What can I say?' I shrugged again, ignoring the reference to the chickens I didn't want. 'My consort is an important woman.'

'This house . . .' But she said it with a smile before she retreated to the kitchen – or to the small room behind it that was hers. I went back to the spoke-shafts, and got two more rough-finished before it started to get dark.

Right after sunset, I pulled out my striker and went into the yard. Three tries convinced me that the big lantern wasn't going to light. I took it down and checked the wick. It needed trimming, but it was also dry, and that meant lugging it out to the shed where I kept the oils, a good fifty cubits behind the shed and off to the side of the stable. If lightning or something happened, like loose chaos, I didn't want the shop or the house burning with the shed. Rissa grumbled about that, and so did I when it was cold or raining or snowing – though that was comparatively infrequent in Kyphros – and I had to get finish oil or varnishes. Luckily, it wasn't that cold or rainy around Kyphrien, but I suppose I would have done the same thing if I had a place in Spidlar or Sligo.

I had just replaced and lit the big lantern when I heard, and sensed, horses. So I waited out in the yard for Krystal and the Finest. Even in the saddle of the big black she looked tired, but she smiled. I offered her a hand down. She took it, which told me how tired she was.

I glanced at the four guards, but none were more than noddingly familiar, then back to Krystal. 'I told Rissa dinner for seven.'

'Good. None of us have eaten.'

'I thought it might be like that.' I squeezed her hand as we walked her mount to the stable. The others followed. Krystal just let me unsaddle her horse and rub him down, while she racked the saddle and poured the feed into the trough.

Then we walked back through the twilight – a few stars had begun to twinkle in the evening sky. As we neared the house, Krystal handed me a heavy leather purse. It clanked. 'Put that away.'

'What's that for?'

'Your traveling expenses from Kasee. Please try to make the coins last. Our treasury isn't exactly the deepest, although Kasee would never say so.'

'I will try to return some, Commander.' I took the purse and bowed.

Krystal hit me on the arm, hard enough for me to wince. 'Sometimes. Sometimes, you are so . . . so . . .'

'Insufferable?'

'Yes!'

'Have you washed up?' I asked.

'No.'

'Neither have I.' I did give her a hug, but it didn't last long.

'You're right. You didn't. And you're still insufferable.'

I turned to Rissa. 'Dinner will have to wait a little longer. At least until we're more presentable.'

'Too much washing is not good for the health.'

'Neither is too little,' I answered.

After I carried the purse into the bedroom and set it in the wardrobe I had made far too quickly – and wished I had taken more time and care every time I looked at it – we went to the rear washroom together.

As I pulled off my shirt, Krystal turned to me. 'What happened to your ribs?'

'Tamra. She showed up this morning, and we sparred. She thought I ought to sharpen up.'

'Being beaten black and blue is going to improve your skills?' Krystal laughed softly as she stripped off her vest and shirt.

At that point I forgot about washing and opened my arms, trying not to wince. She obliged, but only for a bit.

'You and I do need to wash up, and we have hungry troops waiting.'

'Where's Yelena?'

'Getting ready for tomorrow. Have you forgotten so quickly?'

'No. I wish I could.'

After washing quickly, I shaved, and we dried and hurried to the kitchen where, as soon as we entered, all the troopers stood and Rissa began carrying the big casseroles to the table for me to serve.

Dinner was something called burkha, hotter even than the normal chilied foods that the Kyphrans enjoyed so much, and although I gave every trooper a huge helping, they ate it all, and didn't even break a sweat.

I was sweating after three bites, and so was Krystal, and we kept grinning at each other.

'Perron?' Krystal said softly. 'We'll have to leave not much after dawn.'

'Yes, Commander.' He glanced at the two of us, grinning.

'The order-master is my consort, but, more important from your point of view, he has already saved more of the Finest than anyone in Kyphros.'

Perron flinched at the gentle words, spoken quietly, and without edge.

'I never did thank you,' said a woman trooper at one corner.

I looked at her, but I couldn't say I knew her.

'I was the one with the lieutenant, ser. In the vale of Krecia. I'm Haithen.'

'I'm glad I could help, but I was very lucky,' I told her.

'Luck didn't have much to do with it,' she added, directing her words at the squad leader. 'He's the one who took out the white wizard with a staff . . . on a pony.'

Perron seemed to acknowledge that I might have some benefit.

'How did your sparring go with Tamra?' asked Krystal innocently, although I could see the glint in her eyes.

'Pretty much a draw,' I mumbled with a mouthful of burkha. 'I can hit her more often, but she hits harder.' I had to reach for the bread. Redberry alone wouldn't cool the burning in my mouth and nostrils.

'You sparred with the red – the redheaded wizard?' asked Perron.

'About midday. We have on and off for several years.'

'Brave man . . .'

About sparring with Tamra he was certainly right.

After dinner, and more superficial remarks about the heredity and dubious claim of Berfir to the Duchy of Hydlen, Krystal and I took our leave.

After we closed the door and slid the small bar in place, I kissed her.

'We do have some time, Lerris. And I prefer to be close to you without my boots on.' She sat on the edge of the bed.

That was a good idea, and I followed her example, shedding a few other accessories as well.

She stopped and gave me a long deep look, the kind where I almost fell into her eyes. 'You don't have to do this, tomorrow, you know?'

I looked at the floor. What could I say? 'I owe you ... and Kasee ...'

She pursed her lips and laid a hand on my leg for an instant. 'What else happened to you today?' she asked as she eased out of her leathers.

'You know. What happened to you?' I asked, pointing to an ugly bruise.

'Tamra.'

'Darkness, she gets around.'

We both laughed.

Krystal stretched out and lay there in the light of the one lamp. Outside I could hear the faint whisper of the low evening wind. 'You never did answer my question about the day.'

'Not much. I worked on the damned chairs for Hensil. I finally got more of the backs done. It's taking forever, because I don't have enough clamps. Oh ... do you know a woman by the name of Antona? She was familiar with you.'

'Antona?' Krystal laughed for an instant. 'She is the proprietor of the Green Isles. She supplies most of the ... courtesans ... for the more established and wealthy young men – and some of the handsome ... escorts for widows or bored consorts.' Her voice sharpened. 'How did you meet her?'

'She came here this morning and commissioned a desk.'

'A desk?'

'A very tasteful desk. Also very expensive, with a matching chair. I told her it would be fifty golds.'

'She can afford it, but ... still ...' Krystal whistled.

'You told me to charge what things are worth.' I looked at her sheepishly. 'Now I know why she told me not to call her madame.'

'Lerris, you didn't?'

'I did. How was I to know? She was very ladylike about it, just told me to call her Antona. So I called her Lady Antona.'

'You must have made her day.'

'She wanted a desk. I make them.'

'What kind?' mused Krystal. 'Something ornate and elaborate?'

'She had definite ideas and —'

'I'll bet.'

'—she wants black oak, and she wants it simple and perfect.'

'I wonder why. I'm told that's not the style of the Green Isles.'

I grinned at her. 'Because things that are simple and perfect are worth a lot more.'

'I don't know that I like that implication.'

'You are perfect.'

'Oh, Lerris.' But she did open her arms, and I turned down the lamp first, marveling at how long it had taken me to see what she offered, not only each night, but season after season, and how fragile each moment was. And how soon tomorrow would come.

# VI

## Cigoerne, Afrit [Hamor]

The slim bald man in the tan uniform steps from the carriage outside the military gate to the palace of His Imperial Majesty Stesten, Emperor of Hamor, Regent of the Gates of the Oceans, and liege lord of Afrit.

'Marshal Dyrsee, ser, if you would follow me?' The junior officer inclines his head slightly.

Dyrsse nods brusquely in return, but his eyes drift downhill from the green marble palace to the smooth waters of the Swarth River, held in its banks by the levies that stretch from above the capital more than fifty kays down to the great imperial port at Swartheld.

'Ser?'

'Let's go,' Dyrsse says. 'It wouldn't do to keep the Emperor waiting.'

'No, ser. Lord Chyrsse said he was in a foul mood.'

'And he wants to see me?'

'Yes, ser.'

The two march through the gate, past the four soldiers in dress tans who bear dark-barreled rifles, and through the arched halls of pale marble, their boots clicking on the polished stone. The two military men walk past two servers in white who push carts redolent of spiced meats.

An Austran diplomat in dark woolens wipes his forehead as the two officers pass, and an official from the province of Merowey, in flowing white trousers and a peach-colored vest with gold braid, inclines his shaven head. Two functionaries in orange uniforms carrying brown leather cases nod deeply at the marshal and continue away from the receiving halls.

'Did Chyrsse say why?' the marshal finally asks as they approach the northern anteroom.

'No, ser.'

As they step through the archway hung with tan draperies, fringed in gold, a heavyset man in brilliant blue trousers and a matching blue silk shirt, and wearing a heavy gold chain and medallion around his neck, steps forward.

'Marshal Dyrsse, the Emperor is waiting for you.'

'I came as soon as I received the message, but, even with the new river steamers, it takes some time.'

'The Emperor understands that,' replies Chyrsse.

'The Emperor does not have to understand much, Chyrsse,' responds Dyrsse. 'He just has to command.'

'You always understand ... I'll tell him you're here.' After wiping his forehead with a large cotton handkerchief and blotting his damp cheeks, Lord Chyrsse hurries through a small doorway in the corner of the room.

The junior officer looks down at the polished octagonal floor tiles. Dyrsse scans the empty military anteroom, then shakes his head. He sets the marshal's cap on the polished stand by the large doorway next to the two silent guards, wearing swords, in the antique orange and black dress uniforms that date back to the founding of the Empire.

Lord Chyrsse reappears. 'His Excellency is waiting!'

The marshal steps toward the heavy wooden doors warded by the guards, who turn, silently, and open them.

Lord Chyrsse straightens his silks and steps through the double doors before Marshal Dyrsse. 'Marshal Dyrsse, responding to His Excellency's commands!'

Dyrsse's lips barely quirk at the high-pitched squeaking announcement, and he steps into the receiving chamber, where he walks to the orange carpet, turns to the throne and bows deeply. He waits.

'You may depart, Lord Chyrsse.' The Emperor's voice is deep, surprisingly deep, coming as it does from a thin figure with short but thick salt-and-pepper hair and a narrow beaked nose. Stesten's eyes are a piercing light green.

Behind the marshal, Lord Chyrsse bows and walks back through the side doors, which close with a dull thud.

There are no guards visible in the hundred-cubit-long chamber, but the dozen embrasures in the overhead gallery, and the four in the wall that forms a semicircle around the throne, testify to their hidden presence.

'You may approach, Marshal Dyrsse.'

The slim bald man in the tan uniform walks forward until he reaches the foot of the five wide steps that lead up to the imperial throne where he bows again. 'Your Highness. How might I serve you?'

'By doing what you do best.'

'As Your Highness commands.' Dyrsse bows a third time.

'You are to go to Candar, to Dellash. We are going to complete the work there that has been waiting for too long. For far too many ages and through too many insults to the greatness that is Hamor.'

'Yes, Your Majesty.'

'You sound doubtful, Marshal.' The Emperor's voice hardens.

'Your Majesty already has sent two envoys to Candar. Although your wish is always my desire, what could I add?'

'Neither has your understanding of ships, troops, and tactics. And neither has the understanding that Candar merely represents a step toward our ultimate and long-delayed goal.'

Dyrsse spreads his hands, as if in puzzlement.

'You should not question, but you would not be Dyrsse if you did not. That is why you are a marshal and not an envoy. Currently, Candar is relatively orderly. I am led to believe that will change shortly.' A laugh follows. 'Through the infusion of yet more order. We perhaps might even aid in that infusion of order.'

'Us? Infuse order?'

'Let us just say that matters will shortly become very chaotic in Candar. That is, if my scholars are correct, and so far they have been. This will provide us an opportunity to impose our own form of order.'

'The grand fleet?' Dyrsse pauses when there is no answer, but does not wipe the perspiration from his forehead. 'Sire . . . as you know . . . As you know, I have indicated that the forces presently committed to Candar are insufficient.'

'That they are, but, for now, you will carry out the orders of Rignelgio or his successor, as well as you are able.'

'As you wish, sire.'

'It is as I wish, Dyrsse. Remember, one cannot eradicate a nest of vipers without provoking and observing them to determine how widely and deeply they are spread. If I send the grand fleet now, what will it gain me?'

'All of Candar will submit. Or . . .'

'They might put aside their petty quarrels? They might, although

I doubt any, except the autarch of Kyphros, are so perceptive. Better that we continue with the present strategy. Candar will fall, country by country, and then . . . then the black devils will have nowhere to turn.'

'Yes, ser.'

'You are thinking that it is better to strike with a heavy hammer from the first.' There is a sigh from the throne. 'That hammer must be saved until it can be used on the black devils. It would not take the grand fleet to subdue Candar, now, would it, Marshal Dyrsse?'

'I would think not, but it will take more than the twenty-odd warships steaming across the Western Ocean.'

'You will have more ships for Candar, but not the grand fleet. You know that my grandfather would have liked to see that fleet? He especially would have liked to see the shells fall on the black city.'

'Yes, ser.'

Another sigh, theatrically loud, issues from the Emperor. 'I see I must spell matters out, even for the great Marshal Dyrsse. It is simple. You are to take Candar. Ser Rignelgio has already begun the process with the Duke of Freetown. You are to support him. One means of such support is to cut off the Candarian traders from trading with Recluce. The other is to block the Recluce traders from providing support to Candar.'

'The black mages will send out their ships.'

'It is a little-known secret that they only have three. Perhaps you could eliminate one or perhaps two with the ships you will have – on the pretext of our conquest of Candar.'

'Only three? Three ships, and we have worried about Recluce for so long?'

'Those three ships have sunk dozens of our best vessels over the years, because they are quick and cannot be seen. That is why everyone has believed there were more, but . . . we have excellent sources of information, Marshal. There are only three ships. Each formidable, but . . . they cannot cover an entire continent.'

Dyrsse covers a frown with a nod.

'You are beginning to understand. Good. The heart of the power of Recluce lies in the black city of Nylan. When Nylan falls, so does Recluce. And if Nylan is reduced to black gravel . . . do you understand?'

'I understand that Nylan and Recluce must fall, ser.'

'Good. For now, Rignelgio and Leithrrse will direct the efforts in Candar. I rather suspect that they, and most nobles of Hamor, fail to understand the true danger that faces us on the far side of the Eastern

Ocean. You will support them with all your skill. Then will I provide you with the tools to reduce Nylan and destroy Recluce.'

'You do not expect them to fail?' Dyrsse feels his lips drying, but does not moisten them, not with the Emperor studying him.

'They are great nobles of Hamor, and their peers have forgotten that Hamor has lost two great fleets to the black isle, even before the black ships.'

'Ser . . . you tell me that I must support your envoys with all my skill, but that they will not prevail.' Dyrsse bows. 'I am a fighting man, and I will carry out my duty to my last breath, but I must know that duty. I cannot rely on guessing your will, ser.'

'My will is simple, Dyrsse. Crush Recluce. My envoys are interested in growing rich from Candar and making token efforts against the black isle. Sooner or later Recluce will crush them, and you will inherit their authority, an authority I cannot now give you, for the danger is not yet obvious, and even emperors must consider the beliefs of their nobles.'

'Ser, my duty is clear, and I will do my best to carry it out. However, you have pointed out that no one has successfully taken on the black devils and their invisible ships – even if they do only have three. And that does not count their mages. Can you provide some guidance?'

'You are highly recommended. Why must I spell out every detail?'

'So I can do my best for you.'

There is a sigh from the throne. 'After the others fail . . . you will receive my mandate, and you will bring all the powers of Hamor against Recluce. No one has ever before had hundreds of ships of black steel and order. Nor guns that fire five- and ten-stone shells. As for the black mages, they, too, are limited. Never has Recluce had more than a handful, and that handful will not be enough to prevail against the massed order of the grand fleet – when the time comes.' There is a pause from the throne. 'Now . . . do you understand your orders? And your duty?'

'Yes, ser.'

'Then I look forward to the success of your efforts. You may go.'

Dyrsse bows again. Not until he is outside the chamber does he wipe his sweating forehead.

# VII

A gray sky brooded over Kyphros, but the wind was light when Yelena – the squad leader who'd escorted me on the first part of the effort against the white wizard Antonin – and three troopers met me outside the stable. The air smelled more like rain than fall.

Krystal and her guards had left early, far earlier, and I knew she wouldn't have come home the night before – except that I was leaving. Gairloch's saddlebags were full, not only with some apprentice-type tools, but with travel bread and hard cheese. I had some fruit stashed away also, and a heavier jacket, a waterproof, and the bedroll I'd gotten in Howlett when I first came to Recluce. The canteen held redberry, but I knew that wouldn't last. All in all, Gairloch was laden.

For some reason, when I thought of the bedroll, made in Recluce, I wondered about my parents. I could have written, and sent the letter by a trader, but I'd almost felt as if they'd been the ones to throw me out, to send me on my dangergeld. And I'd never even known that my father, the great Gunnar, was a Temple master and head of the Institute for Order Studies.

Should I write? I still didn't know as I stood there in the yard.

'Good morning, Order-master.'

Yelena's greeting cut off my speculations.

'Good morning, Leader Yelena.' I swung onto Gairloch and flicked the reins. He didn't need the hint; he was already moving toward the main road.

*Wheeee . . . eeee.*

'Yes, I know. You thought we'd given this up.' I patted Gairloch on the neck, and he whuffed once.

'One never gives up being an order-master.' Yelena rode up beside me, and I had to look up at the squad leader. Her mount was a good four hands taller than Gairloch.

'Like one never gives up being a member of the Finest?'

'You die with your boots on, anyway.'

'You are so cheerful this morning.' I thwacked Gairloch too hard for a mere pat, but he only whuffed again.

Weldein tried to suppress a grin. Freyda and the other guard – Jylla was her name, if I recalled correctly – rode silently behind us.

My fingers strayed to the replacement staff in the converted lance holder. It was just solid lorken, but bound in iron – without the sort of order infusion that my old one had possessed. Of course, I'd given it that infusion, without really knowing it. As Justen had pointed out, that was one of the problems. Recluce – and my father – hadn't taught me enough, and I still didn't understand why.

'It's better than doing guard duty around the citadel.'

'Speak for yourself,' said Jylla cheerfully.

'Women,' muttered Weldein.

Since we were outnumbered, I saw no reason to comment, but shifted my weight and hoped that the day stayed cool.

I pulled the staff from the holder and began to run through the mounted exercises, since I rarely practiced them, my infrequent sparring being generally on foot.

After a time I replaced the staff, conscious that Freyda had been watching. I raised my eyebrows.

'Only the red bitch is better, I think.'

I tried not to choke. 'The red bitch?'

'The gray wizard's apprentice. The subcommander made us spar against her.' Freyda winced. 'My ribs still hurt, and that was three days ago.'

'You sparred with her yesterday, didn't you, Order-master?' asked Yelena. The question was not quite a question.

'Yes. I think I held her to a draw.'

'She had a few new bruises, I think.'

Tamra? I'd actually bruised her? I shook my head.

Yelena gave me a bemused smile as Freyda and Jylla exchanged glances. I fingered the staff, then concentrated on riding. We had to go through Kyphrien to get to the east road, and the mixed odor of overcooked lamb and goat, onions, and less mentionable items struck me long before we got onto the avenue. The babble was the same as always.

'. . . Mytara, if I've told you once about eggs . . .'

'. . . finest bronze in Candar . . .'

'You'd think that she'd appreciate a solid provider, but, no, she's got to insist on a dandy, one with a pretty face. What will she do when she's got three offspring, and needs money for a serving girl? Does she think of that . . .'

'. . . and you could have walked the lake and not dampened your boots . . .'

'Let Hyrella tell your fortune! A mere copper. Will you grudge a mere copper to learn your fate?'

'. . . best pies in Kyphros . . .'

'Thief! Thief! Get the little scamp!'

My eyes darted to the thin figure who pounded down the cobblestone road, scuttled between two women, and darted into a narrow alleyway leading down toward the river.

The heavyset merchant puffed to a stop and glared at Yelena. 'You serve the autarch, and you let him get away! Why didn't you stop him?'

Yelena reined up, and so did I. Several passersby turned.

'Well, why didn't you stop him?' The man's heavy waxed mustaches waved as he panted out his question.

'I would have had to ride over people,' answered Yelena.

'That's no answer. You let a thief get away! I intend to let the autarch know of this ... disgraceful ...'

'. . . there goes Fuston again . . .'

'. . . too fat to chase anyone and too crooked for anyone to help him . . .'

Fuston turned. 'I heard that. Liars! Liars!'

'. . . too fat . . .'

'. . . too full of himself, he is . . .'

Yelena struggled to keep a straight face, as Fuston rolled his bulk back to face me. 'You! Tell those guards to chase the thief.'

'Me?' I shook my head. 'He's gone. What did he steal?'

'He took some olives, right from the barrel. Scooped them up and ran off.' The fat man waddled toward me.

'. . . kid could have used the olives more than Fuston . . .'

'You're that famous order-master! Why don't you make sure there's order here in Kyphrien?' Fuston's acrid breath hit me harder than his words as he leaned forward, his face less than two cubits from me. Why was it that people like Fuston recognized me and some of the Finest didn't? Probably because Fuston watched parades like the one Kasee gave on my return to Kyphros, and the soldiers were working or on picket duty – or something.

'I presume he was hungry,' I said evenly, letting Gairloch back away.

'So he was hungry! He stole my olives, and what are you going to do about it?' Fuston stepped forward to close the distance between us again.

Yelena fingered her blade, and Freyda and Jylla watched with impassive faces.

'Let me understand this,' I temporized. 'This young thief was so hungry that he took some olives out of the barrel right in front of your eyes?'

'Of course. How else would I have seen him?'

'Does not that tell you something? He is either terribly arrogant, terribly stupid, or terribly hungry. If he is arrogant or stupid, he will try something like that again, and, before long, someone will catch him.' I cleared my throat. 'Unhappily, if he is that hungry, he will steal again also, and he will be caught.' I tried to think through what I should say as the merchant jabbed a fat finger at me.

'You won't do anything? A fine wizard you are!'

I caught his eyes. 'You are wealthy. You are well fed, and you have the means to protect yourself. You are angry because a boy made a fool out of you, and you want to blame someone else. This thief is long gone. I am not a white wizard who sniffs after blood. Nor am I a white wizard who burns people into cinders. What do you want?'

'I want justice!'

I grinned. 'But you have justice. A hungry boy has been fed, and you have warned everyone about a thief. Is that not justice? Or would you call it justice if a white wizard threw a firebolt and turned that hungry thief into ashes?'

'Bah ... the autarch will hear about this ... you'll see ... you'll see ...' Fuston gave me a last glare before turning and waddling away.

'... not a bad answer for a young wizard ...'

'... not that good ...'

'... he's right about Fuston. He's too well fed to chase his young wife around the bed ... forget about thieves ...'

We continued riding along the stone-paved street that would lead to the east road.

'That wasn't a bad sermon,' said Yelena. 'Do they teach you that in wizard's school?'

'There isn't a wizard's school. My father and Justen were always telling me to think before I spoke. People like that merchant don't give you any time to think.' My fingers touched the smooth wood of the staff, and the wood offered some comfort, although I was careful not to put any more order into the staff. You can divide your soul that way. That's really what happens to some wizards, and they don't even know it. I know. It happened to me, but I managed to get it back, mainly because Justen insisted that I reread *The Basis of Order*.

'I don't believe in theft.' I coughed. I wasn't used to talking that much. Woodworking without an apprentice is quiet work. 'But I don't believe that whipping or killing people desperate enough to steal food in the daylight is likely to do much good.'

'No.' Weldein glanced toward the eastern gates less than two hundred cubits ahead.

Jylla and Freyda nodded.

I gave Gairloch another pat and looked back toward the autarch's residence, although I couldn't see it, and then at the road stretching ahead.

# VIII

The tall sandy-haired man with the heavy forearms walked along the pier toward the ship in the end berth. The light wind brought the smell of cooking from the waterfront of Nylan to the pier, mixing the oil with the scents of seaweed and fish. The steel-hulled vessel with the nameplate *Shrezsan* flew the flag of Hamor from a jackstaff above the stern. As he noted the nameplate, a faint smile crossed his lips.

Wisps of steam seeped from the twin funnels. No paddlewheels protruded from the smooth lines of the hull, but the tips of the two big screws were visible just beneath the surface of the gray water in the harbor of Nylan. The tall man stood by a bollard not quite half his height and closed his eyes, concentrating on the ship. After he had stood silently for a time, a steam-powered tractor puffed by, then slowed.

'Is that you, Magister Gunnar?'

Gunnar opened his eyes and turned to the dark-haired woman in black coveralls. He inclined his head.

'Caron. From Sigil. I took your order ethics class at the Temple in Wandernaught.'

'I'm sorry, I did not recognize you.' He gestured toward the ship. 'I'd heard about the new Hamorian steamers, and I wanted to see one.'

'She's a beauty. Fast, too.'

'*Shrezsan* – that's not a Hamorian name. I wonder . . .'

Caron laughed. 'The ship belongs to Leithrrse. He came from Enstronn, but he couldn't finish dangergeld. He's a prosperous merchant in Hamor, sometimes even acts as an envoy for the Emperor – not here, of course.'

'No . . . I suppose not.' Gunnar paused. 'The steel seems almost as tough as black iron, and the propellers are smooth-finished.'

Caron nodded. 'They've built some warships that are even faster, according to the mate, lots of them, with more on the way. He looked over his shoulder when he told me.'

'If they can do this, I'd not be surprised if they're going to arm them with cannon.'

Caron looked down the pier and back. 'They have. Hundreds maybe. That's what one of the sailors was saying in the White Stag.'

Gunnar pulled at his chin. 'Take a lot of iron.'

'Hamor's got a lot.'

'I suppose.' Gunnar looked beyond the ship, out toward the Gulf and Candar.

A steam whistle blew, and Caron flashed a brief smile. 'That's for me. They need to load this up. It was good seeing you, Magister Gunnar.'

'Good to see you, Caron.' Gunnar took another look at the *Shrezsan*, then stepped back next to the bollard and closed his eyes once more.

The steam whistle tooted twice more, and a pair of gulls swooped down and across the stem of the steamer.

A wake left the next pier, a pier guarded and apparently empty, for all that the ripples signified a departing ship.

Gunnar's eyes opened and followed the unseen ship for a time. Finally, he shook his head and walked back toward the shops at the foot of the pier.

# IX

We headed southeast from Kyphrien on a packed clay road wide enough for three horses or a wagon and one horse, riding through the hills of red clay covered with fine sand, patches of grass, and desert olive groves, meticulously tended, their leaves gray in the early winter light. Between the groves were villages, so small they had no kaystones, no squares, just white-plastered houses with red tile roofs and handfuls of children scattered in odd places – on stone walls or tending sheep or driving oxen with long wands.

By mid-morning, the high gray clouds began to break, but the wind remained light, although it had changed direction, coming from the north, and seemed more chill than in Kyphrien.

Riding past the olive trees, I wondered how many of the groves belonged to Hensil, the trader who had commissioned the chair set. Somehow, I liked Antona better than Hensil, although I couldn't say I liked her occupation better. They both catered to human appetites, but I have never liked the idea of any trade in human beings. Then again, just because he was richer, was Hensil any better than Fuston, who had wanted me to punish a starving boy? Food traders withheld food for those who had more coins, and traders in women effectively withheld sex for those who had more coins. Except – I shook my head – women could think, and olives presumably didn't.

'You look worried, Order-master,' commented Yelena.

'Comparing olives and women,' I mumbled.

Jylla and Freyda grinned at each other.

Weldein brushed back his longish blond hair and said softly, 'You have to think about that?'

Even I had to smile.

The olive groves diminished to scattered stands, and eventually gave way to sparser hillsides covered with low and gnarled cedars. The villages grew less frequent, as did travelers. We stopped to water the horses around midday at a narrow stream running between two hills. To our right, downstream, a small flock of sheep had churned the grass around a damp area into a long streak of brown on brown.

'Good thing they're downstream,' offered Yelena.

About to scoop up a mouthful of water, I stopped, deciding a little order-spelling on the water wouldn't hurt. Yelena drank from her canteen. So did Weldein, but I wanted to save the redberry in mine. So I orderspelled some water. I could almost feel the grit and some chaos spill out.

'How can you drink that?' asked Jylla. 'Won't you get the flux?'

'Very carefully,' I told her. 'I wouldn't drink it if you don't have to.'

'But you are.'

'I orderspelled it.'

Freyda and Jylla looked at each other and shook their heads. After that, I stood beside Gairloch and took out the cheese and hard biscuits.

'Would you like some?' I offered a small wedge of the white cheese to each of them. Even the Finest aren't exactly that well off.

'Thank you,' said Weldein and Yelena.

Freyda and Jylla nodded thanks.

'How long will it take to get to Lythga?' According to Krystal, the trip was four days hard riding to Jikoya, and then another two to Lythga and that part of the Lower Easthorns.

'A little over six days,' answered Yelena after swallowing half the wedge of cheese in a single bite. 'The way you're going to Hydlen is almost an eight-day longer.'

'I really don't want to ride up the direct route to Arastia. That's like announcing my arrival with a large trumpet and saying, "Hello, Gerlis, here I am." It's not that healthy.'

Yelena frowned. 'You went up against the first chaos wizard alone.'

'Then I was even younger and stupider. Actually, that was my second. Antonin didn't have an army camped next to him. The first one did, and I ran like hell, and was very lucky to escape.' I didn't point out that being able to shield myself from the troops' seeing me had helped a lot, and they still almost got me shooting off arrows blind. That shielding hadn't worked against the wizard, only the troops, and it wouldn't work against Gerlis himself. 'Also, the point is to get back to Kyphrien with enough information to let the autarch know what is happening.'

That got a snort from Jylla, and I looked over at her, standing beside her mount. She turned pale.

'You made your point, Lerris.' Yelena's tone was dry.

'What point?' I really wasn't that angry, but I had been irritated.

She shook her head.

'I'll still be lucky to get back in one piece.'

'I have great confidence in you, Order-master.'

I was glad someone did.

I packed up the cheese, orderspelled more water, and used some of it to wash my face. Below us, the sheep milled around more, and then drifted farther away from the road.

'I'm sorry,' I said quietly to Yelena as we rode onward and away from the sheep.

'There's nothing to be sorry about.' She paused. 'You know what makes you dangerous, Lerris?'

'Me, dangerous?'

'You,' she affirmed, glancing back toward the three who followed several lengths back and lowering her voice. 'You just do whatever needs to be done. You do it with as much force as you can.'

'That's practical. You do it the best way you can. If you have to do it, then do it. And if you don't, then don't.' I was embarrassed and started looking at the road ahead, for sheep, for kaystones, for anything.

The hills got flatter on the road to Dasir, and the sun got hotter, and the light breeze died down.

*Kaaa* ... *cchwwww!* I rubbed my nose and tried not to sneeze again.

Jylla's sneeze wasn't much more delicate than mine.

With the lower hills, the packed dark clay of the road had turned drier, redder, and dustier.

*Kaaachewwww!!!*

'You have an impressive sneeze,' offered Yelena.

'Thank you.' My nose was running, reddish from the dust that seemed everywhere.

'It's been a dry year, this side of Kyphrien,' she went on. 'That causes the dust. But it's better than the mud.'

Between coughing and sneezing, I wasn't sure that dust was preferable to mud. Being an order-master is helpful for keeping away flies and bugs, but it doesn't do much for dust. I itched everywhere and wondered if *The Basis of Order* dealt with itches. That was the problem, though. When you need to learn something it's late, often too late. I sighed and resolved to read through the book that evening.

With each step, the dust rose. And the dust rose and fell, and poor Gairloch's legs looked like he wore boots made of red dust. I just wore a cloak of the stuff.

*Khhaaa . . . cheww!*

Overhead, the late fall sky had turned a cheerful blue-green, and bright, and the wind had died, making the day seem warmer, warm enough that by mid-afternoon I was sweating, and thin lines of mud ran down my cheeks.

My backside was sore by the time the sun hung on the edge of the low hills behind us. Kyphrien already seemed impossibly far behind. I was still sneezing, and my nose was running red mud. My eyes itched, and I wanted to club Gerlis to death with my staff, just to get things over with sooner.

'We'll stay there.' Yelena pointed to a kaystone on the left side of the road that said 'Matisir.'

I squinted down the road toward a clump of buildings that seemed slumped between two low hills.

'The barracks is right off the square, if you can call it a square.'

Jylla sighed. Weldein flicked his reins.

Matisir contained perhaps ten buildings. One was the barracks for outliers and transient members of the Finest, and one was a long stable. Both were of mud brick covered with a thin layer of white plaster that the red dust and rain had turned an uneven pink. They had red-tiled roofs.

Across the flat grassless expanse that was a square, by the virtue of a large stone tablet commemorating something, was a two-story structure, also of mud bricks, but without the plaster, with a peeling signboard bearing a crude picture of a fireplace.

'That's the Old Hearth,' explained Yelena. 'Local herders go there. New recruits . . . once.'

We rode straight to one end of the stables. I took the smallest stall, and unsaddled Gairloch.

*Kaaachew . . .*

'Still sneezing, Order-master?' asked Yelena.

'Damned dust ...' I kept brushing Gairloch until he looked clean, and until I had a second coat of dust. Then I found some feed for him and a bucket of water. About that time a bell rang. The others – except for Yelena – had left.

'Our rooms are there,' she explained. 'You rate an officer's space.'

The room was narrow – less than five cubits deep and only about ten wide, with a single shuttered window – no glass, no hearth. I set everything on the floor. There was no table, only a single narrow canvas cot. If I had an officer's space, I felt sorry for Weldein, Jylla, and Freyda.

'Dinner won't be long, when the second bell rings.' Yelena left, carrying a bedroll and her knapsack.

First, I beat the dust out of my clothes, standing outside my room.

'You'll just get dusty tomorrow,' observed Weldein from a good dozen cubits upwind.

'That's tomorrow.'

I found the washroom and a pump, and used almost two buckets of water – cold water – to get the dust and mud off me. I blew red mud from my nose, dug red clots from my hair, and washed red mud from between my toes, from dust that had sifted down my boots. Finally, I got clean enough that the world didn't smell like red grit. Then I shaved. As I was drying, the second bell rang, and I had to scramble back into my clothes.

The three trestle tables were mostly filled, although the majority of those eating seemed to be outliers, both from their pale green leathers and shirts and the talk.

'... Gyster ... he says he's desperate enough for the Old Hearth ...'

'... anyone that desperate?'

'... swings a sword like a meat chopper ...'

'... know anything about the new wizard in Hydlen?'

'Berfir is an overgrown herder with a big sword ...'

'... which kind ...'

'... bread, demon-damn it ...'

Yelena gestured to me, and I found a seat on the long bench near the end where an outlier wearing a gold-braided vest sat in a chair.

'This is local leader Ustrello. Order-master Lerris.'

'I appreciate the hospitality.' I inclined my head.

'You are the one who bested the white wizard and discovered the secrets of the wizards' roads, are you not? The ones no one else has been able to ride?' Ustrello appeared short, but broad, with white mustaches and shoulders that many oxen could have wished for.

'I was fortunate enough to do so.' I felt embarrassed about having told Yelena about the roads, and then discovering that no one else could find them. That was another unfinished project, although it had lost its urgency when I had killed Antonin.

Yelena smiled.

Ustrello inclined his head to the woman between us, with hair in which blond and silver intertwined in a long braid piled on top of her head. 'This is my consort – Tasyel.'

'Is this the famous wizard, the one who did all the marvelous things, and the one with the strongest pony in the world?' She looked from Ustrello to me, as if in confirmation.

'Gairloch will be pleased to know that he is the strongest pony in the world, and I am pleased to meet you, Tasyel.'

'Is it true that you have an invisible sack that can never be emptied?'

I groaned, shaking my head. 'You have met Shervan?'

'Shervan?' Both Ustrello and Tasyel looked puzzled. Yelena smothered a grin.

'I stopped in Tellura when I first came to Kyphros. I had ... cast a spell over some of my possessions ... so that I would look like a less tempting target for bandits. When I took something out of a spelled saddlebag, one of the outliers – his name was Shervan – said I had an invisible sack.' I shrugged. 'I tried to explain, but he was telling everyone about my miraculous sack.'

Ustrello laughed. 'I have not met Shervan, but I have met his story. All the outliers tell it. I am almost sorry to learn the truth.'

'There is certainly more that the wizard is not telling, or he would not be a wizard.' The leader's consort winked at me.

'Alas ... the truth is sometimes discouraging.'

'Yes ... but you have not eaten, and we would not let anyone, especially a famous wizard, go away hungry.' She picked up the huge serving dish and thrust it at me. From the smell it was some form of curried goat stew.

'Thank you.' Curried, peppered goat or not, I was hungry and took a helping almost as big as those of the outliers.

Yelena handed me a long basket, and I broke off a suitably impressive chunk of dark moist bread that was still steaming.

'And the olives, they are also special.' Tasyel pressed a small bucket of olives on me.

As I took a handful, absently, I wondered about the little thief that Fuston had wanted me to catch and punish. 'They look special.' I dipped the bread in the goat – it was even hotter than Rissa's burkha. My forehead broke out in sweat, and I noticed that Yelena had taken a small bite, and a much smaller serving than I had. Her eyes twinkled.

'We're famous for our goat!' Ustrello almost had to yell over the voices from around us. 'Nowhere in Candar is it as hot! Tasyel makes the very best.'

Tasyel beamed, and I swallowed, reaching for whatever was in the pitcher in front of Yelena. Bread without the goat and the fruity fermented teekla helped. I only felt as though I had swallowed half a chaos wizard's fireball.

'You like it?'

'I've never tasted anything like it anywhere.'

Ustrello beamed in turn. Yelena covered her mouth. I ate some more of the bread before I took a much smaller second mouthful of the goat. My forehead still beaded in sweat.

'The wizard, he eats pretty good, better than you fancy soldiers.' Ustrello jabbed at Yelena.

'He's a wizard. I'm not,' countered Yelena, chewing another mouthful of the good bread – without spiced goat. 'He's used to dealing with fire.'

I was also hungry. I hadn't eaten that much for breakfast, not as early as I'd gotten up to see Krystal off, and not that much cheese and biscuits at midday. So I kept eating, but had to take another large chunk of the bread.

'He ate it all.' Tasyel gestured for the casserole dish and dumped it back in front of me.

I took a second, smaller serving – and more bread.

'After all, he is a wizard.' Yelena rolled her eyes.

'Where are you going?' Ustrello asked.

In between mouthfuls, I answered, 'To do some wizardly things.'

'That is what one would expect from a wizard,' affirmed Tasyel. 'Wizards must do those things which the rest of us cannot, and that is why they are wizards.'

It made sense in a way. Ustrello nodded at her wisdom, and I kept a straight face, glad to keep what I was really up to not too obvious.

'What do wizards do when they are not being wizards?' asked Ustrello when I had finished the second, smaller helping.

'Different things. I am a woodworker.'

'Do you carve things?'

'I make furniture, mostly, chairs, tables, desks, wardrobes . . .'

'Amazing, he is a wizard who does useful things, too.'

I tried not to choke, and nodded, then took a sip of the pungent teekla.

Eventually, I struggled out of the cheerful chaos and wandered through the twilight back to my narrow quarters, wondering how Krystal was doing.

I got a candle from my pack and, yawning, used my striker to bring it into flame. I began to flip through *The Basis of Order*. As I suspected, there wasn't anything on dust, although there was a passage on itching that wasn't much help, since it pointed out that most itches felt worse with an 'unordered' mind. Great! Itching disordered the mind, which made the itching feel worse. But there was nothing on remedying the causes of itches, at least not from what I could see with a quick flipping through the pages.

For lack of quick results, I decided to go back to the introductory sections, the ones that had bored me so often I'd never really grasped them. The first few pages were still boring, but I did find something more interesting partway into the introduction.

'Pure order cannot nourish life, for living requires growth, and the process of growth is the constant struggle to bring order out of chaos.' I wasn't sure what it had to do with Gerlis, but it had to do with boredom. I'd always seen order as boring, but what if I substituted pure order in my equation? I couldn't make the connection, exactly, but I wanted to think about it.

I didn't get too much farther, ending at a paragraph which concluded:

'. . . order must embody chaos, and chaos order.'

That was too arcane for me, almost a boring truism. After blowing out the candle, I curled up to sleep, ignoring the voices outside.

'. . . excuse for a horse . . .'

'. . . not knock-kneed like yours . . .'

'. . . what do wizards do? You know, Sergel?'

Thankfully, it was quiet when I woke, quiet and gray, with the hint of a chill drizzle from flat clouds.

Breakfast was not quite so noisy as dinner, but with enough of a din that I was glad for the quiet of the road.

On the way out of Matisir, Yelena asked, 'How is your stomach?'

I considered. 'Fine. How about yours?'

'Too much curried goat.'

'You didn't eat that much.'

'You,' she said wryly, 'don't have to eat it in dozens of different ways at every outliers' barracks in Kyphros.'

The mist kept the red road dust down. Gairloch only had a red coating for half a cubit up from his hoofs, but it clung to him more because he was hairier than the sleeker troopers' mounts.

That was the way the trip went. Lots of riding on long roads with few travelers. Lots of quiet, with some words between.

Yelena brought us into Dasir late the next night, where we stayed in yet another barracks with talkative outliers. Dasir was a town, unlike Matisir, and like most Kyphran towns I'd traveled through recently, it had the same roads covered with red dust that clung to everything, even in winter, which was hotter than summer in Recluce. The mist hadn't lasted; the dust had begun to rise again. The white-plastered houses roofed in red tile were generally squarish with few outside windows and centered on garden courtyards, and their white plaster was pink also.

After Dasir, the road got straighter, emptier, and the hills more barren, with a few scattered goats, the kind that made for bounties or dinner, assuming anyone could catch them. That night Yelena supervised dinner – dried meat, cheese, and tea that tasted metallic from the pot – at a waystation in the middle of nowhere. I shared my bag of dried peaches.

'Nice to have dried fruit,' mumbled Weldein.

'There are some advantages to traveling with a craft-master,' suggested Yelena.

I had to orderspell the water twice. That's how brackish it was.

A day later, Weldein pointed to the next kaystone – Jikoya.

'Wait,' was all he said.

A smaller, and poorer, version of Dasir – that was Jikoya. The white-washed plaster of the houses was graying, and the roof tiles were often cracked and some were missing. Some children were barefoot and ragged. I felt my warm jacket and looked at them. Goats ran free.

'What about the goats?' I asked, recalling that uncontrolled goats were food and/or bounty, according to the autarch's laws.

'People here don't pay that much attention to the laws. They're too poor, and the autarch is far away,' said Freyda, riding almost beside me.

There was a barracks – of sorts – attached to a house. I slept on the floor, on my bedroll, rather than trust the vermin-infested straw pallet. Even so, and with what wards I could muster, I had a few reddish bites when I rolled to my feet the next morning. I understood – at least somewhat – the autarch's willingness to trade Jikoya to save trained troops.

Breakfast was hot porridge, and it was hot, which was about all it had to offer. I found grain for Gairloch, and he munched happily enough.

From Jikoya, the old, old road south ran toward Lythga, and that took two days. Camping in the desolate hills with the low wind howling off the not-too-distant mountains was more restful than sleeping in the Jikoya barracks, and not much colder, although I found both Weldein and Jylla shivering and stamping the next morning.

'Cold?'

'You wizards never get cold, do you?' asked the young man.

'Sometimes, but it gets colder than this where I'm from, and it certainly gets colder up north, in places like Spidlar and Sligo.'

'They can have it,' said Jylla, huddling close to the small fire.

I shrugged, wishing I could wash up, but there had been no water, outside of a single plains pothole, since Jikoya.

I did have some of my hoarded redberry and shared it with the others.

'See ... wizards do have some good surprises!' Weldein stated, munching on cheese and spraying some forth with the words.

'This wizard ...' grudged Jylla.

Gairloch wasn't that happy about the lack of water, but he got to drink at another pothole, as Yelena predicted, by mid-morning.

Late in the afternoon, an irregular line of trees appeared on the southern horizon.

'That's the Sturbal River. It's just a stream. Circles west and south around the High Desert. Weren't for that, and the old mines, Lythga wouldn't be there,' explained Weldein.

A good kay outside of Lythga, the narrow road joined a wider one that stretched to the east to the town and southwest along the Sturbal.

Yelena gestured to the east. No kaystone marked the approach to Lythga, and the road was rutted with old tracks. Even the shoulders had deep gouges half filled with red dust and sand. I looked at the gouges and then at Yelena.

'It used to be a mining road. They took copper, and silver, and a little gold from the mines, but it's all gone now. Has been for centuries.'

The gouges looked old, and I probed them with my order senses. I couldn't tell much, only that they had been there for a long time.

After climbing a low hill, Gairloch whuffed, thirsty. On the slope down to the Sturbal and the narrow stone bridge were two roofless log squares that had once been houses. A short cedar grew in the doorway of one. Next to the bridge was an even smaller roofless structure.

'The old tollhouse,' explained Yelena. 'That's how they paid for the bridge.'

On the other side of the stream, a deep gash in the land with only a narrow ribbon of water, were more roofless houses, with desert scrub and cedars growing in and around them.

The road turned northeast, following a twist in the Sturbal, and I glanced from one ruined building to another for nearly a kay. There was a square, with a pedestal that had once apparently held a statue, and three buildings on the northeast side. One had a sign with a pickax crossed over a sword. The second had crossed candles, and the third was boarded up.

Yelena reined up outside the sagging stables behind the Pick and Sword.

Lythga made poor Jikoya look as prosperous as Kyphrien itself.

'Have you been here?' I asked the others.

The three troopers shook their heads.

'It's been five years,' said Yelena. 'I hope it's the last time.'

So did I, especially after a boiled bear dinner that made cold cheese seem wonderful. Weldein and I shared a room whose floor sagged more than a sailor's hammock. But I did sleep – after a lot of work with wards to deal with insects.

Weldein watched my muttering over the wards, shaking his head.

The next morning was gray again, with more drizzle that wasn't rain and that didn't bring much moisture to the ground. I was stiff, but the stiffness left as we rode eastward until almost noon, with brief stops to water the horses. Sometime near noon, Yelena picked a spot on a point that was almost a sandbar in the stream where we could eat and let our mounts graze on the sparse grass and drink. Gairloch preferred the leaves of one type of scrub, but they seemed harmless.

I gave Jylla the last of the white cheese.

'Thank you. You're not bad for a wizard. I can even see why the commander likes you.'

I shrugged. I hoped so.

I was the last, as always, to remount for the ride to the Lower Easthorns, now looming reddish-brown and close enough to touch. It still was mid-afternoon before Yelena reined up – perhaps half a kay from the beginning of the road across the lower pass. The sunlight filtered through thin, hazy clouds above the plains to the west and south behind us, the plains that rose higher to the south until they became the High Desert of southeast Kyphros.

'I hope your task is easier than the last time we parted so.' Yelena inclined her head.

'So do I, Leader Yelena.'

Weldein gave me a salute as they turned away, and I nudged Gairloch toward the entry to the lower pass road. I only looked back once, and they were already dots on the road.

The road at the beginning of the pass was narrow, not much more than a dozen cubits wide before it dropped down into the narrow stream that had so little water that I could have stepped across it. The streambed was a good four cubits below the road surface, and the smoothed and curved surfaces of the boulders and stones around which the stream flowed showed that it often was wild and deep. The road itself bore hoof prints, even an oxen track, and recent droppings.

Gairloch stutter-stepped through the natural rock gates, but the steep rock walls curved away from the road and stream within a dozen rods, and the road began to climb.

*Wheee . . . eeee . . .*

'I know. It's no fun carrying all those tools, and you don't have any company, either.' I patted him on the neck.

On the way, when we got to a straight section of the road, with no one around, I practiced setting up my shields, the kind that shuttled light around me. While no one could see Gairloch or me, I couldn't see anyone else either, and had to use my very rudimentary order senses to feel my way along.

Gairloch couldn't see anything, and he shortened his steps. I patted him again, offering him a little sense of order, but I wanted him to get used to it again before we had to use it for real. The shields only worked for light, and that meant if he whinnied, anyone could hear us. They could also see hoof prints. Magic doesn't solve all problems. It would be nice if it did, but it doesn't.

After a while, Gairloch's stride lengthened a little, and he stopped being quite so skittish. I released my hold on the shields and took a deep breath. We'd covered less than a kay. It was a slow way to travel.

'Good fellow.'

As we climbed and as the sun dropped, the road got colder. Both my breath and Gairloch's began to steam in the late afternoon. Higher in the low mountains, I could see patches of snow. I stopped and pulled on my heavy jacket, although I didn't close it.

After about another ten kays, the road stopped climbing quite so steeply in a long flat valley filled with a mixture of brown grass, short cedars, boulders, and heaps of snow on the north side of the boulders and cedars. The road was dampened clay, and most tracks had faded with the melting of the earlier snowfall. Some of the grass had been cropped short, but in the dimness, I could see no sign of sheep or goats.

Yelena had said there was a waystation, and there was, although the ancient door had rotted off the heavy old iron hinges, and the sod-grass roof clearly leaked when it snowed or rained – at least I assumed the damp spots and depressions in the dirt floor were from natural moisture.

Door or no door, I wasn't that cold. Even a little order-mastery solved that, but cold food was another thing. Cheese was all right cold, and so was the bread, but after nearly an eight-day, I was missing Rissa's cooking. I even missed my own cooking.

I let Gairloch graze for a while, then fed him some grain and led him to the spring behind the waystation. I looked at the road to the east, which continued to climb into the Lower Easthorns, then dragged him back to near the waystation where I unrolled my bedroll in a sheltered corner. I slept, without dreaming.

# X

# West of Arastia, Hydlen [Candar]

Gerlis takes out the small polished glass and sets it in the center of the cream-colored linen that covers the portable table, centering it carefully. Then he walks to the tent entrance and peers out through the canvas flap.

'Orort, I don't wish to be disturbed – except by His Extraordinarily Supreme and Willful Mightiness, the Duke.'

'Yes, ser.' The guard inclines his head, and by the time he lifts it, the tent flap is back down. He swallows.

Inside, Gerlis sits on the polished white oak stool and stares at the screeing glass, ignoring the sweat that beads on his forehead and the heat that slowly builds in the tent.

First, white mists appear in the glass, then a wavering image, which Gerlis studies. Five dusty riders plod down a narrow road. The lead rider is a Kyphran officer, accompanying a figure on a smaller horse.

As the image wavers and fades, Gerlis frowns. 'Danger from a few Kyphrans?' He wipes his forehead. After a time, he stands and walks to the corner of the pavilion tent, where he lifts a bottle of wine and takes a single long drink.

'Turning already . . . curses of the power . . .' He takes another drink before he sets the open bottle back on the top of the closed single trunk that doubles as a second table beside the narrow cot. Then he walks back to the table and sits down.

Again, he concentrates, and is rewarded with the mists, and a second image – that of a slender balding man in a tan uniform with a sunburst pin upon his collar.

Gerlis frowns. 'The sundevils . . . spells trouble . . . but not for a time.' He gestures, and the glass blanks. 'Not until after Berfir holds Hydlen firmly.'

For the third time, his eyes fix on the glass and call for an image – that of a thin man in the colors of Hydlen who sharpens a long knife and looks over his shoulder toward the setting sun.

Gerlis nods at last.

'. . . friend Cennon . . . assassins yet . . .' His words to himself are barely a whisper.

He lifts his left hand and gazes at it. 'The left hand of the Duke, and many will rue it.' Whitish-red fire flickers from his fingertips, and he smiles. Far beneath the meadow, the earth rumbles, and shortly the grasses beyond the tents ripple in the windless afternoon.

# XI

A cold wind blew through the door, and scattered snowflakes danced into the waystation. A thin carpet of snow lay inside the doorway.

I climbed out of my bedroll, somewhat stiffly, and struggled with a few scraps of wood and some twigs I collected from the scrub bushes. Before too long, a small fire burned, heating water in my single battered pot. I needed tea or something.

Gairloch had whuffed and whinnied the whole time I gathered wood and twigs, and I went back out and untied him.

*Whheeeee . . . eeeeee . . . eeee.*

'I should have untied you first? Is that it?' I led him to the spring, and then let him browse as he could while I used my pot to make too-strong tea to go with biscuits that had gotten hard enough to use my chisels on. Instead I dunked them in the tea, ignoring the tea-smoky taste. Then I had some raisins and the last of the olives. Olives don't travel that well, except in brine, and brine's heavy.

My washing up was cursory, with no shaving, since I wasn't likely to sweat, not with the chill wind off the higher peaks and the scattered snow-flakes reminding me that it was almost winter, although the pass was never supposed to be closed by snow. Or not for long, because it was so far south.

I looked at the clouds before I went back into the waystation and stood in front of my little fire. While order-mastery did keep my body from getting too cold, a fire helped, too.

A small piece of older cedar wedged in the corner of the near empty wood bin caught my eye, and I wriggled it free. It wasn't that long, perhaps a third of a cubit and maybe three spans wide, but it had been rough-sawn at both ends, and discarded as too short for firewood, I guessed. The grain was even, and while I warmed myself as the fire died down, I took out my knife and began to experiment. Carving hadn't been my greatest strength, and it could use some improvement.

A face lay under the wood, but whose face it might be remained to be seen as my carving progressed. I couldn't tell with the little I did before the fire died and before it was time to head onward toward Hydlen. Then I fastened my jacket and packed the cedar into one of the bags on Gairloch.

Gairloch whinnied. His breath steamed, and the whiteness mixed with the snow flurries.

'Let's go, old fellow.'

The road climbed gradually, and the snow got heavier. I had a sense that it was not going to get too heavy, but I worried, since it was beginning to stick on the road and especially to build on the scattered patches of grass and on the cedars.

So Gairloch put one hoof in front of the other, and I worried, and we traveled east until we reached the top of the pass. We didn't rest there, not only because of the snow, but because, according to Yelena, the descent was longer, and the road twisted more. I didn't want to be too high in the hills if my senses were wrong about the amount of snow.

For a time the snow got heavier, but the wind dropped off, and the flakes fell almost straight down. A light blanket of white coated just about everything, Gairloch's mane included, until I brushed it off.

Then it stopped, but the air remained still, and the only sounds were Gairloch's breathing, my breathing, and the stolid clop of one mountain pony's hoofs.

The white blanket got blotchier, with boulders sticking through, and the snow began to slide off the bowed branches of the trees, mostly cedars in the higher sections of the road. In time, the way followed another stream, narrow and with only a trace of water, but the trace became a brook, and then a stream as the road wound its way lower.

*Whheeee . . . eeee . . .*

'All right. You're thirsty. We'll stop, but not here. Down there where the bank isn't so steep.'

I guided Gairloch toward a flattened space by the stream, mostly clear of snow. The little that remained was melting away, although the sun remained hidden by the woolly gray clouds.

The earth thrown loosely over blackened branches, the rodent tracks, and the scrapes in the ground showed others had camped there, though not too recently. I walked Gairloch down to a sandy bank, and he lapped the water greedily.

'Easy . . . easy . . . That's cold water.' I knew. I touched it with my finger, and it was cold enough to chill right to the bone, order-mastery or no order-mastery. Cold as it was, it smelled clean, with just a hint of evergreen resin.

After he drank, I gave him a little grain before I remounted and continued downward on the road to Faklaar.

Somewhere on the way eastward, I noticed the change in the trees. On the far west side of the Lower Easthorns had been cedars, twisted low cedars clinging to the reddish and sandy soil between rocks and boulders, with only patches of grass, and scrub bushes.

I was seeing oaks now, black and white, with softer woods, and an occasional lorken tucked into a grove – good supplies and healthy trunks for a woodworker. The trunks were straighter, and some were old – older certainly than the impressive trunks in the woods south of Land's End in Recluce and some of those Recluce trees dated back to Creslin and Megaera – the mythical Founders. The trees in Hydlen felt older, even if they weren't bigger. But the trees of Recluce reportedly had been planted by the ancient order-masters. That would have given any tree a certain advantage.

Trees or no trees, I kept riding, and the clouds eventually broke enough that once or twice in the afternoon there were patches of sunlight.

# XII

## East of Lavah, Sligo [Candar]

After drawing back the drapery that covers the shelves of the rough book-case against the cottage wall, the man in brown smiles.

His eyes stop on each volume, as if to drink the words and the knowledge within.

'What you could tell . . .' He laughs. 'What you do tell. What you are already telling!' Then he shakes his head. 'For so long, so long, you have been hidden.'

The clopping of hoofs on the hard ground outside drifts through the half-open window by the crude door. Sammel lets the cloth drop across the front of the case, leaving what appears as a draped but narrow table.

He turns and walks to the door, which he opens. He steps out and stands on the crude stone stoop, looking westward toward the small river valley that holds the town, although Lavah is more of a hamlet than a town.

On the stoop he waits for the two figures who have tethered their horses to the rude hitching rail beside the first of the irregular stones that form a rough walk to the cottage door. The high thin clouds turn the sun's golden-white light into a bright grayish-white.

'Greetings.'

'Greetings be to you, Master Sammel.' The thin trader walks toward the cottage.

Sammel steps inside and walks to the crude table, where he picks up a single scroll.

'What is there of value in a scroll?'

'This one contains a way of separating natural waxes and fats. It will give you a means to make better candles.' Sammel hands the scroll to the trader.

'Better candles? When they have gas lamps on Recluce? And good oil lamps in Freetown and Hydolar?'

'How many candles are sold every year? How many people buy lamps and how many buy candles?' Sammel shakes his head. 'People will pay more for better candles.'

The thin trader nods his head. 'Aye . . . I suppose so. Theryck would pay for it. He's the renderer in Tyrhavven.' He sets a pouch on the table and steps back.

Sammel leaves the pouch where the trader placed it.

'Master Wizard Sammel, begging your pardon, ser, but what do ye suggest we do about the Duke's taxes?' The shorter trader glances nervously from the man in brown to the doorway of the small cottage.

The cold light coming through the window glistens white.

The trader wipes his forehead and tugs at his salt-and-pepper beard.

'I doubt that Duke Colaris will be worrying about trying to collect taxes in Sligo for much longer.' Sammel's voice is smooth and deep. He smiles politely.

'What's that mean?' The shorter trader halts his pacing by the door to look at the balding wizard.

'Refuse to pay his taxes. He has no claim over Sligo.'

'An' maybe not, but he's got an army, and that's something we don't.' The thin trader studies the white shaft of light coming through the window, and finally lifts his arm through it. The sparkling white dust motes dance, and the sunbeam shimmers enough to cast faint shadows on the dark walls.

'Then wait,' counsels Sammel. 'Make an excuse to his tax-collectors. There will be more than enough chaos in Freetown to keep them and the Duke busy before long.'

'You saying that Duke Berfir's goin' to strip the hide right off old Colaris? Don't see how as that can be, seeing as Colaris's got near on twice as many troops.'

'Then why do you bother to consult me? You know more than I do.' Sammel's voice remains calm, almost soft. He smiles a warm smile, focused into a distance the others do not see.

The thin trader glares at the shorter one by the door.

The short trader looks at the floor. 'Beggin' your pardon, ser. That be not so. You know more, but we don't know enough to know what we don't know.'

'That was well put, Master Trader.' Sammel chuckles, a warming sound, and looks at the hearth, on which the fires seem to intensify their flames and heat. 'Duke Berfir has a strong wizard, perhaps not strong enough for all eventualities, but strong enough to hold the south against the autarch. Duke Berfir also has weapons that spew fire. They are terrible weapons, and little that Duke Colaris has will stand against them in the open field.'

'What's to keep Duke Colaris from making such weapons?'

'Nothing – except he has not the knowledge to construct them. Knowledge is power, especially for a ruler. That's a lesson that has been forgotten.'

The short trader looks at Sammel. 'Why you telling us this? What's in it for you?'

'For me? Call it the love of knowledge. Say that knowledge is a friend who was buried too soon and for too long.'

The shorter trader rolls his eyes.

'Think that I am mad, do you? Watch!' Sammel thrusts a hand, index finger extended, toward the glass of water on the table. From the water a line of fire rises and unfolds into a flower. Then it vanishes. 'All vanishes except knowledge.'

The two traders shake their heads.

Sammel looks at the two, and his deep-set eyes glow. 'You think that I am just a mad wizard.'

The two step back involuntarily.

'What is the knowledge of the price of a spice worth? The knowledge of the value of a cargo? You deal in knowledge, and you cannot see its value? You purchase knowledge, and you cannot see its power?

'Knowledge is my friend, and my ally, and he is far more powerful than any Duke, far more powerful than even the Emperor of great Hamor.'

'Beggin' yer pardon, Ser Wizard . . . we never said it wasn't so.'

'Then I would ask you not to roll your eyes at me, Ser Trader.'

'No, ser. No, ser.'

Sammel watches as the two back out the door.

Once the sound of hoofs fades, he laughs.


# XIII


On my ride through the hills of Hydlen on the road beside what I later discovered was the Fakla River, I was reminded once again that everything took longer than I planned – whether it was a desk or a trip.

The road, despite the intermittent sleet and freezing drizzle, was passable, and with his heavy coat, Gairloch plodded on in stride. I brushed the ice off my cap and jacket, sniffled through the cold, and tried to keep the dampness away.

The scattered trees turned into forests, with clearings, first for grazing, and then for fields, though they were but turned stubble in the winter drizzle. The huts I passed were snug enough looking, with thin lines of smoke from stone and clay-caulked chimneys, but small.

In the air the faint smell of burning wood mixed with the underlying hint of rotten leaves, and, occasionally, the resin of evergreen needles. I rode past one stolid soul, pulling a cart, and nodded. His eyes fixed firmly on the road, he trudged by me, his face blank, his beard tangled, and his boots squshing through the rain-softened clay that was not quite mud. On the cart were two lopsided gourds, one gashed.

*Whufffff* . . .

I patted Gairloch, glad I was riding and not walking, as we continued eastward.

Faklaar stood at the first wide bend in the river, where the hills and most of the woods ended, and the high river plains began. In the late afternoon's winter drizzle, the clump of houses and the inn and store recalled a damper version of Howlett, the town where I had first met Justen. The inn at Faklaar stood in a swamp of churned earth, with muddy planks leading from its main door to the store next door and to the stables behind.

I wasn't thrilled about the place, but I wasn't going to learn much by skulking around, and, besides, people get suspicious of those who avoid other people. So I rode Gairloch past the newly painted sign that displayed a platter heaped with a brown steaming mass and back to the stables.

The stable girl looked at me. 'Pony's same as horses. Two coppers, three if you want a cup of grain.' Her ragged hair barely covered her ears, and her bony knees protruded from holes in overlarge trousers cut raggedly over wooden clogs.

'All right.'

'Before you stable him.'

'I'm supposed to trust you?'

She shrugged. 'I steal from Jassid, and he beats me. Don't take beatings for three coppers.'

I dismounted, trying to avoid the worst of the mud and horse droppings and dug in my purse for the coppers. I gave her four.

She looked at me.

'End stall?' I asked.

'Nope. You can take the corner one there, though. Small enough that Jassid won't double-stall.'

'I'm Lerris.'

'Daria. I'll get you the grain. Good stuff.'

While she walked toward a set of large barrels, I led Gairloch into the low-ceilinged corner stall. Daria was right. The stall was narrow enough for Gairloch, but it was dry, and relatively clean. I racked the saddle and began to brush him, after setting my bags and staff in the corner.

Daria returned with a large measure of grain.

'He bite?'

'He never has.' I paused. 'Except once. He kicked and bit a liveryman who whipped him. That was before I got him.'

'Don't like whips.' She shivered as she poured the grain into the manger.

Gairloch whuffed and began to eat.

'Stableboy! Where's the stableboy?'

Daria scuttled out into the yard.

After brushing Gairloch, and recalling Justen's handling of our stay in Howlett, I checked the hayloft. It was dry, and looked halfway clean.

'What you doing?' demanded Daria as I dropped from the stall half-wall to the ground.

'Checking the hayloft.'

'You've been around.'

'Some.'

'Better than the inn,' she said.

'You sleep there?'

Her eyes narrowed. 'Don't sleep with nobody.'

I shook my head. 'I didn't mean that.'

'No. Live out at the edge of town. Ma cooks for Ystral. The stew's better than the chops.' She left almost before she finished speaking.

I threw an ordered light shield around my staff and supplies. What people couldn't see, they were less likely to steal. Then I walked across the muddy splattered planks to the inn. The door was pine, not evenly planed and not varnished. I knocked the mud off my boots, and used the boot brush no one else had.

A bulky man with a short gray beard and a stained leather apron looked like he owned the place.

'Are you the innkeeper?'

'None other. Ystral, at your service. You don't want a job, do you, young fellow?'

'No. I wanted a meal and a place to sleep.'

He smiled the innkeeper's smile.

'Bed is half silver, and the fare's simple but good. Four coppers for the stew, five for the chops, and good chops they are, too.'

'How about the stable?'

'Three for a horse.'

I smiled. 'How about for me, sharing the stall.'

'Three if you go for that sort of thing.'

I handed him three coppers. 'My horse gets lonely.'

'Takes all kinds.' He took the coins, still smiling, and moved toward two soldiers in crimson-trimmed grays.

I eased away. The public room at the Overflowing Platter was none too large, less than twenty cubits on a side, and the air was greasy, smoky, and reeked faintly of horse and sheep droppings carried in with the mud and dirty boots.

There was a small table on the wall where I could watch the door, and I took it. The table, pine-finished with years of grease, wobbled, and one of the back braces on the chair was cracked.

'Beer or berry?' The woman rubbed a damp hand across a grease splotch on her gray shirt.

'Berry. Stew. How much?'

'Two for the berry. Stew's four, and you get half a loaf.'

'Stew.' I showed a silver, but held it.

'Pay when you get the berry.'

'All right.'

She was gone, back to the kitchen, and I studied the others in the room, trying to extend my hearing to pick up what I could.

'. . . beef pies . . . better than fowl . . .'

'. . . Berfir never hold Hydlen . . . only a herder with a long sword from Asula . . .'

'. . . tell him I want real chops . . . come back and spit him over his own fire . . .'

'. . . pretty face and waggles those lace-covered titties in front of 'em and they think she's a lady . . .'

I tried not to blush or to react too strongly to what I heard, but little had to do with other than the commonplace.

'Here's your berry.'

The mug came down on the grease-polished wood with a slight thump, and I handed over the silver. I did get four coppers back.

'Stew coming up. Next trip.'

As I watched, the two soldiers came in and sat three tables away. I tried to listen, but the serving woman was back.

'Here's your stew and bread, fellow!' She waited and scratched her stomach.

I forced a smile and offered her a copper, getting a smile in return.

'You're all right.'

Daria had been right. The stew was good, and the bread wasn't half bad. The redberry had been badly watered, and I orderspelled it, which made it blander, but safer.

I concentrated on listening, extending my senses toward the two troopers.

'. . . stay away from the chops . . . dog meat from what I hear . . .'

'. . . better than the goat those Kyphrans eat . . .'

'. . . say Berfir's wizard is like the great old ones . . .'

'... Colaris couldn't fight his way out of a Temple ... still wants the valley ...'

'... take the Ohyde over our knives ...'

I frowned and took another mouthful of stew. People were talking, just talking, and there wasn't much to most of it. I kept listening and eating, slowly.

'... Stenafta ... daughter's something, I'd bet, get beneath those stable clothes ...'

Was Daria Stenafta's daughter? I sipped another mouthful of the redberry and tried to hear what the troopers said, but they just ate.

'... these aren't chops! Sliced mutton no matter how you cut it!' The muscular man in a stained blue shirt stood up and flung the platter at the serving woman, spraying her with grease and mutton.

She cringed, and the muscular figure turned without looking at her. Ystral scuttled into the public room.

'Innkeeper! When I order chops, I want chops! Not sliced mutton!' The man in the blue shirt stood half a head taller than Ystral.

'You have the best we have, ser,' Ystral offered evenly.

'Charging for chops! Theft! It's theft!' His hands reached for the inn-keeper, shaking the smaller man. He grabbed for Ystral's neck with a lurch.

As I watched, the big man's hands waved, and his mouth opened with almost a gurgle. Then he sank to the floor, red welling across the blue of his shirt.

Ystral stepped back and wiped the knife on the fallen figure's shirt.

Ystral turned to the cringing serving woman. 'It's your fault. Clean up the mess. Get this carrion out of here.'

Neither soldier said a word. The gray-haired one lifted his mug and shook his head. The younger one chewed on a corner of bread.

Ystral walked out toward the front of the inn, and the buzz of conversation resumed, even while the serving woman tugged at the body of the man who had complained about the chops.

I didn't feel like eating more, but I forced myself to finish the stew, taking one slow bite at a time.

'... don't argue with Ystral ... kill you as anything ...'

'... and I told her we'd go to Sunta, and she could get her finery sewed by the tailor there ... but, no, she said that it had to be Worrak or Hydolar itself ...'

'... say he used to be a trooper ...'

After finishing the stew, I eased back to the stable, having heard nothing useful, at least directly. I was bothered, somehow, that the soldiers had just watched and done nothing. And that Ystral had neither smiled nor frowned.

It was still half light when I pulled my bedroll and *The Basis of Order* up into the hayloft. I could hear the rain falling, again, and I had to shift my bedroll once to avoid the drops from the big rafter.

I used the striker to light the candle and tried to read a few pages.

'. . . the world works to buffer order and chaos, for seldom does it allow unalloyed order to meet the spirit of chaos unfettered by any material. Such a buffer is the basis of life. When the angels and the demons of light fought, their spears were pure, and the very stars in the skies were rent and torn. So is it always when unalloyed and opposing forces meet . . .'

That wasn't terribly interesting. So I closed the book and took out the length of cedar and carved for a time, but it was slow, and I couldn't quite see the face beneath the wood.

Besides, my eyes started to feel heavy after that, and I finally put the knife and cedar away, blew out the candle and put it into my pack. Belatedly, I set wards and went to sleep with the sound of the rain – trying not to sneeze from the hay.

My dreams were strange, something about traveling down roads I didn't know, with a silver-haired woman offering advice I didn't want and couldn't understand.

I woke with a start, the wards tingling in my skull, my fingers grasping for my staff.

Outside, the sky was barely gray.

'Easy!' Daria backed away.

'You surprised me.' I lowered the staff and shook my head.

'Didn't mean to start you up.' Daria eased into a cross-legged position on the planks of the hayloft floor. Her breath steamed.

'What are you doing here?'

'Come early. Ma has to get here. Jassid pays me half copper an eight-day if'n I'm here 'fore breakfast.'

I extracted myself from my bedroll and set aside the staff. After pulling on trousers and boots, I shook out my jacket and put it on. My breath steamed, and I wasn't shivering, not quite.

'You sleep outta your clothes. That safe?'

'Probably not. But it's more comfortable, and my boots last longer if they and my feet get to breathe.'

'Feet don't breathe.'

'Your whole body breathes.'

'You some kind a teacher? You use that staff like they say the black ones do.'

'No.' My stomach twisted at the statement, and I frowned. I wasn't a teacher, but I didn't want to get into explaining about myself. Because I'd carried the black ordered staff of Recluce, I had been a blackstaffer when I'd started my exile, technically a dangergeld where I could return to Recluce if I satisfied the Brotherhood, but I didn't see myself ever doing that. Anyway, blackstaffers weren't exactly popular in Candar. 'I'm a woodworker. Sometimes, I have taught apprentices.' That was certainly true enough.

'You from Kyphros?'

'I just came from there, but I was born a long ways away.' My system didn't protest too much at that evasion. 'Why do you want to know?'

'Ma says women run Kyphros. That true?'

'The autarch —'

'What's an autarch?'

'She's the woman who rules Kyphros. The head of their . . . army is a woman, too. So are most of the officers.' I began to roll my bedroll up.

'Yeah. The black blade. What Jassid calls one of 'em. He was a trooper for the old Duke on the coast. Said she killed couple score. Wish I could do that.'

'Do you want to tell me why?'

She looked at the planks.

'Jassid – or someone else?'

'. . . kill . . . the bastard . . . 'cept Ma have no coins. Khali'd starve. Pa died long time ago. Drowned in a fight.'

'He was a soldier?'

'. . . used to tell us stories 'fore the crops went bad. Signed for the bounty – the rebel Duke on the coast. That was 'fore the new Duke in Hydolar. One duke, another, same thing.'

'Jassid . . .' I mused.

'Don't say nothing. He'll beat me. Ma can't do nothing.'

I thought as I strapped my bedroll tight. 'I promise. I'll say nothing.' But I might not have to say anything.

'Shouldn't said nothing . . .'

I touched her shoulder, briefly, realized that she was older than she looked, and offered a touch of order and reassurance.

'You're one those teacher fellows. I knew it.'

'I keep your secret. You keep mine.'

She nodded, and was gone down through the opening to the stable below.

I carried my things below, shaved quickly at the water pump, quickly enough to cut myself, and was checking Gairloch when a thin black-haired man, his face scarred from old burns on the left side, appeared by the stall. 'You the one who slept here last night?'

'Yes.'

'I didn't see you. I'm Jassid. This is my stable here.'

'I paid Ystral, and I was here. There's my bedroll.' I offered a smile, extending my senses to the man. I tried not to recoil at the amount of chaos in his system. I even reached out with my senses, then drew back. He was so touched with chaos that any attempt to change him wouldn't work . . . unless it killed him.

He just stood there, as if expecting something.

I nodded and put the blanket on Gairloch, then the saddle. When I looked up from cinching the girth, Jassid was gone.

I didn't want to enter the Overflowing Platter again. So I fed Gairloch, and we rode out into the drizzle, leaving Faklaar behind.

Should I have killed Jassid by removing the chaos from his system? Could I have done it? I frowned. Had I done so, would the next stable-master have been any better?

Did I have any right to kill a man because I thought a stable girl had been abused? Did I have any right not to do something?

I wiped the dampness off my face and turned Gairloch toward the muddy track north toward Sunta. The air was still, and the acrid mustiness of graying leaves grew even stronger as the drizzle continued.

Gairloch tossed his head, and I patted his neck.

That I hadn't done anything for Daria bothered me. She'd asked me not to do anything, but it still bothered me. Yet the thought of acting like an ancient angel bothered me. Who was to say my vision of the angel might not be someone else's demon of light?

I watched the road, and Gairloch plodded along, and I continued to think about Daria and Jassid, and Ystral, wondering why some people enjoyed hurting others so much, and having no real answers. I'd already discovered that order and chaos had little enough to do with morality, but more with the mechanics of the world.

*Wheeee . . . eeee . . .*

I patted Gairloch again. What he'd said made as much sense as anything.

# XIV

## West of Arastia, Hydlen [Candar]

The ground rumbles, and a slight swell of earth runs eastward through the valley, swaying tents, ruffling the scattered clumps of grass and the branches of the scrub trees at the eastern end of the narrow valley.

The screeing glass on the table vibrates and hums.

Gerlis rubs his forehead and frowns, glancing over his shoulder toward the northeast. When the shaking of the ground subsides, he looks into the glass again. The mists form, and in their center is the figure of a half-bald, brown-haired man in brown robes, his belt a soft rope tied in an intricate knot. The air around him seems to sparkle, although the man in brown stands in the middle of a room empty except for a draped wooden case filled with volumes of books, a pallet bed, a chair, and a table with a single lamp. His eyes are closed.

The white wizard watches the image for a moment, frowns again, then gestures. The image fades. He looks at the copy of the scroll purchased from the hermit wizard by Berfir, the one with the mixing method for the rocket powder.

'Overgrown herder still . . .' he mutters. 'Thinks a coronet and a blade make a duke. Or that fancy weapons can stand against chaos.'

The rumbling sound of another heavy wagon carrying dried brimstone north to Telsen echoes across the valley, but the wheels do not shake the ground.

Gerlis glances back at the glass, where the mists part to show the image of a young man wearing a brown shirt and brown leather trousers, and riding a mountain pony, a dark staff in place of a spear or lance.

Gerlis shakes his head, almost sadly. 'Poor fools . . . all of them. None can stand against the chaos of the earth . . . nor those who wield it.'

His eyes flick to the charred handle of the dagger on the trunk by his head, and a faint smile crosses his face. The smile fades, and he takes a deep breath. The white wizard's eyebrows knit, and he concentrates once more, this time bringing up the image of a bubbling spring, yellowed steam rising from each set of bubbles.

Another slight shudder rocks the ground under the carpet in the center of the pavilion tent, and, again, the screeing glass hums.

Gerlis smiles momentarily, before his brows knit in further effort, and the ground shakes. In the glass, the spring waters bubble even more furiously, and the surface is cloaked in yellow mists.

The ground beneath the valley groans.


# XV


Sometime around mid-morning Gairloch carried me from the muddy slop of the track from Faklaar onto a firmer road composed mainly of small stones and gravel set in a clay as hard as rock. About then the rain lifted into low gray clouds. The wind picked up, enough that the trees swayed in the wind, but the air still smelled acrid and musty.

Huts gave way to small cottages and stubble-turned fields set off with split-rail fences, alternating with tree-covered hills – presumably local wood lots. In short, the countryside became more ordered, and Gairloch carried me more quickly. The mustiness in the air gave way to wood smoke.

Midday found us just beyond another unnamed village on a hillside over another stream I had never known existed. Gairloch found grass, some actually with a trace of green, and I ate hard biscuits and harder cheese, and the last of the dried peaches. I wished I'd brought more dried fruit, and even dried meat, tough as it could be. Instead, I had hard cheese and biscuits – plenty of both.

Then we traveled on, under a colder, drier wind.

The first hint of a larger town was a brown haze over the hilltop; the second was a line of trees bordering a fair-sized river; the third was a raised causeway leading to a stone-pillared bridge across the river. The stone-paved causeway – wide enough for two wagons abreast – ran through lower-lying fields filled with graying hay stubble.

I edged Gairloch to the right as two oxen pulled an empty farm wagon off the bridge.

'Gee . . . eee . . .' The drover had a light goad, but held it loosely. The oxen seemed to respond to his voice alone, unlike a lot of horses. Gairloch stepped around two women carrying baskets in slings and onto the bridge.

'Handsome lad . . .'

'. . . always looking, Nirda. Clersek is nice enough.'

'You have him, then.'

'And maybe I will.'

From the central span of the bridge, squinting against the sun that hung just above the town, I could see the walls of Sunta, not so impressive as those of Jellico or Fenard, but of solid gray stone. Another short causeway led from the edge of the river across low-lying muddy ground almost to the walls themselves.

The southern gates to Sunta, while guarded, looked almost rusted open, and I doubted they had been closed in years. At the outer gate, one of the guards, a thin man in brown leathers with a crimson sash, motioned to me. 'What do you have there, young fellow?' He pointed to the bigger pack.

'My tools, ser.'

'Tools?' He raised his eyebrows.

'Chisels, planes, a small crosscut saw, an adz head, that sort of thing. I'm a woodworker.'

'Let's see.'

Since he didn't radiate chaos, but more a bored look, I decided not to create shields and disappear. That would certainly have the whole city looking for me, based on my experiences in Jellico. I could always disappear, anytime short of someone putting chains on me.

I got down and started to unfasten the pack.

'That's enough,' he said as the smooth wood of the saw grip appeared. 'Why are you coming to Sunta?'

'To seek out a journeyman position.'

'Pretty young for that, aren't you?'

'I have to start sometime, and there was no room in the village.' I shrugged, then gave a self-conscious grin.

'Good luck, fellow.' He waved me on. 'The craft quarter is off to the right of the main square, just beyond the Temple.'

'Thank you.'

I climbed back on Gairloch and looked at Sunta as if I'd never seen a big town before. Inside the gate, the street was paved in a fashion, with flat stones of all shapes, pieced together and roughly level. Some urchins walked alongside.

'... show you the best inn in Sunta ... just a copper, ser ...'

'... you want more than an empty bed, ser, I'll show you where to find it ...'

'... they're all Kyphran goats, ser,' declared a taller youth with a scar over his eyebrow and a knife at his belt. 'Best you try the Black Skillet.'

I frowned. The older youth didn't press or jostle. I slowed Gairloch

with a gentle tug on the hackamore. 'A Kyphran goat? How is a
Kyphran goat different?'

'You an outlander, ser?'

I nodded. My accent was obvious. 'Montgren way.'

'You got goats there?'

'Mostly sheep. Famous sheep.' I still wasn't about to forget my
work with the sheep of Montgren – or the serious Countess Merella.
I grinned. 'But smelly sheep.'

The youth grinned back, then erased the smile professionally. 'Sheep
or goats, they're the same. The ones that run free, they're the smart ones.
The ones that are penned or slaughtered, they're the Kyphran goats.'

'I fail to see.' I did, but it seemed better to play dumb. I could have
come from Worrak as well as from Faklaar.

'The Kyphran ruler says any goat that isn't penned can be killed or
held for a bounty,' explained the youth slowly, as he walked beside me.
The other urchins had peeled away, waiting for another traveler.

I decided he wasn't exactly an urchin, and let my order sense extend
around him, finding a touch of chaos, and a thin-linked mail vest under
the stained shirt and tattered herder's jacket.

'The Black Skillet, you say?'

'The very best, ser. And tell 'em that Hempel sent you.'

He turned away, but I was bothered. So the autarch's law about
free goats had become the basis for a derogatory term in Hydlen. And
someone was watching the city gates, if casually. All of it was to be
expected, in a way, I supposed, but it still bothered me.

Unlike the houses in Kyphros, a lot of those on the edge of Sunta
seemed to have thatched roofs, although the walls seemed to be plaster
over a basketlike frame of saplings. The plaster walls had a lot of
cracks and patches.

'. . . 'way . . . give way . . .'

I edged Gairloch to the side of the street as a two-horse team
rumbled past us and toward the gate. The slightly acrid odor of
tanned hides remained in the air, mixing with smoke, and other less
appetizing odors, some coming from the open sewer on the other side
of the street.

Gairloch picked his way toward the square, where a handful of carts
were scattered around a patch of browned grass and a few trees in
their gray winter leaves. In the center was the pedestal for a statue,
but no statue. Had it been for the previous duke? Or just empty from
neglect?

Beyond the square I could see two inns – the Black Skillet and the
Golden Bowl.

In addition to the black of the pan on the sign, the plaster walls of the Black Skillet were painted black, imparting a gloomy air to the place that seemed less than orderly. The yard was churned mud, and a smoky haze surrounded the building.

I rode past it and toward the Golden Bowl, which was situated another hundred cubits along the street off the square and seemed slightly higher – or higher enough that the yard was merely damp packed clay. The smoke seemed to come from the chimney, rather than through the windows and doors, and the plaster was dirty beige.

I rode to the back and found the stable. Two men wheeled an empty carriage into the big door at one end.

'Hello, the stable.'

One of the men pointed to a figure in the shadows. The other stable hand was a sullen-faced youngster with a bruise across one cheek. 'Two for the pony double, three single.'

I gave him three and got another corner stall half under the brace posts where a taller animal would have hit its head. Gairloch just whuffed as I unsaddled and brushed him.

I shielded my gear and made my way through the fading light toward the public room. The Golden Bowl appeared at least marginally drier and cleaner, and it hadn't been recommended by a shill – or whatever Hempel might be.

The smoke in the public room smelled like food, rather than pure grease, and there was a table along the wall. I'd gotten very fond of wall tables since I'd come to Candar.

'You're new here, aren't you?' The voice was warm, almost sweet, and the young woman – a girl not much older than I – had red hair and freckles. She also had a nice smile above the wide leather apron. She wore a wide bronze bracelet without ornamentation.

'I haven't been to Sunta. What do you have to drink?'

'Light or dark ale, redberry, green juice, and white thunder.'

'White thunder?'

'If you don't know what it is, you don't want it.' Her smile turned wry.

'I'll have redberry. What's good to eat?'

'Most of it. Tonight the kisha's pretty good, and it's cheap.'

'If you say so. I'll have it.'

'Good choice.' She wiped the table with a half-clean rag and then slipped back toward the kitchen.

I glanced around the room. In one corner were three older men, clustered around what looked to be a Capture board. As I watched, the other serving woman, red-haired also, but older and hard-faced, refilled all three mugs with light ale. She also wore a bronze wrist-band.

A man who looked to be perhaps Justen's apparent age, neither old nor young, sat in the other corner next to a woman with painted lips who leaned against his shoulder, even as they both ate.

The younger serving woman set two crockery platters on the adjoining table. 'That's six.'

'Six ... reasonable, but it must be dog meat,' laughed the thin man.

'No, ser. Not dog, not horse. Teilsyr got a good price on an ox.' The serving girl turned to me. 'Here's your redberry.' She set the redberry on the table, gently, without a thump, and offered another smile. 'That's three. I'm Alasia.'

I set out the coins.

'You come from a long way away?'

'Montgren,' I lied again.

'Are you going back before long?'

'Depends,' I answered.

A wistful look crossed her mobile features. 'Someday, I'd like to see a place like that. Travelers say it's peaceful there.'

'It is peaceful. It's mostly sheep. Sheep and more sheep.'

She offered a quick smile and was gone, responding to the insistent beckoning gesture from the man with the woman clinging to him.

I sipped the redberry, waited for the kisha, whatever kisha was, and listened to the conversations around the room, those I could catch.

'... keeps a nicer place, Teilsyr does ...'

'... fine if you're aware of the tariff ...'

'Try the burkha if you like hot, or the Kyphran chilied mutton ...'

'Real Kyphrans don't eat mutton; they eat goat and beans.'

'... young fellow a soldier, you think?'

'... could be. Trying not to be, maybe. Short hair, no beard to speak of ...'

Half consciously, I ran my fingers along my jaw, fingering the scab I had picked up shaving in Faklaar.

'... anyone could be anything these days ... Duke not much more than a herder with a deadly blade ... white devil at his side ...'

Clearly, the new Duke had some problems, at least with his image.

'Here's your kisha.' With the dish and a small loaf of oat bread, I got another friendly smile. 'That's three.'

I gave her five and smiled back, but she didn't linger long. Wondering if I'd see her again, now that she had my money, I shrugged and began

to eat the kisha, long strips of meat soaked in a mint-bitter sauce and
laid over flat green noodles. Not as good as burkha, but better than
the stew I'd had in Faklaar. As I ate, I continued to listen as well as
I could.

'. . . seen Stulpa lately?'

'. . . just his apprentice . . . said he's gone off . . . left with Duke
Berfir's troops . . . have to keep Freetown from taking the valley . . .'

'. . . need with a chemist?'

'. . . stuff the apprentice gave me . . . didn't work right with the
glazes . . .'

'. . . frig . . . noble Duke Colaris . . . bless his soul . . .'

A clinking sound at the corner of the public room – that and the
look on Alasia's face – alerted me. Three men barged in, and I threw
up shields. That meant I couldn't see anything, but they also couldn't
see me as I stood and edged toward the archway to the kitchen.

'There's a young fellow. Came in here. Brown-haired and wearing
browns. He's a spy. Where is he?'

Their information was right, and their techniques were unsettlingly
direct. I kept edging toward the kitchen, using my senses, and trying
not to touch anyone.

*Clunk* . . .

Someone's mug went over, probably because I brushed it.

'Why'd you do that, Hyld?'

'I didn't do anything! Clumsy oaf.'

I kept moving.

'He was sitting there,' offered Alasia. 'He left a while ago.'

The not-too-sturdy plank floor vibrated as the three stomped toward
the wall table where I had been.

'Sure, miss. His kisha's still hot, and he didn't finish it, and his
mug's half full. Check the back!'

One of the guards went running toward me, and I flattened myself
against the wall as he rushed past. I had the urge to trip him, but
refrained, instead swinging out and following him into the kitchen.

'You! Did you see anyone come this way?'

I could feel the cold iron of his blade as he jabbed it toward the
cook and the scullery maid.

'No, ser. There's been no one here, 'ceptwise Alasia and Rirla.'

'No, ser . . .'

'. . . who else'd be here in this friggin' heat?'

Predictably he marched right out the back door and into the yard.
I followed him.

Unpredictably, he turned around and ran into me.

'Oofff . . .'

His blade whipped through the spot where I had been. Half sitting, half rolling, I scrambled away and a line of fire creased my arm. Lips squeezed shut, I rolled from under his swings and rebuilt my shields.

'Frytt! Son of a bitch's out here somewhere. I sliced him! I know I did. He's another damned wizard! Won't escape cold iron, the bastard!'

I didn't think that it was that dark in the yard. I had seen him with my momentary lapse of shields. Since I couldn't see while holding the shields, and was finding my way toward the stable in my own private dark, I certainly wasn't in any position to know. With the fire in my arm, I wasn't dropping the shield to find out, or to find out why he was so upset.

Trying to step quietly, I almost tiptoed along the stable wall, ignoring the wild swings in the air as the guard whipped his blade back and forth. He headed toward the front of the inn. After all, who would hide in the closed stable?

I felt my way toward Gairloch. Sensing no one else around, I dropped the shield. It was dark, but I could see enough. The slash in my arm was more than a scrape, though not too deep, but there was blood everywhere. I fumbled through my pack and jammed some cloth against the wound. I thought it was a work shirt.

'Search the stable.'

'He's here somewhere.'

I took a deep breath and dropped into the corner under the manger, waiting to raise my shield until I heard steps. Holding shields was work, and I didn't have that much energy to spare. Gairloch snorted, but didn't step on me, tight as the fit was.

'Check the stalls!'

I swallowed and pulled the shield up around me, hoping I didn't have to hold it long, and keeping my lips closed, even as I tried to channel some order into the slice. The damned thing hurt.

'He's not here . . .'

'What about the corner stall?'

I could sense a figure looking into Gairloch's stall.

*Whheee . . . eeeee . . .* Gairloch sidled away from the intruder, shielding me even more.

'Not here. What about the loft?'

More scraping and scuttling followed, and I had to hold my nose to keep from sneezing as hay dust filtered down around me through the gaps in the boards overhead.

*Wheee . . . eeee . . .*

'Stuff it! Make you into dinner!' snapped a guard, so close he could have been standing over me.

So Gairloch whuffed instead. I wanted to hug him.

'Sure he's gone?'

'He's wounded. Would you stay around here? Can't be that good a wizard if he's running.'

'Where did he go?'

'Probably right out the front while you were yelling, Dosca.'

'No stuff in the stable?'

'No. Rudur checked that soon's he came in.'

'They can take care of the damned horse in the morning. He's not going anywhere.'

The voices moved off, and I lowered the shields, and tried to rest for a moment, still holding the shirt against the wound. I heard the stable hands walk by at least twice, but after the guards no one looked into Gairloch's stall.

As I waited, I wondered about Alasia, the serving girl who'd tried to cover for me. I hoped she hadn't gotten punished.

Later, when the stable got quiet and dark, I checked the arm again with my own order senses, using what little reserves I had to force out the traces of chaos. Then I ripped a section off the tail of the shirt and bound the gash.

'You shouldn't make so much noise.'

I looked up. Alasia smiled at me from the stall door.

'Probably not. Did you get in trouble for lying about when I left?'

'No. Not much.'

She was lying, and I could see the bruises across her cheek, and sense those on her arms, although she huddled under a woolen shawl.

'I'm sorry,' I told her. 'You didn't have to lie for me.'

Although I didn't have too much order to spare I lifted my good arm and touched her face, letting a little order trickle into the bruises.

'They said you were a wizard.'

I wasn't sure, but she seemed pale, despite the order I had given her. Was she one of those who were terrified of any sort of wizardry?

'I know just enough to get myself in trouble,' I admitted. 'Most of the time, I'm a woodworker.'

'Are you going back to Montgren?' Her voice was low, and she looked over her shoulder toward the flickering lamps of the Golden Bowl.

'No. I hadn't planned to go that way.'

'Will you take me wherever you're going? Please?' She glanced over her shoulder again, and she was trying not to shiver.

I let my senses run over her, trying not to be too intimate, but learning she was very feminine – and without a trace of chaos. Lack of chaos did not mean she was good – only that she was less likely to be thoroughly evil.

'You supposed to be going to the jakes?'

She nodded.

'Go, and come back.'

She scuttled toward the small building at the end of the stable.

One way or another I wasn't safe in the stable, not any longer. Clearly, they thought I had fled and wouldn't be coming back. Just as clearly, they'd be back to sell Gairloch and all my gear – probably at first light, although I didn't know why they hadn't tried that already, but I wasn't questioning that small bit of good fortune. I quickly saddled Gairloch, and after releasing the shield from around my staff and pack and bags, I hoisted them onto Gairloch. I tried to use my good arm.

As I was strapping down my bedroll, Alasia slipped back. 'You can't just ride out. There are guards there.'

I frowned. 'Why do you want to leave here?'

'You idiot!' She raised her left hand and pointed to the bronze band. 'Don't you know what that means? Teilsyr owns me. If he wants to sleep with me, he can. If he wants me to sleep with someone else, I have to.'

'That's slavery . . .'

'Bond servitude they call it. The Dukes like it.' She glanced toward the inn again. 'Please . . .'

'Are you ready to go?' I asked.

'What are you going to do?'

'You'll fall asleep. Don't worry.' I was concentrating, trying to recall how I had put the officers of the Prefect of Gallos to sleep. This time it was easier, but not much, because I was tired.

'Don't . . .' Alasia slumped into a heap.

With a deep breath I lifted her body, and I sort of enjoyed it, although I didn't have any illusions about her interest in me. I just laid her across Gairloch's saddle. Then I eased open the stall door and led Gairloch to the half-open stable slider.

Again, I raised my shields and walked Gairloch slowly through the yard toward the two guards leaning against the plastered side of the building to the left of the inn.

'You hear something?' asked one of the guards.

'Besides Teilsyr and his whips?'

'How's he get 'em?'

'Geras the leather fellow makes them.'

'I meant the girls.'

'Buys 'em. How else?'

I kept walking, patting Gairloch and trying to reassure him as we edged toward the street. No wonder she wanted out! Whips?

'Sure you don't hear something?'

'Look! Do you see anything?'

Gairloch's hoofs clicked on the stones of the road.

'It's out there. Somewhere across the square. You can hear better when it's dark.'

'I don't know.'

When we got to the other side of the square, I dropped the shield and eased Alasia's limp form in front of me and climbed into the saddle.

I turned Gairloch toward the northern end of the town and hoped that the gates there were as rusted open as the southern ones had been.

They were, and a single guard half watched, half dozed, as I struggled to hold shields around the three of us while we crossed the torchlit space. Gairloch even stepped more delicately, it seemed, but that might have been my imagination.

Less than a half kay beyond the walls, on the northern causeway, I dropped the shield. Although I was sweating, in the cold air, with the effort of almost continual order-mastery, I was exhausted and shivering. I fastened my jacket tightly and kept riding, letting Gairloch pick his own pace. He was the one carrying double.

Although it took a long time, we didn't go awfully far – only until I could reach a woodlot, or a grove – I couldn't tell. The grove was maybe three or four kays beyond the gate and the first one that wasn't close to a hut or a cottage.

I struggled to get Alasia down, perhaps more intimately than I should have. I was glad Krystal and Tamra weren't watching. After wrapping a blanket around her, I laid her on a pile of evergreen needles. I found some cheese and drank the last dregs of the redberry. It was turning fermented-type sweet, but it was still all right.

After a little while, I stopped shivering and started feeling merely exhausted and achy. The smell of the evergreens overhead helped.

'Oh . . . who . . .' Alasia jerked upright. 'What did you do?'

'I put you to sleep. That was so we could get past the guards. You're all right. I didn't do anything except carry you out of Sunta.'

'I don't fall asleep, just like that. And I don't faint. Even at the wrong time of month I don't faint. What did you do?'

'I told you. I helped you go to sleep. That's all.' I tried to make my words gentle, but my arm throbbed, and my head ached, probably from holding shields when I was exhausted.

'Where are we?'

'Probably four kays out of Sunta on the north road.'

She shivered and wrapped the blanket around her. 'I'm not dressed for traveling.'

'You said you wanted to go, and we couldn't exactly wait,' I pointed out. That got a slight laugh, a nervous one.

'How did you get by the guards?' she asked.

'I walked by.' My stomach twisted at the partial truth. 'I tried to make it so they didn't see us. One of them heard me, but the other said he was imagining things. They talked about Teilsyr and his whips.'

'I had to get away ... Rirla, she already has scars.' She shook her head.

'I'm sorry.' I shifted my weight from one buttock to the other, and winced as I put weight on the injured arm. 'Why didn't anyone search the stall?' I asked, trying to change the subject.

'They did – right after you went inside. That's how it works. They didn't see anything; there was nothing in your saddle. So you had to have your coins on you. Teilsyr's men come in. They claim you're a spy from Kyphros, and no one cares what happens.' She shrugged. 'You seemed too nice to be a spy. And too young. I didn't know you were a wizard. Are you really as young as you look?'

There was something she wasn't saying, but I was tired, and I couldn't figure it out, except maybe the distrust of wizards.

'I'm as young as I look. That's why I got sliced up by those thugs.' I yawned.

'You're not some wizened old man?'

'No. I'm a tired, wounded young woodworker who knows just enough wizardry to get in trouble, and I'm doing my best to help you.' I stifled a yawn. 'Are you all right?'

'I don't have any clothes for traveling.'

'I think I've got a shirt you can have. I'll dig it out in the morning. Just wrap up for now,' I told her. 'I need some sleep.'

'Are you sure we're away from Sunta?'

'Not far enough, but I need the sleep, and you could use some.' I yawned again, and my arm throbbed.

'I don't know.'

'Fine. This whole business has worn me out. You stay awake and listen for the innkeeper's guards.' I did set wards, almost out of habit, around the camp and around me. I mumbled 'Good night' to Alasia.

'Good night.'

I could almost feel sleep and exhaustion crashing over me. Almost immediately, I dropped into another dream where the silver-haired woman was trying to tell me something about the earth. She was a druid. At least, in my dream, she was.

*Wheeee . . . eeeeee!!!*

Gairloch's cry roused me straight out of the dream or sleep, but, for an instant, I was so tired that I just lay there.

*Wheeeee . . . eeeee!!!*

'Quiet . . .' hissed a voice. 'Damn you . . .'

*Wheeeee . . . eeee!!!*

I struggled up, just as Alasia climbed onto Gairloch, right beyond the edge of the trees. I hadn't even taken two steps before Gairloch bucked in a way I wouldn't have believed if I hadn't seen his reaction to the stable hand in Freetown when I'd bought him. Alasia hung on for perhaps two heaves before she was on the ground, moaning.

Gairloch settled down, and I gave him a pat on the shoulder.

Alasia tried to sit up, but her shoulder sagged in a way that indicated more than bruises. She wore my waterproof, about the only piece of my clothing that hadn't been within my wards.

'Sit still!' I snapped. 'That is, if you ever want to use that arm again.'

Her eyes were hard, and as cold as the white stars overhead. That I could see even in the darkness, since, like most order-masters, my night vision is good. She had loaded Gairloch with most of the provisions, anything that had been outside my personal wards.

I leaned forward, then away as I saw the glint of a knife in her uninjured hand. 'Do you want me to heal that shoulder, or keep the knife?'

'I'll keep the knife,' she grunted.

'If that's the way you want it.' I started to lead Gairloch away.

She raised her hand as if to throw the knife, but she shuddered and slumped forward. The knife thudded on the hard ground.

I dropped the reins and hurried to her. Between my order senses and my fingers, I could tell that she had broken both her upper arm and collarbone. How she had even moved was a wonder.

It took me a while to find some branches, and cut them. I wasn't exactly happy about using my good saw on resinous evergreens, but I needed to do something. Then I did a quick job of planing and shaping, and cobbled together a sort of sling that immobilized her bones. I offered her a little order for healing, but not much, because I had little to spare after little sleep and the night's events. I also didn't feel that charitable, not after her effort to rob me and steal Gairloch, even if she distrusted men and wizards. I'd tried to help her, hadn't I?

The sky was graying by the time I had eased her out of the waterproof and into the old tattered work shirt that I'd bled over. It might pass for some sort of work smock on her. Then I strapped the splint gadget around her. She moaned the whole time, but she wasn't really awake, either. The bronze bracelet was actually brazed in place, and whoever had done it hadn't been gentle, since there were white scars under it on her wrist. That made me feel worse.

I was still weak. So I did take a chunk of hard cheese and some order-spelled water from my canteen after that.

Then I packed up and lifted her into the saddle. I almost didn't make it, but struggled up behind her limp figure.

*Whheee . . . eeeee . . .* Gairloch pawed the ground.

'I know. She wasn't very nice, but I don't think people have been nice to her, either.' One way or the other, though, if I left her near Sunta, I had the feeling the story would be that I had kidnapped her, and I'd be wanted by more than Teilsyr's hired guards.

Gairloch plodded; Alasia moaned; and I hung on.

By the time the sun actually cleared the horizon, Gairloch was walking steadily northwest on the road to Arastia, perhaps another eight to ten kays away from Sunta. The road ran along the ridge lines, and while the woods came close to the road on the uphill side, the trees had been cut back on the downhill side to allow a view behind us and downhill.

The sky had begun to fill with high hazy white clouds, moving quickly from Easthorns, and the wind was chill. I could see goose bumps on Alasia's neck.

'Let me down! Let go of me.'

I wondered how long she had been awake, but didn't ask. I half let go, holding just loosely enough that she wouldn't fall.

'Oh . . .' She grabbed Gairloch's mane, and he, the ever-obedient pony, stopped. 'Ooooooo . . . bastard!'

I could sense the pain, but I wasn't feeling totally charitable. 'I'm not a bastard. You don't trust men or wizards, and you have decided that I'm both. You don't have to trust me – but you also didn't have to try to steal everything I owned.'

'You're just like all the others.'

'I could have left you. I've splinted and tried to help heal your arm, and I've carried you along as best I could.' I took a deep breath. 'Do you want to walk from here?'

'Where are we?'

'A lot closer to Sunta than we would have been if you hadn't tried to steal everything I own.'

'I did not. I didn't touch anything you wore.'

I laughed.

'It's true.' Her voice was low. 'I just wanted a mount and food to get away from Teilsyr.'

'I would have been happy to help you without being robbed.'

'And what would you have asked of me? Look what you did.'

'I didn't do anything. You did. Your arm and collarbone got broken when you tried to ride off on my pony.' I took a deep breath and swung down off Gairloch, taking his reins. 'I owe you something for trying to help me, but you're making it hard. Now . . . we've got to keep moving, and Gairloch's been carrying double for too long. Hold on.'

Alasia swayed in the saddle, but grabbed my staff for balance as Gairloch started up. She let go almost instantly. Gairloch and I walked onward, the sun at our backs.

'You don't understand,' she said, after a time.

'I do understand. You're indentured to Teilsyr. He abuses you, or threatens to. You want to escape. I agree to help you, which is not a good idea because I could be hung for theft, among other things. As soon as you find out I know something about wizardry, you try to steal my horse and provisions. Then, when I try to treat the shoulder you break trying to steal from me, you throw a knife at me.'

'You make me sound awful.'

'I'm not trying to make you sound any way. You make it hard on me.' I paused. 'Can you get down? It's your turn to walk, at least for a little.'

She let me help her down. She couldn't conceal the wince. 'I'm cold.'

I unstrapped the waterproof from the bedroll and fastened it around her much like a cloak. After standing like a statue until I stepped away, she continued to stare at me as I mounted Gairloch. I had to slow Gairloch because she didn't walk that fast, but I needed a little rest, too.

After another kay or so, round another turn, I heard hoofs and the creaking of a wagon. A bearded man drove the wagon, half laden with what appeared to be cabbages and potatoes, past us without even looking in our direction.

'Friendly fellow.'

'The men here are all like that. Did you expect him to smile and wave?' asked the redhead.

I think I had.

We kept alternating riding and walking, except I walked more than I rode, a lot more, and I had to hold the reins when Alasia rode, not to keep her from riding away, but to keep Gairloch from bucking her off.

Before mid-morning, we came to another stream through the woods. There was an open grass spot, and the remnants of a campfire. Alasia sat on a stump and watched me. I pulled out some cheese and biscuits, and let Gairloch drink and graze.

I didn't even ask Alasia, just set two wedges of cheese and some biscuits by her. She ate them quickly, leaving no crumbs, and I ate two myself.

'Would you like another?' I asked.

'Yes.'

I cut her two more, but she still wouldn't look directly at me.

'What are you going to do?' she finally asked.

'With you? I wanted to help you – that's all. So, I'll get you on the road to Telsen, and let you find your own way home, or wherever it is you want to go.' I sighed. I couldn't just do that. 'And I'll give you a couple of silvers to help, but I'm not going that way.'

'You still don't understand.'

'Probably not.' I ate another thin slice of the cheese and handed one to her.

'What did you do with my knife?' She swallowed the cheese in two quick bites.

'Left it where you threw it, I think.'

'You idiot. That was Teilsyr's. It was worth something. What am I supposed to use for protection?'

'You're probably better without it, then. At least they couldn't hang you for theft if they catch you.'

'Hanging would be fine. Teilsyr wouldn't be that kind. Not after what I saw him do to Rirla.'

'I said I was sorry. I never intended to hurt you.' I still felt guilty. While I didn't like Teilsyr at all and could understand Alasia's need to escape, I hadn't done anything – except put her to sleep. And I'd even warned her, but I felt guilty because she'd been hurt.

I brushed the few crumbs off my fingers and looked at the sun and then in the direction of the Lower Easthorns. All I saw was tree-covered hills. 'Get some water to drink. Wash up. Whatever. We need to keep moving.'

'You don't understand,' she repeated.

I never did understand, except that she thought that most men and wizards were never to be trusted.

I hoped that wasn't true, but it bothered me even as I watched her walk down the road toward Telsen late that afternoon. I'd called, 'Good luck,' but she hadn't looked back.

I'd let her keep not only the shirt, but the waterproof, and some of the cheese and biscuits – and I'd given her two silvers and some coppers.

She just walked toward Telsen, slowly, and she didn't look back once. I finally nudged Gairloch forward and toward Arastia.

What could I say? I'd gotten her free of Teilsyr, and she seemed to think that it was almost her due, as though it were my duty. Alasia wasn't chaos-touched, but, abused as she might have been, I still didn't think she had the right to try to steal everything she could. I wasn't Teilsyr, not even close.

My arm still hurt, and my head ached, and I wondered why I'd even considered traveling such a roundabout way to investigate Gerlis and his magical fires. All I had discovered so far was that sword wounds didn't heal all that quickly, even with order-mastery, and that not everyone liked Duke Berfir, and even fewer liked Kyphros and Kyphrans in general – or wizards. I'd needed to travel for an eight-day to discover that?

# XVI

## Nylan, Recluce

'Gerlis is working with the chaos under the Lower Easthorns. You can feel it from here.' Heldra walks to the window and looks through the wide glass at the Brotherhood's grounds, at the grassy hillside and carefully planted trees. Her fingers caress the hilt of the black blade she wears. Finally, her eyes rest on the harbor of Nylan below, focusing on the black pier and the single shimmering shield that appears as an empty berth to most onlookers in the mid-afternoon warmth.

'He's definitely stronger than Antonin.' Maris's finger runs over the map of Hydlen before him on the table. 'How did he ever come up with the rockets?'

'Gerlis? He didn't. Someone stole the idea and sold it to Berfir,' said Heldra.

'And who stole the idea? Who might that have been?' asks Maris.

'Sammel.' Heldra flushes. 'Sammel. He had the ability to have forged them, but he hasn't set up a smithy. That might be because he's finding it impossible to use order any longer. So I can't prove it. The carts are a local design, but the rockets could be ours, except Berfir's using local steel instead of black iron.'

'It's nice to know the infallible Heldra could have been wrong. Once, anyway.' Maris's voice sounds almost lazy.

'Maybe Berfir found someone to build them.' Talryn sets his goblet on the table with a heavy thump, squaring his broad shoulders. 'Once you have the idea, they're not that hard to make, not like precision cannon. That's why we've tried to keep ideas like that under shields.'

'Like killing that smith in Southport?' Maris raises his eyebrows.

'That was for playing around with cartridges and rifling. Jorol ordered that before I joined the Council. Still, it probably had to be done.'

'I'd still order it,' says Heldra. 'Can you imagine Candar with fire rockets, precision rifles, and white wizards? This war between Colaris and Berfir is going to be a light-fired mess. Even Dorrin had second thoughts about too much machinery loose in the world.'

'Those who followed him claimed that,' mused Talryn. 'I can't say that I've ever read anything that he wrote that states that, and he wrote a lot.'

'It makes sense. What are we here for, anyway? Just to nod and let the world go to chaos?' Heldra squints into the sunlight, then turns toward the two men, although she remains by the window.

'It may anyway, if Cassius is right. He calls it entropy.'

'Another fancy word from where he came from. It still means letting everything go to chaos, and that's not what Recluce stands for.' Heldra walks back to the curved table from the wide window.

'I wish I were as sure as you are.'

'All you have to do is feel the Balance,' snaps Heldra. 'It's real, and it's our job to maintain it.' She looks at Maris. 'Not just to make the oceans safe for traders.'

'I assume that means you'll immediately dispatch an assassin to kill Gerlis or whoever?' Maris fingers his square beard. 'And Sammel?'

'Killing Gerlis right now wouldn't do any good. Too many people know about the idea. But they're costly to make. Once the war's over, we can take steps.' Heldra smiles.

'You're betting that Gerlis won't last too long.' Maris leans back in his chair.

'He won't. The more power he gets, the shorter his life.'

'And the bigger the mess in Candar,' snorts Talryn.

'Unless Lerris dispatches him to save that woman of his.' Heldra walks back to the Council table.

'Krystal? I suppose that's possible,' muses Talryn. 'She might command the forces that would fight Berfir and Gerlis. But what about Sammel?'

'Sammel? I'll take care of it.'

'That's what you want, isn't it?' asked Maris. 'Get rid of Sammel. Have Lerris get rid of Gerlis. Have the autarch take over all of the Lower Easthorns. Have Berfir and Colaris destroy each other, and then send in a black squad to eliminate anyone else who knows about rockets.'

'It's not a bad plan.' Heldra glances back at the window. 'Who will even remember the fire rockets after that?'

'That still leaves Lerris and an even bigger potential chaos focus in Candar,' points out Talryn.

'What about Sammel?' Maris finally asks. 'How did he get into this?'

'He took the books when he left on dangergeld. We didn't think he'd stoop to theft.' Heldra sighs. 'I thought he had some ideals.'

Maris and Talryn exchange glances.

Finally, Maris coughs. 'What if it's gone as far as Hamor? Gunnar stopped by the other day, you know. He says that the Hamorians have improved their steel to where it's almost as good as black iron. Then there's the problem with their traders. Their ships are getting bigger and faster. And they're building a lot of steel warships – some with those new cannon – a lot more than they need on their side of the world.'

'Gunnar's trying to protect his son.'

'He didn't invent the Hamorian steamers, Heldra,' countered Talryn.

'And we have reports about their new cannon. I hadn't thought about the steel, though.' He fingers his chin. 'The traders . . . we can deal with traders.'

'Candar's a long way from Hamor,' states Heldra.

'Not with ships that fast.'

# XVII

After the split in the road, the route to Arastia turned almost due west generally toward the brimstone spring and Kyphros. Heavy wagons had left deep tracks, deep enough to remain after days of traffic.

Less than two kays after leaving Alasia on her way to Telsen, I reined Gairloch over as a pair of Hydlenese couriers rode past, their crimson vests flapping, heading east, probably toward Telsen and then to Hydolar itself. They barely glanced at me, although one checked the hilt of his blade as he rode past.

The hillside farms were more scattered, with larger wooded stands between them. The fields were either cut stubble or turned under for the winter.

I rode on, and wood smoke drifted over the road as Gairloch carried me westward. The road led me to a field filled with stumps with a huge mound of earth, from which the smoke seeped. Beside the mound was a tiny hut, and a man sat on a stool, whittling and watching while the contained heat turned the felled trees into charcoal for the smiths of Hydlen.

I reached back and felt in one saddlebag for the piece of cedar I had started carving and almost forgotten, trying to ignore the twinge in my arm. As I looked at it again, I could sense there was still a face buried beneath the wood and my first rough attempts, but not whose face. I replaced the cedar in the bag as Gairloch carried me away from the charcoal burner's camp.

Occasionally, the meadows scattered between the trees and stubbled fields held sheep, but the small holdings were infrequent, consisting of a hut, an animal barn, and perhaps a shed.

I got another five kays or so before the sun dropped behind the trees. My arm throbbed; my head ached; and my stomach growled. Gairloch was barely plodding along, and occasionally he tossed his head. The road was entirely covered with shadows by the time I found a stream and a sheltered grove that didn't seem to belong to anyone – at least not anyone too close by.

I didn't bother with a fire. After eating another few wedges of cheese and more of the rock-solid biscuits, my headache subsided, and my stomach stopped growling. Then I unsaddled Gairloch, and brushed him, not as thoroughly as I should have, and gave him a handful of the grain.

*Wheeee . . . eeee . . .*

He tossed his head, as if to tell me it was about time.

'I know, old fellow.'

He settled down to grazing and tasting various leaves, and I sat on a stone by the rocky bank of the narrow stream and tried carving the cedar in the dimness. That was not one of my brighter ideas. I had to stop almost immediately as the knife slipped toward my fingers and as the tightening in my wounded arm turned to throbbing. So, after putting the cedar away, I infused the wound with a shade more order, set wards, checked Gairloch, and climbed into my bedroll.

Although I recalled looking at the sky, wondering as the clouds crossed the stars where the angels had come from and what had happened to them, I didn't remember falling asleep. Nor did I dream, unless I didn't remember what I had dreamed. I woke with the gray dawn, and a strong wind out of the west, strong enough to rustle the leaves on the lowest branches and bend the treetops – and a chirping that drilled through my ears.

For a time, I lay there, quiet, but still tired.

*Twirrrppp . . . twirrrppp . . .*

I didn't recognize the annoyingly cheerful birdcall, and only saw a flash of yellow-banded black wings. I pried my eyes open. Gairloch chomped on some leaves from a shrub, some of the clumped grass by the stream. Then he drank.

The yellow and black bird perched on a shrub on the other side of the stream, its head cocked in one of those perky attitudes. People like Tamra who want to talk and sing first thing in the morning look like that damned bird. I got up early enough, but even I didn't feel like singing, especially after suffering through an attempted murder, attempted theft, and gross ingratitude.

'Shut up!'

*Twirrrppp . . . twirrrppp . . .*

Still, it helped get me out of my bedroll and staggering to the stream. The cold water helped more. By the time I could function, after drinking and eating a biscuit, the bird was gone.

I washed up and shaved in the stream, mostly by feel, and only cut myself once, despite the chill of the water. Mist began rising off the trees when the early sun struck them.

I washed out my underclothes and draped them over a bush, something I should have done the night before, but I could spread them across the saddlebags if the day turned out clear and they wouldn't take that long to dry. After dressing, I took out the brush and curried Gairloch again, and he sort of wiggled as I did so.

'I know. You deserve more of this.' With another pat, I put away the brush and began to saddle him and pack up. I had a few more biscuits, but still was in the saddle before the sun cleared the trees and struck the road.

The woods were hushed, and so were the first holdings we passed, although I saw one herder leading sheep to a lower meadow. Mist rose off the grass, indeed off any surface the sunlight touched.

Some of the winter-gray leaves glistened silver in the morning light, and I watched a hare nervously nibbling in a shadowed opening in the trees, his whiskers twitching, head flicking between each bite. Gairloch's hoof crunched on a stone or something, and, with a muffled single thump, the hare was gone.

Faint traces of wood smoke, and the odor of sheep, drifted across the road as Gairloch continued to carry me westward.

Sometime near mid-morning two men in tattered brown coats drove an empty rickety wagon pulled by a bony horse past me. The driver held the whip as we passed, but I could hear it crack in the distance.

I sensed the oncoming forces even before I could hear them, and I edged Gairloch into the trees, far enough in that we wouldn't be seen, but close enough for me to peer from behind a bushy scrub oak whose fall-yellow leaves had faded to winter-gray. My boots slipped and crunched acorns from the taller oaks that surrounded me every time I moved. I also stuffed my underclothes, mostly dry, into the top of my pack.

Three scouts rode over the low rise of the road first. After that came two or three squads of lancers behind a red banner with a gold crown. The lancers talked in voices so low I couldn't pick up what they said. One made some form of gesture, and the two beside him laughed, but the woman blade on the mount behind him unsheathed her blade and thwacked his mount on the rump. He yelled back, but they all laughed.

Nearly half a kay separated the lancers from the draft horses that followed, towing two-wheeled carts that looked like strange cannon, with two squarish barrels side by side. From the woods, I studied the cannon-carts for a long time. They were mostly made of oak, and beside the barrels were long thin boxes. More of the thin boxes were stacked on the wagons that followed.

I tried not to scratch my head, and to keep projecting reassurance to Gairloch, all the while extending my order senses toward the carts. The square-barreled cannon weren't even quite that. They were open at each end.

I reached for the boxes, and my senses touched cold iron. That gave me a jolt, and I almost said something, not that I probably would have been heard, not from more than fifty cubits away.

After trying again, I realized that the cold iron was shaped into cylinders pointed at one end, and blunt at the other, and filled with something that felt like chaos, or stored fire. But it wasn't chaos. There was no iron covering at the blunt end of the cylinder.

I frowned. Cold iron over chaos? Why would a chaos wizard use cold iron? Gerlis probably couldn't touch it, certainly not for long.

The wagons and carts creaked, and the wheels sank into the road, showing how heavy they were. Whatever they happened to be, the deep ruts I had noted earlier had come from something similar.

*Twirrrppp . . . twirrrppp . . .*

The black-winged bird I had seen earlier began to call.

*Twirrrppp . . . twirrrppp . . .*

An officer riding beside one of the carts heard the birdcall and began to look in my direction, then edged his mount toward the trees.

*Twirrrppp . . . twirrrppp . . .*

Muttering, just for good measure, I created a shield – around both Gairloch and me.

The birdcall stopped, and I waited in darkness, my senses extended to see what the Hydlenese officer did.

Someone called to him as he rode closer, until he was at the edge of the trees, not more than thirty cubits away from where I stood behind the scrub oak, holding Gairloch.

Whoever it was called again.

'. . . heard a traitor bird, but it's gone now. Thought someone might be out here . . .'

He swung at the leaves of the front row of scrub with the flat of his blade for a bit as he rode along, before turning his mount and returning to the road.

I took a deep breath and relaxed the shields.

*Twirrrppp . . . twirrrppp . . .*

Traitor bird, indeed. I put the shields back up, and the calls stopped.

The officer turned his mount back toward the side of the road, but more to the east of where Gairloch and I hid.

This time I left the shields up until after most of the carts had passed, thinking nasty thoughts about the aptly named traitor bird.

When I released the shields the last of the heavy wagons had passed, and there was an open space of another half kay between them and a detachment of foot, followed by a rearguard of two squads of lancers, again bearing the crimson banner with the crown.

*Twirrrppp . . . twirrrppp . . .*

Before the Hydlenese got too close, I found a pine cone, the heavy green kind that didn't mature, and threw it at the traitor bird.

*Twirrrppp . . . twirrrppp . . . twirrrppp . . . twirrrppp . . .*

I could see that force would only make the situation worse. I sighed, and put up the shields again, and the last of the Hydlenese forces passed without so much as a glance into the woods.

When I finally dropped the shields, and the road was clear in both directions, I listened for the sounds of the traitor bird, but apparently he had done his duties for the day – or knew I was ready to commit some form of violence.

After I climbed back into the saddle, Gairloch and I continued toward Arastia. Why were the strange carts and forces headed away from Kyphros? If Duke Berfir intended to take Kyphran territory, why were the soldiers headed the other way? Had I gotten turned around?

I looked at the sun, then at the hills. Was there a hint of higher ground, of the Lower Easthorns ahead? Once again, things weren't making much sense. First, the strange cannon devices ... devices I knew I should recognize, knew I knew, but couldn't quite figure out. There was something about the contained chaos and the iron ... something somewhere I had read ... but I couldn't remember.

I patted Gairloch, and my arm twinged. Most of the time, I just felt a dull ache. Once we were back on the road, I laid out the slightly damp clothes across the packs.

Close to midday, I saw the gray kaystone proclaiming that Arastia was three kays ahead and confirming that I had been going in the right direction. The road wound slightly uphill to Arastia, where the houses and buildings were all of dressed logs or planks, not plaster or brick.

The central square had a dry-goods store, a harnessmaker's, and the equivalent of a chandlery, plus an inn, bearing a sign of a huge white bull with fire coming from his nostrils.

I decided against eating in the White Bull, since my luck in inns hadn't been exactly wonderful, and tied Gairloch outside the chandlery.

Inside the red-painted double doors were the usual arrays of saddle-carried gear, which I walked past, glancing from one side to the counter along the other. A woman with brown hair piled on top of her head stood behind the counter, while a girl closed the door to the iron stove in the middle of the store. A faint heat radiated from the stove. The heat reminded me that the day had not been that warm, but the wind and chill hadn't bothered me that much.

'Travel rations?' I asked.

'Stranger, aren't you?'

I nodded.

'Thought so. Know most folks round here. Where you be from?'

'Out Montgren way.'

She frowned. 'You have much trouble on the roads that way?'

'I didn't come direct, but I saw a lot of lancers and carts on my way into town. I heard there was trouble.' I wandered over to the table that had cheese sealed in wax, and dried meat, stuff tougher than leather that had to be boiled to avoid breaking teeth, and a barrel of dried apple flakes. I almost drooled over the dried fruit. I'd gone through mine too quickly, and brought too little.

'Aye, the new Duke has his troubles.' She laughed. 'Old or new, there's always someone to fight.'

I shrugged. 'Why now?'

'There's those that say Duke Colaris must prove he is strong and take the mines in the hills south of the accursed ancient city. And there be those who say that Duke Berfir must slake the blood lust of them that gave him the gold circlet.' She snorted, and gestured toward the girl. 'Makes no difference to us. Our menfolk and the young girls who like the blade – they die no matter whose tale be right.'

'I haven't seen many dukes die in battle.'

'Aye, and ye never will.'

The brown-haired girl sat down in the corner next to a graying dog, which licked her face.

I grinned at her and the dog, but she didn't notice. I picked up a package of waxed white cheese. 'How much?'

'Two.'

'And the dried apples?'

'Penny a scoop, and a penny for a waxed bag.'

I took three scoops of the apples, as much as would fit in one of the bags, a bag of hard biscuits, the cheese, and four large grain cakes for Gairloch – bound in twine – and laid everything on the counter.

'Have any redberry or something like that?'

'I don't run an inn, young fellow.'

'I could hope.'

She reached behind her and produced a pitcher and a mug. 'Water's good, and it's free . . . leastwise for customers.'

I laughed. 'My thanks.' It was cool and good, and I drank it all. 'How much for this?'

'That'll be nine.'

After fumbling through my purse I came up with a silver. Most of the golds were in hidden slots in my belt. It doesn't pay to carry a heavy purse that clanks.

She took the coin and slipped it into her own purse, and handed me a single penny back. 'You traveled a long way, have you not?'

'Longer than I'd like,' I admitted.

'Be longer than that if you're a-heading to Kyphros.'

'Trouble there?'

'Aye. They closed the road to the brimstone spring. I used to take Varsi, there, for baths when she was a child. A sickly little thing she was, and the spring helped. The Temple ladies, they helped, too.' She shrugged. 'I'd guess they're all gone or killed. I hope Varsi doesn't need no baths this winter.'

I glanced toward the corner, but the dog and the girl had left.

'The older I get, the stranger things get.' She frowned. 'The new Duke, he's got his men, and ours, in the north and here in the west. Here, it makes no sense. That woman in Kyphros – she never started anything, but there's a new prefect, they say, in Fenard. That's because the old one lost the war he started with her. And this Duke Berfir, he's going to fight her and the fellow in Freetown together. Makes no sense, but what do I know?'

'When you put it that way, I can't give an answer. Dukes and folks like that don't think like us.' I had to shrug and smile. I picked up my purchases and turned.

'They don't think.' She paused. 'Well . . . take care, young fellow.'

'I hope to.' I closed the red-painted door carefully. After folding up the dry clothes, probably somewhat dusty, I packed my added supplies into one of the saddlebags – all but one grain cake and a handful of the apple flakes. Gairloch got the grain cake, and I ate the flakes on the spot. I dug out the older biscuits and gnawed through one and pocketed another before I mounted Gairloch.

On the way out of Arastia, I let him stop at what seemed to be a town watering trough and let him drink. As I stood there, I saw Varsi throwing a stick for the old dog, who didn't look quite so old. I watched, and Gairloch drank. Then we headed west.

That Gerlis or the Duke had closed the road to the spring didn't exactly surprise me. The next problem was getting around the guards.

Still, I rode nearly five kays without seeing any soldiers or guards. I passed homesteads, a handful of women walking toward Arastia, a youth leading a cart and horse – but no troops.

As the end of the valley began to narrow, I passed a crossroads that led south – presumably the alternate and rougher route that Ferrel had started out on.

I got halfway up the next hill before I ran into trouble. Three lancers stood under the tree. Another was mounted by the road.

'You can't go this way, fellow. The road's closed.'

'How am I supposed to get to Kyphros?' I asked.

The lancer smiled and shrugged. 'I'm sure I don't know. Not this way.'

The three under the tree laughed.

'So be a good fellow and just turn around.'

I didn't even argue. Instead, I rode Gairloch back down the road until it curved enough and I was out of sight. Then we went into the woods and stumbled uphill and around thickets. We even rode across some poor holder's fields, but at the edge, and no one came out, although I could see wisps of smoke from the chimney.

It took three times as long to cover the distance off the road, but eventually I got back on it beyond the sentries. I also had sap on my shoulder and a scratch on my cheek. I brushed leaves out of Gairloch's mane, and picked off the burrs I could reach as he carried me upward along the road toward the spring.

My ears and senses were alert, since there had to be more sentries, and if I ran into them I certainly couldn't play dumb again, not without running the risk of incurring some form of grave bodily harm.

At that point, I realized that, effectively, I was now a spy, and could be treated like a trooper – or worse. As a woodcrafter or even an order-master, I hadn't really thought about that. I should have, but I hadn't wanted Krystal to get fried like Ferrel, and I'd been able to handle the white wizards, hadn't I?

This was different. I had to find out something, not just escape or avoid the Hydlenese troops, and what I found out would affect a lot of people. I wished Justen were around. Instead, I took a deep breath and patted Gairloch. He whuffed, which wasn't that much reassurance.

It was late afternoon before I neared the valley that held the spring, and the odor of brimstone from the Yellow River had become particularly obvious in the near windless conditions.

The road began to climb steeply and bore right as it neared the opening to the valley holding the brimstone springs. I didn't wait to get too close to any sentries guarding the valley. Gairloch and I went into the woods on the left side of the road. My perceptions told me that the rise wasn't that steep, and that the underbrush wasn't especially thick.

Still, the sun had dropped behind the hills, or low mountains, when I peered through the last of the scrub oaks at the valley itself.

Under the rocky outcroppings at the west end of the valley, where the road from Kyphros – and Jikoya – entered the spring valley, was the spring itself. Beside the spring were the two stone buildings. One of them had probably housed the Temple sisters. I could sense tents and bodies there, but not well, because another low rise separated the grassy meadow just in front of me from the other end of the valley. Low cedar trees, no more than ten cubits high, covered the rocky ground.

I glanced around, then decided to wait until twilight arrived. So I tied Gairloch to a tree and dragged out some of the apple flakes, biscuits, cheese, and my canteen. The canteen held only orderspelled water, unfortunately. I sat on a rock and ate. I did give Gairloch some apple flakes, and he licked them from my hand, greedily.

When it had gotten darker, a soft almost purple darkness, filled with scattered insects, rustling leaves, and the ubiquitous smell of brimstone, I untied Gairloch. After drawing my shields around us while we crossed the meadow, I dropped them as soon as we reached the cedar trees, not wanting the white wizard to sense my use of order, especially after we reached the top of the low rise.

I stopped partway down the western side of the rocky rise, easing Gairloch behind a wide cedar. Almost a kay from us, still to the east of the spring, was a level space filled with tents. In the middle of the tents was a larger pavilion tent, one that radiated chaos and that ugly whiteness I could sense but not see, although it almost glowed in the darkness.

A low growling rumbled through the valley, and the tents swayed, and the ground under Gairloch trembled. I grabbed Gairloch's saddle, and he whuffed, though not loudly.

The rumble contained and radiated from chaos. What exactly was Gerlis doing?

Despite the growing coolness of the evening, I had to wipe the sweat from my forehead. I could feel the power welling from the white tent, and I was more than a kay away. So much power there was that I doubt he even could have sensed me, my poor abilities lost in that wave of chaos. I swallowed.

What could I do against that kind of power? Antonin had swatted me aside at first. Even in the end, I hadn't faced his awesome power, not really, only cut him off from its sources, and hung on until he died. And, in a way, I'd done the same thing with Sephya.

Gerlis had enough power in himself to fry me, even if I could contain him in an order bound. What could I do?

I kept thinking, but as the evening deepened I got no answers. Overhead, a patch of stars brightened as the clouds thinned. Cold and distant, they offered no solutions, and they almost seemed to say that they had no interest in me, or in Gerlis.

Looking back toward the camp, I began to probe around. There were still almost a dozen of the square muzzled cannon tubes, with the thin boxes of cylinders, and there was a space near the stone buildings, well away from everything else, where long flat pans, partly filled with brimstone water, lay on the ground.

I could also sense a huge stack of charcoal, and something else. All that confirmed that Gerlis, or the Duke, was using the brimstone to make powder. But what was the powder being used for?

Sensing around more, I could sort of trace the powder – and from what I could tell, it was mixed, then wet, and ground, then placed in the thin steel cylinders.

'Oh . . .' I felt like kicking myself. The cylinders were rockets, the kind used to destroy the white fleets centuries before. Or something like them. What had happened that Recluce no longer had mighty fleets? That was just another of the questions that hadn't been answered by either my father or the Brotherhood.

Did the Brotherhood still have rockets? Why were they showing up in Hydlen now?

Firebolts? No . . . Ferrel had been killed by rockets. I couldn't prove it, but it seemed all too likely. Rockets would be deadly in a confined space, like a mountain road or pass. With enough of them, the Hydlenese wouldn't have had to be particularly accurate.

As I considered the rockets, the valley floor groaned, and another trembling wave rumbled underfoot.

I didn't like it, but I sent my own perceptions beneath the valley, not that I could go very deep – just deep enough to sense the webs and flow of chaos that seemed to surround both the springs and the Yellow River itself.

Between whatever Gerlis was doing with chaos beneath the valley and the whole idea of scores of fire rockets, I just wanted to run, to ride like the demons of light were after me, but that wasn't likely to do all that much good.

I tried again to sense what the white wizard was doing, but could only gain the impression of shifting rocks and heat and more and more chaos, mostly natural.

In time, I rubbed my forehead, aching in rhythm with the throbbing in my arm. Gently, I turned Gairloch back the way we had come, back across the meadow and over the next wooded hill and down the road toward Arastia, and around the guards near the crossroads, although they weren't good guards. All of them were sleeping when we eased past sometime near midnight.

Then we took the side road, along the way Ferrel had probably intended to come. In that sense, I felt safer. The cause of her death wasn't unknown. It was just terrible. But with the wizard in his valley, and night all around me, I didn't fear the rockets.

I still didn't understand why the Duke of Hydlen was sending troops away from his border with Kyphros or what Gerlis was doing in the brimstone valley, but staying around might not answer the question, and might well lead to him noticing me.

So I rode slowly and quietly through the hills, trying to put distance between me and Gerlis. Overhead, the cold stars and their indifferent light began to vanish behind the growing clouds.

# XVIII

## East of Lavah, Sligo [Candar]

'Honored mage.' The taller of the two men in green bows, and almost clicks his heels. He glances around the modest room, taking in the table with the oil lamp on which some stacks of paper rest under a smooth stone, the draped bookcase, and the pallet bed and chair. 'I see no . . . apparatus . . .'

'Nor will you. I offer knowledge.' Sammel nods. 'What is your master's need?'

'The Viscount of mighty Certis has no needs,' says the shorter man.

'I beg your pardon. What might he desire of this humble seeker and disseminator of knowledge?'

'It is said that you may know ways of making firearms more dependable and of assisting the Viscount in the defense of his people.'

'You wrote something of the sort, did you not?' asks the short man.

'In a fashion,' answers Sammel. 'In a fashion.'

'So what have you to offer?'

'That would depend on the Viscount's needs and some small remuneration.'

'The Viscount does not pay. You serve.'

'In Sligo, the Viscount rules? I was not aware of that.' Sammel clears his throat.

'He will soon.'

The taller man gestures to the shorter. 'What Hendro means is that the Viscount may be forced to take measures against Duke Colaris to ensure the safety of his people.'

'I am sure, and I am also sure that he would not grudge a poor seeker of truth a handful or two of golds for knowledge that would help him achieve that.' Sammel steps forward to Hendro. 'Might I see your knife? The little one.'

Hendro looks to the tall man, who nods, and then extends the knife to Sammel.

Sammel takes the knife carefully, by the leather-wrapped hilt, holding it between two fingers. His eyes close, and a halo of white surrounds the blade, which begins to glow, rising quickly from orange to cherry-red to a white that begins to spark. Sammel opens his eyes, bends, and gently tosses the sparking blade into the cold logs in the hearth. Flames flare up, even as iron droplets fall through the grate onto the stones.

Hendro backs away.

'That is what one can do with knowledge.' Sammel smiles politely.

'I daresay you have made your point, Ser Sammel,' says the taller man. 'I know of no other wizard who can burn cold iron.' He looks to Hendro. 'I do not think the Viscount would grudge the mage his livelihood.'

'How would your . . . knowledge help . . . defend Certis against Duke Colaris?'

Sammel turns and lifts two scrolls from the table. Each is tied neatly with twine. 'This describes a way to preserve food.'

'Food! What does that have to do with firearms? This mage may be powerful, but what help is that, Julk?'

'How much time do your troops spend foraging?' asks Sammel. 'What if all they had to do was to open a container from a wagon? With food from the fall harvest – even in midsummer?'

'How much metal does that take?' Julk twists the corner of one mustache.

'Glass is better. The process is there for that, too.'

'But you mentioned firearms?' persisted Hendro.

'I did. Those ideas are less valuable, but since you do want them . . .' Sammel picks up a third scroll. 'This tells how to keep chaos from firearms, so that they may be used in all battles. It also allows faster recharging of both cannon and hand-held weapons.' He presents the scroll to Hendro.

Hendro looks at it, but does not open it.

'I will let you take those, and, if you are satisfied, you may reward me as you see fit. If not—' Sammel shrugged. 'I will provide knowledge to those who value it more.'

'I think that is more than fair, ser mage.' Julk bows, straightens, and takes the third scroll from Hendro, who blinks. 'I am certain you will be receiving the Viscount's thanks in a way that will ensure your continued . . . supply of knowledge.' Julk bows again, and so does Hendro.

'The preservation of food . . .' Sammel adds.

Both men straighten.

'It could prove useful in laying away supplies for a cold winter.'

'And a siege?' asks Julk.

'There will be no long sieges.'

The two from Certis exchange glances and bow again.

Sammel watches, a sad smile crossing his lips.

# XIX

After all – or what little – I'd discovered, I kept riding, until I could barely stay in the saddle. By then Gairloch was tired, too. I camped in the trees, between scrub and cedar, on the uphill side of the road, and took off his saddle. But I wasn't about to brush him. I used the wrong arm to carry the saddle, as the pain immediately reminded me.

How there would be anyone else on the road I didn't know, except locals headed to Arastia, and they would scarcely be traveling in the middle of the night. Still, some caution was necessary, and I had selected a spot not visible from the road.

I woke not much after dawn, stiff as a chair spoke. My head ached, and my arm throbbed and itched – at the same time. Gairloch was already chomping through the greenish leaves of the one kind of scrub bush he liked. It looked like a greenberry, but it wasn't.

*Wheeee . . . eeee . . .*

I could tell he was thirsty. So was I, but I could drink from the canteen and he couldn't, not as much as he needed. So I saddled him and packed everything together and rode until I found a brook another kay farther on. While he drank, I orderspelled more water for the canteen, and then washed and checked my arm. There was no sign of chaos, but the whole area around the scabbing gash was black and green. I added a touch of order and pulled my shirt back on. The itching got worse, and that meant that it was healing and that I wanted to claw it.

The overcast skies, the gusting wind, and the dampness of the air forecast rain. Before Gairloch had carried me another five kays, the first droplets fell out of the gray clouds. Another kay, and the drizzle turned into light rain. I started to look for the waterproof, before remembering I had left it with Alasia. I was going to get wet, but would the redhead have even cared? I still had trouble understanding how she, or anyone, could attempt to steal Gairloch without a trace of chaos. I also felt bad that I hadn't done something about the stable girl in Faklaar who had asked for nothing except understanding.

All the while the road turned and twisted uphill and generally west, though it twisted back east one cubit for every two cubits west it carried me. The air was thick and smelled of damp cedar and rain.

In time, the rain became a steady sheet of water, and we plodded onward. There was no reason not to keep traveling, since no real shelter appeared and both Gairloch and I would be almost as soaked standing under a cedar inadequate for shelter as plodding onward. One advantage was that if Gerlis had been following us with magic, he certainly couldn't so long as the rain lasted. White magic doesn't work well through falling water, but then, neither did a drenched woodworker and a soaked mountain pony.

The water seeped everywhere, down my neck, through my shirt, and off my knees and into my boots. Each hoof squushed, and each toss of Gairloch's head threw more water in my direction.

In retrospect, would it have been better to take the shorter route both ways? I didn't know. Some of what I had learned had come from meeting with people, sensing how the people reacted, although I would have been pressed to explain what that had added, and why. The shopkeeper in Arastia had told me about the troop movements, but the autarch had her own ways of discovering that sort of information.

I wiped the water off my forehead and out of my eyes. One thing I did know. A quicker return was safer, now, and that would get me back to Krystal sooner. I had no illusions about my getting back to my workshop for long. This latest white wizard was going to prove costly for woodworking, I feared, and I didn't really want to think about how it might affect Krystal.

The rain kept falling – through the morning, through the day, through the afternoon. As Gairloch carried me higher and deeper into the Lower Easthorns, the stream got noisier and wider from the rainfall, though the road was built at least three cubits above the top of the stream at the lowest. Some places, there was a drop-off of nearly ten cubits.

The rockets seemed like the least of the problems facing me. How could I deal with that much chaos? And what on earth had Gerlis been doing in that valley, to make the earth heave? Why?

Plodding through the rain, I worried that I hadn't found out more, but I'd been concerned about being discovered and not getting back with the information. As I worried, I got wetter, and the rain just kept falling.

Somewhere on the road, under a twin-peaked mountain, I found a way-station, like the first one I'd used on my way into Hydlen, without a door and with a sagging roof.

With the rain pelting down, it was definitely an improvement over camping out. I took one dry corner, and gave Gairloch the other.

Since there was some wood, I made a fire and had tea. The chimney didn't draw that well, and smoke swirled around – but didn't get too thick, since fresh damp air poured in through the open doorway.

I shared some of the apple flakes with Gairloch, along with a grain cake. Then I had to walk him down to the stream, and we both got wetter. After that I took off my clothes and wrung them out and draped them around, hoping that the air and the heat from the fire would dry them out some. My shirt, trousers, and drawers were soaked, as were my boots. My arm throbbed, and the scab itched.

After eating I found a part of my corner out of the wind and lit my candle. I opened the book – *The Basis of Order* – and huddled inside my bedroll in my corner. My staff was right beside me, since I didn't have to worry about innkeepers. I read for a long time, trying to find a key as to what I could do if I had to deal with Gerlis.

There were some hints – things like, 'there is power, and the control of power. Chaos unchecked can obliterate its would-be user. So can order. What an order-master must do is channel that power . . .'

Fine, I'd known that with Antonin. Knowing something is so doesn't necessarily help much. That was still the problem with the book, Justen, and my father. Everyone was perfectly willing to tell you the problem, and even what needed to be done – often in boringly detailed ways. They just weren't much help in telling you *how* to solve the problem. Just like the old children's tale about crossing the torrent on a rope. All they needed was a rope across the river. But no one knew how to swim the torrent to carry the rope across.

Great. I needed to channel power. How did one control and channel power? I went to sleep trying to figure that one out.

The rain still fell the next morning, but more like a heavy mist than a rain, and the stream wasn't as high. My shirt was dry, or close enough, but everything else was damp. I had spare drawers, those dried on the ride, and there was only a slight stain from the leather of the packs. Who looked at drawers? Drawers were like wood glues – necessary and boring.

Gairloch got two more grain cakes while I was dressing and packing

up, and I brushed him hurriedly before saddling him and leading him
out to the stream. He did drink a lot, and so did I.

I mounted. He whuffed.

The road twisted and turned, and got rougher, with more and more
potholes. The stream got narrower.

The cedars got shorter and farther apart, and no one rode or walked
the road besides Gairloch and me.

The drizzle turned into winter mist again, and the ice-damp wind
blew around and through us. The road twisted and turned, and rose and
fell. Finally, when it got too dark to see, we stopped and camped.

The next morning I got up, and started all over again. I fed myself
and Gairloch, washed up, brushed him, and packed up.

I mounted. He whuffed.

The potholed road twisted and turned, sometimes with cubits-wide
sections having slid into the stream. The stream got even narrower.

The cedars got shorter and so far apart that they looked like squat
sentinels, rather than trees.

The winter mist swirled, dropping occasional snowflakes, and the
ice wind blew around and through us. And the road twisted and turned,
and rose and fell, and the stream became a narrow trickle.

After a while, each section of the mountain-trail road seemed to take
on a certain boring similarity to the section before – until the valley
of death.

Even the mist that hung over the place seemed tinged with
chaos, and nothing moved. The sole sounds were the wind over
the rocks, Gairloch's hoofs, and my breathing. It reminded me of
Frven, except worse.

Piles of ashes had drifted on each side of the road, half frozen into
wind-sculpted mounds. The narrow stream had cut but a thin channel
through the layer of ash that covered all the ground, and that ash
muffled even the sound of the water over its rocky streambed. The
reddish rocks on the valley floor were cracked, as though they had
been baked in an oven. But, in places, along the walls of the narrow
valley – more like a gorge – were huge black smudges as if greasy
fires had burned there.

Gairloch's whinny took on a plaintive air, echoing back and forth
between the bare rock walls.

'Easy . . . easy . . .' I wanted out of there, too. Nothing lived in the
valley. Not a tree, not a bird, not a blade of grass. Just ash, and rock,
and hard-fired soil, and a dead stream. The mist should have softened
it, but it didn't, only made the unseen flames of chaos dance with a
more sinister grace.

I tried not to shudder and urged Gairloch on through the ashes and chaos, looking at the greasy black splotches on the rock walls, almost hearing screams.

Then I swallowed, and my eyes burned. I had found Ferrel's grave – and ashes.

I patted Gairloch, even as I let my senses take in the devastation. The squads with Ferrel had been attacked with rockets. Those who had survived that, if any, had probably been murdered under the blade, and Gerlis had turned his awesome firebolts on the entire valley – just like the first white wizards I had run into had charred meadows into the same dead ashes.

As I kept Gairloch on the road, I kept riding and thinking. None of it made much sense. Why did they use so much power? How could I – or anyone – stop them?

*Wheeee . . . eeee . . .*

I patted Gairloch again, saying nothing until we passed out of the valley of death. The road turned northwest. I kept thinking, trying to get the smell of ashes and death out of my mouth and my mind.

Finally, I stopped at a spring that seemed to be the headwaters for the stream. With snowflakes drifting around me, and a light white carpet on the ground, I washed my face and eyes, and rinsed my mouth. It helped, but I could still taste ashes. Then I checked my arm. The scab itched, but I couldn't sense any chaos, and the bruise around the scab was now totally green and yellow.

Gairloch drank his fill while I looked back to the southeast.

Finally, I gave him the last grain cake and had some cheese and biscuits and apple flakes.

What controlled chaos? Iron and black iron. I didn't have any black iron, and there wasn't a smith outside of Recluce, not that I knew of, who could forge it. I might be able to make some out of some weapons steel, by concentrating on ordering it, but it would be a very small piece of black iron, and it would take a lot of effort. For what?

On the other hand, Recluce was supposed to be orderly because of the iron that ran beneath it. How did the earth contain chaos? With pockets of iron ore? Why did the brimstone and fire springs only flow forth in some places?

I ate without really tasting what I put in my mouth, realizing again just how little I knew about how the world really worked.

I walked toward the spring and looked at it, trying to duplicate what I had felt that Gerlis had done, trying to trace its roots into the rock. The rock seemed to block me, but I could sense the water, the branches and the flow, and I had the feeling that I could have traced it, had I only known how. But *The Basis of Order* didn't mention that. At least, I didn't recall anything like that.

When I finally shook my head, snow flew, and a thin layer had fallen on my saddle. Absently, I brushed it away.

I couldn't follow chaos lines, but I could follow water. Was water more orderly?

Gairloch whickered.

'Sorry, fellow. It's snowing, and we're in the middle of the mountains, and I'm just standing here. Not very bright.' I mounted.

The trail road I had followed joined the main road, or what I took to be the main road, to Kyphros less than two kays farther on.

Gairloch and I turned due west and headed downhill. The snow stopped, but the wind picked up, and the late afternoon got colder.

That night, in a waystation with a door, I went through more of *The Basis of Order*, trying to read between the lines, under the lines, find hidden meanings in the words. Even when I thought I'd found something, I wasn't sure what I'd found.

'... iron has a grain, and through that grain can order be stored as in a warehouse, both in tools and even deep within the earth ...'

'... separating order out of chaos is like forging a fine pair of blades and giving each to twin sons of the ruler at his death ...'

Twin blades? What did that have to do with how to contain chaos?

The last one I read seemed to offer a glimmer of an idea.

'... too much order, or too much chaos, may recoil upon the user and consume him as fat in a smith-fire ...'

How could I help Gerlis obtain too much chaos? What would happen if I helped him get more chaos, and he just used it on me? That seemed dangerous, demon-damned dangerous.

I finally blew out my candle stub and tried to go to sleep, but the wind howled, and my mind turned and twisted like a mountain road. And I remembered Ferrel and the glint in her eye when she had handed back my knife.


# XX

## Dellash, Delapra [Candar]

Dyrsse steps out of the full sunlight of the courtyard, crosses the covered veranda, and walks up to the table set on the corner to catch the breeze from either the bay below or the low forested hills to the west. He glances back down on Dellash and the black ships anchored in the bay. From only one funnel rises a thin line of smoke.

Turning his eyes back to the dark-skinned man who rises from the table, Dyrsse bows. 'Marshal Dyrsse at your service, Ser Rignelgio.'

'You come highly recommended for your military skills, Marshal Dyrsse.' The black-haired man smiles politely, but his eyes remain like blue ice. 'Please have a seat.' His square and blunt-fingered left hand gestures almost languidly toward the wooden armchair that matches the one in which he sits.

Dyrsse sits down heavily, and the chair creaks. 'I am only here to serve the Emperor and you.'

'That's an interesting way of putting it,' observes the envoy, the half-smile remaining on his smooth-shaven face as he reseats himself.

'I always put the Emperor first.' Dyrsse laughs. 'It is not only fitting, but far safer.'

'Spoken like a true marshal of the Emperor, and one who has obviously worked closely with the throne.' Rignelgio lifts a pitcher. 'Delapran wine. It's not bad, and Delapra's one of the few places in Candar you can get any kind of decent wine. Would you like some?'

'Half a glass.'

Rignelgio fills the glass precisely half full. 'There. One must try to retain some semblance of civilization, especially since Candar is far indeed from Cigoerne.'

'Not so far as it once was, Ser Rignelgio, nor so close as it soon shall be, in either distance or culture.' Dyrsse sips from the clear goblet. 'This is not bad, indeed, though I am not one to judge wines.'

'It is rather good, in a quaint fruity way, like some aspects of Candar.' Rignelgio takes another sip, though his lips barely smudge the edge of the crystal. 'Your words seem to imply that the grand fleet might be assembled and sent here. Do you really think so? I doubt that the Emperor will commit those resources so far from Hamor.'

'I do not know of the grand fleet, but I do know that another score of the iron cruisers will be here within the eight-day. That is why you must prevail upon the Delaprans to furnish more coal.'

'Ah, yes, the Delaprans. They often seem less and less cooperative, and it may be difficult to persuade them.' Rignelgio smiles again.

'You are the envoy and the master of persuasion. I will defer to your knowledge and expertise. You are the mouth of the Emperor, and I am here to serve you. That is my duty. His Majesty made that quite clear.' Dyrsse takes a second sip of the wine. 'It does seem like good wine, but, in this also, I must defer to you.'

'I do appreciate your deference, Marshal Dyrsse.' Rignelgio stands. 'I think perhaps I should introduce you to several others, especially Leithrrse. He was born in Recluce, you know.'

'Recluce has produced some fine citizens of the Empire.'

'Including the Emperor's grandfather, a fact which bears on the Emperor's concerns about Candar and the black isle – not to mention your devotion to duty, does it not?' Rignelgio smiles again.

'Let us say that the Emperor was reflective about the . . . sentiments . . . of his grandfather.' Dyrsse lifts the glass toward his lips, but does not drink, instead inhaling the aroma of the wine.

'Leithrrse is quite competent. He is one of the more successful traders in Hamor already, and the Emperor has requested he serve as an envoy to assist me.' The envoy stands.

'I will serve him as I serve you.' Dyrsse sets the glass aside and also stands.

'Oh, please do.'

The two men descend the wide brown-tiled steps. A faint breeze crosses the veranda, bearing the slightest odor of ashes.

# XXI

Gairloch and I trudged back through Kyphros, another five days in all before Kyphrien spread out from where we rode through the hillside olive groves. Five days of dampness, chilied goat at outliers' barracks, and five more nights reading *The Basis of Order*. I was sick of all three.

And five more days of looking at the cedar length that held the face that my mind was too dull to find and my arm too sore to carve more than fitfully.

In the end, Gairloch and I still had to plod through Kyphrien itself. Should I stop at the barracks and try to find Krystal? I wanted to see her.

So I stopped, left Gairloch with the ostler, who said nothing, and marched up to her door.

Herreld wasn't exactly helpful.

'She didn't say where she was going, ser.'

I looked at him.

He backed away. 'She really didn't, ser.'

Next I went down to the barracks, where the smell of oil and metal and leather was almost a military incense, to find Yelena.

'Yelena's off duty, ser. She said she was going to the marketplace.'

Tamra? Well, she wasn't there, either.

'The red ... the apprentice? She's gone, not that many'd mind, ser.'

Tamra was still making friends, I could tell.

So, much later, I rode into my own yard where the big lantern had been lit, and still flickered with the wind that gusted through the fittings that held the glass around the wick.

Krystal came out, almost running, and half hugged me, half carried me off Gairloch. I'd forgotten how strong she was.

'You're back.'

'Careful of the arm. It's still tender.'

So she kissed me instead. The kiss alone was almost worth it.

'... didn't miss each other much ... not at all ...'

I ignored Haithen's wry comments to Perron, who had pretty much replaced Yelena as head of Krystal's personal guard.

Finally, we let go, and I carted in my gear. Haithen offered to stable Gairloch, and I let her. Gairloch seemed agreeable.

'You could use some food,' my consort observed.

'I could use cleaning up.'

Krystal wrinkled her nose with a grin. 'I suppose so.'

'Dinner'll wait a while. It's waited enough already,' added Rissa. 'I cook for numbers I do not know. I cook and do not know when people will be here to eat ...'

Krystal and I grinned at each other, but she came with me to the wash-room, where I stripped off my close-to-filthy clothes.

As I washed, she studied my arm. 'How did that happen?'

'Some innkeeper's bully boy, looking for a guest to rob. I didn't dodge quickly enough.'

'What about your staff?'

'I wasn't carrying it. People get unhappy when you carry a five-cubit length of wood. They think it's dangerous. Of course, carrying a blade is respectable.'

Krystal snorted. 'Maybe you ought to carry a truncheon.'

'That's not a bad idea.' I hadn't thought about it, but the idea did make some sense. 'There are maybe tenscore troops around the spring, and they've got rockets.'

'Rockets? Like Recluce used on Fairhaven in the old days?'

'Not quite. Berfir's got steel casings, I think, or thin iron.' I began to shave away the stubble I hated even worse than shaving itself.

'You're going to shave before dinner?'

'You want me to afterward?'

'You are impossible.'

'Only sometimes.' I switched the razor to the other cheek and jaw. 'That wizard – Gerlis – is stronger than Antonin was.'

'Let's talk about that later.' Her fingers brushed the faded yellow and green of my wound. 'How long ago did this happen?'

'In Sunta. So, let's see – not quite an eight-day ago.'

'It looks older.' She frowned.

'Order-mastery has some advantages.'

'Don't let it blind you. Some wounds you won't be able to heal.'

She had a point, and I finished shaving and washing as quickly as I could. But my stomach still growled as I pulled on a clean shirt.

'Some things haven't changed.' Krystal shook her head.

'A lot of things haven't changed.'

We walked past the door to the back porch I hadn't sat on since summer and into the kitchen. No sooner had we stepped inside than Rissa was setting things on wooden holders all around where I sat.

'Serve it before it gets colder,' suggested the cook.

Perron and Haithen grinned.

Everything was steaming, enough that I almost burned my left hand, but I didn't argue. I served one of Rissa's favorites, a chicken thing with dumplings, green noodles, mint leaves, and a pepper sauce nearly as hot as burkha.

'How was your trip?' asked Haithen.

I looked at Krystal, then smiled. 'After I tell the commander, I'll let you know.'

Perron shook his head.

'The olive grower – Hensil, he said his name was – stopped by last eight-day,' announced Rissa into the silence. 'He started to complain, but I told him – just as you had told me – that you were on business for the autarch. And he said that was fine, but the autarch didn't make good chairs, and you ought to stick to chairs and not the business of ruling.'

I swallowed a mouthful of too-hot chicken dumpling before I spoke. 'What did you say?'

Rissa shrugged. 'I told him that he was right, and that we all would be happier if we did what we did and not what others wanted us to do.'

'Of course,' pointed out Haithen, her mouth full, 'he probably wants the master-crafter to do his chairs.'

I kept eating. There was no way I was going to win that sort of argument.

After dinner, Rissa shooed us out, and we didn't protest, not for an instant.

Krystal closed the bedroom door. 'Business or pleasure?' She smiled.

'Business first. Then we can get to the important part.'

Except we both knew that the business part never went away, no matter how hard we tried.

So I told her everything, even the bits about the two girls and my feeling bad about the stable girl.

She shook her head. 'You would think that, but you also have to think about why you were there.'

She was right. Getting caught or calling attention to the fact that I was a wizard of sorts wouldn't have helped anyone, and I still didn't see how I could have done anything to Jassid except kill him, one way or another.

'You're worried about Gerlis?' She sat on the edge of the bed, so close I could sense her with every sense I had, without even trying.

'Yes.'

'Can you do anything about it tonight?'

'No.' I had to admit that.

So . . . that night we mostly just held each other. Not totally – but the holding was the important part, and I remembered that was how it had begun back on Recluce, even before I knew I loved Krystal, when, facing dangergeld, she had asked me to hold her, and I had.

# XXII

Gunnar walked up the stone-paved lane from the road toward the black stone building that covered the crest of the low hill. Several scattered chirps rose from the thin and graying leaves of the trees in the cherry and apple groves on each side of the lane.

He turned and glanced eastward, in the direction of Wandernaught, noting the single rider on the road from the town to the Institute for Order Studies. Then he turned and continued walking through the fall wind and the rustling of the dry leaves toward the solid black stone archway that defined the entrance to the Temple portion of the Institute. Behind him, a flurry of wings rose above the faint hissing of the breeze as the birds headed for stubbled fields farther downhill from the groves.

When he could hear the chatter of hooves on the road, he turned.

The rider was bareheaded – a tall and slender woman with slightly silvered blond hair. As she drew abreast of the tall mage, she reined up and dismounted.

'Elisabet! I hadn't expected you.' Gunnar offered a quick hug to his sister.

*Whuff!*

A single look from Elisabet quieted the stallion.

'You should have. Even I can sense the conflict.' The breeze rippled through her short hair. 'But I always have to come find you.'

'Even you could sense it?' Gunnar laughed. 'You'd be the first to sense that.'

'Not always.' In three quick turns, she wrapped the leathers around the iron ring on the hitching post. 'And the time will come when you'll have to seek out others.'

'Perhaps. You may be right.' Gunnar glanced toward the young man and woman who approached from the doorway that led to the smaller meeting hall.

'Magister Gunnar,' asked the redheaded woman, 'have you read the essay?'

Gunnar nodded. 'I'll have to talk to you about it later. You're still having a problem in confusing order with an abstraction of "good." Order is not necessarily good. Nor is evil necessarily dependent on chaos. You think about that . . .'

'But I did, ser.'

Gunnar took a deep breath. 'I'll talk to you in a bit.'

'Yes, ser.'

The man looked hard at Gunnar. Gunnar caught his eyes, and the young man paled, then turned. The two walked quickly back toward the lecture room.

'You do that so well, Gunnar. You end up terrifying them all.' Elisabet finished her sentence with a gentle laugh.

'Hardly. Half of them hate me, probably including my own son. That doesn't include the Brotherhood. Talryn thinks I set up the Institute as a rival to the Brotherhood – as if I'd ever wanted to get involved in politics.' He gestured to the stone-paved path to his left. 'Let's walk down to the garden. We're less likely to be interrupted.'

'I don't think Lerris hates you. Not any longer. You were hard on him, but it was better that way. So was Sardit. I think it bothered him to be so strict about the woodworking. But understanding and explanation don't always work. Sometimes, children have to face the hard consequences of their actions. After all, you tried to explain everything with Martan.'

'And you never had children.'

'I had you and Justen.'

'Little sister . . . that was your choice, Elisabet, and, in some ways, I suspect you're the happier for it. How is Sardit?'

'Well. He enjoys the order of the wood so much. How is Donara?'

'Well. She still enjoys creating order with the pottery.'

They both laughed as they walked toward the black stone bench that overlooked the waist-high hedge maze whose outer border had been grown and trimmed into the outline of Candar. Below the flat area that held the maze, a stretch of short grass perhaps a hundred cubits wide separated the maze from the slope where the orchards resumed. Above the bench, another slope of grass rose gently to the wide windows on the south side of the main Institute building.

Elisabet settled onto the east end of the bench, tucking one trousered leg crossways under her.

'I've never been able to understand why you do that,' said Gunnar.

'Just because. It's comfortable.' She squared her shoulders. 'You're busy, and I won't take that much time. But you wouldn't volunteer to tell me.' She grinned at her older brother and cleared her throat. 'Neither you nor Justen ever did. So I came to find you.

'Chaos is welling up everywhere, and I don't sense any great increase in order. Has the Balance stopped functioning? I thought that was impossible.'

'It's functioning.' Gunnar sat heavily on the other end of the bench and looked at the maze. 'I don't know where the additional order is, but it has to be somewhere. There's no sense of imbalance. You already know that.'

Elisabet nodded. 'I worry about Lerris and Justen. Most of the chaos seems to be in Candar.'

'I worry, too.' Gunnar's eyes flicked toward the clouds rising above the low western hills.

'What can we do?'

'What we must.' The tall mage shrugged. 'What we must.'

'Times are finally changing, I think.'

'They are, especially in Hamor, and things will not be the same. The Council doesn't seem to understand that.' Gunnar stood as three black-clothed figures scrambled down the path toward them. 'They and the Brotherhood will be out to blame the Institute or me or Lerris.'

'Have you talked to them?'

'Unfortunately. They still seem to think I want to take their positions. As if I couldn't have been on the Council years ago.' He snorted.

'If you hear from Lerris or Justen . . .'

'I'll let you know. You know I'd let you know.'

Elisabet rose and gave her brother a quick hug. 'Your students seem to have found you.'

'They always do.'

The two walked up the path toward the three who had sought out Gunnar.

Behind them, the wind whispered through the hedge grown into the maze that represented Candar.

# XXIII

The next morning found Krystal and me both in the autarch's private study where Kasee, again, had dark circles underneath her eyes and disheveled hair. The piles of papers and scrolls around her were even deeper than before. The glass on one of the lamps was almost totally black with soot.

'What did you find out?'

'Ferrel's dead. I found where it happened . . .' I explained about the valley of death and then about the terrain of the spring and where the Hydlenese had placed their troops. I couldn't explain, not in any real way, how terrifying that valley had been or how much power Gerlis really had.

Krystal had heard it all and listened.

'So . . . there are really only a comparative handful of troops guarding the brimstone spring.'

'For Berfir, ten-to fifteenscore might be a comparative handful. That's still more than fifteen squads.'

'There were a lot more before,' Kasee said.

Krystal frowned. 'Did the Duke move them out?'

'Some, but I couldn't find out how many there really were to begin with. There are still about fifteen squads in the valley, with another two squads scattered along the roads. That's not the problem.' I cleared my throat, feeling as if I were fighting off both a chill and chaos infections.

'What about the firebolts? Was it chaos-fire?'

'No . . . the Hydlenese are using something from the old days –

rockets. They're like self-propelled cannon shells, and the powder is encased in iron. When they hit, they explode in fire. The wizard used firebolts afterward.'

'Rockets,' mused Kasee. 'The old histories mention them. They were used by Recluce before the fall of Frven. The idea is simple enough, but there seems to be a trick to making them.' She brushed a lock of black and silver hair over her forehead.

From things I had half heard, and recalled, as a child or later, I wasn't sure that the Brotherhood had lost that trick, not after the three black ships I had seen in the harbor at Nylan.

'People don't like to use powder much because a wizard could touch it off,' mused Krystal. 'There aren't that many white wizards. It's a risk, but not that big a risk.'

'Would you do it again?' asked Kasee.

I looked blankly at the two of them.

Krystal looked at me and smiled. 'Not if I had any choice.'

I felt complimented without knowing why, but I went on. 'The powder's pretty much inside steel casings. That's close enough to cold iron that you'd have to have a strong wizard to get it to explode from any distance.'

'There aren't that many chaos wizards any more.'

I frowned, glancing at the overbalanced desk again. 'There's something else that still bothers me.' I went on to explain about all the troops and rockets moving north.

Kasee pulled at her chin, half nodding. Her hair was tousled, almost as though she had been tugging at it. 'It's probably not that big a mystery. We can't afford a big attack on Hydlen. Berfir has to know that. Either a small body of troops can hold or they can't. Either way, we're not about to rampage across southern Hydlen.'

'But why did he even take the spring?'

'To get the brimstone for the powder to build the rockets to use against Duke Colaris,' answered Krystal. 'Colaris has been recruiting for over a year. A lot of soldiers left Gallos after Antonin died, and I've had some reports that there's a new prefect.'

'I heard that in Arastia,' I admitted.

'We don't know if it's true. But Duke Berfir's biggest problem is Colaris, not Kyphros.'

Something about it all still bothered me. Finally, I spoke up. 'All of this makes sense except for one thing. Why did Berfir or the wizard or whoever it was use rockets on Ferrel?'

'Maybe it was a mistake,' suggested the autarch. 'Sometimes, hotheads don't do as they're ordered.' She and Krystal exchanged faint smiles.

I wondered. Should we just leave the spring alone?

'No.' Krystal answered my unspoken question. 'If we intend to act, it should be now.'

'I would tend to agree,' said Kasee. 'Why do you think so?'

'Berfir's in no position to block us with much force. If he fails against Colaris, we don't have to worry much. If he's successful with those rockets, he can bring them back south. If we can take the spring and fortify the area, the rockets aren't likely to be nearly as successful against fixed emplacements – if he has any left. They can't be that easy to make.'

I understood that logic ... sort of. There was another problem. 'How do we handle Gerlis?'

'We don't. You do, if you can. If you would.' Kasee paused. 'I can't command you, but we have to try, one way or another.'

I had this feeling I'd been conscripted again. But if she were going to order Krystal into battle against Gerlis, what choice did I have? 'And if I can't? He's even more powerful than Antonin.'

'We try to avoid him. Wizard fire isn't much good against rocks. It works best in the open field, and we aren't going to give him that. His rockets won't be that much good against scattered scouts, or troops trained to take cover using the terrain.'

The idea was all right for avoiding rockets and firebolts, but how did you command troops scattered all over mountains? I also was worried about Gerlis. They hadn't felt his power. I had, and merely saying he was more powerful than Antonin didn't exactly convey the feeling of that power.

'Tactics ought to be simple enough,' Krystal noted. 'If we hold in emplacements, something like stone shelters or fences —'

'Caves?' asked the autarch.

'No,' Krystal and I said simultaneously. I shut my mouth.

Kasee smiled with a twist to her lips. 'When you both talk like that, I have the feeling that I made a real mistake.'

'Powder and fragments do a lot of damage in confined areas. If this wizard could guide a rocket into a cave, I don't think anyone would survive, not unless it were a very deep cave. Then, how would the troops do us any good?' asked Krystal.

I just nodded.

'You need a barrier, almost flat, that the rockets don't penetrate.'

'What about doing what Lerris did again, with fast squads?' Krystal looked at me. 'Would you mind leading them back the short, roundabout way?'

'Not if you're leading the main body.' I forced a smile.

So did she.

Kasee looked at me, then at Krystal. 'You're not happy about this.'

'I have to do what works. Does it matter whether I like it?'

'No,' answered the autarch. 'We have to do something. The last time someone started raiding the borders, we didn't do anything, and look what happened.'

Krystal looked at me. I shrugged. I couldn't fault the logic, but I thought there was more behind Berfir and his white wizard than I really wanted to know, and I still didn't have an answer, not one that I liked.

'How do you think we ought to take the spring?' asked Kasee.

'If we have to take the spring, we should take it from behind, if we can. Yelena can lead a force with Lerris from the east. Berfir just doesn't have that many troops. I don't think, white wizard or not, that he can hold on two fronts.'

'You question whether retaking the spring is wise?'

Krystal shrugged. 'There's no easy answer. If we let Berfir hold the spring and he does prevail against Colaris, he can use the brimstone against us. If Colaris destroys him, then we may have lost a lot of troops for nothing.'

'What if we wait?' asked the autarch.

'Unless we can be assured of knowing what happens in Freetown almost instantly, Berfir can probably reinforce the spring faster than we can get there and take it.'

Put that way, even I wasn't sure that going ahead wasn't the best way.

'We'll need to protect the Finest and the outliers we use as much as possible. But we can combine that with taking attention away from Lerris and Yelena. We advance the main body slowly along the direct road, with vanguards way in front of us. That serves two purposes. It makes Berfir, or his wizard, or whoever's in charge, worry about the main body. Lerris, and the others, will take the circular route – not quite so circular as the one he took getting to Hydlen – and hit them from behind.'

'What if there are too many?'

'That's for Yelena and Lerris to find out. If there are, then they don't attack. Lerris can see beyond his eyes a little,' Krystal pointed out.

'A very little,' I confirmed.

'We get close enough to monitor his attack. If they're distracted, that gives us an advantage. We'll need a lot of archers, though, as many as we can find.'

Mainly, from that point on, I listened.

'Lerris . . .'

'Huhh?' I sat up. I must have been dozing.

Kasee winked at me. 'Take him home, Krystal. One day won't destroy our plans, and he needs the rest anyway.'

'I'm fine.'

They both looked at me.

Krystal took my arm and walked me out past the guards. 'You need rest. You look like a scarecrow. I'm sorry I dragged you here.'

'I'm fine.'

'You will be.' Krystal shook her head. 'Do you see how loose your trousers are?'

'Tamra said I was getting fat and sloppy, anyway.'

'When did you start listening to Tamra?'

I shrugged. I was clearly going to get some rest.

As we walked toward the stables, she squeezed my hand. 'I'm glad you're back.'

So was I. I just wished it would be longer before we headed out again.


# XXIV

The four druids and the ancient stood in the time-draped grove of the Great Forest and watched as darkness and light boiled across the sand map of Candar.

Of the silver-haired druids, only the eyes of the youngest, a woman scarcely appearing more than a girl, were upon a tiny point of blackened sand separate from the darkness that seemed to envelop both ends of the sand map of the continent. Two flares of white sand erupted from the eastern section of the map.

'The darkness of this order has no soul,' stated the ancient, 'only the cold ordered iron of those who fell before the demons of light. Even the Great Forest fears such order.'

'It has no song,' said the frail silver-haired singer.

'You always speak of songs, Werlynn.'

'And you, Syodra, forget the songs.'

'Some of us have to live them,' said the youngest druid. 'And the price is high.' She looked away from the map.

'So are the joys, Dayala,' points out Syodra.

'They are,' admitted Dayala, but her green eyes bore a darkness as they flicked to the single isolated point of black on the sands. 'But joys end more quickly – and more painfully.'

'There is always a price,' intoned the ancient. 'This one will be greater, far greater, for order without soul is terrible, indeed.'

'They have not heeded the songs,' added the sole male, 'and the truth of their notes.'

'Leave it to the Balance,' suggested the druid who had not spoken.

'Leave it to the Balance? Yes, Frysa, leave it to the Balance. We, and generations, are still paying for the last decision we left to the Balance.' Dayala took a deep breath. 'The Balance works, but it is far from kind. Nor is it always merciful or just.'

'And did we not pay more dearly for those we did not leave to the Balance?' asked the ancient.

Dayala's eyes dropped to the sands again and to the spreading darkness.

# XXV

After Krystal ensured that I got some rest, although certainly not all of that could have been called rest in any language, by the next day I was looking over my workshop, and she was back hard at work in Kyphrien.

While Krystal and the autarch and the new subcommander, a woman named Subrella, who'd been the district commander in Ruzor, worked on the logistics and the detailed plans for exactly how to recover the brimstone spring, I went back to the chair set for Hensil.

Before I'd left, I'd gotten all eight chair backs done, rough-finished, at least, and it was time to start in on the seats and legs. The leg design was all turning, rather than steaming or bending, and time-consuming. I had to use the first chair as a sort of template for the rest of the set. In between times, for a break, if harder work were really a break, I went back to the time-consuming chiseling of the insets for the diamond-shaped backplate with the inlaid initial *H*.

Of course, the turning part got delayed because the band on the foot treadle broke. After I fixed that, I had to stop to sharpen the chisels. I'd been gone long enough that it seemed like every edged tool in the shop needed to be sharpened.

About then, I wondered when I was even going to start on the desk for Antona. I hadn't even figured out what I'd need for the woods, let alone the bracing and thickness. I took a deep breath, and wiped the sweat off my forehead. While it might be chill outside, I'd built the shop snug, and the hearth helped, not only for heating and mixing glues or steam, but for keeping the woods from getting too hot or cold.

Rissa hammered on the door. 'Master Lerris?'

She stepped inside and held a stool with a broken leg.

'Can't it wait?'

'It's been waiting since the day after you left, nigh on three eight-days, and I need this to get to the higher shelves. I told you those shelves were made for a giant.'

I took a deep breath. 'Set it over there.'

'Thank you, ser.'

The stool leg was easy enough, and I even had a leftover piece of oak that I turned down quickly. Then it was three holes with the brace and bit, some smoothing, and some more cleaning out, and then the glue.

It wasn't a problem, but I knew I'd spend more time dealing with Rissa's gentle reminders than it would take to fix the stool if I didn't get it done soon.

Then I went back to turning down and shaping the chair legs. I looked at the only partly begun cedar carving, but it would have to wait. Carvings didn't pay for wood or tools or food.

Then I thought about my parents, again, and the letter I hadn't written. I took a deep breath.

It was almost mid-morning before Rissa tapped on the door again.

'Ser, we're near out of stove-length wood. I can split, but —'

'You can't saw,' I finished.

I didn't have time to saw, either, and I'd need someone on the other end of the big blade anyway. With another breath, I unlocked the storeroom and rummaged in the hidden cabinet for some silvers. After locking up again, I handed her four silvers. 'See if you can get Gelet and Hurbo to saw the second stack behind the stable. Or someone else.' I paused. 'Take the stool. The glue needs to set until tomorrow.'

Rissa looked at me for a moment. I looked back. 'Sawing wood does not finish chairs. If I don't finish these, I don't get paid. If I don't get paid, I can't afford the food you want to cook on that stove.'

She took the coins, not quite rolling her eyes, and I went back to the turning. When my foot got tired, I took out the narrow chisels and started the inlaid channels on the third and fourth backplates.

Rissa put her head in the door.

'I'll be taking the mare to find Gelet, Master Lerris.'

I just nodded, not taking my eyes off the chisel.

'I said I'd be taking the mare —'

I had to look up. So I did. 'Fine, Rissa. Take the mare.'

'I hope it doesn't take too long to find someone to do the wood.'

So did I, or I'd be getting reminders for days. I really wanted to get as much done on the chairs as I could. For however long the campaign for the spring took, I wouldn't be doing woodwork, and those would be days where no coins were being generated. I had some coins left from Kasee's purse that I hadn't given back, more than a few, but I felt bad about keeping them in some ways.

That was another thing I needed to talk to Krystal about – among other things – if we ever got much time together. Sometimes, we were just too tired to talk. Sometimes, we did a lot of holding, and that was good, too. But we weren't talking about what the white wizard was doing, and that wasn't good.

I took a deep breath as I heard the mare carry Rissa out of the yard and readjusted the foot treadle before I went back to turning the chair legs. Even with sharp blades on the chisels, it was a slow, slow business. Cherry is tough. That's what makes it good furniture wood.

By the same reasoning, that was what made reading *The Basis of Order* valuable. It was tough, and I still didn't understand half of what was in it. I understood that there *might* be an order-based way to use chaos on Gerlis, if I understood what the book said, if I could figure out how to make it work, if I could survive to get close enough to Gerlis to try it . . .

I readjusted the chisel and pumped the foot treadle. Turning cherry – tough as it was – was a lot easier than handling order and chaos.

# XXVI

The eight chairs, all rough-finished, sat in a line across the workroom floor. With fine-shaping, a bit tedious, and some polishing and finishing, they'd be ready for Hensil. As it was, an apprentice, a careful one, could have finished them. Of course, I didn't have one, and no prospects at the moment. That was my own fault, though. I hadn't really looked for one, and finding a good apprentice was hard, as I had illustrated for both Justen and my uncle Sardit with my failures.

Still, I looked at the lines of the chairs and smiled – for a moment. Even unfinished, they showed quality. I hadn't quite finished Kasee's wardrobe, although it looked finished, and I had the two desks to complete. The one for Werfel was a simple single-pedestal desk in red oak, less than an eight-day from completion. Antona's I hadn't started. I hadn't even done wood selection.

The patter of a light winter shower came and went, and I could sense horses on the road. Rather than start something else, I went out into the yard and waited. The damp smell of barely wetted clay disappeared in the light cold wind as the clouds carrying that rain moved eastward. The sky toward the Westhorns was clear.

Before long, Krystal and her guards rode into the yard.

Perron had pretty much replaced Yelena as the head of Krystal's personal guard, because Yelena was being groomed for more leadership, especially for the attack on Hydlen. After Krystal's quiet words, he had been even more deferential than Yelena had been. He nodded at me from the saddle. 'Good evening, Master Lerris.'

'Good evening, Perron.'

I held out a hand for Krystal, but she ignored it, her mind clearly elsewhere. I took the reins and led the black into the stable where we both unsaddled him and took turns brushing him down.

I patted Krystal on the shoulder once or twice, but she didn't want to say much, perhaps because she was thinking about everything that was threatening.

When we walked into the yard from the stable and past the end of the building that served as a bunkhouse, Krystal looked at me. 'Let's walk up on the hill.'

Behind the house, the trees rose to a low hill beyond the flat part that had once been a sheep meadow before Kasee gifted me the land – it had reverted to her when something strange had happened to the previous owner. The land had been part of my reward for taking on and being fortunate enough to eliminate Antonin.

Someday, I intended to use the small stream for my own millrace, and cut and season my own wood. There were all three kinds of oaks, and even a handful of lorken, although they only grew near the very top of the hill.

Krystal's eyes were darker and more serious, and there were deep circles under them, and her hair was showing streaks of silver. I needed to work on that, too, like everything else. She still wore her gold-braided jacket, and I had sawdust on my sleeves.

I brushed off the sawdust and took her arm as we walked up the path. It ran next to the covered water line that fed the house from the pond I'd made on the hillside. The gray leaves of the oaks rustled in the light and cold winter wind, and the sky was a velvet purple, with a trace of pink along the western hills. The air was damper on the hill, with the acrid scent of winter leaves.

Neither one of us said anything as we walked through the trees. There was a cleared spot at the top of the hill, and we looked down at the house, the attached shop, and the stable and shed. A line of smoke rose from the kitchen chimney, and I could smell the wood burning. The pile of new-sawn wood was stacked by the shed, and a smaller pile of partly split stove wood was heaped by the back door. I grinned, recalling Rissa's efforts to get me to saw it.

Krystal squeezed my hand.

'Lerris . . . you don't have to do this.'

'Do what?'

'You know. You always act dense when it's difficult for you. I meant leading Yelena's force to the white wizard.'

I squeezed her hand in return, but I kept looking down at the house. I hadn't quite thought of it as leading Yelena's force. 'You'll be right behind me.'

'That's not answering the question. You still won't admit it if you are worried or if you need help. Don't make me guess how you feel. Not now.'

'Krystal.' I paused. 'We don't have any choices. You're the commander, and being who you are, you won't command from Kyphrien. That means the Hydlenese will throw rockets at you – unless someone stops them. Or diverts them.'

'Yelena could go without you,' she said quietly.

'She could, and a lot of troopers could get killed.'

'They will anyway.'

'You risk your life a lot, and I craft wood most of the time these days.'

'No. I don't risk my life very often, not any more. I'd rather not.'

I could sense the smile, and I gave her hand a squeeze. She returned the pressure, and we looked at the violet sky turning black, and the stars flickering into tiny lamps.

'Lerris . . .'

Krystal was quietly determined, another reason why I loved her, and she wanted an answer, not an evasion. Evasions were sometimes easier for me, and she knew that.

'I don't like it. Gerlis is stronger than Antonin was. He's got those rockets, and he's a lot smarter.'

'Because he's surrounded himself with an army?'

I nodded. 'He's not as arrogant, I don't think, and he dug up the idea of the rockets from somewhere. Or Duke Berfir did. I wonder if they've found out something else as well.'

Krystal put an arm around me, and I put one around her as we looked out toward Kyphrien.

'You didn't say much to Kasee . . .'

I tried not to shrug. 'What could I say? If you have to lead the forces against rockets, and I sit here because I'm no soldier, how will I feel if anything happens to you?'

Another silence fell.

'How will I feel if you die doing my job?' she asked.

'What I have to do isn't exactly your job. And it is your job to use what you have to,' I said slowly. 'Kasee was right. We just can't let things happen. Things always get worse. The thing that bothers me the most is not being with you.'

'It bothers me. A lot.'

It bothered me a lot, too. How I felt about separations was strange. Once I'd wandered all over Candar without her, without even knowing that I missed her, and now I disliked every small separation.

'I said it bothers me, and it does. But it won't go away, either. What you've planned makes the most sense, but I don't have to like it.'

'Thank you.' Her voice was soft, and she put both arms around me, and we held each other.

# XXVII

## East of Lavah, Sligo [Candar]

The man in the cyan sash looks at the drawings on the sheets before him. 'How will this help us against the red demon? Or to reclaim our heritage in the Ohyde Valley?'

'Knowledge is always helpful, Ser Begnula.' The man in brown smiles and his eyes turn to the window, where the season's first snowflakes drift lazily by the glass. 'I offer knowledge. You and your master can use that knowledge or not.'

'And who will you offer it to, if we do not? The red demon?'

'Like everyone, I must eat, and knowledge is my trade.' Sammel offers a shrug as he turns away from the window.

'A chaos wizard like one who serves the red demon could explode the powder with one firebolt.' Begnula licks his lips nervously. 'For this, you expect golds?'

'If you keep the powder in the iron magazines and load the guns right from the magazines, nothing will happen. That is how the black folk have handled powder for centuries.'

'You are sure this will work?'

'How else has Recluce ruled the seas?' The man in brown nods.

'Still, the duke could not afford . . .' Begnula's voice turns reluctant.

'I would suggest that your master talk to the envoy from Hamor, assuming you have not already. The Emperor would be more than interested in developing new weapons for his campaigns.'

'And seeing them tested, no doubt, far from Hamor?'

'There is that. But you asked for a weapon to counter the chaos wizard. These will do that. You can even cast hollow shells filled with powder and use them. Or thinner shells filled with smaller lead pellets.'

'They are the demons' weapons.'

'That may be, but you are fighting a demon, you say.'

'You serve both chaos and order. How can that be?' asks Begnula suddenly.

'Knowledge serves no one. Knowledge rules both order and chaos.' Sammel smiles. 'Whoever controls knowledge controls order and chaos. I offer your master knowledge. He may use it as he pleases.'

Begnula rolls the sheets into his dispatch case, then takes his purse and pulls three golds from it. He places the coins carefully on the edge of the table. 'I trust . . .'

'As you see fit, Ser Begnula.'

Begnula looks at Sammel and adds another gold.

'Thank you. I am always happy to provide knowledge.'

The functionary of the Duke bows. 'Good day, ser wizard.'

'Good day.'

Sammel crosses the room and opens the door.

Begnula bows again after he leaves the cottage.

The wizard smiles as the other man mounts and wipes his forehead before chucking the reins of the gray gelding. Then he closes the door.

Sammel walks over to the hearth, where he places another log upon the coals, and then another. He straightens and frowns, his eyes glazing over as if he listens to a distant conversation.

He takes the glass that had been upon the table and crosses the room, where he sets it on the floor in the corner. He purses his lips and stares. A fountain of unseen chaos flows from the glass, then ebbs, then flows . . .

Sammel concentrates once more, and the glass appears to vanish, but a wavering curtain of mist or heat appears in the corner.

With a faint smile, Sammel walks back to the hearth. After a time, he wipes his damp forehead and waits. Abruptly, he vanishes from sight, and the cottage appears empty, low flames from the coals in the hearth the only motion.

The faintest of scrapes whispers from beyond the closed front door.

The door bursts open, but no one enters.

For a long moment, the door wavers in the wind, and the hearth coals flame up in the breeze that sweeps into the cottage.

*Whhhst! Whhhsttt!* Two small rockets burst in the corner, sending up a sheet of flame.

*Hhhsstt! Hssttt!* The firebolts slash from the unseen figure that stands before the stones of the hearth, and two charred figures fall through the doorway.

The flames begin to rise in the corner, then twist and die amid the shards of glass.

The wind gusts through the open door, and the door bangs against the wall, then slams back against one of the bodies, then crashes against the wall again.

Sammel reappears before the hearth and wipes his forehead on his sleeve. Then he crosses the cottage and studies the two black-clad bodies. Both clutch stubby weapons that look like tubes atop rifle stocks. More standard blades lie tangled in burned trousers and legs.

The wizard lifts one tube weapon by the wooden stock and sets it on the table. Then he concentrates once more, and the bodies turn to white ashes, as do the blades and the remaining tube weapon. He turns toward the corner of the cottage, and the blackened wood and darkened rough plaster flake away, leaving the wall apparently untouched. Sammel looks at the blackened floor planks and a thin layer of ash appears over now-unburned wood.

With a deep breath, the white wizard closes the front door before he walks to the single closet in the cottage where he extracts a willow broom. He begins to sweep all the ashes toward the hearth.

'Mere black iron will not prevail against knowledge . . .' He shakes his head, but he looks first at the weapon on the table and then toward the east, and he frowns.

After he finishes sweeping, he replaces the broom, then draws back the cloth covering the bookcase and looks for a time at the volumes.

He reaches out to touch one, then draws back his hand. 'To come to this, where each touch shortens your life, dear volumes . . .'

# XXVIII

'If anyone comes, Rissa, tell them that I won't be back for at least three eight-days. I'm under the autarch's command.' I kept strapping my bedroll and waterproof behind the saddle. My saddlebags had a lot more dried fruit than on the last trip – a lot more food, and not tools.

'You just got back from one o' those, Master Lerris, and here you go again. No way for a craftmaster to work.' Rissa held the lamp in one hand. The other hand was on her hip. 'What's a body supposed to do if you don't come back and the commander doesn't?'

'Then, you're free to do as you like.' I finished strapping the bedroll in place and set the staff in the lanceholder.

'Master Lerris, you joke about those things too easily.'

'What else can I do?' I took a deep breath. 'I didn't exactly volunteer to be a soldier or a soldier's wizard.'

Rissa shook her head, and she was right. I had volunteered. Was I a fool, knowing that Krystal could die if I didn't help? Or was I deluded? Krystal was the professional soldier, not me, and maybe it was more likely I'd be the one doing the dying. I tried not to shiver at that.

We both worried about each other. Was that love? Did order or chaos really care about love? I knew the answer to that one, not that I liked it.

My stomach tightened as I realized I had answered – maybe – one of my own questions about my father. If order did not care about love, then had he had any choice? That bothered me. Could I do what I felt was right, whether it was orderly or not?

With no pleasing answers in mind, I led Gairloch out of the stable and into the yard, still before dawn, and barely light. A chill blustery wind whistled out of the west, bringing the icy chill of the Westhorns, and whipping through my hair. I felt in my belt for the knitted cap. I didn't like to wear it, but I wouldn't freeze my ears either, not if it got that cold. But, thankfully, I didn't need it yet.

I patted Gairloch and climbed into the saddle.

'Wizards . . .' mumbled Rissa.

I looked down and realized she was holding back tears.

'We'll be back, Rissa. Make sure everything's in good condition for us to come back to.' I bent down in the saddle, awkwardly, and touched her shoulder, letting a bit of order flow into her.

She started to sob, and I understood once more how much I didn't understand. I patted her shoulder again, but she only sobbed more. 'Just . . . you . . . be going . . . Master . . . Lerris . . . be . . . all right . . . here . . .'

Finally, I nudged Gairloch toward the road, and toward Kyphrien and the barracks of the Finest, where I was to meet Yelena. Krystal had left even earlier, but neither of us had wanted to give up the last night together.

The sky had a few high and puffy clouds moving eastward quickly, and that probably meant a long bright day that would be cold indeed.

The road to Kyphrien was untraveled. Most of the streets there were deserted in the dawn light, and even the market square was almost empty, except for two women who carried buckets of water up the stone-paved avenue. I saw the flickering of a handful of lamps, and smelled wood smoke from the chimneys.

Weldein was waiting for me by the gate to the Finest's barracks.

'The others are at the outliers' barracks toward the eastern gates, Order-master.'

'Am I late?'

'No, ser. The force leader left to ensure the outliers would be ready.'

I rode through the eastern section of Kyphrien, down the lower avenue, without saying much. I would have liked to have ridden with Krystal, but, as a practical matter, moving all the forces at once through places like Dasir and Jikoya would have put too great a strain on the local facilities. So Krystal and the main forces would follow a day later.

I hurried along to meet up with recently promoted Force Leader Yelena and three squads of the Finest and two squads of outliers – one of them Tellurians, the other Meltosians.

The sun had barely edged over the horizon when I reined up Gairloch in the yard in front of the outliers' barracks. A number of the outliers were still strapping packs and bags on their mounts.

Yelena was mounted, talking to the squad leaders, who had circled their horses around her.

'There he is! See ... there is the wizard, the one with the invisible sack.'

The voice was familiar, and I didn't quite groan. Instead, I eased Gairloch toward the Tellurians. Shervan – the very first outlier I had met when I came to Kyphros, the one who still told of my 'magic sack' – waved from the third row. The squad leader looked at me.

I doubt that I looked very impressive, not in browns and carrying only a staff.

'Greetings, Shervan.' I nodded to the man mounted beside him. 'It's good to see you, too, Pendril.'

The squad leader edged his mount toward me and away from Yelena. His eyes flicked between me and Yelena. For some reason, Yelena was smiling.

'This will be an adventure, following the wizard. Did I not tell you, Pendril?'

Pendril grunted, and I approved.

'And wait until I tell Barrabra ...'

'Shervan,' I said clearly, 'first we have to go where we are going, and then we have to come back. You cannot tell anyone unless you come back. The more attention you pay to your squad leader, the better your chance to come back. He is a fighter. I am a wizard.' I saluted him and turned Gairloch back toward Yelena and Weldein, nodding to the squad leader as Gairloch carried me past him.

'... see. I told you he was a wizard, and a smart one ...'

'Shervan, be quiet – for once,' said Pendril in a tired voice that carried. 'Or what I have to say to Barrabra will make what the wizard said sound like love talk.'

I grinned, but I could do that since I was looking toward Yelena.

'Listen up,' snapped the Tellurian outliers' squad leader, a stocky man with a brush mustache.

I reined Gairloch up beside Yelena.

'Not bad. What made you think of that?' asked Yelena.

'I don't know, except it sounded like Shervan would be blabbing about how he knows me all the way to Hydlen. That wouldn't help him or his squad leader.'

'You might actually make an officer someday.'

I doubted that. I just let Gairloch keep pace with Yelena and her staff as we headed out in the dawn over the east road toward Dasir and Jikoya and, unfortunately, toward Hydlen and one white wizard.

# XXIX

Behind Gairloch, I could hear the sounds of hoofs, harnesses, and the occasional clink of metal on metal. I felt like someone was looking at me, but my senses didn't feel anything like chaos, and I hadn't seen any vulcrows. I turned in the saddle, surveying the rocky walls, the stunted cedars, and the narrow ribbon of water to the right of the road. Nothing.

I looked up, but the sky remained misty, with flat gray clouds hanging over the Lower Easthorns. Nothing flew in the misty drizzle, not even a vulcrow.

My gloved fingers brushed the wood of the staff, but it remained merely wood bound in iron. I wiped the dampness off my forehead with the back of my glove.

Now less than a day behind us, but too far behind for me to hear or sense, followed Krystal and the larger force. I hoped that they stayed far behind – far enough behind that the wizard looked for us – even though that wasn't exactly Krystal's or Kasee's plan.

'How far before we get to this turnoff?' I asked.

Yelena turned in the saddle. 'We'll stop here. Let them water their mounts.'

'Hold up! Stand down . . .'

'Water your mounts by squads . . .'

'. . . leave the upper part for drinking . . .'

The quiet commands still echoed through the dampness and the grayish mist. Almost-freezing mist was worse than snow in some ways. I never got quite warm, and with my order-control I couldn't quite complain about freezing, even to myself.

In the middle of the mist that wasn't quite a drizzle, Yelena spread the rough map on the boulder. 'Here is where we are. It's about ten kays up this road from where we entered the Khersis Gorge. If we followed the river, we'd end up at the pass here, and then it's only a few days down to the brimstone springs. We could save some time if we take the cutoff just below the pass rather than the earlier one up ahead.'

'Is that a good idea?' I asked.

'That's closer to where the springs are.'

'That's also closer to where Gerlis is, and he's bound to be waiting

for some sort of response to incinerating the commander of Kyphros.
I would be. He hasn't shown much respect for boundaries so far.'

'But . . .' Weldein started to speak, then stopped as both Yelena and
I looked at him.

Since riding up the direct road to the valley in which the spring lay
was as good as blowing on a loud trumpet to announce our arrival,
we were looking for the side road that I had taken on my way back
that would provide us with a more roundabout approach.

I studied the map, looking for the trail. It didn't look that far ahead on
the gorge road. 'We take this trail to this pass here, under these —'

'The Two Thieves, they're called,' interposed Yelena.

'—and then take this road here . . .'

'That's almost eighty kays, and we'll end up in Hydlen south of
Arastia. It's less than ten kays difference if we take the one just below
the pass.'

'That's just too close.' I waited, but they all looked blank. It seemed
simple enough to me.

'What's the one direction that Gerlis won't expect an attack or
scouting force to come from?'

'From inside Hydlen. That's clear enough,' said Yelena. 'But do you
think his troops are just going to let us ride through Hydlen and do
nothing?'

'Probably not.' I forced a smile. 'Would you prefer to face the wizard
coming up this road?' My finger outlined the road ahead. 'Or possibly
run into some Hydlenese troopers on this trail? Do the Finest patrol
all the back trails in Kyphros?'

'Of course not. The outliers do some of it.'

'And five squads aren't a match for a squad of whatever the
Hydlenese use as outliers?'

This time Freyda grinned at Yelena. The force leader, a dubious
promotion under the circumstances, shook her head. 'We'll still be
lucky to get back in one piece.'

'I know. This way there's a chance.' I looked around. 'How long
before we reach that trail?'

'It should be just a few more kays.'

'It's on the south side,' offered Freyda.

I had to trust their judgment, since I was no scout and had only
taken the road once, and then I hadn't been in the best physical or
mental shape.

No one said anything else, and Yelena folded up the map and put
it into her case. 'Mount up!'

'. . . mount up . . .'

'. . . finish up . . .'

'. . . not in the water, you idiot!'

I climbed back on Gairloch and turned him to continue up the canyon in a generally eastward direction.

The clink of metal and the sound of hoofs echoed back through the gorge, and the low murmurs of wet troopers underlay it all. I looked back to see if I could hear Shervan or Pendril, but through the drizzle, one outlier looked like another.

Gairloch seemed to have covered a lot more road than a mere two to three kays before I pointed to the left. 'Is that it?'

'That looks like it,' admitted Yelena. 'It's headed toward the Two Thieves.'

The trail was the same trail – just a trail, but where it left the main road it was still wide enough for two horses abreast.

'It can't be that easy,' mumbled Weldein.

It wasn't. In the first place, the drizzle turned into rain, and then into a light snow that didn't stick. In the second place, the trail hadn't been maintained in a long time, if ever, with pits and potholes everywhere. I had noticed that before, but it was worse with a whole force. Gairloch did fine, and no one said a word after Freyda's mount came up lame from stepping in a puddle that had a pit in it. The injury was more like a sprain, and I managed to infuse it with a little order, but that meant Freyda had to take one of the few spare mounts and lead her mount for the rest of the day.

Then we hit the valley of death, with wet ash and more ash, with the smell of wet fire and death. And with the sense of death and gloom.

'Shit . . .' mumbled Weldein.

'. . . hell of the demons of light . . .'

Yelena looked at me and rode closer. Her voice was low. 'You didn't tell me about this.'

'I told the commander and the autarch.' I swallowed. 'I'm sorry.'

She surprised me. She just shook her head sadly. 'Was this where . . . Ferrel . . .'

'Yes, but there's no way to prove it.'

'You came through this, and you're bringing us back through it?' asked Freyda.

'It's the best way.'

'. . . take the best way through demons' hell . . .' muttered Jylla, a shade paler.

The talk died into silence when the outliers followed us into the narrow valley. I tried not to think about the power involved, but that didn't really work when I could feel the remnants of chaos creeping out of the rocks.

Gairloch put one foot in front of the other, and I hung on.

When I saw the first clump of grass at the other end, I took a deep breath. Weldein took one as he passed the first scrub cedar on the left side of the trail.

I kept thinking about using order to strengthen chaos to defeat Gerlis, and it almost seemed insane. Maybe it was. Maybe the whole order-chaos conflict was insane. I didn't know. All I did know was that Gerlis was waiting for me in the valley of the brimstone spring.

Not long after we passed the ashes, the rain came down in sheets, just long enough to soak us. Then the sky cleared, and the cold wind picked up.

That night, we camped in a narrow valley with water, and some grass, and it was cold, not chill like in Kyphros, but almost winter-cold, for all that we were in the southern part of the Easthorns that weren't that much more than hills, probably not much taller than the Little Easthorns that divided Kyphros and Gallus.

'No fire?' I asked.

'No fire,' Yelena affirmed.

All of the Finest were bundled up in their riding jackets, and the outliers wrapped themselves in blankets as well. I wore my jacket and cap, but I wasn't huddled into a ball the way most were.

Weldein looked at me. 'Aren't you cold, Order-master?'

'No.' I wasn't cold, at least not miserable, freezing cold the way they all were. I supposed that the one advantage of the mist was that the chaos wizard would have a hard time finding us. Even as I thought about it, though, I wondered about the uneasy feeling that had come and gone in the last few days. Was Gerlis somehow watching us?

# XXX

## West of Arastia, Hydlen [Candar]

Gerlis looks up at the sound of heavy footsteps. For a moment his eyes flick to the iron dagger with the charred handle that rests on top of the closed trunk.

'I don't care what he said! I am the force leader, and I will see Master Gerlis! And I will see him now!'

'Master mage,' announces the guard at the front of the pavilion tent, 'Force Leader Cennon be here to see ye.'

The white-clad magician frowns, and the white mists vanish from the glass on the table. 'Bid him enter, Orort.' Gerlis stands and steps toward the tent flap as it opens.

'Bid me enter, will you?' Cennon, unruly black hair bound with a silver band, marches into the tent. 'Bid me enter?'

Gerlis looks for a moment at Cennon, then turns, and walks to the trunk, his back momentarily to Cennon, where he picks up the dagger and a small wooden platter before facing the force leader. 'Why, yes. I did bid you enter, in all courtesy.'

'You and your talk of courtesy.'

'Would you rather I talked of power?' Gerlis steps forward and sets the dagger by the blank screeing glass, and balances the platter in his hand. A fireball appears on the tip of his index finger of his free hand.

'Charlatan! A child's trick, unlike the rockets. They are real.'

'You believe what you must, Force Leader Cennon.' Gerlis tosses the platter and releases the fireball.

*Hssstttt!* White ashes drift downward, and the odor of burned wood and grease fill the tent.

'Had I hit you with the full firebolt, you would be a grease spot . . . or less.' Gerlis looks at the carpet that covers the earth. 'I prefer not to soil my carpets.' He picks up the long knife from where he had set it next to the glass, careful to hold it by the burned leather of the hilt, rather than let his fingers touch the cold iron blade. 'I believe this belonged to one of your men.'

'Hardly. One of mine would not have lost his knife.' Cennon does not reach for the charred hilt.

'I admire such certainty, Force Leader Cennon.' A smile follows, one showing wide white teeth, as Gerlis sets the knife aside. 'You wished something?'

'Why have we waited while the Kyphrans dawdle their way through the Lower Easthorns?' Cennon brushes away the drifting ashes. 'We should strike them before they expect us.'

'I doubt seriously if you can surprise them again. You might have noticed that they are sending a great number of advance scouts, and those scouts are rather thorough. The autarch is cautious.'

'We surprised them once.'

'On her lands with no warning,' points out Gerlis. 'You might also note that most of the rocket carts have been sent to the border with Freetown, since Duke Colaris is a rather more imminent threat.'

'I could still destroy the Kyphrans without your infernal wizardry.'

'Duke Berfir believes that also. He also believes, as he pointed out to you, that such destruction should take place somewhere reasonably close to his lands, or at the very least those lands which he claims.'

'That I have to obtain your approval . . . my father will hear of this – soon!'

'I presume that your messenger will reach him shortly. I also presume that he will understand Duke Berfir's logic.' Gerlis smiles with his mouth.

'Someday . . .'

'I agree.'

Cennon looks at the white wizard for a long time, his fingers flexing around the hilt of his own cold steel blade. Then he turns and marches out into the windy morning, where ragged clouds scuttle out of the Higher Easthorns to the north, as if fleeing from the northern winter.

'Fool . . . not to see your own limits . . .' Gerlis turns back to the table and the glass and reseats himself. After a time, and concentration, Gerlis watches an image emerge from the screeing glass – seeing again the five squads of Kyphrans and the young man in brown who accompanies them.

The white wizard smiles, with his entire face and eyes, and the image, and the mists, vanish. 'Yes, Cennon, you will find your limits, poor hero. And you, too, little black mage.' His eyes lift to the banner in the corner, the one with the crown on it. He shakes his head.

After a time, he looks at the glass once more, where a bald man in a tan uniform appears, crossing the deck of a warship. Gerlis purses his lips and concentrates once more. In time, the valley floor grumbles, and shudders.

# XXXI

I sat on the edge of the boulder and looked out toward the east, where the sun barely had cleared the trees. The ground dropped away from the goat trail that continued to masquerade as a road. Each series of hills lay slightly lower than the previous one, dropping away to the north where a brown smudge rose amid the lower hills.

'That's Arastia.' I pointed, then tried to shift my weight with my hands, but the crumbling edge of the stone gave way under my left hand, and I sat back down – hard – on the same rock edge that had been cutting through my trousers. 'Oofff.' I wanted to rub the sore spot, but didn't.

'It should be,' confirmed Yelena.

'It is.'

I concentrated, but could sense nothing nearby, except a few goats. The trail wound north-northeast generally. If I recalled the route accurately, it would interesect the road from Arastia to the brimstone spring within five or six kays, although distances are deceiving from heights, and I didn't remember the distances that well from my single trip. Then it had been dark when I had taken the road before us, and I had had my mind elsewhere, to say the least.

'I'd say it will be another six kays as the vulcrow flies —'

'You haven't seen any, have you?'

'No.' I didn't mention that continuing sense of unease, as if I were occasionally being watched. How would that have sounded? But I tried to be alert to any sense of chaos.

'Good,' mumbled Weldein.

'Sooner this is over the better . . .'

'. . . what is the miraculous wizard doing now . . . and he is miraculous . . .'

I eased off the boulder, wishing Shervan's voice were not so penetrating and his admiration of me were far less vocal. I brushed the sand and rock from my trousers and massaged what was probably going to be a bruise.

Gairloch whuffed as I checked the saddle and patted him on his shoulder. The trees bordering the overlook weren't the dense forest south of Arastia, but a mixture of scrub, stunted oaks, a few taller but twisted cedars – just enough to give the illusion of cover. I looked back up the road where the more than five squads waited.

'We'd better get moving.' I climbed back onto Gairloch, trying not to wince as my backside contacted the saddle.

'You're the wizard.' Yelena didn't smile, and I knew she was worried. So was I. Who wouldn't be, with five squads of Kyphran troops inside the borders of Hydlen with a powerful white wizard somewhere ahead? Even if we were circling back toward Kyphros?

Once again, distances were deceiving, and the road was slower than I had hoped. It was past mid-morning before we looked down on the beaten clay road winding through the low valley that gradually narrowed as it neared the western border of Hydlen – and the brimstone spring where we were headed.

'I think this is the right place.' My nose twitched at the faint odor of brimstone. Below, on the other side of the road, ran a narrow stream. A faint trace of steam rose from its waters, more noticeably in the places shadowed by the hills.

'The official border is, what, say ten kays up the road?' I turned to the tight-lipped force leader. I'd never bothered with borders on my scouting trip. I supposed it still didn't make any difference.

'If the hills, there, are the ones I think they are, that marks the border. Less than ten kays.'

'We've got about fifteen kays to go.'

Yelena nodded.

Ahead, the valley narrowed into a gap formed by the Yellow River. After winding uphill for three kays, the gap again widened into a small circular valley. At the western end of the valley – closest to Kyphrien – were the brimstone springs. The eastern end had a rise that was half grass, half cedar trees, and the Yellow River wound through the northern side of the valley. The idea was to cross the scrub forest to the south, leaving the road before we reached the valley, and then use the rise for cover for the force – when we got there. That assumed we did get there, and I was worried about that.

Again, I got the sense of being watched, and I scanned the area around us, looking for vulcrows, scouts, anything. Then I sent out my own modest perceptions, which were now reaching out almost a kay. I could sense nothing, at least nothing of excessive order or chaos, just animals, and trees.

I took a deep breath as I retreated into myself. I had to grasp Gairloch's mane to steady myself as I waited for my eyes to readjust. When I could make out the grayish leaves of the trees beside the road, I let go and patted him on the shoulder.

'Are you all right, Order-master?' Yelena eased her mount closer to mine.

'Yes. I was just . . . searching.'

'Did you find anything?'

I shook my head.

Yelena gestured, and we headed downhill toward the main road, which ran on the flat beside the Yellow River. The southern side, just beyond the road, was wooded, mostly with softwoods, very little oak or good material for a woodworker. That was a problem – good furniture wood also made good firewood, and most farmers or peasants didn't much care about saving the good wood for crafters. They cared about such things as heat, warmth, and food – or the coins that would buy them.

I kept looking and sending out my perceptions, but it took a while to find the guards near the actual crossroads, since they were almost a kay farther up the road. I guess that made a sort of sense. In the narrower section near the hilltop, they wouldn't face attacks from two sides, as they could at the crossroads. Also, the crossroads section was relatively open, with no trees for several hundred cubits. So there was nowhere to rest or sit, and no shade.

'The guards aren't at the crossroads,' I said.

Freyda, riding almost abreast, raised her eyebrows.

'I noticed,' was Yelena's comment. 'Do you think they pulled back?'

'They're up the road. We can get almost to the crossroads without being seen, maybe farther. The road curves.'

'Do you think so?'

I nodded.

'You're the wizard.'

I laughed. 'You're the force leader.'

'Just remember that.'

We rode downhill slowly, and I kept checking for the sentries. We finally reined up nearly half a kay beyond the crossroads.

'There's a patrol uphill just around the curve. Three of them, I think. This is as far as we can go without being seen.'

Yelena looked at me, as if asking for suggestions. I looked at Weldein. He was the closest of the troopers I knew.

'Weldein, how about trusting your friendly order-master?'

He did gulp when I explained. 'I'm going to lead an invisible horse and rider – that's you – right up to these outlier patrols. Then, I am going to attempt to unhorse and otherwise disable them. Your and my job is to keep them from fleeing up the road to warn the wizard's forces. While we're trying to slow them down, Leader Yelena and some of the fleetest riders will come to our aid.'

'That's a stupid plan,' offered Freyda. 'What if they chop you up?'

'Very stupid,' I admitted. 'Do you have a better one? Do you want to take Weldein's place?'

She ignored the question.

So I went on. 'Those three riders aren't terribly alert. One of them is sitting on a log or something. The other two are mounted. It's a bit far for arrows, and not many here are archers.'

'It's still stupid.'

'Does anyone have a better idea?' I asked again. 'If we try to go through the woods and underbrush, they'll certainly hear us before we ever get close.'

Despite my explanations, I didn't have any real answer to Freyda's

question. If they were good with blades, I was in trouble, but if I
didn't do something Krystal would be in trouble. So I waited. No one
offered a better plan. That might have been because I was the one
out in the open.

'How will this work?' asked Yelena.

'I put a shield around Weldein and his mount, and lead him up
the road, pretending that I'm leading an invisible horse to Kyphros
to sell. I hope they'll think I'm mad, and let us get close enough to
stop them from warning the wizard, or slow them down enough so
our faster riders can catch them.'

'I don't know,' said Yelena slowly.

'If they're here as scouts, they must have fast horses,' I pointed out.
'What would you do if five squads of strange horsemen appeared?'

'Run like the demons of light were chasing me,' offered Jylla.

Yelena glared at her.

I turned to Weldein. 'All right. You won't be able to see. That's
all right. I can't see either behind a shield. That's why I'll lead your
horse.' I concentrated.

'He's gone . . .'

I could hear the indrawn breaths.

'. . . son of a bitch is a wizard . . .'

'. . . not so loud, idiot . . . want him to do it to you?'

'Weldein, don't do anything until you can see, but have your blade
out of the scabbard and ready to use.'

'How can I do anything?' he muttered. 'I can't see shit.'

'You will.' I swallowed and fumbled around until I grasped the
leathers of his reins. 'Let's go.'

As we stepped out, Yelena slowly began to bring the Finest as close
to the guards as she could without getting into their sight.

'Easy, Weldein.'

'I'm here. Where that is, is something else.'

His mount whickered, but that didn't matter, because the guards
wouldn't notice the sound didn't come from Gairloch until we got
too close.

I rode past the last stand of trees separating me from the patrol.
The two mounted riders watched as I whistled my way toward them.
I think I was off-key.

'What are you doing, fellow?' asked the one who rode toward me.
He was a skinny little trooper with a wispy beard and little eyes, and
that probably meant he was as good and nasty as the demons of light.
'How did you get past the guards at Arastia?'

'I'm leading my invisible horse. I won him at the market in

Sunta. I'm going to take him to sell in Kyphros.' It sounded logical to me.

'Invisible horse? Well, you need to take your invisible horse and turn around and head right back to Sunta.' He put his hand on the hilt of his blade.

'But I can't go to Kyphros that way,' I protested, letting go of the all-too-real invisible bridle, and edging forward. I needed to get closer to the other mounted trooper.

'You can't go this way.' He insisted.

'It is the road to Kyphros, isn't it? I am on the right road?' I put a whining tone in my voice as I edged Gairloch to the side of the road and forced the trooper to follow me.

He drew his sabre. 'You just turn around right now.'

'But I can't sell my invisible horse unless I go to Kyphros.'

The other two troopers were smirking.

'You won't sell that horse anywhere!' He spurred toward me, lifting the sabre, and I urged Gairloch toward the other two, who had burst into laughter at the spectacle of the poor mad fool fleeing the trooper.

Then, I pulled out the staff, and, somehow, held on to it as I brought it across the chest of the other mounted trooper. She went down like a flour sack, even as I released the shields around Weldein.

The first trooper didn't even see Weldein, so intent was he on spitting me. His blade flashed. I did parry it, even though he took a chunk right out of the hard wood, and shivered my arms. Gairloch backed around, without much guidance from me.

Another wild swing followed, and this time I slid his blade rather than taking the impact. My fingers still tingled from the first one, but I got the staff back in position to counter another hacking blow.

'Get you ... get you yet ...' he grunted as he took an even more forceful cut.

The last wild blow left him off balance, and I countered with a perfect blow across the face as he was bringing his blade back up. The blow sounded half dull, half gonglike from where the iron ring on the staff hit his plate skullcap.

He slumped in his saddle, his sabre clattering to the ground, and a wave of whiteness struck me, almost as hard as his blows. I knew he was dead.

His horse stood motionless, and I tried to project some reassurance to the beast. Dead? Had I struck that hard?

Weldein galloped up in time to keep the third trooper from mounting. The unmounted man looked from me to Weldein and his sabre and back to me, but didn't say anything.

The woman trooper struggled to her knees, clutching one arm. I could feel the pain.

'Are you all right?' I asked stupidly.

'Bastard! Go ahead and kill me . . . go ahead . . . Frigging invisible horse . . .'

I half expected tears, but she remained hard-eyed, standing in the dirt of the road. Her mount had stopped on the shoulder of the road nearest the river.

The two remaining troopers watched, almost blank-eyed, as the rest of the Kyphran troopers rode up.

'. . . shit to pay, Murros . . .' mumbled the woman to the sole uninjured Hydlenese.

'. . . white wizard'll take them . . .'

'. . . maybe . . . maybe . . . you want to tell him what happened?'

Yelena surveyed the carnage, shaking her head. 'Did you really need any help?'

If I'd been able to shield more people, I might not have needed to kill anyone. But I couldn't. I slowly replaced the staff in the lanceholder, and wiped my forehead, not realizing until then that I'd been sweating.

'Bind them,' commanded the force leader.

'Wait a moment,' I found myself saying as two troopers dismounted and stepped toward the injured woman. I climbed off Gairloch and handed the reins to Jylla. She took them gingerly.

'Frig you . . .' the injured Hydlenese trooper muttered as I walked forward.

I could sense the dislocated bone even before I got too close.

'If you don't mind, trooper,' I said, 'I'd like to set that break so it heals right.'

'Why? You caused it, you dumb bastard.'

'Call it fortunes of battle.' I nodded to the two troopers. 'Hold her. It's likely to hurt for a moment.'

She spat at me, but she didn't scream, although I could feel how much it hurt. She slumped, not quite unconscious by the time I applied a touch of order binding, and strapped her arm in place. I hoped riding wouldn't reinjure it, but that was the best I could do. Then I wiped my face.

I checked the break again after they boosted her into her saddle, but my rough setting and the order patch had held. She still glared at me, and I couldn't blame her.

Two other troopers had cut a shallow trench in the ground by the stream while I had worked on the woman's arm, and a squad was piling rocks over the body to create a rough cairn.

I swallowed, unable to see for a moment. None of it really made sense, but more people would die if the wizard had been warned, wouldn't they?

'Mount up,' ordered Yelena after a while.

I rode in silence at the head of the column; Yelena rode beside me. A good three lengths separated us from the others. The road continued to climb, but so gently that the only way I could tell was to look back.

The road ran beside the curves of the Yellow River, the winter-gray trees, interspersed with a scattering of evergreens, to the left of the packed clay that bore traces of more heavy carts headed back into Hydlen. Rocket-carts?

'You are terrible, you know,' offered Yelena after we had covered another two kays – without seeing any other sentries.

'Yes. I'm terrible at fighting.' And a few other things. Could I have talked more, and stalled the Hydlenese troopers until they were surrounded? I wished I'd been a stronger mage and could have cloaked a whole squad. Then no one would have been hurt.

'You're rather good at it once someone attacks. That's unfortunate for you.' Yelena paused. 'And for them.'

Armsmaster Gilberto had been right. My body had known when to attack, but I felt almost betrayed by it. And yet what choice had I had? When people started fighting, people died. Ferrel had only gone out to investigate, and she was dead. I still didn't understand why, and I didn't think anyone else did either, except maybe the white wizard.

'I said you were terrible,' continued Yelena. 'I meant it. It is terrifying to see a gentle man destroy people. It is terrifying to see an honest man use deception.'

Terrifying? I wouldn't have used the term. Miserable, unhappy, unfortunate, and stupid, yes. Terrifying, no.

We rode on, and I still felt as though someone were watching, but there were no vulcrows, no sentries, nothing but the sound of gray leaves in the light breeze, rushing water, hoofs upon a damp clay road, and low voices muttering about the fortunes of battle.

# XXXII

Sometime after a quick midday watering and an even quicker gulping of rations, we passed the boundary stone clearly flaunted by the Hydlenese – the one that stated 'Kyphros.' Someone had thrown or kicked horse droppings at the letters on the gray stone marker.

No one said anything, but Jylla looked at the defaced kaystone for a long moment as she rode past.

The road rose more steeply and bore right as it neared the valley holding the brimstone springs. The wind carried the faint scent of brimstone along with the dust that indicated it had not rained recently, maybe since my hurried departure from Hydlen.

Yelena held up a hand. The column came to a halt.

'. . . we there yet . . .'

'. . . riding in circles, it seems like . . .'

'Quiet.' Yelena's calm command carried as she looked at me. 'There have to be more sentries.'

'They were just inside the valley last time.' I nodded and sent out my perceptions, trying to sense what lay over the low rise around the curve in the road. If I were the Hydlenese, I'd have had sentries on the top of the rise to give them more than a kay's warning. That was where the sentries had been before, and they still were.

When my eyes refocused, I looked at Yelena. 'The sentries are at the top of the rise around the curve. Except it's not really a curve, but it looks that way because the trees grow closer to the road there.'

'Are you up for another invisible horse, Weldein?' asked Freyda.

Jylla laughed.

'That won't work,' I added. 'There's more than half a squad, and they can't be more than two kays from the edge of the Hydlenese camp lines.'

'Can you tell how many troopers are in the main body?' asked Yelena.

'Not from here. The camp looks about the same, though. Probably not more than ten- or fifteenscore.'

'Just between two and four times what we have. Enough to make it interesting,' mused Freyda.

'What about going through the trees, the way we planned?' asked the force leader, after a sharp look at Freyda, who had ignored the glance.

'It looks all right, but let me go a little farther.' I edged Gairloch off the clay to the left – the south side of the road – and through the scrub and cedars. My nose twitched at the acrid odor of winter leaves and the underlying pungency rising from the cedar fronds left beside the road by a Hydlenese firewood detail.

Just as I recalled, the slope was gentle, and the trees far enough apart for mounted troops, even with their larger horses, to pass easily.

Without really trying, I could also feel the presence of the white wizard, the unseen chaos boiling out of the valley.

I was going to try to confine a white wizard more powerful than Antonin with a special order bound? And use order to turn chaos against him? Did I really have a choice?

When I returned, Yelena looked at me.

'It should work. There's no one stationed at the bottom of the rise, and you can't see the far south side of the first meadow from the road where the sentries are. The scattered trees on the rise reach almost to the plain where their tents are.'

Yelena looked at me. 'Are the commander's main forces close enough to see us?'

'I can't tell from here. We'll have to get into the trees on the rise before I'll be able to tell.' I pursed my lips. 'I'm sorry, but I can't sense things that far away.'

'. . . sorry he can't see more than a kay away over trees . . . glad he's on our side . . .'

I hoped the unknown trooper would feel that way later.

'We'll be exposed.'

I knew that, but there wasn't much else I could do. So I started Gairloch through the trees. Yelena must have motioned, because I could hear the sound of hoofs behind me. I kept Gairloch moving, slanting southward, until we emerged onto the meadow almost in the corner where the south valley walls started rising. There was a fine haze of dust rising behind us, and I hoped that no one happened to be looking closely in our direction, although the dust couldn't have been seen from the main camp. I rubbed my nose to keep from sneezing, as I sat on Gairloch and sent out my perceptions again.

The meadow and the trees beyond on the rise seemed clear, and I started across with Gairloch.

Yelena pulled up beside me. 'You don't have to lead a charge.' Her tone was only partly serious.

'I think they have to see their wizard sticking out his scrawny neck.' I shrugged, trying to loosen the tightness in my shoulders. I could feel my stomach tightening as well.

'You will let my squads lead the charge on the Hydlenese?'

'Yes. I'll need to find a white wizard.'

I slowed halfway down the far side of the rise, where the trees and the shadows from the mid-afternoon sun were still thick enough to provide cover. Wood smoke from cook fires or something drifted our way, mixing with brimstone.

'Now?' asked Yelena.

'Hold on a moment.' After reining up Gairloch next to a cedar tree, perhaps the same one I had used more than an eight-day earlier, I sent out my perceptions, not toward the Hydlenese, but toward the road beyond, trying to find any sense of where Krystal and the main forces might be.

I thought I sensed some Kyphran scouts, but I couldn't tell. What I could tell was that there were a good five squads of lancers drawn up in a rough formation near the western exit to the valley, even beyond the far end of the valley where the brimstone springs flowed and the low stone buildings stood. There were only a dozen or so of the rocket carts, from what I could tell, and they were lined up at the western edge of the tent area, pointed roughly toward Kyphros, and toward where Krystal's forces would be if they left the cover of the gorge and reached the road.

Krystal had been right about that, and it would take time to turn the rockets back toward us, if they could be turned and moved at all during a quick attack.

I had another problem. If I couldn't hold off Gerlis with my order shields, was I willing to use order to funnel chaos to him? I let my perceptions drift below the valley, using the water flows, rather than the rocks, seeking that white-hot-redness of natural chaos.

The sweat beaded on my forehead. There was a lot of natural chaos, perhaps more than that focused in Gerlis. Did I want to try? Would I have any choice?

'Are you all right?' asked Weldein.

I nodded and took a deep breath. I also lied, and that didn't help the twisted feeling in my guts.

Yelena had drawn up the Finest and the outliers behind me in a rough line. Below us to the west of the rise was the flat plain where the tents of the Hydlenese forces were set out. Beyond where I watched lay the last part of the rise that dropped a good fifty cubits in less than half a kay.

'Well?' asked the force leader in a low voice.

'I *think* there are some scouts out there. The Hydlenese have about five squads stationed near the valley entrance, and they seem to be waiting.'

Yelena shifted her weight in the saddle and studied the flat beyond the rise. 'That would leave ten squads standing down in the area around the tents.'

I waited.

Finally, she gave me a grim smile. 'Can you keep the wizard out of our hair?'

'I can only try,' I admitted. 'And I'll have to get a lot closer.'

'The opportunity's just too good.' She looked at me again. 'Where are those devices?'

'At the west end of the tents. There aren't many Hydlenese around them right now.'

Yelena turned to Weldein and Jylla. 'You two guard the order-master. Try to keep him out of too much trouble. He's going to find the white wizard.'

Weldein grunted.

'You're so generous to share the joy of single combat, Weldein,' murmured Jylla, her low voice carrying.

Yelena glanced down the hillside again. 'We'll have to hit the troops they've got drawn up first, but I'll send the outliers through the tent area, and hold the second back.'

She rode toward a small thin subofficer and began to explain something, then rode on to another subofficer, and another, until she had covered all the squad leaders.

The first and third squads lined up quietly on the left, while the two squads of outliers formed up on my right. One squad of the Finest – the second – remained in the center behind the other four groups.

Yelena eased her mount up beside me. 'Are you ready?'

I wasn't ready. My guts were twisted, and my heart was pounding. Reacting, as I had with the white wizard on the road, was much, much easier than deciding to ride down on an armed camp and a white wizard powerful enough to swat me aside like a fly.

I felt like the third wheel on a two-wheeled cart, better at watching, and only able to get in the way if I tried anything. But I had to try something.

'First and third. Now.' Yelena raised her hand, then dropped it.

The front four squads charged – except it wasn't a charge. There were no trumpet blasts, no yells, just horses trotting down through the scattered cedars and out onto the plain.

Yelena's troops moved out quickly, drawing well ahead of the rest, and leaving a fine cloud of dust that drifted toward us. I coughed, more than once, as I bounced along between Weldein and Jylla, slightly behind and to the left of the outliers. Their longer-legged beasts drew ahead of Gairloch and me. That was fine for me, trying as I was to locate Gerlis without alerting him. The location wasn't that hard, not with that tower of unseen white pouring from his pavilion tent near the far end of the encampment. Dust rose around me, and I tried not to cough.

My fingers gripped the reins in one hand and the staff in the other, although what good the staff might do was another question. My palms were sweaty, and my heart thumped faster than I thought it could.

Once on the browning grass, Yelena's squads pulled away toward the road, still quiet, and still trotting.

Then a single trumpet sounded, three quick blasts. The signal repeated itself, once and then again.

More than half the Hydlenese around the road hadn't fully turned when Yelena's squads hit them. By then, the outliers and I were almost on the tents, and the confused Hydlenese there.

Dust and more dust swirled up into my face, and my eyes stung, and my head swam because I was watching half with my eyes and half with my mind, and two sets of images flashed before me.

Somehow I'd gotten the staff into a pattern. I felt like I was flailing, except I saw one woman go down before her blade reached me, and I rocked back in the saddle, half turning before I could get Gairloch headed down the space between the low tents of the Hydlenese troopers and on toward the wizard's pavilion tent.

In the background, there were more trumpets, interspersed with heavy drum rolls, and yells, clashing metal, curses, and the screams of dying souls and horses.

*Hhssttt! Hssstt!!!*

Two firebolts spewed past me, close enough that I could feel their heat, close enough that I could smell singed hair and scorched flesh.

'Aeeiii . . .'

'. . . oh . . .'

Another firebolt hissed overhead, and I ducked. 'Come on, old fellow.'

*Wheee . . . eeee . . .* Complaints or not, Gairloch cantered forward, and I lurched along with him.

'Follow the wizard . . . follow the wizard . . .'

Why Shervan was telling the outliers to follow me made no sense, but Gairloch had begun to canter. I could not only sense the wizard's tent, but see it.

'Follow the wizard . . .'

A distant wavering trumpet seemed to echo from the hills, just as another firebolt flared around the shields I hadn't realized I'd raised – not light shields, just the kind of order barriers I'd used against Antonin.

'Get the rockets! The rockets!'

At that cry, my eyes glanced beyond the wizard's tent.

A handful of men were using something like torches, and the smell of another kind of flame swirled through the tents to me.

With a whistling hiss, a rocket dug into the far hillside beyond Yelena's forces, and the brown grass began to burn out in a circle.

More rockets arched out into the west, toward the road to Kyphros.

The heat and sound of a wizard's firebolt jerked my eyes back to the white tent.

The next firebolt shivered against my staff, so hot and hard I almost dropped it. From the side two men in red tunics slashed toward me, while another half squad ran up from the left.

Two of the outliers spurred their mounts up on the right to shield me, and one went down under the brutal slash of the leading Hydlenese lancer. A spray of blood cascaded across my arm. My guts wrenched, and I dug my heels into Gairloch, although what I was doing charging with only a staff was another question. I recalled that I'd done it before, without a lot of success against such things as arrows.

More mounted Hydlenese appeared, all seemingly headed toward me, and it seemed as if Gerlis's tent were still kays away, as if Gairloch and I were hardly moving forward, as if I were making every motion through water, ever more slowly.

*Whhhsttt . . . Whhhsttt . . .* The line of fire from the rockets was so bright that my eyes followed them for a moment, and my mouth dropped open as they flared right through the center of the Hydlenese lines, one exploding almost at the crimson banner with the sign of the golden dagger.

Then I was trying to unseat another Hydlenese trooper, and the dust and noise swirled around me.

Half ducking, I deflected another firebolt.

'Second!' screamed a distant voice, and the trumpet called again.

Weldein slammed past me, slashing at a trooper I hadn't even seen, and the way to Gerlis's tent, less than fifty cubits ahead, cleared.

Through the cleared space, Gerlis hurled another firebolt, like a spear, one that flew wide of me, but the outlier on my left went up in flames, so quickly he or she didn't even scream.

I pulled aside another flaring and hissing firebolt, and through a gap in the dust and smoke I thought I saw the green leathers of the Finest – more of them – charging from the west.

Gerlis turned, and another pair of firebolts flew – not toward me, but toward the Finest – and Krystal.

I urged Gairloch forward, toward the wizard, somehow throwing what seemed to be a bolt of pure order at Gerlis.

I was less than twenty cubits from the tent when the figure in white turned.

'Oh, the little black mage!' Gerlis seemed ten cubits tall, and he smiled as he leveled his hand at me.

*HHHHHHHHHHHSSSSSSTTTTT!*

A line of white fire burned at me, and flared around my shields, almost crumpling them and halting Gairloch in his tracks.

'You foolish little black mage . . .'

I didn't feel like answering. I just held my seat on Gairloch with my sweaty knees, holding my staff in slippery sweaty hands, again urging Gairloch forward.

Another massive firebolt, almost a wall of flame, slammed toward us. That blast staggered even Gairloch, and my staff went flying.

I tried to reach the chaos deep below the valley, using my own shields to channel it toward Gerlis, not less than twenty cubits from me, across a gulf that seemed a kay wide and even deeper, though the gulf had to be only in my mind.

'. . . shouldn't do that, little mage . . .'

And it seemed as though I should not have, for he seemed to tower out of the tent, standing shimmering there as the white canvas burned away, lifting his hand toward me.

'Save the wizard!'

A blade – a cold iron blade – went flying by me, spinning end over end, and it seemed to turn ever so slowly as it arched toward Gerlis.

His eyes flickered from me to the blade, and another flash of flame darted toward the spinning blade.

With a shrieking hiss, the blade was gone, and my whole body rocked, as though I'd been picked up by the wind and smashed against a stone wall. I had to blink through burning eyes, but I was still in one piece, if barely breathing, and still moving toward Gerlis.

Frantically, I tried to channel more of that awful chaos toward him, without being too tainted by it . . .

. . . he took it, greedy for the power it held.

Another fireball flared past me toward an outlier.

'Aeeeiiiii . . . save . . .'

The whiteness of death rolled around me, as another trooper screamed, and my knees clutched Gairloch more tightly, but he stepped forward, carrying me on a platform as stolid as a rock, and I wanted to hug him and cower, all at the same time, even as I used my last vestiges of order control to smooth the path of chaos to Gerlis.

I never even saw the blade of the Wizard's guard, but Weldein did, and he parried it, and riposted, or whatever it's called, and another body tumbled into the dust.

Around me, I could feel the disjointed rhythm of blades hacking, chopping. Grunts, screams, yells, and curses, loud as they were, seemed to retreat as I struggled with order and chaos.

More rockets flared in the background, out toward the west, although some felt far short of the Finest.

I threw the last of my own order bolts at Gerlis, tempting him to call on that awful power, and he grinned an awful grin, sucking in that power, and looming out of the ground as though he wielded all the power of the deep earth's chaos.

*HHHSSTTTTT . . . CRRRRRUUUMPPTTTT!*

The whole valley groaned, and the earth heaved, and I went flying out of my saddle, and a sheet of flame cascaded toward me. I tried to raise a shield, or I thought I did. It didn't stop the ground from coming up hard. I lay there, with white fire burning through my leg.

Under me, the ground heaved, and tents and their poles swayed, the canvas in flames. Brimstone mists sheeted across the sky, and brimstone rain began to fall – instantly.

Gairloch whinnied and pawed at the ground, somewhere.

The whole valley seemed to heave and spin, in time to a distant trumpet, spinning like the iron blade that had momentarily saved my life, and I thought I heard a faint voice saying, 'So much for the Balance.'

The blackness came down like instant night, like an avalanche of sleep that burned through every bone in my body. I tried to scream, but the words froze in my mind and my throat . . . and I could feel myself falling into a deep gulf, the gulf of chaos.

# XXXIII

The *cracccckkkk* of lightning snapped through my ears.

With a deep roaring, the earth seemed to move under me, and the rain poured down, but I could not move.

My left leg seemed snapped, and I could not lift my right arm. I smelled singed hair, and flesh, and feared that it was mostly mine. My breath came in little gasps, and each gasp seared fire into my lungs.

I opened my eyes, at least for a moment, and screamed, because the white fire of chaos burned them, and that awful white darkness reached out of the earth and seized me, and dragged me back into the depths where the earth roiled and churned around me.

Later, someone in green leathers stood over me, and looked for a long time, or so it seemed. It wasn't Krystal. My eyes burned, and I still couldn't see. The air was damp, and I could hear rain.

I didn't recall anything after that until I woke, lying or riding on a cart of some sort, and every sway and creak of the wheels hurt.

I could hear the rain on a canvas over me, and some of it slipped under the cart's awning and cooled my face. The canvas flapped and cracked like a whip, and the sound slashed my ears.

'You awake?' asked someone.

I tried to open my eyes, but that blinding whiteness threatened to creep in. Then I tried to speak, but all that came out was a croak. I tried again. 'Yes.'

'Tell the commander he's awake.'

I think I dozed for a moment.

'Lerris . . . Lerris . . .'

'Mmmmm . . .' I tried to swallow. 'Water . . .'

I got a trickle of greenberry or something, but it was enough.

'Can you hear me?'

Krystal's voice seemed to echo and come through layers of blankets wrapped around me, but she was there.

'Yes.' I nodded, too, but the effort was too much, and I dropped under the white blackness.

When I woke again, I was still on the damned cart, but it wasn't raining, and the cold wind felt good on my face. I felt as if I were burning up, and I knew I ought to be doing something with order to heal myself, but I couldn't. I opened my eyes, and they only burned.

Krystal was there. Maybe she hadn't left, but she was riding beside the cart.

'Sorry . . .' I mumbled.

'Oh, Lerris . . . you're sorry?' She bent down in the saddle, and her fingertips brushed my forehead. They felt cool and good.

'What . . . happened?'

'Yelena cut down half the lancers on the road. Their own rockets got most of the rest. You . . . the white wizard . . . there wasn't much left. Maybe two score of the Hydlenese survived.'

'Shervan . . . saved me,' I mumbled. 'Threw his sword . . .'

The cart bounced again, and the knives shot through me for a moment.

'. . . good for something,' mumbled Jylla from beyond Krystal. Her arm was strapped tight to her body, and her face was a mass of red lines and bruises. The upper tip of her ear was missing.

I didn't see Freyda.

'... the spring ...' I still was having trouble talking and see-ing.

'Don't talk. Please don't talk. I'm right here.'

I thought that was funny, and I wanted to laugh. The commander riding beside the wounded wizard. Commanders should be in charge, I thought.

'... spring ...' I gasped.

'We took it back. There's more brimstone than ever, and some of it keeps spouting into the sky ...'

I must have slipped off because I didn't hear anything more.

After that, I kept waking up on the cart, and not being able to say anything.

Krystal was there, and she was crying, and I had never seen her cry, and then I couldn't say anything anyway because it hurt so much just to breathe.

I did wake up again, and I was in a bed in a big room, and there was light everywhere, and I felt like I was burning alive.

Justen was looking down at me.

'... how ...?' I croaked.

'When you do something, you make enough of a dent in the order-chaos fabric to ring the whole world like a bell. I was already on my way back. Now ... let me work.'

'... wrong ...' It still hurt to breathe and talk, but not so much.

'Outside of a leg with two snapped bones, chaos infections, bruises * on every muscle in your body, a broken rib that almost got your lungs – not much.'

He seemed to age, even as he looked and worked on me.

'Demon-hell time to have to do order-chaos balances ... idiot nephew ...'

I thought about thanking him, but even my thanks wouldn't have been pleasant to his ears. Where had he been when I was taking on Gerlis? I never got the words out, though, but passed out or slept or both.

When I finally did wake up, Rissa was sitting there, and she had deep circles under her eyes.

'Rissa ...' I managed to croak.

'It's about time, Master Lerris.' She leaned over me holding a cup, and her words seemed to come from a long ways away. 'The old mage says that you have to drink this stuff if you wish to live.' I drank. Whatever it was tasted vile and smelled worse. But I drank. I lay there for a time, I think, but apparently drinking had exhausted me, because I went back to sleep.

The next time I woke Krystal was there. She looked as if she had been facing the demons of light.

'. . . love . . . you . . .' I managed, not wanting to waste words, wondering if I had many left.

She put both hands on the sides of my face, gently, and kissed my forehead. 'I know, and I love you.' Then she had the damned cup in her hand. 'You need to drink as much of this as you can.'

So I did, and I didn't fall asleep. I just looked at her. She wore the green shirt and leathers, but not the vest, and the shirt was wrinkled, and her eyes were tired.

She looked at me, and finally she smiled. 'Do you want some more to drink?'

'No. Will . . . though . . .'

She held the cup steady with one hand, and my good hand with her other, and I drank, and I thought it helped. Then she sat beside me and held my hand until I fell asleep again.

# XXXIV

Never shall darkness nor light prevail, for one must balance the other; yet many of light will seek to banish darkness, and a multitude shall seek to cloak the light; but the balance will destroy all who seek the full ends of darkness and light.

Then shall a woman rule the parched fields and dry groves of the reformed Kyphros and the highlands of Analeria and the enchanted hills; and all matters of wonders shall come to pass.

In the fullness of time, both order and chaos shall rise again. Those who seek order shall follow chaos, and those who follow chaos shall seek order, and none shall know which path to tread.

The sword called knowledge shall be unsheathed, and scholars and soldiers shall both proclaim its virtue and trumpet how it shall bring prosperity out of want, and plenty out of drought. Yet its blade will cut deep into the land and burn into the heavens, and many will turn from its terrors unto their own weapons.

Terrible indeed shall be those weapons – one shall be like unto the swords of the stars that are suns, and another like unto the lances of winter and yet another like unto the mirrored towers raised by the demons of light.

Dark ships shall speed upon the waters, and destruction shall fall from the heavens, shattering the greatest of walls, and even the weakest of those who bear arms shall strike with the force of firebolts . . .

*The Book of Ryba*
Canto DL [The Last]
Original Text

# II.

---

# FINDING
# KNOWLEDGE

# XXXV

## The Black Holding, Land's End [Recluce]

'Did you feel what happened in Hydlen?' Heldra steps onto the ancient terrace.

'Yes, and I didn't like the feel of it.' Talryn walks along the wall that edges the terrace.

'It felt ugly, but Candar's always been a mess.' Heldra glances from the black stones cut centuries earlier to the oak that spreads far above the terrace and then to Talryn, who nods.

'Why are we here?' asks Maris.

'Because this is the Founders' Shrine and because the rules of the Council say we have to meet here once a season.'

'It's creepy, like Creslin's looking over my shoulder.' Maris turns toward the ancient house, its stones still crisp and locked in order.

'That's the idea. What we do is supposed to reflect their ideals.'

'That was a thousand years ago. This is now.' Maris sniffs.

'As Heldra pointed out,' responds Talryn,' some things don't change. Candar is still a mess. There's a lot of chaos floating free. Lerris did something to Gerlis. There's no chaos focus left there. We've had order and chaos focuses for that whole time, and we still don't have a good way to deal with them.'

'Pretty spot. I can see why Megaera liked it.' Heldra turns from viewing the Eastern Ocean. 'Lerris did a lot more than something. I can still sense the reverberations.'

'So what will happen?' Maris studies the window and peers into the old Council Room. He shivers.

Talryn shrugs. 'I suspect that Berfir will cede the spring and some land to the autarch. At some time in the future, once he's trounced Colaris with his rocket carts, he'll repudiate the agreement and try to take it back.'

'You think the autarch will let him? And what if Colaris finds some new tricks of his own? They really want that Ohyde Valley back.' Maris still peers through the window at the old Council Room. 'Is that blade Creslin's?'

'Yes. This is your first time here, isn't it?'

Maris nods.

'They say he never wore that blade after he destroyed the great white fleet. Probably just another old tale.' Heldra pauses. 'I've held the blade, though. There's . . . something . . . there.'

'Maybe. You and your blades.' Maris fingers his beard. 'You might be right. Truth is sometimes harder to believe than lies. What about Cassius? Who would believe a man from another – what does he call it? – another universe . . . coming through an order/chaos flaw? He's here, though. What if Lerris created something like that? What if the next visitor isn't so friendly?'

'Those things don't happen often.' Talryn half laughed.

'Then there's Sammel. Antonin, Gerlis, Sammel, Lerris, and that doesn't even include Justen and Tamra.'

'Sammel?' Heldra opens the door and holds it. 'What about him? His problem is that he loves knowledge more than order. That's not exactly the same as Antonin or Gerlis, who were out to create chaos for their own power.'

'He's setting himself up as something.' Talryn follows Heldra inside the Black Holding.'Have you heard from the black squads?'

'No. That bothers me a bit.'

'A bit?' asks Maris. 'How many did you send?'

'Just two, with the rocket guns. They didn't have to get close.'

Talryn frowns. 'I can still sense Sammel. We may have a problem there.'

'He might be a bigger problem than young Lerris, a much bigger problem,' suggests Maris. 'And what if this war between Berfir and Colaris drags on? And what if Sammel and Lerris and Justen and Tamra all get involved? Then what do we do?'

'Candar – always a mess. What else has happened there since the fall of Frven? Justen destroyed the old white empire, and melted it into slag, and it didn't affect us. We can certainly handle this one. We'll let Colaris and Berfir fight it out, and I'll take a squad after Sammel personally.' Heldra closes the outside door, and then leads the way to the black oak door to the old Council chamber. 'I'm more worried about the growth of machines and all those new ships in Hamor . . . and that steel that's nearly as good as black iron.'

'You just don't want to admit you were wrong about Sammel,' says Maris.

Heldra's hand eases around the hilt of the blade.

'Just joking,' adds Maris quickly.

# XXXVI

## Northwest of Renklaar, Hydlen [Candar]

The first rocket flares toward advancing Freetown troops led by the white and cyan banners. As it passes above them, a few soldiers glance upward, but most continue to march up the gentle slope toward the shallow trenches of the Hydlenese.

Another wave of rockets flies downhill toward the mass of Freetown troops. One smashes into the ground less than a dozen cubits before the left edge of the attackers. Scattered fires flare through the troops, and two fall. One man becomes a bonfire. Several others try to roll on the ground to extinguish the flames that threaten to consume them.

More rockets flash downhill from the Hydlenese emplacements, exploding almost in the center wedge of the attackers. Cyan-clad troops lie scattered across the hillside, where bodies, scrub bushes, and browning grass all burn. Plumes of black, white, and gray smoke entwine and circle skyward.

After yet another volley of rockets, a trumpet sounds, urgently, and the attackers begin to retreat, first at a walk, then a run, but another flight of the rockets follows them.

With a series of whistling hisses, another round of rockets flies.

'Archers!' commands Berfir.

Shafts in waves arch downhill, their heavy triangular and barbed heads slashing through flesh and light chain mail.

The black, gray, and white smoke plumes circling upward from the lower part of the hillside thicken.

Another trumpet sounds, and this time, a good dozen squads of horsemen wearing the gold and red plaid of Yeannota swing off the opposite hillside at an angle.

'Shot rockets! Shot rockets!' orders Berfir, but the rocket officer has already turned the carts with the crimson stripe toward the lancers.

Another flight of rockets slams into the retreating foot, followed by a last volley of high-arching arrows.

More than tenscore bodies lie below the shallow trenchworks of the Hydlenese.

Berfir watches as the Freetown mercenary horse reaches the flatter slope on his left flank. He nods.

Two heavier rockets arc the short distance toward the horse.

*Crummmmptt!!! Crummptt!!*

Iron discs scythe through the lancers, and the screams of men and horses drown out the sounds of the next set of disc shot rockets.

The heavy-headed arrows pick off the handful of lancers on the hillside, and less than a half squad of stragglers and survivors struggle back to the Freetown lines.

Berfir gestures to the rocket officer, and the rocket-cart launching tubes are angled higher.

The next set of rockets arches into the troops on the other hillside. Another set follows. Shortly, smoke begins to rise from the Freetown emplacements, joining the clouds that have already begun to dim the sun.

Berfir smiles as the cyan and white banners retreat.

'Got 'em good this time, ser,' rasps the rocket officer.

The smile fades from the Duke's face, and he looks tired. 'This time, Nual, this time. Thanks to the rockets.'

'You think they'll be getting rockets soon?'

Berfir looks to the northeast, in the general direction of Freetown, although the foot of the Great North Bay on which the port sits is more than a hundred kays away. 'Colaris will come up with something. He always does.'

'Mean bastard, he is.'

'In these times, everyone is.' The Duke straightens. 'Get the launchers reloaded.'

# XXXVII

The winter sunlight pouring through the window of the autarch's guest quarters didn't warm the room that much, and I was glad for the heavy quilt, except where it pressed on my left leg. Order-mastery or not, it was hard to stay warm when I was hurt, and shivering sent waves of pain up from my leg, but the more I shivered, the more I hurt.

The big bed was comfortable, and the dark-stained cherry headboard not a bad piece of work. The wardrobe, the bedside table that held the lamp, and the small chair were all the same dark-stained cherry, and the work of the same crafter, although I didn't recognize the style. Uncle Sardit might have, but I didn't have his experience.

For lack of anything better to do – that I could do – I'd prevailed upon Krystal to reclaim my *Basis of Order*. At times, though, my eyes still burned when I tried to read, and parts remained insufferably boring, especially the rhetoric at the front. That had to have been tacked onto the book later. It didn't even sound the same as the parts that explained what, and how, and why.

'Order is the basis of any community.' Why was that even necessary? Anything with more than one part had to have order to work, and any group of any animals that stayed together had to have some degree of order. Ants did. Sheep did. Geese did – sometimes. So what was different about people?

The door opened, and in stepped Justen.

'Let's see how well you're healing.'

I didn't have that much extra energy, but I'd used what I had to keep any traces of chaos infections away, and encourage some healing. More than encouraging it wasn't good, according to both Justen and *The Basis of Order*. I set the book on the table.

He drew back the quilt and started with my arm.

'Hmmmmm . . . not bad. That won't be long.'

Long for what? I wondered. His voice seemed to get louder and then die off, but it was probably my ears.

'. . . really did mangle this . . .'

That was my leg, strapped up in wood and leather. All in all, I managed to lie still as Justen probed at my body, but it wasn't easy, not with half of it yellow and green from bruises, and an arm and a leg not working all that well. His fingers were light, but I could feel them.

'You'll live.'

'Is that all you have to say?'

'Lerris, with the shape you arrived in, that is saying a great deal. Bruises, burns, broken bones —'

'Burns?'

Justen shook his head. 'You turn a simple brimstone spring into a boiling inferno, and you're going to get burned.'

'I didn't know I did that.'

The gray wizard took a long and elaborate deep breath. 'You tapped elemental chaos beneath the earth and channeled it directly to the surface. Elemental chaos is hotter than forge fires. What did you think was going to happen?'

'From the book' – I gestured to *The Basis of Order* – 'I figured that if I gave Gerlis enough chaos, it would overload his ability and destroy him.'

'You did, and it did.' Justen shook his head. 'It also turned the valley into a small version of the demon's hell, and killed most of the Hydlenese troops. From what I can tell, you put up some sort of shield that saved the Kyphrans around you.' He snorted. 'You are lucky. I'll give you that. Most of the other Kyphrans, including Krystal, were far enough away to avoid that first flame blast.'

I shrugged, and it didn't hurt too much. 'What was I supposed to do? Let Gerlis burn everyone alive, including me?' Sometimes, Justen was a pain. Just like Talryn and my father, always saying what was wrong with what I'd done. Where had he been? Off somewhere with some woman, and now he was complaining – again – about how I'd botched things. All the magisters were like that. Talryn, Lennett – they'd say that if you made a mistake, you'd pay. The problem was that they usually didn't tell you what was a mistake until after you made it.

I frowned, recalling Tamra's point about the order tie, and I squinted, and tried to concentrate on really seeing Justen, with order senses and all, and though the effort sent little knives through my eyes, I kept at it.

He looked different – like his whole body were made up of little blocks of chaos coated in order. Tamra had been right. There was a hint of an order-tie trailing off to somewhere. Maybe . . . he had a consort. Justen with a woman – permanently? I wondered what else I didn't know, or hadn't seen.

'You could have left him alone. Chaos-masters don't live that long. The chaos would have diffused eventually.'

'When? After Berfir came back south with his rockets and took over Kyphros?'

'That wouldn't have happened.'

Justen always had answers. It was tiresome and predictable, and they always involved patience, which, in a warlike place like Candar, wasn't always possible for those of us who weren't gray wizards who would live forever. Except, even as I thought that, my stomach twisted a little. By handling chaos, even with order, wasn't I becoming a gray wizard?

Justen turned his eyes directly on me. 'We need to talk more, when you're feeling better and not so sorry for yourself, and when I have more patience, and when I'm not so tired.'

Why was he tired? He hadn't been fighting chaos and battles. My eyes hurt, and his words got louder still and then died away.

'I'm tired because I've been trying to save all those wounded and burned troopers. You weren't the only casualty, you know. You're just the only one who gets a fancy sickroom.'

'I'm sorry.' I felt about one finger high, but what else could I say?

He shook his head again. 'I'm being too hard on you. You did the best you could. This isn't the best time to talk.'

His hair was streaked with silver again. That showed he was too exhausted to keep himself young, but I hadn't really noticed. Maybe he was right. Maybe I was feeling too sorry for myself and bored.

'Could I go home?'

Justen studied me. 'If you get someone to lend you a carriage. You'll get bounced too much in a wagon, and a horse, even a gentle one like Gairloch, is out of the question.' He coughed before continuing. 'It might be better. I can't do anything more for you that you can't do for yourself now.'

Without asking why it might be better, I just nodded.

'We will talk.' He turned and was gone.

I looked at the cold light coming through the window for a time, then at the cover of *The Basis of Order*. How many people had died? Had I really killed them? Had it been necessary?

I rubbed my forehead gently, feeling the flaking skin and the stubbly hair growing back in from where it had been burned away. I thought it had just been cut while I had been unconscious in order to dress a slash or something. Burns?

Krystal was the next visitor, wearing her training garb, stained gray shirt, worn leathers, and her blade. She was sweating, despite the faint chill in the room.

'You've been busy.'

'We still don't have enough trainers. Tamra helps them get used to a staff, but good blades who understand what they're doing are hard to find.' She bent over and kissed me, and I kissed her back.

'You are getting better.'

'Justen told me I'd live.'

'For a while, none of us were sure.' She pulled the single chair right up beside the bed and sat down.

'I'm tougher than that.'

'You're a hero of sorts, not because you defeated the white wizard, but because you've survived the wounds.' Krystal laughed softly. 'Enough of the Finest saw you on that cart. Not one in a score survives that kind of beating. You're not only the order-master. You're the toughest order-master anyone has ever seen, and you're their order-master. You fought a wizard, and you fought blades.'

'I don't much feel like a hero. Justen was just here.'

'He has that effect.' Krystal laughed, with a bitter note. 'He asked if this whole business had really been necessary.'

'I've got some of the same questions. How many died?'

Krystal's face went almost blank, and there was a pause.

'That bad?'

'It was pretty bad for the outliers. Only the half squad closest to you made it through, and one wounded Hydlenese. He's mad though – just keeps weeping about you. He calls you the terrible wizard, and then he weeps.'

Me? A terrible wizard? 'What about Weldein? He saved me a couple times.'

'He was banged up and took a deep thrust, but Justen pulled him through.'

'Freyda was killed.'

Krystal nodded.

'Jylla?'

'Her arm and shoulder were crushed. No thrust wounds. She won't fight again, but she'll keep the arm.'

'Yelena?'

'She's fine. But I sent her to Ruzor to take over Subrella's old job. Kyldesee didn't work out. I didn't think she would, but we had to try. She's a friend of Mureas's.'

Politics again.

'What about Shervan? He died, didn't he? So did Pendril, I think.'

Krystal nodded.

Wonderful odds. Of the half dozen or so I'd known and ridden with, three were dead, one crippled, one wounded. My throat felt thick, and my eyes burned. It had seemed like a good idea. But if our plan had been a good one, what would have happened with a bad one?

'That's what happens when people fight, Lerris.'

It had seemed so easy, so clean, dealing with Antonin. Poof . . . fire, struggle, and white ashes. Was that why wizards were so dangerous? Because they never saw the bodies and the blades? Never knew the people?

I swallowed. 'What about the Hydlenese?'

'Worse. We sent back maybe one squad, mostly wounded.'

I shivered. 'I think it's time to go home.'

'You don't like the autarch's hospitality?'

'She has been more than gracious.' And she had. She'd stopped in to see me more than a handful of times, and had even insisted on pressing another bag of coin on me, claiming that coins were a poor reward. Not knowing when I'd be able to go back to work, I'd taken them. They were still tucked under a corner of the mattress.

I looked back to the window and the cold light still streaming through.

'What does Justen say?' Krystal's voice softened, or faded away some.

'If I can get a carriage to take me, it would probably be better to be home. He didn't really say why.'

Krystal fluffed my hair gently, and kissed my cheek. 'Because the wood will help you heal, I think. First bloody battles are hard.'

'Was it hard for you?'

She squeezed my good hand. 'Hard enough, but I'm older. I've seen a lot more violence than you have.'

'Do you get used to it?'

'I hope not.'

I looked at her face, with the fine lines running from the eyes and the streaks of silver in the dark hair. Behind her dark eyes was another kind of darkness, a darkness I thought I was just beginning to discover. Like Justen, she looked tired.

I eased both hands around her hand, ignoring the discomfort in my right arm, and she stayed for a long time. She didn't say anything, but she didn't need to. Neither did I, and at some point, I fell asleep.

# XXXVIII

I was stretched out in my own bed, with my back propped up with pillows against the headboard, reading and trying to recover from the carriage trip home the day before. Despite Justen's approval, it had hurt, and tired me. Even my eyes had gone back to hurting; so I'd slept most of the time since.

Then Tamra marched in. 'So how's the cripple? Feeling sorry for yourself?' Tamra wore the blue scarf that matched her eyes. She plopped into the wooden armchair, her back to the window.

Outside, I could see the blue sky and the scattered trees waving in the wind. Even the clouds were moving fast. 'No. Just sore all over.' I set down *The Basis of Order* and took a half-deep breath and closed my eyes for a second. That helped. My chest and ribs still ached with really deep breaths.

'You think you'll be up before long?'

'I don't know how long. Justen says the ribs are mostly healed, and the arm's coming along. It's the leg.' I wasn't about to mention the eyes or the sometimes fading hearing. I figured they'd get better with rest.

'Justen's your uncle. He's too nice to you.' Tamra smiled brightly and shifted her weight in the chair.

'He was nice to you when you needed it.'

'I think you'll look good in gray,' Tamra announced as if she were telling me about the weather. 'If you'll ever get off your ass, anyway.'

'Gray? I've never worn gray, and I never will.' Even as I said the words, I wanted to take them back. 'Never' is a dangerous word, especially for me. So I changed the subject. 'Some wizard you are,' I snapped back. 'You just criticize. What can you really do?'

Those blue eyes turned the color of slate, and the whole room darkened, and the shutters banged, and a cold winter wind whipped across me and ripped at the coverlet.

I swallowed. Tamra had definitely learned *something* from Justen. 'All right. You can throw the winds around. What do you want?'

'First, I want some respect. You, and all men, seem to think that if I don't parade my power, I don't have it. Second, I want you to show some real strength. Are you going to throw away everything you've learned because you're stubborn? Are you going to lie in that bed until someone begs you to get out of it? Is the poor little order-master so beaten up . . .'

I sat up, despite the pain in my leg and arm, and swung my good leg around and sort of dragged the other. I had to hold on to the headboard for a moment.

'Not bad. Justen didn't think you had enough strength for that. But he's a softie.' Tamra grinned, and it reminded me of Gerlis.

'You really are the red bitch.' The words came out between waves of white pain.

'Now, if you do that more often, you'll be up and around a lot sooner.' She looked at me. 'You really did get beaten up, didn't you?'

I had to lean back against the pillows before I fell over. 'You really did get into trouble with Antonin, didn't you?'

'Good!' Tamra was all businesslike. 'Kasee needs to throw more of a scare into Berfir's envoy. He'll be here in another eight-day, and you should be moving around by then. That type always needs reminding. That's why you're going to wear grays to the audience.'

'I don't wear gray. I wear brown.'

'You want to let Krystal down? Or all the troopers who died? You want this envoy to walk all over Kasee?'

'No one walks all over the autarch.'

'That's not what I meant. She doesn't have that much of an army, and any envoy who comes here will know it. What does she have? She's got me and you and Krystal and a good small bunch of mercenaries. So you have to be there and look impressive, and browns don't look impressive.'

'How am I even going to get them on?'

'Rissa says you'll have to put buttons in place of the seams on the left trouser leg, but that's no problem. You'll have to do that anyway.'

'Fine. I'll go to the meeting, the audience . . . whatever. I'll wear browns. And someone can wheel me in on a cart. I'll really look impressive.'

'I'll get another staff made. You'll hobble in before the envoy gets there, and you'll stand there with that staff and look most impressive in grays.'

'I'll wear grays the day Justen shows up for this meeting.'

'Good. He's coming. Three of us will have to be enough. I brought the gray leathers and some gray cloth. Rissa said she'd make the trousers and shirt, and you'll pay her.'

'I already pay her.'

'Pay her more. You got more golds from Kasee.'

'Ha! If I don't get back to work soon, we'll all be starving.' It wasn't true, not yet, but Tamra made me angry.

'Then you'd better work harder on healing yourself, hadn't you?' Tamra stood up. 'I'll have Rissa start right away. She'll have to measure you, and don't throw some sort of fit.'

She gave me a last smile and was gone.

I glanced at *The Basis of Order*. Finally, I picked it up and started to read, not that the words made all that much sense.

'. . . the order of the earth is the order of order within and around chaos, and he who can order the earth can order the world, would he bear the weight of the sorrow he would cause . . .'

Sorrow? Every sort of order seemed to result in sorrow for someone? How come there wasn't a book for chaos-masters that warned them about sorrow? Was that because they didn't care? Did all order-masters really care?

Too many questions, and I finally put down the book and dozed.

It was late when Krystal came in, well past dark, but she walked into the bedroom with her jacket and blade still in place.

'How are you doing?'

I sat up, and again managed to turn and dangle my legs, good and bad, over the side of the bed, except the splinted left one really didn't dangle but sort of stuck out and hurt. 'Getting better.'

'That's good.' She touched my cheek and gave me a quick kiss.

'How are you doing?'

'It could be worse. Yelena sent us some recruits from Ruzor. A couple actually look pretty decent. They're from Southwind. They still have most of the ancient military traditions – not so good as Westwind was, but close, and we can use that.'

'A couple? That's good?'

Krystal pulled the chair close to me and sat down with a deep breath, then answered. 'We're getting interest, and that's good. I understand there's an entire squad coming from Spidlar. The traders are cutting back again.' She sighed again. 'The idiots. Didn't they learn from the time of Dorrin? Of course not. It's just a matter of coins.'

'Tamra was here today.'

'She said she'd stopped to see you.'

'Did she tell you about her idea for impressing Berfir's envoy?'

'She's still rather abrupt, isn't she?' Krystal's laugh contained a rueful note.

'She always will be.'

'What do you think?' asked my consort.

'She's probably right.' I shrugged, if carefully. 'Kasee doesn't have that big an army, and someone like Berfir is more impressed with a show of some kind of force.'

'I think so. Can you do it?'

'I'll have to, won't I?'

'You're getting better.'

'Long day?' I fought dizziness for a moment.

'Very.'

From the higher position on the bed, I could reach down. So I stroked her cheek and kneaded her too-tight shoulder muscles. After a little bit, I had to use just my left hand. The right arm hurt too much for me to keep it up.

Krystal just dropped her head forward and enjoyed the neck and shoulder massage, and so did I.

# XXXIX

The next morning, while Krystal was pulling on her uniform, I hobbled out to the table, dark as it was outside. After Tamra's visit, it didn't look as if I were going to have that much time to lie around.

Besides, I was well enough that I didn't feel like lying in bed once Krystal left for the barracks, no matter how early it was.

I worried, because she probably wouldn't have been home, except I was hurt, and the getting home late and the getting up early meant she didn't get much sleep. But I liked having her sleep beside me.

Rissa set a cup of herb tea down. 'You look like you need this.'

Whether I needed it or not, I was going to get it. It didn't taste like much, unlike the awful stuff they had poured down me to get me to heal.

Then Rissa set the bread down, just moments before Krystal sat down, her short hair in place, her vest on, and her blade clanking against the chair.

I patted her leg and got a smile as she reached for her own mug of tea.

From the darkness in the yard came the sounds of horses being saddled and readied. Rissa set a bowl of dried peaches and pearapples between us.

'You go first. I'm not exactly going anywhere.' I nodded to Krystal, and she smiled again.

'It won't be that long before you will.'

Perron came through the door, and Krystal motioned to the table. 'Have them all come in and get something to eat.'

'Yes, ser.'

After he stepped into the yard, Krystal added, 'They all want to see you anyway.'

'Me?'

She snorted.

'Greetings, Order-master,' Perron said.

Haithen, another woman, and a man walked in and sat at the table. Rissa set out two more bowls of dried fruit and two more loaves of the dark bread.

'Herbal tea?' asked the woman trooper I didn't know, a brunette with a sharp nose, as she broke off a chunk of bread.

'It doesn't taste like much, but it's supposed to help.' I took some bread and a handful of dried peaches. 'Is there any cheese?'

'It's only the yellow stuff, Master Lerris.'

'Better than nothing,' I groaned. 'Let's have it.'

After Rissa set the block on the table, I cut two slices, left-handed and a bit awkwardly, then passed the yellow cheese to Krystal.

There wasn't much left, large as it had been, after Krystal's guard took their slices, a reminder that being the commander's consort was costly in not-so-obvious ways.

Haithen finally spoke. 'How come you can't heal yourself?'

The other guards looked as if they had wanted to ask the same question.

'I could . . . but I couldn't do much of anything ever again, and if I ever got tired, I'd fall apart.' I tried to explain. 'Order-mastery takes strength and skill – just like handling a blade. Haithen, why don't you carry a two-hand blade?'

'It's too heavy, especially riding. I'd lose my balance.'

'The same thing's true about wizardry. When I went up against the first white wizard, I only had to touch him with my staff after I cut him off from his power. With his power gone, he was already dying. If I used pure order to heal myself, if I ever lost my power or strength, I'd fall apart. When I got older, I'd die.' I held up my good hand to stop the objections. 'Now, another wizard could help a little, and that's what some healers do. I can use order to keep chaos out of my body and to help the bones knit. I'll heal faster than I would otherwise, and the bones will knit straight.'

'Is that why healers can't help very many wounded?' Haithen asked.

I nodded. 'Each time you try to heal someone, it takes energy. A healer can use so much order that it can kill the healer and save the patient.'

'That's why you carry a staff?' Perron frowned.

'It's not that simple. You can't kill or hurt someone with order – not directly. They say that a storm-wizard can use order to create a storm, and the storm can kill people. That takes time, and it wouldn't work very well in a battle.'

'But you killed the white wizard.'

'No. I helped him kill himself.' I forced a laugh. 'You also may have seen what a mess it made.'

'. . . still don't understand . . .' mumbled the other woman. 'You destroyed a whole valley, and you have to carry a staff to protect yourself?'

'What am I supposed to do if a trooper comes swinging at me with a blade? I can't turn chaos on him.' I looked at the woman. 'Or her. And I don't know how to create storms.'

'But you did. It rained for days.'

I had to grin. 'How much good did that do me?'

Haithen laughed, at least.

'This is interesting,' said Krystal, 'but the autarch is expecting me right after morning muster.'

They all gulped down the remnants of whatever they were eating, as if it were their last meal. Then they headed for the yard, bowing to Rissa.

'Thank you, Rissa.' Perron gave her a deeper bow.

'Thank you.' Rissa – no-nonsense Rissa – flushed.

Perron grinned and turned.

As Krystal stood, so did I, even if it took levering myself up on the table and holding tight to a rough cane.

'You don't —'

'I can't lie around forever.' I hugged her.

'I don't want you limping for life to prove something. You don't have to be a hero at home.' She did kiss me, though.

I stood in the door as she swung into the saddle and rode into the gray of the dawn, back toward Kyphrien, and training sessions, logistics, planning, politics, discipline – all the details that took so much more time than fighting.

After that I hobbled back to the table and sank into a chair, while Rissa put things away.

'I'm doing more bread, Master Lerris. Any kind you want more of?'

'I'm partial to the dark.'

'I know. Like Commander Krystal.'

'That's not —'

'You're too serious for a young fellow.' She laughed.

I did smile.

'And have some more cheese and bread.'

'Yes, Mother Rissa.'

She sniffed, but she sniffed with a smile.

After cutting a thick slice of bread and a wedge of cheese, I ate and sat at the table for a time, letting my fingers trace the design. The curves with the curlicues had been the hardest part, and I had vowed to avoid that kind of elaboration again. If I looked at them sideways, they looked almost chaotic.

Woodwork can't be chaotic, not really, but the swirls reminded me of the intertwined order and chaos I had felt, felt and tapped, beneath the brimstone spring. Were order and chaos really intertwined that closely?

I recalled those few words Justen had said to me when he had started to heal me – something about a demon-time to do order-chaos balances. Idly, I let my senses focus on my arm. It was still tender, and bound in heavy leather, but the bone hadn't snapped the way my leg had. Part of the arm had a strange design, almost as if the chaotic tiny bits that exist within everyone were imbedded in larger pieces of order.

I swallowed, recalling that Justen's whole body had been like that when I had looked at him with my order senses.

'Rissa?'

'Yes, Master Lerris?'

'Would you come here?'

Lifting her eyebrows, Rissa stepped closer to the table.

'Just put your arm next to mine.'

'That's all?'

'That's all.' I compared the two. Parts of my arm were different, seen that way, just like the way I had seen Justen's.

'You done? I still have bread to bake.'

'Oh . . . yes. Thank you.'

'Wizards . . .' Rissa left with a flip of her short hair.

Could I reorder the arm, all of the part around the healing bone, the same way? I concentrated, and a tiny little section seemed to change. My fingers shook, and my eyes burned. I stopped because I had to put my head down on the table.

'Master Lerris! Master Lerris!'

'I'm all right. I just got tired.'

'You get up and get back in that bed. You almost died, and here you are trying to pretend you're all healthy.' Rissa marched up beside me. 'There's nobody looking, and you don't have to show all the Finest that you're the toughest wizard ever. Lean on me, and we're getting you back to that bed for some rest.'

So I did, and it felt good to lie down. I even dozed off. Maybe I did have to lie around a little longer.

# XL

## Northwest of Renklaar, Freetown [Candar]

The body of the Hydlenese forces grinds to a halt near the hilltop, and Berfir rides to the fore of the main group, one hand straying to the hand-and-a-half blade across his shoulders. He glances down the slope and notes the three horses on the ground, one screaming. One rider lies facedown, unmoving.

A puddle spilling over from marshy ground has flooded the main road and the grass on each side with a sheet of muddy water twenty or more cubits wide, but less than a few fingers deep.

Another lancer eases his mount off the road, but the horse takes no more than a few steps before it screams and bucks. The lancer hangs on, as the horse settles, but holds a forefoot high. She leaps from her saddle back toward the dry ground, holding the reins.

As she bends down to study something in her mount's hoof, even as Berfir watches, a hail of arrows streams out of the hillside, seemingly from nowhere. More lancers fall, and the others look indecisively, then spur their horses back uphill, trying to escape the arrows. The injured horse takes several arrows and breaks away from the lancer, splashing through the puddle, and collapsing with a shrieking whinny.

The lancer on foot goes down.

By following the arrows, Berfir finally sees the archers, concealed on the side of the hill behind what had seemed to be low bushes. After a last volley, they scramble uphill and out of sight.

The Duke rides down toward the retreating lancers, and horses and riders move from his path as the massive sword comes out of the scabbard. He holds it easily in one hand.

'What happened?' he snaps at the subofficer.

'Caltrops . . . hundreds of them.'

'On the road? You couldn't see them?'

The lancer gestures to the water, and Berfir's eyes flick to the downhill end of the marshy area. In hindsight, the earthy berm that had looked natural is clearly a dam.

Shortly, another lancer approaches and offers a rusted caltrop for the Duke's inspection.

'Rusted? Iron doesn't rust that fast.' Then he nods. 'They rusted them first.'

'I would say so, ser.'

'You'll pay for this, Colaris.' Berfir looks to the northeast and his blade rises. 'We didn't want this . . . war . . . but you'll pay for it.'

The lancers shrink away from the big blade, but Berfir only swings it back and into his scabbard. 'Go on! Clean it up.'

The Duke turns his mount downhill and rides slowly along the edge of the muddy water, studying it.

The lancers head back downhill after him. Shortly, two have pried open a hole in the earth berm and the road is clear of water. Hundreds of pointed brown iron objects lie on the muddy stones.

Berfir snorts in disgust.

Before long the rusted caltrops rest in a cart brought from the rear of the force, and the Hydlenese forces surge up the low hill on the far side of the valley, beginning the slow march toward Freetown.

# XLI

At least Kasee sent a covered carriage for me – or Tamra did in the autarch's name. Tamra also sent the iron-bound staff she had promised, and I rode in style through the heavy winter rain. Kyphrans complained about the winter rains, but compared to those on Recluce, or those I had experienced elsewhere in Candar, they were mild, indeed.

I wore a brown cloak over the grays, and carried my new staff, using it as support to climb into the carriage. The staff barely fit inside, and I had to sit sideways because of the splint on my leg.

Other than the words of greeting, neither the guard nor the driver spoke, but I wouldn't have either, not while they were getting soaked and I wasn't.

Even with the carriage springs, the bumps still hurt some, and I wondered how long it would be before I could ride poor Gairloch again. He'd been burned too, but when I'd looked at him earlier in the day, he seemed to be healing well.

The coach pulled up outside the main door to the autarch's residence, where I was greeted by Jylla, her shoulder braced and bandaged.

'Greetings, Order-master.'

'Greetings.' I looked at her shoulder. 'I'm sorry.'

She stepped into the long hall before she answered. A guard in greens closed the door behind us.

'Don't be. I'm lucky enough in one way. I'll get a yearly stipend, and I'll get out alive. The gray wizard says I'll be able to use the arm, but not for heavy carrying.' Her eyes flicked across me. 'You took as much as anyone. You looked like dead meat on that cart.'

I had to grin. 'I felt like dead meat.'

'You looked better fried than some chops I've eaten.' She paused. 'The envoy won't be here for a bit, but the commander said you could sit in the corner of the audience room until everyone arrives.'

'That's fine.' I had to walk slowly toward the audience room, and the staff helped. That made my third staff since I'd gotten to Candar. One staff lasts most people a life, but I was on number three in less than that many years. 'Where can I leave the cloak?'

'There are some pegs in an alcove by the chamber.'

'You're not moving much faster than I am. We make quite a pair.'

'You love her, don't you?'

The question caught me off guard. 'What?'

'The commander. You love her. I heard you on that cart. All you mumbled about was how you had to stop the rockets and the wizard.' Jylla slowed and pointed to the dark space on the side of the hallway. 'She loves you, too, you know. She rode the whole way back beside the cart. She gave all the commands on horseback beside you.'

I took off the cloak and started toward the alcove.

'I'll take it.'

I didn't protest.

'That's why,' Jylla continued as she returned, 'everyone would die for her.'

'Because she loves me?' That didn't make sense.

Jylla shook her head. 'Because you love each other so much, and because you both fight, in your own way. You have more to lose than any of us. And you come from afar. How can anyone refuse?'

I had to shake my head. In one way it made sense, and in another it was crazy. We could have been mad, and maybe we were. Being mad and in love didn't make good leaders. And I wasn't a leader. Krystal was, but I wasn't. Maybe Tamra was.

'I'm not the leader type.'

'You are. You will learn that. Who led the charge?'

That just confirmed that I was crazy.

We walked up to the double doors. Jylla opened them, and I tried not to hobble too much. Inside, the oil lamps on the walls were lit, probably because the rain made the day dark, and not enough light came through the long narrow windows behind the line of columns on the outer wall. We were the only ones in the room that stretched at least sixty cubits from the doors to the hangings behind the autarch's chair.

The inside walls were paneled in dark wood. The end of the chamber held a dais raised not quite two cubits above the polished green marble of the floor tiles. A long green carpet ran down the center of the hall and led up the four steps of the dais. The dais was carpeted in the same green. The sole piece of furniture on the dais was the autarch's chair – a light wood, probably white oak or young cherry, stained green. The chair had too much in the way of fanciful carvings wound into the arms and the back to be a simple chair, but it wasn't quite bulky and impressive enough to be a throne. The only simple part seemed to be the plain green cushion.

I sat down on an armless chair tucked behind one of the columns and stretched out my splinted leg. 'How long before this starts?'

'Who would know?' Jylla started to shrug and winced.

I understood that feeling.

I heard the doors open and peered around the column to see two other figures in gray. Justen and Tamra crossed the chamber. The corners of Justen's mouth were turned down, and his eyes were bleak.

'How are you?' he asked. 'Don't get up yet.'

'I'll manage.' I didn't get up.

'You shouldn't really be here.' He glared at his apprentice.

Tamra smiled. 'Lerris is stronger than you think.'

'Hmmmphh.' He studied me. 'We need to talk before too long. When you're fully healed.'

The doors opened at the far end of the audience hall, and a full squad of the Finest marched in, led by the thin subofficer who had led the first squad of Yelena's force.

After he lined them up, each half fronting a side of the dais, he put them at rest and crossed the green carpet that led to the chair. He nodded to Justen and Tamra, but walked up to me.

'Greetings, Order-master.'

'Greetings.' I stood. Using the staff helped, and I did make it up halfway gracefully, ignoring Justen's frown.

'I am Nusert, ser. I wanted to tell you that we are all in your debt, ser.'

In my debt? I tried not to swallow my tongue. 'I appreciate the thought, Nusert.' What could I say? 'But ... you and your troopers did what had to be done. I am pleased I was of some help.'

'You are gracious, ser.' He bowed. 'I must go.'

He crossed the room and took a position at the end of the line of troopers closest to the door.

A bell chimed, and the doors opened once more.

Several dozen functionaries flowed into the chamber and stood farther back, the Finest holding the space open between the dais and the spectators. Some of the latest arrivals I did recognize – like Liessa, the autarch's sister and heir; Mureas; and Public Works Minister Zeiber. Most I had never seen.

'It's time for us.' Tamra gestured.

I levered myself along with the staff, and walked slowly, and stiffly, after Tamra and Justen. Climbing the four steps was awkward, but the staff helped, and we lined up slightly behind and to the left of Kasee's chair.

'You stand closest to the autarch,' hissed Tamra.

I did.

A small door I had not noted earlier on one side of the dais opened, and Krystal stepped out, followed by Kasee. The autarch wore green silks and a stark but shining gold coronet. Krystal was in somber greens, except for the dress braided vest. Her blade was her fighting blade, as always.

I settled myself and looked toward Krystal. I did get a quick smile from her, and a quicker one from the autarch. Then both their faces grew stern as the bell sounded once again, and their heads and eyes turned to the back of the chamber. Kasee sat squarely in the high chair, and Krystal's hand was on the hilt of her blade.

'Arms,' said Nusert. The Finest slipped to attention.

A single muted trumpet sounded, and the chamber doors opened.

'The honorable Thurna, envoy to Duke Berfir of Hydlen.'

Thurna, a broad-shouldered beefy man with ragged blond hair, marched up the green carpet, carrying a single scroll as if it were a naked blade. Three troopers in crimson followed.

The Hydlenese guards stopped just before Nusert, but Thurna went on to the bottom step to the dais. There, he bowed low before the autarch, so low that it was almost comical. 'Your servant, Most Honored Autarch.'

'You humble yourself too much, ser.' Kasee's tone was dry.

'I offer you only your due.' Thurna straightened. His eyes flicked toward Krystal.

Krystal's face remained impassive. She stood a half step forward and to the right of the autarch, as silent and as deadly looking as a well-used blade.

Thurna finally looked in our direction. So did the three guards who stood back by Nusert.

Thurna's deep-set eyes studied Justen, Tamra, and me – and passed back to Kasee.

'Your honored counselors?' he asked politely.

'They are certainly counselors.' Kasee's eyes twinkled. 'Might I present to you the gray wizard Justen, the mage Tamra, and Lerris. Lerris is the youngest, as you may note, but his skills were, I believe, more than adequate at the brimstone spring.'

One of the guards looked at me, and I looked back at him. He was a big fellow, a good half head taller than either Thurna or me. But I kept looking. That I could do, despite the discomfort in my leg. His eyes finally caught the staff, and he went pale, and his legs crumpled. He went forward like a statue, and all that metal clanged when he hit the carpet. I winced. The marble underneath that thin carpet was hard.

'Autarch . . . I must protest—' the Hydlenese envoy began.

'Your man will be fine,' Justen said. 'I doubt he expected to see young Lerris again.'

Envoy Thurna looked, apparently to see if the soldier was breathing, and then offered a faint and polite smile. 'Such matters do occur.'

'That is true,' said Kasee. 'Like many young wizards, Lerris has a habit of overdoing things.'

I had to hand it to Kasee. She was adept at using the tools at hand.

'His Mightiness Duke Berfir would convey to you his deepest wishes for peace and tranquility along the borders.'

'At least while he's engaged with Duke Colaris?' asked Kasee.

'Your Mightiness misinterprets the Duke's desires.' Thurna bowed again.

'I would certainly not wish to misinterpret his desires. Might you have a representation of those desires?'

Thurna extended the scroll. Krystal stepped down and took it, opening it easily, handing it to Kasee, and stepping back.

Everyone waited while Kasee read the document.

'His Mightiness the Duke is most generous in his reparations. I regret that he lacked the understanding to avoid the need for such reparations.' Her eyes went to me, pointedly, before returning to Thurna.

'I am certain that he understands that need now, Your Mightiness.'

'We look forward to a time of continued understanding, ser, and we accept the Duke's offer in the spirit in which it was offered. We trust the remainder of your stay in Kyphros will be pleasant and enlightening.' Kasee smiled and stood.

Thurna bowed, and stepped back without turning.

The big guard refused to look in my direction at all as Thurna backed out of the chamber, followed by his guards. Some of it seemed silly. Thurna couldn't turn his back on the autarch, but his guards could? They weren't considered important?

The trumpet sounded once again.

'The public audience is ended,' announced Nusert.

The onlookers filed out, except for Liessa, and then the Finest departed. Almost as soon as the doors closed, Kasee got up and began to grin. She walked toward Tamra and me. 'I thought I was going to laugh, especially after that guard looked at Lerris. Sweet Lerris – and he thought he'd seen the demons of light.'

Justen looked at her with a wry grin. 'He didn't see the Lerris you see. He saw a madman with a staff who had turned a peaceful valley into a brimstone-spewing hell.'

Behind Kasee, Krystal nodded, but she gave me a quick soft smile.

'Well—' Kasee turned to Tamra. 'You were right. It worked. All Thurna wants to do is to leave us alone – for now.'

'For now,' pointed out Krystal. 'Over the long run, he'll want Berfir to destroy us, and the story will get out that you have three deadly wizards. Probably they'll be claiming that Lerris killed that guard with a single look. Stories have a way of getting out of hand.' She looked at me. 'Try not to believe them when you hear them.' The amusement in her voice had a slight edge, and I wondered why.

'I know.' Kasee nodded in agreement. 'But that is not all bad. We still needed to buy time.'

'I hope the price wasn't too high,' said Justen.

'So do I,' added Liessa, a younger-looking version of her sister, with the same high cheekbones and dark hair, without the silver-gray.

So did I. I needed to sit down, and I used the staff to clump over to one of the chairs along the wall, where I sank into the seat and stretched out the still-splinted left leg.

'How does it feel?' asked Justen.

Tamra was saying something to Krystal about the Viscount of Certis, and Kasee was listening, but my hearing was fading in and out again, and I didn't catch much.

'Uncomfortable. It twinges; it itches —'

'That's good.'

'I know. It's healing.'

'It is healing. You figured it out, didn't you?'

'The order-chaos balance? Yes. I haven't been able to do much except think.'

'You should finish healing in another few eight-days, but don't use too much order. The bones will knit better if you just use the order to encourage the regrowth. Don't substitute order.'

I had figured that out. I could have literally held the bones together with order, but if I got tired, they'd probably separate with much stress.

'Why did you agree to come here?'

'Tamra.' Justen laughed. 'She bet me. I said that she'd never get you in grays.'

I laughed. Some magic had nothing to do with order or chaos.

# XLII

## East of Lavah, Sligo [Candar]

The two men stand in the small room warmed by a fire comprised at least half of white-hot embers.

'The Duke has not had time to employ the devices whose design you provided last season, Mage.' Begnula inclines his head politely.

Sammel gestures at the scrolls on the table. 'Knowledge is the key to his future.' He smiles. 'Or someone's.'

'You are not suggesting that you would turn that knowledge over to the red demon? You presume too much.' Begnula takes a step forward, and his hand touches his blade.

Sammel gestures with his index finger, and a ball of fire appears, then drifts toward Begnula. 'Do I presume too much? How then shall I presume?' His eyes drift momentarily to the corner of the room where the wood, plaster, and floor planks are somewhat lighter colored.

Begnula steps back. 'Ser Mage . . .'

'Do not tell me that knowledge is not important, Ser Begnula. Nor that it is not useful. I will have this knowledge' – Sammel gestures toward the scrolls – 'spread throughout Candar and used. For too long, people in Candar have been kept in the dark.' He laughs gently, and lowers his hand.

'Even now, the black mages would have this knowledge suppressed. If it is valuable enough to be suppressed by Recluce – then is it not of value?' He points to the tube weapon mounted on the wall. 'Do you know what that is, Ser Begnula?'

'Ah . . . no.' Begnula takes another step back, a deep breath, and wipes his forehead.

'A pity. Definitely a pity. It is one of the tools by which Recluce has kept Candar in darkness.' Sammel turns back to face the envoy.

'How did you . . . ?'

'You might say it was presented to me, in a manner of speaking. Of course, it was supposed to depart with its presenter. A pity there, too, but these things do happen when one denies the value of knowledge – or tries to suppress it.'

Begnula wipes his forehead again. 'Ah . . . yes . . .'

Sammel turns, bends, and eases another log into the fire on the hearth, where it bursts almost instantly into flame. Then he straightens and smiles again, waiting.

'What . . . what knowledge do you offer the Duke now?' asks Begnula after a long pause.

'A way to spy out his enemy's positions nearly instantly, yet from a distance.'

'In one device?'

'It takes two, but one is very simple, merely a tube and two special pieces of clear and finely polished glass. The other takes silk or another finemeshed fabric and wax. These are easier than the cannon. They will also make the cannon more useful.'

'If these are so simple, why have they not been used before?'

Sammel smiles. 'Who ever said they had not been?'

Begnula looks down.

Sammel's eyes flicker toward the door, glazing over as though his senses were elsewhere. Behind him, the light seems to glimmer on the polished steel of the rocket gun.

# XLIII

By the time I could get around, even hobbling with the splint on my leg, my arm was healed enough for most woodworking. I finished the light polishing necessary for the autarch's wardrobe. I should have completed that before I'd gone traipsing through the Lower Easthorns, but I hadn't. My frailty reminded me of the need for coins, and I sent a message through Krystal before she departed on her inspection tour of Ruzor.

Lo and behold, both a large wagon and a purse with twenty golds arrived, and the wardrobe disappeared in the direction of Kyphrien. I felt both better about the coins, and somehow guilty. So I went to work on completing the chairs for Hensil, which wasn't all that hard. It took a little longer, but it was too cold to sit on the porch, and watch the rain fall, and that would have just been boring. Being so slow, knowing I could have done it faster, was boring too, but I was getting something done.

For a while, using the foot treadle to turn spokes and shafts was out, even though my right leg was fine, because I couldn't get the good leg on the treadle without bending the broken one, and the splint stopped that. Without the splint, I couldn't move without reinjuring the leg.

I could have rebuilt the treadle system, but I gave up on that, and concentrated on healing the leg, and on doing the woodwork that didn't require turning. There was more than enough of that.

One day, when I needed a change of pace, I did the sketches and plans for Antona's desk, and used the cart to get to Faslik's to discuss the wood I needed, except Faslik's sister had died, and the mill was closed.

The jouncing hurt some, but I wasn't going to get better doing nothing. If it really hurt, I carved the cedar limb I'd found on my first trip to Hydlen. I still couldn't make the face emerge from the wood, and ended up working on the figure's cloak – he or she was wearing a cloak. That I knew.

That afternoon, my leg was better, and with my leg stretched out, I worked on smoothing the second chair in Hensil's set – until my hips began to cramp. Then I hobbled over to the desk I had started for Werfel and had kept putting off. I traced out the dovetailing on the inside joints for the second drawer, and then the third.

With the wood vise and the big clamps and the small sharp saw, that went cleanly. There was only one tiny joint on the back inside edge of the second drawer that wouldn't match quite as well as I would have liked, but Werfel wouldn't know, and more important, he wasn't paying for that level of perfection. It still bothered me, and I finally took a deep breath and went back and looked it over. I couldn't redo it, but I could recut one side so that I had a clean edge, and fill it with a matching piece. It would be the same strength, but it would look better. I still didn't like the compromise, but I told myself it was an inside back corner that no one would see.

I could imagine Uncle Sardit telling me that I would know. I understood that better now. I sighed, wondering if I'd always have to accept the wisdom of others – like Justen, or my father, or Uncle Sardit, or Aunt Elisabet.

As the sound of horses in the yard seeped through the closed door of the shop, I finished clamping the back of the second drawer together. I forced myself not to hurry, and not to twist the clamps too tightly. Then I walked out in the cold drizzle of late afternoon where Justen and Tamra led their mounts through a cold drizzle and into the stable.

'Do you have a kettle on?' I glanced at Rissa, who stood under the small overhang that protected the door to the kitchen.

'In this weather, I always have a kettle on. Even wizards need hot tea or cider. And you certainly will if you stand in that cold rain any longer.'

'All right. Some warm bread and cheese would be good also.' I walked across the yard to the stable.

Justen was settling Rosefoot into the stall beside Gairloch. Gairloch whuffed, and Rosefoot whuffed back. The two had always gotten along and had shared a stall more than once.

'Rissa has a kettle on.'

'Rissa always has a kettle on, I'm sure.' said Tamra. 'Not that it won't be quite welcome.'

'These old bones could use the warmth.' Justen's smile was lop-sided.

'Poor old, tired Uncle Justen . . .'

'Just be kind to your elders, Lerris. This one's been kind to you.'

Even Tamra laughed, and Justen looked sheepish.

While Justen had been kind, in many ways he hadn't been particularly helpful. Kindness is like spice – making life far more palatable – but kindness didn't go that far when I was the one getting torn up by the white wizards like Gerlis.

'I am. I asked Rissa to make sure there was warm bread and cheese.'

'Good. I'm hungry.' The redhead tied her mount in one of the stalls used by Krystal's guards, certainly not a problem since Krystal was inspecting the harbor defenses in Ruzor and wouldn't be back for at least an eight-day.

As we crossed the yard toward the house, Justen gestured toward the shop. 'Do you mind if I look in? I'd like to see how you're progressing.'

'Suit yourself.' I held open the door as they stepped inside, wondering what exactly Justen had meant about how I was progressing.

He shook his head as he looked across the room. '. . . the extravagance of youth . . .'

Working hard to make a living was an extravagance of youth?

'Before we take advantage of your hospitality, I want a last look at that leg,' stated Justen. 'We're headed off to Vergren.'

'Here?'

'Why not? Sit down on that stool.'

I didn't have an answer. So I sat. 'I think the bone's mostly healed, but the muscle's weak. You going off to heal the sheep again?' I shifted my weight on the stool. 'You can stay for dinner, can't you?'

'I didn't say that we were going to rush across Candar. I leave that for you younger types.'

Tamra looked at the chairs. The light stain I had applied earlier was their final shading. 'These are actually decent, Lerris.'

'They're better than decent. Not great, but better than decent.' Tamra still bothered me, still trying to cut down everything I did, or show that it wasn't all that important.

'These chairs are better than decent, Lerris.'

'Thank you. Your staff work is better than decent also.'

'With most people,' Justen mumbled as his fingers ran along my leg. Had Tamra flushed?

'Are you still helping train the Finest?' I asked her.

'Yes.'

Justen grinned, then frowned as his fingers stopped over the healing lower break, and I could feel the flow of order. Rather than follow what he was doing, I concentrated on Justen, trying to see how he had ordered himself.

He raised an eyebrow. 'There are certain dangers to that, you know.'

'Dangers to what?' interrupted Tamra.

'Self-healing,' I answered. 'I've been careful. I haven't used order to hold anything together.'

'I noticed. Try to be more elegant. Brute force – even order force – can't heal by itself, or hold things together. We all need some chaos in our systems. The key is to twist the chaos so that its forces help sustain order.'

It was my turn to frown.

'Someday, I'd like a desk like this – if I ever have a place to put it. Would you make me one then?' Tamra's eyes didn't leave Werfel's desk.

'When you're ready, I'd be happy to.' That was as close to an apology as I was likely ever to get from Tamra. 'I was thinking about taking the splint off. What do you think?' I asked Justen.

He pursed his lips and frowned. 'If it were my leg I'd wait an eight-day, but you are younger. I'd give it a few more days, and take some longer walks and see how it feels.'

'That makes sense.'

Justen stood. 'You mentioned a kettle?'

'Coming up.' I closed the shop door behind me, after adding a log to the fire and checking the water in the moisture pot. It's not the cold or the heat that bothers wood, but the changes in heat and moisture in the air – especially sudden changes.

Tamra and Justen washed up, and so did I.

By then, Rissa had set three mugs of steaming mulled cider on the table, followed by a basket with a small but warm loaf of bread.

'Thank you, Rissa. Your bread always smells so good.' I raised the cider and let the apple-spice aroma wreathe my face.

'Bread should smell good. Dinner will not be for a while, but it is good for you to have company.'

'Krystal won't be here?' asked Tamra.

'No. She's inspecting harbor defenses in Ruzor, and there's a dinner there for the envoy from Southwind.'

'Why not here?'

'Something about trade, and Ruzor being the main port.'

'Ha! The Southwind envoy just doesn't want to travel an extra eight-day for ceremony.'

'It could be.' I shrugged and looked at Rissa. 'What is dinner?'

'The good fowl soup with leeks and lentils and even some quilla.'

'Quilla?'

'They had some in the market, and it was cheap. So I got it. You may be a hero, Master Lerris, but the winter has been long. With the chills, there is nothing like fowl soup – it helps mend the joints and the bones . . .'

Quilla was a crunchy root that tasted like oily sawdust. It used to be common on Recluce before the great change, and even the Founders had eaten it frequently. That probably made them better people than I was.

'Soup does help,' offered Justen.

'Quilla tastes like sawdust.'

'Nothing I cook tastes like sawdust. You think that cooking is easy, now, in the winter, when the vegetables are withered and the meat is strong . . .'

'You cook wonderfully,' I protested, wondering how the vegetables could be withered when I'd unloaded so many recently.

'Sawdust, you said —'

'I said quilla tasted like sawdust, but that wasn't what I meant about your cooking.'

'If I cook, it will not taste like sawdust, Master Lerris.' Rissa turned back to the pot on the stove, shaking her head.

Tamra, her back to Rissa, was grinning. 'The same old tactful Lerris.'

'You're going to Vergren?' Changing the subject seemed belatedly wise.

Justen sipped his cider before setting it down and nodding. 'As I have told you before, Lerris, even gray wizards must support themselves. I do not have your abilities with wood, so . . .'

Tamra broke off a good-sized chunk of the steaming bread and began chewing a healthy mouthful.

'So you're going off to make sure next year's lambs are healthy?'

'Among other things. We'll probably go to Certis after that – oil pod seeds, you might recall.'

'I never got to doing oil pod seeds. That was when I did some unplanned healing – if you recall.'

'Planning hasn't been your most notable characteristic,' Tamra added, after swallowing the bread and following it with a sip of hot cider.

'And you planned that well?'

'I had some good ideas.' Tamra flushed.

'So did I.'

'Children . . .' said Justen sardonically. 'Children . . .'

We both glared at him. Then Tamra laughed, and I had to as well.

'Dinner – it is almost ready,' announced Rissa.

For Rissa, dinner was simple – the big dish of soup in the brown crockery pot and another loaf of bread in the basket.

After a mouthful of the chicken and the potato slices, I bit into a still-crunchy quilla root. My memories had been correct. Even in leek – and onion-laden soup, it remained crunchy and oily, although the sawdust taste was masked by the onions or something. Still, the soup was good.

'You see? I do not cook food that tastes like sawdust.'

'I am sorry I ever made you think that, Rissa. The soup is very good.' The comparatively thinner soup was also welcome relief from the array of thick stews I had been eating recently.

'Very,' mumbled Tamra.

Justen just ate methodically, as if food were another necessity.

'This soup is almost as good as my mother's.' Rissa beamed.

'Was she a good cook?' asked Tamra.

'A good cook? She was a wonderful cook. How else would I ever learn?'

I shrugged. What had I really learned from my parents? Woodworking had come from Uncle Sardit, and my studies had come from tutors like Magister Kerwin.

'She must have been very good,' said Tamra.

'Good – that was not the word. From stones she could make soup, and from a few bones a wonderful stew fit for a feast. A cook like my mother there has never been.'

'That sounds more like wizardry,' offered Justen dryly.

'And your mother, Lady Wizard?' asked Rissa.

'I don't know. She left when I was young,' Tamra admitted.

'Then who taught you to cook?'

'No one. I can't cook – not well.'

'Oh, that is such a terrible thing. it is bad when a man cannot cook, but for a woman ... What are parents for, but to pass on what they have learned?' Rissa sniffed. 'Terrible it is, too, when you outlive your children and cannot pass on ... what you know ...'

'You're hardly ancient,' said Justen.

'Perhaps your wizardry will help me find another man?' Rissa lifted her eyebrows. 'What about you, Master Mage? Would you not like someone ...?'

Justen squirmed in his chair, but I saw the glint in Rissa's eyes.

'My lady is far from here, but I doubt she would appreciate —'

'You wizards are so serious.' Rissa laughed. 'One day, Kilbon, he will ask me. Still, it is sad, Lady Wizard, that you did not know your mother. Or that she does not know you are grown and powerful.'

I didn't even know who Kilbon was, and wondered if Tamra's mother had been like Tamra – not willing to be tied to any man unless she had the upper hand. I also wondered exactly where Justen's lady was.

'I don't know that she cared,' said Tamra slowly. 'Or even if she is still alive somewhere. Some parents don't care that much.'

'That is terrible.'

I wondered. Had my parents cared that much?

'Have you ever let your parents know you're all right?' asked Justen, almost as if he had seen my thoughts.

'I'm sure they know.'

Justen nodded.

'It's not the same thing,' Tamra objected. 'You have parents. There are ships from Ruzor to Nylan, sometimes even to Land's End. How long has it been – more than three years, isn't it?'

I nodded.

'That's a decision you have to make.' Justen laughed, a trace of bitterness in the sound. 'I'm not one to judge.'

For a time, the only sounds in the kitchen were those of eating and the faint whistle of the cold wind that had driven off the drizzle.

After dinner, Tamra and Justen and I sat around the table. Rissa finished cleaning up and slipped out to the front room, with a comment about not wanting to know too much about 'wizards' business.' Of course, she sat there and knitted, listening to every word through the open door.

'Lerris?' asked Tamra. 'Did you ever find out where that wizard found out about those rockets?'

'Gerlis? No.' I pulled at my chin. 'I couldn't say why, but I don't think the wizard had much to do with them. He seemed much more involved with handling chaos, and he used that – not the rockets. The Hydlenese troops used the rockets.'

'Rockets used by regular troops – that is bad,' mused Justen. 'They haven't been used that way since before the fall of Fairhaven.'

'Fairhaven?' Tamra raised her eyebrows.

'Frven,' I explained.

'What's a name, anyway?' She sniffed. 'The old chaos-masters are dead, Fairhaven or Frven.'

'Why not?' I asked Justen. 'They seem simple enough to use. Good steel seems to shield them against chaos.'

'Now . . . but chaos and order were both much stronger then.'

'That doesn't make sense. If they were stronger in the old days, why were they used then and not now? It seems as though it ought to be the other way around.'

'Then, only the black mages – the engineers – could forge black iron to make them and use them. No one else knew how. When order and chaos were weakened by the fall of Fairhaven, black iron became harder to forge and depleted total order too much for widespread use.' Justen spread his hands and then took another sip from his mug. 'Now, it seems odd.'

'Odd?'

'Tamra, why don't you get the mounts ready? I need a word with Lerris.'

She raised her left eyebrow, a trick I'd tried and never mastered. 'Do you want me to handle Rosefoot?'

I swallowed. Justen clearly wasn't going to say any more. Why not was another question, but I had an idea that he knew a whole lot more than he was saying, and that bothered me.

'If I don't get there before you finish with your mount.' Justen nodded at his apprentice.

Tamra left, with a trace of heaviness to her step that suggested anger. I tried not to grin. Again, Justen was restricting knowledge to those he thought could use it or needed it. Was that a habit with all older mages? While I didn't want Tamra knowing everything about me, I also thought Justen was being unfair.

'You know, Lerris,' began Justen.

I tried not to wince at his tone, which screamed of the paternal 'uncle knows best.' If Tamra had been there, she would have been smirking, and I almost wished she were.

'Yes.'

He looked sharply at me and took a deep breath. 'That won't work. It didn't work with my father, and it won't work for me.'

I waited.

'Once upon a time, there was a young soldier. These days his story is not told much. He was not the heir to the family title and lands, and he left his family to avoid an arranged marriage that would have left him rather comfortable. He had a number of adventures, which are relevant to his life and times, but not to us at the moment. Then he was faced with a decision. Should he undertake a great task – one he believed would save the world? He listened to those around him, who counseled caution, but in the end, he opposed their pleas for caution. He was successful in his great task. He saved the world, and thousands upon thousands died in battles, storms, and fires. He was considered a great man.'

'Justen, this sounds familiar.'

'There are two other stories. Do you want to finish them?'

I shut up.

'Another young man resolved to build his heart's desire. He was a metalworker, and those who learned what he wanted to build cast him out. He was exiled to a far land, and, there, he finally built his heart's desire. One ruler conquered an entire country to try to take the thing he built. But the metalworker took his heart's desire and cast down both his enemies and triumphed over those who had exiled him. And, again, thousands upon thousands died because of what he built, and the lives of all those in the world were changed.'

Justen smiled wryly, as if to challenge me to speak, but I nodded for him to tell the third story.

'The third young man had no idea what he wanted.'

I must have frowned at that, for Justen smiled. 'Not all young men know what they want, or, in your case, what they don't want. This young man was coerced into a war, but he, like the second young man, was a metalworker and he began to build devices that were terrible. He and his brother, in one great battle, cost the enemy almost two-thirds of their armies – but the enemy prevailed, and he fled into the hottest and driest desert in the world. When he was rescued, he learned what he thought was the truth of the world, and he resolved to bring that truth to his enemies. He was successful – so successful that his name is never spoken by those who knew what he did. He was so successful that he destroyed the mightiest empire known and the most powerful city of his own people.'

I waited.

'That's all there is, Lerris. Just three stories.'

'The first one is the story of the Founders.'

'Creslin, actually.'

'And the second one is Dorrin, I'd guess. I didn't know that he created such destruction.'

'He did, but it wasn't as instantaneous or as direct. He just changed the world with his steam-chaos engines. And people always suffer more in times of change.'

'You seem to be saying that people who try to do great deeds create disaster.'

'I have noticed that the two appear to go hand in hand.'

'You must be the third.'

'The names aren't the point.' Justen shrugged. 'The point is that when great deeds occur – either planned or unplanned – the whole world suffers. I have a certain aversion to great deeds.' He offered a sardonic smile.

'I am not exactly fond of them.'

'No – but you're the most dangerous type of all. You would do anything for love, and you love Krystal. The angels save us all.' He stood. 'Keep that in mind.'

'You can stay tonight,' I offered.

'No. We need to pack up things.' Justen grinned. 'Especially Tamra.'

I walked out to the stable with him. Tamra gave me a look that was almost a glare. As for Justen, there was no 'almost' involved.

He ignored it and looked at Tamra. 'Time to go.'

She glanced at me and shook her head. I shrugged, and then watched them ride into the evening rain.

After I climbed into a cold bed, wishing Krystal were there, Justen's – and Tamra's – comments about my parents drifted into my thoughts. A letter wouldn't hurt. I could stay angry forever, but they were still my parents, and they had done what they thought best.

Recluce – and the Brotherhood – that was another matter.

# XLIV

## Nylan, Recluce

The man in the tan uniform bows and remains standing before the curved black wood table. His wide brown leather belt bears only a short blade on the left, a small purse, and a lighter-colored patch of leather on the right, where a scabbard would rest for a cross-drawn left-handed blade.

Just inside the door the two soldiers in tan, with the orange starburst on their right shoulders, remain motionless.

'Welcome, Ser Rignelgio.' The silver-haired Talryn gestures to the chair. 'Would you have a seat?'

'I may not be here that long.' Rignelgio offers a self-deprecating smile.

'You asked to see us?' asks Heldra.

'That is correct, Ser Heldra.' The envoy shifts his weight on the hard black oak to face the three councilors.

The sound of the high surf ebbs and fades, ebbs and fades. Maris glances at the open window to the south, then back to the Hamorian envoy.

'The Emperor has become more and more concerned about the continuing lack of stability in Candar of late . . .'

'As are we,' offers Talryn.

'But not, we believe, for precisely the same reason.'

'Oh?' Heldra inclines her head.

'Some have led the Emperor to believe that Recluce has come to foster disorder as a means to increase its own order. The Emperor would like to believe that such a charge is baseless. He would also dearly like to believe that Recluce has merely confined its attentions to its own lands and that the chaos that has developed in Candar is without the interest and blessing of Recluce.' Rignelgio holds up a hand, as if in apology. 'You understand, I am the mere messenger of such concerns.'

'We do understand your position as a messenger, Ser Rignelgio,' answers Talryn smoothly.

Under the edge of the tabletop, Maris rubs his thumb and forefinger together. His other hand strokes his beard for a moment, even as his eyes stray to the two soldiers in the functional tan cotton uniforms.

'Then you can also understand why I might have some concerns about not being understood.'

Heldra and Talryn nod.

'Understanding is often only the first step.' Talryn's low voice almost rumbles. 'Even when two parties understand what is, they may not agree upon the meaning of that understanding.'

'Yes, there is that. Perhaps that is not necessarily so great a barrier, however. At times a course of action can be agreed upon without a sharing of understandings or motivations. The Emperor would be most pleased if the amount of untoward chaos in Candar were to decline.' Rignelgio smiles politely.

'Untoward chaos – that is an interesting term,' says Maris. 'Might there be such a thing as "toward chaos"?'

'Probably not, which is why we might reach an understanding.'

'What sort of understanding?' Heldra's voice is diffident, almost detached.

'Why . . . you are the wizards of the black isle. Understanding I must needs leave to you. I can only say that the Emperor, like you, is most interested in the enhancement of order, throughout the world, but particularly in Candar. He is most concerned, and he wished you to know that.' Rignelgio smiles and rises. 'I said I would not be long.'

'A moment, Ser Rignelgio,' says Heldra. 'You have expressed the Emperor's concerns, but you have failed to suggest what might allay those concerns.'

'Hamor has always been interested in free and open trade, and disorder hinders such trade.' The envoy bows. 'As I said before, I would not presume to suggest specific actions.'

'I would presume,' says Maris coldly, ignoring the sidelong glance from Talryn. 'You hint, and you bow, and you talk about open trade. In my experience, Hamor's "open trade" means open only to Hamor, with restrictions on Recluce or Austra. Are you telling us that Hamor intends to make Candar a trade colony and not to interfere?'

The smile leaves Rignelgio's face, and his expression is blank as he replies. 'As I indicated earlier, the Emperor has expressed his concerns. I would not presume to go beyond my charter in conveying those concerns.' He bows stiffly.

'We appreciate your concerns about exceeding your charter, and your diplomacy,' acknowledges Talryn, rising in turn. He is followed by Maris and Heldra.

'And I yours.' Rignelgio's voice remains cool.

The soldiers by the door stiffen as the envoy turns.

After Rignelgio has left, Heldra reseats herself and looks at Maris. 'Was that called for?'

The trader walks to the window, looking down at Nylan. 'Yes. I can't play word games.'

'Well . . . that was interesting,' reflects Talryn. 'I suspect something more than the usual is going on. Rignelgio clearly didn't want to deliver an ultimatum, and someone wanted him to.'

'The Emperor?' asked Heldra.

'Telling us to please stop meddling in Candar?' suggests Maris. 'We're supposed to let Hamor take over control of all trade.'

'I didn't get much hint of a request there,' rumbles Talryn. 'I think we'd better look more closely into how the Emperor plans to accomplish this. Rignelgio isn't at all comfortable with his position, and that could mean trouble.'

'We can't afford to knuckle under to him,' says Heldra. 'I won't knuckle under.'

'Your attitude and your blade, even your squad of marines, can't stop the changes in the world,' observes Talryn. 'Or the entire Hamorian fleet.'

'The old values are important,' responds Heldra. 'If they aren't, why are we here? Are we just supposed to be facilitators of trade?'

'Don't sneer at it, Heldra,' replies Maris. 'Trade pays the bills.'

'You both have good points,' interjects Talryn. 'We do need to remember that the Brotherhood doesn't exactly have the world's largest standing army, and, even with our armed merchant ships, Hamor's fleet greatly outnumbers ours.'

'Most of them half a globe away.'

'They won't stay that far away.' Maris rubs his thumb and forefinger together.

Talryn nods. 'Perhaps not.'

'Traders . . .' mumbles Heldra, mostly under her breath.

Maris and Talryn exchange glances.

# XLV

Three mornings after Justen and Tamra left, I took off the splint. It didn't hurt, but I could feel the weakness of the muscles, and only time and effort would cure that. Then I went back to work on finishing Werfel's desk. Of course, the glue in the pot had hardened. That meant chipping it out and using a mortar and pestle to powder it for a base for a fresh batch.

When I carried the pot into the kitchen, trying not to limp, Rissa looked up from slicing various vegetables.

'More of the awful-smelling glue, Master Lerris?'

'More of the awful-smelling glue, Rissa.'

'Dinner, it should not carry the odor of animals' hoofs.'

'I do need it for the desk I am working on.'

'You have a hearth.' Rissa sniffed.

'It's hard to heat this properly near a fire. A stove works better.' I changed the subject. 'What's for dinner?'

'A mutton-spice stew.'

I nodded. Rissa's spiced stews were hot enough to make me forget the taste of mutton, but she wasn't through talking.

'I was talking to Verillya at the market, and she has to cook for Hunsis. He has the hauling yard – the big one off the west highway before you pass the mill road. You know, Master Lerris, you ought to talk to Hunsis. His woman – that's Freka, and she is the one who Verillya really works for – she, I mean Freka, likes fine furniture, and Hunsis certainly brings in enough coins. His wagons run all the way to Sarronnyn now that folks can take the old direct roads, thanks to you . . .'

As she talked, Rissa kept chopping vegetables and potatoes into the big pot, her fingers almost as quick and deft as Krystal's – almost.

'That is a thought, Rissa. Except I'm having trouble finishing the work I have now.'

'Of course it is a thought. But you should get some help – an apprentice. And you might have more time if you did not travel over and through the mountains . . .'

'I also might not have a consort, and I might have a very unhappy autarch. But I could use an apprentice.'

'There, there is a point. I will talk to Freka at the market about an apprentice for you.' She paused. 'And you should not try to be a hero. If you are both heroes . . .' Rissa stopped chopping. 'I will talk all morning, and then you will not get any woodworking done.'

'Thank you.' I left the pot on the corner of the stove to heat. With Rissa talking about an apprentice, I had no doubts youngsters would start showing up. I worried more about the hero comments. Did I have some sort of sign on me that said I was trying to be a hero? Heroes got killed, in the end. I hoped Krystal didn't want to be one, either.

Back in the shop, I began smoothing the drawer fronts, forcing myself to take my time. I added a log to the coals on the hearth, trying to keep the temperature even, and poured some water into the old iron pot on the hook over the coals. That was another one of those things Uncle Sardit had taught me. Wood works better if the air has some moisture in it.

Wondering didn't create desks, or chairs, and I took the smoothing blade in hand and went back over the front of the top drawer, careful not to nick the edges where the grain can splinter. I had gotten to working on the second drawer's front piece when Rissa banged on the door.

'Master Lerris, your glue's a-bubbling, and I don't want the dinner to smell like glue.'

After setting aside the smoother, I reclaimed the glue from the kitchen and put it on the smaller hearth hook, folded nearly against the side bricks, just so that the fire would keep the pot warm while I brushed the glue over the pegs and eased the top into place.

Then, while it set, because Gairloch needed exercise, and I wanted to see how the leg did riding, I curried Gairloch. I'd told Rissa I'd ride out the west road to Brene's – less than three kays – for some eggs.

'Now, Master Lerris . . . no more than a copper for the eggs. Brene, she has more eggs than she could ever do with, and that's lucky for us, having no chickens of our own.' Rissa looked out toward the stable. 'If we had chickens . . .'

'No chickens.'

'Brene will be pleased to see you, and then she'll look poor and won't take your coppers until you have to force them on her, and that's how she always gets more.'

I nodded as I half fastened my jacket and edged back out to the yard where Gairloch's breath steamed in the chill.

'No more than a copper, Master Lerris . . . mind you.'

'Yes, Rissa.'

*Whuuuffff* . . . was Gairloch's only comment.

The cold air felt refreshing, and I let Gairloch take his own pace as we headed west. Despite the chill, I could see chickens everywhere once I turned Gairloch onto the drive that led to the small house. Chickens perched on the rail fence that surrounded the hog pen. Although some of the rails had but one end in place, the hogs seemed to be confined to the pen. Then again, maybe some had left. The smart ones?

Another flurry of chickens scurried away from Gairloch as I reined up outside the weathered plank-sided house.

*Whuffff . . . uffff . . .*

'I know. I don't like them much either, except to eat.'

The door opened, and Brene waddled out. 'Master Lerris! I'd be guessing that you came for some eggs for Rissa. Kind of you to fetch eggs for your own cook, but that's what makes the world turn. Kindness, that is and a poor place the world would be.' She lifted an empty basket. 'I'll be just a moment. Wouldn't be wanting to send you off without the freshest eggs . . .'

She waddled toward the low chicken coop, the gaps between the roughcut boards filled with what appeared to be a moss-and-mud mixture. The boards had to have been sawmill rejects, but chickens didn't care, I supposed.

I climbed off Gairloch and tied him to a slanting post that propped up one corner of the sagging porch.

'. . . just let Mother Brene . . . don't need all those eggs anyway . . .
more than enough chickens here . . .

. . . *awwkkkk . . . awkkk . . .*

I grinned, glad Brene had the chickens and I didn't.

Before long, the portly figure in the mismatched leathers and woolens, sprinkled with feathers and fragments of feathers, waddled back
from the coop and presented me with a basket filled with eggs.

'Thank you.' I took the basket and set it on the porch next to the
beam to which Gairloch was tethered. 'They're large.'

'Good hens I've got, maybe the best west of the city. You know,
you have to talk to them, helps them get into laying . . .'

I extended a copper.

'What? No . . . we do fine, and I'd scarcely be a neighbor if I took your
coins, with all and what you've done for everyone, Master Lerris.'

I held back a grin. 'If you don't have some coppers to buy feed for
the chickens, then you won't have eggs to share. It's little enough, but
you'd do me the pleasure of taking a small token at least – for the
chickens, anyway.' I felt that, so long as she had chickens, I wouldn't
have to have any.

'No . . . I couldn't, not being a neighbor.'

I shook my head. 'Being your neighbor, I have to insist. It's a pittance
for such fine eggs, and they are fine eggs.'

'Aye . . . well, I do say they're good eggs.'

'That they are.' I put the copper in her palm and closed her fingers
around it. 'Have you heard from Kertis?'

'Oh, such a lad. He's working hard in the warehouse there in Ruzor.
Bursa came back last eight-day to tell me. Bursa travels the Ruzor
road for Rinstel. Kertis sent a shawl with Bursa, a warm black one.'
Brene smiled. 'Bursa says that afore long Kertis will be traveling with
him, maybe to Vergren on the wool-buying . . . almost as good as the
wool from the black island . . . what Kertis says . . .'

'I'm glad he's doing well.'

'Aye, and I am, too. Never meant to be a holder, the lad, likes the
city too much, and the sea's in his blood, just like his father.'

I untied Gairloch and picked up the basket. 'What about the
basket?'

'You just bring it back next time, or have Rissa do it.'

'We'll bring it back.' Of course, Rissa or I would have to bring it
back with something in it – a loaf of special bread or something.

'Take care, Master Lerris. Tell Rissa that Kertis misses her black
bread. There's nothing like it in Ruzor. Don't you be forgetting
that.'

'I won't.' I had to mount carefully, because of the basket and my leg.

Brene stood in front of the sagging porch until Gairloch turned back north on the main road. The trip home was warmer, or seemed so, because the wind was at my back.

When I reined up outside the stable, I had to hold on to the saddle for a moment after I dismounted. The leg was fine, but I could tell my thigh muscles hadn't been quite ready for a long ride, although Gairloch and I had certainly taken it easy on the way back. I didn't want to break the eggs in the basket – and we hadn't.

After setting the basket on the stall wall, I unsaddled Gairloch.

*Wheee . . . eeee.*

'Not enough exercise . . .'

I fed him a grain cake, but he ate it in three bites, as if it were only his due. He didn't complain when I left, though, and I picked up the basket and carried it across the yard and into the kitchen. 'Here are the eggs.'

'Thank ye, Master Lerris. If you'd set them on the table . . .' Rissa did not turn from the bowls and flour before her.

'I only gave Brene a copper. Kertis sent word through Bursa. She says that Kertis misses your black bread. There's nothing like it in Ruzor.'

'There is nothing like my black bread in Kyphrien or Dasir or Felsa, and all the world knows it . . .'

'I certainly know it.' The kitchen smelled good, and I contented myself with half a mug of redberry, knowing that our supplies had to last until late in the summer.

'And so does Brene, and she'll be wanting me to put a small loaf in the basket when next I go for eggs.'

'I got that impression.'

'She's a sly one, Brene is, for all that she's a good woman.' Rissa cleared her throat.

I retreated from the kitchen to the workshop where I did a last polishing of Hensil's chairs before I loaded them on the wagon, padding each one with lint and rags, and covering them with a waxed canvas, just in case it rained.

Then I sat down for a while to rest, just to catch my breath. I didn't sit down long, because I could smell the hot metal of the dry moisture pot, and I had to refill it. Then I fastened my jacket back on and went out to the stable. After harnessing the cart horse, I guided the horse and wagon out into the yard, limping a bit because my thigh was getting tired. I'd started with the cart, but then Rissa had told me about a spare wagon Hunsis had, and the cart hadn't been big enough. So now I had both cart and wagon. Somehow, I was always ending up with more.

Gairloch whinnied when I took the cart horse.

'You never liked being a cart horse. So don't complain.'

He whinnied anyway, and I felt a little as if I were deserting a friend as I eased the wagon out into the yard.

'Now where are you going?' demanded Rissa, thrusting her head out the kitchen door.

'I'm delivering the chairs to Hensil.'

'You take off that device from your leg, and you are well?'

'Well enough to deliver these and get paid.'

'You men . . .' But she went back into the kitchen.

I set my staff along the side of the wagon bed where I could reach it. I doubted anyone would want to steal a load of chairs, even expensive chairs, but these days I was discovering all sorts of new and unpleasant truths.

I released the brake and flicked the reins, and nothing happened. I snapped the reins a bit harder. As the wagon lurched forward, I was glad I had padded the chairs. At the end of the drive the wagon half turned, half skidded onto the west road leading into Kyphrien, because I hadn't swung wide enough. Why was it that everything I hadn't done a lot before I seemed to have trouble with?

Krystal was still in Ruzor, or on her way back, and Justen and Tamra were somewhere on the road to Vergren. Although it would be eight-days yet before spring, Justen needed to be there before the ewes were bred. I didn't quite understand the timing because in Recluce, breeding occurred earlier. Were the sheep in Montgren different?

There was still a lot about Candar that I didn't understand – like why Kyphrien was the capital city of Kyphros and so far from the ocean. Of all the countries in Candar that had access to the sea, only Kyphros and Sarronnyn had capital cities that weren't seaports or on major rivers navigable by seagoing vessels. Was it coincidence that both were matriarchies?

The wind was a low moan, coming out of the Westhorns, cold as the ice that it had swept over on its travels from the Roof of the World to the sea.

I flicked the reins gently, not wanting to move the cart horse into a trot that might jolt the chairs – and me – but wanting to move more quickly.

Despite the chill and the recent rains, the road into Kyphrien was fairly smooth. I waved as I passed Jahunt, the old one-eyed peddler who hawked things like scissors and pins for Ginstal.

'Good day, Ser Lerris. Watch for the rain.'

'Good day, Jahunt. The clouds are pretty high for rain.'

'Not high enough, young fellow. Not high enough.'

'We'll see.'

I did try to sense the weather, but didn't have much luck. I'd never had much success with the high winds. I suppose that was why I'd been more than a little surprised, in reflection, on my ability to sense the energy flows beneath the earth. Who'd ever heard of an earth wizard? Then, outside of finding metals, what use was an earth wizard who was an order-mage? Maybe that was me, master of mostly useless order magic.

Farther toward the city, two guards and a huge wagon covered with canvas, but only half full, passed me. Both guards wore blue surcoats and light chain mail under the coats – enough to stop casual brigands, I supposed, but not much match for a good blade or even a good staff.

The white-bearded guard glared at me, and I glared back, but he didn't lift a blade, and they rode past. I cast out my senses to see what the wagon was carrying that was so valuable. Only the sense of clothlike tubes came back to me. Then I nodded to myself – carpets, carpets from Sarronnyn. That explained the blue surcoats and the guards. The patterned Sarronnese carpets were among the best in the world, if not the very best.

The west gate – really the southwest gate, but everyone called it the west gate – was unguarded, but all the gates to Kyphrien were unguarded. Why not, if an enemy had to travel days just to get there?

Cold or not, the marketplace was filled, and I could hear the usual commotion from three blocks away – which was as far as I could keep from the square. The only circular roads in Kyphrien were inside the city, from military planning, I guessed.

'Fresh chickens!!!! Get your fresh . . .'

'. . . spices . . . spices straight from the docks of Ruzor . . .'

'. . . corn flour . . .'

Two youngsters glanced at the wagon, then at me. One frowned, then shook his head at the other, and they slipped into an alley. I glanced down at the staff, glad I had brought it.

I found the south road and turned onto it, looking back for the young thieves, but caught no glimpses of them, as the wagon gently shook its way over the stones.

Once past the southern gate to Kyphrien, the clamor died away, but the roughness of the ride did not. Especially after I guided the wagon over the stone bridge of the Ruzor road, the clay ruts on the southern road were frozen into joltingly uneven obstacles. With every bump my leg twinged, and I wished I were riding Gairloch.

The ruts evened out as I headed south into the hills that held the faded gray-green leaves of the olive groves. Hensil's house sprawled over the hillside amid those groves – a low and white-walled building that seemed to take as much space as a small grove.

All the bumps stopped once I drove past the twin posts that marked the beginning of the drive up to the stables that served the house. The drive was graveled and graded smooth, and I shook my head, deciding that I should have asked for more for the chairs.

Two guards stopped me a good hundred cubits from the main yard. One held a crossbow on me – stupid, in a way, because it's only good for one shot. The other waved a blade that I could have taken away with one blow of the staff.

'What's your business?'

'I'm Lerris, the woodcrafter. I'm delivering the chairs that Master Hensil commissioned.' I gestured toward the back of the wagon.

He lifted several rags and sacks before pointing toward the yard.

It wasn't that easy, not with the half-dozen guards in the yard, all of whom had to check that the chairs were indeed chairs. What else did Hensil do besides grow olives?

The carved double doors with the inlaid glass panels didn't diminish my suspicions, nor did the long stable, or the golden-oak coach being polished by three grooms. Of course, olive-growing could have been highly profitable.

Hensil, almost overflowing his brilliant blue tunic and trousers, and bulging over a silver-buckled belt that barely held his trousers closed, arrived even before the last guard had finished inspecting the chairs.

He bowed with that excessive gesture that signified no respect at all. 'Ah, Master Lerris.'

'The same.' I inclined my head. 'I have delivered your chairs.'

'I can't say as I expected them so soon.' Hensil looked at the wagon.

His consort, a graying woman as slender as he was ample, stood under the portico, saying nothing, a heavy green woolen shawl wrapped around her.

'A man of your eminence should have his commissions when they are ready.'

'I had heard that you were injured.'

I inclined my head again. 'I was, but the leg injury left me more time to work on the detail you requested.'

He finally nodded. 'Well, let us see if they will do . . .'

I bit my tongue and climbed down off the wagon seat, having already set the brake earlier. I slowly removed the canvas, and then the chairs, carrying them up the three steps one by one onto the covered porch.

Hensil watched, trying to keep his face impassive, but his eyes glittered, especially when they rested on the inlaid *H* in the back of each. His consort looked at each one, then at the olive grower.

Finally, as I carried the eight one onto the porch, she slipped up to him, and he bent down. I strained for the words.

'. . . beautiful . . . but they make the table look poor.'

'Cover it with linen,' he mumbled back, straightening.

Then I watched as he inspected every join, every angle. He didn't look at the way the grains matched, and that bothered me, because that was really the hardest part, to make each part seem to flow together.

'They seem adequate,' the grower observed.

'I think you will find them more than adequate, Ser Hensil.' I gave him the overly deep bow he had used earlier.

He started to scowl, then smiled, looking more like a hungry mountain cat than a man, but I really didn't care. I knew the chairs were good.

'We'd agreed on fifteen,' he finally said, his voice jovial.

'We did.' I smiled back, adding, 'And that's a bargain. You did well, Master Grower.'

'. . . uppity crafter . . .' The mumble came from one of the guards.

'. . . idiot . . .' hissed another. 'He's a black mage, too, that one is.'

I heard a swallow, but Hensil ignored it.

'One moment, Master Lerris.' The olive grower walked back into the house.

His consort looked at the chairs, looked at me, and smiled briefly. She still said nothing to me, although her eyes flicked toward the guards. Under the circumstances, it was probably better.

From what I'd seen, even as rough as I was with the staff, I probably could have taken any of the guards, but not the whole dozen – but Tamra and I might have together – if my leg had been fully healed.

Hensil returned with a leather purse. 'Here you are.'

As I took it, I could sense the golds, and there were sixteen. 'Thank you.'

'You didn't count them.'

'I appreciate the extra, Ser Hensil.'

There was another swallow from the guard nearest the steps.

Hensil actually laughed. 'I might like you yet, Master Lerris.' He gestured. 'Send back a small barrel of the black olives with the craftmaster. He deserves some of our best. We've his.'

He had style, and I grinned back at him with a headshake.

Even his consort smiled faintly.

The small barrel of olives was the size of a flour barrel and probably worth two golds itself. Hensil and his consort and the chairs had disappeared through the glassed doors before the olives and I rolled down the drive and back toward Kyphrien.

Once I was clear of the estate, I did check the purse, and there were sixteen standard golds. I looked at the staff. I now had a reason for it, but the barrel of olives might actually deter thieves, since they might figure I had no coin, only olives. I hoped so.

Jahunt had been right, of course. No sooner was I back on the Ruzor road toward Kyphrien than it began to drizzle, almost an ice mist that froze my lungs and created a deep aching in my leg.

The rain also deterred would-be thieves, or maybe my totally bedraggled appearance did. By the time I bounced back to the house, my jacket was damp through, and ice flakes were crusted into my hair, while my ears were freezing. I didn't have that much order strength left, I'd discovered.

Rissa, of course, greeted me.

'Master Lerris.' Rissa shook her head. 'For a craftmaster, you'll be having no sense at all. Out in the rain yet, and that leg is still not healed. It won't be healed when you're old and gray the way you treat it.'

'It was clear when I left.' I glared at her. 'And if I don't deliver my work, then I don't get paid, and we don't eat. I like eating better than not eating.' I pointed to the olive barrel. 'For a bonus, Hensil sent a barrel of black olives, the good ones, he said.'

'Olives are well enough, and we can use them, but coin is better.'

'There was also a one-gold bonus.'

For a moment, only a moment, she was speechless, since a gold was half a season's wages, and I paid better than many. 'Best you get that poor horse into the stable and come into the kitchen. A kettle of warm cider I'll have on the table, and there's a loaf of black bread just ready to come out of the oven.'

I thought that meant she approved.

After eating, I decided I didn't have to go to work immediately, not on crafting, not on Werfel's desk. That could wait. Instead, I took out a quill pen. I dreaded writing the letter, but my parents did deserve that.

'Good,' stated Rissa. 'You work too hard.'

In one way, Rissa was right, and the kitchen was warm, and my leg and muscles were sore. In another way, she was wrong. Writing the postponed letter was scarcely going to be easy.

She continued to work on the next loaves of bread as I wrote. Sometimes, I stopped and just let the smell of yeast and fresh damp dough roll around me.

I had more bread, and I actually finished a whole loaf myself.

Later, I looked at the letter. Deciding to write had not been easy, nor had the words come easily, but my parents at least deserved to know that I was well and prospering – at least relatively. My eyes skipped down the pages.

> ... regret it has taken me so long to send word ... hope and trust you are well ... for a time was an apprentice to your brother Justen ... then Uncle Sardit will be relieved, I hope, to learn that I have returned to woodworking ... a journeyman in Fenard for a year or so ... now have a small shop in Kyphrien ... need to seek an apprentice ... that should give Uncle Sardit a laugh ...
>
> ... have joined with Krystal, from Extina ... beginning to understand something about love ... she is commander of the autarch's blades ... share a home when she is not planning campaigns or fighting them ... even have learned to ride a mountain pony named Gairloch ...
>
> ... have had some adventures with various white wizards ... recovering from assorted injuries ... and concentrating on woodworking more now ...
>
> ... still do not believe that order is of necessity boring, but that there is far too great a danger in failing to explain what order is and what it means ... telling a youngster that order is important is meaningless without showing why – and Recluce is so ordered that the dangers are not at all obvious ...

I didn't know if what I had written about order was quite right, but the general idea was. No one likes to accept 'because that's the way it is' as an answer, especially young people, and while people like my father and Justen with vast experience found certain aspects of the world obvious, the rest of us didn't.

'Won't be long 'fore dinner, Master Lerris.'

I took the hint and folded the letter. Then I went back to the workshop and put my seal across it, and set it aside in the box for my papers – who would have thought that being a woodworker meant keeping stacks of papers?

I shook my head. Tomorrow I'd have to ride into Kyphrien to arrange for it to be carried to Recluce. Probably one of the wool merchants – like Clayda – could do it.

I checked the water in the moisture pot and added a log to the shop hearth before heading back to the washroom.

# XLVI

Werfel's desk, like everything else, was taking longer than I planned. This time, again, it was the glue, which I'd neglected, and needed to remake. The problem with glue is that it hardens, usually before the joins are ready. So I was chipping and grinding, and heating more water when there was a rap on the shop door.

Three people stood there – Rissa, another woman, and a black-haired youngster – presumably the first response to Rissa's efforts in informing all of Kyphros that I was seeking an apprentice. All she had needed was my admission that I needed one.

My leg no longer twinged when I walked across the shop, but it did tremble if I put weight on it for too long, although the bone seemed completely healed.

'This is Master Lerris,' said Rissa. 'Wendre thinks Callos would be a good woodworker.'

I inclined my head to Wendre, a stout woman with long brown hair wound into a bun. 'Sometimes, woodworking is difficult.'

The youngster looked up at me. He wasn't as tall as I am, but most Kyphrans aren't. 'You're a wizard, aren't you?'

'At times, but I spend more time doing woodworking.'

Rissa tugged at Wendre's arm. 'I have some fresh bread. Let Master Lerris talk to Callos.'

Wendre let herself be tugged out of the workroom.

'Come over here.' I walked toward the bin that contained my odd-sized pieces – too big to burn and too small to use except for boxes, breadboards, inlays, or small decorative items – except for the inlays, things that would have been done mostly by the apprentice I didn't have. After fishing out a piece of cherry, I handed it to Callos. 'What can you tell about this?' He took the wood, but he looked at me as if I were crazy. 'It's wood. It's a piece of wood. That's all it is.'

'What would you do with it?'

'Make things, I guess. Isn't that what you want an apprentice for?'

'What does it feel like?'

He shrugged, his black eyes puzzled. 'It feels like wood.'

'Is it smooth or rough? What does it smell like?'

'Smooth, I guess. It smells like wood.' He handed it back to me.

I did not sigh. 'Why did you come to see me?'

'My mom, she said I'd better do something, and you're not just a craftmaster – you're a wizard. I want to be a wizard.'

'I had to learn to be a woodworker first.' I wondered how to tell him that it just wouldn't work.

'I don't think I'd like that.'

'Maybe you ought to think about it some more.' I set the piece of cherry back in the bin and led him to the door and through the drizzle up onto the porch and into the kitchen.

Rissa's friend looked from me to her son. So did Rissa. Neither said a word.

I swallowed. Finally, I said, 'I don't think Callos is really interested in being a woodworker.'

Wendre glared at her son.

'It's not something that you can force,' I added. 'Some people are good with stone, others with blades . . .'

Wendre's glare softened somewhat, but Callos stayed by the door.

'Thank you.' I slipped back out the door and toward the shop. Had I been that indifferent? I didn't think so. Sloppy? Yes, I had been sloppy, and careless, and I recalled Sardit's frustration and anger, but the wood had always felt good in my hands. Was I asking too much? Probably, but Bostric had felt the woods, and even Brettel the millmaster had been able to feel that in Bostric, that gangly apprentice I had trained for Destrin and had married to Deirdre.

I swallowed, wondering how Deirdre and Bostric were doing, whether they had children, and whether Deirdre had been able to keep her father alive. Destrin hadn't been that good a crafter, but even he had understood woods.

With another deep breath, I went back to turning the legs of the desk chair for Werfel. On the second leg the chisel slipped, and all I had was a piece of firewood, or perhaps the leg of a working stool. I shook my head at myself, both at the waste of wood and the lack of concentration.

Rissa slipped though the door and stood at the back of the shop.

'Yes? Are they gone?' I asked.

'I told Wendre that Callos would not be a good woodworker.'

'Then why did you have her bring him?'

'Would she listen to me? I am not the woodworker.' Rissa shook her head. 'I see you look at the wood, and it is not just wood. You touch it, almost like a lover. Callos – he would strike it with a hammer to see if he could make a hole in it.'

I took a deep breath. 'Are there any youngsters who like wood – young women, too? Men aren't the only ones who could be woodworkers.'

'That I do not know. But I can ask, and see if there are those who might feel that way. I will have to tell them that is what you want. If I say that – they will think Rissa has gone crazy, but wizards and mastercrafters are all crazy. So no one will think anything about it.'

'That's why you had Callos come in ... so that everyone would learn that I'm impossible?'

Rissa didn't smile, but her dark eyes did sparkle. 'Callos was already talking about how you wanted him to feel the wood and smell it. Soon everyone will know.'

'Wonderful. All of Kyphros will think I have lost my mind.'

'No, Master Lerris. No one presumes to know a wizard's mind, and so who can tell whether he has lost it or not?'

An impossible, inscrutable wizard yet – but it was better than being thought mad or chaos-tinged – and I wasn't that much past the score mark in years. For some reason, I recalled my father and wondered what he would have thought. Probably he would have delivered a long moralistic explanation. Uncle Sardit would have understood, though, and I still would have preferred being the eccentric craftmaster to the inscrutable wizard.

'Well, this crafter is going back to working on a desk that should already have been finished.'

'Never ... never do you stop unless you are hurt or ordered by the commander or the autarch.'

'Can you think of any better people to obey?'

'Men ...' sniffed Rissa as she left.

As for me, I still didn't have an apprentice, and I still didn't know when Krystal would return, and I was beginning to worry. Going out on a routine trip and not returning – that was what had happened to Ferrel.

I went back to chipping and grinding old glue, and boiling water.

# XLVII

## South of Hrisbarg, Freetown [Candar]

From behind the revetment at the top of the hill, Berfir looks at the round object hanging in the sky over the hill on the far side of the valley. There Colaris's forces have dug themselves in behind heavy trenchworks. Two black lines run from a basket beneath the elongated ball to the ground.

A puff of grayish smoke belches from a hole in trenches of the Freetown forces. Berfir forces himself not to duck at the whistling of the cannon shell, and at the dull thud that accompanies the gout of earth and grass that erupts from the hillside below.

The Duke studies the flat ground below the hill where the crimson banners of Hydlen hang limply. Dark lumps lie in the dust of the flat land that had been a grain field seasons earlier. A few high browned shoots remain, after-harvest weeds. Beyond the flats that had once been grain fields, another long and low hill rises. To the left is a small stand of trees, a woodlot. To the right, fields stretch out to another set of hills in the distance.

In the fields are far too many of the dark lumps, and, Berfir reflects, far too many had worn the red and gold plaid of Yeannota.

Another shell pounds the hillside, this time turning a small pine into a spray of kindling, less than a dozen cubits below the left end of the trenches of the Hydlenese forces.

Duke Berfir studies the balloon hanging in the sky and the mirror flashes from the basket. '. . . telling the gunners where to aim,' he mumbles to himself.

'I beg your pardon, ser.'

'Nothing. Nothing.'

. . . *eeeee . . . eeee . . . crump!* Yet another shell erupts below the Duke, gouging out the soil below the center of his troops' earthworks.

'We need to see if we can guide the rockets into their gun emplacements.' Berfir turns and strides across the hillside, not remaining all that close to the revetments.

'Ser . . .'

As the shells continue to fall, the Duke continues onward, toward the rocket emplacements.

The rocket officer looks up at the Duke.

'Ser?'

'Lift the launchers, Nual.'

'What?'

'Point them up.' Berfir's hand describes an arc. 'So they drop down over the Freetown revetments.'

'We'll waste rockets.'

'We're wasting rockets now. Unless we can get to those cannon, they'll push us right back out of Freetown, and before long they'll hold the Ohyde Valley, and they'll be knocking at the gates of Hydolar and Renklaar.'

'Yes, ser.'

Berfir watches as the rocket crews struggle to wedge the launchers into higher positions than the equipment had ever been designed for. All the time the cannon shells creep closer.

# XLVIII

The heavy clouds that had rolled in that afternoon led to a dark night, really black. I lit the lantern outside the shop, and then went back inside to work on the supporting aspect of Werfel's commission – the chair – since it definitely needed to be sturdy to bear his weight. Why was it that most of the patrons who could afford good woodcrafting needed chairs capable of handling heavy loads?

After having finished gluing the legs of the desk chair into their sockets, I was cleaning up the glue pot and adding some water before setting it back on its tripod by the hearth. Outside, distant thunder mumbled, and rain splattered against the outside walls and the back window.

I kept casting my senses out. Krystal should have returned days earlier, and I had heard nothing. I felt she was getting near, though, and finally I could sense the horses, and hear them through the dampness, long before they reached the yard. I had put down the glue pot and was out in the slashing cold rain even before Krystal and her guards pulled up outside the stable.

Perron had the stable door open, and Haithen stood in the mud and held his mount's reins. The other two guards were dismounting.

I held out a hand to Krystal, but she didn't need it as she vaulted clear of the saddle. She did need it to keep from skidding in the mud.

'You shouldn't be out here.' Despite the concerned tone, she gave me a smile that was worth the chill.

'I'm a lot better, and I missed you, and I should be here. And I've been worried,' I admitted, even as I was hugging her and ignoring the blade that dug into my good leg.

'I'm glad.'

Then we didn't talk for a moment.

'How can you stand me? I smell like a stable.'

'I hadn't noticed.'

'More needs healing than your leg.'

'You can help,' I offered.

Perron grinned, I thought, although I really couldn't see in the darkness and the rain. The night was so dark and the rain so heavy that even the big lantern didn't help that much.

'I'm soaked, and standing here won't help you.'

She was right about that, and I grabbed the reins and followed Haithen and her mount into the stable, glad that I'd insisted on raising the clay floor when it had been built. I lit the stable lantern.

'Lerris, your stable is drier than some inns,' offered Haithen, her short hair plastered flat against her skull.

'I do what I can to encourage the commander and her guards to stay here.'

'I don't think she needs much encouragement.' That was a low-voiced comment from Perron.

Krystal actually blushed. I coughed.

By the time we got Krystal's mount rubbed down and her saddle and gear wiped dry and clean, and headed for the house, big wet flakes of snow had begun to fall, interspersed with the rain that seemed more like ice.

'A real winter's on its way.'

'It looks like it.' I squeezed her hand and then held the door for her.

Rissa was standing there, her hands on her hips, stains on her apron, and a scowl upon her face. 'Lamb stew will have to do. Thank the darkness I baked today. If only I could know when you would be here, Commander . . .'

'Lamb stew is fine, Rissa. It is far better than march rations or inn fare, especially at this time of year.' Krystal smiled and stretched. 'It's good to be home.'

'And your guards, where are they?'

'Hanging out their gear to dry in the stable. The ride back, especially from Felsa, was through the rain.'

Rissa looked at us. 'Drowned rats – they look drier.'

We looked at each other. She was right.

So we went into the bedroom where I stripped off my soaking work shirt, and Krystal pulled off her tunic, and I dropped the wet shirt and hugged her again. Her damp skin was chill, but she felt so good.

She kissed me, and we hung together for a few moments – until her stomach growled.

'I haven't eaten since breakfast . . .'

I got her an old heavy work shirt, and an older one for me, and followed her back to the kitchen where the guards stood waiting.

'Sit down.' Krystal gestured.

Rissa set the stew pot on a breadboard in the middle of the table and a basket filled with three loaves of warmish bread beside the pot.

'. . . better than the barracks . . .'

'. . . best food . . . anywhere . . .'

'Stop mumbling with your mouth full, Jinsa,' admonished Perron.

Rissa put down mugs. 'Herbal tea or dark ale I have.'

'Ale,' said Krystal firmly. 'It's been a long eight-day.'

Haithen and I had tea; the others had ale.

By the time I'd sipped half a cup of tea and felt warm, Krystal and her guards had each had at least two helpings of stew, and Rissa had put two more loaves of bread in the basket.

I was full with one solid helping, but I'd had bread and cheese at mid-day, and I hadn't been riding through an icy rain.

'How were the harbor defenses?' I asked after swallowing my last mouthful of stew.

'Ruzor really doesn't have any.'

'No defenses? What about all those walls?'

Krystal took a mouthful of stew without answering. Perron looked down at his bowl.

'Might I have some more bread?' asked Haithen.

I looked at the basket, not believing it was empty, but it was.

The two other guards looked at each other and down at the table.

'Have as much bread as you want,' offered Rissa. 'Of bread, we have plenty.'

'I see,' I offered. 'Against Berfir's rockets, the walls aren't that much good?'

'Nor against the Hamorian long cannon, apparently.' Krystal stopped and took a long pull of the dark ale. 'The old fort sits on the breakwater, and that's too exposed.'

'Did you get that from the envoy from Southwind?'

Krystal took a deep breath. 'Hamor has a squadron of a dozen steel-hulled steam cruisers at Dellash and more on the way.'

'Dellash? Where's that?'

'You know the island opposite Summerdock?'

'That's in Delapra, but Delapra's almost part of Southwind.'

'Not any more. There's a big Hamorian trading station in Summerdock, and the Hamorian traders use the port year-round now.'

The picture got very clear. Hamor was using Dellash, wherever that was, as a naval base to 'protect' its trade in Candar.

'So that was why the Southwind envoy came to Ruzor and not Kyphrien?' I asked.

'She wasn't an envoy.' Krystal's tone was openly sarcastic. 'She was merely taking a pleasure trip.'

'A pleasure trip? With a staff of a half score?' suggested Perron.

'"Just a simple traveler I am, Commander Krystal ..."' Krystal snorted, then emptied the mug. 'I'd like some more . . .'

Rissa nodded and brought her the pitcher.

Krystal filled her mug to the very top, then had to sip quickly to keep it from overflowing.

'She talked a great deal about the Hamorian cruisers, their draft, their guns, their displacement, their armor, their marine contingents, and their proximity to Summerdock.' My consort took another deep swallow from her refilled mug. 'Dellash used to be a fishing village. It now has a deepwater stone breakwater and three piers, not to mention a huge mountain of coal that magically appeared from nowhere.'

I was getting a sinking feeling in my stomach as Krystal talked, one that wasn't helped by the way the guards looked at the table and not at either of us.

'Why hasn't anyone heard about this?'

'Obviously, the Emperor didn't want it to be heard. Not until now, anyway.'

I liked that even less.

'Does Kas – the autarch know?'

'Not yet. But there's little enough she could do tonight.'

I glanced toward the window, and the heavy flakes of snow that continued to fall.

'There's little enough she could do anytime,' offered Perron.

Krystal took a long slow breath and another deep swallow of the ale, while Perron refilled his mug.

'How is Yelena doing?' I finally asked.

'Everyone respects her,' Krystal said with a faint laugh, 'especially after she discovered on the first day how Kyldesee diverted funds into her own purse.'

'A lot of things reappeared in the armory and the storerooms,' added Haithen. 'Especially after word got around that she knew you, Master Lerris.'

'Somehow, I doubt that my name had a lot to do with it. Yelena is more than competent without having to rely on third-rate wizards.'

'You'll notice how he's finally given up denying that he's a wizard.' Haithen winked at Perron.

'Denial would be hard now, even for Lerris,' added Krystal. 'He's known as both a hero and a wizard.'

'You're supposed to be on my side,' I protested.

'In matters of state, my loyalty is to the autarch.' She actually managed to say it with a straight face. Then she grinned.

We talked for a time longer, but not much longer, because everyone was yawning, me included.

Haithen left first, peering into the yard. 'There's a span of demon-damned snow on the ground. Snow? This early in Kyphrien?'

'You have your boots on. You want help getting them off?' Perron leered at her.

'You'll have more than enough trouble with your own.'

The other male guard shook his head. The woman – Jinsa – grinned.

Krystal stood up, and so did I, leaving them to their own devices.

Later, once the bedroom door was closed, I asked, 'Why was this traveling envoy there to warn you about Hamor?'

'Lerris . . . think about it. If Southwind is so worried that they can't even send an official envoy to Kyphrien, but only an unofficial traveler to Ruzor, what does that tell you?'

'They don't think they can afford the slightest affront to the Emperor. They're worried that Hamor will use any pretext to take over Delapra and Southwind.'

'In practical terms, Hamor already controls Delapra. Early in the fall, when we were worried about Hydlen, they sent a ship – one ship – off the breakwater at Summerdock. It reduced the lighthouse to rubble with three shells from their new long cannon.' Krystal hung her jacket on one of the pegs in the closet, then sat on the edge of the bed.

I pulled off one boot, and then the other, taking the liberty of massaging a shapely calf.

'I need a shower.'

'After this weather?'

'I can't stand being this filthy.'

'You look good to me.'

'Lerris . . .'

'It's cold.'

'I need a shower, and you can warm me up.' She smiled, and I had to smile back.


# XLIX


Krystal left early the next morning, through the slush that the night's snow had become even before the sun rose. Her departure, with her guards, was through a yard that had become an expanse of freezing mud.

I edged along the front of the house and shop and circled through the virgin slush to get to the stable to groom and feed Gairloch and the cart horse.

Gairloch pranced a bit in his stall.

'You may want to be ridden, but we're not going anywhere until this slop freezes or dries out.'

*. . . eeee . . . eeee . . .*

'No.' I did pour a few more oats into the corner of his manger.

*Whuffff* . . . Whatever that meant.

While he ate, I mucked out the stall, and then repeated the process with the cart horse, and with Krystal's stall.

I looked at the guards' stalls. They were filthy, too. I looked for a while, then picked up the shovel. At least we were getting a lot of manure for the gardens, and Rissa didn't mind it at all, for which I was grateful.

All that cleaning meant washing up in too-cold water before I went back to working with light and fine-grained woods – manure and dirt do stain, contrary to some beliefs. I shivered as well, and the shivering meant my leg twinged again, and I had to sit in front of the shop hearth for a while to warm up.

There I saw the moisture pot was dry, and I needed to add some water to the glue pot, and by then I realized I had to bring in more wood for the hearth, and I dragged in dirt and mud, and that meant sweeping the floor.

Some mornings went like that, and the sun was well clear of the horizon before I was actually at work, accompanied by the dripping of ice and slush falling from the eaves outside.

I'd resumed work on Werfel's desk – the chair, actually – when a catching of the smoothing blade told me it needed sharpening, and since I was sharpening, I did the chisels, which had gotten too dull, and the knives. Before long it was mid-morning, and I hadn't really done any work at all, but the shop looked good and the tools were sharp, except for the saws, but I let Ginstal do that. A bad sharpening job will ruin a good saw faster than just about anything, and I had too much in the saws, and too little confidence in my ability there.

I had finally gotten back to smoothing the desk chair for Werfel when I heard another rap on the shop door.

Rissa stood there with a young man. Mud dropped from his worn boots all over the entryway . . .

'This is Turon . . .'

I sighed. 'Have him brush his boots off.'

Rissa shook her head and handed the youth the boot brush. He looked at it. She made a brushing motion.

'Ah . . . clean the boots.' Turon smiled broadly and took the boot brush.

I did not shake my head as he used it to fling mud everywhere around the doorway. I didn't even wince when one glob landed on my good varnish brush. I just set down the smoothing blade and walked across the shop.

Rissa smiled and stepped outside, shutting the door behind her, leaving me with the young man. Turon was big for a Kyphran youth, almost as big as I was.

'You want to be a woodworker?'

'Yes, master.' He grinned, a wide ready grin, and an empty one.

'How do you know you want to work the wood?'

'Because, the woods, I love them. They smell so good when they are cut, and the smooth woods, like there, they are like a girl's skin.' He pointed toward the desktop.

I handed him the block of cherry, and his fingers caressed it. 'What is this?'

'Good wood, hard wood, and you will make many things with it?'

'It's small for many things.'

'You could make a whistle. I made a whistle. See?' He extracted a crude wooden whistle and waved it.

'Usually, I make larger things.'

'I see the chairs.' His dirty fingers gently touched the curve in Werfel's desk chair, and I tried not to flinch. 'They are pretty. Stasel has no chairs like these.'

'Most people don't. They're hard to make.'

For a long moment, Turon looked at the chair. Then he put away the whistle and his eyes flickered toward the plank floor. 'Even the floor is clean.'

'A woodcrafting shop should be clean.'

He smiled sadly. 'I am sorry.'

So was I. The problem with Turon wasn't his feelings, but his brains. Why couldn't I get an apprentice who could sense the woods *and* think?

After Turon trudged out and back down the road to wherever he had come from, I got out the big broom and swept all the mud back out into the yard. Then I cleared off the boards leading to the workroom. I hated mud in the house or the shop – my Recluce heritage again.

Rissa reappeared as I completed sweeping. 'He is a good boy.'

'He is good. That I could tell. And he would work hard. But ...' I paused before continuing. 'He could not learn what he would need to learn.'

'It is not easy to be a woodworker.'

'No.' Then, I wasn't sure it was easy to be good at anything, let alone outstanding. I did good woodwork. Not as good as Uncle Sardit, and maybe not always as good as Perlot in Fenard, but good, and people were already seeking me out. Was the world that short of people able to craft well and willing to work hard enough to turn out good products?

'It is sad,' Rissa said slowly. 'The good ones, they have no brains, and the smart ones, they will not work.'

'Sometimes the smart ones get around to learning they must work.'

'Seldom, I think.'

'I didn't like to work.'

'I think not, Master Lerris. I think not.' She frowned. 'Poor Turon ... it is sad.'

I felt sorry for the eager-faced youth, but all my pity would not give the boy the understanding needed for what I did. He could have made crude benches for Destrin, but I didn't make crude benches.

Still ... I felt badly. In time, after cutting off a slice of white cheese and munching it with a crust of dried bread, I walked back to the shop. My hair got wet from the melting slush dripping off the roof.

After spending all afternoon on the finish for Werfel's desk and chair, I was more than ready to put away polishing rags and oils by the time Krystal arrived.

'You smell good,' she said.

I hadn't hugged her because my hands were oily, and they would have left rather permanent marks on her greens. 'Finishing Werfel's desk.'

'You still smell good.'

I grinned.

'Perron and the others are eating, or will be.'

'You want a private dinner?'

'We have some things to discuss.'

My face must have fallen. 'What did I do?'

'Oh, Lerris.' Her laugh was a little sad. 'You didn't do anything. Except sometimes I worry that you're going to go off and be a hero again. And sometimes, I like to be alone with you, and sometimes . . . I just don't want them knowing everything.' She perched on the stool. 'Finish up what you were doing.'

'I was almost finished.' I spread out the rags to dry – on the stone slab well away from the hearth and with plenty of space. Many a woodcrafter had lost a shop to a rag fire, and I didn't want to be one of them.

Perron stood as we entered the kitchen. 'We're almost done, Commander.'

Krystal nodded, and we walked back to the washroom.

She washed, but left her greens on, but I was grimy enough that it took more time. I also changed into a clean brown shirt.

When I got back to the kitchen, Rissa had set the brown plates on the table, and with roasted chicken halves for each of us, garnished with the good black olives.

'Chicken?'

'We could have chicken more often if we had our own chickens,' Rissa pointed out.

'No chickens.'

Rissa shrugged. 'Not so many chicken dinners, then.'

As Krystal filled her mug with the dark ale I had bought with a small portion of the proceeds from Hensil's chairs, or, if I counted it that way, from the autarch's wardrobe, she laughed. 'You two . . .'

I poured some redberry into my mug, and began to dismember the chicken, even before Rissa set the bowl of buttered beans between us. Then she put down the bread basket and two jars – one of greenberry conserve and one of apple butter – before slipping out of the kitchen and closing the door.

'Berfir has set up guard stations on all the roads into Hydlen.' Krystal took a deep swallow of her ale, and used her belt knife to dissect the chicken in the effortless way I had always envied. My chicken already looked like the result of a mountain cat's attack. 'He's not stopping anyone yet.'

I nodded, taking a sip of the redberry. Then I massaged my left leg. It still got tired too quickly. 'How is his war with Colaris going?'

'His troops crossed the hills north of Renklaar and started across the farm valleys south of Freetown. Then Colaris got organized, and nothing much seems to have happened, except a bunch of battles that no one is winning. I got word today that Berfir's raising another set of levies out of Telsen.'

'He isn't going to try to use the Frven road, is he? That belongs to Montgren.'

'The Countess has rather less ability to defend herself than Colaris.'

'Berfir wants to take over all of eastern Candar, is that it?'

'If he could. Hydlen has always worried about Freetown, even when it was Lydiar, and Colaris started the war.' She shrugged. 'The olives are good.'

'Hensil's best. A little bonus.'

'Oh, Lerris. Somehow, there's always something extra with you.'

I decided to change the subject. 'What stopped Berfir?'

'We think Hamor sent some gold, and Colaris is getting some advice from another wizard.'

'Wonderful.'

'It's our friend Sammel.'

'Sammel? From Recluce? He didn't seem the chaos type. Not at all – he seemed more like a hermit or a pilgrim.' I recalled Sammel in sandals and brown robes, with a soft voice. He'd been older than any of us, almost in his forties, but with a gentle commanding sort of manner.

'What did Tamra think of Antonin to begin with, with his feeding of the poor and all that?' asked Krystal.

'There is that.' I took a deep breath. 'Still, that bothers me. Why would he adopt chaos?'

Krystal took another sip of the dark ale and broke off another corner of the bread. 'We don't know that. We just have word that he has given some rather special scrolls out – not just to Colaris, but to the Viscount, and even to Berfir. Kasee thinks some have even gotten as far as Hamor.'

'That sounds like chaos – or setting up chaos.'

'Maybe he's selling knowledge to support himself. Justen does that, as you've pointed out.' She had an amused look on her face.

'It's different with Justen.' I slathered some greenberry conserve on the dark bread.

'It probably is.' Krystal winced. 'How you can do that . . .'

'Sometimes, tart stuff is good.'

'I wish you hadn't said it quite that way.'

I almost choked.

'The Viscount of Certis has pledged his support to the Countess,' added Krystal conversationally. 'He's issued a call for a levy in the spring.'

'Shit . . .' I mumbled through the mouthful of chicken. The more I heard, the less I liked it. And I had thought the war between Gallos and Kyphros had been bad.

'Kasee would like you to come to an audience sometime about an eight-day from now.'

'Me? A mere woodworker?'

'She wants you to wear grays again.' Krystal snorted. 'You haven't been a mere woodworker in years, and everyone in Kyphros has known it for seasons.' She paused to slice up another section of the chicken, then she refilled her mug and took a deep swallow.

'So why am I slaving at doing things like Werfel's desk?'

'Because great wizardry doesn't pay as well as great woodworking?'

'I'm not sure great wizardry pays at all.'

'Kasee has paid you.' Krystal paused. 'I almost wish she hadn't, except for the wardrobe.'

'Why?'

'Because . . .' She shrugged. 'You want to please too much, and I worry that you'd kill yourself being a hero again just to please me or her.'

'Not her.'

'Well . . . if you please me otherwise . . .'

I groaned. 'Why does she want me at the audience or whatever it is?'

'Because she's seeing an envoy from Hamor. A real one. That's why she's requested you wear grays.'

I really wanted to groan then, but I'd already groaned too much. That's the trouble with complaining too early. When you really need to, no one will listen. 'I'll really have to wear those grays again?'

'Yes.'

'What about Tamra and Justen?'

Krystal shrugged, and I knew what she meant. They were somewhere in Montgren or Certis, but who knew where?

'So I have to play at being court wizard?'

'Is it really playing?'

She probably had me there.

I watched as she took another swallow of the ale.

'That's a lot of ale.'

'I know.' She gave me a sloppy smile. '. . . thought it might help . . .'

At least I had enough sense not to ask what it would help with, and it did – later.

# L

Tamra slowed her mount well back from the edge of the trees and waited for Justen. The older man in gray drew up his pony beside her as perhaps two squads of horse troops rode down the road and passed from sight, the hoofs of their mounts clipping on the old stones.

Behind the cavalry-led van followed a column of figures, also clad in a grayish cyan, marching southward on the old straight road. A single cyan banner with a hawk's claw clutching a sheaf of golden grain fluttered intermittently in the light but cold breeze.

The hills to the west beyond the road bore traces of white near their crests.

The dark-haired older man patted Rosefoot on the neck as he and Tamra studied the passing soldiers.

'. . . had a girl and she was mine . . .

. . . had a fire and a cot . . .

. . . had a horse and he was fine . . .

now a blade is all I've got!'

'Colaris's forces heading out to invade Hydlen from the north?' she asked.

'Probably.' He nodded. 'But they'll have to take the Hydolar Road, and that runs through Certis. The Viscount might have some objection.'

The soldiers in the column carried what appeared to be thick staffs, resting them against their shoulders as they marched southward.

She squinted, and her eyes seemed to focus into the distance. After a moment, she shivered, and she looked at Justen. 'Rifles? They can't be carrying rifles, can they? That's what they feel like, with all that iron . . . but Berfir has a white wizard.'

'They're rifles,' affirmed Justen with a sigh.

'How?'

Justen paused before answering, his voice low. 'Try to sense what is in their belts.'

After a long silence, Tamra straightened in her saddle. 'Little metal – steel – canisters.' She swallowed. 'Will the steel shield them from chaos?'

Justen nodded. 'Miniature shells, rockets . . . for their guns. No more powder flasks.'

'Why . . . why now?'

Justen shrugged, his eyes still on the long column of soldiers.

'Is this because of Lerris?' Tamra's whisper was sharp.

He responded with a sad shake of the head. 'This started long before Lerris.' As Tamra's mouth opened, he added, 'Long before. But someone has rediscovered what was thought to be safely hidden. Nothing stays hidden forever.' He took a slow deep breath.

Behind the soldiers came heavy, creaking wagons, each pulled by a four-horse team.

Tamra and Justen waited and watched, watched and waited.

## LI

The man standing at the shop door came to my shoulder, and his rabbittrimmed green cloak and polished boots indicated a limited prosperity. 'Master Lerris?'

'Please come in.' I glanced at Werfel's completed desk. I was getting ready to pack it up into the wagon once Rissa's friend Kilbon arrived to help me. 'What might I be able to do for you?'

He stepped inside and closed the door against the chill. 'Durrik. I trade mostly in spices.' He brushed his thinning dark hair off a browned forehead and cleared his throat. 'I do supply some spices to Hensil, and . . . well . . . Verin told me about the chairs.'

'You would like some chairs?' I asked.

Durrik laughed. 'Chairs like that – or a desk like that? I couldn't possibly afford or justify them. No . . . I was wondering about an upright chest, one with compartments . . .'

'To store your rarer spices in? Ones you would prefer to keep in the house or office?'

'Exactly . . .'

'That could present a problem.'

Durrik pursed his lips.

'The woods ... and the finish. You'd need a hard finish, at least in the storage compartments, that wouldn't add or subtract from the spices. Right?'

'I hadn't thought about that, but it makes sense.'

'How big would you want the compartments, and how many?'

'I brought a list of the spices.'

'How many, roughly?'

'Say ... between a score and a score and a half.'

I pulled out some sketch sheets and set them on the bench. 'Some you'll want more space for than others ... what about bigger spaces in the base and smaller ones on top?' I began to sketch. 'This isn't what it will look like, except for the general shape.'

The spice merchant watched, his dark-haired head tilted at an angle. 'Hmmm ...'

'Do you want doors or drawers?' I paused. 'Or some of each?'

He pointed at the sketch. 'What if the top ones, on each side, here, were small drawers? That would work for the rarer ones that you need only a little of. And two rows of smaller drawers here ...'

I could see some problems with his arrangement, because lots of little drawers weigh more than a smaller number of larger ones, and the chest could get unbalanced. 'I'd have to balance this somehow. A lot of drawers in the top, unless I make the base wider – like this – will make it top-heavy.'

'I don't know as I'd like that,' Durrik said slowly. 'Isn't there another way?'

'There are several. Each has advantages and disadvantages ...' I sketched out several rough design, beginning with a straight-sided chest where the larger drawers flanked smaller center drawers and ending with a larger piece with open shelving that could be used for books or display.

While he looked at them, I added some water to the moisture pot and the glue pot, then brushed a trace of sawdust off the desk chair.

'I had not thought commissioning a simple chest to be so complex.'

'Simple chests aren't. You want a chest with all the drawers the same size, and you can have it – but you waste space, and there's nothing particularly special about it.'

'I don't need a work of art, Master Lerris, just a chest.'

'Fine.' I sketched out a simple twelve-drawer chest. 'What about this?'

'That's too squat.'

I gave him a fifteen-drawer one, thinner and taller.

'I don't know . . .'

I laughed. 'You say you just want a chest, but when I give you a plain chest, you don't like it.'

'I can't afford a work of art, young master.'

'Part of the cost is wood. It's less costly to work in softer woods and use a harder varnish. Of course, softer woods will get dented more quickly.'

'Are you trying to sell me the most expensive chest possible?'

I shook my head. 'You misunderstand. A more expensive piece from a good craftsman will be a better piece. You know that. You want the best you can get, but you fear the cost.'

He nodded. 'Indeed I do.'

I took a deep breath. 'All right. Let's start with what you would really like. I'll tell you about what it will cost . . .'

'About?'

'I'll give you a firm price once we work out what you want. The amount of turning and carving can change the cost of the same-sized chest a great deal. So can any metalwork or ornamentation.'

'Then . . . proceed.'

I must have used nearly ten sheets of sketch paper, more than a few coppers' worth, before we agreed on a basic design – a variation on the original sketch with the larger drawers on the outside, except that I put in a single shelf in the center of the upper part – for balance and display.

In the end, we did agree.

'Eight golds . . . the golden oak, and at least three coats of the hard varnish, and this design. No cracked wood, mind you.'

'No cracked wood – and if you don't like it, you don't have to take it,' I added.

'Do you tell all your customers that?'

'Yes.'

Durrik shook his head. 'The confidence of youth . . .'

I didn't know as it was confidence. I thought my work was good enough to sell to someone else – but even if it weren't I wasn't about to force customers to purchase woodwork they didn't like. They wouldn't feel good, and neither would I. 'I would not force anyone to buy . . .'

'I hope you will always feel that way.' He smiled, almost sadly, before asking, 'When might the chest be ready?'

I had to think for a moment. 'It might be four eight-days or a season. I don't have enough oak, and that means seasoning so it will not split.'

'I would hope not more than a season.' He pulled his cloak around him and turned toward the door.

'So would I.' My voice was dry.

'Good day, Master Lerris.'

'Good day.'

I finally did manage to pull out the plans for Antona's desk and start on the sketch for the bracing – unlike Uncle Sardit, I had to sketch some things out. Then, maybe he did when he was younger, too.

Kilbon arrived on a thin and bony brown mare right before midday. The sound of strange hoofs brought me to the shop door, but not any sooner than his mare brought Rissa to the kitchen door.

Kilbon's face was as thin as the mare's, but he smiled when he saw Rissa, and inclined his head to me. 'Master Lerris?'

'Kilbon. I appreciate your help. I'm working on getting an apprentice, but since I don't have one . . .' I shrugged.

'Good help is, mayhap, hard to find.'

'Especially if the master wants a bright lad who can also sense the woods with more than clumsy hands,' added Rissa.

'Ah, Rissa, lass, were I Master Lerris, that I'd want, too. I can't use a lad who can't find and bend the rushes without breaking them.'

Rissa looked from Kilbon to me and back again.

Kilbon, thin as he was, had a wiry strength, and we had the desk and chair in the wagon in no time. It took me longer to pad them and cover them with the oiled canvas. I even remembered my staff.

I offered Kilbon two coppers, but he shook his head.

'Rather trade a favor for a favor . . .'

I smiled. 'Fair's fair.'

'. . . and some warm food from the lass.' He winked at me and smiled fondly at Rissa, putting his arm around her shoulders.

She actually smiled back at the basketmaker.

'You sure you won't be needing me on the trip?'

'Enjoy the warm food from the lass,' I suggested.

'Master Lerris . . .' Rissa actually blushed.

I flicked the reins and ignored the muffled *whuff* from the black mare. The wind continued to blow cold out of the northwest, and it felt as if I were in the Westhorns themselves even before I drove the wagon into Kyphrien.

A guard outside the autarch's palace waved to me as I passed, and I waved back without recognizing him. There were getting to be far more people who knew me that I didn't know than the other way around.

Werfel had his house and hauling business northwest of Kyphrien on the road to Meltosia. As I guided my small wagon up the hard-packed drive, a blue-sided hauler's wagon easily twice the size of mine rumbled by. The driver tipped his hat. The blue side panel bore a picture of two horses and a wagon, more of a black outline really – with the name 'Werfel' underneath.

The white-walled structure sat on a very low rise, just enough to ensure good drainage really, and formed a square around a central court. Two sides of the square were for the dwelling, and two for the stables and wagon-barns. The hauling sides opened outward, while the dwelling sides opened onto the courtyard.

There were no guards around – unlike Hensil's establishment – but a broad-shouldered hauler who looked as though he could have eaten most of Hensil's guards for breakfast without taking a breath directed me.

'Looking for Master Werfel? He's in the office, round the corner.'

I flicked the reins, gently, not wanting the wagon to jerk, and guided the horse around to the south side of the building. By the time I had set the brake and gotten down, Werfel was standing by the heavy, iron-banded front door.

'Master Lerris . . . you'd deliver to a hauler?'

'Why not? I'd have to come out to tell you it was ready.'

Werfel laughed and turned to the big hauler who had followed me. 'That's a good crafter, not willing to waste his time.'

Then he gestured and the big hauler and another man walked into his office and carried out a flat table, setting it outside the door. They lifted the desk out of the wagon as easily as if it were a saw or a basket of potatoes, and the desk wasn't light. That oak was solid.

They carried it into the office and set it down about four cubits out from the wall, right in front of the iron-barred door. Werfel followed them, and I brought the chair in and set it down.

The haulers nodded to me, and left us in the office, a white-plastered room perhaps ten cubits deep and fifteen in width. The single window, though nearly two cubits wide and three tall, was protected with heavy iron grillwork on the outside. The desk dominated the room, as I realized Werfel must have intended, although the hauler himself would have dominated any room. He was a head taller than me, all lean muscle.

Werfel said nothing, but he had a fixed frown on his face as he studied the desk. He ran his fingers along the beveled front edge. Then he kneeled down and glanced up underneath at the joins from beneath.

He opened each drawer, and ran each of the three back and forth several times. Then he took out each in turn and examined the back and inside. After that he sat in the chair, forward and backward and on the edge. Finally, he straightened. 'There's only one problem ...'

I tried not to swallow, and I didn't know whether to brain Werfel or not.

'You haven't put a maker's mark anywhere.'

I hadn't even thought about a maker's mark. Sardit had marked his better pieces, but Destrin certainly had not. Then again, who cared about the maker of cheap tavern benches?

'I hadn't thought about it. Each piece I do is unique.'

Werfel laughed. 'Don't worry about it. I was just giving you a hard time. To me, it doesn't make a difference. You might think about it, though.'

He opened the iron-barred door behind the desk and disappeared for a moment before returning with a leather purse.

'It fits well, I think, Master Lerris. Don't you?'

I smiled. 'I think so, but I may not be the best one to ask.'

'Who else could I ask?'

He had a point there. Good crafters and traders are harder on themselves than most others.

He counted out the golds – ten of them – and laid two silvers beside them. 'There. The silvers aren't much – but times haven't been what I'd hoped for. But I will praise the piece to others.' He gave me a wry look. 'Although I think it can speak for itself.'

'Troubles?' I asked, feeling uncomfortable with the praise, and wanting to change the subject. My work still wasn't as good as Uncle Sardit's. 'Hamorian traders?'

'No. Not yet. Poor harvests. Do a lot with cabbage, fruit, potatoes, and the olives, especially the olives.'

'You said "not yet." That sounds like you expect problems with the Hamorian traders.'

'Not the traders themselves, Lerris, but what follows them. They've got cheap cloth, made with those power looms, and pretty soon they own the dry-goods business. Then come cheap tools and cheaper glassware and pottery. Pretty soon, they start their own hauling businesses, and their own mills and you name it.' He snorted. 'Saw it happen in Austra, and south Nordla. It's happening now in Delapra.'

'What happens if the Duke, or whoever, won't let them?'

'Tariffs, taxes – that sort of thing?' He snorted. 'They still find a way.'

I nodded.

'Then they start bringing in their troops and ships. Figure that's what's happening in Freetown. Colaris can't stand up to Hydlen, nor to the Viscount. Hamor will support him, but only if he lets their stuff in. Won't be long before they own him.' He smiled grimly. 'Not that there's much a hauler and a woodcrafter can do. Could be hard on your consort, 'for long, though.'

'It could be.' Anything ended up being hard on Krystal – or me – or both of us these days.

'Glad it's not me.' He looked toward the door.

I took the coins, and the hint, and bowed. 'Thank you.'

'Thank you. Fine desk. Always wanted one like this. Might as well enjoy it while I can.'

He sat and enjoyed the desk while I walked out and reclaimed the wagon. I checked to see if the staff was handy, but it was right where I left it and where I could reach it instantly.

While I didn't need the staff on the trip home, I had the feeling it might be necessary sooner than I wished.

# LII

The next morning, after Krystal left for Kyphrien, I trudged out to the stable. After feeding and grooming Gairloch and the wagon mare, I set up a sandbag on a long rope from a rather and began a few exercises with the staff. Then I worked on hitting the bag as it was swinging.

Before long I was panting, but I kept at it until I overreached. The staff hit the stall wall and snapped back against my weak thigh. I went down in the straw, trying not to moan. When the stars cleared, I checked my leg with my order senses, but I hadn't broken anything. I would have a huge bruise.

*Whufff ... ufff ...* That was Gairloch's reaction as I limped out of the stable and closed the door. He'd wanted out, but I was in no shape to ride at that point.

I limped back toward the shop, but Rissa was sweeping things out the kitchen door. 'You go out to the stable, and you limp back. You do too much too soon. You and the commander, unless you slow your steps, you will not live to see thirty summers, or to see children look up to you.'

'If I slow my steps, Rissa, I won't live to see next fall.'

'You must run and limp from the stable to the house – that will help you live longer?'

Put that way, she had a point, and I had to grin.

"You ... you do much, and you craft wonderful things, but will those things you make love you?"

'Rissa ...'

She gave a last brush with the broom and closed the kitchen door, getting in the last word by saying nothing.

After I refilled the moisture pot and reracked a saw, I pulled out the sketches for Durrik's spice chest. Then I worked a while on translating the sketches into a working plan – figuring out the bracing and the support, and how to do it with the same woods. If I could avoid it, I wouldn't put lighter or cheaper wood anywhere in the piece, even inside where few see it. Some crafters can work out those kinds of details in their head, but I couldn't – not for a new design anyway, and I hadn't been crafting long enough to have seen all types of work.

Once I had that mostly figured out and the throbbing in my thigh had subsided into a more normal bruise, I saddled Gairloch. I needed to ride in on the western road to see Faslik about the woods I'd need for Durrik's chest and Antona's desk. Somehow, what with my injuries, the death of Faslik's sister, that desk kept getting put off.

Depending on what Faslik had and what it cost, I might have to rework the plans for one or both of the pieces.

A winter wren chirped once as I turned into the hard-packed damp clay road leading uphill to the mill, then flitted into the regrowing trees on the south side of the drive.

I tied Gairloch to the post by the millrace, then walked down toward the mill, glancing at the water as it churned in the narrow stone trough toward the undershot waterwheel.

The moss-covered stones above the waterline in the millrace testified to how long the mill had been in Faslik's family. The whine from within the stone walls of the mill testified to the continued operation of the sawmill, and that the miller, or someone, was present.

I found Faslik at the blade, where a young man, broader across the shoulders than even Talryn, guided the logs toward the saw. Rather than bother him, I walked toward the racks where the planks and cut timbers were stacked, pausing to check the stocks. Of red and white oak and pine and fir there were plenty, but there was little lorken, less cherry, and no nut woods at all.

Another broad-shouldered young man, with short brown hair, limped toward the rack of drying oaks, most of them small, barely a dozen spans in breadth. From their size, I guessed they would be cut for timbers, rather than planks. My own thigh still throbbed from the morning's mishap with the staff, and I nodded sympathetically as he planted his weight on his good leg and levered down the uncut oak onto a handcart.

When the whine of the blade stopped, I limped back toward Faslik. The younger man was cleaning the saw pit, and two other young men were stacking the planks. Faslik was walking back from the north door, presumably from closing the millrace.

I couldn't help sneezing with all the sawdust in the air.

The millwright raised a hand in greeting. 'Master Lerris, what sorts of woods you be wanting?'

'Golden or white oak and cherry. Enough for an oak chest and a cherry desk.'

'You looked over the racks?'

I nodded.

'Show me what you need, and we'll see what we can do.'

We walked down past the racks.

'The wide cherry. Eight of those, and five of the narrow beams here.' We walked over to the oak. 'Six of the planks, and six of the beams.'

Faslik frowned and was silent for a moment before speaking. 'For the cherry, I'd guess three golds . . .'

'That's a great deal for young cherry.'

'Young cherry?'

'The grains are wide-spaced . . .'

Faslik frowned and spit into the clay floor. 'For a young fellow . . .'

'I had good training.'

'I can't do less than two and a half.'

'Two and a half, then.' As an outsider, I still didn't like to press too much, and cherry was scarce. 'And the oak?'

'What would you say was fair?' Faslik smiled at me.

I hated beginning the bargaining. I frowned. 'The white oak, here, is fair, but you've got a lot of it, and not many people want it in the spring, when coins are short. Say eight silvers.' I was aiming for a gold.

'Not a copper less than a gold and three.'

I shrugged. 'Nine silvers.'

'A gold and two, and that means my family will have to eat maize bread.'

'A gold, and that means my pony will have to graze at the roadside, for I won't have enough coins to buy hay or grain.'

'A gold and one, but only because you've been fair, and I want to keep selling to you.'

I sighed, mostly for effect. 'A gold and one.'

Faslik took my hand. 'Done.'

'I'll pick it up later today, if that's all right. I didn't bring the wagon with me.'

He nodded.

'Ma . . . maa . . . ster . . . ?' asked a voice.

Beside me stood the young man with the clubfoot.

'Yes?' I tried to make my voice gentle as I turned to him.

'Don't be bothering the mastercrafter, Wegel . . .' said Faslik gently.

'It's no bother.' I looked at the youth, more of an overgrown boy. 'You had a question?'

'Ab-bout . . . cra-cra-cra . . . fting . . . ser.' He looked down, then pulled a small figure from his tunic, a winged figure with a woman's face and long flowing hair. 'Do . . . do . . . you . . .' He stuttered and fell silent, then thrust the carving at me.

'He's always been like that, Master Lerris, a good lad, but not quite able to say what he means. He's a good lad.'

I took the carving and studied it, far better than anything I had been able to do. Every line matched the grain of the wood. My eyes almost burned, and I shook my head.

'You did this?' I asked.

Wegel nodded.

'He's a good lad,' said Faslik. 'A good lad.'

I shook my head again. 'No . . . you don't understand. This is so much better than anything I could do.'

Faslik gaped. So did Wegel.

'I can make furniture, and I know it's good, but . . . art like this . . .' I looked at Wegel. 'If you want to work hard, I'll teach you what I know about woods, and crafting. It's often very hard, and it has to be done right. I don't like sloppy work. And sometimes, it's just plain messy. A crafter's shop has to be kept clean, and we have to wash it a lot to keep the dust down. Will that be a problem?' I watched his face.

'N-nn-noo . . . m-mm-ii-II . . . clean.'

He looked at his father.

So did I. 'With your blessing . . .'

'You don't have to, Master Lerris.' The millwright looked down.

'Don't have to?' I laughed. 'Together, we could do things I've only dreamed about. I've sent word all over Kyphrien that I needed an apprentice, and I never looked among those who work most closely with the woods.' I swallowed. 'But . . . would . . . I mean, what about the mill?'

'Bro . . . brothers . . .' stammered Wegel.

'His brothers . . .'

Faslik's eyes narrowed. 'What's the apprentice fee?'

I shook my head again. 'No . . . it would be good if you would help him with a few tools, though. I really don't have enough for two.'

'Everyone says you're a good man, even if you're an outlander and a wizard,' Faslik said slowly.

'I don't eat apprentices, and there will probably be times when he'll have to mind the shop while I'm gone.' I frowned. 'You'll have to bunk with the commander's guards for a while, until we can build you your own room. They're not there all the time, but —'

'You be sure about this, Master Lerris?' asked the father. 'About his foot . . .'

'I'm sure. If he can lift your timbers, his foot certainly won't be a problem. All he needs is one good one for the foot treadle.'

'You be sure . . .'

'You don't believe me, draw Rissa aside and ask her.' I handed the carving back to Wegel. 'Keep this safe, Wegel.'

Wegel looked at me, eyes wide.

'How soon can you start?'

He shrugged and looked at his father.

'Be taking a bit to work this out, get tools he needs . . . say an eight-day?'

'Fine.' I smiled at the young man. 'I'll see you in an eight-day.'

'Th-th-thank . . . y-y-you . . .'

'I'm glad I found you.'

I was whistling as I walked back to Gairloch, certain that Faslik was shaking his head. Maybe I could even learn about carving by watching Wegel and feeling how he did it. If not, he could carve, and learn cabinetry. Someday, he might even be better than I was.

Gairloch *whuffed* at me, maybe because I was whistling, or just to put me in my place.

Rissa was out when I returned, probably getting eggs from Brene or flour from Hirst's mill, or something else that I hadn't the faintest idea we needed.

I stabled Gairloch and waited until she got back, with a basket of eggs.

'You did not tell me you would need the wagon.'

'I didn't know whether Faslik had the wood ready.'

'Will the commander be here for dinner?'

'She said she would. I haven't heard otherwise.'

'Strange it is, cooking here.' She shook her head and walked into the kitchen.

I climbed up on the wagon and flicked the reins.

When I got to the mill, Wegel loaded every scrap of wood as though it were gold. If I could have caught his face in a carving, it would have made me an immortal artist, but I couldn't, and I didn't.

I did say, 'I hope you like working with me. It's not always easy.'

He just looked down for a moment. Finally, he handed me the carving. I couldn't refuse, but I decided it would still be his – that I would only hold it for safekeeping.

I could see the tears seep down his face when I looked back, and I felt as if my own eyes were burning. How terrible it must be to be so overjoyed that just a single person valued your skills.

When I got back to the house, I put the carving on the table in the bedroom. I wanted Krystal to see it first. Then I unloaded the wood.

Perron and Krystal entered the stable while I was still grooming the cart mare.

'Don't you ever stop?'

At least she was smiling, and I hugged her.

'Where have you been?'

'Getting wood for my next projects . . .'

'The lady's desk?'

'And the spice merchant's chest,' I added, setting aside the curry brush and closing the stall door.

We groomed her mount together, and then washed up while Rissa set out the dinner. Except I lit the big lantern and then washed up, but she wasn't finished, and she stood and watched as I shaved.

Perron and the three guards waited until we returned and sat down at the table.

'Did anything interesting happen to you at the mill?' asked Krystal.

'Well, I did find an apprentice . . .'

Rissa gave me an appraising look as she set the big pot on the wooden server in the middle of the table. 'Where did you find such a wonder?'

Perron just looked at the loaves of bread in the basket that Rissa had left by the oven. Jinsa grinned at Dercas.

'At Faslik's . . . Wegel – his youngest.'

'Ah . . . the one who carves . . .' murmured Rissa.

'You knew about him?'

'He is a carver. Was I to know that you wanted a carver, an

artist?' She shrugged as if to indicate that somehow I had failed to communicate.

'Rissa . . .' I began.

Jinsa laughed softly. Krystal shook her head, and I stopped talking. Nothing I said would change Rissa's mind.

'You can't win,' mouthed Perron.

'He'll start in about an eight-day.'

'Will he be happy doing the drudgery that goes with woodworking?' asked Krystal.

'I don't know, but he's doing drudgery at the mill for his father. Here, at least some of his carving will go into things people use.' I cleared my throat, and took a sip of the cold water. We'd run out of redberry, and at the out-of-season prices I wasn't about to buy more. 'You're the one who said I needed an apprentice.'

'I did, and I am glad you'll have someone else to help. Just don't take it as an excuse to go off doing wizardry.'

'Me? I'd rather stay home and do wizardry.' I ladled out a heaping dish of yet another variety of goat stew for Krystal, highly spiced, then one for myself, before passing the ladle to Jinsa, who took an even bigger helping. I looked at Krystal, hoping to change the subject. 'Have you heard anything from the olive growers?' Olive growers came to mind because I'd delivered the chairs to Hensil.

'The olive growers are worried about pirates. So are the wool merchants. They claim that the autarch cannot protect their shipments to Biehl or to Jera, let alone to Nordla.'

'The autarch isn't responsible for the sea. Does she even have a fleet?'

'That was the point,' said my consort after swallowing a mouthful of stew and washing away the steam with a mug of dark ale.

'Oh . . . you think Hamor is planting the idea that rulers should be able to protect their trade anywhere?'

Her mouth full again, Krystal nodded.

'So . . . next the autarch will hear from the handful of copper miners? Or will it be the vintners in the south?'

'The vintners were in to see the autarch last eight-day,' Perron said dryly.

I glanced at Krystal. She nodded.

I decided to eat, and reached for the bread.

After dinner, I followed Krystal into the bedroom, lit the lamp with my striker, and watched as the light fell over the carving of the ancient angel.

'Lerris . . . where? It's beautiful . . .'

'It's not ours, but I'm keeping it for Wegel.'

'Wegel?'

'He gave it to me because I wanted him for an apprentice. It's too good for me to take.'

Krystal looked at me, and moisture seeped from the corners of her eyes. 'I love you, you know.'

'Why?'

'Just because. Because you see, and because you care.' Then she hugged me, and I held her for a time. Finally, she stepped away.

'I need to get out of this uniform.' Even as she spoke, Krystal sat down, pulled off her boots, and tossed them into the corner. Then she stripped off her uniform, and, in rather efficient motions, pulled a robe around her before she plopped herself on the bed, propped up against the headboard.

I was still standing there in my trousers.

'Anything else new today?' I managed to ask.

'Not much. Berfir and Colaris are still at it, but there's something happening in Certis.'

'How did you find out?'

'Kasee got a travel-scroll – unsigned, but probably from Justen.'

'Justen?' I sat down on the edge of the bed and pulled off my boots. The thigh still hurt. When was I ever going to learn?

'He and Tamra are on their way to Montgren. The scroll said that the Viscount is making something disturbing, and to watch the borders.'

'So very helpful,' I grumbled. 'Just like Justen.'

Krystal raised an eyebrow. Lying there on the bed, she looked so desirable, yet distant, warm yet cool, competent yet vulnerable.

I stopped talking and looked. Then I did more than look. I eased up beside her and kissed her.

Her lips were warm for a moment before she eased away and asked me, 'Have you noticed that Justen disappears whenever things seem to get dangerous?'

'I don't think it's fear.'

Krystal pursed her lips, and I brushed them with mine.

'You are impossible.' She smiled and kissed me back, just kissed me for a time. Then she reached over and twisted down the lamp wick.

'You're the impossible one, woman.'

'What I want is very possible.'

I didn't argue.

# LIII

Smoke drifted across the small valley, smoke heavy with the odor of brimstone and nitre, and the rattling sounds of rifle discharges echoed back up along the hillside trail where the two riders paused.

Justen surveyed the smoke-shrouded land. On the eastern hillside controlling the road from Montgren into Certis, cyan banners flew from staffs planted in the earthen barriers before the trenchworks. On the trampled grass of the hillside, once a meadow for sheep, lay dark figures in green or with green sashes.

'The Viscount's troops are getting slaughtered. The idiots,' said Tamra.

'For getting slaughtered? I doubt they had much choice,' reflected Justen.

'They could have just let Colaris's troops head into Hydlen.'

'Pride often triumphs over rationality,' said Justen dryly.

As they watched, the green banners waved, and another wave of pikes struggled up the hillside. The rattling fire of the rifles increased, and pikes and troopers fell in uneven rows across the bloody grass. Then all but one green banner dropped. The pike line broke, and more figures lay sprawled across the slope.

'Pride,' snorted Tamra. 'They're not even trying to use wizardry against the rifles. They could try.'

'Those cartridges are made of steel, and no one except a strong chaos wizard could ignite them, and no strong wizard would choose to work for the Viscount.'

'You think that Colaris will take over Certis and Hydlen?'

'He has an advantage now.' Justen shook his head. 'Before long, they'll all be using rifles with cartridges – if Hamor will supply them.'

'If not?'

'The Emperor may send his own troops, and this will seem like a pleasant excursion by comparison.'

'Are you sure?' Tamra snorted. 'Won't they all huddle behind trench-works, and nothing will happen?'

'Hardly. The way things are going, we'll probably see big cannon hauled in.' He lifted the reins, and Rosefoot carried him westward. 'And things will get even worse. They usually do, I've found.'

After a frown and then a long glance back at the smoke-covered valley, Tamra urged her mount to follow Justen. She frowned, and a slight breeze swirled around her, providing a momentary respite.

# LIV

Krystal, and her guards, left early the morning of my audience with the autarch and the envoy from Hamor, an audience scheduled for just before noon, and one to which I was not looking forward.

After brushing and feeding Gairloch, I went out to the shop and surveyed the layout. If Wegel were to have space to work, I needed to rearrange some of the benches – and the wood I had picked up from Faslik for Antona's desk and Durrik's chest. It took a while to move everything around. In moving things, I discovered some chisels that needed sharpening, and not to mention some wood that I'd tucked behind one of the benches. So when I had things the way I wanted them, it was time to get ready for the audience, and I'd gotten no real crafting done at all.

I washed up and shaved. Shaving scraped my skin, but not shaving made my face itch, especially in the summer and if I worked near the hearth.

When I walked into the kitchen, Rissa looked up. 'You look good. Young for a wizard, but wizards can look any way they please . . . so that is all right.'

'I'm glad you approve of the way I look, since I don't know of any real way to change it, except by growing a beard, and I hate beards.'

'It would make you look older and more distinguished.'

'No beards.' I broke off a corner of not-quite-stale bread and began to chew. Who knew when I'd get to eat once I got to the autarch's palace? Matters of state usually took precedence over food.

'Do not get crumbs all over your new grays.'

'They'll brush off.'

'Master Lerris . . .'

I finished the bread and brushed off the crumbs, then made my way out to the stable to saddle Gairloch.

*Whufff . . . uffff . . . ufff . . .*

'Yes, we're actually going somewhere. Not far, but somewhere.'

The sun was trying to break through the hazy overcast when I climbed on Gairloch, wearing the grays under my brown cloak. I still didn't have a gray cloak, but the envoy wasn't about to see my cloak. I had gotten Rissa to sew up the leg that had been buttoned together so that I didn't feel like quite so much of an invalid.

While the day held a hint of nip, I could almost sense spring building under the brown ground. I was more than ready for it, more than a little tired of the cold rains and ice, although the deep snowfalls had been few indeed, mostly during the time I had been recovering from my encounter with Gerlis.

I stayed away from the market square, going down the artisans' street instead, wishing, in a way, that I could afford the jewelry I glimpsed between the bars of the goldsmith's window. Krystal couldn't wear it in uniform, but I would have liked to have been able to give her something that wasn't a necessity.

Shaking my head, I rode on to the autarch's palace, still concerned about jewelry I didn't even know she wanted or would wear.

Haithen was mounted and waiting outside the gates. 'You have a stall in the Finest's stables.'

'Since when?'

'Since we all decided that it was stupid for you to stable Gairloch with the mounts of all those clerks and functionaries. You're more of a fighter than a courtier.' She grinned at me. 'I knew that from the beginning. It took longer for the others to find out.'

I followed her to the rear stables, a slightly longer walk back to Krystal's quarters, but at least I wouldn't have to deal with the uppity ostler in the front stables.

'Should have done this a long time ago,' said the bull-necked woman who ran the guard stables. 'No sissy wizard here.'

Compared to her, I felt rather slight in build, but I nodded. 'I do appreciate it. Gairloch would be more at home here. So am I.'

'Thought so.'

Haithen remounted and saluted before riding somewhere, and I crossed the well-swept stones of the yard between the stables and the main barracks.

Several guards nodded to me. Some, like Jinsa, I knew. Others I didn't. Weldein glanced at me as I passed him in the corridor, his collar showing the silver pin of a squad leader. 'You're not quite so stiff, Master Lerris.'

'Next time, I'll let you lead the charge. Or maybe I'll make you Tamra's permanent sparring partner.'

He did grin, after a fleeting expression of surprise, and I nodded and continued on to Krystal's door, where Herreld stood squarely. Some things hadn't changed, but, in a way, I was glad that he protected her access so carefully.

'Is she ready for me, Herreld?'

'I will check, Order-master.'

'Thank you, Herreld.'

He reappeared instantly. 'She asked if you would wait just a few moments. She is meeting with Kyldesee and Finance Minister Mureas.'

'Under the circumstances, it's better we both stay out here.'

Herreld actually gave me a faint smile.

Shortly, the blocky Mureas emerged, her square-cut white hair glued in place, followed by a younger woman, also with square-cut hair – brown – wearing the greens of the Finest.

I nodded politely. 'Good day, Minister Mureas.'

I got a curt nod in return from the minister, and the two were gone.

Herreld gave the faintest of headshakes, and Krystal motioned me into her office/palace quarters.

Only when the door was shut did she shake her head. 'I hate that . . .'

'Mureas leaning on you?' I kissed her cheek.

'She was expressing her concern that the Finest were not employing Kyldesee's talents to the degree possible.' Krystal grimaced. 'Kyldesee can handle a blade fairly well; she's a decent squad leader; and a first-class lightfinger. Yelena still hasn't figured out where all the coins went while Kyldesee was in charge of the Ruzor district.'

Krystal's table was heaped high with scrolls, and so was the bed in her sleeping quarters. One lamp mantle was sooty, the sign of oil having burned down too many times without the reservoir being cleaned.

'You couldn't tell Mureas that, I take it.'

'Light-demons, no! We can't even prove Kyldesee was the one who did it. But if Mureas weren't her aunt, I wouldn't have to.'

'Mureas is important, of course.'

'She is if we have to fight the war I think we're going to have to fight.'

'War? Which war? Berfir? The Viscount? Hamor?'

'I think they're all parts of the same war. Light! Recluce has made a mess out of Candar. And we're the only ones who seem to see it or care.' She straightened her gold-braided vest. 'Kasee wants to talk to us, mostly you, before the audience with the envoy from Hamor.'

'Me?'

'As I keep pointing out, you're the only gray wizard she has left. And the only one she really trusts.' She bent forward and gave me a kiss. 'We need to go.'

'She doesn't trust Justen?'

'She doesn't distrust him . . . but you do live here, and you don't have this habit of vanishing. Even if you do have a hidden hero desire.'

'I don't like being a hero. It's dangerous.'

She raised her eyebrows as she opened the door and stepped out into the corridor. 'Herreld . . . it will be some time before I'm likely to return from the autarch's audience. If someone has a real problem, tell them to see Weldein. If he can't handle it, he can find someone who can.'

'Weldein. Yes, Commander.'

Krystal was moving before Herreld finished acknowledging her instructions, long legs carrying her down the dark-walled corridor toward the narrow stairs. I followed, almost running for a moment to catch up, and trying not to limp at the same time.

Two more sets of guards snapped rigid as we passed before we entered the wide-windowed and tapestried hall outside the autarch's study.

The taller guard of the third pair of guards opened the door into the study, and closed it just as quickly once we were inside.

'Greetings. We only have a little time before I must array myself for our honored guest.' Kasee set the pen in the holder and leaned forward across the overbalanced desk. Someday, when I felt truly brave, I was going to suggest she pay me to craft a decent replacement. So far, that day hadn't come, and since she had ordered and paid for the wardrobe, I wasn't about to hurry it.

As usual when in private, the autarch's black and silver hair was disarrayed, and the left side of her forehead was smudged with either ink or charcoal. I suspected her maids, valets, or whoever helped her dress for functions did a lot of despairing.

'I asked you to come, Lerris, because you've had the closest contact with what happened in Hydlen, and because' – she shrugged – 'somehow I felt that you could help. Also, we don't know much about this envoy. The rumors are that he is an exile from Recluce, and that might be true, because he's not the envoy that the Emperor just sent there.'

'Isn't it strange to send two envoys a quarter of the way around the globe?' asked Krystal.

'Candar's a big place,' pointed out Kasee.

Perhaps, but it seemed to me that it was getting very crowded very quickly.

'Then there's the mess in Freetown . . .' added Krystal.

'I thought Berfir and his rockets would roll over Colaris,' admitted Kasee, 'especially once he could divert troops from the south. And he might have, but some long-range cannons have appeared, and a thing that carries an observation basket into the air to guide the cannon fire.' She picked up the pen and chewed on the end.

'It sounds like a balloon of some sort, like in the old books.' I watched as a drop of ink landed on the blotter, amazed that it hadn't hit her green silks.

'Lately, Colaris's troops have been using rifles,' the autarch added.

'Rifles – but can't some third-rate wizard ignite the powder?'

'They're using steel cartridges. They're hard on the barrels, but it would take a first-rate wizard to set them off, and since each one is separately packed . . .'

I got the picture. It was like combining miniature rockets with cannon, and it's difficult to use a sword on troops who can kill you before you can reach them. 'What about archers?'

'A good archer's probably as good as a soldier with a rifle, maybe a better shot, but it takes longer, a lot longer, to train an archer,' Krystal pointed out. 'Also, you can carry a lot more cartridges than arrows.'

'Did the rifles come from Hamor?'

'Where else? They're using steam-powered machines to make the cartridges.' Kasee looked at a scroll on the side of the desk. 'That's what the traders tell me, anyway.'

'What about the balloon?'

'That's from the new wizard in Sligo. This Sammel's not that far from Freetown and Montgren – or even Certis. All sorts of new ideas, all very neatly set out in ink, have been coming out. A lot of gold has gone into his coffers, and we know that some of these ideas have even gone to Hamor – such as some of the improvements to the cannon. The Empire did come up with cartridges themselves.'

Krystal looked to me. 'How can this happen? Why doesn't chaos tear them apart?'

I had to shrug. 'I don't know. Maybe, if you break ordered things into small enough pieces, like the cartridges, it's harder for chaos to disrupt. Maybe good machining, like good woodwork, can hold chaos off. That ought to work in theory. But I really don't know.' I was getting the beginning of a headache. Gerlis – one white wizard working for a second-rate duke – had been bad enough, but the picture I was getting was worse. Sammel had had some training in the basis of order and chaos.

'How does this Sammel compare to Gerlis?' asked Kasee.

'When I met him in Recluce, I wouldn't have even guessed that he'd become involved with chaos. He looked more like a hermit, and his voice was thoughtful. He couldn't handle edged weapons, either.' I shook my head. It was still hard to believe that Sammel was tied up with chaos. 'But he probably understands the basics better.'

'Sammel seemed to be the type who really believed in what he did,' added Krystal. 'If he believes in what he is doing . . .' She spread her hands.

'It will be worse than the Hydlen mess, you think?' asked the autarch.

My consort and I both nodded slowly.

'I thought you might say that.' Kasee straightened and stood. 'I need to be made presentable. Krystal, why don't you and Lerris go down to the audience room? Use the side door, and I'll meet you there.'

After she left, Krystal led the way through the back corridors I wouldn't have even pretended to know. My night vision did keep me from stumbling as I followed the surefooted Krystal through the dim, but not dusty, passages.

Once in the audience chamber, we sat on two stools behind a pillar.

'Do you understand what she wants?' asked Krystal, glancing toward the dais and the empty green-upholstered chair.

'For me to stand there and look interested, add what she wants added, and try to figure out what is really happening.'

'Don't try to figure anything out at the audience. Just try to feel whatever you can. You can sort it out later. I think your feelings are important.'

'All right.' I grinned and squeezed her knee. 'I'm glad you do.'

She blushed slightly. 'That wasn't what I meant.'

'Oh?'

'Sometimes . . .'

'Good!'

At that point the door opened, sooner than I would have expected, and Kasee emerged, with hair in place and smudges removed.

We walked to the dais, and Krystal stood to her right, slightly in front of her, while I was on the left. Kasee sat in the chair, waiting.

The bell sounded and she straightened in the chair and looked at Krystal and then at me. 'Here we go.'

The double doors opened, and someone announced, 'The Most Honorable D'ressn Leithrrse, envoy of His Imperial Highness Stesten of Hamor.'

Leithrrse bowed once as he entered, walked forward, and bowed again at the steps below the dais. The Hamorian envoy was lighter-skinned than most Kyphrans, and could have stepped off the Feyn River plains. If he were from Hamor he hadn't, but Hamor was home to ambitious exiles from the world over. The few Hamorians I'd seen were generally as dark as Kyphrans, but I supposed there were people of all complexions in any country.

He also didn't wear jewelry – just a plain tan tunic with a silver arrowhead at the collar, and tan trousers, with a silver-studded belt and a short sword and a pistol. The pistol bothered me, because it, like the envoy, was short and businesslike, though he wouldn't have had the chance to use it, not with the two archers behind the slits in the walls flanking the dais, nor with Krystal standing there.

'You bring tidings from the Emperor?' asked Kasee.

'That I do, Honored Autarch.'

'Pray tell us.'

'The Emperor trusted we would find you in health and prosperity. He will be pleased to learn that you are indeed in health, and that your people are prosperous and well fed at a time when troubles have besieged many in Candar. And he sends his greetings and respects.'

I had the feeling that Leithrrse had oiled his way to his present position, oozing charm from every pore as he made his way across every type of floor. He was the kind I disliked almost on sight.

'We have worked hard, and we have been fortunate that our work has been rewarded some of the time. As the angels know, hard work is not always rewarded with prosperity.' Kasee smiled.

'Prosperity comes more often to the righteous, and to those who work hard,' returned the Hamorian.

'At times. At times, prosperity follows trade, and trade can often follow the swiftest sword, and it has been said that the swords of Hamor can be swift, indeed.'

'The Emperor believes in peace and trade, and in trade that is peaceful. Much like the island of Recluce, you know, the Emperor is greatly interested in the peaceful expansion of trade . . .'

Although I could not see Krystal's face, Kasee nodded, and I waited for the barbs that would probably follow.

'The Emperor believes that trade between countries is a benefit to all people. Because high customs levies stop trade, they can lead to conflict between countries that would otherwise be friendly. And then trade ceases or is no longer friendly. And all suffer.' The envoy paused.

'I think that translates into a veiled request that I consider reducing the tariffs levied against Hamorian manufacturers.' Kasee smiled.

'What about the Hamorian tariff against Kyphran fruit and olives, or against our southern linen? Does the Emperor propose reductions in his tariffs?'

'You misunderstand, Honored Autarch. The emperor merely has stated his beliefs about how trade should be improved. Hamor makes no requests of Kyphros. It would not be proper for him to presume to tell an equal how to rule.' Leithrrse gave a slight bow.

'What do you think, Lerris?'

I inclined my head, trying to look sage, although how anyone so young as I could look sage in the setting was beyond me. Still . . . I had to say something, and the fact that Kasee had dumped it on me was indication enough that she wanted confirmation of her statement.

'Presumption comes in many forms, Honorable Leithrrse.' I paused and let my order senses touch him, recognizing that he had both order and disorder within him, twisted together in a way that would have caused exile or dangergeld in Recluce. 'A statement that would seem innocent enough if uttered by a merchant may have a greater meaning if uttered by an envoy of a mighty ruler. A general word of caution may have the force of a threat.'

Leithrrse inclined his head in the slightest, as if to dismiss me, before continuing. 'Those of Recluce, they have fine words, and their ships do but prosper, especially in trade with Candar.' He smiled a charming smile at Kasee. 'Yet is it not passing strange that Recluce has often cast out its best, like the mighty Dorrin and the gray wizard Justen?'

At that point, with Kasee's information and the veiled bitterness in his words, I knew, knew that he must be the Leith mentioned by the young woman I had met on the first day of my trip to Nylan years ago.

'Strange?' mused Kasee. 'I think not. A pearapple does not grow well on an olive limb.'

'Nor a pearapple tree well in an olive grove.' Leithrrse bowed very deeply. 'The Emperor would wish your olive groves well, for they endure unto the generations.'

He bowed again, signifying, I thought, that he had said all he had to say.

So I added my bit. 'By the way, Leith, Shrezsan wishes you well.'

He stood stock-still for an instant, only for an instant, before responding to Kasee, rather than to me. 'And the Emperor would wish you well in the choice of the gardeners for your groves.'

Kasee held back a smile, I thought, but answered solemnly, 'And

I wish him well, and we will send back with you a barrel of those olives that he appreciates so much.'

'I am certain he will enjoy such olives, not only this year, but for many years to come.' Leithrrse bowed twice. 'And I will convey your good wishes and the olives to him in the spirit in which they were offered.'

Kasee rose. 'I do so hope.' Then she waited until he backed down the green carpet, gave a last bow, and left the chamber.

'Back to my study,' suggested Kasee.

That was where we went, and there were, wonder of wonders, some crackers, cheeses, and dried fruit on a platter.

'Please have some. It has been a long day.'

I didn't hesitate and was crunching my way through a small wedge of cheese and a cracker when Kasee raised her eyebrows.

'What did that comment about Shrezsan mean, Lerris? For an instant, he wanted to kill you. If he were a chaos wizard, you would have been covered with firebolts.' Kasee shook her head.

'I was fairly certain that I met a former love of his, years ago, when I first traveled to Nylan on my dangergeld. She asked me to say that if I ever met him.'

'But how did you know he was the one?' asked Krystal.

I looked at the autarch. 'You said that he was an exile from Candar, and there aren't that many. Most of them are pretty able, and the odds that he'd have the same name were slim.'

'I still don't see . . .'

'It felt right.' I had to shrug. 'And Krystal and you said I should follow my feelings.'

Kasee laughed. 'It certainly didn't hurt. He wouldn't have changed his message, and this way perhaps the Emperor will be more cautious.'

'I doubt it.' Krystal shook her head.

So did I.


# LV

## Nylan, Recluce

Maris bows deeply, until his beard almost touches the council table, then hands the dispatch case to Heldra. 'My fellow counselor, I bring you tidings of great import.'

Heldra sets the case on the table without extracting the scroll inside. 'Such great deference . . . such courtesy . . . such hypocrisy . . .'

'All right. I'll try it another way. What are you two going to do? The price of our wool in Summerdock has continued to drop,' Maris declares. 'It's the same way in Southport and in Biehl.'

'Wool? Is that all?' Heldra's response contains mixed tones of laughter and annoyance. 'I thought we were meeting on the problem of Hamor.'

'Wool? Is that all? Is that all?' Maris's hand slams the table.

Heldra stands, and her hand is on the hilt of her blade. 'You forget yourself, Maris.'

'I think you both have made Maris's point,' rumbles Talryn as he motions Maris away from Heldra and the table.

'What point? Trade isn't exactly the reason for this Council.'

'About wool and woolgathering, and about iron and steam, and care and carelessness.' Talryn pauses. 'Maris is ready to risk getting spitted on your blade, Heldra, because wool is important to him, and to Recluce. You find wool far less of a concern than Hamor, but you're both talking about the same problem.'

Heldra and Maris wait.

'The Emperor has dispatched a second squadron of those iron-hulled monsters to Dellash.'

'A second squadron?' Maris's eyebrows lift. 'What does that have to do with the price of wool?'

'There was already a squadron there. That was one of the reasons why the price of your wool is falling. The Delaprans are buying Hamorian cloth; it's cheaper.'

'Of course it's cheaper. They've got slaves to grow cotton in those hot deltas, and since that inventor came up with a carding machine . . .'

'And since they're using steam engines to run their looms,' finished Talryn, 'and steam to power their merchant ships, our wool is more expensive.'

'Ours is better cloth.' Maris rubs his thumb and forefinger together.

'The average peasant or clerk could care less. Cotton is less scratchy, and it's cheaper, and for someone who doesn't have much coin . . .' Talryn shrugs.

'And I suppose the warships are there as a gesture of good faith?' snaps Heldra. 'Or just to drive the price of our wool down?'

Talryn laughs, a short, rumbling bark. 'They flattened the old lighthouse off Summerdock with three shells from their new guns.'

'Rignelgio's visit makes more sense in that light,' said Heldra. 'It's more than wool or trade.'

'Of course, dear Heldra,' murmurs Maris.

'He was probably surprised that we didn't know, or felt we were insufferably arrogant,' Talryn says quickly.

'Gunnar appears to have been right,' ventures Maris.

'Wool . . . and Gunnar . . . Gunnar.' Heldra stands and walks toward the window overlooking the Eastern Ocean, a bright blue-green that foreshadows the coming spring. 'Are we never to be free of his heavy hand?'

'I'm more worried about Hamor's heavy hand right now.' Talryn leans forward and puts both hands on the back of the heavy black wooden chair. 'It would take us years to match what the Emperor has sent to Candar.'

'I still think the mighty trio could sink most of those squadrons,' points out Heldra.

'Do you want war?' Maris's voice is high, almost squeaky. 'Do you know what that will do to Recluce?'

'To your precious traders, you mean?' asks Heldra.

'No,' counters Talryn, 'but do you think we really have any choice? I think it's time to have the Brotherhood act.'

'What do you have in mind?' Maris fingers his beard.

'Follow Heldra's suggestion. Have the trio pick off every Hamorian warship that leaves Dellash. If they have to stay there, then that neutralizes them.'

'What about their traders?'

'Leave them alone . . . for now.'

'And Sammel?' asks Heldra. 'I had planned to take —'

'I think Sammel is the least of our problems. Besides, do you want to take one of the trio out of action for three eight-days to transport you and a black squad? Right now, the ships are needed more off Delapra. In any case, if chaos and order focuses attract, Lerris may solve that one for us.' Talryn straightens and takes his hands off the chair.

'I don't know . . .' muses Heldra.

'I don't either, but I don't think you should be wandering through Sligo at the moment. As for using the trio, what's the alternative? Wait until Candar is run by Hamor with dozens of those steam cruisers?'

'I don't understand,' protests Maris. 'How can they build all those machines? I thought the amount of order in the world was limited.'

Talryn laughs. 'They're using the other side of the balance. If order is limited, so is chaos. Cassius suggested this could happen. Their machines are made of steel, and they've made so many that they've stretched out the destructive aspects of chaos. If Cassius is right, at some time, there will be a rebound, but it won't happen immediately, and it won't do us much good if Hamor holds Candar before it happens.'

'But how could this happen?'

'How does anything happen? People make it happen, and we let it occur.'

The Eastern Ocean glitters bright blue and green as the three glance to the east, in the direction of Hamor.

# LVI

Since Krystal was in Dasir – some sort of shake-up with the outliers and some problem in the region involving the local and the regional commander – I was up early. I'd fed and groomed Gairloch and the mare. After feeding the two, I took out my staff and worked a little with the exercise bag, until I was sweating. By then I felt guilty for taking the time. I always seemed to be rushing from one thing to another.

By the time I actually got to woodwork, my tunic was damp, not from exercise but from crossing the yard to and from the barn in the rain – four times – to clean the stables and feed Gairloch and the mare, and because I'd had to get some oil from the far shed.

Outside the shop the rain continued to pelt against the shop windows. Chilly as it seemed, it was warmer than it had been, and in Kyphros no one said anything about the late winter and early spring rains because there was seldom much moisture after that – not until the next winter.

The little details ate into my time at every opportunity. If it weren't the need to get finishing oil or lamp oil, it was time to sweep the floor, or refill the moisture pot, or sharpen the chisels, or take the saws to Ginstal for sharpening, or reformulate the glue, or fix a stool or chair for Rissa. That didn't even include such problems as lying flat on my back for nearly a season, or trying to improve my staff skills. With the chores held at bay, I was working on Antona's desk, muttering to myself, because the way I'd drawn the framework for the pedestals wasn't going to work. Like a lot of things, the plan looked good, but sharp edges weren't good planning because they get chipped or they hurt people. Rounding corners is better planning, but every piece has to be double mitred. Some crafters don't – they just use a forty-five-degree angle and then plane the angles down. When I tried that, each one looked subtly different, and I wasn't about to charge fifty golds for a desk with different roundings. With a simple-looking piece, for the wood surfaces to fit, I had to trim each internal brace piece exactly the same – for the entire two-plus cubits. It was easy enough, but time-consuming. Cherry is hard, and the least impatience usually ruins the wood under the blade.

As I'd suspected, Antona's desk was going to be more involved than I had figured – even though I'd thought that when I had priced it.

'Master Lerris – someone's driving into the yard,' Rissa announced from the door to the shop.

'I'm coming.' I set down the calipers and walked right onto the step under the front eave. A well-kept covered trap, with polished brasswork, was pulling into the yard. The driver wore both a waterproof and livery. Anyone who had a two-wheeled carriage also had a full-sized carriage, and anyone who could afford both was clearly wealthy.

The thin and white-haired man who stepped from the carriage and walked up to the narrow porch created by the overhanging eaves and the wide stone step was Finance Minister Zeiber. The first time I'd met him had been at the dinner where I first met the autarch, and Minister Zeiber had suggested my approach to Antonin had been too theoretical.

I still didn't like him, but I opened the door to the shop and gestured for him to enter. 'Please come in, Minister Zeiber.'

Rissa stepped back and headed for the kitchen, not that I blamed her.

I followed him inside and closed the door.

'You are said to be a fine crafter.' Zeiber's deep-set eyes did not meet mine, but traversed the shop, settling for a minute on the partly completed framework for the desk pedestal. 'What is that?'

'That's the beginning of a double-pedestal desk.'

'Hmmm . . .' He cleared his throat and looked back to me.

I couldn't really sense much in the way of disorder about him, but he made me feel uneasy. Was there such a thing as ordered-dishonesty? Or dishonesty that didn't involve chaos?

'I would like to commission a simple bookcase.'

'Do you have any idea of exactly what you want? Size, number of shelves, height of shelves? What type of wood?'

'It does not have to be large . . .' His eyes roamed back across the shop, stopping on the moisture pot. 'What is in the pot?'

'Water. It keeps the wood from splitting if I keep the air a little moister. In the summer, I don't need the pot, but I hang damp cloths around.'

Zeiber nodded. 'You are very thorough as a crafter. Surely, you could use your . . . other abilities . . .'

I laughed – softly, I hoped. 'That takes a great deal of effort. What counts is how the piece looks in your home, not how it looks here.'

He waited.

'Do you want me to sketch some rough ideas for you?'

'Oh, no. I want a case with four shelves. Each shelf would be three-quarters of a cubit above the one below. The bottom shelf should be a half cubit off the floor, and the legs should be strong enough to bear four stone worth of books. The wood should be the strongest possible.'

'For a bookcase, I'd suggest red or black oak. Lorken is too brittle, and cherry isn't strong enough. The nut woods could be rather expensive.'

'The case should be dark.'

'Black oak?'

'How much would that cost?'

'First, let me sketch what you told me.'

The public works minister frowned, but I sketched, until I had the piece laid out on paper. 'Is this what you had in mind?'

'Are the legs thick enough?'

'That's why I planned to slant them in the arcs. The weight is gradually shifted to the bearing surface.' I used the quill to point out what I meant. 'Here the weight rests across the entire top of the leg piece. What you don't see is that I'll run another piece of oak all the way around the inside here to reinforce the legs. That way, you'll have grace and strength.'

'You would use oak where it cannot be seen?'

'Minister Zeiber, you wish a strong case, do you not?'

'How much?'

'Eight golds,' I told him. 'If you are not satisfied when it's done, you do not have to accept it.'

'And lose my deposit, I suppose?'

'No. There is no deposit.'

'How do you make coins, young fellow?'

'Frankly, if you don't want it, I could probably sell it for more to someone else.'

'Oh . . .' Zeiber looked positively disappointed, and he stood there for a long moment. 'You will inform me when it is complete?'

'I will deliver it when it is complete – if that is agreeable?'

'Oh, most certainly.' He nodded. 'You do run a different business, crafter, but to each his own. Good day.'

I barely got to the door before he did, and I watched as the trap carried him out of the yard and back toward Kyphrien.

The whole business bothered me more than a little. Minister Zeiber was in charge of public works, basically the main roads and bridges – mostly the metaled ones. I'd bid the bookcase low because I felt Zeiber had commissioned it not because of my skill, but because of my consort. There was no way I wanted it construed as an indirect bribe. He'd been surprised at my indications that I had bid lower than the going price. The whole thing bothered me. If I didn't take the work, then I was too good to do it, and that caused problems. Besides, Krystal was important enough that I'd run into the same problem with anything I did. That meant I had to do good work, and even then I wasn't going to be certain if I were getting the commission because of my skill or contacts.

Still, I needed work at the moment, and puzzling about the customer's motivations wasn't going to get the commission started.

I had just finished sketching out the last of the details for the bookcase for Minister Zeiber when I heard another horse. After setting down the quill, I walked to the door. The rain had completely stopped earlier, but the yard was muddy.

The small man on the horse wore a peaked cap of green and white plaid wool, and a quilted brown waterproof over it. Clearly at home in the saddle, he vaulted down with an ease that equaled Krystal's, tied the horse to the post with three quick turns, and bounced up to the step.

'Master Lerris, I trust?'

'I'm Lerris. How might I help you?' I held the door and gestured.

'Thank you. Thank you. I'm Preltar. I'm a wool factor – the man who deals mostly with the Analerian herders.'

That explained his ease on horseback. According to the history I'd learned from Lortren and the Brotherhood, Analeria had been the high plains region between what were now Gallos and Kyphros, when they all had been ruled from Fenard. Then Jeslek, the High Wizard of Fairhaven, had raised the Little Easthorns, driving the nomadic herders – those that survived – into the high grasslands of southwest Kyphros. The Analerians lived on horseback, and distrusted those who did not or could not ride.

'I take it that you want some woodworking done?' I closed the door.

'Quite so. Quite so.' He unfastened his jacket, rubbed his hands, then pulled off the wool cap. He had a shiny bald head and bushy white eyebrows that gave him a hawkish look. 'A dowry chest. Yes, a dowry chest.'

I drifted toward the bench that held my makeshift drafting board. 'Do you have any idea of what you want?'

Preltar wandered toward the beginnings of the frame of Antona's desk. 'This? What might this be?'

'It's the beginning of the left pedestal of a twin-pedestal desk.'

'I see. But you're using cherry for the frame?'

I nodded. 'Good crafting starts on the inside.'

'Good crafting starts on the inside! Ha! I like that. I do like that. Good crafting starts on the inside.'

I waited.

'Ah, yes, a dowry chest. It must be a quality chest, and of course it has to be of cedar, to keep the woolens and the linens, you understand, and the hinges must be beautiful and brass. Brass doesn't rust, and, if it's lacquered . . . but you understand all that. Hylera is marrying – we're old-fashioned, you know, and the ceremony will be in the Temple. Most folks don't think all that ceremony is necessary, but blood will tell, you know?'

Blood probably did tell, but that wasn't anything I'd choose to explore.

'Well . . . blood is blood, and Jisrek – he's Kilert's father – trades more in the southeast off the grasses at the edge of the High Desert. The wool is tougher there, but who wants clothes as tough as cordage? Kilert is more into the factoring – he spends most of his time in Ruzor, and since he and Hylera will be moving to Ruzor, she must have a good-quality dowry chest. Hensil, except it was really Verin – she told Mura, and Mura, well, it wouldn't do that anyone but you craft the dowry chest. Ha!'

I was breathless by then, and I hadn't even done the talking. 'Hylera is your daughter. You want a dowry chest for her. It should be made entirely from cedar, preferably using the most aromatic wood to line the inside, and the hinges should be both strong and decorative, and they should be of brass?'

'Exactly! Just so. Just so. Verin said you understood what she needed, and she never talked to you even.'

'How big a chest?'

'How big? How big? Hylera . . . she never said, but she will be getting linens and woolens and darkness knows how many cloths and things. How big do you think it should be, Mastercrafter?'

'If it is a decorative piece, it should be smaller – probably no more than three or three and a half cubits, and a cubit to a cubit and a half high.' I bent down and used my hands to indicate the approximate size.

Preltar frowned.

'I could make it bigger, but the bigger it is the heavier it gets.'

'Heavier ... yes ... but she will have much to store in it.'

It was his chest – or hers? 'How about this big?' I motioned again, using my hands to draw in the air a piece a third again the size of the first.

'Much better. Much better.'

I turned to the drawing board and dipped the quill, then sketched out a simple design. 'How about something along these lines?'

'Hylera said something about a bumper rail ... a bumper rail ...'

'Yes. You run a coping around the edges at the top and bottom.' I sketched those in.

'Better. Better. And what about the hinges?'

In the corner of the paper, I drew several types of hinges – strap hinges, inside hinges, and big decorative butterfly hinges.

'Those. Yes, those are it exactly.' He pointed to the decorative butterfly hinges. 'And it should be appropriate to their station, and their entrance into Ruzor. Yes ... most appropriate ...'

I'd have to get a coppersmith to do the too-elaborate butterfly hinges on his daughter's chest. That might be a problem because I didn't know any of the coppersmiths that well. So far, I'd gotten by with ironwork from Ginstal.

Borlo did good work, supposedly, but outside of three words once, I'd never really spoken to him. There was also a woman – Merrin – who had come from Southwind. I took a deep breath. I probably needed to visit them both if I needed metalwork. Like everything else, one thing led to another.

'This will be too much, Mastercrafter? Too much? You sighed.'

'I did sigh, but that was not for this chest.' The lie tightened my guts, and my head throbbed for a moment. 'I was thinking about other items not within my control. I apologize. Is there anything else you would like? Or that your daughter would need in this chest?'

'Two compartments – one for linens and the other for woolens. Yes, I should have mentioned that. But ordering chests, I don't do that often, although I will, I suppose, next year again, when it gets to be Gresta's turn, and two years after that ... you see, Mastercrafter, you could see many chests.' Preltar beamed. 'Is it possible to get this chest for five golds?'

The hinges would probably cost me close to a gold with the

decorative nature. If the top were too heavy, I might have to reinforce them with inside hinges, although I hoped to avoid that. Cedar wasn't cheap, either.

'Alas, no. The materials alone might run that.' That was an overstatement, and, again, my guts protested. This part of the business I did hate, because bargaining is based on deception of sorts, and deception is more than a little hard on me.

'I see. I see, and the look on your face tells me that it must be close to true. Fine, yes, fine, and the word is that you are honest, as honest as any, more honest than any, in fact. You tell me what a fair price might be.'

'One last question, Master Preltar. You want two compartments. Do you want separate flat lids inside?'

'Oh, yes. Of course. One would not want anything to mix from the linens to the wools. Yes, very separate compartments.'

'Eleven golds, and I'll deliver it anywhere around Kyphrien.' With his mention of Ruzor, I wasn't about to commit to that.

His lips pursed for a moment. 'More than I had thought, yes, more, but Hermiel had said it would be fifteen and not a copper less.' He smiled. 'In these things, she is often closer to the coin than I. Done for eleven, and I would hope that it could be done before the harvest.'

'I would hope so, also.'

'A pleasure doing business with you, Master Lerris. A pleasure, indeed, and if you need the finest and softest wool in Kyphros, Preltar will have it. Yes, indeed, we will have it.'

After he rode off I wiped my forehead and took a deep pull of cold water, afraid that my tongue might race away after listening to his rapid words.

I finished sketching what Preltar wanted before I went back to the design for Minister Zeiber. Then I harnessed the cart and drove down to Faslik's. I didn't see Wegel, but one of Faslik's older sons helped me. The wood for both pieces came to nearly seven golds, although that really wasn't right, because I'd have some left over, and in time, the remnants were often sufficient for smaller pieces. At least they had been when I had worked in Destrin's shop, and Uncle Sardit had assured me that such was often the case.

That night, after I unloaded and racked the wood, with Krystal gone, Rissa and I had leftover stew with fresh bread. I climbed into bed early to get the weight off my leg.

I didn't drop off to sleep immediately, not with my mind going over Minister Zeiber's commission. Why had he done it? Was he trying to get around Mureas and to Krystal through me? Talkative as he had been, Preltar had almost been a relief, although his tactics had probably gotten him the chest cheaper than I would have offered. The next time, if there were to be a next time, would be different. I just hadn't run into a Preltar before, and I learn better from experience, as I had unhappily discovered. Others' words didn't always mean something to me, unfortunately, as both Justen and my father and Uncle Sardit – and I – had discovered.

*Grrrrrurrr* ...

Although the rain had stopped, the wind had picked up after I had put out the lanterns, and sometimes the house timbers groaned in the wind. I hadn't noticed the sound at dinner, but in the darkness I did.

The sound seemed familiar – familiar beyond even the sound itself. Certainly, the groaning happened in any high wind, but, as I lay in my bed wishing Krystal were there, the repeated groans reminded me of something else.

My father had always made me try to follow the winds, but the winds didn't sound like that. I lay in the darkness and tried to recall where that sound had come from. The house had certainly groaned in the wind many times before, but I'd never had the feeling before. Why not? What had happened?

*Grrrrurrrrr* ...

Gerlis! The feeling beneath the ground in the brimstone spring valley! The groaning of hot molten rock and fire ...

I cast my thoughts downward, and let my mind follow my senses through the clay, through the rocks, this time not forcing them, but following the broader paths of order. It seemed almost effortless – until deep below Kyphros I could feel the mixing of iron and chaos, chaos and iron. And the iron held the chaos, no matter how much the chaos twisted.

Beneath the earth, the intertwining of order and chaos seemed more complex. Why was the Balance more simple in the open air than beneath the surface of the earth? Or was everything more complex beneath what seemed to be?

I tried to let my senses pass through the subtle mixtures of ordered red and white iron and white-red chaos that seemed pure fiery destruction. Mixtures of order and chaos, patterns intertwining, caught my senses, and I felt myself drawn to them. There – an upwelling of pure black, somehow brilliant white-red simultaneously, twisted around a fountain of white tinged with red, and beyond it a rhythmic pulsing of smaller order-beats against a squarer kind of chaos, like a level almost, except how could chaos have any order or form? How could chaos be like a level?

Had there always been such an intertwining of order and chaos? I tried to let myself drift along the lines of order, along the forces that made Gerlis's and Antonin's powers seem small, toward a small fountain of blackness that somehow seemed to geyser deep out of the melting rocks far below, far below Kyphros. Even as my senses drew near, the fountain changed, and a torrent of white boiled around the blackness, and red chaos oozed, then spurted forth.

A cool thread of black beckoned, and for an instant, I felt as though I almost understood the interweavings of the patterns, like the grains of a perfect inlay on a lorken table.

A line of molten chaos, red with dull white, lashed from nowhere, and needles like knives burned through me. Another, thicker band of white began to twine around my senses, dragging me deeper into the depths. Realizing that I could get trapped within the depths, like Justen had somehow trapped the wizards of Frven, I tried to wrench free – even as another thinner white line slashed at me again, moving impossibly quickly in the deeps.

A band of black, ordered iron, ripped at me, and another line of white, tinged with red, slashed, and my soul and my face burned. Beneath Kyphros, in those depths, I struggled, recalling belatedly, again, Justen's cautions, and lessons.

I forced myself, my senses, into a ball of self.

*I am me! I am Lerris! Lerris . . . Lerris . . . LERRIS!!!!*

The lashes of chaos and order continued, but I could feel their powers weakening, and I redoubled my efforts, trying to master myself before chaos and order did.

*I am me! Me . . . me . . . ME!!!!*

An image formed – one that I knew was not real – and yet it was.

A figure in green stepped forward, out of the depths, lifting a blade. I strained to see the face, but shadows remained across the face of the soldier who carried no shield, only the short cavalry blade. Then, out of the shadows, two soulful eyes pierced me.

*I died for you, and death is chaos. You, the great wizard, and you have left me in the depths, and I followed you and saved you. You have multiplied death, with fire and brimstone, and never will I see Barrabra again.*

Though I could not move, though my senses and body were separated, I shuddered, then tried to look through the figure with my order senses, but only the tiniest pulses of energy appeared behind the image that extended a blade that became a staff as it was extended – a staff filled with the fire of chaos.

*Take it ... it is yours ... great master of chaos ...*

Master of chaos? Never! I tried to push the staff away.

*... take it ...*

The figure of Shervan hurled the staff at me, and a dull aching smashed across my chest.

*... it is yours, great wizard, great master of chaos ...*

The image of the outlier faded, but another appeared, that of a dark-haired woman in white. She smiled, and beckoned, but an ugly burned slash across her neck looked like a second mouth, gaping, opening ...

*... oh, Lerris, you loved me, or you loved the body I held, and you killed me ... you loved me ... and I suffered this from your love ... I gave up my life so that your love could live, and you threw it away ...*

No! I did not love you. I never loved you.

*... but you did, and you hated her ... and you twisted her and killed me ...*

You killed yourself. You took what never belonged to you!

Those white-clad arms grasped for me, and I threw up a shield, but a finger, impossibly long, reached out and seized my left arm, and those nails flared fire, and I could feel my flesh sizzling, smell the stench of burned flesh.

*... you loved her, and your love killed me ... and will kill her ...*

I pushed away the image of Sephya, and yet another rose out of the endless depths beneath Kyphros – a sandy-haired woman in green leathers with a jagged scar across her cheek urged her mount toward me, then reined up. Her shortsword jabbed at my breast.

*... great wizard, great warrior ... the greatest in all Candar ...*

Great warrior? Not me! Great wizard?

*... the greatest ... for who else has dared the depths and survived the firebolts of chaos? Who else ... tell me that I did not die for a weakling. Tell me I did not die for nothing ...*

With all the burning and pain, I could feel tears. Had Freyda died for nothing? Had Justen been right? No! I refused to accept that, and I thrust her away. But before she faded, the flat side of the sword, thrown in disgust, slammed against my right arm. Flat side or not, it hurt.

*... come ... great bearer of destruction ... join us ...*

Another figure rose from the swirling fog of order and chaos – a man cloaked in white, who smiled, and his smile was sparkling dust, as were his body and his garments down to his white boots.

Behind him, I could feel rising hordes of the dead, could feel the crimson- and green-cloaked soldiers, the white-cloaked figures of chaos wizards.

*. . . join us . . .*

Red-whitened ashes flowed from one arm . . . while the other bore four blackened spots, burned through white cloak and skin and flesh, burns aching with the pain beyond pain.

*. . . join us . . .*

I looked dully at the wizard. What couldn't I see? Why did every figure I thrust away bring up another, and more pain, more injuries?

*. . . join us . . . great wizard . . . join us, for you deceive yourself as you believe we deceived you . . . believer in order alone, believer in deception . . . deception . . .*

A firebolt seared my chest. Smoke rose, and I could smell signed hair – mine.

*. . . join us . . . you cannot escape . . . you are a hero . . . and heroes never escape . . . they must always save someone else . . . until they are lost . . . and you will be lost to your heroism, great wizard . . . join us . . .*

. . . cannot escape . . . cannot escape – the thought hammered at me. Cannot escape . . . what couldn't I escape? Being a hero?

Then I swallowed, and ignored the burns, the smoke, the pain, and I held out my arms, inviting the dread figures to me, for they were me, and I was them.

A dull wailing rose and fell somewhere in the depths . . . and the depths rumbled.

I dropped the frail shields I had raised and waited.

*Grrrurrr . . . rrrrrurrr . . .*

Order and chaos swirled through me, and I knew – knew that they were not separate, but two sides of the same coin, knew that one could fight neither chaos nor order, but only those who misused one side of that coin. I knew, too, that the evil fostered by Recluce would be countered by an equal evil, and I shuddered.

So did the earth.

The chaos and the order slashed through me, burning, but both were mine, and could be no one else's.

Finally, I lay there, sweating, for a long time before I lurched upright and lit the lamp. I could feel my eyes widen as I took in the singe marks and burns that outlined where my body had rested on the sheet, and the burns on the quilt.

I staggered toward the small mirror. My body was crisscrossed with burns, and blisters crossed my reddened face. My head throbbed, as though it had been squeezed between the jaws of my own wood presses. Small sharp knives stabbed through my eyes.

Finally, while I felt like shaking my head, I dared not, for I felt as if it would have fallen off.

Slowly, I trudged to the kitchen and lit a lamp. Then I pumped some water and slowly blotted my face and the burns on my body. A heavy dark welt was turning into an ugly bruise on my right arm, as was another across my chest. Five oozing burns marked my left forearm.

With what little order strength I had left, I tried to keep chaos from the wounds as I washed away the stench of brimstone in the dim lamplight. I kept bathing the worst of the burns in cold water until the fire subsided.

'Master Lerris . . .'

I didn't even realize I was naked as I turned.

'Ohhhhh . . .'

Rissa went down like an unsupported sack of flour. Did I look that bad? I was certain it hadn't been my naked body. She'd clearly seen naked males before. I looked down.

I didn't look wonderful, with welts, burns, bruises, cuts – and all from just lying in my bed and speculating and seeking out order in the depths beneath?

No wonder a lot of mages didn't survive very long.

I pulled on an old shirt, which was loose enough not to bind, before I blotted Rissa's face.

She finally sat up, shuddering.

'I'm sorry, Rissa. I didn't mean to disturb you.'

'What . . . be . . . you . . . doing?'

Her words seemed to waver in and out of my ears, but I caught the general idea and answered. 'Learning about being a mage – the hard way. I don't seem to be able to learn any other way.'

'Oh . . . Master Lerris . . . when will you be learning not to meddle?' Rissa straightened herself and got to her feet.

'Probably never.'

'Darkness help those around you. Darkness help us all . . .' She swallowed. 'Like the commander says, you were born to be a hero, and that is a terrible burden.'

'I'm all right,' I sighed. 'And there's nothing you can do tonight.'

'Darkness . . . cook for a wizard . . . and he boils himself . . . terrible world we live in . . . terrible . . .' She walked toward her room at the back of the house, and I set down the damp cloth and headed for the bedroom. I'd worry about cleaning things up in the morning – assuming nothing else rose out of the depths to smite me.

I eased myself back into bed – on Krystal's side – the unburned, unsinged side. Tomorrow, I'd have to send Rissa to buy linens.

At first, I couldn't sleep, not with the aches and pains, nor with the endless questions, although it helped to leave my eyes closed. Why was seeking order and chaos in the ground easier? By rights, it ought to have been more difficult, since earth and clay and rock were far heavier than air.

I tried in the smallest way to sense the winds and the clouds overhead, and my head began to throb. I felt that, while such sensing was perhaps a shade easier than when my father had first insisted, sensing what lay beneath me was far, far, easier.

Was I really an earth wizard? I'd never heard of an earth wizard. Why not? I didn't have an answer, and all the order-searching had left me bruised, beaten, wounded . . . and tired.

So finally I fell asleep to the creaking of the house timbers.

# LVII

Justen moaned in his sleep, then bolted upright, his blanket dropping away. Tamra screamed.

A faint groaning in the ground echoed in their ears, as if from an imposibly distant source.

'Justen!'

'Darkness . . . darkness . . .' muttered the older mage.

'What . . .?' gasped Tamra.

'Lerris, the idiot.' Justen struggled out of his bedroll and eased a log into the coals. He rubbed his forehead.

Tamra rubbed her own forehead. 'My head hurts. Worse than after chasing storms.'

'So does mine.' Justen offered her his water bottle.

She drank, then looked at the fire, at the cold stars overhead, and at last toward the northwest and toward distant Jellico.

*Grrrrurrrr* . . .

They both winced.

'What about Lerris?' Tamra handed the water bottle back to the gray wizard.

'I didn't think he was . . . this far . . . he didn't tell me everything.'

Tamra looked at Justen. 'That's because you didn't tell him every-thing. You hide too much. You didn't trust Lerris fully, and you trust me even less. You sneak around in the shadows cast by your own past.' She massaged her forehead again. 'Darkness, my head hurts.' She glared at Justen. 'It hurts even to try and sense what's out in the darkness. I'd hate to try to read the weather now.'

'There's no weather underground.'

The log on the coals burst into flame.

'Stop being obscure. That's just another form of distrust.'

'I suppose so.'

'I know so,' snapped the redhead. 'Just because you hide things doesn't mean they stay hidden. So tell me what Lerris is doing, and why it's disrupting order and chaos all across Candar. It's not in the air. I could tell if it were.'

'He's challenging the Balance, and he's doing it deep within the earth. I didn't know he was an earth wizard.'

'An earth wizard? There are earth wizards?'

'There haven't been before, not full ones, not any I heard of,' admitted Justen. 'But that's what he's doing.'

'You aren't an earth wizard?'

'I can do a little there, like Lerris can do a little with the winds, but the forest and living things, and metals, are what I know best.'

'You know metals and aren't an earth wizard?'

'I was a smith once, and metals above the earth are easier. With ... help ... I can do ... some things below the earth.'

'You're not telling me everything. Again!' Tamra massaged her forehead. 'Everything you say leads to more questions.'

*Grrrrurrrrr ...*

With the distant deep rumbling, Justen pursed his lips.

'So am I an air wizard? Or can I just sense things in the air like you can in the earth?' Tamra took a step back from the fire.

'You're an air wizard, but how strong I don't know.' Justen shrugged, sadly. 'No one seems to be able to tell until things like this happen. Some wizards never really find out.'

'You're being obscure again, and I don't like it.'

'All wizards have to go through a personal trial – if they want to be full wizards using order. You will, too – probably not for a while yet, though. That's what's happening to Lerris.'

'What will happen to him?'

'If he survives, he'll be on the way to full control of his abilities, but he'll probably be pretty beaten up.'

'Pretty beaten up? He almost died already. What do you expect of him? What do you expect of me!' She started to glare again, then held her forehead. 'Men! Idiots!'

'I don't expect anything,' growled Justen. 'You seem to think that, because you can see the storms, call up a breeze, or move a cloud or two around, you're a full wizard. It doesn't work that way.'

'How does it work? What does this have to do with the Balance? Tell me, and don't be so demon-damned obscure.'

'All wizardry involves the Balance.' Justen pursed his lips and looked at the fire.

'And?'

'The greater the use of either order or chaos, the more likely a wizard will upset the Balance. When that happens, he has to right it, especially in himself. If not . . .' Justen shook his head.

'Why will it be a while before I face this . . . whatever it is? I'm older than Lerris.'

'Because you're an air wizard, you might not. My brother Gunnar never did. Creslin lost his sight, but he was older, I think.'

'You think? Don't you know?'

Justen looked back at the fire.

'Don't you know?' Tamra massaged her forehead again.

'No. I'm sort of a jack-of-all-trades wizard. I'm not an air wizard.'

Lit by the flickering red of the fire and by the cold light of the stars, neither mage looked at the other, but far beneath Candar the ground rumbled . . . and rumbled.

# LVIII

## East of Lavah, Sligo [Candar]

After stepping inside the cottage, the man in the tan uniform carefully folds the heavy brown cloak over his arm and offers a half-bow. 'Honored Mage, might I introduce myself?'

'You might.' Fire glitters on Sammel's fingertips, then fades.

'D'ressn Leithrrse, envoy of His Imperial Highness Stesten of Hamor.' Leithrrse bows again.

'My, that is an impressive series of titles.' Sammel offers an exaggerated bow in response. 'How could this poor seeker of knowledge possibly offer anything to such an exalted personage?'

'You already have rendered some services to the Emperor, at least indirectly.'

'Ah, through Duke Colaris . . . I cannot say I am surprised.' The fire flares momentarily on Sammel's fingers, then vanishes. 'And I am vain enough to appreciate a little recognition of the power of the knowledge I provided.'

'The Emperor does recognize the power of knowledge. Knowledge can change the world, and doubtless that is what you hoped, even expected.' The envoy sets his carefully folded coat across the back of the crude wooden chair. 'In fact, you might even have been said to have ensured it.'

'It was clear that Begnula was on your payroll. Knowledge I provided somehow appeared in Hamorian form before it was ever used in Freetown, and that says a great deal when that knowledge must travel the oceans.'

'I am what I say, an envoy of the Emperor,' mock-protests Leithrrse.

'Who was born in Recluce and who has adopted the Hamorian form of naming.'

'I remain the envoy of the Emperor.'

'Then, perhaps you will do me a favor.' Sammel turns his back to Leithrrse. 'Take one of those metal cartridges and place it on the hearth – away from the fire.'

'As you wish.' The shorter, slender man extracts the metal cylinder from his belt and sets it on the stone, stepping back past the chair that holds his cloak.

Sammel's eyebrows lift, and a thin funnel of white appears around the cartridge.

*Wwhhhhssstttt!!!* A cone of flame flares upward and vanishes. White smoke swirls around where the cartridge had been. When the smoke dissipates, no sign of the cartridge remains, only a smear of blackness on the stone.

Although a film of perspiration coats Leithrrse's forehead, he does not reach for the linen handkerchief folded inside his tunic.

Sammel smiles. 'Now, you may continue.'

'For all your recent wealth and for all your power' – Leithrrse gestures around the cottage – 'this is still a cottage, and only a handful of people know of your prowess.'

'Public reputation is scarcely desirable for a mage,' returns Sammel dryly. 'Private recognition and remuneration, yes, but not public acknowledgment.'

The envoy's brows knit for an instant, before he laughs. 'You surprise me. I thought you would protest. I thought you would claim you do what you do solely for the love of knowledge.'

'Love of knowledge and a desire for remuneration do not exclude each other.' Sammel walks toward the hearth and frowns. The black splotch on the stone vanishes. 'Especially as one grows older.'

'I understand that,' admits Leithrrse, holding up a hand. 'And so do you. Recluce does not. Let me be frank, since you appear to appreciate that. If you remain here, certainly Recluce will send someone after you. How many times in the past has knowledge been discovered, and then extinguished by the black isle?'

'More than a few.' Sammel's voice remains dry. His eyes flicker to the tube gun mounted on the wall.

'In fact,' continues Leithrrse, his eyes following Sammel's, 'it appears that the black mages may have preceded me.' He clears his throat, then continues when Sammel does not speak. 'Powerful as you clearly are, alone you are vulnerable. You have to sleep at some point. Now ... the Emperor is a great supporter of knowledge, and Hamor would be far more receptive to what you offer.'

'At least so long as my knowledge furthers his conquests?'

'My, you are cynical.' Leithrrse inclines his head slightly.

'No more so than you. Recluce does breed a certain caution.'

'You wish to see knowledge available to all, and you wish some limited recognition and more than limited remuneration. Why not help accomplish all these at once? Become the head of the great Library at Luba.'

For a moment, Sammel continues to look out upon the land beyond the window, where areas of browned grass are beginning to appear through the snow. 'If the Emperor's other voice – the other envoy – is willing to make such a proposal, I might ... might consider it.'

'I will have to discuss it with him.'

'Do so.'

'I will, Honored Mage. In the interim, you might consider that the Library would be less able to afford a new supervisor if the cost of the conquest of Candar becomes prohibitive.' Leithrrse bows, then extends a leather pouch. 'A token of esteem and recognition. Just a token.'

'I am honored.'

'The Emperor would hope that you would honor him.' The envoy reclaims his cloak.

'You speak well, Leithrrse, and so does your coin.' Sammel laughs softly.

'Knowledge is always valuable, and only a fool disregards its value. The Emperor has high regard for knowledge, and is certainly no fool.' The envoy smiles. 'After all, I am here, offering recognition of such a regard.' Leithrrse turns at the doorway and bows a last time.

'I appreciate your interest, Honorable Envoy.' Sammel inclines his head. 'I do, and look forward to your return.'

'Good.'

As Leithrrse walks toward his mount, and the troops who have waited, Sammel nods and speaks to himself. 'Head librarian . . . a title better than most . . . Talryn, you think knowledge can be buried?' He closes the door and laughs. 'Or that mages must bow to Recluce or remain penniless?'

# LIX

In some ways, I was glad Krystal had to stay in Dasir for a while, since I looked and felt like a vulcrow's carrion for a while. The slashes, cuts, burns, and bruises weren't that bad – especially not compared to the injuries I'd sustained in Hydlen, but even with some order-mastery and a lot of self-pampering, they still hurt, and ached, and slowed me down. Sometimes I just had to close my eyes to shut out the stabbing, but those spells didn't last long. I did have to give up the morning staff practice for a few days, and that bothered me because I'd just been getting back to where I was improving.

For a time, I just worked on Durrik's spice chest, because the golden oak and design were more forgiving than the cherry of Antona's desk or the dark oak of Minister Zeiber's case. Besides, Durrik had commissioned his before Zeiber.

I had more than enough time to finish Preltar's chest – assuming something else didn't come up, but it doubtless would. Life was turning out that way. Then, maybe it always had, and I just hadn't realized it.

Two mornings after my encounter with the Balance – I guessed that was as good a description as any – I had just about finished the last of the internal framing for Durrik's chest and clamped it in place to dry.

I had also finished up the last of the glue, and that meant brewing more.

When I took the pot into the kitchen, Rissa was less than enthused.

'My kitchen is for food, not for smelly glue.'

'This smelly glue is what helps pay for the food.'

'Then I will take the mare and the wagon and fetch some eggs from Brene. We have no chickens, and no eggs. If we had chickens, I would not have to drive through the mud and the rain.'

'No chickens.'

'If we had chickens, I could make chicken soup, and that would be good for your bruises and soreness.' She shook her head. 'Wizards. How can a man nearly be killed in his own bed with no one around? I thought the commander lived a dangerous life. It is good you two have each other, for who else would dare to live with you?'

'That might have been a problem.' I put another length of wood into the firebox of the stove.

'A problem? The only thing worse would be two wizards. Why, then, no house would we have. No food, no shelter . . .'

I stirred the mixture in the pot.

'Already, my kitchen is smelling foul.'

'Not so fowl as it would if we had chickens.'

Rissa mock-glared at me as she pulled a cloak around her. 'Wizards!' She headed to the stables. She was strong enough, and knowledgeable enough, and the mare was docile enough, that she had no trouble, for which I was grateful.

I broke off a crust of not-quite-stale bread and chewed on it as I continued to stir. While the afternoon drew on and the pot heated, I watched the liquid swirl, and my thoughts turned to the depths below. In a way, the depths swirled much the way the heating glue did. Was the center of the earth like a huge chaos-fire?

I shivered, not exactly liking the idea that the world was composed of chaos-fire contained by a shell of order. If that were so, of course the Balance would have to hold. If order triumphed, then the world would freeze, and if chaos triumphed, it would explode.

Once I had the glue basically made, I took it back to the shop, and began to measure and cut more of the framework pieces for Antona's desk. I tried to keep in mind Sardit's admonitions about measuring twice before cutting—' Measure twice; cut once. Measure once; cut twice – and waste wood.'

Cutting matching lengths exactly is important because trying to trim off fractions of a span can bruise or splinter the wood, and I certainly wasn't in a position to waste high-priced wood. It was a long afternoon, and I didn't go out when Rissa returned, just kept on with trying to be exact.

With my various aches and pains, I was slow – and careful – and hadn't even quite finished when I heard the second set of hoofs. I racked the wood and headed out to the yard, pausing to light the big lantern on the way.

There was a splotch of mud on Krystal's cheek. She looked wonderful, and I gave her a big smile.

'What on earth happened to you?' Her eyes raked over the healing blisters on my face. 'Did you put sawdust in the hearth?' She swung out of the saddle and onto the ground, wincing as she did.

'I wish it had been that painless.'

I took the reins and led her mount toward the stable, again conscious of the dull aches that seemed to surround me.

Perron followed closely, with his mount, and Haithen wasn't all that far behind.

'Well?' asked Krystal gently, brushing my cheek with her lips, as if she were almost afraid to touch my blistered skin.

'It's not a long story, but' – I looked over my shoulder – 'more than a few people seem to want to know. Could I wait a bit until we eat?'

Krystal raised her eyebrows. I sighed as I tied her mount – a black gelding this time – in place in the stall. Krystal undid the cinch as I reached for the brush.

'All right,' I began.

'No . . . don't let me hurry you.'

I glared at her, and she grinned.

'The simple answer is that I got caught in the workings of the Balance.' I began to brush the gelding.

'Where did you go?'

'That's the worst part. I didn't go anywhere.'

'The rest of us have to travel to find trouble. I thought you'd be half-safe here.' She sat down on a bale of hay.

'You need to eat. You look exhausted.'

'I am tired.'

I glanced at Perron over the stall wall, but he looked away. I finished the mare with a too-quick brushing, and we walked out of the stable and across the yard to the house.

'Noodles and sauce – that is all I can fix when no one tells me anything,' protested Rissa.

'That will be fine,' we both said. Then we looked at each other and smiled.

'Noodles . . . it is not fine. If we had chickens, now . . .'

'No chickens . . .'

'If we had chickens, a real meal with no notice, it might be made . . .'

I kept walking toward the washroom. So did Krystal.

In the washroom, she eased out of the vest, gingerly.

'What happened to you?' I let my senses range across her body, but I didn't have to probe much to find the slash/bruise on her left shoulder. 'How did that happen?' Even as I talked, I let some order flow into the area, around which the slightest hint of chaos flickered. How had I missed her wound? Was it because I had been too wrapped up in my own injuries?

'That feels good.'

'Good. Now, what happened?'

Krystal eased out of her shirt, and I tried not to wince at the slash and the bruise – or the crude stitches. Instead, my fingertips brushed the wound again, forcing out chaos infection.

She started to shrug, then thought the better of it. I pumped more water, and began to sponge her off, gently, very gently.

'We had a problem in Matisir, not Dasir. This subleader, a woman named Frinekl, basically ambushed the local outlier's leader. Ustrello, I think. She claimed he'd tried to rape her, and that she'd defended herself.'

'Nasty business.' I frowned, trying to recall Ustrello. 'He was older. I met him, and his consort. He didn't seem the type, but I suppose you never know.' I kept sponging and patting.

'Ooooo . . .'

'Sorry.'

'Don't be. I wanted to get home . . .'

She had turned pasty, and I sat her on the stool, patted her dry and loosely wrapped my robe from the peg on the door around her.

'You need to eat.' I offered a shade more order, not that I still had much to spare, but it removed some of the gray from her face, and helped her back into the kitchen, where I took the bread off the table and broke a chunk for her.

Rissa took a look at me, then Krystal, before saying, 'The noodles will not be too long, but here is some cheese, the white kind.'

Krystal ate bread and cheese, and sipped some cold water, slowly, silently, as the guards straggled in and sat around the table. Finally, she pushed away the last crust. 'That's enough for now.'

I touched her wrist again, but she seemed a little stronger.

'What happened with Ustrello?'

'He died before anyone else got there.' Krystal took a slow even breath. 'This Frinekl . . . it makes me so mad . . .'

'What happened,' said Perron apologetically, 'is that the bitch played on the commander's sympathies until the commander happened to examine the leader's body closely.'

'He couldn't have been facing her,' Krystal said. 'And he could have been running away, but the footprints didn't fit that. Nothing fit, and when I asked her, she picked up Ustrello's sword – to demonstrate – she said . . . stupid, I was just stupid.'

'I don't understand this,' protests Heldra. 'How can they do this under the Balance?'

'They are, aren't they? I told you how earlier. Besides, that's not the question. What do we do? Surrender all interest in Candar?'

'According to your logic,' observes Maris, 'we don't have any choice.'

'But how can they?' questions Heldra again.

'They're mechanically increasing the amount of order in the world. The Balance is mechanical. Our predecessors restricted the growth of order so as to limit the growth of chaos. Hamor has never had such scruples. Also,' adds Talryn with a smile, 'after Justen's demonstration of the full power of order, no one on Recluce was exactly too enthused about creating an equal amount of chaos. Even his brother turned away from him on that.'

'But . . . what's happening? If Hamor is putting that much order into the world, and Candar, isn't there going to be a huge chaos focus – somewhere?' Maris sets the scroll on the table.

'Of course. We were talking about that before you got here.' Talryn nods toward Heldra. 'Chaos is seething beneath Candar, even beneath the Gulf, I think. If you send out your senses, it doesn't take much to find it. There's even some building beneath Recluce.'

'Great,' mumbles Heldra.

'I'm not a mage,' snaps Maris. 'I wouldn't know.'

'Take my word for it.'

'So why don't we have wizards and chaos focuses popping up all over? According to your lectures, that's usually what happened in the past.'

'Let's see,' muses Talryn ironically. 'Antonin almost destroys the midsection of Candar. The conflict between Lerris and Gerlis turns a valley in the Easthorns into the equivalent of the demon's hell, and the entire world hears the reverberations. Sammel is now wielding enough chaos power to burn water, and all of Candar is rumbling with chaos deep beneath the earth. Does that answer your question?'

'Just what are we supposed to do, then?' asks Heldra.

'Have the Brotherhood build some more black iron destroyers, and beg Gunnar for help. Or Justen.'

'Justen? Do we want that kind of help?'

'Can we survive without it?'

'And how do we pay for all of this?' protests Maris.

Both Heldra and Talryn just look at him.

Perron shook his head. So did I.

'No one else would have stood a chance,' added Haithen. 'The commander had to kill her on the spot, of course.'

'Stupid bitch,' muttered Jinsa.

'I should have seen it,' repeated Krystal.

'There are lots of things we should see and don't.' I reached out under the table and squeezed her thigh, just to reassure her, and because her arm wasn't in any shape to be touched. Krystal hadn't seen Frinekl's deception because of the events that had led to Krystal's own exile from Recluce.

'There's truth to that,' stated Rissa as she put the noodles and sauce on the table and the rest of the bread, and more cheese. The guards waited until Krystal and I took a helping, although Krystal only took a small one.

We did not linger long at table, nor did the guards. Everyone was yawning – except Rissa. Tired or not, the four guards had ensured that the noodles and sauce had disappeared, as though by chaos magic. Dercas and Jinsa left first, then Perron and Haithen.

'Shoo!' was all Rissa said, and it was all we needed.

When I had shut the bedroom door, and lit the lamp, Krystal sat on the edge of the bed. I pulled off her boots, knowing bending over would hurt her.

'New bed linens,' Krystal observed.

'The old ones got a little warm. But since you're such a skeptical woman . . .' I pulled down the charred sheet and quilt from the top of the wardrobe, and laid them out across the new quilt. I hadn't been that thrilled with the broken-wheel pattern on the new one, but that was all Rissa had been able to find.

'Oh . . . Lerris.' She forced a smile. 'What were you doing that was that hot in bed?'

'Not what I'd like to have been doing.' It was a little forced, but she needed it, and so did I.

She looked at the quilt again.

'Let's get you off your feet and into bed, and I'll tell you.'

'You don't look any too healthy yourself, Mastercrafter.'

So we pulled off clothes and put them where we could and curled into the cold newer linens and quilt.

'Now?' she asked, with a yawn.

'I was thinking about the groaning of the house timbers in the wind, and it reminded me of the groaning deep under the brimstone spring. So I sent my order-senses down into the earth, and I discovered that I'm probably an earth wizard. I also discovered that I didn't know as much as I thought, and that, in some places, careless intruding is the same as upsetting the Balance.'

'Can't you even be safe in your own bed?' She shook her head slightly, and I stroked her hair.

'Oh . . . I'll be safe enough now. I just had to pay for the privilege.'

'We're always paying for something.'

'We always will be.'

'I'm tired of paying.'

There wasn't much I could say to that. She had paid more than I had, a great deal more. Instead of speaking, I kissed her cheek. Then I lay beside her and held her hand.

'I don't see you for days, and when I do, neither one of us is worth a demon's damn.' Her words were low.

She sighed, softly, and I squeezed her hand again, then kissed her cheek, and lay there as she dropped off to sleep.

*Grrrurrrrr . . . rrrrr . . .*

The faint rumbling I heard was not in the timbers, for the winds were still, and the night quiet. Should I investigate – send my senses out? I licked my lips, and Krystal rolled over, snuggling against me, and I put an arm around her.

'Mmmmmmm . . .' Her breathing smoothed out and lightened.

Had the earth always rumbled, and I hadn't been aware enough to sense it?

Finally, gently, I let my senses creep into the depths, slipping around the intertwinings of order and chaos.

I never did reach the source of the deep groaning and heaving, but I could tell it originated somewhere to the northeast, probably beyond Freetown and in Sligo. There was so much I didn't know, and that wasn't so bad, except that every time I learned something, I learned that there was even more I didn't know.

After hugging Krystal again, with care to avoid her bruised and slashed arm, I rolled over onto my own unbruised side and slept.

# LX

## Nylan, Recluce

'Y ou can almost hear the chaos buildup in Candar . . . I can sense it from here.' Heldra looks toward the half-open door. 'Where's Maris?'

'Picking up a message from the traders. He shouldn'[t] Talryn fingers the black ceramic mug. 'I can sense th[e] asked Gunnar about it. Even he's worried. He thinks th[e] high as when Fairhaven fell. Maybe higher. I wouldn't he's rather older than we are.'

'He claims he's survived through the working of ord[er] wonder about that explanation,' muses Heldra.

At the dull clunk of the outer door, both council Maris steps into the Council Room, glances around t[o] besides the other two Council members are there, an[d] door behind him.

'Hamor has invaded Candar. More than twoscore ship[s] ones – hold Freetown. Colaris and his personal guard we[re] executed. More troops and ships are expected.'

'Almost twoscore ships in Freetown? You're certain?' [A] flick from Talryn to Maris and the scroll he holds. 'All and steam-powered?'

'That's the report. The Emperor's regent holds Freet[own] strokes his beard, his fingers fluttering nervously.

'What will your traders do?' Heldra turns her back on below and the flat blue of the sunlit Eastern Ocean fra[mes] Council Room window, waiting for Maris to answer for th[e]

'What can we do? Avoid Freetown, but we're blocked fr[om] and Southwind. Freetown is the biggest port on this end of and with Hamorian warships there . . .' Maris shrugs and tu[rns] Talryn. 'What about the Brotherhood? Can we build anothe[r]

'In time to do any good? I doubt it.' Talryn picks up black ceramic mug and examines it.

'Avoid Freetown? Is that all you weak-kneed traders can snaps Heldra.

'We could transfer our shipments to Renklaar.'

'And what will happen to costs?' Talryn's rumbling voi[ce] almost indifferent.

'They'll be forty percent higher,' admits the former trad[er] have to use riverboats to get to the Jellico road above Hydol[a]

'I rather doubt that trade is our most immediate problem,' Talryn. 'Hamor now has almost fourscore warships in an[d] Candar. Our trio may indeed be able to pick off the dozen Dellash. Then, if they can race eastward to Freetown in what days in good weather – they can try to bottle up the Hamorian Great North Bay. That leaves Summerdock, Southport, Biehl, all under Hamorian control when the next fleet arrives – and

# LXI

Krystal's arm was better in the morning – sore, but with no signs of chaos – and I bandaged it loosely before she rode back to Kyphrien to report to Kasee. Then I went to work on Durrik's chest, but not for long.

Wegel showed up – a day earlier than I'd thought. Faslik brought him, and the young man actually had two saws, one a good crosscut blade, a smoothing blade, and chisels, although the largest chisel was really too big, more suited to working for a shipwright than a crafter. I didn't say anything about that, and he could probably trade it for something smaller in time.

'You sure about this, Master Lerris?' Faslik asked for the fourth time as he sat on his wagon seat, ready to leave. 'He's a good lad.'

Wegel stood by the walk to the shop, looking down.

'I'm sure. He gets his lodging, his food, and a copper an eight-day for now – and half of the proceeds after the wood costs of anything he sells.'

'How long before he can be more than an apprentice?'

I had to shrug. 'I can't say. Two, three years if he's good.' It might be sooner than that, but I'd decided it was better to promise less. 'It's not just talent. Talent he has.'

Wegel smiled shyly at that.

Faslik nodded. 'He's a good lad.' Then he lifted the reins and drove off, his bearded face looking back with every other step of his horses, and his wagon creaking all the way out to the road.

Wegel swallowed, and I patted his shoulder.

'Let's get you settled.' I led him to the long bunk room at the end of the stable. I'd surveyed the stable and guard area earlier, and had figured out how to build a small space for Wegel. I'd help a bit, but he was going to do most of the work. In the meantime, he'd just have to take one of the bunks. It was better than I'd had when I'd started with Destrin. There were six bunks anyway, and Krystal almost never brought more than four guards, but, as in everything, I'd overdone the design – Krystal was pointing that out to me more and more. I wondered why it bothered her so much. She'd paid for the materials and a lot of the work I couldn't do. Sometimes, as with Wegel, it worked out.

He looked around the space with the small table, the stools – quick, crude efforts on my part – and the three sets of bunks.

'You want an upper one or a lower one? The upper ones are a bit warmer, which might be better now. We'll have you in your own cubby before the weather gets too hot.' I thought about his foot and added, 'Some people worry about falling out of the top ones, though, and some like it colder when they sleep. You ought to take one of the end ones – either the top one or the bottom. That way, when the commander's guards are here —'

'C-c-c-c-com . . . ?'

'I told you. When Krystal – she's my consort, except she's really more important than I am, so perhaps I'm her consort – is here, her personal guards sleep here. They're good people. Krystal wouldn't have it any other way.'

'Y-y-you k-k-k-illed the order wiz-z-z . . .'

'I did put an end to a couple of wizards, but it wasn't all that heroic. After the last time, I couldn't walk for a half-season, and I still limp.' I snorted. 'Crafting's a lot easier, hard as it is, and generally a lot more rewarding.'

Because he still had that inquiring look, I kept talking. 'Pick a bunk and put your pack and stuff there. Not your tools. We'll put those in your racks in the shop.'

Wegel just stood there, short brown hair straggling down across the top of his forehead.

'Wegel – don't believe everything you hear. Most of the time I'd rather be doing woodworking than wizardry.' I patted him on the shoulder, even if he were nearly as tall as I was and broader across the chest and shoulders. 'We need to get you started. There's a lot of work to do.'

Finally, he swung his gear onto the top bunk at the end and followed me back across the yard. Before we went into the shop, I brought him into the kitchen, where Rissa was scrubbing the stove.

'Master Lerris . . . the floor needs scrubbing, I do not have —'

'Rissa, I just wanted you to meet Wegel. He'll be sleeping in the guard quarters until he can build his own space in the stable building.

'Wegel, this is Rissa. She fixes wonderful food, runs the kitchen, and lets us all know what she thinks. She's right enough that I'm very careful about disagreeing with her.'

'Master Lerris . . . you be making me into a spite-cat willing to chew this poor fellow up.' She put down the blackened brush and turned to Wegel. 'Faslik's boy, aren't you? The one with the good knife? Someday, if Master Lerris doesn't work you into the ground, I'd like you to carve me a wooden chicken. Of course, he won't work you as hard as he works himself, but that sometimes doesn't help much. But maybe you can do me a chicken.' She looked at me. 'Carved ones likely be the only ones we get around here.'

'Rissa. No chickens.'

She glanced back at Wegel. 'You look hungry.' She crossed the kitchen, bringing back a good half loaf of bread. 'It's cool, but it's good enough. Go ahead. Master Lerris won't mind.'

I nodded. 'When you finish eating, bring your stuff to the shop, and we'll get it racked. Then we'll start you in.'

I left the kitchen and went to the drawing board in the shop. While Wegel finished eating the bread, I sketched out a rough drawing of a box just like the one I had built for Uncle Sardit. Like I'd had to do, Wegel was going to keep notes on woods and projects. And like Uncle Sardit, although probably not nearly so well, I was going to have to teach him what I knew. I took a deep breath. Uncle Sardit would have laughed.

The two additional commissions I'd gotten just before Wegel had arrived weren't exactly ideal for starting Wegel. He might be able to help on the case for Minister Zeiber. Then we'd see about the dowry chest for Preltar's daughter. I sighed, thinking about the hinges I needed to commission.

As I was finishing the sketch of the box, Wegel peered into the shop.

'That rack's yours. When you aren't using a tool, it goes back in the rack. Understand?'

He nodded.

I wasn't about to start Wegel on a desk like Antona's, although I would have him carve the inlaid A – he could clearly do that better and more quickly than I, even in the dark lorken, and there was certainly no sense in my spending forever on something that would take him perhaps a morning, a day or two at most.

So I had him start on his note box, interrupting him as necessary to help hold and position the work I was doing on Antona's desk.

'Gluing and fitting cherry is even harder than oak. Oak is heavier, but, in a way, it has more give. Cherry tends to be more brittle, and it requires more care. You just can't force it, and you have to be careful with the grains.' I edged the pieces together as I talked.

'You can't force a join, just like you can't force a carving.' I lined up the clamps for the pedestal bracing, and tightened them slowly.

'See ... you only want enough pressure to hold the wood in place ... with just enough glue there ... the wood and the pins carry the weight. The glue is really to keep the pieces in position so that the supports do carry the weight ...' I looked at Wegel. 'Do you see ...?'

'I ... sss ... eeee ...'

I shook my head and grinned. 'You don't have to talk. Just nod yes or no. Unlike some people, I think I can understand, and I don't want you wearing yourself out when you don't have to. Save your efforts for the wood.'

Wegel nodded, then turned away.

I touched his shoulder. 'If you want to talk ... that's fine, too. All I meant was that you don't have to if you don't want to ...' I hadn't meant to hurt his feelings, but talking was such an effort for him at times that I didn't want him wearing himself out trying to please me.

Wegel nodded at me with a half-smile.

'Can you write?'

'A l-l-l-little.'

'Good. When you feel like taking a break from the box, I want you to do two things. I'll give you some thick paper, and the first thing is to write down what you know about cherry, and anything you learned today. After that, I'll show you how to do breadboards. Every apprentice needs to do a few. Rissa could use one or two, and you might be able to sell some others for a copper or two. Some of the extra wood can't be used for anything else, and at least that way it won't cost you. Then, in your spare time, I want you to sketch out the design for an *A*.'

Wegel raised his eyebrows.

'The desk here. It will have a small carved *A* that I'll inlay in the corner. You carve better than I do. So you can take the first cut at the design. After you carve it, I'll chalk it and cut the grooves.'

'M-m-m-me?'

'Why not?' I grinned. 'The design has to be carved – it's really cutting as much as carving. And you can't hurt the desk because you're working on a separate piece. I'll show you how I want it set so the wood grain runs in the right direction.'

'G-g-g-rain?'

That question led into an explanation of wood grain, and how the grains have to match, unless you're using the grains as a pattern in themselves. I was a little surprised that Wegel didn't know more about grains, and woods, but I had the feeling he had been doing the drudge work at the mill.

Still, he seemed to understand.

# LXII

## South of Hrisbarg, Freetown [Candar]

As the sky lightens, the Duke watches the far hillside, but the balloon does not rise with the dawn, nor does the smoke from the Freetown cookfires. Only a handful of cyan banners drop in the still air. No fog created by the breath of troops wreathes the hill from where the Freetown cannon had fired their deadly shots the day before.

'Scouts!' demands Berfir, pushing his mount to the crest of the hill, from where he can survey the Freetown position.

'Ser?' asks the stocky officer who rides up beside him.

'Colaris's forces have abandoned their position. That's what it looks like.'

'Why would they do that?'

Berfir nods grimly, his eyes flicking back to his own most recent trench-works, the thin lines of red-clad troops – and the rows of mounds that lie on the downside of the hill. 'I don't know. The cannon are gone.' He gestures. 'It looks like they even left supplies, and if that's so . . .'

'I understand, ser.' The stocky man salutes.

'We may reach Freetown yet.'

'If they don't have those demon-damned long guns, ser . . .'

'Or if we can overtake them and capture them,' suggests the Duke.

'Wouldn't mind having a few, ser, long as they're pointed away from us.'

Berfir's laugh dies away as he purses his lips, studying the seemingly empty Freetown position. 'Why . . . ?'

The scout officer waits.

'Check if it's clear to take their position – and those supplies. Then we'll see . . . then we'll see.' He fingers his salt-and-pepper beard, before his fingers go to the captured pistol at his belt. 'We'll see . . .'

# LXIII

After Krystal left for Kyphrien, still favoring the injured arm, and trying not to, I fed Gairloch and the mare. Then I went back into the kitchen.

'Master Lerris, how can I clean if everyone —'

I stopped just inside the door. 'Do you know where Merrin – the coppersmith – is, or Borlo, the other one?'

'Merrin? She is the queer Southwind woman who works with copper?' Rissa pushed back her hair off her damp forehead with one hand, and set the broom against the side of the wall with the other.

'That's the one. I need hinges for a chest.' I'd kept putting it off, and now the chest might even be late if I didn't get on with it, but I hated to depend on others.

'Most crafters use Borlo, and he has lived in Kyphrien for a long time. His shop is off the market square on the artisan's street. Now, his father! Neltar was a coppersmith, and the kettles he made! Guysee, when times were better and she was Morten's housekeeper, she showed me one of those kettles. Morten, he had three of them, and one of them whistled a simple tune.' Rissa offered a half-smile and shook her head. 'How things change, but that kettle, I never did hear . . . and oh, what a kettle it looked to be . . .'

I held up a hand. 'What have you heard about Merrin?' I'd heard enough about Borlo. When someone praises a crafter's father, it usually means that the younger crafter isn't nearly so good.

'That one! She dresses like a blade or a man, and perhaps she was, for there are blades upon the wall, and once she ran the merchant Fuston out of her shop . . .'

At that point I was almost ready to hire Merrin. I hadn't cared much for Fuston the one time I'd run across him, either.

'. . . and they said that the heir, the one called Liessa, she has commissioned works from the woman.'

I nodded. 'Where might I find Merrin?'

'Always, always, you look for the troublesome ones, Master Lerris . . . Borlo is a nice man, always so polite . . .'

'I want the best one.'

Rissa sighed and lifted both hands into the air.

I waited.

'She has her shop on the south side of Kyphrien, below the river bluff, and the back wall is part of the old city wall that was destroyed by Fenardre the Great ages and ages ago ...'

The directions weren't that bad, and I went back to the shop, where Wegel was working on carving the too-ornate top for a breadboard. I could tell that if I weren't careful, he'd do more carving than anything. Then, he had talent there. I tried not to sigh.

Instead, I looked around. 'Wegel, when you take a break, the floor needs to be swept. The stalls need mucking, and the lamps need refilling.' I fumbled in my purse and handed him two silvers. 'We need hay. Rissa will tell you who is likely to have some, and once you unload it, make sure you replace the stuff in the stables.'

My apprentice looked up with that dumb, desperate, obedient look that they all have when confronted with the unpleasant. He didn't groan, though. 'Y-y-yes, s-ser.'

'I'm going to make arrangements for the brass hinges for Preltar's chest. I hope it doesn't take too long, but I want all that done before you do any more carving.'

'Y-y-yes, ser.'

I almost whistled as I saddled Gairloch, until I bent too energetically in reaching for the saddle and my assorted bruises and burns reminded me that I still wasn't totally healed from my last encounter with chaos.

As a matter of habit, I did stick the staff in the lanceholder before leading Gairloch out into the yard.

Rissa came out of the kitchen. 'Leastwise, you're taking your staff. Southside is filled with ruffians and thieves. You use Borlo, and you don't worry about taking your life in your hands ...'

'I'll be fine, Rissa.'

'And you were fine taking on all the wizards, and you were fine even in your own bed ...'

Clearly, what I said wouldn't matter. So I smiled and climbed into the saddle.

'Just be ready to use that staff, now.'

'I will.' I tried not to sigh.

Gairloch almost pranced along the road to Kyphrien, and I felt a little guilty that I hadn't ridden him more recently. Poor pony – he either got ridden practically to death or not at all.

I hadn't been in the old southern section of Kyphrien, where the streets were almost narrow enough for me to reach out and touch walls with each arm.

Twice I had to ask for directions of a sort, because all the streets wound in and back on each other, but I finally got it sorted out, and my nose got accustomed to the sourness and the accumulated odors that hung in the older quarter. Fenardre the Great might have done everyone a favor if he'd been more energetic in removing buildings and walls all those years ago.

An outsized copper kettle over a heavy iron-banded door was the only indication of Merrin's location or occupation. The building was a narrow two-storied brick dwelling with a cracked tile roof and a single wide window on the second level – at least in front.

After tying Gairloch to the iron ring on the stone post by the single stone slab that was the front stoop, my staff in hand, I rapped on the door, hard.

'Coming! Coming!'

The door came ajar, and I could see the glint of the blade and the dark iron chain even before I saw the short gray thatch of hair or the highcheeked and slightly wrinkled face. 'Who are you?'

'I'm Lerris. I'm a crafter, and Liessa had suggested you might do the kind of brasswork I need. You are Merrin?' I asked as an afterthought.

'I'm Merrin.' Her eyes scanned me, and she muttered something about a staff and pony. Then the chain snicked, and the door opened. 'Come on in.'

Inside the stone floor was clean, and a desk or worktable stood on a braided rug. The building was deeper than I had realized, and I could see a hearth and something that looked like a stove, not to mention some crucibles, hammers, small anvils, and other tools whose function I could guess at.

High side windows provided more light than the single front window. A brass or copper lamp sat next to a sconce of some sort. Neither was swirled or ornate, yet there was something distinctive about each, something I couldn't pin down. The smell of hot metal, and an incense, just tickled at my nose.

'Sit down.'

I leaned the staff against the wall and sat.

'I'd offer you tea, but I haven't made any.' She laid the blade aside. 'So . . . you're the famous Lerris? The wizard who loves wood.'

'Not famous.' I shrugged. 'I came because I need some heavy decorative brass hinges for a dowry chest.'

'Why didn't you try Borlo?'

'Because' – and I tried to capture Rissa's tone – 'his father, he made wonderful kettles . . .'

Merrin laughed, and her wrinkled face crinkled a shade more.

I extended a sheet of paper. 'This is a rough drawing of the sort of hinges I need.'

She took the paper and frowned. 'Are these real hinges, or are you going to put iron inside the chest?'

'I don't like false work. If you think I have to, I will, but I'd prefer that your hinges do the work. If I can afford them.'

'Afford me?' She laughed again, then looked at my sketch. 'I won't do these. You let me design my own, and you can have them for five silvers. That includes the matching screws, and those are a pain.'

'All right, but I think the hinges will need to be that large. It's a heavy chest.'

'You did these the size you wanted?'

'They could be larger here' – I pointed – 'but that's the thickness of the chest top.'

'I'd make them larger.' She nodded. 'You willing to trust me? Sight unseen?'

I was, though I couldn't say why, perhaps because of the lamp and sconce. Or because Liessa did. I nodded.

*WHHEEEE ... EEEEE ...*

I grabbed my staff and ran for the door. Merrin snatched a blade from somewhere and followed.

A young fellow in not much more than gray rags lay against the far wall, and another in a ripped and stained shirt had lifted a length of wood – a rough staff. He'd hit Gairloch once.

'... demon beast ...'

His eyes flicked up, and I was almost on top of him. With a clumsy swing, he tried to slam my midsection, but my staff was quicker and heavier, and his frail weapon went sailing. Then I thrust and twisted, and he went down like a sack of spilled flour next to the other man. Both groaned.

'Yense! I warned you.' Merrin stepped forward with the unsheathed blade toward the one Gairloch had knocked into the wall.

I glanced up the narrow street. A white-haired woman peered out from a half-open door, and a small boy, dressed in trousers and a rough tunic shaped from some sort of sacking, watched from a step across the narrow lane, his eyes darting to the partly open door behind him.

'Wasn't meaning trouble for you, Merrin ...'

'You're an idiot. You're almost a dead idiot, too.' The blade flicked, and a line of red marked Yense's cheek. 'That's my promise. The next time, you'll be dead. Get up, both of you!'

Both Yense and the man I had knocked down struggled to their feet. Something felt wrong, and my staff flicked almost without my direction.

*Clung! Clank!*

The unnamed man held his broken wrist and the long knife he had drawn from his ragged shirt lay on the uneven street stones.

'Don't you two ever learn?' snapped Merrin. 'This man is named Lerris. Does the name have any meaning? No, of course not. There's one wizard of that name in the city. He's killed a few dozen troops and several wizards with that staff. He's the only one in the whole city who rides a mountain pony, and you two are dumb enough to try to steal it. Neither of you is worth trying to save. Get out of here!'

The hatred in both sets of eyes seemed overlaid with fear, and then they stumbled down the lane, one blotting his cheek, the other holding a broken wrist.

Merrin reached down and scooped up the knife. 'Not bad work. Stolen, of course.' She looked at me. 'Shall we finish?'

I patted Gairloch, and offered a touch of order-healing to the welt on his flank. 'All right, fellow . . .'

*Whufffff . . .*

'If we leave the door open,' I said.

'Fine.' She shrugged. 'But no one around here will mess with you now. That's one reason why I put on the show. It works better than killing them, most times anyway.'

As I shook my head, I got the definite feeling that there had been a few dead bodies at her door.

'For a man who's certainly a warrior, you don't seem that pleased.' She stepped back into the shop.

I glanced back at Gairloch and moved the chair so I could see him through the open door. 'I'm not.'

'Neither am I, but some people only respect force. Like that idiot in Certis. Or Hamor. Or poor dumb Yense.' She set the blade down. 'Now . . . how thick do you want these hinges?'

As we talked, and negotiated, I kept looking out at Gairloch, but no one came anywhere close.

I left three silvers for a deposit.

'You'll like them. I promise.' She watched from the door until I was riding Gairloch uphill and away from the south bluff section. Behind me, the heavy door shut with a dull clunk.

Force – why did some people only respect force? I shook my head and kept my hand on the staff as I rode slowly back through Kyphrien.

# LXIV

Dayala – silver-haired and her age distinguishable from that of a young girl only by the darkness behind her pupils and the barely visible fine lines radiating from the corners of those too-wise eyes – stood before the sand table of the Great Forest of Naclos.

'What will be, will be, but let me see the course of the Balance and the vision of the sands.' She bowed, then straightened.

She stopped speaking and concentrated on the sands. In time, a map of eastern Candar began to appear. Piercing green eyes fixed on the sands, and sweat beaded on her forehead, though her hands remained by her side, seemingly relaxed.

In time a small spike of sand appeared on the thin line of darker sand that represented the road from Weevett through Certis to Jellico. She nodded. Patches of ugly reddish sand continued to churn up around the Great North Bay and at a point in Sligo that bordered Freetown.

For several long moments, she studied the map before taking another deep breath and concentrating once more. A wave of darkness spread from the southeast and began to creep toward the chaos. Another appeared at the edge of the Great North Bay and began to creep westward.

Then, the sand sprayed into the air in a column, with the force of a contained explosion.

Dayala stepped back, then turned away, and rivulets of tears streamed down her cheeks as she walked out into the ordered darkness of the grove beyond.

# LXV

I had sketched out the plans for Wegel's room, and gone over them with him before I went back to work on Antona's desk. 'I'll help when you need it, but it's basically your job.'

Wegel had just nodded.

'You're going to do most of the work.'

'F-f-fine.'

'Now ... let's get on with this. While I'm setting up, you can bring the fire up and sweep out the sawdust and small scraps.'

He looked at the floor and then at me.

'I know. It's cleaner than most places, but I like it cleaner than that. It also means that we don't get sawdust in the glue and that we're not sneezing nearly as much. Besides, I get upset when things aren't neat.'

Wegel shrugged and limped over to the corner alcove where the broom was racked on pegs.

I checked the plans again, and then began planing and smoothing the next set of drawer guides for the left pedestal. I kept glancing at Wegel, but he seemed to work with a will. An apprentice? It was hard to believe.

Wegel had just finished with the hearth and the sweeping when the enclosed gray carriage with the matched chestnuts rolled across the drying mud of the yard and stopped outside the walk to the shop. No insignia marked the glassed door, but I knew who the occupant had to be.

The driver and the guard wore heavy quilted jackets. The guard still carried the crossbow, but also a blade and a heavy pistol. A long spear was set in a holder behind his shoulder. I'd seen more pistols in the last eight-days than I had in years, and I didn't like what that foreshadowed. If people were using more pistols, it meant that firearms were working better, and that meant more order in the world. Somehow, I felt that had something to do with the groaning chaos beneath Candar, but how had I really had enough time to figure it out?

Antona stepped out, not wearing the fur coat I had half expected, but a long green quilted coat.

'Lady Antona ...' I bowed. After all, she had commissioned a fifty-gold desk set.

'Master Lerris?' She laughed. 'Must you persist in according me undeserved honors?'

'Any customer is due honors.'

'Especially when one has not delivered?' she asked mildly, the stonegray eyes raking over me.

'Especially.'

She walked toward the shop, and I walked beside her, not really having any choice. I could have trailed her, but that didn't appeal to me.

'You're no longer limping.'

'Not until I get tired.' I opened the door for her.

She looked around the shop, and then at Wegel, who was refilling the moisture pot.

'That Faslik's boy?'

'Yes. That's Wegel. I've been looking for an apprentice for a while.'

'Good help is hard to find ... even in my enterprises. Or perhaps I should say, especially in my enterprises.' The coat fell partly open in the warmth of the shop, and I caught a glimpse of the same green silk shirt, or another like it, the brushed gray leather trousers and vest.

'Since I am not familiar with your enterprises ...' I inclined my head without finishing the sentence.

'Every business takes help and talent.' Her eyes took in Wegel. 'You choose carefully, don't you?'

An odd comment, since she clearly knew of Wegel, and his misshapen foot and limp were obvious as he carried the bucket back to the shelf in the corner and racked it.

'I try, Lady.'

'What do you have to show me?'

'Not so much as I would like, as I suspect you know.' I led her toward the flat board at the end of the bench that served for my plans and rough drafting. It took a moment, but I lifted out the plans and the sketches.

'You have only sketches?' Again, her voice was mild.

'No.' I laughed. 'But I want to show you how it is being put together, and the sketches help.'

I smoothed the papers on the flat wood. 'Cherry is not quite so heavy as oak or lorken, but it is not a light wood, either, and the proper internal structure and braces are important. Here are the four main internal beams for the pedestal – it's the same on each side. Each has to be notched just so, and —'

'I think I can see that.'

'Fine.' I walked to the corner where her piece was taking shape, more slowly than I would have liked. 'Here are the pedestals ...'

'They look like the drawing.'

I certainly hoped so.

'What will you do next?'

'The drawers.'

'Why don't you do the top part first?'

'That comes next. In a way, I have to do the fronts of the drawers and the top together. That's so all the grains match.' I nodded toward the wood racks. 'There is the wood ...'

'That looks like more than you'll need.'

'It is, and it isn't. You're paying for a perfect piece, or as perfect as I can make it.' When she offered a faint smile at the term 'perfect piece,' I tried not to hesitate. 'That takes more wood, because I want to keep the grain widths the same on all the exposed surfaces. It sometimes takes a while to select the wood. Good crafting starts with good wood.'

Behind Antona, Wegel nodded.

'Everything starts with good material.' Antona smiled. 'I learned that early enough.'

Not knowing what to say, exactly, I just nodded.

'You have managed better than I would have expected, given the reports of your exploits, Master Lerris. Have you other exploits planned?' Her eyebrows lifted.

'I have no others planned, but I didn't have the last set planned, either. I must bow to the needs of the autarch.'

'And her commander, no doubt.' She smiled. 'Wise man.'

How wise I really might be was another question, but I nodded and followed her back out to the coach and waited until it was out of sight and headed back to Kyphrien.

After that, I went back to drawer guides, and explaining what I was doing to Wegel. Then I let him work on possible ideas for carving the *A* for a while before we took a break for a midday meal, which we shared with Kilbon, who had stopped by to deliver some potatoes, except we all knew he'd come for more than potatoes. Wegel and I left Rissa and Kilbon in the kitchen.

By mid-afternoon, I finished the last of the drawer guides on the left side. Since I was getting bored – I still did sometimes – I decided to take on Durrik's chest for a change.

'Wegel. I'm going to work on these.' I pointed to the blanks that would become drawer fronts for Durrik's chest. 'There's not much for you to do. So you can start on the framing for your room. You'll have to lay the sills . . .'

He looked blank, and I tried not to sigh, instead adding, 'Let's go out to the stable building.'

After I showed him what he needed to do, he smiled. I knew I'd have to check up, but he might as well have something he was responsible for from the beginning.

I could hear the noises of the saw and of the hammer as I continued with the drawer fronts.

Every so often, I trudged across the yard, which was finally drying out in the warming winds that preceded spring, to check on Wegel. I made him reset one sill, because it was clear he hadn't really used the level – probably because he needed to chop through a ridge of clay and lay another line of stones – but he got the idea, and only looked somewhat sheepish.

Both Wegel and I were tired, long before I lit the big lantern, and long before Krystal rode in, but he kept working and so did I – but only until I heard the horses.

Krystal looked tired, too, and I could sense the dull aching in her arm as she dismounted.

'Long day?'

She shook her head, and I hugged her gently. Then she looked down at the tracks in the yard. 'You had visitors today.'

Wegel smiled from the kitchen door, as did Rissa.

I gave a wry grin. 'Antona. She was not totally pleased, I think, at my progress on her desk – even if she did say something about being surprised at how much I had done given my exploits. At least, she didn't come two eight-days earlier.'

'Sometimes darkness does favor you, Lerris.' She shook her head, taking the reins and leading the black gelding toward the stable.

'Sometimes?' asked Jinsa from the shadows.

'You want to be "favored" the way he was in Hydlen, Jinsa?' asked Haithen.

'I take that back.'

'You'd better,' said Perron with a half-laugh.

After I helped groom the gelding, both Krystal and I washed up, and then headed for the kitchen. My stomach was growling. So was Krystal's.

'A long time since you ate?' I asked.

'Breakfast.' Krystal sank into the chair at the end of the table. 'I need to enjoy this while I can. The demon's hell has opened up in Freetown.'

'Not that it could happen to a finer place.' Rissa set the platter of sliced mutton on the table, and followed it with a bowl heaped high with noodles and a dark gravy. 'What with all those dukes that love to fight and kill.'

The four guards leaned forward, but waited for us to serve ourselves.

Krystal helped herself, and I followed before passing the platter to Wegel and asking, 'What happened in Freetown?'

'Hamor. Nearly threescore ships and five thousand troops. They executed Colaris.'

'Executed him?' I asked.

'Good stuff,' mumbled Dercas, grabbing for the bread.

'If it's hot, you think it's good,' said Jinsa. 'This is really good. You don't know how lucky you are.'

'I do,' said Haithen quietly, giving me a wink.

Krystal caught the wink and smiled.

Haithen swallowed and flushed.

'I understand,' was all Krystal said, but the hand in her lap reached across and squeezed my thigh.

'Understand what?' mumbled Dercas.

'Like every man, you miss it all.' Jinsa laughed.

'What about Freetown?' I asked.

Krystal shrugged. 'We don't know everything. Hamor pulled its long guns from Colaris's troops – the ones fighting Berfir. Most of the officers left, and the troops retreated. Who wants to get killed fighting for a dead duke? The better officers and their forces have thrown in with Hamor. The others have scattered, but Berfir is, or was, marching toward Freetown. Maybe he thinks he can take the place before Hamor is fully in control. I don't know.' She stopped and took a long deep swallow of the ale.

'This makes things difficult for you.'

'You don't know how difficult. With all those Hamorian ships, I can't pull troops out of Ruzor. Do we reinforce the port and hope we don't need the troops along the Little Easthorns?' Krystal set the mug down.

'Do you think the Prefect of Gallos will try something?'

'I don't think so. Then, I knew Hamor was up to something, but I hadn't figured on an invasion of Freetown. It makes sense, though.'

'How?' asked Perron quietly.

Krystal took another pull of ale before answering. 'Colaris had all his forces out to the south trying to stop Berfir. Because Hamor was providing the long guns and supplies, no one probably paid much attention to the first Hamorian ships, and by the time they did, it was too late.'

'A lot of the folks in Freetown probably weren't all that fond of Duke Colaris anyway,' added Rissa.

'After what he did to Duke Holloric's people, I can't possibly see why,' said Haithen dryly.

'Good sauce,' mumbled Dercas.

'All you think about is food,' said Jinsa.

'Got to eat.' Dercas sounded indignant. 'Can't do much about invasions and ships. I can enjoy food, though.'

Rissa nodded, and I had to agree with at least part of what he said.

'Going to be a real mess around Freetown,' observed Perron.

'I hope we don't have to head there anytime soon.' Haithen broke off a chunk of bread.

Krystal ate deliberately, without speaking, and even her strokes with her knife were slow, a sure sign that she was exhausted.

'Think Berfir will pull back once the Hamorians get organized?' Dercas spat out bread fragments with the question.

'Dercas!' snapped Jinsa. 'You're disgusting.'

'That's being too nice,' added Haithen.

'Autarch doesn't pay me to be nice ... pays me to fight and guard the commander.'

'Enough.' Perron broke off a corner of bread with a crack.

Wegel seemed to sink lower with each bite of lamb and noodles, and dinner was over before long.

Krystal trudged to the bedroom, and I followed.

'You're going to Ruzor, then?' After helping her pull off her boots, I set them in the corner by the wardrobe.

'Before long. It makes sense.'

I understood. Except for the south, all Kyphros's borders were defined by mountains, and much of the terrain near those borders was less than hospitable. The Little Easthorns were the least defensible, but even the new Prefect of Gallos probably wasn't insane enough to start another war with Kyphros with the Empire of Hamor knocking at the door.

With the size of the Hamorian fleet, Ruzor was clearly the most vulnerable point, and Kasee had less than a handful of ships, none really more than steam-powered and armed merchant ships.

I thought for a moment. 'Kyphros really can't be the first target.'

'No. Hamor will take the trading ports first, then slowly choke the rest of us.'

'It'll take a long time to choke Kyphros.'

'That's why Kasee's worried.'

'Oh.' I understood, or I thought I did. By the time Hamor got to Kyphros, Kasee would have no allies and no negotiating room. And Leithrrse would know that – so Hamor could put a lot of early pressure. If Kasee refused to submit, then Hamor would make an example – assuming the Emperor were successful in overrunning the rest of eastern Candar. If he could put nearly threescore ships in the Great North Bay, I didn't have any doubts that there were a lot more ships and men on the way – and a lot more cannon and cartridges.

'She won't negotiate. She can't.'

'No. She'll hope for a miracle.'

I didn't like that, especially since people in Kyphros looking for miracles seemed to head in my direction.

'There's another problem that might affect you,' she added.

'I need another problem. I really do.'

'One of Kasee's more reliable sources says that the Hamorian envoy has made several visits to Sammel.' Krystal struggled out of her leathers.

'That's interesting.' What was I supposed to do about that? If Krystal wanted some help in Ruzor ... that was one thing, but wandering all over Candar wasn't going to finish desks and chests or bring in the coins to keep things going. And what could I do with Sammel, anyway? Try and stop him from providing information and scrolls? With Hamor in Freetown, it was somewhat late to worry about the past spread of once-hidden knowledge.

'I hoped you wouldn't be that interested.' She pulled on an old soft shirt and turned back the new quilt.

'It is interesting,' I admitted. 'But I don't see what I can do. So far as we can tell, even if there is a lot of chaos around Sammel, nothing else is happening, and any white wizard is going to gather chaos.'

'A lot of the devices seem to have been his idea.' Krystal stretched out on the bed.

'What can I do? Everyone seems to have already used the ideas. I can't make them disappear.'

'I don't know. I don't know.' She sighed. 'I do know that nothing I can do will be enough to save Kyphros once Hamor really brings in troops and those new rifles. Kasee knows that, too. I just hoped you might have some ideas.' She added. 'Just ideas. Just ideas.'

Ideas? I had lots of ideas, but most of them dealt with making desks and chests – or getting Wegel to finish his own spaces. Sammel wasn't raising an army, and for the first time in seasons, no one was directly attacking or threatening Kyphros.

'Can Kasee get some rifles?'

'Right now, to outfit just the Finest would cost more than the Treasury. They'd all have to be smuggled in. Mureas is looking into it, though.'

'Oh ...' I sat there for a moment. Then I snuffed the lamp and pulled the quilt around me, before leaning across the bed and kissing Krystal's cheek. She seemed so exhausted.

'Hold me. Just hold me.'

My consort? My competent consort who carried powder across Kyphros on her mount and risked being blown skyward at any moment? The woman who had survived double-crosses and rigged duels? I just held her.

After a time, she shivered once, and wrapped her arms around me. 'Sometimes, Lerris, I don't say what I feel. I see you here, and you're so solid, like the very darkness itself. You deal with everything from chaos to chickens, and you care for people like Wegel and Rissa.' She shivered again. 'All you ask – but you don't ask, you hope – is that I love you. I do love you. Sometimes, though, sometimes, I get afraid.'

I held her without asking why.

'I worry that you don't understand how everything can change in a moment. We never think. Ferrel had a daughter. Eldra's just joined the Finest. I never knew Ferrel had a daughter. One day Ferrel rode out, and she never rode back. We don't have children, and I hope we can. But I can't now, not right now. Kasee needs me, and we don't have anyplace else to call home.'

'Things are getting better, now, with the crafting.' Still, I had to wonder. Would I have gotten the commission from Zeiber if Krystal hadn't been the commander? Preltar was another question. I doubt he even knew Krystal and I were consorts. Antona? I really didn't know. But just as things seemed to be looking up, here came the invasion of Freetown by Hamor – didn't anything ever settle down?

'And as soon as they do,' Krystal said, with another shiver,' something like this mess with Hamor happens. Won't it ever end?'

I didn't have any answers, not any that I wanted to voice. So I kept holding her in the darkness and tried not to think about Hamor and Sammel. Or the cost of smuggled rifles. Or the need to make powder. Or the chaos building below Candar.


# LXVI


The Countess of Montgren – a white-haired, lean, and tanned woman in spotless light blue leathers – waited by the edge of the corral filled with sheep. Beside her stood two guards, carrying rifles and wearing short blades.

Justen brushed back short hair that bore more than mere traces of silver. Tamra took a deep breath, trying not to sag against the fence rails, then brushed away a large fly that circled back toward her again.

*Baa . . . baaa . . . baahhh . . .*

Behind the two mages, the sheep continued to mill in the corral, and the odors of raw wool, dust, and dung accompanied the noise.

The redheaded mage sneezed and wiped her nose, then wiped it again.

'Is it almost as bad as three years ago?' asked the Countess Merella of Montgren.

Justen blotted his forehead. 'Worse, I think. Or I'm older and more tired.'

Tamra took another deep breath, letting her senses flick across the animals in the corral, feeling the scattered white chaos.

'What happened to your last apprentice?' asked the Countess.

'He's done fine ... if you consider destroying three white wizards and nearly getting killed twice a form of success. He's a woodcrafter in Kyphros most of the time.' The gray wizard looked at the Countess, then around the area. The bodyguards stood well back from the three. 'What are you going to do about Hamor?'

'What can I do?' The Countess shrugged. 'My guard is less than twentyscore, and I could raise perhaps a thousand in levies, as the Hamorian envoy has been so kind as to point out.'

She smiled bitterly. 'My daughter and son both died, not long after Herril, and I have no direct heirs. That makes it easy. My nephew is not pleased, but he understands.'

'You name the throne of Hamor as your heir, and you administer Montgren for the Emperor?' asked Justen.

'You have a better answer, Mage?'

Justen shook his head slowly.

'That way, my people don't suffer again the way they did when mad Korweil defied Frven. The hilltop where his keep sat still won't grow more than thistles and grass.' Her eyes twinkled for a moment. 'As for wizardry ... I have no desire for Vergren to look like Frven or the deadlands – assuming I could find a willing wizard.'

Tamra's eyes grew hard, but she said nothing, even after the Countess turned to her.

'There's an obligation to ruling, Magistra, just like there is an obligation to magic.' Merella nodded curtly, and turned to Justen. 'Tomorrow ... the pens outside Vergren?'

Justen nodded.

After the Countess and her guards had left, Tamra asked, 'What was that business about mad Korweil?'

'Korweil was the Duke who gave Creslin and Megaera sanctuary – you know, the Founders of Recluce. He thought he could hold off the wizards. They burned most of the meadows, killed most of the flocks, and leveled his keep.'

'Could Hamor do that?'

'There's not much difference between a firebolt and a good cannon – not now, except that all those ships and cannon create free chaos through the Balance, a great deal more than I – or Recluce – ever anticipated.'

'Can't you use order to control it?'

'Absolutely.' Justen offered a hard smile before asking, 'Do you want to be the one who tries to channel it? That's what Lerris did, you know.'

'Oh . . . Will he try it again?'

'Given Lerris, probably. But I don't really want to be anywhere near when he does.'

'Will we have a choice?' Tamra persisted.

Justen lifted his shoulders and dropped them. 'We've got a lot more sheep waiting. You can start.'

# LXVII

Krystal had been in Ruzor for more than an eight-day when Durrik the spice merchant rode up one morning, early enough that Wegel was still attending to his chores, and I had barely gotten into the shop after practicing with the staff in the stable. I was getting better at hitting the moving bag more times in a row. With a soft cloth I was dusting away a thin coat of the red dust that had begun to drift into the shop with the warmer weather when I heard hoofs and went out into the yard. Outside the shop, the sky was clear and bright, and the first blades of grass were peering from the fields and around the yard.

After Durrik reined up and dismounted, I escorted him into the shop where his chest was taking shape, alongside Antona's desk, and Preltar's daughter's dowry chest. It was amazing how much work I was able to get done when someone else did the chores and when I wasn't riding all over Candar.

'There's your chest.' I gestured at the light oak chest, almost completed except for the finishing. It was farther along than any of the others.

'It's . . . striking . . .' Durrik's fingers brushed the wood, and I could tell he was pleased. He walked around it and looked, finally turning to me. 'It's better than I paid for.'

He was right, but young crafters are usually underpaid, just as some older ones are often overpaid.

Then Durrik looked at Wegel, who was racking the broom. 'Young fellow, if you can learn half of what your master has already learned, you'll never have to starve anywhere.'

Wegel gave Durrik a slow smile. 'Y-y-yes, s-ss-ser . . .'

Durrik's fingers brushed the wood on the side of the chest again. 'I wish I could offer you more, but times are hard, and getting harder.' The spice trader wiped his forehead, although the shop wasn't that hot – not yet.

'The Hamorian traders?' I asked.

'That . . . and spice prices. The ones that come by sea – they're hard to get, and the prices keep going up. If I don't charge what they cost me, I lose coins. If I do, only the wealthy can buy. Even some spices from Sarronnyn are getting dear.'

'From Sarronnyn?' I'd opened the mountain roads three years earlier. Why were Sarronnese spices getting dearer?

'They've got the same problem I do. You can't make coins on high-priced imported spices, and so you up the price where you can. I'm selling tresselwood needles at twice what I was a year ago. I don't like it, but what can I do?'

All that because Hamor controlled perhaps five ports? Except the ports weren't the problem, but the shipping.

'It's going to get worse. The Hamorian fleet is intercepting ships headed to Recluce.'

'They can't get every one,' I offered.

'They don't have to. Who wants to take that kind of risk when the Hamorians pay fairly well?'

'I'm surprised Recluce has not done something.' And I was. Recluce needed trade. Why hadn't the Brotherhood struck back?

'They may yet,' Durrik said with a half-shrug. 'If they don't . . .'

I understood the shrug. If Recluce didn't do something fairly soon, whatever the Brotherhood did would probably be too late, although I wasn't quite sure what they could do – or if I wanted to know.

'I was glad to see the chest, but that wasn't why I came.' Durrik handed me a flat envelope with a black wax seal. 'This is a letter from your family, and I said I'd get it to you.'

'What do I owe you?'

'Nothing. It's always paid on the other end.' Durrik grinned. 'Even if it weren't, I couldn't take anything after looking at the chest.'

He clapped me on the shoulder. 'Best I be going. You want to send a letter back – I'll find a way to get it there. Might be roundabout, but I can do it.'

'Thank you. I'll let you know.'

After the spice merchant left, I walked out into the yard and halfway up the hill – just to be alone when I opened the letter. I wasn't totally alone, though. A big horsefly kept circling around, an omen of what might be a long and hot summer.

I swatted at the horsefly, but it kept circling. So I had to set a low-level ward before it buzzed off to bother someone else. The black wax of the seal cracked evenly, and I opened the envelope and began to read.

Dear Lerris,

Your letter was most welcome, and your father and I were glad to hear that you are well and prospering. I told Sardit and Elisabet about your work as a crafter, but Sardit just smiled. Apparently, your name is somewhat known in the woodcrafting circles already. That may be why he has always insisted you were fine. He said to tell you that Perlot was both relieved and sad that you had left Fenard.

Corso and Koldar also send their best. She had a daughter last fall, and named her Betina. Your aunt Elisabet was amused and pleased, I think.

Your father says that these are troubling times, and that Recluce may be caught between the chaos of Candar and the forced order of Hamor . . .

I shook my head. The chaos of Candar had been and continued to be a creation of Recluce. For my father to deny that was . . . I didn't even quite have the words for it.

. . . neither of which will be good for the Balance. He said to tell you that the Balance works both ways, and that it does not matter whether order or chaos comes first – there will be a balance . . .

I frowned at that. My father, even as relayed by my mother's hand, was sounding suspiciously like Justen. Then why shouldn't he? They were brothers.

. . . when the time comes, you may need to come to Recluce, but that must be your choice . . .

Of course it would be my choice. Who else's would it be?

The trees bore well last year, even the sourpears . . .

When I thought about it, I hadn't seen either sourpears or chrysnets in Candar. Were they something that the old order-masters had created for Recluce, back before the great change?

The rest of the letter dealt with more routine news, and I read through it quickly before I folded the letter back into the envelope and walked back to the shop, where I tucked it into the box with my other papers, wondering why my father's secondhand words had upset me.

'Wegel . . . let's look at that cedar. We'll start with the inside frame sections on this dowry chest . . .'

He only scratched one section by trying to smooth it too quickly, something I'd done more than once for Uncle Sardit.

Just after I clamped the corners on one inside frame, the creaking of the wagon, and Rissa's words to the mare came through the open window beside the door.

'Now, you be stopping right where you are, you old woman . . .'

Long before she could have stabled the old mare, she marched into the shop.

'No chickens, Master Lerris?' She lifted the basket of eggs. 'Eggs is all I can get from Brene, now. No chickens. If we had our own, it'd be a different story. Even at a silver a chicken she won't sell, maybe three for a gold, but I wasn't about to be buying chickens for golds. Not me. Not without talking to you.'

'Three chickens for a gold?'

'Everything's like that. People are getting a-feared of the Emperor.'

I didn't understand at all. It would take well over a year for the Hamorian forces to reach Kyphros, even if Kasee had already dropped dead. Who knew what would happen in a year?

'That's madness. There aren't any Hamorians within six hundred kays.'

'That might be so, Master Lerris, but folks are scared, and scared folks think with their hearts and not their heads. Sometimes they think with their feet, too. Like Brene. Old Brene's talking about selling her chickens and going out to visit Tyglit —'

'Tyglit?'

'That'll be her oldest. Tyglit lives out in the trade village near Upper River, toward the Westhorns. That be one of those places where the grasslands people trade come winter. Anyway, Tyglit lives out there, and not even the Hamorians like those grasslands.' She lifted the basket. 'Makes no matter. She goes, and we got no eggs, either.'

I surrendered.

'How many chickens can you buy?'

'If I bought a couple of hens and a young cock, Brene might let'em all go for a gold.'

'Fine. I'll get you the coins. Just keep them out of the shop.'

'You be asking me to head right back out to Brene's, after I just been there?'

'You've been asking me about chickens for nearly a year, and now you practically tell me we're in danger of going hungry if we don't get chickens . . .'

'Master Lerris . . . some days, I never be understanding you.'

I went into the bedroom and dragged out my purse. There was enough there without going into the strongbox hidden behind the storeroom wall off the shop.

'Here is a gold and three silvers. Try not to use the silvers.'

'I'll be a-trying everything.'

I didn't watch her drive back out the southwestern road, but went back to mixing the finish for Durrik's chest.

Wegel set down his knife.

'Let's see what you wrote on the cherry, Wegel.'

He brought over his box, and I flipped through the cards. 'Cherry . . . hmmm . . . why didn't you write anything about how brittle it is?'

'Br-br-brittle . . . ?'

I looked at him. 'Get me a scrap of cherry – a little one.'

He looked down at the floor, which needed sweeping, and then trudged over to the scrap box.

'Take your knife. Try to cut it. No, not at an angle; just saw it . . .'

He looked horrified, as well he might. I was asking him to break a blade.

'Don't you see? You have to work the grain. It's too hard . . .' Finally, I could see he understood. 'Now, that's what I want you to put on the card.' I handed him his box back.

At that point, I let Wegel go out to the stable and work on putting up the wall boards. The floor was in, although it needed smoothing, and so was the door to the yard. Later, Wegel could put in a window, but I'd have to buy the glass, and he'd have to make his own bed.

Still, he whistled at times when he worked, and he always watched closely when I asked him to.

I went back to work on Preltar's chest – until Rissa returned. I still needed to do more on Zeiber's case, but that would have to wait.

'Master Lerris . . .' said Rissa.

*Braaaawkkk . . . awwkkkk . . . aaawwwk . . .*

'You got the chickens, I hear.'

'Seeing as you had the extra silver, I got four hens and a scrawny young cock – just for a gold and a silver.'

She handed me back the extra silvers, but I let her keep one, and I tried to ignore the squawking and clucking.

'Master Lerris, we'll need a coop or a henhouse for them. I can put them in the stable now, but won't be long 'fore the cats and —'

'I understand, Rissa.' Of course, no one had mentioned a coop, but I should have figured that out as well.

That night, after having to stop work on the dowry chest to help Wegel with the corner framing that he hadn't done right, after drawing a rough plan for the henhouse, after listening to Rissa's praise of chickens, and the distant *braaawkk . . . brawk* from the stable, and finally eating something that was hotter than burkha and heavier than leaden oak, I washed up in cold water and sat on the bench on the porch for a while, looking at the stars above the horizon and wondering.

Life wasn't supposed to be quite this way. I was older, but I didn't have as many coins, not really, as when I'd been a journeyman for Destrin. I'd found someone I loved, but it seemed like I saw her less and less. I was becoming known as a crafter, and yet I had to bargain more and more, rather than less and less.

Since I was tired, and my leg still ached when I was tired, I stood up and headed inside to the empty bedroom, where I undressed slowly.

With another deep breath, I turned back the quilt and climbed into bed, looking toward the other side, the empty other side. Krystal was still in Ruzor, and probably would be for a time, maybe a long time. So was Kasee, and so were most of the Finest, trying to ready the city against the Hamorians.

I took another deep breath, trying to ignore, for the moment, the distant order-chaos rumbling.

*Grrrurrrr . . . grurrrrr . . .*

Deep in the night, deep beneath Candar, chaos and order warred, and I tossed in an empty bed.


# LXVIII

## Nylan, Recluce


The former trader strides into the Council Room.

'You look upset, Maris.' Heldra pours greenberry into her mug, then wipes her forehead with a white cloth. 'Darkness, it's hot this spring.'

'I am upset. Worrying about the weather! At times like this?'

'It's hot everywhere, Gunnar says. Underlying chaos, he claims.' Talryn fingers his mug.

Maris turns and steps up to the window. Beads of sweat ooze from his forehead, but he does not wipe them away. Finally, he turns back to face the other two. 'Those Hamorian warships ... now, they're intercepting traders from Candar.'

'And what might they be doing with those traders, eating them for breakfast?' The short and broad mage sets down the mug.

'This is serious.'

'Oh, I agree,' says Heldra, before taking another long swallow of the cold juice.

'They're paying half the declared value of the shipments to Nylan – or throwing them overboard.'

'That is serious.' Talryn leans back in his chair.

'You two, you don't understand,' snaps Maris. 'That means Hamor gets the goods at half price and the traders from Candar still make some coins. They'll bitch, but they won't risk smuggling or breaking the embargo.'

'I said it was serious,' points out Talryn. 'I might as well joke a little. There's not much humor anywhere right now.'

'They sank the *Grestensea*.'

'I presume because the captain didn't want his cargo tossed into the Gulf and tried to outrun them.' Talryn takes the greenberry pitcher.

'Everything he owned was on the ship. You think it's funny? I don't understand you two. I really don't. Enough is enough.'

'Oh, I see,' says Talryn. 'You want us to send our mighty trio up against – what is it now? – fivescore armored warships, and say, "We won't put up with this anymore"?'

'You're saying we can't match their ships?'

'We've had the trio there for half a season, and we've gotten four of their ships. They've added a score more. You can figure the arithmetic,' answers Talryn.

'Or perhaps,' adds Heldra, 'you think we should take our two thousand-odd armed Brothers and marines and send them out against the close to ten thousand Hamorian soldiers already in Candar? They should charge the Hamorians – using good black steel swords – and let themselves get cut down by those nasty new Hamorian rifles? That's good arithmetic, too.'

'What are we going to do?' demands Maris. 'All you do is ask impossible questions.'

'You want direct action, like everyone new to the Council does,' points out Talryn, 'like I once did. But we don't have the resources for the actions you want. We can whittle away at Hamor, but we never have had the resources to take on the Empire directly, at least not since the fall of Fairhaven.'

'Impossible questions are important.' Heldra smiles. 'They lead to answers.'

'Sometimes,' adds Talryn. 'But we try.'

'What have you two come up with now? Do I want to know?' Maris slams his hand on the table. 'No. I'd be a fool to want to know.'

'We'll have to take the fight to those who count.' Heldra draws her blade, almost carelessly, and sights along the edge.

'Your black squads?' demands Maris. 'Is that wise?'

'Hardly, but we're beyond wise choices.' Heldra looks at the blade and replaces it in the scabbard. 'We were selected, like you, Maris, to preserve order with a minimum of taxes and resources, and to avoid changing our society much. Every time we suggest something, you ask how we'll pay for it. Until it affects you traders, and now you want us to act – immediately. Well ... we'll act, as best we can, with three ships and a relative handful of troops.'

'You're going along with this?' Maris asks Talryn.

'Rignelgio or Leithrrse?' Talryn asks Heldra, his tone somewhere between disgusted and idle, as his eyes ignore Maris.

'Both, and the commander of the Hamorian forces in Freetown. Also the Hamorian fleet flagships. Of course, it will require pulling one of the trio off station for nearly a season. You'll recall' – she turns to Maris – 'that was why we didn't send another set of black squads against Sammel. It would have taken one of the trio away from Dellash for three eight-days, and we thought that destroying Hamorian warships had a higher priority. We might have been wrong, but' – she shrugs – 'it's so much easier to decide that after you've made the wrong decision.'

'What are you two talking about?' asks Maris.

'Holding those who make decisions or who are responsible for carrying them out personally accountable for those decisions,' says Heldra.

'You're mad.'

'No,' says Talryn slowly. 'Not mad. Just late.'

'Would you mind explaining? I'm just a dumb trader, here because the Guild would like to know what happens before it happens – at least once in a while.'

Talryn leans forward, and his eyes darken. 'One of the problems in dealing with empires and large countries is that those who make the decisions never suffer the consequences. One way or another, we have been moderately successful in visiting consequences on those in Candar who create unfortunate circumstances, such as the previous Duke of Freetown. You may recall that Duke Colaris did not attempt to repeat the policies of Duke Halloric toward us. Unfortunately, Hamor is more than a third of the globe away. Now that the Emperor has sent senior commanders and envoys, they shall have the opportunity to experience the same treatment as they have visited on others.'

'You are mad,' whispers Maris. He turns to Heldra. 'You're going to lead them, I suppose?'

'No,' says Talryn. 'Before long, we'll probably still face an attack here. We don't need counselors running all over the Eastern Ocean. We'll also probably have to explain this to the Guild and the Brotherhood. Everyone wants explanations when there's trouble. They can't be bothered otherwise.'

'You're both mad.'

Talryn shrugs. 'No. If we do nothing, Hamor will own Candar over the next five years. If we try to fight directly, we will be overwhelmed. So . . . we fight those who make decisions, and those who command.'

'But there are others who will take their places.'

'For how long?' asks Heldra.

# LXIX

'That's it. Hold it there.' I hammered the plank in place, and the back wall of the henhouse was complete. After taking a deep breath, I wiped the sweat off my forehead on my ragged sleeve.

The *braawkking* of one of the hens seemed but cubits away, even though all were somewhere on the other side of the stable.

'Th-this side?' asked Wegel, brushing away a large horsefly. The horsefly circled back in for another nip, and Wegel smashed it flat against the bracing timber, then wiped his hand on his trousers.

'Might as well. I'm tired of tripping on chickens, even if I do like eggs. Maybe we'll have enough to eat a few by fall. Chickens, not eggs.'

Wegel grinned.

'Get another plank.'

He kept grinning, but we only got two more planks done before we heard hoofs.

I recognized the small man with the peaked cap of green and white plaid wool, even before he vaulted from his mount – a big white stallion of the kind I never wanted to ride. Preltar tied the horse to the post with quick turns of the leather reins.

'Master Preltar. Have you come to inquire about the progress of your daughter's dowry chest?'

'Quite so. Quite so.' He rubbed his hands together, then followed me into the shop where he pulled off the wool cap and held it in both hands.

Wegel followed us inside and looked at his carving. I nodded. He might as well do some work on it while I talked to the wool factor. He couldn't put the heavy planks for the henhouse in place by himself.

Wegel wiped his hands on a rag, sat on the stool, then looked back down at the wood in his hand, without moving the knife.

I pointed to the chest, such as it was. 'I've refined the plans and set up the framing here, and cut the wood. Here are the inside sections . . .'

Preltar nodded as I explained. 'You're coming along well, Master Lerris. Yes, well. I must be frank. Frank, of course. The chest will be superb, I'm sure, but I would like something quite different. Quite different, and as soon as you could do it practically. I would pay a bit of a bonus. A bonus, you see.' He gestured with the cap, his bushy white eyebrows and unfocused expression giving the look of an absentminded hawk, were there such a bird.

A bonus I could deal with. 'What is this you would like?'

'A traveling storage chest, and I would like two of them. Two, if you please, and very functional, and light, but strong.'

'How large?' I went over to the drawing board.

'Most of the time they would be carried by wagon – but a horse should be able to carry one in an emergency.'

'Probably not much more than two cubits by a cubit and a half, and a cubit deep?' I used my hands to indicate a rough size.

'A shade bigger. Could they be a shade bigger?'

I laughed. 'They can be any size you wish. I was thinking about a horse having to carry one. I'd use fir, I think. That's the best for strength when you're worried about weight.'

'Fir?'

I shrugged. 'It's softer, and it will get dented and banged up more easily, but you'll save more than a stone in weight for a chest that size. That's one of the reasons sailing ships' masts are usually fir.'

'Ah, weight. Yes, they must be light. And so must the chests.'

'Fir,' I affirmed.

Preltar twisted the green and white wool cap in his hands, and I noticed that the moisture pot needed refilling, although it would not be long before the real heat would begin. That meant letting the wood dry over the summer, not something I was thrilled with, but a necessary concession to the climate.

'How soon could you finish these chests?'

I frowned. I was still working on Antona's desk, and Durrik's chest, and I still hadn't done much on Zeiber's bookcase. The traveling chests would be easy, and I knew Faslik had plenty of fir. Besides, a good shop has half a dozen pieces working at one time. Of course, I wasn't anywhere near that good. 'Three eight-days, perhaps sooner.' I should have been able to finish them in half that, but I was learning to give myself some margin.

'Three eight-days. Oh, that would be superb. Just superb.' The bushy eyebrows under the bald head knitted, and the hawk looked a lot less absentminded. 'The price. We did not discuss the price.'

'No, we didn't.'

'Fir is less expensive, is it not, and you did not mention ornamentation.'

'True. A chest that size in oak or cedar, as you know, would run close to ten golds.'

'But these are smaller than Hylera's chest, perhaps two thirds that size, and the fir cannot cost what the cedar does. It cannot. No, it cannot.'

'You are correct, Master Preltar, and I certainly never said that one of these chests would cost what Hylera's chest will. I presume you would want brasswork for the lock plates and hinges, and good crafting.'

'Ah, yes, good crafting. That was why I came to you.'

I shrugged. 'Five golds apiece.'

He didn't blink an eye, and that bothered me.

'Five apiece, yes, yes, we find that fair. Very fair. And, Master Lerris, if they are ready in three eight-days or less, a gold extra for each.' He beamed at me.

I liked that even less, but I bowed. 'We will certainly do our best.'

'And Hylera's chest ... when might that be ready?'

'I might, *might*, be able to have that ready around the same time.'

'Oh, superb . . . just superb. That would make matters so much simpler. Yes, simpler. Then, she could take . . . ah, but there's no reason to bore you with the details. Not the details. A gold extra for that if you could have it ready in no less than four eight-days.'

Preltar was in a hurry, a definite hurry.

'I take it that the Hamorian traders are on the move.' I smiled politely.

'The Hamorians? Their traders . . . terrible people, you know. Their cotton is cheap, not enduring like good Analerian wool, and they are so . . . demanding . . . very demanding.' He replaced his cap on his head, and bowed, then extended a gold to me. 'A token, just a token deposit, but . . . yes, just a token.'

I did take it, and nodded again. 'I'll be getting right on it, Master Preltar.' And I would be, in more ways than one. 'These chests . . . there seems to be a certain urgency about them.'

'Urgency. Well, Master Lerris, one must shear, yes, shear, when the wool is ready.'

'I've heard some people are worried that Hamor may move beyond Freetown and Delapra. What do you think?' I tried to make the question offhand.

'Me? Think? A mere wool factor, Master Lerris? How would I know?' He gave a jerky shrug. 'The Empire keeps growing, they say . . . yes, growing, and the Hamorians have warships in Southwind and Freetown, and who knows . . . who knows where they may go. I'm sure I don't. I'm sure I don't.' He put the cap on his head and bowed.

I inclined my head to him and followed him to the door.

'A good day, yes, a good day to you, Master Lerris.'

I tried not to shake my head until he was out of the yard on the big stallion. Then I walked back to the door of the shop and called for Wegel. 'Come on. We need to finish the demon-damned henhouse.'

'Master Lerris, ser . . . I'd thank you not to call down the white forces on our chickens . . .' Rissa stood by the kitchen door, broom in hand.

'Sorry, Rissa.' I wiped my forehead. The day was already hot, and it wasn't even midday, and still relatively early in the spring. And now the wool factor was worried enough to order shipping chests without really haggling over the costs.

That meant another trip to see Merrin, and more brasswork to pay for, and who knew what else.

# LXX

## Freetown Port, Freetown [Candar]

'Hamor! Hamor!' The chants rock the marketplace.

The dark-haired man in the tan uniform bows and raises his right hand as he steps forward onto the stones of the public stage. His wide brown leather belt bears only a short blade on the left, a small purse, and, on the right, a heavy short pistol in a leather holster that matches the belt perfectly. He is flanked by two soldiers carrying the cartridge rifles of Hamor. Behind him flutters a pale blue banner bearing the orange starburst of Hamor.

'Hamor! Hamor! . . .'

Less than twenty cubits away stands a slighter, fairer man, under a thin traveling cloak that covers also the uniform of Hamor. Unlike the man upon the stage, Leithrrse carries no knife, but both pistol and shortsword, and he studies the crowd for a time before turning his eyes to the stage. '. . . strut and prance your time upon the stage, Rignelgio.'

'Friends! Friends! This is a great day for Freetown and for you. No more endless wars between Freetown and Hydlen, no more conscriptions by yet another plotter calling himself the Duke. From here on, the forces of Hamor will protect you and yours . . .'

The light wind off the Great North Bay brings the smells of the sea, drying seaweed, sewage, and the smoke from the engines of the Hamorian warships.

Leithrrse snorts quietly as the speech continues, and his eyes study the crowd. He squints for a moment, as the scene beneath the market stage appears to waver before his eyes. He rubs his forehead, then blots away the sweat brought on by the intensity of the midday sun, despite the light breeze that sweeps through the square.

He looks back to the stage.

'. . . clothing that does not cost a fortune . . . goods that every family can purchase . . .'

'Hamor! Hamor! . . .'

*WHHHHSSSTTT!* A miniature sun flares from the crowd beneath the stage and explodes across the chest of the Emperor's regent, leaving an instantly charred mass of flames, that wavers, and then pitches forward into the crowd, which scatters away from the feebly flailing column of charcoal.

'Eeee . . . eeee . . .'

'Magic!'

'Demonspawn!'

Leithrrse flings off the cloak and bounds up the stone steps.

'Fire! There!' He points toward the slight wavering in the air that seems to flow even faster than the fleeing crowd.

'Ser?'

'NOW!' His pistol is in his hand, and he cocks and fires the weapon in the direction he has pointed. *Crack!*

*. . . crack . . . crack . . . crack . . .*

The volleys go on for a time, and bodies fall across the marketplace under the searing sun.

Then, when all that remain beneath the stone stage are a charred corpse and half a dozen bodies strewn across the stones, Leithrrse nods to the guard, and, accompanied by three guards, the envoy and now-acting regent walks the marketplace, finally stopping and standing over one figure – a black-clad blond woman still clutching a stubby, wide-nozzled device that looks like a miniature cannon of sorts – the same sort of rocket gun he has seen on the white wizard's cottage wall.

'Demon-damned Brotherhood . . . they'll pay for this.'

'What . . . ser?' asks the guard serjeant.

'Recluce. Their black marines, sent by their black Brotherhood. Their turn will come.' He ignores the looks that pass between the guards.

'Tell Marshall Dyrsse that we need to make some changes.'

The guards exchange another look.

# LXXI

Despite the henhouse, the chores, and woodworking, Wegel, with some help from me, got his own narrow room finished enough to use. He would have plenty of chances to improve his craft, since he needed just about every item of furniture, although Faslik brought over a nice single bed. I did provide a lamp, and the oil, which was another item getting dearer by the eight-day. A lot of the increased prices and shortages weren't the result of real shortages, but of greed and fear. It would be seasons, if ever, before the Empire could take over Candar,

although the black Brotherhood of Recluce had done precious little.
Somehow, I didn't think that would last.

I'd managed to ride down to the south side of Kyphrien and
commission some more hinges from Merrin – far less elaborate and
expensive. I hadn't seen Yense or his accomplice, but I'd left Merrin's
door open just in case.

After wiping my forehead and looking around the too-dusty shop,
I took a long drink from the pitcher – the dry heat of Kyphros pulled
water out of my body like an oven-dried bread dough. I offered the
pitcher to Wegel, but he shook his head. He didn't seem to need the
water as much as I did, but then he'd been born in Kyphros.

'Sweep up the chips and the damned red dust, first . . .'

'B-but . . . M-m-master Lerris . . . it'll just . . . just g-g-get d-d-dusty
again.'

'I know, but I believe in struggling against disorder even when
it's futile.'

The blond young man shook his head sadly and picked up the
broom. I picked up a soft rag. The red dust was gritty, and it had
a tendency to stain the light-colored woods if it got damp. The way
I was sweating, even wiping my forehead continually wasn't enough
to keep some moisture from hitting the wood. I was making it a habit
to dust anything I worked on before I started.

After the dust from the sweeping settled, I was going to put a finish
coat on Durrik's chest. I shook my head. The finish coat should be the
last work of the day, when no more dust was being raised, and when
the wind died down. Thinking? What about thinking, Lerris?

Instead of working on finishing the chest, I smoothed the inside
lids of the dowry chest until there was space enough for a finish
coat there.

Plane and wipe my forehead. Plane and wipe; plane and wipe . . .
the pattern was tedious, but it worked.

After that, we cut the last of the planks for another set of traveling
chests – not that we had a buyer, but if Preltar were that nervous,
there had to be others, and the chests weren't that difficult to make.
Wegel could do a pair while I did more finish work on Antona's desk
and on Zieber's case.

'J-J-Jahunt b-be here,' said Wegel.

'Jahunt?' I set down the plane on the bench and walked out onto the
porch where the one-eyed peddler stood. Even with the light breeze,
the morning was hot, nearly as hot as in midsummer, and the grass
in the meadow beyond looked more like midsummer, and ready to
brown. 'Greetings.'

'Greetings, Master Lerris.' The peddler looked down at the stone underfoot, then back at me. 'I was a-thinking . . . ye being a mastercrafter . . . well . . . would ye be having small things I could peddle for ye?'

'Small things?'

'Breadboards? I seen those at the craft fairs, years back. Or napkin rings, carved ones?'

'M-m-master Lerris . . .' stammered Wegel.

'You have some things like that, Wegel?'

'A f-few.'

I pursed my lips. 'Jahunt. Most of what we craft here is furniture. I don't do many things that small. Wegel does a few . . .'

'But . . . an apprentice, beggin' your pardon . . .'

'Wegel is better at carving than I am. If he's willing to let you hawk what he has, count yourself lucky.' I cleared my throat, dry from the heat and the dust. 'Why are you asking us? You used to hawk scissors for Ginstal.'

'Ginstal went to Hrisbarg, ser.'

'Hrisbarg?'

'Now that the Empire has Freetown, and the regent there has reopened the old iron mines . . . Ginstal said they'd be needing a good ironmaster who knew the mines, and that's where he learned the trade. His brother lives there, someplace called Howlett . . .'

I recalled Howlett, not exactly favorably.

'. . . Ginstal was saying that the new steam pumps would let them dig deeper, and he was a-tired of wondering what the Empire would do . . . or who was going to attack Kyphros next.'

I wondered how many people in Candar felt that way. Was that what the Empire counted on?

'Begging your pardon, ser?' said Jahunt.

'Oh, nothing.'

'You had that faraway look, ser.' The peddler shivered and looked at Wegel. 'He looks like that, young Master Wegel, and I'd not be in his way.'

'N-not me . . .'

The squawks from the henhouse told me that Rissa was feeding chickens or collecting eggs. A crow from the young cock – perched on the top rail of the fence by the henhouse – confirmed that someone had invaded his territory.

'Young cocks . . .' I muttered.

'Not being so old, yourself, Master Lerris,' cackled Jahunt.

Maybe not, but at times I didn't feel all that young, either.

'I'd guess I'd be pleased to have any woodwork things young

Wegel might offer, leastwise till the Hamorians show up,' Jahunt offered.

'You may have a long wait,' I suggested.

'You going to take them on, then? Folks say you be a mighty mage.'

'Just mighty enough almost to get killed a few times. No . . . I wasn't thinking about that.'

'If'n folks like you don't stop them, who will?' asked the peddler.

Wegel looked at me, and I didn't have an answer.

'A good question, but I don't have the answer.' I turned to Wegel. 'You can work out something with Jahunt, but it's on your free time, not mine.'

'T-t-thank you.'

I smiled. 'I don't know thanks are necessary. Double work isn't much fun.' While Wegel stammered and Jahunt dickered, I went back to the shop, where it was already hotter than outside, despite the open door and windows that meant more dust and grit. Again, I felt as if I couldn't get ahead.

There I began on the notching and dovetailing for the traveling chests. With the way Jahunt was talking, there might be quite a market for traveling chests, though I still didn't see the Hamorian sunburst entering Kyphros anytime soon, not with Krystal holding and fortifying Ruzor.

Wegel came back before long, smiling, at least until I put him to work on a traveling chest – a simpler version.

Later, just before dinner, I had him clean the shop, and then I did the finish work on Durrik's chest so that it could set undisturbed overnight.

Dinner was some type of chilied eggs, wrapped in peppers. Even Wegel was sweating after two of them, but like all youngsters, he ate five. I stopped at three, and ate more maize chips than I should have, and drank a lot more water than was wise.

I curried Gairloch after dinner, and he was skittish, probably because of the early summerlike heat that was creating a high haze in the sky and large numbers of hungry flies that seemed to buzz everywhere.

The chickens . . . they just *brawwked* and generally made noise and messes, but we did have eggs.

The night was warm, but dry as it was, falling asleep wasn't that hard. Staying asleep turned out to be somewhat harder.

*Grrrurrrr . . . eeeeeeeEEEEEE!*

I sat up in bed, shaking from the mental force of the reverberations of chaos. Without probing, not that my senses would travel that far, even underground, even if I were a reluctant earth wizard, I knew that the brimstone spring had exploded in chaos – that fire and steam cascaded down the Yellow River into Hydlen.

I huddled on the bed, suddenly cold in the warm evening, with the quilt gathered around me.

Where would chaos strike next? Would it all form around Sammel? Could he avoid it? More important, how could he refuse such power? But if he were accepting it, why was it erupting in Hydlen? And where was all that chaos coming from?

Unbidden, the words of my father's letter slipped into my thoughts: '. . . the Balance works both ways . . . it does not matter whether order or chaos comes first . . .'

I knew Recluce wasn't creating that much additional order, not unless things had changed more than I could believe, and I was in Candar, and neither Justen, nor Tamra, nor I were adding that much to the order forces. So who or what was?

Hamor? But didn't there have to be order to make steel or black steel? Not if my father were right. Justen, if he and Tamra weren't still traveling somewhere in Certis or wherever, could have confirmed that, but I really didn't need confirmation.

I took a deep breath, and shuddered under the quilt, while hundreds of kays away fire and steam cascaded down the Yellow River.

# LXXII

## Northwest of Renklaar, Hydlen [Candar]

Berfir waits behind the heavy earthen revetment as the latest barrage from the Hamorian long guns walks its way up the left side of the trenchworks. The shells are lofted, falling from the heavens like the thunderbolts of the long-dead angels – or like the spears of the demons of light.

The screams and moans of the Hydlenese troops are lost in the pounding explosions of the cannon.

*Crumpt! Crumpt! Crumpt!*

With each explosion, dry soil geysers into the sky, and a plume of dust drifts back almost into each shell crater in the hot stillness of midday.

Overhead, the white-gold sun burns in the bright blue-green oven of heaven, and the dust drifts slowly southward in the light wind, over the red-clad troops, bringing with it the odor of dust, of blood, and corruption.

A rocket arches into the sky, then drops toward the western Hamorian gun position, falling short by a dozen cubits, and spraying flame across the earthworks. Soldiers duck, then reappear, untouched.

Nearly a dozen rockets arc toward the Hamorian guns before one hits, and a wedge of flame and black smoke flares skyward on the west flank of the Hamorian position.

'Take that, sundevils!' Berfir smiles, and his hand strays toward the hilt of the big blade he still wears in the shoulder harness.

Now the shells walk toward the Hydlenese rocket batteries, even as more rockets impact uselessly on and around the earthworks that protect the two Hamorian batteries.

*Crumpt! Crumpt!*

The big shells drop inexorably closer and closer to the Hydlenese rocket launchers until they finally strike the emplacement. Soil, rag-doll figures, dirt, and smoke erupt into the sky. Then, fire, sparks, and smaller explosions wash across the left side of the Hydlenese lines.

The Duke sprints toward the carnage, ignoring the still-falling shells, his blade out for emphasis as he bellows orders. 'Re-form with the right battery. Re-form at the right!'

Soldiers stagger past him, blank-faced.

Berfir thwacks one – not a solid Yeannotan, thank darkness – with the flat of the big sword. 'Re-form with the right battery! Now!'

The soldier reaches for his own empty scabbard before his eyes refocus on the tall Duke. 'Ah . . . yes, ser. Yes, ser!'

Slowly, the serjeants repeat the refrain, as the two remaining rocket officers and a handful of soldiers trudge southward behind the remaining earthworks toward the heavier earthworks of the right rocket battery.

The Hamorian guns continue to boom, and the shells scream downward, creating a zigzag pattern of craters across the front of the Hydlenese earthworks, as the shells walk back toward the other rocket battery.

With the impacts, more dust drifts across the Hydlenese lines.

Berfir turns and walks back from the turned soil and torn bodies of the left rocket emplacement to the command revetment, ignoring the handful of officers who await him. He looks down at the big sword, helplessly, and then resheathes it. He walks to the crude slit embrasure in the earthworks.

The plumes of smoke from the distant hillside drift across the churned ground of the field, across the abandoned cottage and the shattered remnants of a small barn.

'Ser?' The words rasp from the officer in red, his uniform coated in dust, who stumbles up to the Duke. 'The scouts report . . . they're bringing up another battery of the guns.'

'When will they be in place?' asks Berfir tiredly.

'Probably not until late today, maybe early tomorrow.'

'Should we pull back now, or wait for darkness?' Berfir blots the dirt and sweat off his forehead with the forearm of his left sleeve.

'Ser . . . if you wait much longer . . .'

'I know . . . I won't have any troops left.'

'Yes, ser.'

'Sound the retreat. Try and keep them on the river road. I'd like to have some forces left by the time we reach Hydolar.'

'Hydolar?' asks the officer.

'You think we can defend Renklaar with all those ships they brought to Freetown?'

'Hydolar?' repeats the officer. 'That means we're giving them the Ohyde Valley?'

'Hydolar – unless you can find a way to lead a successful charge against their guns and rifles.' Berfir looks back through the slit. The shell explosions continue their slow walk across the hillside.

# LXXIII

Early summer had struck Kyphros like a hammer, the sun burning through the blue-green sky and searing the land into stunted grasses and dusty roads. In the midst of the heat and dry winds, Durrik had collected his spice chest. I had collected the hinges from Merrin in time to finish both the dowry chest and the travel chests for Preltar and collect his proffered bonus.

Zeiber had even accepted his case and offered a gold bonus. I'd reluctantly deferred. There was no way I could take a bonus from Zeiber. He'd even looked pleased at the case, touching it and shaking his head.

After that, Wegel and I had completed and sold four more travel chests. I was even getting close to finishing Antona's desk, and Wegel had placed a few small carvings with Jahunt, but the peddler was having trouble selling much of anything. That was what he told us, anyway.

Wegel was sweeping up the shop in the late afternoon while I was racking and organizing fir lengths for another travel chest when Krystal rode back into the yard, leaving a trail of dust that hung in the air for kays, turning almost pink in the twilight.

*Braaawkkkk ... brawkkk ...* Two of the hens pecked away at the hard, cracked ground around the side of the henhouse.

'No chickens?' Krystal brushed road dust from her leathers even before she swung down from the saddle.

I shrugged. 'Rissa was persuasive.'

'Ah, no, Commander. Only when Brene would sell no chickens, only when she was ready to pack up her house and leave to visit Tyglit, only then would Master Lerris consent to the chickens. And now – now we have chicks that will be dinners before fall, and now we have eggs, plenty of eggs.'

The cock announced his presence from the rail near the henhouse.

'And too much crowing,' I said.

Krystal laughed, but I could see the lines around her eyes, the additional silver hair, and the looseness of her leathers.

'Do we get chicken tonight?' asked Perron.

'You would have chicken tonight if Master Lerris had seen fit to buy the chickens earlier.' Rissa went back into the kitchen.

Krystal and I walked across the yard to the open stable doors, leading her mount.

'You're staying here, I hope?'

'There's really nowhere else to stay. Only one wing of the barracks is open, and that's to support Liessa.'

'Showing the flag?'

Krystal nodded. 'The heir stays here to reassure the people, but any attack will come at Ruzor.'

'Is it that bad?'

She nodded, but said nothing, and I got the message. It was bad enough that she didn't even want to talk in front of her personal guard.

I got out the curry brush. 'Durrik picked up his spice chest, and Preltar paid for his dowry chest and a couple of others. Zeiber offered a bonus, but that I turned down.'

'It sounds as though you've done well.' Krystal loosened the girth and removed and racked the saddle. 'You were right about Zeiber.'

'We haven't done badly for a while. Wegel's sold some carved pieces through Jahunt.'

'Jahunt?'

'The peddler. He used to sell stuff for Ginstal, except Ginstal moved back to Hrisbarg. Jahunt said he was a master miner years back.'

'They closed the mines before I was born,' said Jinsa from the middle of the stable.

'Before I was born, and that's something,' added Dercas. 'What be for dinner?'

'Food? Finish grooming that nag, and clean up before you worry about food,' advised Perron. 'There's always good food here. There's even enough for the rest of us after you eat.'

Jinsa snickered.

'Man has to know the important things. Good food, good mounts, and Barrel's no nag.'

'Enough,' said Perron quietly.

Haithen unsaddled her mount without a word, and I could sense her discomfort from halfway across the stable, mirroring Krystal's. How women put up with it, I didn't know, but I was more than glad I didn't have to endure the pain and discomfort firsthand. Secondhand and removed was disconcerting enough, especially with two of them in the same state.

After I finished currying the gelding, I stepped behind Krystal and rubbed her back, especially the lower part.

'That feels good.'

'Good.'

Rissa had a mutton curry dish with noodles and bread steaming on the table almost as soon as Krystal and I were washed up.

'Good stuff!' Dercas licked his lips.

Jinsa glared at the other trooper.

'Please sit down,' said Krystal.

I sat and served her, then me, and passed the noodles to Wegel, then dished out the mutton and sauce. Wegel took a substantial helping, just short of being too large. Dercas did the same.

'It would be nice if you men left some,' said Haithen, her voice sharp.

I looked at my plate.

'I don't mean you, Master Lerris.'

'You'd better not be,' added Rissa, 'since he's the one providing the table.' She set down a second loaf of bread in a basket.

For a moment, no one said a word.

'I like being here better than in Ruzor.' Jinsa brushed her short hair back off her forehead.

'Doesn't the sea make it cooler?' I asked.

'Not that much, and it's damp. You sweat, and you're never dry, and pretty soon everything smells like mold unless you wash it all the time, and if you do nothing really ever gets dry.' She shuddered.

'Beautiful Ruzor by the sea,' added Krystal. 'Keeping supplies and food from spoiling is one of Yelena's biggest problems. Besides getting them.'

'How is she doing?' I broke off a corner of bread and passed the basket to Wegel, who took a much smaller chunk, after a quick glance at Haithen.

'Yelena? Like the rest of us, she has too much to do and too little time to do it. I think she misses being in the field. She's spending what little free time she has practicing.'

'That's probably what I should be doing.' I'd done some, but I still felt rusty, especially without Tamra to keep me on my toes.

'You two . . . all this talk of weapons practice and preparation. Many seasons will pass before any Empire takes Kyphros, for that is what the Book of Ryba has said, that no man will take Kyphros.' Rissa stopped abruptly as Perron looked at her.

'Prophecies are only as good as those who enforce them.' That was the lanky soldier's only comment.

'We're pretty good, then,' barked Dercas.

'At eating, anyway,' added Jinsa.

Neither Krystal nor I added much to that, and, after dinner, we retreated to the bedroom, where I helped her pull off her boots and rubbed her back.

'Does that help?'

'You know it does. You just want me to tell you.' Her voice was muffled because she lay facedown.

'We men need to hear we're appreciated.'

She rolled over and threw a mock punch at me, mock enough that I managed to duck. If she'd been serious, I would have been nursing a bruise somewhere.

'Careful . . . I'm a fragile man.'

'Fragile? Ha! I've roasted meat less than that wizard roasted you. Don't tell me you're fragile.' She grinned, momentarily, before her eyes focused a thousand kays away.

After a long silence, I asked, 'How are *you* doing? You seem kays away.'

'This preparing for the coming of the Hamorians . . . it seems endless.'

'I wonder if it's not more like the coming of the demons.'

Krystal raised her eyebrows, then stretched out on the bed on her back. 'Darkness, this feels good, almost as good as having my back rubbed. What did you mean about the coming of the demons?'

'There's a lot of chaos rising, all over Candar. Preltar bought traveling chests, and didn't even quibble over the prices, and he's the type that quibbles over everything. Brene – Rissa told you about her. It doesn't make sense. Nothing's going to happen that soon.'

She shook her head. 'It has. The Brotherhood assassinated the first regent – Rignelgio, not Leithrrse. They've also sunk at least three Hamorian cruisers, iron-clad or not, and one of them had the Hamorian fleet commander on board. Leithrrse has taken command of everything, and he seems to know what he's doing. Renklaar just fell, and supposedly the harbor waters were as red as the banner of Hydlen. The Hamorians landed another five thousand troops in Freetown, and they're marching on Hydolar. Montgren has surrendered to the Emperor's regent, and the Viscount of Certis has sent out notices for all his levies.'

'That's worse than I thought.' I'd been thinking more in terms of chaos, but the physical impact of the Empire was something again.

'It will get worse.'

'Has Leithrrse sent any messages to Kasee?'

Krystal shook her head.

I waited, then added, 'I think the brimstone spring exploded two or three eight-days ago. The impact of the chaos woke me up.'

'Kasee got a report that about half of Arastia was destroyed by the fires and steam. The river's still steaming.'

'I can still hear the chaos groaning.'

'Can you do anything about it, Lerris?'

'I don't know what. Too much chaos really means too much order.'

'Too much order? There can't be that much order in Recluce.'

'It's not all coming from Recluce. I got a letter from my parents.'

'You did? I'm glad you wrote them.' She grinned. 'Tamra would be, too. I haven't heard from either Justen or Tamra. Have you?' She shook her head. 'I'm tired, and I'm not thinking too clearly. What did your parents say?'

'My mother did the writing, but she said my father said the Balance worked both ways. It seemed odd at first.'

'That does seem odd.'

'But I figured it out. Recluce limited the amount of order in both Candar and in Recluce to limit the amount of chaos. Hamor is using tools and machines to create order . . .'

'And that creates more chaos?'

'I think so.'

'Darkness help us all.' Her eyes refocused in the distance, and I held her hand for a time, leaving her in her thoughts.

Then, when she was almost asleep, I helped her undress. Through the night, I held my commander close, and I could almost ignore the deep groanings of chaos surging beneath Candar – almost.

# LXXIV

## East of Lavah, Sligo [Candar]

The man in the tan uniform knocks three times at the cottage door. Behind him, surrounding the small cottage, and creating a blanket of dust that seems to flow downhill toward Lavah, two horses wait with empty saddles and nearly fivescore mounted troopers.

'Honored Mage?' Leithrrse says as Sammel appears and opens the door.

'It's you again. What might you want this time? To offer me the position of the Emperor of Knowledge of Hamor?' Sammel wipes his forehead and steps out into the glare of the sun. Then, he squints and retreats into the dimmer space of the cottage. 'Come on in. No sense in discussing things in front of the world. They'll find out soon enough.'

Leithrrse follows the white wizard inside. He blots his forehead with a cloth. Despite its open windows, the cottage is warm in the midday heat.

'Actually, I was going to appeal to you to help us reclaim some lost knowledge.' Leithrrse bows again.

'Exactly what lost knowledge? Why are there so many troops out in the yard? And don't bow so much. That's false humility, and it doesn't go with an envoy from Hamor. I doubt there's much humility there.'

'Perhaps not. All of this' – Leithrrse gestures toward the tan-clad troopers—' is somewhat tied together. As you may have heard, a Recluse assassin killed Regent Rignelgio. Likewise, the invisible warships of Recluse have sunk a small number of our ships. Unfortunately, Fleet Commander Kuliorrse was aboard one of them. So, for the moment, I am more than a mere envoy, a situation that the Emperor will doubtless rectify shortly. But for the moment —'

'For the moment,' chuckles Sammel,' you personally would prefer that the Hamorian leadership in Candar not be further decimated. Clearly, I am being even more honored than upon your last visit.' He offers a slightly exaggerated bow. 'And what is this "knowledge," and how might I possibly be of assistance to your mightiness? Or to His even more Supreme Mightiness the Emperor?'

'The Emperor is mighty . . .' begins Leithrrse, then shakes his head. 'You are getting impudent, Mage.'

'You are getting more desperate, Honored Envoy. The knowledge you would like me to recover?'

'Once there were great highways all the way from Freetown to Frven and from thence through the Easthorns. We believe we can locate those highways, and would like to restore them, by removing obstacles, and then use them.'

'With your armies leading the way, no doubt.' Sammel blots his forehead again.

'Unfortunately, we have neither scholars nor engineers at hand.'

'And you're getting tired of dealing with Recluce on the ocean . . . so you figure you'll suffer fewer losses on land.'

The envoy waits. His eyes flick to the rocket gun on the wall, and his lips twist.

'And what will you do if I say no?'

'At this point . . . nothing.'

'That sounds suspiciously like a threat.'

'The Emperor remembers friends.' Leithrrse shrugs. 'He also remembers others.'

Sammel strokes his chin. 'Well . . . restoring roads. That is a form of knowledge.' His eyes follow the envoy's to the rocket gun, then drop back to Leithrrse. 'Last time you mentioned remuneration. What did you have in mind?'

'I left a token upon my departure. It was only a token, and the head librarian's position remains open. In addition, traveling with an army might be somewhat . . . healthier . . . these days,' points out Leithrrse.

'So long as the other was but a token.' Sammel laughs and wipes his forehead. 'And the Easthorns are definitely cooler now.'

'I did take the liberty of bringing a mount, in case you had none.'

Sammel smiles wryly. 'Let me gather a few things before we start on this quest for knowledge. And you can gather up the latest "token."'

'Of course.' Leithrrse nods. 'Of course.'

# LXXV

'What are you doing today?' As I glanced toward Krystal, I lifted the mug of redberry, early redberry, and expensive, but I was tired of water and had broken down and bought a keg of the juice. I'd also, to be fair, bought a keg of light ale for Krystal, although she only would drink that at night.

The remnant of a gust of wind, hot and bearing dust, sifted through the open door. Rissa closed it with a thud. 'Leaving the door open . . . we lose all the cool of the night too soon.'

'I'm sorry.' Then I looked up. Why was I sorry? I hadn't been the one who left the door open. It had been one of Krystal's guards, going out to saddle up and get ready for the ride to Kyphrien. Or maybe it had been Wegel. 'What are you doing?' I asked again.

'Playing politics again.' Krystal smiled wryly, setting down her mug. She looked more rested than when she had arrived two days before, although I hadn't seen much of her between breakfast and sunset. Still, while she'd gotten more sleep, there were still lines running from the corners of her eyes, and circles under them. 'Getting advice from Zeiber, and even paying a call on Father Dorna, and trying to keep the followers of the one god happy. I've already met with Mureas twice.'

'Isn't that Kasee's job?'

'She'll be here later today, and she'll do the same thing, starting tomorrow, but this way she'll have an idea of what they're thinking, and they'll be flattered that we both value them.'

'Won't they know that's what you're doing?'

'Of course. But the form of the flattery counts. It says they're important enough for both of us to talk with them. They can't resist telling everyone, and that shows that Kasee cares about Kyphrien and the people. That's very important, especially when it comes time to raise levies.'

I shook my head. Wizardry was sometimes, maybe always, less convoluted than politics.

'What about you?' Krystal finished the last of her redberry and set her mug on the table.

'Me? We'll finish the two travel chests, and I'll smooth out Antona's desk chair. By tomorrow, I'll be ready to start the finish work on the set.'

'After that?'

I had to shrug. 'There isn't much else. Everyone else with coins has either left or is hoarding them.'

'It's like that everywhere.'

'I know, but I don't understand.'

'It's simple. The wealthy determine prosperity. At least, according to Mureas,' she added dryly. 'If someone commissions a piece, you buy lumber from Faslik, and Faslik pays his family or his mill hands. They in turn use their coins to buy wool cloth or food or what they need. Now, what happens if you don't get commissions? You don't buy lumber . . .' Krystal stopped.

'But I still buy food and clothes,' I protested.

'You don't buy as much. Then the merchants either don't make as much, which means they can't buy as much, or they charge more, and that means others can't buy as much as they used to.'

It made a sort of sense, and I sat there for a moment and thought. I already worried about fewer commissions.

*Chirrrppp* . . .

The cricket's call was cut short by Rissa's strong arm and a rolled rag. 'Bugs . . . the heat, it brings them inside. They look for water, and then they eat anything.'

Krystal and I grinned at each other. Then Krystal stretched and stood up. 'I've enjoyed myself too long this morning.'

'So you're going to punish yourself?' I got up and hugged her, then let my fingers walk up her back, massaging muscles that were too tight.

'That feels good.'

'You still want to leave?'

A horse whinnied in the yard before she could say anything.

'I think that's my answer.'

After massaging her shoulders for a moment, I kissed her and let go, watching as she shrugged on the worn braided vest and belted on her blade.

'I'll be late tonight, way after dinner. Kasee's coming in, and we're going to eat with Liessa and a few others.'

'More politics?'

'What else?'

She gave me a hug before she left, and I watched from the kitchen steps – after Rissa shut the door behind me – as she and her guard rode northeast to Kyphrien. Lately, she hadn't said too much about my trying to be a hero, but why was it that she could ride off and do things, and it was all right?

Wegel had finished sweeping the shop and was smoothing a brace for the travel chest when I came in.

'T-this all r-right, M-m-master L-L-Lerris?'

'That's fine. You keep working on those. I'm going to do the last touches on the cherry desk.' My fingers crossed the inlaid A. The combination of Wegel's carving and my grooves had worked. 'I like the A.'

Wegel bobbed his head and smiled, and I smiled back, happy that I'd found someone who actually understood the woods.

After taking a deep breath, I cleaned the smoothing blade and checked the edge, knowing that I had to be careful . . . very careful. I wiped my already sweating forehead and used my order senses on the wood, trying to detect even the smallest patches of roughness in the cherry.

There weren't many, and I was almost finished, although it was near noon, when a low murmuring seemed to whisper in from the yard, and I set down my chisel, and walked quietly to the door. Wegel looked up for an instant, then went back to smoothing one of the braces for the travel chest for which we didn't have a buyer – not yet.

Two children stood on the stone step outside the kitchen door, looking up at Rissa. A thin woman, a ragged gray cloth tied loosely over her hair and forehead to protect her from the sun, stood on the other side of the yard, in the small patch of shade cast by the thin oak I had planted after I'd finished building the shop nearly three years earlier.

'Please . . . we're so hungry . . .' The plea from the dark-haired older girl was barely loud enough to reach my ears. 'Mama . . . said you had food.' She looked at her younger sister. Both children seemed clean, but dressed in rags, and those clean faces were far too thin.

I eased back into the door before Rissa looked in my direction.

'Just a bit . . .' Rissa's voice was uneven, not exactly harsh. 'Master Lerris cannot feed everyone.'

'We're not everyone,' said the smaller girl. 'You know us. I'm Jydee, and she's Myrla, and we don't have enough to eat.'

'I'll see . . .' Rissa's footsteps faded as she walked into the kitchen.

Were things so bad that children were going without food? And begging at my door, not just in the poorer quarters of Kyphrien? I'd expected my work to dry up, but I catered to those who had extra coins.

'Here . . .'

'Thank you, Mistress Rissa . . . thank you . . .'

'Don't thank me. Give thanks to Master Lerris. It's his larder.'

I eased back to where I could see. Each girl had half a loaf of nearly stale bread and some olives. They walked slowly across the yard to their mother, their bare feet lifting red dust as they walked.

Jydee, the smaller one, slowly put an olive in her mouth and then began to chew on the corner of the bread.

The mother raised her hand to Rissa, and the three walked down the drive.

I walked up to the kitchen.

'Master Lerris . . . Guysee is a good woman . . .'

I held up my hand. 'I'm not complaining. Those children looked loved and cared for – and very hungry.' I nodded toward the table in the kitchen and shut the door behind us, to keep out both the heat and the red dust.

I took a pitcher from the cooler and poured some redberry. 'Who is the woman?'

'Guysee? I have known Guysee for many years. Her man was Wylbel. He worked for the old wool factor Sinckor. He died before —'

'Isn't he the one who owned this land?'

Rissa nodded. 'His home and warehouse burned down, and he died in the fire, and a terrible fire it was, with flames as high as the trees. Some say Histel – that was his only son, and an evil one he was, beating the girls until his own father turned him over to the autarch's guards – some say Histel killed him for his gold.' Rissa shrugged. 'No one ever found Histel or the gold. Wylbel tried to save Sinckor, and he was burned and never could work a day again. He died in the great rain three years ago. So Guysee, she ran Morten's household until that black-haired woman came and the times became hard and the hussy could persuade Morten to let Guysee go.'

'Where do they live?'

'Where they can.'

I swallowed, then took a sip of redberry. The extra silvers I'd paid for the keg seemed truly luxurious.

'They come here to you often?'

'I always tell them you are the generous one, and you are, for it is your food.'

'Even if I didn't know it?'

She shrugged. 'She is a good person, and there is no work, and her family, they are dead.'

Now what was I going to do? It was easier when you didn't see people's troubles. Maybe . . . maybe . . . but I couldn't solve everything overnight.

'For now, you can be a bit more generous. Let me think about them.'

'You are a good man.'

I shook my head. I didn't feel good. A little extra food for a homeless woman with two children made me good? 'Is it like this all around Kyphrien?'

'Food, it is getting dear.'

'Why . . .' I stopped. 'I didn't notice it because, with Krystal gone most of the time, we're not feeding as many mouths.'

'That is true, and we are eating more maize and old mutton and olives.' Rissa smiled. 'I try to be careful with your coins.'

'I'm grateful for that.' I finished the last swallow of redberry and stood. 'I need to think and work.'

'And you should. Many people, they depend on you.' Rissa gave me a broad smile.

I didn't need that. I had a snug house, a wonderful consort, food, a good pony, and a craft I enjoyed. What did people like Guysee and her daughters have?

Back in the shop, I looked at Wegel. 'Do you know Guysee?'

'Wh-wh-who?' But he flushed.

'What do you know about the woman?'

'N-n-not m-much . . .' Between stammers, he explained that he and his brothers had sneaked her food for a while, until their father had caught them.

'So . . . what can she do?'

'Sh-sh-she sews . . .' Guysee had been good enough to be a seam-stress.

I shook my head. 'Fine. You started this. You can finish it. You get to turn the henhouse into a cot with three beds – we'll worry about a hearth later. Then you get to build another henhouse. I'll pay for the lumber.'

'Wh-wh-why?'

'Because . . . if I don't do something, who will? I can't save the world, but maybe we can help a poor woman for a while. And don't tell Rissa or Guysee! Not until you finish that cot. Tomorrow, we'll have to get the lumber from your father's mill. Now . . . finish that chest.'

'Y-yes, s-s-ser . . .'

Was building a cot just something to make me feel good because I couldn't figure out what to do about the bigger problem that seemed to face Kasee, Krystal, and Kyphros? Did I have to be a hero of sorts in someone's eyes?

I didn't know, but my eyes lighted on an object in the corner behind the drafting table – the old piece of cedar I'd started to carve I didn't know how many times. There was a face in the wood, but I still couldn't see whose face or what it was, not clearly.

After studying it for a while, I set it aside and picked up the smoothing blade. I needed to get the desk ready for the finish.

Wegel hummed while he worked on the travel chest. I began to study the desk and to smooth it, and the unfinished carving seemed to reproach me in a sightless way – although I didn't understand how, since it had no more than a rough outline of a face and no eyes at all.

# LXXVI

## Hydolar, Hydlen [Candar]

Smoke puffs from the Hamorian emplacements, and the dull impact of a shell against the wall beside the city gates follows.

'The demons' cannons. Always the demons' cannons!' Berfir looks to the hills just beyond the outskirts of Hydolar, then back at the clouds of dust rising from the low walls.

*Crumpt!* Another section of stone wall perhaps thirty cubits to the Duke's right fragments and slides down into the dry moat below with a dull rumbling almost lost in the unceasing roar of the cannon. The dust wells up into the stillness of the day.

'Where do they get all the powder?'

'Ser?' asks the squarish officer with heavy braid upon the shoulders of his red vest.

'Never mind!' The Duke strides along the top of the walls, heading east toward the growing breach that the Hamorian cannon have targeted. His fingers tighten around the captured pistol, and he finally jerks it from the holster.

*Crumpt!*

More stone slides earthward, widening the gap in the walls opposite the highway that leads north and across the hills to Jellico.

The Duke steps up to the nearest stone crenelation. He points the pistol toward the Hamorian positions, cocks the hammer, and fires.

*Crack.*

He reloads and fires again. And again.

The cannons continue to fire into the widening breach in the city walls, and with each shell more stones crumble and slide into the growing pile at the base of the outer wall.

The Duke stops, and takes the last cartridges from the belt. His fingers twitch, and one cartridge bounces along the stones. 'Demon-damned weapon. Woman's tool!' he mutters as he scoops up the errant shell and fumbles it into the pistol. 'Nothing man to man, just like the wizards. No skill . . . no strength . . .' He grunts.

Then he straightens and studies the line of earthen revetments that the Hamorian troops have thrown up just beyond bowshot. Not a single sundevil uniform is visible – just the smoke of cannon and the blank earthen walls.

Finally, he holsters the pistol and turns to trudge back along behind the battered crenelations of the city walls toward the barriers on the west end of the north wall where the last of the Hydlenese rocket guns rest. As he walks, the Hamorian shells begin to fall around the northeast tower. Berfir looks back to see the outer crenelations split into stone dust and gravel, before falling out of his sight toward the base of the outer wall. His fingers seem to move toward the hand-and-a-half blade, but he jerks them back as he reaches the rocket emplacements.

'Nual?'

'Yes, ser.'

'Put everything you've got left on the guns. Just the guns.'

'We been trying, ser. It's a hard target, ser.'

'Just do it.'

'Yes, ser.'

As Berfir steps back, a rocket from the Hydlenese battery hisses northward toward the cannon, but it explodes in a cloud of flame against the outer earthen walls protecting the Hamorian artillery.

'Higher!' yells the Duke. 'Arch them.'

'Yes, ser.' Nual motions to the rocket crews.

*Whhstttt! Whhhsttt!* More rockets arch northward, dashing themselves against heavy earthen barriers, though one drops behind the barriers, but no smoke or flashes result.

The Hamorian gunners continue to throw shells at the remnants of the northwest tower, and Berfir watches as the second-level galleries are exposed, and a handful of archers' bodies slide down into the rubble.

Then the shells resume their assault on the walls beside the gates.

Berfir looks toward the smoke from the guns, then walks swiftly down the open stone steps. 'Derbyna! Derbyna!'

'Yes, ser.' The white-haired officer in a red vest meets him at the base of the steps.

'Get the irregulars and my Yeannotans.'

'Ser?'

'We're going to mount an attack on the guns. The Yeannotans are the only mounted troops left, and they'll follow me.' Berfir glances in the direction of the stables, then wipes his forehead.

With the impact of another shell, fine grit sprays across the two men.

'But, ser . . . those rifles . . .'

'The walls can stand against rifles. They can't stand against those guns.' Berfir strides toward the stables where far too many horses have been crowded. 'Yeannota! To me!'

By the time he has mounted, and waits for the guards to crank open the gates, almost threescore Yeannotans and a handful of irregulars gentle their mounts behind the Duke.

'Open them!'

Slowly, the gates creak open.

'Halfway! Just halfway!' yells Berfir. 'Now!' The big chestnut carries him out onto the cratered road and around a low heap of stone. Behind him follows a line of troopers, most in the red and gold plaid of Yeannota.

*Crumpt!*

A shell slams into the wall to the left of the Hydlenese, and more grit and fragments rain across the road and into the dry moat that has slowly filled with shattered stone, and occasional bodies.

'Move it!' commands Berfir, turning in the saddle and motioning the others to follow. His eyes fix on the smoke that rises from the high earthen mound that lies nearly a kay away. 'Yeannota! To me!'

He holds back the chestnut until the line of riders catches up with him and regains some semblance of order.

The first bullets from the Hamorian troops begin to raise puffs of dust from the dirt between the green wheat stalks.

*Spanng!* One bullet ricochets off the stone of the road.

Ignoring the Hamorians' fire, the Duke raises his hand and thrusts it toward the smoke-crowned earthen revetment that lies nearly a kay from the walls of Hydolar. 'To the guns! The guns!'

'To the guns,' echo the Yeannotans, flourishing the big blades that mirror the one still in Berfir's shoulder scabbard.

*Spanng! Spanng!* More bullets whisper past the charging Hydlenese.

To the right of Berfir, a horse staggers, then falls. One Yeannotan, then another, falls.

The hail of bullets thickens.

'To the guns!' Berfir pulls out the pistol and levels it toward the nearer earthworks, from which the Hamorian rifles fire, squeezing the trigger once, twice, again, and then again, as he rides northward toward the guns.

Three more riders fall, and, at the end of the line, an irregular turns his horse eastward, ducking and urging the animal toward the river.

The pistol clicks on an empty chamber, and Berfir looks down at the empty cartridge belt. Then he flings the useless pistol, and it turns end over end before dropping into the trampled wheat.

Another horse and rider crumple, almost where the pistol fell.

'Come on and fight!' yells Berfir out toward the Hamorian forces, swinging his heavy wide blade from the scabbard.

Less than a squad remains riding abreast of the Duke, and foam flies from the mouth of the big chestnut as the horse strains to carry the Duke toward the cannon.

*Crumpt! Crumpt!* Behind the charging handful of riders, the high-angled cannon shells continue to pound the walls of Hydolar.

'Come on and fight, man to man!' screams Berfir, swinging the heavy blade. 'Come on, you cowardly bastards!'

As the bullets whistle around the Duke, yet more riders fall.

Behind the Duke, the shells still fall, continuing to widen the gap in the walls as yet more shattered stones slide down, exposing archers' galleries and passages.

'Come on, devils! Stop hiding!'

*Spanggg!* A bullet splatters on the road stones less than two cubits from the Duke. Another bullet rips through Berfir's sleeve, leaving a red line on his left arm.

'Cowards!' Berfir swings his blade again. 'We're almost there!'

Smoke from the cannons drifts downhill almost to the Duke, and less than a hundred cubits ahead looms the base of the earthworks that shield the deadly guns.

*Thwuuuck!*

The Duke pitches forward onto the dust-covered green wheat stalks, his half-helmet blown off his head by the impact of the bullet through his skull.

Three riderless horses circle, aimlessly, in the trampled wheat, while the cannon shells continue to pound the walls and the city, and dust surrounds the walls like fog. And stones continue to shatter and fall into the dry moat below the outer walls.

# LXXVII

Krystal didn't return until well after dark, and we sat alone on the back porch, waiting for the evening breezes to cool the house and the bedroom, looking at the clear and distant stars, and talking.

'I don't know. I don't like giving things to people,' I said slowly, 'but somehow just saying that it's bad luck or their fault doesn't solve things. Neither does handing out a few coppers to make me feel better.'

'That's life,' Krystal said, leaning back in the chair. 'That sounds . . . wrong. I mean . . . some people make bad decisions or have bad luck, and they die or get hurt. Magisters like Lennett or Talryn want to make it so cold. If you make a mistake, you pay. If you say that every woman must pay for the stupid things she did . . .'

'That's just it. It balances, but is it fair? Take Guysee – her consort was hurt trying to help someone. Was it a bad decision for him to try to help? Talryn would say it was. No one paid him for that, and she and their children paid for his decision. I've been lucky. Kasee paid me for helping the Finest, but no one paid Shervan or Pendril – at least not much beyond a gold or two.'

'Two golds,' said Krystal. 'That's the death payment for the outliers.'

'Two golds.' I shook my head. 'I probably owe my life to a dozen people, maybe more, who are dead. If I paid their families even that, I couldn't keep a roof over our heads.' My guts tightened at the statement. 'Well . . . I couldn't keep more than the roof of a cot over our heads.'

'You're also keeping a roof over the heads of Rissa and Wegel and me.'

'I like you under my roof, but you don't exactly need my help —'

She squeezed my hand.

'—and, I don't know, but the Balance doesn't really care about people, or about whether children go hungry.'

'That was what got Tamra in trouble,' pointed out Krystal. 'She still had trouble with the lack of justice in the Balance. So do you, or you wouldn't be turning a henhouse into a cot.'

'Wegel's doing the work.'

'You're buying the materials and paying him.'

'That bothers me, too, in a way.'

'Nothing says you can't work on it.' She laughed, and I hugged her, because she was right, and we held each other in the quiet and the light breeze for a time.

'I worry, too, you know.' Her voice was low, barely audible above the rising whisper of the strengthening breeze. 'You don't carry a blade every day.'

I swallowed. Here I was worrying about being too charitable or not charitable enough, and Krystal carried forged death at her hip just about every waking moment. 'It bothers you.'

'Sometimes. Kasee's pretty good, and most of the time we do more good than harm.' She paused. 'But I have to ask why so often everything has to be decided by force. The one-god followers talk about goodness. I haven't seen much goodness that wasn't backed with steel.'

'Kasee's a good ruler, as rulers go, but Hamor doesn't seem to care about that.'

'Their leaders are very shrewd. They're a lot more experienced than we are.' She shook her head. 'They've already got the support of most people in Freetown and Montgren. Certis probably won't last long – half the people hate the Viscount, almost as badly as the Gallosians hate their Prefect. With the Hamorians' new weapons, who can stand up to them in battle? We've barely been able to purchase a score of those new rifles, and not many of the cartridges – but they're sending every foot soldier to Candar with one.'

'You make it sound impossible.'

'Well, dear man, just how do we stop an empire? And when I ask that, it bothers me, because it sounds like I'm asking you to go out and be a hero, and I don't want you to.'

'Why not?'

'Because ... heroes really aren't very nice people, and I'm afraid that you'll change.'

'Maybe that's why Justen avoids things,' I said. 'He was a hero once, maybe more than once, and he never wants to do it again. That was a long time ago, and they didn't have machines like Hamor does. He destroyed Fairhaven, and everything else collapsed.' I laughed. 'If the Hamorians had any idea of what he'd done, I don't think that they'd ever let him anywhere close to their capital or their emperor. Not that he'd go. Anyway, the machines change everything.'

'I wonder,' mused Krystal. 'Do they? Really? You keep talking about the boiling chaos building beneath Candar. That sounds to me like something's upset the Balance.'

'It has. My father thinks that it's mostly Hamor.'

'Don't order and chaos have to balance? Won't it strike back at the Empire?'

'How? Hamor is a third of a globe away, and the chaos is here.' I frowned. Krystal had something, something so obvious that I couldn't quite figure it out.

'I don't know. You're the order mage. I'm just a professional soldier.'

'Just? Hardly.' I ruffled her short hair.

'You're the one who bought me my first blade.'

'Because you needed it.'

'Oh, Lerris . . .'

'We can't solve all the world's problems tonight. And you're leaving tomorrow.'

'You could come to Ruzor.'

'What would I do, besides get in your way?'

'You never get in my way. Are you worried about losing the crafting business?'

'A little – except I don't seem to have much left.' And I didn't. Commissions seemed to have vanished.

'What about the desk?'

'We're just about through with it.' I shrugged. 'After that . . .'

'Then you could come – you could bring tools, couldn't you?'

'I could . . .'

'You don't sound like you want to.' Krystal's voice carried a slight edge.

'It's not that, not exactly. Going to Ruzor doesn't feel quite right, but I don't know why, and it bothers me because I don't. I don't like your being there, either.' I laughed. 'Then, I don't like your being away so much, anyway.'

'You have to trust your feelings,' she said slowly. 'But you could visit, couldn't you?'

'I'd at least have to finish the henhouse.'

She laughed. So did I, and we left the cooling winds and the cold stars for a warmer bedroom.


# LXXVIII

The three druids stood in the grove of the ancient one, watching the sands that depicted all of Candar shift and boil.

The youngest druid held her lips tightly, recalling another time when she had watched the sands, then in hope. In the space before her, under the ancient oak that was older than Recluce, older than the citadel of Jellico, older even than ancient and departed Westwind, she watched the sands boil, changing from white to black and black to white.

'The angels will not return, not for all the songs, not for all of the cold iron of the machines,' said the male druid. His thin silver hair, his thin face, both topped a frame so frail that it seemed closer to vapor than flesh and bone.

'The price will be paid,' stated the other woman. 'None have paid this price in generations, and the arrogance of the Emperor will ensure that his pride will be laid low.'

'His will not be the only pride laid low,' said the youngest druid.

'Oh, Dayala, never has it been easy for you and Justen.'

Dayala smiled, sadly. 'I will be with him this time, Syodra. I will leave the Great Forest.'

'I thought you would be, should be.'

'All songs are sung a last time,' offered the old singer. 'A last time when the words regain their purity and power.'

'In Balance, no less.' Syodra laughed, but the tears flowed from her eyes as her fingers stroked the smooth-gnarled bark of the oak.

Dayala's lips brushed the fingers of the singer, and her fingers squeezed those of Syodra, before she walked away from the grove and toward the river, and the boat, that would carry her to Diehl – and the journey beyond.

# LXXIX

After Krystal left for Ruzor again, the weather got even hotter, and the dust got drier and redder, and I took a lot of cold showers for a lot of reasons, but the effect wasn't all that lasting.

What was lasting was the continuing distant rumbling of chaos from beneath eastern Candar, almost as if it were moving closer to Kyphros, but I still couldn't tell except that it seemed stronger, louder, as it echoed through the depths. Either that, or I was becoming more adept at reading and sensing the depth.

That morning, more than an eight-day after she had left, hot as it was, I got out the staff again and trudged to the stables, raising a slight cloud of dust, and trying to ignore the *brawwking* of the chickens.

After feeding Gairloch and the mare, I began to practice, trying to step up my speed against the demon-damned swinging bag, as I did most mornings. One good thing about the bag was that I didn't have any restraints against delivering really hard blows. That way I could get some exercise and work on delivering more power. Somehow I worried that I might need it.

After a long series where I actually got the better of the heavy sandbag, stopping its swing cold without totally shivering my own arms, I paused to catch my breath and wipe my forehead. Of course, it came away muddy from my sweat and the reddish-brown dust that seemed to be everywhere.

'It is a bad time when good men practice with weapons,' said Rissa from the open stable door.

I wiped my forehead again.

*Whhheeeee* ... That was Gairloch's only comment on the matter.

*Braawkk* ... Even the chickens seemed to have a viewpoint of sorts.

'It's worse when good men are bad with weapons.'

Rissa shook her head, and, at that point Jydee and Myrla skittered out the door behind Rissa, giggling as they went. My audience had been larger than I'd thought, and that was bad and good. Good because I'd been wrapped up in exercising. Bad because I hadn't sensed them. Did that mean that when I was exercising hard, my order senses were blunted?

Not that long after I'd put away the staff, I began to work on plans for a tall storage chest for clothes – a bigger and deeper version of Durrik's spice chest – not that I was getting anything from it, since I hadn't the faintest idea who would buy something like that.

Finally, I put down the quill and studied Antona's desk and chair. I hadn't attempted to deliver them. First, I didn't know where to cart the two pieces, exactly, and, second, my making inquiries about the Green Isle would have set off a few rumors I would rather have avoided. So I had offered Guysee a few coppers to deliver the envelope the day before.

That gave her coins, and I certainly didn't want to send poor tongue-tied Wegel off to Antona's establishment. If he wanted that kind of pleasure, he'd have to find it himself, not through my assistance, indirect or otherwise.

My fingers brushed the cherry. I'd miss both of the pieces, because

I had done – or we had – good work, and the carved and inlaid A was far better than I could have easily done.

After Guysee had returned the afternoon before, she had solemnly informed me that the lady in green had taken the envelope and laughed. 'So cautious is Master Lerris!'

Cautious? In some ways, I guessed. Was I too cautious?

With a deep breath I picked up the quill again and dipped it in the ink, but I hadn't drafted four lines before there was a clatter of horses in the yard. Antona and her carriage, and a wagon that bore the painted black outline of two horses and a wagon – Werfel's sign – rolled into the yard. Werfel was not driving the wagon, but a thin gray-haired man was, accompanied by a younger and burlier fellow.

I went out into the heat of the yard. 'Greetings, Lady Antona.'

'You are always so polite, Master Lerris. Let us see your master-work.'

I inclined my head and held open the door.

After she entered, Antona looked at Wegel, steadily, until he blushed.

'Don't be embarrassed, young fellow, just because a bawdy old woman enjoys the sight of you. Your master's too cautious. Besides, looking that way at him could cost me my head, and I'm right fond of it.'

Her head? Surely, Krystal wasn't that jealous.

'I wouldn't bet on that,' said Antona. 'You might, but I wouldn't.' She walked toward the desk, sitting in the open space back from the door, her fingers slipping over the finish of the desk and the chair. Her eyes rested on the inlaid carved A where the darker lorken stood out – but not ostentatiously – from the lighter cherry.

'Why did you make the inlay darker, rather than lighter?'

'It's less obvious, Lady. I didn't think you would wish to flaunt it.'

She laughed. 'Master Lerris, you're a wise man.'

'Only about some things.' I still recalled her veiled reference to Krystal.

'But you understand your weaknesses, and that makes you stronger.'

'You're far too kind.'

'Me? Kind? You are the charitable one.'

'For doing what I like to do?' I tried to change the subject.

'You like to craft. Few people truly enjoy what they do.' Her gray eyes sparkled for a moment before she asked, 'Would you do a dining set for me? Chairs like you did for Hensil, and a table?'

'Now?' I couldn't help the surprise. No one was commissioning anything in Kyphros, which made a strange kind of sense. A good piece of woodworking will last for generations, but people don't make that commitment when they aren't certain about the future.

'Don't sound so surprised. My business, unlike most, does better in hard times. People need consolation.'

I nodded. That made sense. 'It would be costly, and it would take longer.'

'That would be fine.' She frowned. 'The chairs cost Hensil sixteen golds.'

What didn't the woman know? 'That was rather a bargain.'

'I won't quibble. Say thirty golds for the chairs, but I'd like twelve. Then another fifty golds for a table to the standard of the desk.'

I thought. I'd never had anything close to a commission that huge. Eighty golds! 'I will have to have a deposit on something that large, Lady, if only for the wood. And it will probably take most of a season to obtain and season enough cherry.'

'Always honest, Master Lerris. That's what I like about you. Are you that honest in the bedroom? No, don't answer that.' She laughed. 'That wasn't fair. Fun, but not fair.'

I knew I was blushing.

She handed me a purse with two hands. 'There are eighty golds there. Fifty for the desk and chair, and a deposit for the dining set.'

I tried to take the heavy leather bag graciously, but it's rather hard to take a bag that weighs more than half a stone gracefully.

I tucked it inside the empty moisture pot for the moment when Antona went to summon the carters, and while Wegel opened the other half of the door, the half that usually was closed except when we lugged in lumber or eased out finish work.

'Easy with that desk. It's a masterwork, and you dent it or scratch it, and Werfel won't be able to find a hole deep enough to hide you,' announced Antona politely, without raising her voice. Of course, I could have used her tone to etch designs in brass, but she didn't yell or shout, and I had some idea that she expected to be obeyed.

The two carters loaded the desk, and I helped pad and anchor it.

Guysee, Jydee, and Myrla watched from the end of the yard next to the rough cot that the henhouse had become. The second henhouse was rougher, much rougher, than the first, probably because Wegel had done most of it, but the hens didn't need crafting. They needed protection, mainly from wild dogs and mountain cats, although I hadn't seen many cat traces.

Both girls watched with wide eyes, Guysee with a certain sadness, as Antona's carriage bore her back to Kyphrien.

I sent Wegel out to the shed for some lamp oil and to check how much grain was in the feed barrel. I didn't need either, but I wanted to get the golds into the hidden strongbox in the small storeroom as quickly as possible, all but a few, anyway.

After that, since we didn't have any other great and pressing work, I harnessed the mare and took the wagon and Wegel with me to Faslik's to see if the millmaster had any more cherry for Antona's dining set.

He didn't, and, like me, he wanted a deposit. I gave him five golds and a promise of five more in an eight-day.

When we got back to the shop, I handed Wegel several sheets of paper. 'You sketch a design for the chair backs – one that we can make and one that fits with the desk and chair we just delivered.'

'M-me?'

'Why not? I'm not saying we'll use the design. That depends. But you need to practice that now, too. Any half-decent journeyman can join wood smoothly. What you make when you join it is what determines how good you are.'

'B-but . . .'

I held up my hand. 'I've watched you carve. You have a feel for design. You just have to work on showing it on paper, not in the wood. How else will you learn crafting? The knife or chisel doesn't always lead you there. Sometimes you have to see what you want in your mind, and then you have to put it on paper so that others will know what you are thinking.'

Half the time, I suspect my sketches had sold the pieces, and I really wasn't an artist, but most people just can't visualize what something will look like, whether it's a chair or a painting.

Wegel's brow knitted up, but he didn't say anything.

I gestured to the paper again. 'Go ahead. It can't hurt.'

# LXXX

'Quiet.' Justen eased Rosefoot along the narrow road, bordering the walls of Jellico. Unable to see with his eyes, he let his perceptions guide him and his pony toward the western road and away from Jellico, away from the Viscount and the coming battle.

Behind him, Tamra struggled to sense her surroundings, struggled to keep her shields in place and her mount from betraying her location while following the gray mage.

*Click . . . click . . .*

'You hear something?' echoed a voice from the wall overhead.

'What? You think the sundevils are already outside the walls?'

'Who knows . . . wish I were out there.'

'You leave, and the Viscount'll have your guts for bowstrings. He's not letting anyone leave.'

'Tell me . . . the merchants are screaming . . .'

'There's something down there.'

'What? A stray dog? Go ahead. Waste a quarrel, but you'll wish you had it when the sundevils get here. See that dust? That's them. Won't be long before the thunderguns are booming.'

'Shit.'

'It is, isn't it?'

Justen smiled tightly in his cocoon of darkness.

Tamra wiped her forehead, struggled with her shields, and tried to keep close to Justen and Rosefoot.

*. . . click . . . click . . .*

'. . . swear I heard something . . .'

'. . . forget it . . .'

As the two mages slipped through their own darkness toward the south-west, the heavy cloud of dust rolled toward Jellico.

# LXXXI

I picked up the cedar length from the back of the bench, glancing across at the drawing board where Wegel was sweating over the chair designs for Antona. He was beginning to discover the difference between creating what was easy and creating what was necessary.

I looked at the roughed-out figure. A face existed somewhere inside the old cedar, but I hadn't found it yet. So I sat on the stool and trimmed away a bit more of the wood, bringing out more of the general shape of the face.

*Grrrrurrr . . . rrrrr . . .* Setting the cedar down, I stood. Thin shiverings of . . . something . . . seemed to echo through the ground and stones beneath Kyphros, almost as if ripples of chaos ran through the ground. Ripples of chaos? From where?

I set down the knife beside the cedar and steadied myself with a hand on the edge of the workbench.

'M-m-master L-L-Lerris . . .'

'I'm all right. Just a bit hot.' I walked slowly out of the shop and then back through the empty kitchen to the rear porch where I plopped down onto the bench.

I tried to let my thoughts follow those waves of chaos, focused chaos, back through the ground, but I lost them beyond Kyphrien, somewhere short of the Little Easthorns.

Somewhere short of the Little Easthorns? Not bad for someone who couldn't tell what was in the upper air within a few kays. Then again, I wasn't an air wizard, and it appeared as though I might indeed be an earth wizard of sorts.

*Braaawkkk . . . brawwkkk . . .*

'Shoo!'

The chicken *brawwkkked*, but just kept scratching at the ground.

An earth wizard who couldn't even shoo away a chicken, I decided. I shivered as I recalled the power of chaos in the last tremor I had sensed. Chaos coming from the Easthorns, and seemingly moving westward.

It had to be linked somehow to Hamor. Hamor was using the mechanical order and the Balance. Logically, it made no sense that chaos was involved, and my father would have told me so. But chaos seemed always to hover around violence and conquest, and Hamor was certainly involved in that. And besides, it *felt* as if Hamor were involved. And Krystal had told me to trust my feelings. Even the autarch had.

I wiped my forehead, glancing toward the west and the Westhorns I could not see, but only sense vaguely. The sun, reddish in the late afternoon, hung over the top of the hill.

Krystal and Kasee had planned the defense of Kyphros on the assumption that Leithrrse would use the Hamorian fleet to reduce Ruzor. But by now Leithrrse had to know about that defense. If he learned about it, wouldn't he change his plans? I knew I would.

Were I in Leithrrse's shoes, I'd use the wizards' roads through the Little Easthorns and come down through Tellura and Meltosia. Whether Leithrrse knew that most of the northern outliers had been wiped out in the battle for the brimstone spring was another question, but I doubted that the outliers at full strength could have stopped the Hamorians and their rifle-armed troops. Kasee's troops were too few and too spread.

Yet the chaos hadn't come from the Little Easthorns, but beyond, farther to the east. Also, I doubted that the wizards' roads were passable farther east. Otherwise, Antonin would have used them.

I swallowed. Was someone – Leithrrse? – using chaos to restore all the old roads that the white wizards had used to dominate ancient Candar? Or could they just march over the blocked parts? Then Hamor could move armies quickly down the center of Candar, or by sea.

The wizards' road left Tellura and Meltosia open to the Hamorian troops ... I frowned. The road also left Gallos open, and wouldn't Leithrrse take Gallos first? But why? He could use Ruzor to reinforce a conquered Kyphros and outflank the Prefect on both sides. Certis would fall, or had it already? There was so much I didn't know. Still, once the Hamorians had Kyphrien, they could use the river and the river road as a highway right into Ruzor.

The wizards' roads were one of the tools that the ancient white wizards had used to bring most of Candar under their rule. So far, the Hamorians hadn't missed a trick. Why would they now?

Had Krystal or Kasee thought about that? I took a deep breath. Maybe I was going off on feelings I couldn't even trust.

Another rippling shiver of chaos seemed to echo from the rocks below. That I wasn't imagining.

I could run off, or I could take a little time and go to Ruzor. Besides, I wanted to see Krystal, especially before I went off investigating more chaos and the person – or people – who wielded it. I also wanted to think more about it, and to talk to Krystal. Was it all in my imagination? If it weren't, though, Kyphros was facing an even bigger problem.

I stood up and looked toward the coming sunset.

'Rissa!'

One way or another I couldn't do anything to help Krystal by staying in Kyphrien, and it would be at least several eight-days before Faslik had anywhere near enough cherry for Antona's dining set and chairs.

'Rissa!'

I walked back to the kitchen to start getting ready for the morning's trip.

# LXXXII

Gairloch almost pranced as I saddled him and strapped my gear in place. I took my staff and a few tools, including a small saw.

When I walked Gairloch out into the yard, I didn't see Guysee, but Jydee and Myrla sat on the crude bench outside their cot. I had to admit that they kept it clean – even the jakes that Wegel had built, although he'd grumbled about where I'd insisted it be. I wasn't about to have it too close to the house, even if the water were piped from the hillside'spring.

Jydee gave me the smallest of waves as I led Gairloch over to the house, where I had left the bag of provisions by the kitchen step. Wegel stood outside the shop door, broom in hand. I didn't even have to ask him to keep the shop clean anymore, and I'd left him with the responsibility for another travel chest and the design for the dining set, plus whatever he could provide to Jahunt. I'd also suggested he think about a window for his room. It probably wasn't enough, but it was all I could think of, and I didn't want to commit us to making too much when no one except Antona was buying.

'G-g-good l-l-luck, s-s-ser.'

'Thank you, Wegel. I'm not sure luck is really the answer. I probably won't be back in less than an eight-day, and it could be longer, much longer.' After strapping the provisions bag behind the saddle, I glanced at Rissa. 'You have enough to keep things going?'

'Now that we have chickens, and eggs, if I can't keep this place going for two seasons on ten golds, you should have me hung, Master Lerris.' She gave me a smile. 'Some goats or a cow, and I could make my own cheese.'

I shrugged. 'How much for some she-goats?'

'He's worried, boy.' Rissa looked at Wegel. 'When a crafter doesn't fight against his housekeeper spending hard-earned coins, he's worried.'

'You do have a good sense of when to ask me.'

'And I'd not be the woman I am if I didn't.'

'How much?'

'She-goats are cheap, and the cheese is the rank stuff.'

I got the message, dismounted, and tied Gairloch to the post outside the shop. In the end, I gave her ten more golds to see if she could find someone who could spare a heifer that could become a milk cow. Knowing Rissa, I suspected she could. Somehow, things kept getting more complicated. The two girls pretty much watched the chickens and gathered the eggs for Rissa, and Guysee helped clean the house, and she'd even started mucking the mare's stall. I'd never asked her, but she felt better doing it, and it certainly had left Wegel more time for helping me.

I finally managed to get back on Gairloch.

'You be careful, Master Lerris,' Rissa warned.

'I'll try.' I wasn't that confident about my success in being careful, not the way things seemed to be headed in and around Kyphros, nor with the ideas I needed to talk over with Krystal and perhaps the autarch.

'Try,' snorted Rissa. 'That was what Faras said.'

I didn't answer, since it was the first time she'd mentioned the name. I wondered if Faras had been her consort, the one murdered by bandits. Instead, I smiled and waved, guiding Gairloch across the yard and toward the road.

Like all my recent trips in Kyphros, I began by riding into Kyphrien. The marketplace was perhaps half-full, less noisy than usual.

'. . . and I said to her, Hezira, how could you expect to keep that high house and all those gowns? She only had her face and a narrow waist and smooth skin, and all of that goes when you eat rich foods and have children. So, I said, Hezira, best you get that figure back, or you'll be on your back at the Green Isles working for Madame Antona . . .'

'. . . a lady Antona is now . . .'

'. . . such a lady, with a mind like a blade . . .'

'. . . best sweet breads in Kyphrien . . .'

'. . . all she sees is a ready smile and blue eyes . . . can you expect of a girl . . . who will bring in the coppers for the bread . . . and coppers be getting hard to find these days . . .'

'. . . spices . . . preservatives for your larders . . . work even in the heat of summer . . . spices . . . preservatives . . .'

'. . . old bread, hard bread, but good bread! Half copper a loaf! Just a half copper! . . .'

'Steel! Good steel blades . . .'

'. . . said the sundevils hold Jellico now . . . won't be long afore they're looking this way, autarch and her wizards or not . . .'

'. . . mighty wizards they are, though . . .'

'. . . 'gainst cold steel devices?'

I didn't feel like a mighty wizard, and what I did hear in the marketplace didn't cheer me that much, nor did the sight of the autarch's palace on the hill with the windows I knew were dark. At least, Liessa hadn't shuttered them.

The gate to Ruzor was the south gate, really the southeast gate, that led to the river road. A boat would probably have been faster, at least to Felsa, and the cataracts there, but the Phroan River was too shallow for most of the way for larger boats or barges broad enough to carry cargoes – or mountain ponies. So how would I have gotten back without paying a fortune?

Most of the river road was metaled, but narrow, with the width of the paving stones barely enough for two wagons to pass side by side. Then, except in the winter, the roads in Kyphros were seldom muddy.

Dust was another question. I tried to keep Gairloch on the stones, but even in the center of the road, dust rose with each step, and the fine red powder hung in the air and clung to everything.

Even before we reached the first bridge, less than twenty kays along the road, where the Mildr joins the Phroan River, the old square from a work shirt that I used for a handkerchief was more red mud than the clean gray cloth I had put in my belt that morning.

Red mud streaked my cheeks, the result of dust and sweat. Even though I washed hands and face, and my kerchief, what seemed every few kays, my reddish muddy sweat clung everywhere, even though we saw almost no one on the road, save for an occasional farm wagon, usually empty, headed away from Kyphrien. Only the olive groves seemed unchanged, with their leaves greened out, but olives seemed to outlast everyone.

Gairloch snorted and snuffled, but carried me southward.

The first night found me at a waystation below a town called Hipriver. From what I could tell, few had visited the waystation recently. There were only a scattering of tracks in the dust on the road, and since we hadn't had any rain in more than a handful of eight-days, the weather hadn't destroyed the evidence of travelers. More likely, there were few indeed in recent days.

Sometimes, fear of violence is more deadly than the violence itself.

After long, steady riding, I reached Felsa around noon on the fourth day. Felsa sits on an arrow-shaped point of hard rock where the Phroan River is joined by the little Sturbal River. Right below Felsa the Phroan plunges through the Gateway Gorge and down onto the delta plains.

Although Felsa's walls are not that high, they don't have to be, not to defend against attacks from the water, since the cliffs are almost twenty cubits high and made of sheer, but crumbling, rock. Supposedly, parts of the walls have to be moved and rebuilt every few years, and the town is said to be nearly two hundred cubits narrower today than when it was ruled from Fenard.

The north walls, guarding the road from Kyphrien, were higher and thicker, but they wouldn't stop an army. Then, in more than ten centuries no one had marched an army downriver. That wouldn't stop Leithrrse, though.

A single guard nodded as I rode Gairloch through gates that seemed rusted open.

The market, like the one in Kyphrien, was more than half deserted.

Unlike Kyphrien, there was little chatter, just a few murmurs here and there. After stopping in the shade of the public fountain and rinsing my face, I took Gairloch to the watering trough. Then I remounted Gairloch and took the east gate out over the bridge.

From Felsa, there are two roads to Ruzor – the mountain road, which winds along the north side of the gorge and then the high cliffs, and the water road, which circles the gorge on the south and then follows the twists of the river on the river plain where a strip of fruit orchards separates the river from the grasslands that stretch west and south, getting drier and higher each kay from the river.

I decided to follow the general rule, even though I had never traveled either road before. Since it was summer, I took the mountain road, a winding strip of paving stones barely wide enough for a single wagon except for a scattering of turnouts.

Despite the clear sky, mist rose out of the gorge from where the river was threshed by the rocks, seeping up almost like fog. It shrouded parts of the road – a welcome relief from the heat I had encountered all the way from Kyphrien. Kyphrien is actually cooler than Felsa or the grasslands, something I had heard. Finding it out in person was a dubious pleasure.

Once I left the gorge behind, the mist vanished. The sun continued to beat down, and the dust rose, but the air was so dry that the dampness from the mist left my clothes before the dust could even reach me.

Because the High Desert rises right off the cliffs on the east side of the river below the Gateway Gorge, the road got hot – and hotter, and I went through the water in both bottles before long. There was only one waystop that whole afternoon and evening, and to get water there, I had to use a bucket and a rope that must have been nearly fifty cubits long – twice, once for me and once for Gairloch. And I had to orderspell both buckets' worth.

I finally stopped in the second waystop, barely before full night. My legs ached, and Gairloch was plodding. He drank two buckets of water, but I didn't let him gulp them down all at once.

The next morning we set out again, finally reaching the outskirts of Ruzor around mid-afternoon.

Ruzor sits on the east side of the river, a city seemingly backed against the cliffs that contain the High Desert and keep its sands and waterless rocky hills from spilling into the Southern Ocean. The road wound down from the cliffs onto a lower plateau, fortified by recently repaired and extended stone walls. A small section of the city was lower still, barely above the waters of the bay.

The upper gates had a pair of guards, who only nodded at me. What harm could a single dusty traveler on a pony do? From there I found the main square and asked an off-duty trooper where the Finest were quartered.

'The Finest?'

I nodded.

'The green devils. Ah, you want the green devils and their commander. The demons help you, fellow. Still, I'd not gainsay a man a choice of his death. Aye, and death it will be when the sundevils bring their iron ships and death cannons to the bay and send their thundershells into poor Ruzor.'

'The Finest?' I prompted.

'The east road, by Haras's place – the Golden Cup – stay on it until it nears the seawalls and look for the iron gate and the mean-looking women with their blades. Yes, mean-looking, and if you tarry too long, I'll be behind you, little as I like it, for I'm as much a fool as ye.' He laughed, loudly. 'For I'm as much a fool as ye.'

'I thank you.'

'Don't be a-thanking me, fellow.' He bowed, with an exaggerated sense of care, then winked before straightening.

With a nod to the trooper, I turned Gairloch toward the sign of the Golden Cup, trying not to frown. Was Ruzor as doomed as the trooper thought?

I tried to extend my senses in and around the city, but found no chaos, no disruption – more a sense of calm, or peace, bolstered by the order of the reinforced walls and the discipline of the Finest.

I couldn't help frowning as I rode Gairloch eastward toward the seawall, noting little of the laughter and chatter common to the towns and cities of Kyphros.

'. . . way for the cart . . .'

'. . . sea salt, fine sea salt . . .'

'. . . way for the cart . . .'

I doubt I could have missed either the iron gate or the heavy gray stone walls of the barracks, or the banner of the autarch flying from the building farther up the hillside from those barracks.

At the gate was a single broad-faced and dark-haired guard. I dismounted and walked up to him, leading Gairloch. He didn't acknowledge that I was standing there, and I'd never seen him. He looked right through me, as if I didn't exist. While I might have been dusty, I was certainly there.

'My name is Lerris, and I'm here to see the commander.'

'No one sees the commander without a pass.'

I nodded. 'Who gives out the passes?'

'The commander or the district commander.'

'I suppose the district commander is Yelena.'

'Leader Yelena to you.'

I decided I hadn't learned enough patience, because I wanted to pick up my staff and thrash the idiot. I didn't. Instead, I asked politely – at least I thought it was politely – 'Where might I find Leader Yelena?'

'You need the permission of Subofficer Thrilek.'

I wiped my forehead. Why did these sorts of things happen to me? 'And where do I find Subofficer Thrilek?'

'Serjeant Hissek might know.'

'All right. Where is he?'

'He's in the main hall.'

I started forward.

'You can't go in there without a pass.'

'Look. The commander happens to my consort, and I've fought in more battles than you've clearly seen. I'd really appreciate seeing someone like Yelena.'

'I don't know you, and you're not going in.'

'Could you call someone?'

'I can't do that. I'd have to leave my post.'

'To call someone?'

'I'm not yelling just because you say so. You're just some tradesman, anyway.'

'All right.' I stepped back and pulled the staff out of the lanceholder. 'Do you know what this is?'

'It's a long piece of wood.'

I shook my head. 'It's a staff. It's the third one I've had since I came to Kyphros. I broke the first one against a white wizard. The second one got burned to a cinder against another white wizard.' I tried smiling. 'I'm not a tradesman. My name is Lerris, and I'm the commander's consort.'

'I don't care what it is or who you say you are. You're not going into the barracks without a pass.'

I stepped forward, and he reached for his blade.

I saw red – or white – or something, but the staff cracked him across the wrist hard enough that he dropped the blade. He was dumb enough to reach for a knife, and I knocked that away.

'Help! Murder!'

The man could bellow, and suddenly there were three other young troopers with blades, and they didn't even ask what I wanted, and I was too busy defending myself to explain, and it seemed like whenever

I knocked one down, there were two others trying to hack at me. So I ended up with my back to the wall, knocking around troopers I didn't even know.

'HALT!'

I recognized the voice, and so did most of the troopers except the one who decided that when I stopped defending myself, he'd gain some glory by slashing me up. Except I'd gotten a little more cautious, but I still wasn't quite expecting it. So I had to hit him harder, and I could hear the bone crack.

'Halt!' snapped Yelena again. Two other officers stood with her, but I didn't recognize either.

'Ser!' screeched the guard who had started the whole thing. 'That man attacked me.'

'Shut up, trooper!' She turned to me. 'How did you get in this mess, Master Lerris?'

I lowered the staff and shrugged. 'Well . . . I was tired and trying to find Krystal – or you – but apparently I needed a pass to see either of you, and this fellow wouldn't let me see anyone who could give me a pass. He also wouldn't call anyone who might help. I've been on the road almost six days, and I was a little hasty and tried to walk in. He pulled his blade and tried to hack me apart. I tried not to kill anyone, but it was getting pretty tense.'

Yelena smiled. It wasn't exactly a pleasant smile, but I smiled back. She looked at the dozen or so guards. 'You are all idiots. You're also lucky you aren't dead. Might I have the pleasure of introducing you to Master Lerris. In addition to being probably the best woodcrafter in Kyphros, he is also the gray wizard who defeated the Hydlenese white wizard and who killed somewhere in the neighborhood of ten squads of Hydlenese troopers by himself.' She nodded. 'All by himself.'

'But he didn't have a pass,' protested the first trooper. The others looked at him as if he were crazy.

'Did he tell you who he was?'

'He said he was the commander's consort, Lerris.'

Yelena shook her head and turned to the subofficer beside her. 'Thrilek, is this man yours?'

'Yes, ser.' Thrilek was sweating.

'Good. I'd like to see you both in my office after I escort Master Lerris to the commander. Did I mention that she is his consort?' She paused. 'By the way, I seemed to notice that Lerris was holding off about a dozen of you. Didn't any of you think? If a man with a staff is good enough to keep that many of you occupied, don't you suppose he's good enough to kill a bunch of you?'

Surprised eyes met surprised eyes.

*Whheeeee . . .*

I looked at Gairloch.

Yelena grinned – for an instant. 'You!' Her hand jabbed at a dark-haired trooper. 'You can stable Master Lerris's mount, in the stall next to the commander's, and I don't care whose mounts you have to move.' She turned back to Thrilek. 'Wait with your trooper outside my office, and I also don't much care how long you have to wait.'

By then they were both sweating.

I unstrapped the bags and pack and threw them over my shoulder, but I did keep hold of my staff.

Yelena turned to me and lowered her voice. 'You know, Master Lerris . . . you have this knack.'

'Of getting in trouble?'

'Things do get interesting whenever you're involved.'

I glanced back at the dispersing troopers. 'Did I make a mess of this all by myself, or are they as dumb as they seem?'

'I won't comment on your actions. I'd get in trouble either way. Your judgment of the quality of our forces is close to true – unhappily.' Yelena wiped her forehead. 'The commander will be happy to see you, I think.'

After my entrance I wasn't all that sure.

Of course, Krystal was off somewhere in the upper building with the autarch, and Yelena ended up escorting me to Krystal's quarters, guarded – still – by good old Herreld, who filled up most of the narrow space between the dark stone walls. The only light came from a thin embrasure opposite the door, although there was an unlit lamp in a brass bracket on the left side of the doorway.

'Greetings, Herreld.'

'Greetings, Master Lerris. She'll not be here.'

'I'll just wait.'

'She'd not mind if you waited within, Master Lerris.' Herreld actually opened the door.

'Thank you.' I tried not to gape, but I did catch a hint of a grin from Yelena.

'The word is that you taught the locals a lesson, ser.'

'I don't know about that. I broke one fellow's wrist – he didn't give me much choice.'

'That be Unsel – he'd have ye believe no blade matches his.' Standing in the doorway, Herreld gave me a smile.

'Master Lerris?' asked Yelena.

'Yes?'

'Once you are rested, in a day or so perhaps, would you consider a little sparring, the way the red . . . the other mage did?'

'I'd be happy to, Yelena.' Tamra was never going to escape being the red bitch, I suspected, and if I could somehow manage to help Yelena . . . even if I weren't as good with a staff as Tamra, well, I suspected I owed it to her.

She bowed and was gone.

'There'll be more than enough wash water, Master Lerris, and I'll have more sent up for the commander.' Herreld nodded and left me in the corner tower room.

Krystal only had a single circular room in Ruzor, perhaps twenty cubits across, with a bed, a washstand, a desk, a conference table with six armless wooden chairs, a wardrobe, and a small table beside the bed that held an oil lamp with a burnished reflector to help with reading.

The stacks of papers on the battered plank desk and the small square table beneath the narrow window were familiar enough, as were the stained exercise leathers strewn across the unmade bed.

After setting down my packs, I hung up her clothes, either on the wall pegs or folded them and set them on the shelves on the one side of the wardrobe. Then I made the bed, and straightened things up – except for her piles of papers. Those I didn't touch. There wasn't as much dust in Ruzor as in Kyphrien or on the road, and what dust there was happened to be grayish.

I took my own decent browns and hung them up, hoping that the hanging would get rid of some of the wrinkles. Then I stripped down to my drawers and shook out my clothes before I washed up. The water turned dark, of course, by the time I was finished washing and shaving, but I felt a lot better, even though I would have preferred a shower.

Later, when I was sitting on the bed, reading through *The Basis of Order*, still hoping to find another clue as to how I could deal with so much chaos, there was a rap on the door.

'Yes?'

'Fresh water, ser.'

'Come on in.' I hadn't bolted the door.

An older woman marched in, opened the window, and threw the water in the washbowl out, letting it cascade down the wall. Then she refilled the bowl and pitcher from a large bucket, nodded brusquely, and left.

I picked up *The Basis of Order* again, absently wondering when I might see Krystal.

I had reread most of the introduction and was puzzling over another one of the more obscure passages.

> . . . order and chaos can be linked, and twisted, into smaller and smaller segments, as the sands of the beaches are the result of the constant pounding of chaos against order. Even the greatest might find despair in building pure order or chaos from such sands . . .

Could someone take Justen's technique and refine it until order and chaos were fragmented into the tiniest of bits? What would happen then? Would anything?

The door opened, and Krystal stepped inside and closed it in a single motion. She shook her head. 'Only reading?'

After we held each other for a time, she kissed me for a longer time, then gently disengaged herself. 'You do have a good sense of timing. Yelena also told me you made a theatrical appearance.'

'As usual, I wasn't as forebearing as I could have been.'

'From what I heard, the guard wasn't particularly helpful.'

'No, but somehow I didn't think, and then I just had to defend myself.' I hugged her again.

'How was the trip?'

'Dusty.' I paused. 'People are worried everywhere. They don't buy my crafting. Prices are going up, and I think a lot more people are going hungry. I'm worried. There's a lot of chaos building in the north . . .'

'That's why your timing is good. Kasee would like us to dine with her this evening.' She smiled. 'But I'm glad you came to Ruzor.'

I hugged her again, and, after a moment, she stepped back, shaking her head. 'You did manage to order everything here.'

With a shrug, I managed an embarrassed smile. Probably I did order things too much.

'I need to change, but I won't get very far unless you let me.'

'I don't know that I want to let you.'

So she didn't get very far beyond undressing, and I was glad I had straightened the bed. Krystal was, too.

'You are impossible!'

I kissed her, and then we didn't say much for a long time.

Later, when the light through the window had dimmed, she rolled over and shook me awake. 'Now . . . we do have to get dressed.'

She dressed a lot faster than I did, but I managed to struggle into the browns and pull on my boots.

Herreld didn't blink an eye when we left, not even a wink.

'Just Kasee?' I asked as I followed Krystal down the narrow

steps and across a courtyard toward the taller building behind the barracks.

'I think so. She looked relieved when she heard you were here.'

I wasn't sure I liked that.

Krystal didn't even have to knock. The guards opened the narrow, iron-banded door, and we walked right into a room no bigger than Krystal's, although all the walls were lined with dark wooden bookcases filled almost to overflowing. I hadn't seen so many volumes since the Brotherhood library in Nylan. Even with four oil lamps, the room seemed dim.

'Impressive, aren't they? Unfortunately, most of them are too old to be useful – those that are readable.' Kasee stood on the other side of the circular table and nodded to me as the doors closed behind us. 'It's good to see you.'

'I apologize for the delay . . .' Krystal flushed.

So did I.

Kasee laughed. 'I wouldn't have expected less, and in these uncertain times, it would have been foolish for you not to spend at least a little time alone together.'

That didn't help. We both blushed more.

'Before we get started, let me call for dinner.' Kasee lifted the brass bell and rang.

Two serving women brought in two trays, a basket, two pitchers, three mugs, and left us in the lamplight of the library.

Dinner was simple, very simple – slices of mutton, brown spice sauce, bread, and fried sliced quilla. I never thought I'd see quilla on the autarch's table, even on a conference table in an ancient stronghold.

Krystal poured Kasee and herself some sort of ale, and I filled my mug from the pitcher of redberry I had to myself.

'A drink to your safe arrival, Lerris.' Kasee lifted her mug, and we lifted ours and drank.

The redberry was good, properly tart, and I sighed.

'I hoped it would be good,' said the autarch, serving herself two slices of steaming mutton from the platter and edging it toward Krystal.

'It is.'

Kasee cut her meat and took several bites before speaking. 'In one way, things don't seem too bad. Hamor has made no moves toward Kyphros. In another way, things are bad and getting worse. Almost all sea trade has been cut off, and our olives, dried fruits, and wool can only be sold through Sarronnyn. That means that what we get is going down while Sarronnyn gets the extra.'

The autarch took a quick sip of ale, and I munched on the

heavy dark bread to take away the spice of the brown sauce on the mutton.

'Hamor controls all the important parts of northern Hydlen, and the explosion of the brimstone spring and the Yellow River have ruined Arastia and Sunta. So Faklaar and Worrak are really the only places of any size left outside of Hamor's control in Hydlen. Montgren has surrendered, as have the traders of Sligo.

'The Viscount of Certis is fighting a losing battle, and Jellico will probably fall before long – if it hasn't already.' Kasee shrugged.

Krystal looked at me, and I swallowed the meat in my mouth, wincing as a too-large chunk scraped my throat.

'That bad?'

'Too big a bite.' I took a sip of redberry. 'I can't add too much, except that I think – I think – that Hamor is using a chaos wizard, maybe Sammel, to reopen all the old wizards' roads through the Easthorns as a quick way to get to Gallos and Kyphros. That way, they could march —'

'—right down the road through Tellura and into Kyphros,' finished Krystal.

I nodded.

'How do you know?' asked Kasee.

'I don't *know* it. I *feel* it.'

'With anyone else, I'd question that. Can you tell me more?'

Nodding, I quickly chewed and swallowed. 'There's chaos coming from the Easthorns. It's somehow tied to Hamor, but I can't explain how. It's growing, and it's moving westward.'

'You think we should reinforce Kyphrien, rather than Ruzor?' asked Krystal.

'No.' I swallowed. 'I think I probably ought to find the wizards' road and travel backward.'

Krystal paled.

Kasee shook her head.

'Why?' Krystal finally asked.

'Because I don't see how you can defend Kyphrien against both Hamor and chaos. If I can figure out how to stop them from using the road, then they'll either have to attack through Ruzor or through Gallos. At the least it will buy time. If you abandon Ruzor ...' I shrugged. 'I don't know exactly if that makes sense, but it feels right.'

Krystal pursed her lips.

The autarch sipped from her mug, and the library was silent for a time.

'Are you saying that you can stop the Hamorian armies?' Kasee finally asked.

'No. I think I *might* be able to deny them the use of the wizards' roads, at least those that are blocked.'

'How many troops should we send with him?' asked Kasee.

'A squad?' Krystal suggested.

'No. The last time I took a squad or more, most of them didn't come back. If I can't handle this with a handful, I can't do it at all. Four is all I need in Kyphros, and two squads couldn't protect me if we run into a whole army. I might be able to hide three or four others.' I thought. 'Just three. That's all I know I could shield.'

'That seems to be settled,' Kasee observed dryly. 'Lerris will attempt to use his skills to force the Hamorians to fight their way through Gallos first, and we hope that he can.'

I looked at her. 'It's that bad?'

'It's worse. Leithrrse just got another five thousand troops, and more of those rifles for his Candarian allies. Right now, with levies, we could raise perhaps eight thousand against a force that could be three times that, and we'd have to fight with swords and arrows. There's not a crafter in Kyphros that could forge either their cannon or their rifles. We've managed to buy from smugglers – and others – threescore of the rifles and less than a thousand cartridges.' The autarch took a deep swallow from her mug.

'Geography helps us here,' Krystal added. 'The main channel into Ruzor is long and narrow. That means they can't bring many of their ships into range of the walls at any one time, at least not more than a half score, and rifles don't help that much against thick stone walls. Ruzor's not like Renklaar or Worrak where a lot of deep water runs close to shore.'

I hoped that meant that Krystal and Kasee could hold Ruzor, at least for a time, and that would make Hamor's efforts in Gallos difficult. That assumed that one Lerris could keep the wizards' roads blocked.

'Can you do it?' asked Kasee.

'I won't know if I don't try. And I can't try if I don't get moving.'

'Not tonight.'

'Hardly.'

At least, we agreed on that. Even Kasee gave us a wan smile as we left the library.

On the way back to Krystal's room, under the dim light of scattered oil lamps, we didn't even talk about not talking about the future.

With her door closed behind us, and bolted, there were tears, and holding, and words meaningless to all but lovers facing desperate, and separate, battles. And, as I had come to expect, her pleas for me not to be a hero.

In the end, we slept, but neither long nor well.


# LXXXIII

## The Black Holding, Land's End [Recluce]

'Jellico has fallen.' Talryn walks into the meeting room of the Black Holding. He wipes his forehead. 'So has Hydolar.'

'So quickly?' Maris steps inside from the east-facing terrace and out of the faint summer breeze. 'How did you find out?'

'Nordlan traders.' The broad-shouldered magister picks up the pitcher in front of Heldra, sniffs it, and sets it down. He wrinkles his nose. 'It doesn't take that long when you have cannon throwing five-stone explosive shells and when the defenders are fighting with swords and arrows against those new rifles. Berfir's dead, and Hydlen's a mess. So is Certis.'

'Cold steel seems to have lost its strength.' Heldra lifts an empty mug. 'To the age of new order.' She pours ale from the pitcher into the mug.

'You've been drinking.' Maris glares at her.

'Can you think of anything better to do? Meeting this far from Nylan?'

'We haven't exactly lost yet,' observes Talryn. 'The trio are still intact, and the *Llyse* is back on station. To date the three have managed to sink more than a half score of the Hamorian ships. The Brotherhood is close to completing another warship.'

'So glorious, so glorious . . .' Heldra hiccups. 'Threescore warships . . . and we have destroyed ten.'

'Twelve,' corrects Talryn. 'And the Prefect of Certis may have lost Jellico —'

'—and his life.'

'—but that cost Hamor nearly five thousand casualties. Hydlen didn't do so well. Hamor used more cannon there.'

'Neither Kyphros nor Gallos can put up that kind of resistance.' Maris paces back and forth across the end of the table. 'The last war bled them both dry.'

'The fruits of our success!' Heldra thumps the mug on the ancient table. 'The fruits of our success . . .'

'Shut up, Heldra.'

'Don't tell me to shut up.' Her hand reaches for the blade. 'Not so drunk I can't carve you into dog meat.'

Maris steps back. 'That's easy. Just chop me up. That won't stop Hamor.'

'Don't tell me when to stop talking.'

'Hamor is the problem,' interjects Talryn.

'All right,' concedes Heldra. 'Just keep this frigging trader civil.'

'Heldra . . .' Talryn draws her name out like a threat.

'All right, I said.'

'Why don't we ask Gunnar for ideas or help?' Maris paces to the east window and turns.

'Him and his hidebound Institute? What help will they give? He's the one who's stopped the work on machines. Better we ask the Founders.' Heldra gestures toward the ancient blade on the wall. 'It's almost as hot as when they got here.'

'Gunnar is still a great weather mage,' Talryn reflects.

'Who hasn't raised a storm in generations,' answers Heldra, lifting her mug and taking another swallow.

'He might now,' points out Maris.

'Might he now?' Heldra raises her mug. 'Then here's to the great storm wizard. To the great storm wizard.'

# LXXXIV

Either Krystal or Kasee arranged for sweet rolls and hot cider to be sent to Krystal's room, and we sat beside each other at the small table, with the hot light of morning pouring through the window.

Outside, the air was still, without even a hint of a breeze off the ocean or the bay, and the heat seemed to ooze into the room. Light bounced off the wall, glinting from the sand in the plaster.

Krystal reached out and held my hands, saying nothing.

Did I have to go? That wasn't the question, and we both knew it. We could wait until things got worse, until the armies of Hamor were actually in Kyphros and I could do nothing.

I shivered.

'What's the matter?'

'I wonder. I hope that I didn't wait too long. Maybe I should have gone straight to the wizards' roads.'

'You didn't know what was happening.'

'I still don't.'

'Don't worry about the timing, Lerris. Jellico hasn't fallen yet ... not that we've heard, and armies don't move places overnight.'

'Neither do I.'

She raised her eyebrows, and I blushed.

After a while, Krystal spoke in a low voice. 'Lerris. I know what has to be done, but I don't have to like it. First, there's this Antonin, and you come back from your fight with him with bruises all over your body. Then, you have to take on this Gerlis, and you come back on a stretcher, with burns, and broken limbs, and you don't even recognize anyone for days. You're finally well and strong, and now there's another chaos wizard who's even stronger than the first two and he's knocking down mountains to make way for an army to roll over Kyphros. I don't know and you don't know if you can stop him, but if you can't, we don't have the troops to.' Krystal looked at the faded and cracked inlay work on the table. 'One of these days you won't come back.'

I looked at the table myself. What could I do?

Hamor might impose order on Candar, order that the place needed badly, but that order would be clasped on the people like steel fetters, and the chaos beneath the rocks would flare – and each new chaos wizard would be stronger and that would allow greater order – and restrictions – to be created by Hamor.

We couldn't go back to Recluce. The Brotherhood wouldn't take either one of us – not a lady blade like Krystal nor a gray earth wizard like me. We couldn't surrender, not without being put to death or imprisoned, although I thought imprisonment was highly unlikely. Rulers are rather skeptical about whether anyone called a wizard will stay put.

Yet, if we fought ... how many more would die? How many more Shervans and Pendrils would there be? That was one reason why I really didn't want to take many troopers with me.

'I'll be back.'

'Lerris ... please don't be a hero, and you know what I mean.'

I nodded and clasped Krystal's hands again before I said, 'I'd better get ready.'

She nodded, and we stood and held each other.

Outside, the sunlight and the heat built, and heat waves shimmered across Ruzor, promising only more heat through the long days ahead.

# LXXXV

I seemed to be moving more quickly up the road to Felsa than on my descent, but whether that was because of the escort or because I was committed to getting myself into more trouble was another question I wasn't sure I really wanted to answer. The older I got, the more questions like that seemed to pop up.

The sun was hot, and the road was dusty, with the red dust clinging to everything. Gairloch plodded along, keeping right up with the bigger mounts carrying Weldein, Berli, and Fregin.

To the left, beyond the low wall on the edge of the road, the cliff dropped down to the narrow line of silver that was the Phroan River. Ahead, I could see the mist spilling out of the Gateway Gorge, just as it had only a few days before. The one thing about the burning summer heat of Kyphros was that there weren't that many flies – and no mosquitoes, except near the rivers and ponds, and there weren't that many of either.

Weldein rode beside me, and he hadn't said much. I had noticed that his once-long blond hair was shorter, much shorter, more military. Somehow, Weldein had also become more military, more focused. Perhaps the times were forcing that kind of change on all of us.

He glanced at me, then up the road.

'I know. It's a fool's errand.' I forced a grin at him. 'But it's a chance to get out of Ruzor and away from the bugs.'

After a long moment, he grinned back. 'You always know how to cheer a man, Master Lerris.'

'Yes, me and my trusty staff.' I pulled it from the lanceholder and twirled it a bit. Then I put it back in the holder and shifted my weight in the saddle. When I did, I saw that Berli and Fregin had ridden up closer behind us, as if they wanted to hear the conversation.

*Wheeee ... eeee*

'I know it's hot,' I muttered to Gairloch, 'and it's going to get hotter before we reach the Gorge.'

'I'd forgotten how you talk to your pony.'

'Why not? He doesn't argue back, at least not much, and he goes where we have to.'

'The pony carried him against – what – three wizards?' Weldein offered the statement to Berli and Fregin.

*Khhhcherwww* . . . 'Demon's dust,' muttered Fregin.

'Two, actually.' I rubbed my own nose to keep from sneezing. 'I tied him up when I went into Antonin's castle.'

'You walked into a chaos wizard's castle on foot?' asked Berli.

'I know better now.' I shrugged.

'Was that when you rescued the . . . the redheaded mage?' Weldein had a glint in his eye.

'Yes. I wasn't sure she was there, but I had to do something.' I wiped my forehead. Dry or not, I was still sweating.

'What about the time you rescued Haithen? Didn't you charge into a whole squad of Gallosians?'

'Someone had to do something.' I didn't mention that I hadn't exactly meant to charge the white wizard. The idiot wouldn't let me try to avoid him.

*Kkkchewww* . . . Fregin sneezed again. 'Wish you could do something about this friggin' dust.'

Berli laughed for a moment, then said sweetly, 'I take it, Weldein, that you are trying to let us know that Master Lerris is both more formidable and more dangerous than he looks?'

'I'm not sure I'm all that dangerous, but being around me could be.'

'I was at the brimstone spring,' said Berli.

'What brimstone spring?' asked Fregin.

Berli shook her head.

Fregin sneezed once more. '. . . friggin' dust . . .'

I wiped my forehead once more, hoping that it wouldn't be too long before we reached the Gorge. Even a short period of mist and cool would be welcome.

I tried not to think about the days and days ahead.

# LXXXVI

Despite the low clouds, the light wind out of the south was hot. Sweat dripped down the inside of Justen's shirt, and his collar was dark with moisture. After wiping his forehead, he patted Rosefoot on the neck.

Somewhat behind him, Tamra rode silently, her eyes partly glazed over, as though her mind or sense were elsewhere.

A not-too-distant explosion echoed through the hills, then another, but the two continued to ride to the southwest, away from Jellico.

In time, Justen reined up behind the wreckage of a mountain willow. The entire tree had been bent and smashed flat by the heavy limb of an oak that had fallen across the top of the willow. Where the trunk of the willow had bent was a mass of twisted and splintered wood.

Justen looked up and studied the whitened section of the oak from where the branch had fallen, his eyes taking on a faraway cast.

'What is it?' asked Tamra.

'Cannon shell.'

She glanced from the tree to Justen and back to the tree.

*Crummppt!* Less than four hundred cubits below them, sod and scrub brush erupted into the sky.

In the valley to the southeast, patches of smoke as thick as fog had begun to drift across the low hills and grasslands. At the east end of the valley, behind the handful of sunburst banners, the flashes of the cannon continued.

Dirt and sod and grass spewed into the sky where the heavy shells from the Hamorian guns continued to explode just in front of the Certan troops, lying flat behind hastily dug embankments that offered no real protection against the explosions. Their green banners lay scattered, as if no one wished to raise one as a target for the deadly cannon.

Justen pointed to the west and to the back side of the ridge. 'We'll need to circle around this and take the back trails. It will take more time.'

'Won't we run into more troops?' Tamra looked from the distant cannon to the scattered troops below. 'They seem to be everywhere.'

'Hamor doesn't work that way. They take the roads, the cities, the trading points, and wait. Eventually, people give up. These troops didn't take any of the main roads, and that's a problem.'

'Why?'

'I don't know, but I'd bet that the Hamorians are rebuilding or clearing the old hidden roads of Fairhaven. I don't see any other way how they got all these troops into Certis so quickly and unseen.'

Justen rode for a while, then continued. 'That gives us two other problems. Do you see?'

'They'll use the roads to take the middle of Candar, and the seas to take the ports?' asked the redhead.

'That's one,' pointed out Justen. 'And with the ports in their hands and the roads, that doesn't leave much.'

'I can't see the autarch giving up. Or Lerris.'

'That's going to be the second problem, especially if we don't get to him.' Justen nudged Rosefoot away from Tamra and down the far side of the hill, away from the troops and the falling shells. 'A real problem. Can you see why?'

Tamra took a last look back at another geyser of soil and cloth fragments, then spurred her mount after Justen. 'What could Lerris do to stop an army?'

Justen did not answer, even when Tamra pulled her mount alongside his, though his face remained grim.

'Why won't you say? You're hiding things again.'

'How do you think Hamor is clearing the roads that quickly? Haven't you heard the groaning in the earth?'

'Chaos? And Lerris will try to stop it? Like he did in Hydlen? Oh, darkness . . .'

They kept riding.

# LXXXVII

With each step, Gairloch looked more like a small roan horse than a pony, and the rest of us like dust-covered statues – except for the sneezing.

No matter what I tried, I kept sneezing, and so did Weldein and Fregin. Fregin's nose was as red as a hearth, but somehow, Berli had managed to avoid the sneezing all through the long ride.

My rear was sore, and I'd already forgotten how good it had felt to sleep in my own bed the one night we had stopped at home, rather than in the barracks in Kyphrien. My own bed or not, though, I missed Krystal. I hadn't missed the *brawwking* of the chickens.

Wegel had looked so mournful in stammering through his explanations of what the little girls needed that I'd let him use scraps and mismatched lumber left over to see what he could do to make a table and stool for the cot. I also suggested he try to get some leftovers from his father. It had been his idea, and it wasn't a bad one, but he needed to do some of the asking as well.

Rissa had just shaken her head when we rode out, and the two girls had watched wide-eyed. Wegel had waved the broom, and I'd wanted to tell him that we weren't exactly on the most glorious of quests, that getting tied up with the collision between order and chaos was going to be messy, and, if I weren't lucky and careful, possibly fatal. The disturbing thought that followed was that it could be fatal even if I were lucky and careful.

Still, the ride north had been quiet, almost too quiet, with the marketplace in Kyphrien a hushed shade of its former self, and the roads deserted and the dust thick and sometimes undisturbed.

*Kkhchewww!* I looked up.

'You sneezed. You actually sneezed.'

Berli looked embarrassed. Then she shrugged.

'. . . don't believe it . . .' muttered Fregin. 'Friggin' dust finally got to her.'

I patted Gairloch on the neck and wished I hadn't as more dust swirled up into my nose, and I sneezed.

'See?' Berli said.

The kaystone on the right side of the road announced that Meltosia was three kays ahead.

We stopped there for a midday meal at Mama Parlaan's, where we ate more burkha, as hot as I'd ever had, and where everyone was quite polite, and all too quiet. I began to dread reaching Tellura.

The dust hung over everything, and seemed baked on me as Gairloch carried me northwest toward the small town and outpost where I had first entered Kyphros at a time that seemed so long ago. Sometimes, three years is more than a lifetime.

I wasn't too thrilled about stopping in Tellura, not with the casualties I had created, and I especially wasn't looking forward to seeing Shervan's sister Barrabra. But it was the last place to resupply before we reached the wizards' road, and I would have felt wrong in avoiding Tellura, hard as I knew it was going to be.

The outliers' station looked the same – soft white plaster walls, red tile roof, sitting in the midst of red dust and more red dust.

We reined up outside the front of the covered portico.

*Whuffff* . . . Like the rest of us, Gairloch snorted out dust.

'The Finest! The Finest!' A small girl ran up inside the building.

I dismounted and handed the reins to Weldein.

'But . . .'

'I need to do something.'

Barrabra's ample figure stood silently under the archway in the late afternoon sun. As I walked up the three steps, I could see thin streaks of white in the blond hair, and lines in her face.

'Master Wizard . . .' She inclined her head, but there was a darkness in her once-happy Kyphran eyes that had not been there before.

'Barrabra . . . I am sorry.' I bowed my head. 'Words don't mean much. There's not a lot I can say or do to take away the pain. I wanted you to know that I owe my life to Shervan and the others.'

For a long time, she looked at me, just looked, before she asked, 'Why are you here?'

'I'm going to try to stop the Hamorians. They're going to use the hidden wizards' roads to take over Candar.'

'Ah . . . if it is not the Prefect of Gallos, then it is the Emperor of Hamor . . . why will they not leave us alone?'

'I don't know, not really. People talk about order and chaos, and sometimes they are just names without meaning when those we love die.'

'You are older.'

'Perhaps.'

'You will age even more.'

'Probably.'

'Tell me . . . how did Shervan save your life?'

'There's not much to tell. We charged a chaos wizard, and he threw his sword at the wizard. The wizard had to stop the sword, and that let me do what I had to do.'

'I see.'

'No . . . lady . . . you don't.' Weldein stood behind me. 'Lerris led the charge on his pony. He carried only a staff. The chaos wizard broke Lerris's arms and legs, and half his body was burned. Shervan and Lerris saved hundreds of troopers. I was one of those they saved. They carried Lerris back to Kyphros on a cart, and no one thought he would live. Now he's going out to face an army alone – except for us.'

Barrabra looked at Weldein. Weldein met her look.

Finally, she looked down, then gave me a wan smile. 'I knew you were unlike the others, but we had hoped so many would not die.'

'So did I. So did I.'

'Pendril died. Niklos died, too.'

Nothing I could say would change that. For a time, the three of us stood there. Then Barrabra shrugged, a shrug of resignation, sadness, acceptance, and called, 'Cirla!'

The young blond woman – barely beyond girlhood and wearing the same maroon trousers and shirt she had more than a year earlier – rushed from the doorway.

'You remember the wizard?'

Cirla looked down at the tiles that comprised the floor of the covered porch.

'Would you show them where to stable their horses? They need rest before they go out to fight.'

Cirla looked up. Her green eyes met mine, without resentment, and I turned and followed her, reclaiming Gairloch.

Grooming Gairloch seemed to take forever, and I felt as if there were twice as much dust on me when I was done. I tried to brush off the worst of the dust once I stepped out of the stall.

'Why did Pendril have to die?'

I hadn't realized Cirla had just waited outside the stall.

I swallowed. Finally, I answered her. 'It didn't have to be Pendril; it just happened that way. When battles or wars are fought, troopers die.'

'The blond Finest' – her eyes flickered toward the corner where Weldein was wiping off his saddle – 'he said you almost died. Is that true?'

'Died? That's what they told me. I don't remember much until probably three eight-days after the battle. I couldn't walk for a while, and then I had to use my staff.'

'Why did you go out to fight?' Her eyes were open, and she wanted an answer.

'Because I was afraid my consort – I thought she might be killed if I didn't do what I did.'

'What's her name?'

'Krystal.'

'Your consort is the commander, and she might have been killed?'

'The autarch's commanders fight. The last one was killed in the battle before the one where Shervan and Pendril and Niklos were killed.'

'But the Emperor of Hamor doesn't fight, and the Prefect didn't.'

'Should the commander ask outliers like Shervan to fight and maybe die if she always is safe from harm?' I knew Krystal felt that way.

'Do you feel that way?'

'No. He's worse,' said Berli, racking her saddle. 'He's tough, our wizard is, but he won't ask anyone to fight unless he's in twice as much danger.'

Cirla looked from the dark-haired woman to me, then shook her head. 'No one ever told us.'

'I wish I had, earlier,' I admitted. 'I mean, about how brave Shervan and Pendril were.'

'I never thought of Shervan as brave. He always talked a lot.'

'He was brave.' I closed the stall. 'He never looked back, never complained.' He'd probably been too brave. 'And he did talk a lot. I missed it when I learned he had died.'

A single bell rang.

'Dinner is ready,' she announced, turning back toward the wing of the building with the big dining room.

Berli, Fregin, and Weldein followed me into the long room. The same place at the head of the table was empty. I slowly took it, and Barrabra took the place on the left, the same spot where she had been seated when I first met Shervan.

'Would you . . . ?' asked Barrabra, turning to me.

This time, I did have something to say.

'When I was last here, I prayed that right-thinking people would have the will to bring order from chaos, and around this table were many right-thinking people who did just that. They brought us order at the cost of their lives, and yet, chaos again threatens. Chaos will always threaten, and order often requires all that we have to give. May the sacrifices and the hopes of all those who have made our lives a better and more ordered place always be remembered.' I swallowed and looked at the table for a moment.

'He sounds like a wizard now,' coughed the old woman. If I recalled correctly, she had said I hadn't sounded like a wizard the first time I had come to Tellura.

Cirla brought in the casserole this time, and the aroma of spices filled the room – chilies, and who knew what else.

'Smells good,' whispered Fregin.

Barrabra lifted the basket of bread and held it before me. I broke off a chunk and then held the basket for her.

'Thank you.'

I passed the basket to Berli and waited to serve myself some of the casserole. Weldein took a heaping measure, as did the young outlier beside him, before the dish reached me. I hadn't felt that hungry, but the lamb and spices prompted me to take a normal helping before passing the dish to Barrabra. She took a small portion.

I tasted the chilied lamb, the same dish I'd had before, but it didn't seem nearly so spicy, and I was far hungrier than I had first realized.

Slowly, slowly . . . the conversation picked up at the far end of the table.

'According to the peddler . . . dreadful doings there was in Freetown . . . the Regent turned into flame and a Hamor warship went up in flames, almost at the pier . . .'

'The black devils, it was, with one of their invisible ships.'

'The mighty *Drakka*. All her armor didn't stop the black devils.'

'A terrible time it is, these days,' offered the older woman in yellow, making the sign of the one-god worshipers, 'like as to the end of the Legend when chaos dies . . .'

'How can chaos die?' Cirla looked toward me.

I had to swallow a mouthful of lamb before I could answer. 'The only way I know is if order also dies. The Balance seems powerful enough to ensure that.'

'Could order die?'

Could it? What would be the death of order – or chaos? 'I suppose anything is possible, but right now, I can't think of a way to destroy either.' I had to shrug again.

Cirla pursed her lips.

'They say that the wizard has killed three chaos-masters.' The low comment came from the other end of the long table.

'You believe in that?'

'Why not? It's a good story.'

'It's also true,' added Berli.

'You saw this? With your own eyes?'

'I saw the third wizard perish, and a friend was saved when he destroyed the first one.' Berli shrugged. 'As for the second one . . . he doesn't exist anymore, but I wasn't there.'

'What do you know about the wizard?' the young outlier asked of Fregin.

'Don't know about any wizards,' mumbled Fregin with a mouth full of lamb. 'Saw him break a trooper's wrist with a staff while he held off a dozen armed men with that piece of wood. Saw the toughest officer of the Finest bow more to him than the autarch. That's enough for me.'

'The wizard is what the wizard is,' announced Barrabra. 'Enough of such foolishness.'

Even Fregin paused from shoveling in food, but not for long.

'How are the groves?' I asked.

'They are dry, and we are lucky that the winter was so wet, for the summer will be longer and hotter yet, and perhaps the fall, too, according to the ancient.'

'I am not that old,' snapped the elderly woman in yellow. 'It takes no idiot to recognize that heavy winter rains can only lead to dry summers and drier falls. The clouds, they hold only so much rain.' She turned to me. 'Is that not so, Master Wizard?'

'Each cloud can only hold so much rain, but the winds and the oceans tell how many clouds there will be.' I didn't wish to contradict her, but clouds alone did not hold the answer.

'And the winds, they are from the dry north, and not from the wet south. So we will have no rain.' She gave the outlier a sharp nod.

He shrugged.

After dinner, I sat in the dimness of the portico.

'Master Wizard?' Barrabra stood under the archway behind me.

I gestured to the bench across from me. 'Please sit down.'

'I would not wish to disturb you . . .'

'Please sit down.'

A single birdcall echoed from somewhere, and I listened, but the call was not repeated.

'You are sad to see us.' She brushed her hair back off her shoulder, and I noticed that she no longer wore the green combs. 'The combs – Niklos gave them to me.'

After a time, I answered. 'It hurts to come back here. When I was last here, people sang, and they laughed. Now . . . you are unhappy, and I helped cause that sadness.'

'But you came.'

'I should have come sooner.'

'You came when you could, and that is all we could expect of a great wizard.' She brushed her long hair back again, and I thought of the green combs of Niklos and knew she would never wear them again.

'I am not a great wizard. I'm just a man – one who's not very old – who's trying to do what's right. That's hard because no one can tell you what is right and because, if you're honest, you have to question even your own idea of what is right.' I snorted. 'And then you have to act, and that's when everyone gets hurt.'

'You are older than you think. What you do will make you wiser and older before your time. Niklos and I had time to be young. I fear you will not.' She sighed. 'I was angry at you, and then I saw you, and the faces of those who came with you. Now I am not angry, and I am glad I have lived as I have, and loved as I have, and I am even glad Shervan was with you.' She stood up, and brushed back her long hair yet again. 'And Pendril. And even Niklos. They did not have to carry what you carry, and what you must.' She laughed a soft laugh. 'I hope you will remember what it is to be young and to love. It does not last long, and less for the mighty.' She took a step and added, 'Best you sleep while you can, Great Wizard.'

For a time, I sat alone. Me – a great wizard? Barrabra acted as though I carried the fate of Candar on my shoulders. All I had to do was go out and block the wizards' roads to buy Kasee and Krystal some time to figure out another way to stop Hamor from overrunning the rest of Kyphros. Just that.

When I did climb onto the hot narrow pallet in the narrow room and lie back, I still could sense the groaning of chaos beneath Candar, and the growing nearness of the chaos wizard. Even the mountains seemed to shift in the darkness. Though I fell asleep quickly, I did not dream, not of silverhaired druids offering advice or chaos boiling from the depths, and for that I was glad.

# LXXXVIII
## East of Yryna, Gallos [Candar]

The quiet sound of soldiers shifting in their places echoes through the chill air of the deep canyon. A huge pile of rock that has collapsed from the cliffs to the left of the old road blocks the canyon. The old paving stones seem to march right up to the rubble.

Behind the troops stretch perhaps fifty kays of canyon that had once held the great Easthorn Highway. The base of that highway had been formed from the mortared and fitted stones that linked the foundation blocks. Each long section was straight as a quarrel, a segment of the road that had once run from ancient Fairhaven to Sarronnyn, a road that the white wizards had planned would run from Freetown – then called Lydiar – through the Westhorns and Sarronnyn and on to Southwind.

Now, yet another wall of fallen stone bars any passage, and the Hamorian troops wait once more. Scattered cedar trees and scrub oak dot the rocky mass that blocks the western end of the road. Beyond the piled rocks, the canyon continues westward.

A single figure in brown – brown sandals, tunic, and trousers – stands well before the Hamorian troops and studies the rock. The watercourse beside the uncovered section of the road holds a long narrow expanse of water, blocked by the fallen rock and the thin soil of centuries from its descent to the plains of Gallos.

Finally, the wizard turns to the man beside him who wears the tan uniform of Hamor and a heavy pistol on his wide leather belt. 'I can do it, but it will be even more dangerous than any of the rock piles I removed earlier. You need to march the troops back a good kay.'

'Where will you be?'

'Almost that far back,' Sammel says with a smile. 'There's more than enough chaos to work with.'

Leithrrse shudders.

'Don't shudder. You're the ones who created it with all those ordered ships and weapons.' Sammel's tone is matter-of-fact.

The Hamorian envoy turns to the officer with the silver braid upon his vest. 'You heard the wizard. Move them back.'

The troops turn and march back along the paving stones, so recently scoured clean of debris with the lick of chaos flame.

After a time, they halt and wait, and low voices exchange comments.

'. . . bigger than anything he's tried so far . . .'

'. . . looks so kindly . . .'

'. . . kindly, like a hungry mountain cat's kindly . . .'

A flash brighter than noonday sun, sharper than the closest of lightnings, flares across the stone mass.

*RRRRRurrrrrr . . . rurrrr . . .*

The ground heaves, and the rock mass shifts, and shifts . . . and a chasm opens where the drainage way had been. Steam flares into the air, bearing brimstone.

Rocks and stone more than a hundred cubits high splinter, shatter, and slide northward into the maw of chaos.

In time, the flames and heat subside, and the wizard in brown trudges over to the ancient kaystone. There he sits down, holding his head, ignoring the letters graven on the stone: 'Yryna 75 K.'

'When can we march?' asks Leithrrse.

'Let it cool a bit.' Sammel does not look up.

Where the rock had been a flat expanse of smooth stone, melted as smooth as glass, stretches half a kay to where the old road resumes.

The soldiers mutter and shake their heads.

Leithrrse drinks from his water bottle and wipes his forehead.

Deep beneath the rocks, chaos rumbles still, and the ground trembles.

# LXXXIX

Dayala stood for a long time at the single pier at Diehl, just a step away from the plank leading up onto the *Eidolon*. A thin wisp of smoke trailed from the single green-striped black stack of the old Nordlan half-steamer, though the paddles were stilled.

The silver-haired and youthful-looking woman turned for a last look toward the valley of the Great Forest of Naclos. She turned back, took a deep breath, picked up her pack, and walked up the plank to where the mate with the short blond beard and muscled arms waited.

'My name is Dayala.'

'Yes. You are the druid. Captain Heroulk said you should have the second cabin to yourself, Lady.' He bowed.

She waited, not knowing where the second cabin might be.

The mate smiled, then gestured to the sailor behind him. 'Jelker, show the lady to the second cabin.'

A blond-haired and slender youth stopped coiling a line and stepped up with a bow.

'Thank you.' Dayala inclined her head to the mate.

'Our pleasure, Lady. Druids bring good luck, or at least, keep away ill fate, and that's the same for any sailor.'

'Steam up! Plank up! Cast off!' ordered the mate, after turning from Dayala.

She followed Jelker down the ladder and into the small cabin, where she set the pack on the lower bunk. Her toes wiggled on the hardwood, and she repressed a shiver.

'Are you really a druid?'

'I am.'

The ship swayed, and a dull thumping sound reverberated through the hull.

'I mean, do you talk to trees . . . ?'

She shook her head. 'Trees don't listen. Sometimes, we listen to them, or to the rest of life . . .'

'Do you . . . I mean . . . is it . . . just trees?'

With a laugh, she answered. 'No. I have a man. A mage who is also a druid.'

'Oh . . .'

'Don't sound so disappointed that an old woman like me—'

'Old? You can't be more than eighteen.'

'If you knew how old I really was . . .' She gestured toward the cabin door. 'I'd like to go up on deck.'

He stared down at her boldly.

Dayala sighed and looked back at the young man for a long moment, feeling the darkness well from her, feeling the age and the power of the Great Forest surge forth.

The youngster paled. 'I'm sorry, Lady.'

She touched his shoulder lightly. 'I did warn you. Let's go.'

Jelker hurried the three steps to the ladder and scrambled up, leaving Dayala to make her way topside alone. After shaking her head, she took her time.

Later, standing by the port rail, she watched the shore fall away, her eyes focused beyond Diehl toward the Great Forest.

Once the *Eidolon* cleared the bay, the dull thumping stopped, and the ship shivered into full sail before the wind.

Dayala kept one hand on the poop railing as the *Eidolon* gently eased over a low wave, and a small spray of white outlined the bow. In the late afternoon light, the ship steadied, quieter than ever.

The paddles still, the great ancient steam engine cooled. While the wind held, and it would, the captain needed to burn no coal.

'Always get a good wind coming out of Diehl,' observed the second mate, pausing beside Dayala for a moment, his short brown hair disheveled by the wind. 'Most times, anyway.' He glanced at the browns Dayala wore and then at her bare feet. 'You a druid and traveling? That doesn't happen much.'

'Only when it is necessary. Very necessary.'

'And this is very necessary?' A smile played around his lips.

'If you do not want the world to belong to Hamor and for chaos to perch on every hilltop.' Her tone was light.

The man's eyes flicked to hers. Then he looked down at the planks. 'I guess it must be important. Druids don't lie.'

'Sometimes it would be easier.'

He shivered, and then bowed. 'Need to be getting on, Lady.'

A faint and bitter smile crossed the druid's lips, and she turned her eyes to the northeast, toward Kyphros and Ruzor. Toward where she would meet Justen.

# XC

I slowed Gairloch to a deliberate walk as the road dipped into another small dry valley in the Little Easthorns. Around us were rocks and more tree-covered rocks. Most of the rocks in the Little Easthorns were red and black, and rough, unlike the heavier and grayer rock of the Easthorns and Westhorns.

As I studied the flat area in front of me, I wished I had a better memory for details.

'Is this the one?' asked Weldein for at least the third time, running his fingers through his short blond hair.

'I don't know yet. I was only here once before, and that was almost three years ago.' It felt as if a lot longer than three years had passed.

*Kkhhcheww* ... 'Friggin' dust ...' mumbled Fregin.

'We know,' snapped Berli. 'We know.'

I paused, sensing the aura of chaos. On my left seemed to be a thick and intertwined grove of scrub juniper bushes, while on the right was a large gray-white boulder that blocked the view to the north.

Slowly, I eased Gairloch toward the apparent boulder, reaching out with my senses. I nodded. 'This is the place.'

'Just a bunch of boulders that way,' mumbled Fregin, reining up behind Weldein.

Berli had dismounted and brushed at the reddish-white dust of the flattest part of the road.

'Stop raisin' dust.' Fregin sneezed.

I concentrated on the illusion, although I could tell it was fraying, tracing back the lines that held it together, half marveling at the fact that even Antonin had had to use order to serve chaos. That use of order was how and why the illusion had lasted, of course.

Finally, I traced back the webs and slowly separated them, breaking them into smaller and smaller segments of chaos within order, much in the same way as I had finally reordered myself to match the pattern that I had seen in Justen, except this time I was almost working in reverse.

'Demon-damn! Where'd that road come from?' asked Fregin.

'It's always been here,' answered Berli, straightening up. 'See. Here are the outlines of the paving stones.'

Weldein shook his head. 'I've ridden this road a dozen times and never seen this.'

'You weren't meant to. The illusion was strong enough to hide it from anyone but a mage. Kry – the commander sent some people to find this, but they never did, and somehow I never did get out here to find it – something always kept happening.'

'Imagine that,' said Berli dryly.

'Anyway, it will stay like this now.'

'Is that good?' asked Weldein. 'You said the Hamorians were using it.'

'They're starting at the other end. If they get this far ...' I shrugged.

'I see what you mean.'

Before we left, I studied the dry wash again. The spot had actually been a crossroads of sorts, because a covered drainage way ran under the north-south road that Kyphrans had used for years. The top of the drainage way was part of the other road itself – the road between Gallos and Kyphros and the one we had just ridden up from Tellura.

I wondered why people hadn't used the wizards' road before Antonin hid it, but maybe that was because it didn't lead anywhere nearby. Still, that didn't make sense. The white wizards had built the road to be the shortest east-west highway across Candar.

Berli slipped back into her saddle, and I turned Gairloch east and onto the dust – and dirt-covered paving stones. There was a shallow set of ruts where Antonin's carriage had passed. At the bottom of the rut, I could see traces of the paving stones beneath, unmarked, uncracked.

Whatever else they had done, the white wizards had built well, as I knew from the part of the road still used from northwest Kyphros to Sarronnyn.

We traveled another ten kays before I found out why the part of the road we traveled hadn't been used before Antonin arrived. The faultless stone-work of the old road, concealed as it was by a thin layer of dirt and some scrub brush, ran right up to a huge pile of red and black rocks tumbled together, a pile nearly forty cubits high. The rocks had apparently peeled away from the cliff above the road and buried it, perhaps for centuries.

Why hadn't anyone tried to reopen the road before Antonin? I frowned, then nodded. It was a military road. It didn't improve travel between Gallos and Kyphros. With the use of steamships, trade was easier by river and the ocean, and, probably most important, it would have taken hundreds of workers a good season to move just the pile of stone in front of me.

Even Antonin had only created a stone-fused narrow passage through the rock pile. The lingering feel of chaos surrounded the narrow passage.

*Wheee . . . eee . . .*

'I know. It feels terrible.' I patted Gairloch on the neck.

*Kkcchew!* 'Damned dust is white now,' muttered Fregin.

'The chaos wizard did this?' Weldein pulled up beside me, and we were almost shoulder to shoulder. I could have reached out and touched the fused stone wall. It would have been a tight fit for Antonin's carriage.

'The second one – Antonin. The feel of chaos is fading, but it's still there.'

'He burned through this, and you defeated him?' asked Berli, close behind, her words echoing from the stone.

'Sometimes, luck and order can overcome brute force.'

'Prefer the brute force, myself,' grumbled Fregin. 'Can't always count on luck.'

I appreciated that sentiment, especially since the growing rumbles of chaos from the depths to the east of us indicated that the chaos wizard ahead had much more brute force than Antonin or Gerlis had possessed. How had Sammel gathered such force? Was it because he knew the basics of order? That would explain a lot.

'Gettin' right thirsty,' Fregin said to Berli.

'Who isn't?'

'Hungry, too.'

'You're always hungry.'

We stopped in the shade of a cliff another two or three kays farther east along the road. I offered slices of the white cheese and the bread that Barrabra had pressed on me the morning before when we had left Tellura.

Food wasn't the problem. Water was. The summer had been so dry that there was no water in the drainage way beside the road, and we'd only passed one spring.

I wiped my forehead . . . then paused. If I were such an earth wizard, why couldn't I look for springs and the like?

Sitting in the shade, I let my senses try to seek out water. I'd sought and found iron before, deep beneath the earth. Water shouldn't be that hard.

It probably wouldn't have been, had there been any to find, that is, any that wouldn't have taken a team of miners to get to. Absently, thinking of miners, I wondered how Ginstal was doing in his efforts to rebuild the Hrisbarg iron mines. Not too well, I hoped, since that would only strengthen Hamor's hold on Candar.

I chewed through the bread and cheese and moistened my mouth with some water from my water bottle. There was less than a quarter left, and Gairloch hadn't drunk since morning, and even in the shade he was hot and panting. After putting the food back in the left saddlebag, I took another deep breath and concentrated on trying to find water.

'I'm not sure,' I told Weldein, 'but there might be a spring another kay or so ahead.'

He nodded as he mounted, as if my announcement were only to be expected.

I wasn't quite as accurate as I'd hoped. It was more like three kays, but no one could have missed it, because it was more like a stream that flowed into the drainage way and then slowly vanished into the ground beneath the stones lining the drainage channel.

Still, everyone got plenty to drink, even Gairloch, although I made him take it in steps, and we refilled our bottles before we set out again.

'Some advantages to being with a wizard,' conceded Fregin.

'Tell us that when chaos-fire is flying around our heads,' suggested Weldein.

That night, I didn't even have to find another spring. We camped in a long-abandoned, stone-walled waystation with a flowing spring. The roof had ages-since turned to dust, but we didn't exactly have to worry about rain or cold.

I didn't sleep all that well, not with the feel of chaos growing stronger and deeper with each kay we moved eastward, but what good was it to tell the others that I was sensing chaos that they couldn't feel or hear?

The next day was pretty much like the previous one.

We found another, smaller rock pile where Antonin had burned a passage, and the carriage tracks pointed eastward. Most of the time, the wizards' road was surprisingly clear, and from the carriage tracks, the dried horse droppings, and the lingering hints of chaos, it was clear that Antonin had indeed used the road frequently.

Late in the day on the second day on the wizards' road, we came to a grove of scrub junipers, planted right in the middle of the road, and totally blocking it.

'Where'd that come from?' demanded Fregin.

'It was probably always here,' answered Berli.

I shook my head. The grove felt wrong, but I was tired, and it took a moment for me to realize that it was another illusion. After fumbling a bit, I dissolved the illusion as well.

There was another crossroads, and even a weathered kaystone that announced, 'Yryna – 10 K.' I'd never heard of Yryna, but the placement of the stone on the northern side of the crossroads seemed to indicate that the town was somewhere in Gallos, and I thought I would have heard of it somewhere had it belonged to Kyphros.

'Yryna?' asked Fregin.

The rest of us shrugged.

As Gairloch carried me eastward along the wizards' road, I realized two things. First, the cliffs around the road were higher, and, second, there were no carriage tracks on the road.

'Somewhere ahead, the road must be blocked.'

'No tracks?' asked Weldein.

'That's good and bad. It means the Hamorians haven't gotten the road unblocked yet, but I don't know if we can get through, either.'

'What do you want to do, Master Lerris?'

I shrugged again. 'Go on.'

From my own experiences in the deadlands, I suspected that the road got worse and hadn't been used, even by Antonin, nearer Frven.

Otherwise, why would he have used the muddy and boggy roads around Howlett?

Most of the paving stones had remained generally in place, although a thin layer of soil covered many areas, and there low bushes, brush, and scrub oak had started to take hold, more than in the section of road we had already traveled.

We camped at another abandoned waystation that night, with yet another spring that seemed to flow into the ground.

The rocks and the cliffs beyond the road had turned into a heavier gray, and I hadn't seen the sharp-edged red and black rocks, not since we had left the crossroads five or six kays behind.

We finished the last of Barrabra's bread and the white cheese, leaving only hard travel bread, some dried mutton, and yellow brick cheese.

Again, that night, my sleep was fitful at best, and I woke up twice in a hot sweat, feeling as though chaos – formed of snakes of molten iron – were stalking me. The wards I had set didn't help much against nightmares, or against my own fears.

The second time, I walked out to the spring, where a mountain rat scurried away. Overhead, the stars glittered blue-white and cold, and even my breath seemed to steam. I splashed my face with the cold water, and that helped, but I still woke before dawn.

The next day, as we moved into the Easthorns, the canyon walls got higher, and, except around noon, the road was generally shaded. That morning, it had been chill enough that Weldein and the two guards rode with their jackets fastened.

The ground seemed to shake underfoot, but I said nothing, and Gairloch picked up one hoof and then another, placing each carefully. The sense of chaos had grown nearer and nearer, and I uncapped my water bottle and took another swallow, glancing down at the dry drainage canal beside the road.

As we rode eastward in the early afternoon, in the distance ahead, I could finally see another slumped mass of rock, even larger than the first mass, that turned the road into a dead-end canyon. I kept riding until we reached the tumbled stones that had peeled off a cliff that seemed more than a kay high and cascaded across the old highway.

'Doesn't look as though we can go too much farther.' Weldein wiped his forehead and unfastened his jacket.

I fingered my staff.

Still, I could sense the nearness of chaos, and a whispering sound that suggested troops ahead – a lot of them.

*Whhnnnnn* . . . A mosquito whined past me, presumably toward Weldein, who offered a more tempting target.

I looked at the pile of rock that had fallen across the old stones of the road. A few had bounced even farther westward, creating a rough dam, and turning the stone-lined drainage channel into a semistagnant pond. The dried algae on the rocks showed the water was lower, much lower, than normal. That was also probably why there was one lonely mosquito whining through the hot shade of the road canyon and not an entire swarm.

Somehow I was glad that the heat was hard on mosquitoes also.

The ground shivered underfoot, and Weldein looked at me.

'Stay there,' I told Weldein, as I dismounted.

'What are you doing?'

'Climbing a rock. So I can see them.'

'See who?' demanded Fregin.

'The Hamorians on the other side of the rock pile.'

'Won't their wizard see you?'

'Not while he's handling that much chaos.' At least I hoped Sammel didn't. So I clambered up the rocks, carefully, slowly, sweating every cubit of the way, trying not to hold my breath, while still grasping my staff. If I needed it, I didn't want to have to climb down and up again.

I almost laughed when I got to the top and looked eastward.

Beyond the huge pile was a flat expanse – two hundred cubits or so of untouched road – and then another pile of rock almost like the one where I perched.

Looking upward, I could see what had happened. An entire cliff had collapsed and fallen down over a slight ridge that had split the rock flow into two avalanches, leaving a section of good road between the two piles of rock.

Then I frowned, and concentrated, trying to trace the chaos ahead.

*Rurrrr . . . Crackkk!!!!*

The ground shivered underfoot, and several smaller stones bounced downhill, away from Weldein, thank the darkness.

Beyond the second rock pile, chaos was working and building.

Dust flared into the sky, and I could see the pile begin to move, almost to shrink. Stones, some larger than a hut or a hovel, tumbled downhill, northward into a caldron of what seemed to be molten chaos, a seething lake of fire.

The heat made noonday Kyphros, even in recent days, seem cool.

White lines of chaos lashed at the rocky rubble. The few small cedar and scrub junipers that had clung to the rocks flashed into ashes that fluttered skyward with the smoke and white dust.

'What is it?' called Weldein, his voice barely audible above the roaring and the whistling of the wind.

'More demon dust!' screamed Fregin.

'Is it the chaos wizard?' yelled Weldein.

I gave him an exaggerated nod, then waved him away from the rock pile on which I perched before turning back toward the slowly shrinking pile of rock.

*GGRRRRurrr* . . . More rocks bounded down away from me.

I glanced up toward the cliffs up to my right, grayed and weathered rock that looked none too steady. Even as I watched a small fragment of the cliff cascaded away and downward.

The falling stones flared into white powder, and began to pelt down like fine stone mist.

The blue-green of the sky was disappearing behind a mist of stone dust, chaos-fire, ashes, and who knew what else. I wiped my forehead, and the back of my hand came away gritty.

What could I do?

I shook my head and began to climb across the flat section of the rubble, and then down toward the short piece of the old highway.

Let Sammel spend his time and energy on removing the first pile of stone. I'd certainly have a better chance if he were tired, but I had to hang on to the top of a large boulder as the ground rumbled, and more stones shifted around me.

The day seemed dimmer, almost like twilight, as I struggled downward, trying to make sure I was never in a crevice between two stones.

I climbed across rocks and down, and the ground rumbled, and the stones on the once-enormous pile melted or flared away.

By the time I stood on the old highway and looked eastward, the last fragments of stone were melting away. I took one deep breath and then another, and carrying my staff, began to walk toward the smooth expanse of cooling flat rock that had replaced the old road.

Through the fog of dust and fine white ashes, I could see, well back, a few sunburst banners, and sense several thousand troops.

Before them was a pillar of white – Sammel. Now I could see him.

I stopped just short of stones hot enough to burn through my boots.

Sammel stood on the other side, still in his brown robes, almost looking like the kindly hermit I had once thought him. Although I couldn't see his face clearly through the chaos fog, I imagined that his eyes were still sad and the top of his skull bald.

Even from nearly two hundred cubits away, what I did see was the total power of chaos surrounding the man. He flared with power, and his whole body radiated the white of chaos so deep that it was that ugly reddish-white.

What should I do? Even if the order-encircling technique would work – even if I did cut him off from the outside chaos forces, there was enough force within him to fry me into burned bacon or the human crisped equivalent.

Yet I had succeeded in wrestling the Balance, and survived. So how could I use what I had learned against Sammel?

'So! You would challenge the power of knowledge?' His voice rang like a trumpet.

Challenge the power of knowledge? I really hadn't thought of it that way. My fingers felt slippery on the staff, and I laid it down on the road, knowing that it could not help me.

'Come! Join me! Spread knowledge to the starving world.'

Why was it that all the chaos wizards wanted me to join them? Or did they think I was stupid enough to believe that anyone possessed by chaos could share anything? I waited, building my own shields, quietly.

'Can you not see, young Lerris, that Recluce has tried to destroy Candar by denying the people knowledge?'

I could see that, certainly. That had been my own complaint. My father and the Brotherhood had denied us all knowledge. I found myself nodding.

'And can you not see that nothing will change Recluce? Recluce will not save Candar, or your beloved Kyphros.'

How did he know I had made my home in Kyphros? He was with the Hamorians. Did that mean their envoy – Leithrrse – had told him?

'The Black Brotherhood preaches order, but to keep Recluce ordered, they create disorder in Candar, and cast out anyone who would question them.'

All of what Sammel said was true, but it didn't matter.

'Only through knowledge can people advance. And only Hamor will allow knowledge to be used to help people.'

'Like your rockets helped people? Or your rifles. Or your—' I couldn't finish the sentence because I really didn't know what other devices he had turned over to Hamor.

'It is too bad you do not understand.'

I extended my senses toward Sammel and the figure in tan behind him.

'Be done with him ... he's only a young wizard, and not that powerful—'

'I will do as I choose.'

A long silence followed, while I struggled. I did not want to unleash chaos, nor did I want Sammel unblocking the road and opening Candar to the well-armed and effective soldiers of Hamor.

*Crack!*

As I had struggled with my own thoughts, the firebolt flared past me and flattened around the shoulder-high boulder to my left. The rock flamed, and just slumped like a candle set next to the hearth might ooze into a lump.

Another firebolt whistled by me, and although my shields deflected it, I still staggered under the force thrown at me – and that was after Sammel had reduced half a mountain to nothing.

Two more firebolts seared toward me, and flared around my shields.

I took two steps backward, while I sent my senses downward, down to the depths, seeking iron. Iron was the key – or copper – or some rocks like that – anything that could contain the power of chaos.

*Whhhsssttt! Whsssttt! Crack! Crack!*

Then, even as I danced aside, trying to deflect another wave of those already endless-seeming firebolts, I sweated, struggling to open up an order channel from the depths and through the ground. With the first effort, my thoughts bounced back as though they had struck a metal shield, and my mind went numb, just like my arm did when Tamra hit my staff at the wrong angle.

For a moment, I just stood there on the ancient highway, looking blankly into space, sweat pouring down my face.

Another firebolt jolted me back, and I tried to ease my thoughts into the depths, sideways, trying to reach that deeper level, as I had in Hydlen, and as I had that night when I had wrestled the Balance.

'Mere rote order cannot prevail against knowledge!' trumpeted Sammel. He followed his florid words with two additional flashes of chaosflame.

More rocks in the pile behind me turned into stone replicas of melted wax, and I could feel the heat building around me, as the stone dust and chaos fog rose even more thickly around me.

Stone splintered around me, fragments flying like the bullets from the new Hamorian rifles.

*Crack!* More stone splinters flew from the impact of another firebolt, and I ducked in spite of myself, knowing that ducking wasn't going to help – only my control of order and chaos would really help.

I staggered again as chaos and stone slammed against me, and reeled from the smell of burning leather, burning cloth, and singed hair – all mine.

Finally, struggling deep beneath Candar, while fending off firebolts, and feeling torn into pieces, I wrapped my senses around that mass of near molten iron, that reservoir of order that created the Balance and made chaos in Candar possible, trying to guide it upward, toward the channels that Sammel had already used.

As the next fireball arched overhead, slower than the last, I continued to struggle to free the deep and ancient iron from its bounds.

Through the smoke fog and stone haze and the flickering energies of order and chaos, I could sense the Hamorian troops backing toward the east and toward Certis, but I knew that direction would change if I failed.

The next fireball seemed smaller, slower, showing that Sammel was tired. So was I, but I kept struggling to ease open, force open those channels, to let that upflowing well of molten order, imbued with the fire of chaos, seethe toward the twilight, toward the ancient road where we struggled.

*Whsst!*

I pushed the small mass of flamed chaos aside.

The road trembled underfoot in the momentary silence while Sammel wiped his face beyond the haze of smoke and stone dust that separated us. As I tried to guide, to order the chaos I had freed from its iron bonds, I could hear the rumbling . . . and I had to shift my weight as the ground trembled again, and the trembling was my creation.

Another firebolt, larger, slammed into my shields, and I danced aside, trying to keep my senses wrapped around the rising column of order-circled and chaos-fired iron, trying to keep channeling more and more of the deep chaos into that column.

The ancient road stones creaked, and at least one cracked like one of the Hamorian rifles. The trembling grew, and the whole road shook.

Even without throwing another firebolt at me, Sammel abruptly turned and began to run, back toward the Hamorian troops.

The ground rumbled, again, almost belching, as a column of molten ironstone burst up from the road, literally beneath Sammel. Even before the molten iron reached him, a web of chaos interlocked with order formed around him, shielding him from the heat and chaos.

The iron-based lava fountained into the afternoon shadows, filing the canyon with a reddish glare, and the odor of brimstone slashed at me.

Yet Sammel remained untouched within his web of order and chaos.

I turned the fountain toward him, surrounded him, but his shields held. Unfair as it might be, I knew I must destroy him, or within days the road to Kyphros would be open. And I could see the bodies strewn across Kyphros, bodies like Shervan's and Pendril's, bodies like Krystal's. Wincing at the heat and the pain, I forced more fountaining iron into the twilight sky, until heat and molten stone rained down on Sammel and the Hamorians.

Yet, as I did so, I was aware that the sundevils were fleeing pell-mell eastward, out of the range of the heavy iron. Not all of them made it – that I could tell from the wave of whiteness that whispered back toward me, whispered of deaths that beat against my shields.

Despite the growing heat and the pile of already cooling iron lava, Sammel still persisted, and his shields held off the chaos and the heat that surrounded him.

So I reached out with my senses into the mountain walls sheered smooth by the ancient white wizards, and somehow undid the bonds holding the canyon wall above, almost like pulling out ancient pegs from a tall, tall dresser created by a mastercrafter.

With a whispering that crescendoed into an earth-shaking roar, gray stone crumbled, then cascaded downward, some of it hitting the old ridge line and bouncing toward me, and I cast up yet another shield, throwing what seemed to be every bit of energy I had around me.

Despite the shields a wave of gray stone surrounded me, and I felt as if I had been thrown against the canyon wall and bounced back and forth between the gray slabs of stone that flanked the road. Then I staggered and half fell, half sat, as chaos rained around me, holding tight to my shield until I no longer could and until blackness fell across me.

I woke up to raindrops falling on my face. When I looked back east, the small sharp knives I thought I was through with jabbed at the back of my eyes, but I could see steam hissing off hot rock. I couldn't hear the hissing, or much of anything, except intermittently. My face was wet and cold, and rain was splashing into puddles. Trying to move reminded me that I'd been bounced against something, or many things, that were hard.

'Uhhhmmm . . .' I rolled over onto my knees and finally worked myself into a sitting position.

Rain splashed down from gray clouds, not low thick ones, but clouds high enough that I could see the tops of the cliffs. The rain was letting up because, I suspected, there just hadn't been that much water in the air – assuming the explanations in *The Basis of Order* were correct.

My legs felt stiff, and so was my back.

Before trying to stand, I looked to the east – and shivered. A steaming mass of black and gray rock blocked the canyon, reaching almost to the bottom of the ridge that had split the original rock fall. The darker gray of the south wall showed where the rock had sheared away.

Clouds of steam still billowed off the black and gray – and I could feel the heat, not surprisingly, since I was less than two hundred cubits from the western edge of the hot rock.

Scattered smaller boulders lay on the expanse of old road where I sat. I used a nearby one, more than a cubit high, to lever myself to my feet. Then I looked for my staff. For once I felt I needed it, just like an old man might, to help me along.

It took a while, but I found it, partly buried beneath dust and smaller rocks. After that, I stood and surveyed the mess, closing my eyes occasionally to relieve the pain of seeing.

I had no strength left for order sensing, but I was already sure that Sammel hadn't survived, and there was no way that the Hamorians were going to use the wizards' road anytime soon – not with the mass I had created and the older and smaller – but still large – rockfall behind me.

More importantly, they wouldn't know how many other rockfalls remained to be cleared, or whether I might be able to destroy an army with another rockfall.

The raindrops' steaming continued, although the rain was tapering off, and I could see gaps in the clouds to the north.

With that, I turned back toward the older rock pile and hobbled toward it, then slowly eased my way upward. I'd gotten perhaps halfway to the top when I saw a bedraggled figure in greens waving.

Weldein was saying something, but I couldn't make out the words, as he clambered down toward me.

'Weldein?'

He answered, but I couldn't hear the words.

'Don't worry about it. I'll be there in a moment.'

I was wrong. Climbing the rest of the rock pile took longer than a moment. In fact, it was almost dark by the time we struggled back down to the other side.

Berli had a small fire burning, and Fregin lay on his bedroll beside it, his left leg at an angle.

'It hurts . . .'

'. . . boulders . . . hit him,' explained Berli. 'Can't . . . heal him?' Her words were far away, and I had to squint and look at her face to make out what she said. Of course, that meant my eyes hurt even more.

I just looked at her through the darkness. 'Not now. We can straighten the leg. He won't die, and when I've got some strength back, I'll set it, and then heal him enough so it won't fill with chaos.'

Weldein said something, I thought, about what I had done.

'How much did you see?' I asked, watching him closely.

He shrugged, and I saw for the first time the cuts and scrapes, and the shredded leathers over his left arm.

'Let me see that.'

'It's nothing.'

Weldein's injuries weren't that bad, surface cuts and deep bruises, but some of those bruises, especially the big ugly one across his arm and shoulder, had to hurt.

*Grrrrrrrr ... rrrrr ...*

I found myself swaying in the aftershock of the chaos-order quake.

Berli put an arm out to steady me. She and the staff helped me get over to the stone coping on the side of the road, where I eased myself down.

Weldein studied me for a long moment, then shook his head, and muttered a few words.

'What?' I concentrated on him.

'You look older.'

'I feel older. I feel like an old man. Everything aches.'

Fregin snapped something from beside the fire, and Berli answered.

I turned to catch Fregin's response, then realized he was talking to me.

'... leg ... fire ... like ... you ... do something?'

Weldein glared at him. 'He knows ... last battle ... wizard ... snapped bones ... burned ... body ... you ... good ... die ... heal you ...' Once more I could only catch some of the words and guess at the others, and squinting and concentrating hurt.

'... hurts ...'

The ground shivered, more gently.

Fregin closed his eyes and moaned.

Berli shook her head and grinned wryly. I found myself grinning without really knowing why. After a moment, Weldein shook his head also, and offered a grin.

I sat on the stone coping of the old road and slowly ate cheese and travel bread, interspersed with water. Water hadn't tasted that good in a long, long time.

'What happened?' Berli asked more than that but I missed it. Weldein explained something with both words and gestures. I thought he was saying that I dropped a mountain on Sammel, but he could have been talking about anything.

'. . . never . . . stand . . . your way,' said Berli.

'It wasn't like that,' I protested. 'I figured out how to turn his chaos against him, and to bring up more order and chaos from the earth. But it wasn't enough, and I was afraid he'd escape and open the road.' I shrugged and wished I hadn't. 'So I managed to unbind some of the stones up there. It wasn't anywhere close to a mountainside.'

'It looked like it.' Weldein sipped from his water bottle. '. . . rock and . . . mountain . . . huge hill . . .' He gestured again and looked at Berli, and I had no idea what he said.

I tried to raise order senses, but I couldn't. 'I can't do anything tonight.' My eyes seemed hard to focus, and Berli seemed very close and then very far away, and I started to topple over.

Someone caught me, and laid me out on my bedroll, and I slept.

# XCI

## Nylan, Recluce

'How could you three have let such a disaster occur?' The big man with the nearly jet-black skin circles around the end of the table. 'Do you have any idea what happened in Candar last night? Any idea at all?'

'Some,' admits Talryn.

Maris lifts his hands. 'Someone could tell me.'

'Don't play "poor trader" now,' mutters Heldra.

Cassius's eyes seem to flash red as they sweep across the two men and the woman. 'Another few moments, and there would have been an order-chaos portal, and who knows what could have happened? Or what creature could have appeared from where?'

'Order-chaos portal?' Maris fumbles out the words.

'Where do you think I came from? Where do you think the angels came from? Does anyone else on this planet have truly black skin? Didn't Talryn tell you?'

'I forgot.' Maris looks down.

'I forgot?' Cassius snorts and looks at Heldra. 'Did you forget too, counselor?'

'We had hoped Lerris and Sammel would cancel each other out.

Sammel already killed both members of a black squad.'

Cassius shakes his head. 'Do you know what happened?'

'Not exactly, Cassius.' Talryn shrugs. 'We're convinced that Lerris and Sammel ran into each other. Lerris prevailed, but we're not sure if he survived. Sammel didn't. There's no chaos signature left.'

'They just . . . fought . . . and wrenched order and chaos every which way in half of Candar? And you don't know what happened?'

Heldra looks blankly at the heavy morning clouds over the Eastern Ocean. Maris stares at the polished tabletop.

'It may be worse than that.' Talryn wipes his forehead. 'There really wasn't any change in the total of order and chaos. It seems as if Lerris used the forces behind the Balance itself. If you will, he drew from both sides and played them against each other.'

'Mother of—' Cassius stops and waits.

'Because there wasn't that much change, that means that much of the Hamorian army remains intact. I'd have to surmise that Lerris found some way to block them. There were reports that Sammel was using his powers to reopen the old wizards' roads to help the Hamorians get to Gallos.'

'I could feel the deaths. The whiteness was strong enough that there had to be a lot of soldiers dying.' Cassius shakes his head. 'Lerris diverted them, killed off part of an army, and probably blocked off whatever road they were using. You've been fairly successful in picking off their ships. Do you have any idea what conclusion the Emperor of Hamor is going to reach?'

'I'm afraid so. We should have another two ships ready.'

'Two ships!' Cassius laughs. 'Much good they'll do. I'd suggest you mend your fences with Lerris, and his father, and Justen.'

'But—' protests Heldra.

'But?'

'Lerris and Justen are as gray as wizards can be.'

'So? You want to be spotlessly pure black and dead?' Cassius shakes his head.

Heldra looks helplessly toward Talryn. Talryn offers a crooked smile. Maris looks back down at the polished tabletop.

# XCII

By the morning, I felt better. Still creaky, still sore, still bruised, and still smelling like burned clothing and hair. My eyes burned, mostly,

rather than stabbing all the time – but I could use my order senses
... barely. In some ways, certainly, Krystal had been right. Being a
hero – or even a second-rate wizard with an idea – definitely had
disadvantages.

After eating and washing up in a clear pool of rainwater, I changed
into my other shirt. Then, the three of us worked to set Fregin's leg so
that it could be splinted. I had just enough order strength left to drive
out the worst of the chaos. I sat down and rested after that. Later, it
took both Weldein and me to get Fregin into the saddle, where he sat
looking morose.

'Cheer up,' said Weldein. 'One broken leg for stopping the armies
of Hamor. You're a hero, and we won't even tell that you were hit by
a boulder.'

His words, everyone's really, were still far away, and I really had
to concentrate to make them out.

'Thanks. It wasn't your leg.'

'The rain took care of the dust,' offered Berli. 'You won't have to
sneeze all the way back.'

'So friggin' cheerful you are, Berli.'

'Like you said, Fregin, it wasn't my leg.'

Weldein looked at me as the ground trembled.

'It's going to keep doing that, I'm afraid.' As I rubbed my forehead, I
could feel the stiffness in my shoulders. 'There's probably more chaos
than ever under Candar.'

'After all that fire yesterday?'

'All that happened was that Sammel and I fought over control of
chaos. We really didn't do anything to change how much there was.
Not very much anyway, unless a few of the Hamorian rifles were
destroyed, and even a few hundred wouldn't amount to much with
the tens of thousands they've created.'

'The rifles are a creation of chaos? I knew it,' grumbled Fregin.

'No.' I sighed. 'The rifles are a mechanical creation of order by Hamor.
Creating more order also creates more chaos. That's why Recluce has
opposed machines for centuries.'

'Shit. We're in big friggin' trouble then, with all those machines
Hamor's buildin'.' His words were still far-off sounding.

'That's a fair statement.' I had to agree with Fregin's conclusion. I
felt like shit, and I really hadn't done that much, except postpone the
seemingly inevitable invasion by Hamor. Leithrrse would probably try
something else, although what that might be was another question I
hadn't had time to consider.

Weldein and Berli looked at me.

'Oh . . . we're heading back to Ruzor. It should take several eight-days for Hamor to backtrack and even get into Gallos – longer if they want to slog through the Easthorns directly.' Personally, I doubted that Leithrrse was dumb enough to take an army through the Easthorns without using some form of road, and all the other roads to Kyphros led through either Gallos or Hydlen.

I nudged Gairloch, and he started forward gently. My back still twinged.

We had almost reached the crossroad to Yryna when I saw two mounted figures riding toward us – one on a pony, and one with red hair.

'It's Justen – and Tamra.' I wiped my forehead. The brief rain of the night before hadn't done anything to reduce the mid-day heat.

'You've done it this time, Lerris,' Justen grumped at me, even before we got within ten cubits.

'Done what?' I reined up, trying to ignore the half-stabbing, half-burning behind my eyes.

He studied me for a moment. Then he shook his head silently.

'Oh, darkness . . .' Tears were actually flowing down Tamra's cheeks.

I shook my head. 'I'm all right.'

'No . . . no, you're not,' Tamra choked out. 'You . . . just look . . . at yourself.'

Weldein glanced from me to Tamra, then back to me. He tried to keep his face immobile, but I could sense he was disturbed, but I couldn't tell why.

Finally, I looked at Justen.

Justen fumbled with his pack, twisting in his saddle, and finally bringing out a mirror. 'Look into this, Lerris.'

The image in the mirror wore the same browns as I did, but the man's face was heavier, somehow, and he was definitely a man. Faint traces of gray touched his temples, and his shoulders were broader. The man looked like me, but was at least a good ten years older. I wiggled my shoulders. So did the image in the mirror, and the fabric felt tight across my own shoulders, and the tunic had been loose when Deirdre made it, loose from my recovery after the fight with Gerlis, and even when I had set out.

'That's not me. That's some kind of magic.' Except I knew it wasn't, especially when I looked at Justen.

'Anyone but you would have died of old age,' he said. 'Even you can't use order to channel chaos without paying a price.'

The ground rocked gently again, but not so strongly as before, and I could tell the chaos tremors were beginning to subside.

'You never do things by halves, do you?' asked Justen. 'There's still chaos welling up.'

'I haven't been given much choice.'

Justen looked like he might dispute that, but instead, he gestured back toward the pile of stone and rubble already in the distance. 'I presume you blocked the road?'

I nodded. 'I doubt anyone will unblock it soon.'

'No one'll ever unblock it,' snapped Fregin.

Everyone looked at the trooper.

'Well, they won't. He sealed the place with the fires of the demons' hell.'

Justen raised his eyebrows. 'Just how much chaos did you use?'

'A lot,' I admitted. 'I channeled it through order.'

He shook his head. 'You may be the greatest gray wizard ever, but if you keep this up, you won't last a season.'

I sat there for a second, half stunned by the matter-of-fact statement by my uncle. He'd brought down Fairhaven, and he was telling me that I might be the greatest gray wizard ever?

'Don't you see?' asked Tamra. 'Even with all that power, you can't save yourself from the touches of chaos.'

'I'm getting that impression.' And I was, but the problem was that no one else seemed to be able to do much to stop Hamor, and everything I did pushed me farther into the gray, and that meant I was stuck in Candar, and that meant more use of order and chaos, and that meant . . . I shook my head. It ached, more than I'd realized. Me, a great gray wizard? It didn't help the aches, or the seeing that hurt, or the sometimes-fading hearing.

'You know that pile of rock won't stop Hamor?' said Tamra.

'I know. They'll probably attack Gallos next.'

'Why do you think that?' asked Justen, whose face held a bitterly amused smile.

'It's about the only way they can get to Kyphros.'

'Why would they want Kyphros . . . at least now?'

I had to shrug. 'Isn't it obvious?'

'I don't think so.' Justen wiped his forehead. It was hot, and still getting hotter. 'We can talk as we ride.' He turned Rosefoot around. 'You're going back to Ruzor?'

'Yes. I can't do much more here. Not now.'

'No, you can't.' He laughed, but there was an ironic undertone.

Tamra and Weldein rode behind us, side by side, and close, as if they were straining to hear. I could have laughed, because I was straining also.

'Friggin' heat,' mumbled Fregin from the rear.

'Stop complaining. You're a hero now,' said Berli. 'Act like it.'

Justen said nothing for nearly a kay, even when the ground trembled with the unease of the chaos beneath Candar.

Finally I asked him, since he wasn't going to say anything unless prompted, 'Why don't you think Hamor won't attack Gallos?'

'Because it would be stupid, and the Hamorians aren't stupid. Greedy, yes. Warlike. But not stupid.'

'All right. Why would attacking Gallos be stupid?' Ahead, heat waves danced across the side road to Yryna. 'Did you come down the crossroad there?'

Justen turned in his saddle. 'Yes. You did a good job of removing the illusion, but you certainly didn't conceal that you'd done it.'

'It was rather obvious,' added Tamra.

'Everything's obvious to you two, but neither one of you seems to be around when something has to be done.'

'No ... we were healing sheep and finding out what was going to happen, and trying to warn the Viscount,' answered Tamra. 'Then you showed up, and killed off another white wizard without learning anything except how to make a bigger mess.'

I had to admit she was right about that. The ground still heaved, and I hadn't really stopped Hamor – just delayed one army and probably made Leithrrse madder, but I was stubborn enough that I didn't want to admit it – not then. I just closed my eyes for a time, and that helped a little.

We passed the crossroad in silence and kept riding.

I had to ask again. 'It may be obvious, but why would attacking —'

Justen sighed. 'Think about it. If Hamor can open the old road here, then they can march right into Kyphros without attacking Gallos. They can use their fleet on Ruzor, and force the autarch to spread her forces. If they take Worrak, then they could use the passes through the Lower Easthorns as well. Without the old road —'

'That means fighting someone else,' I said. 'But Hamor's out to take all of Candar anyway.'

'You should have noticed,' said Justen, 'that they try to attack at one point at a time. They haven't attacked Kyphros yet.'

'Then, there's the problem of Recluce,' put in Tamra, adding more that I didn't hear.

Justen frowned, but said nothing.

'What?' I asked, turning to concentrate on her words.

'Lerris . . .' Tamra sounded exasperated. 'The Hamorians have been losing ships to Recluce. You just stopped an army and probably killed at least several hundred troops, and they have to know you're from Recluce. They're going to think Recluce is behind all of their troubles.'

I nodded. 'Oh, did you know that the Brotherhood – or someone – got the Hamorian regent?' I asked, rather than directly telling Tamra and Justen. After all, Justen wasn't volunteering much, just silently judging me.

'They did?' he answered. 'Well, that just makes it worse. The idiots.'

'They also sank some ships – the iron-clad warships.'

'I knew that.' Justen looked at me. 'Tamra was right. They know both of you are from Recluce.'

'So you're saying that they're going to see Recluce as playing the same old manipulating game?' I asked.

'If you read the histories, you might recall that the white wizards tricked Hamor into attacking Creslin – twice. It cost them a great deal, and I doubt they have ever forgotten.' His words wavered, but I got them.

'You're saying that Hamor wants both Recluce and Candar,' I said flatly, 'and that they'll take the tools wherever they can – whatever tools they can.'

'Brilliant,' added Tamra.

'Thanks,' I said. 'You seem to be saying that Hamor will be worried about Recluce, but they have to know Sammel was from Recluce, and he was on their side,' I pointed out.

'What about all the devices Hamor and the dukes were using? They were Sammel's doing, weren't they?' asked Tamra.

'Really, how much good did Sammel's devices do Hamor?' asked Justen. 'The devices stirred up chaos, and they probably made the conquest of Hydlen a lot harder and bloodier, but Hamor could have taken over Freetown and Montgren anyway.'

'Without Sammel's knowledge?' asked Tamra. 'Then why was he with them? And why did he decide to help them?'

'Hamor has always been opportunistic. Wouldn't you rather enlist an ally than have a wizard who might turn unfriendly?' Justen rubbed his chin and shifted in the saddle.

'That explains Hamor,' Tamra pointed out. 'But what about Sammel?' Justen looked at me.

'I don't *know*,' I began, 'but he delivered a little speech asking me to help him overthrow Recluce's hold on knowledge. He said he wanted to bring that knowledge to the "starving world" or something like that. When I didn't accept his generous offer, he started throwing firebolts.'

'Knowledge doesn't feed people,' snorted Tamra. 'Food does.'

'That was just an excuse,' I answered. 'He was angry because . . .' I didn't finish the sentence. Sammel had been angry for the same reasons I had been, because Recluce had insisted I find my own answers, rather than laying them out. And I was still angry, but not angry enough to turn to chaos.

'Because?' prompted Tamra.

'He thought Recluce didn't have any business hiding knowledge.' I patted Gairloch on the neck, and he *whuffed* back.

'There have been a few reasons for that policy,' Justen added. 'At least it's taken Hamor some centuries before they could build all those ships.'

In a way that made sense, but why hadn't anyone wanted to explain why? I almost shook my head. Of course, the explanation would have revealed the existence of the knowledge to every dangergelder for centuries, and made Recluce even more of a target.

'You still didn't answer my question about the magic devices,' said Tamra. 'Recluce certainly didn't supply them.'

Justen looked at me, and I looked at Justen. Then I nodded to him. He knew more than I did, and he could explain.

We rode a while longer, and I wiped my forehead.

'Friggin' heat,' muttered Fregin. 'No damned wizard . . . leg hurts.'

'Just keep riding, hero,' said Berli.

I looked over at Justen. 'Devices? Recluce? Were they something you thought up, years back?'

'No. Recluce didn't make a one, except for the rockets.' He laughed sadly. 'Some of them Hamor developed by itself, and most of the others were based on ideas Sammel just stole from the hidden shelves of the Brotherhood libraries. Maybe Hamor stole the ideas from the Brotherhood, too. It's certainly possible.'

Tamra flushed. 'Hidden shelves? Those . . . those hypocrites.'

Justen went on. 'I suppose you've guessed something like this, Lerris, but did you know that there's a whole section on inventions and ideas that Dorrin developed?'

I hadn't guessed, but I wasn't about to admit it. So I nodded.

'Dorrin?' Tamra's eyes flickered from me to Justen.

'The founder of Nylan – the magic engineer.'

'What about you?' Tamra's voice almost cracked. 'Is Lerris right?'

'Me? In a way, but most of the ideas were there before I was born.

I can't say I was much better, except I didn't write it down to hide in the libraries.' Justen wiped his forehead. 'I did manage to develop a system to focus order.'

'That was how you brought down Frven?' I asked.

Justen nodded, then added, 'And destroyed about half the order and chaos in the world. That's why the Brotherhood didn't want any more machines. They concentrate and build order, and the Balance allows more chaos then.'

Behind me, Weldein swallowed. Berli and Fregin just rode, and I couldn't tell whether they looked puzzled ... or if they were even listening.

'You were an engineer-smith?' asked Tamra.

'Yes.'

'What else did you build?' I asked. 'Besides the device to focus order that destroyed Frven?'

'Not much. Wasn't that enough?' Justen shrugged. 'I suppose I should add, while I'm confessing, that I also built a land-engine that crossed Candar faster than the fastest horses. It used the same sort of turbine that the Mighty Ten have, except it was smaller. It was the only one ever built, and Lerris's father helped me.'

That did follow, unfortunately. My father was probably the only one Justen could have trusted.

'And you helped them keep all that hidden?' asked Tamra. 'Why?'

'So much knowledge. So much of it could have made life easier for people. But it isn't that simple. It never is.' Justen spread his hands. 'And what did we all do? We hid it away. Recluce did it because the Council members honestly thought that limiting order-based knowledge would limit chaos. And I? Well, I tried to help Candar stop the festering of chaos ... and it worked for a while.'

'Until someone in Hamor figured out that the Balance works both ways?' I asked.

Justen nodded. 'Now things will have to change, and I don't imagine anyone will be happy with the results.' He gestured at me. 'Look at you, Lerris. Was stopping Hamor worth ten or fifteen years of your life? It might be more, you know. How much order is it taking to hold your appearance?'

I thought. Was I using order? Finally, after trying to study myself, I opened my eyes again. 'None.'

'That's good. But what about the next time?'

I didn't have an answer, but for the moment, at least Krystal wouldn't have to worry about looking older than her consort. Then again, I'd hear about being a hero. As I thought about it, I realized that Krystal was likely to be less than thrilled. In fact, she could be very upset. I took a deep breath. Everything was getting more and more complicated.

Tamra brushed her hair off her forehead. Weldein looked at Tamra, then away. Fregin mumbled something I couldn't hear as we rode westward toward the crossroad for Tellura. I closed my eyes and let Gairloch carry me, because my eyes were filled with white fire from the effort to hear and read lips.

Beneath us, the ground trembled, ever so slightly, as a reminder that order and chaos remained far out of balance.

# XCIII

As we rode downhill from the Gateway Gorge toward Ruzor, Justen became more and more silent. I looked toward him, but Tamra glared at me as if to tell me to leave him alone, and I did, and we rode silently through the heat of the morning, and the even greater heat of the afternoon toward Ruzor, stopping only briefly and quickly for water.

At twilight, in the dust and the heavy stillness that blanketed the road before the sea breeze would offer some slight relief, we approached the gates to Ruzor – on the eastern side.

Krystal was waiting, mounted, well before the gate. Her guard waited also, a good hundred cubits back, accompanied by a silver-haired woman who did not, from a distance, appear as old as Krystal. The woman looked like the one in my dreams, the one who had been giving advice I hadn't understood, and that bothered me.

Since we had traveled quickly, certainly as quickly as any messenger, although I certainly hadn't sent any, I suspected that the silver-haired woman had something to do with Krystal's appearance.

My consort rode forward slowly, as did I, until our legs almost touched. For a time, we shared each other's eyes. Then she reached out. Her fingers brushed my face before they took my hand. Her face was wet, and she swallowed, but said nothing.

'I don't think Hamor will invade from the north for a while.'

'I heard . . .' She shook her head, and swallowed again, then squeezed my hand. After a moment Krystal turned to Justen. 'There's someone waiting here for you. I trust you knew already?'

Justen nodded stiffly.

'You don't sound happy,' observed Tamra.

'Dayala's never left Naclos. She's a druid.' He shook his head and rode forward toward the silver-haired woman.

'So are you, really,' answered Tamra, but Justen did not acknowledge her words as he approached the druid.

My eyes bounced back and forth between Justen and Dayala, while my senses tried to follow the unseen line of order that linked Justen to his druid. I realized it was the first time I had heard her named, and it sent a shiver through me, as though her name were a portent of something even more ominous than the might of Hamor.

'A real druid . . . silver hair and all . . .' said Fregin.

Justen and Dayala never actually touched one another, but the order bond between them flared so brightly with energy that I looked around. Only Tamra saw it, and she nodded at me, as if to acknowledge that she also had seen it.

I swallowed, feeling even more dread from the power of that shared bond than I had when I had first heard Dayala's name. So much power, and she had come to seek him out.

'Are you all right?' asked Krystal softly, reaching out and touching my hand again.

'Yes.' I took a deep breath.

She looked at me.

'I'm tired, and we'll talk about it later. And I don't like playing like a hero. It hurts.'

That got me a nod and a faint smile.

We rode silently and slowly back to the barracks building. I didn't realize how tired I was until I found myself letting Krystal help me unsaddle and groom Gairloch.

'You shouldn't be doing this. You're the commander.'

'And all the times you did it for me don't count?'

I leaned forward and brushed her cheek with my lips.

'Someday, you just might learn to receive, as well as give.' Krystal turned for a moment. 'There's dinner for everyone in the autarch's small dining hall. Anyone who wishes to wash up . . . please make haste.'

'Food . . . could use some food,' announced Fregin, leaning against a stable stall while one of the ostlers unsaddled his mount.

'That's a surprise?' asked Berli, who had already unsaddled and groomed her mount.

So I made haste, but I did wash off the worst of the dust and grime. Then we did walk side by side into the small dining hall, where Kasee waited, alone, except for the servants.

'Oh . . . shit . . .' Fregin's whisper carried through the silence.

'I hope not,' said the autarch politely.

I tried not to grin as I inclined my head.

'Just sit down.' The autarch sounded faintly exasperated. 'I shouldn't be intruding on your dinner, for a great many reasons, but, unfortunately, what I do depends on what you have done and what you can tell me.' She paused. 'I think you had better eat, first.'

On the platters passed around the table were thick slices of mutton, smothered in a brown sauce. The bowls contained white strings of something, sprinkled with cheese, and the baskets had loaves of bread. There were also pitchers of redberry and dark ale. I had redberry, and Krystal had ale.

Down and across the table, Weldein filled Tamra's mug with redberry, and a puzzled expression crossed her face. Weldein smiled politely, and nodded, then filled his own mug. Tamra then offered Weldein the platter of mutton, and he served them both.

In time, I helped myself and served Krystal. For a moment, her eyes twinkled, and she reached out under the table and squeezed my leg. A serving girl placed a plate in front of Dayala. On her plate were nuts, cheeses, and bread – only foods from plants, trees, and milk. Someone had seen to that. Krystal? I looked to my consort, and her eyes met mine.

'You need to eat.'

I did, not that I'd get any younger, but I might get less stiff and sore with food and rest. I had to use my knife with a fair amount of vigor to cut the meat. It was chewy, quite chewy, and only the spicy sauce made it palatable. The white strings were shredded seaweed with spices and goat cheese. The bread was warm and tasty, anyway.

I paused in mid-chew, then swallowed. If tough mutton was being served at the autarch's table, what were the poorer folk eating? I looked to Krystal.

'Food is hard to get. It's mostly because of hoarding, but Kasee doesn't want to use troops yet.' She refilled her mug with more ale; I hadn't realized she had drunk the entire thing.

I could understand where that would go, and yet, if the autarch had to pay higher and higher prices to feed her forces, then taxes would have to climb, and soldiers might be needed then.

After everyone had eaten at least something, Kasee inclined her head to Justen. 'Where do you think Hamor will strike next, Mage?'

Justen finished taking a drink of the dark ale. 'This is good ale, Honored Autarch. Would that my speculations were as good – or as certain.'

Tamra frowned, and I pondered. On the road, Justen had implied that Hamor would strike Recluce next. Why would he not tell the autarch that?

Beside Justen, Dayala sipped water.

The autarch waited, and Justen finally cleared his throat.

'I don't know. I had thought that Hamor would strike Recluce next, but Dayala seems to think that is not so, that Hamor will strike once more at Kyphros, although not until the sundevils hold Hydlen.' Justen shrugged.

The autarch turned to Dayala. 'Lady druid, might you enlighten us?'

'The sands do not tell all,' Dayala began, her voice like husky silver bells, 'but the webs of order and chaos remain in Candar. The ships will come from the sea to finish Hydlen first, and then they will come to Ruzor, even as the armies of the sun will cross the Lower Easthorns.'

'How do you know this?' asked Kasee, her voice conversational, but with a hardness behind it.

'I know what I know,' answered Dayala apologetically.

'Logic would say she is right,' added Krystal from beside me. 'Hamor has not that many ships in Candar now, and twice in the past has lost fleets to Recluce. Why would the Emperor start another war before finishing the one he is about?'

That made sense, but Justen had made sense on the ride back from my contest with Sammel. I blinked.

Kasee turned to me. 'Lerris? You have been silent.'

'I don't know. I can make a case for Hamor attacking either Kyphros or Recluce, and I feel that before it's over attacks on both will occur. As for which comes first, I don't know. I think we have to prepare to be attacked. Perhaps, as we prepare, matters will become more clear.' I hoped they would, but I didn't have much confidence of that.

'You don't sound entirely convinced of your own wisdom.'

'I am convinced that an attack on Kyphros will occur. I am not convinced that matters will become more clear. Things always seem to be more confusing, not less.'

'Always like that . . .' muttered Fregin into the silence.

'Yes, it is,' said the autarch with a slightly forced laugh.

At the end of the table, Weldein refilled Tamra's mug, and she said, 'To what do I owe such attention?'

While he flushed slightly, he answered. 'Only to being yourself.'

'And what am I to the Finest, ser?'

He smiled politely and said, 'Do you wish to know?'

Her eyes turned icy.

'The red bitch,' Weldein said even more politely.

Justen almost choked, and Kasee covered her mouth.

'He has nerve,' Krystal whispered in my ear.

Nerve he had, but at that point I wasn't sure about intelligence.

Tamra laughed, and everyone else let go of their breath. Then she added, 'You're the only honest one in the bunch, except maybe Lerris, and Krystal's responsible for that.'

'Honesty doesn't always guarantee survival,' Weldein pointed out.

Tamra had lifted her mug, but paused before drinking, as if she really hadn't considered the point before. Then she turned to Justen. 'That's it.'

'What's it?' asked my uncle.

'Existence – life – honesty, order . . .'

'Of course,' Justen said.

Their words had me lost – either that or it was so obvious that I'd never voiced it. Order couldn't be managed on a large scale without honesty because the order handler had to be honest with himself to avoid overextending himself and getting destroyed – or aged, I reflected. In a way, though, the same was true with chaos, except, since chaos was so much more destructive, the process happened faster.

I frowned. Theoretically, that meant that an order-master could wield more power than a chaos-master. So why had chaos usually won, except at the end of every conflict? Survival? It fit in a strange way. Wielding great powers resulted in great costs, and an order mage would know that, and, being honest, would probably not want to be forced into self-sacrifice unless absolutely necessary. Chaos mages could deceive themselves about the prices; so their works were more obvious.

I shook my head. Parts were missing, but the general idea was there.

'Lerris?' asked Krystal softly. 'Are you all right?'

'Oh . . . yes. I was thinking about honesty.'

She shook her head and took another pull from her mug.

'Commander?' asked Kasee. 'Where do you think the attack will come?'

'Against us, but I could not explain exactly why I think so, except we are weaker, and their fleet seems determined to bring all outside trade to a halt.' Krystal shrugged.

'In time, we shall see.' Kasee smiled tightly. 'In the meantime, enjoy the table.' She lifted her mug, then added, 'To your return.'

We all drank, and then we had some fried cakes.

After the dinner, Krystal and I walked through the narrow stone-walled corridors and up the stairs to her room, where Herreld waited.

'Evening, Commander.'

'Good evening, Herreld.'

He turned to me. 'Heard what happened, Mage. We're glad you be back.' He nodded.

'Thank you.' I nodded to him, and we entered the room. Krystal bolted the door, not that I thought anyone or anything would pass Herreld.

The quilt on the bed was even straight, and the papers were stacked in neat piles around the conference table. Krystal took off her blade, but not her boots.

Because my feet ached, I pulled my own boots off and just sat on the edge of the bed, looking out through the narrow window at the darkness, and the few lamps in the distance.

Krystal eased down beside me, but she was stiff.

'You're upset?' I guessed.

'How did you guess? My consort has gone out to stop another wizard, and he comes back aged more than a decade, and I'm supposed to be calm?' Her voice rose at the end. 'I'm supposed to be calm?'

'I did the best I could.'

'I didn't want you to be a hero. I wanted you to come back safe.'

'I did. I'm just older.'

'Older!' she exclaimed. 'What about . . . ?' After a moment, she sighed. 'Never mind. It doesn't matter.'

What could I say? It wasn't as though I'd gone out and aged myself on purpose. 'It does,' I answered, 'but I didn't get older on purpose. I was trying to keep the Hamorians out of Kyphros, and they had more—' I took a deep breath. Nothing I said would change things, and she'd still be angry. 'Never mind . . . I didn't mean to do it.' And I hadn't.

After a time, Krystal sighed once more and ran her fingers through my hair. 'There's only a little gray.'

'Yes. I suppose I could be like Justen, but the idea of using order to keep myself young doesn't sound quite so good now.'

'Why not?' She kissed my neck gently, not insistently, just gently.

'Like a lot of things . . . it doesn't feel right.'

'How did it happen?'

I laughed, and the sound was harsher than I intended. 'I don't know that, either. I was getting beaten around so much I didn't even feel the aging.'

'I don't understand. Justen is a gray wizard, and he's lived for centuries. You do one thing, and you age.'

'I think it has to do with how I did it, not what I did. If I understand

Justen correctly, he used order to focus more order on chaos. When he did that, he reduced the amount of both order and chaos in the world. I used order to focus chaos back on Sammel, and I didn't reduce, not much anyway, the amount of anything. That's why the ground still trembles. There's a lot of chaos still beneath Candar.'

'That's not fair.'

'No. But the Balance has nothing to do with fairness. A purely ordered life will last longer. My father looks younger than Justen, and he's older, not a lot, but older, and it takes Justen more use of order to maintain himself. That might be why Justen avoids chaos.'

'Too much contact would kill him?'

'You see what happened to me, and I used order to channel it.' I wasn't about to mention my failing hearing and the pain of seeing, not as we were finally getting back to some semblance of closeness.

'Oh, Lerris.'

Her arms went around me, and mine around her. At that point we didn't need words. We needed to be close.

# XCIV

## Worrak, Hydlen [Candar]

The staff on the breakwater flies the crimson banner of Hydlen, a banner ragged from the rock chips and shell fragments flying around and through it. A squat stone-walled fort rises from the middle of the breakwater.

In the nearly flat blue waters of the Gulf of Candar circle the steel-hulled ships, plumes of smoke from their funnels identifying them as steam-powered, the golden sunburst on the pale blue flag identifying them as from Hamor.

Another shell arches over the breakwater and into the fort that guards the harbor entrance. Stones cascade down from the breech in the wall, rolling into the oily water of the harbor. The crimson banner of Hydlen, more ragged, continues to flutter in the sea breeze.

With the regularity of a pendulum, the shells leave the guns of the Hamorian squadron, and with nearly equal regularity slam into the fortifications that bar the invaders from the port of Worrak.

On the bridge of the *Frentensea*, Leithrrse smiles as he watches the progress of the guns in hammering down the barriers to the harbor.

'Won't be long now, ser,' advises the captain. 'Not long at all before we can steam right in.'

'Good. Good. Teach those Hydlenese a lesson. And the black devils hiding on their island.'

The captain glances seaward, frowning. 'Something out there. Maybe they're not hiding any longer.'

'Out there?'

'I'm more worried about Recluce than Hydlen, ser.'

'The unseen ships?' Leithrrse laughs.

'Unseen, mayhap, but those unseen ships have sunk near on a dozen of ours so far.' The captain squints. 'See ... there's a wake out there. Low one, and it's headed our way.'

'Guns!' yells the envoy and acting regent, gesturing toward the wake.

'How do you hit a ship you can't see?' asks the gunnery chief.

'There's a wake there. Use the wake,' snaps the captain. 'Aim right ahead of the wake. Use enough shells and you'll hit it.'

'But don't they have magical armor?'

'Demon-damn! No magic is going to stop a five-stone shell! Stop bitching and start aiming. Leapfrog the guns if you have to.'

'Yes, ser.'

Once the gunnery officer has left, the captain wipes his forehead.

Leithrrse smiles as the gunnery officer begins to bellow orders and the turrets turn.

Geysers of water raised by the Hamorian shells begin to appear in the offshore waters in front of the thin line of white that marks the track of the unseen attacker.

After a rocket slams into the thicker armor above the waterline of the *Frentensea*, flames cascade up over the side of the Hamorian ship, even as the dull impact of the rocket echoes through the hull.

More shells track the invisible attacker, and more water geysers up from the flat shallow waves of the Gulf around the Recluce vessel that the Hamorian gunners cannot see.

A thin haze of gunpowder smoke creeps across the sky, then drifts shoreward, where it combines with spray off the breakwater to shroud the battered harbor fort.

The *Frentensea* shivers as her bow explodes in flame.

'Keep shooting!' yells Leithrrse.

More columns of water flare into the sky, then collapse into themselves in a mass of spray on the nearly calm waters of the lower Gulf of Candar.

Two rockets strike the smaller ironclad beside the *Frentensea*, and

flames race across the forward decks and around the main turret.
Another set of flames licks the superstructure.

*CcccccRRRuMMMMMPPPTTT!* Chunks of iron and wood fly skyward with the explosion of the smaller ironclad.

Leithrrse ducks behind the iron shielding on the *Frentensea*'s bridge,
but the fragments from the smaller Hamorian ship clatter against
the hull harmlessly, and the flagship leaves the widening oil slick
behind, a slick that oozes over wood fragments, and a few struggling
figures. Flames lick at the oiliest parts of the slick, creeping toward
the survivors.

The *Frentensea*'s big guns continue to lead the curving wake of the
unseen Recluce vessel.

'Ser! There's another one!' The lookout points astern, where a wake,
almost foam-white, arrows toward the big Hamorian cruiser.

'Guns! Keep on the outboard one!' snaps Leithrrse. 'Get him first!'

A huge fireball blossoms in the middle of the seemingly empty sea,
and then a low black structure appears, breaking into fragments as
Leithrrse watches, the flames raging across the waters as the wreckage
plummets from sight.

'Now . . . the other —'

*WHHHHHSTTTTT! CRUMPPTTTT!*

His words are cut off as the *Frentensea* explodes into an inferno of
flame, flying metal, and chunks of meat that had once been sailors.

# XCV

Dark ships shall speed upon the waters, and destruction shall fall
from the heavens, shattering the greatest of walls, and even the
weakest of those who bear arms shall strike with the force of
firebolts.

For every shield shall there be a greater sword, and for every
sword, a swifter quarrel to bring it low. For every firebolt shall
there be a higher wall of ice, and for every wall of ice, a ladder
of fire with which to scale it.

For every prophet shall come another who says the opposite,
and whoever shall offer his words last shall the people follow, and
they shall turn one way and then the other, for no road shall offer
certainty, nor peace, nor rest. And none shall sleep easy.

Men and women shall question, and so shall the angels. Yet for every answer shall they find a score more of questions, each with yet a score more answers, until their words and their reason be stopped with words whose meaning escapes even the highest.

The dark ships shall cover the oceans, thick as sands upon the shores, and they shall come from the end of the earth to the city of black stone, north of the sun and east of chaos.

Those of the black city will cover their faces and wail loud lamentations, claiming that they had ever stood against chaos, and the dark ships of the sun shall neither heed nor turn from their course.

And on the shores of truth shall stand those serving neither order nor chaos, yet both, and without trumpets, without firebolts, shall they sow confusion upon the waters.

From that confusion, shall the dark ships of the sun seek refuge, but neither the mountains nor the oceans shall provide succor. Mountains shall be rendered into dust, and oceans shall be burned and boiled, and ashes shall cover all, and chaos shall die . . .

*The Book of Ryba*
Canto DL [The Last]
Original Text

# III.

---

# FINDING
# THE BALANCE

# XCVI

'What brings you here to Mattra, Gunnar? Usually, I'm the one who has to seek you out.' Elisabet opened the door and stepped aside.

'This.' The sandy-haired man held up a scroll. 'Might I come in?'

'Certainly. I'll even get some redberry. It must be something to pry you out of Wandernaught. For once, I'm not chasing you.' She grinned and headed for the kitchen.

Gunnar pursed his lips, but followed. His sister set a pitcher and two mugs upon the table. Gunnar looked at the pitcher, then sat. Elisabet filled both mugs before seating herself.

'The Council has learned that the Emperor is sending his fleets against Kyphros,' said Gunnar after taking a short swallow of redberry. 'This is good.'

'Thank you. It's fresh.' Elisabet offered a brief smile that faded all too quickly. 'I would have thought they were going to send a fleet against us. After all, Recluce has kept Candar weak and fragmented. By opposing any real changes within the isle, the Council has kept us from getting much stronger, and that means we're comparatively weaker. So why is Hamor going to attack Kyphros?'

'Lerris and his consort Krystal have apparently thwarted their takeover of Candar.'

'I'm afraid your son's taking more after Justen than you, Gunnar.' Elisabet laughed. 'But that doesn't make much sense. Didn't the trio sink nearly a third of the Hamorian fleet before the fleet sank the *Llyse?*'

'You knew about the *Llyse?*'

'Gunnar, I listen to the winds as well as anyone.'

The sandy-haired mage shook his head. 'That's probably why. They don't have enough ships around Candar to feel safe about attacking Recluce. It wasn't a large fleet anyway, not compared to what they have and what they're building.'

'It's already built,' pointed out the sandy-haired woman. 'It has to be, from all the growth of chaos. That means the Council wants Kyphros to be our buffer?'

'It's more complex than that. I think the Emperor knows that Recluce has never had more than a handful of powerful mages, and most of those are now in Kyphros. The royal house there has carried a grudge against us since even before the present Emperor's grandsire was exiled.'

'Now that Austrans bow to his every whim, the Emperor is ready to expand Hamor's control in our part of the world?' Elisabet pulled at her chin. 'And his scheme is to weaken Recluce before they ever attack us directly?'

'Exactly. And that's the way the Council would have it. They'd be happy to have Kyphros and the rest of Candar fed to the mountain cat first, but I'm going to Kyphros.'

'You really are, aren't you?'

He nodded.

'Justen said something about that once, about Candar being the shield of Recluce in the end.' The sandy-haired woman looked off the porch toward the shop where the sound of a crosscut saw is followed by the susurration of finishing cloths. 'I'm not sure that Justen's not right.'

'You always did stand up for Justen.'

'Gunnar, you're too old for self-pity and "Elisabet loved Justen best." You have to believe that Justen was right.'

'Oh?'

'We've used what he taught you, haven't we? Otherwise we'd long since be buried with the High Wizards of Fairhaven – excuse me, Frven.' She offered a sad smile. 'Actions tell where the heart is.' She poured more of the cold redberry into his mug.

'They're worried.'

'Do tell. They want you and Justen and Lerris to rescue them again. Is that why you're doing it?'

'If I don't go, Justen will slip away, and Lerris will have to save Ruzor alone.'

'Getting soft in your dotage, aren't you?' Elisabet smiled at her brother.

He grinned at her. 'A little.' The grin faded. 'Lerris is on the way to finding out how to destroy us all. Put him and Justen together ...' He looked down at the table.

'You knew it would happen sooner or later. How long did you think what Justen discovered could be hidden?'

Gunnar laughed. 'Not as long as it was. The Council was more adept —'

'More ruthless,' snapped his sister, 'and Hamor wants a reckoning in blood.'

'I suspect Dorrin was right.'

'Much good that will do us now. Do you want help? I can go with you.'

'Not now. Perhaps later.'

She smiled. 'If there is a later.'

'There will be.' His eyes lifted to the mug of redberry. 'There will be.'

'Yes. That reckoning has been waiting for a long time, hasn't it?'

'Since Dorrin.' He nodded. 'Maybe since Creslin and Megaera. Maybe since the angels.'

# XCVII

## Worrak, Hydlen [Candar]

'You summoned me?' The thin officer in tan steps into the room. His holster is empty. Behind him the two guards stand outside the open door. One holds the officer's sidearm.

'I did, Force Leader Speyra.' Dyrsse gestures to the table in the middle of the spacious room, and to the map upon it. 'Please sit.'

The door closes with a dull thud.

Speyra purses his lips and sits on the edge of the seat of the carved chair. Behind him, the hillside villa's window frames the placid harbor waters – and the battered breakwater and the pile of stone that had been a fortress. Black-hulled ships brood over the harbor, some with thin plumes of smoke trailing from their stacks.

'You see here – the Fakla River?' The marshal traces the line of the river west from Worrak.

'Yes, ser.' Speyra nods and straightens in the chair.

'You will be taking the second army up this road, through the vale, here, and into Kyphros. Take the road north from Lythga and then west into Kyphrien.'

'All the way to Kyphrien?'

'All the way. Do what is necessary. The Emperor and I have absolute confidence in you, Leader Speyra.'

'You're not coming?' asks the officer.

'You are perfectly capable, Force Leader Speyra, and you will be provided more than enough cartridges and even some mobile field pieces.' The marshal smiles. 'Someone has to watch for another strike from the nest of vipers. And coordinate your support.'

'No one has yet taken Kyphros.'

'Fenardre the Great did, and so will we. For the Emperor. The most force the autarch can muster is less than eight thousand outliers, levies, and her Finest.' Dyrsse wipes his balding head with the fine white cotton handkerchief.

'I believe it only took one wizard and a handful of troops to block the Easthorn road.'

'We lost less than a third of our troops in that effort. We also enlisted the help of another wizard and cleared the old highway into Certis. That gives us a more direct way to move troops at least as far as the Easthorns.' Dyrsse smiles again, briefly, and studies the map on the table before him.

'Ser ... have we not lost a number of commanders ... and the wizard?' The force leader purses his lips and shifts his weight from one foot to the other.

'We have. Good commanders, and two regents. And if they were willing to risk their lives for the Emperor, then ... can we do no less?'

'Yes, ser. I mean, we can do no less.'

'Good. You will have four thousand troops. You will see less than a tenth of that, even if you march all the way to Kyphrien. The autarch's forces are all in Ruzor. Kyphrien is your destination. You will have more than enough force to accomplish your mission.'

'Yes, ser. Then what?'

'The usual. You hold the city for the Emperor and follow the established practices. In the meantime, the fleet will be reducing Ruzor, and then attacking up the Phroan River. Because Ruzor is where most of the autarch's troops are, you will see few, indeed.'

'And if I do?' A faint sheen of perspiration coats the force leader's forehead. 'If I do?'

'You won't. But if you need reinforcements, you shall have them. Don't worry about that in the slightest.' Dyrsse smiles.

# XCVIII

More than two eight-days had passed since we returned to Ruzor, and I had finally recovered from my stiffness, and I could hear, although sometimes people's words faded in and out, sometimes my eyes still hurt. The sun continued to beat down, and the dust continued to coat everything. Krystal continued to train and plan, and Kasee to persuade and to gather supplies.

Few ships reached Ruzor, and what they brought was dear, indeed. Even the smugglers could find no more Hamorian rifles or cartridges, at any price.

I started joining the Finest at their morning exercises and training, since I couldn't really do much woodwork, outside of some simple repairs. At times, I wished that I'd at least brought the cedar limb to carve, but I hadn't thought about that.

That morning, after I loosened my shoulders, I finally picked up the staff. Then I wiped my forehead, even though I had only been in the mid-morning sun for a short time. Krystal stepped forward, the blade-shaped wand extended. Her exercise shirt was damp as well. I bowed, and so did she.

'He's a mage, but he's going to be in trouble now . . .' murmured someone from the side of the courtyard.

'. . . don't know. Staff is pretty long.'

Her wand snaked out, and I parried . . . and parried . . . and blocked. So long as I wove a defense, she couldn't touch me. But I couldn't do much on the attack. So, eventually, I tried to touch her.

We went at it until we were both soaked, and I got a few bruises. So did Krystal, but hers were lighter. I just couldn't strike that hard in practice.

'Enough . . .' I finally panted. 'You're more in practice. You do this all the time.'

'All . . . right . . .' She was breathing almost as hard as I was.

We stepped into the shade and watched some of the others practice. Weldein was using a wand against Tamra, and actually holding his own.

'Does Weldein spar with Tamra a lot?' I asked.

'No one else comes close to her with a blade.'

'Except you and Yelena?'

'And Weldein – now,' Krystal added. 'He didn't at first, but he kept at it.'

'Brave man.' In more ways than one, I thought.

I watched for a while longer. 'He's not as good as you are.'

'Close,' Krystal commented.

He was probably stronger than Krystal, but not quite as quick or as deft. Then I supposed that was how I'd have described the difference between me and Tamra with the staff, although I was definitely a great deal quicker than in the beginning, when Tamra had beaten me black and blue.

'You're as good as she is,' Krystal added. 'Different style, but as good.'

I didn't believe it, but it was nice to hear.

Haithen nodded as we passed, and so did Berli, pausing from a stretching routine.

'Commander . . . ?'

Subrella stood in the archway, a scroll in her hand, and circles under her eyes, though they were certainly no deeper than those under Krystal's eyes.

'I'll see you later,' I said.

Krystal gave me a wry smile, and I grinned, and made my way toward the wash house. After washing up, I carried the staff and my damp shirt up to Krystal's room.

Herreld opened the door for me.

'Show 'em how, Master Lerris?'

'I think the commander did that. I managed to stay in one piece.'

'More than most folks, these days.'

I spread the shirt on the sill beneath the open window where, in the heat, it would be dry long before noon. Then, bare-chested, I sat on one of the chairs and read more of *The Basis of Order*.

Krystal arrived later, much later, around noon, bearing two pitchers and some bread and cheese.

'Nice view.'

'I try.' But I had cooled down a bit and pulled on a shirt before I sat down with her at the table.

We ate without saying much. We were both hungry.

'More problems,' she finally explained. 'Bandits on the south river road, not more than ten kays from Ruzor. So I sent Weldein and his squad out, along with a few others. Then, the Nordlan ship sent word that they wouldn't unload unless we sent a guard detachment. Beggars and people screaming for passage all over the piers.'

'We don't even have any real idea if Hamor will attack.'

'You don't believe that, do you?'

'No,' I admitted. 'They'll attack. That's what they do. Evil is as evil does.'

'Are they evil or just greedy?'

'Does it make any difference?' I swallowed some redberry. 'I mean, in a way, Sammel was the same. He was greedy for knowledge . . . and he couldn't stop using it even when he knew it was evil.' I was trying to explain to myself as much as to Krystal.

'Why was Sammel so evil?' Krystal sipped some of the amber ale, then some more. 'You said that he was mostly trying to share knowledge. Why was that evil?'

'He was treating knowledge as if it were order – or chaos – itself.'

Krystal got this puzzled expression that told me that I wasn't making much sense. She set the mug of ale on the table.

I tried again. 'One of the big differences between order and chaos is that it's almost impossible to create pure order. You have to order *something*, but a chaos-wielder can throw chaos-fire at people – and that's close to pure chaos. Well ... Sammel was just providing what he thought was pure knowledge – and pure knowledge is a lot like pure chaos – an awful lot of it's used for bad purposes.'

'Are you sure? It seems to me that knowledge isn't good or bad. It's like a sword – you can use it to protect or kill.'

I laughed. 'That's a better explanation than mine.'

'Why?' Krystal took a sip from the mug.

'Because ...' I dragged out the word. 'When you lift a blade for real, someone always gets hurt – whether you're protecting or killing. Knowledge is like that.'

'Ooooo ... That explains a lot.' She frowned. 'If knowledge always means someone gets hurt, that creates chaos, and that means Recluce has to oppose new knowledge, doesn't it?'

'Oppose or hide?'

'It's the same thing,' she pointed out.

'There's another problem with knowledge. When you write out a way for using powder, like Sammel did for Berfir, it doesn't tell you what happens to people.'

'But it could mean good things as well as bad,' protested Krystal.

'The *results* could be good or bad.' I nodded in agreement, then added, 'But the idea is bad, like chaos, because when you give someone written knowledge – words or diagrams on a scroll – you separate the knowledge from its effect on people.'

'How is that different from a blade?' Krystal looked toward the window. 'There's still no sign of rain.'

'There won't be for a while,' I said, adding, 'When you use a blade, you know, after the first time at least, that someone will get hurt if you use it.'

'But you can threaten with a blade.'

'That's why it appears more effective than knowledge. How can you threaten someone with knowledge? You can't, not without using it.'

'Oh. And if you use it, then anyone can – so the use of black steel to confine powder went from rockets to cannon shells to rifles.'

I frowned. 'Not exactly.'

There was a rap on the door. Krystal opened it, and the autarch stood there, a scroll in hand. Krystal stepped back, and Kasee stepped inside and shut the door in Herreld's surprised face. Then she slumped into the empty chair beside Krystal.

'What is it?' Krystal took out a spare mug and poured some of the ale into it, extending it to the autarch. 'You look like you need this.'

Kasee straightened up. 'Thank you.' She took a swallow from the mug. 'I need to talk to both of you.'

We sat and waited. Kasee took another sip.

'Hamor has Worrak, and their forces are massing to march up the Fakla River.' She glanced around. 'I wanted to talk to you two, and if I summoned you, then everyone would be there before I had a chance to think.'

That made sense. Everyone always watched the autarch.

'Apparently, Recluce took on the Hamorian ships, and destroyed several, including the flagship, the *Frentensea*. Leithrrse was on board, and there were no survivors. Someone called Marshal Dyrsse has taken over command. He has a reputation as a rather bloody but effective commander. The remainder of the Hamorian fleet is resupplying, and will be headed here within an eight-day.'

'They want to hit us before harvest,' said Krystal.

'Dyrsse has requested more ships and troops, but is proceeding.' Kasee looked at me. 'Things have become more clear.'

I shrugged. 'I guess I'm off to the Lower Easthorns again.'

Krystal paled, but she said nothing.

'I don't want a decision this afternoon.' Kasee looked from Krystal to me and back to Krystal. 'I want you to consider the best course.'

'We can't wait too long.' Why I pointed that out I had no idea, since I certainly wasn't enthused about wielding chaos to destroy another army and myself in the process. Maybe it had something to do with knowing that I couldn't do anything about a fleet and feeling I had to do something.

'Let me know what you think tomorrow.' Kasee stood and took the scroll with her as she left.

'Could you and Justen and Tamra talk this over?' asked Krystal.

If he doesn't decide to disappear, I thought. 'You definitely ought to be here, too.'

'And Dayala.'

So she sent poor Herreld off to round up everyone, and we straightened up the room and dragged out two more mugs and some more redberry and ale.

Tamra arrived first. 'What's this all about?'

'Hamor.'

Then came Justen and Dayala, looking slightly disheveled. I had to repress a grin. At his advanced age, yet. Then I thought again – at their advanced ages, yet.

'You requested us?' Justen asked.

'Hamor holds all of Hydlen. The new marshal is sending ships and troops to take Ruzor, though probably not for an eight-day, perhaps two. Another army will be marching up the Fakla River and through the Lower Easthorns. We don't have the forces to send to Lythga, not and still hold Ruzor.' Krystal sat down in the corner chair.

For a moment, there was silence.

'I suppose Lerris wants to go out and save Kyphros again?' Tamra leaned back so her chair was on two legs.

'He had mentioned something like that,' Krystal said. 'It's something he feels compelled to do periodically.'

'Do you want to die that badly, Lerris?' asked Justen.

I glared at them both. 'You both make me ill. All you can do is tell other people what not to do. Fine. Are you suggesting that the autarch surrender Kyphros to Hamor? After all, probably fewer people – or at least fewer troopers – will die, and who cares about anyone else, anyway?'

'No one died in Montgren,' said Justen.

'Montgren didn't have any army at all and no wizards,' pointed out Krystal. 'That meant the Countess had no choice. We do have a choice.'

'The machines should not prevail,' said Dayala softly.

Justen looked at her, clearly surprised that she had spoken.

'Order should not be embodied in cold iron. It is against life and against the Legend.'

'That seems to settle that,' said Tamra, looking at Justen, then at me.

The way Dayala said it . . . I had to agree, but I looked at Krystal, and she nodded.

'So we can't allow order to be embodied in iron,' I began, 'but the problem is that pure chaos can be concentrated and developed without being attached to anything.' That seemed clear enough to me.

'Of course.' Justen sounded exasperated. 'That's the way the world is. Order has to be able to order *something*. You can't have pure order because order means the organized arrangement of something. Chaos is disorganization.'

'But it has to disorganize something,' said Tamra.

'But even chaos has some organization when it's used by the white wizards.' I knew I was on to something. 'When they throw firebolts, what are they doing?'

Dayala nodded.

'Throwing firebolts organized with a minimum of order,' answered Tamra. 'That doesn't change the fact that you need to duck if you don't want to get fried. Unless you have a better *practical* solution.'

I knew I was right about this one. 'When I destroyed Gerlis, what I did was let chaos build inside channels of ordered rock holding lots of little bits of iron —'

'Iron ore. It generally works that way,' Justen agreed. 'And if you can go deep enough, you can find it in most places.' He took the last of the ale Krystal had left and swallowed it. Then he poured more from the second pitcher. 'Warm, but good.'

'But . . .' I pointed out. 'The molten rock was still rock. That means that —'

'That's right.' Justen nodded as if he'd known that all along, and I wanted to brain him with my staff. 'Pure chaos isn't usable. I suppose you could create it, but it has to be tied to something because you need some way to control it.'

'This is simple stuff,' protested Tamra. 'That's why Sammel was so dangerous. He knew some of the basics of order. What's your point, Lerris?' She grinned, and I wanted to brain her.

'A sword is simple.' Krystal paused and smiled. 'In the right hands, it kills people very quickly.'

'What did you do to defeat chaos?' I had a good idea, but I wanted Justen to tell me.

'Concentrated order through a fire-eye lens. It took most of the sun's light. Putting that much order in a small place created too much order, and that order tore apart anything it touched.'

'That's what melted Fairhaven?' asked Krystal.

Justen nodded. 'Mostly.'

'Couldn't we use that on the Hamorians?' I asked.

'No. It took a year to build the device, and a lot of free order that doesn't exist. Even if it did, or you could free it, which I wouldn't be surprised if you could, we don't have the time.'

'So what do we do?'

'I don't know.' Justen shrugged.

We talked a lot more than that, until dinner, but never came to a resolution clearer than the four of us would have to go to the Lower Easthorns and do something. What that might be, none of us would say, probably because we all feared it meant using order to raise chaos to destroy an order based on machines. And that would make a light-fired mess.

Then, after everyone else left, things got worse.

Krystal bolted the door and sat down at the table. She didn't look at me, and it didn't take much imagination to figure that she was angry.

'What's the matter?' I asked.

She didn't answer, just kept looking out the narrow window. I folded the shirt I'd left there to dry and put it in the wardrobe.

'You don't want me to go?'

Still no answer.

I straightened a stack of papers in the corner and looked back at Krystal. She hadn't moved.

I waited for a while, looking out the window at the stars above the sea. Despite the warmth of the night, they looked cold and distant. After a while, I touched her shoulder, and she pushed my hand away.

'Please don't touch me.'

'I can't fix whatever's wrong if I don't know what's wrong.'

'Fix things? You fix things? You are the most arrogant, self-centered —Sometimes, I hate you!'

'Hate me? What did I do?'

Krystal finally stood, almost crackling with power of some sort, and I backed away as she walked to the window.

'Do I have to spell everything out one letter at a time? You could tell I wasn't happy about your . . . exploit with Sammel, but you seemed to understand. I thought you did. But you didn't. That's clear enough.'

'But —'

Krystal didn't even listen to my objection and went right on. 'First, you go off and defeat one white wizard and rescue Tamra. That wasn't too bad. Then you set up a house and woodworking shop, and you condescend to maintain the house, and the quarters for my guards, and feed them. Then you charge off and defeat this Gerlis, and almost get killed in the process. After that, you can't wait to go out and get aged ten years! I thought that might have taught you something, but, no, here we go again. Lerris, the hero, off to save Kyphros and Krystal once more!'

'I don't understand.' And I didn't. It seemed simple enough. Krystal didn't have enough forces to hold Ruzor and fight off the sundevils coming through the Lower Easthorns. There was a lot of chaos under Candar, and a lot of rocks and stones in the mountains, and three wizards and a druid at least had a chance of stopping that army.

'Lerris, your body may have aged ten years, but your mind has a lot of catching up to do.' She turned to look at me, and her face was stone-cold in the light from the single wall lamp.

'It might help if you'd give me some idea of why you're so upset.' I bent down and smoothed the coverlet on the bed.

'It might help if you tried to understand instead of — Oh, what's the use?'

'Understand what? That you can't do it all? That I don't want to see you run over and destroyed by various wizards —'

'What you want to do is smother me! If there's any danger, let Lerris try to reduce it. If there's a problem, let Lerris try to fix it. Being a blade is dangerous. You can't protect me from everything, and I'm so tired of your guilty, hang-dog look when you feel you haven't been able to save me or do as well as you think you should. Darkness! You muttered all the way back from Hydlen about how sorry you were. Death is part of life. People die. I may die. But stop taking on the weight of the world. Stop jumping in and throwing yourself in the fire – sometimes to save people who could care less. Who will care in a hundred years if you get ground to powder in the Lower Easthorns?'

'I care now. I care because you don't have enough troops to fight two battles at the same time. I can't help you here, because anything I tried to do near a city would destroy the city and kill a lot of people – maybe you.'

'Why don't you say it that way . . . instead of just pretending to be high and noble?'

'I wasn't pretending anything.'

'Oh, Lerris.'

We didn't fall into each other's arms, but at least she didn't yell at me anymore, and the room wasn't quite as cold as the Roof of the World in winter, but I didn't sleep that well, and I don't think Krystal did, either.

# XCIX

'When do we talk to Kasee?' I asked Krystal.

Even right after dawn, even with fall approaching, the morning was hot enough that I had been sweating as soon as I had climbed out of bed.

'Dayala told her to wait.' Krystal's voice was still cool – not as icy as two nights earlier, but cool.

'Fine.' We'd been waiting for two days. I straightened my shirt and peered out the window at the calm waters of the harbor. A ship lay berthed at the main pier, the only one in days, bearing a Nordlan ensign. 'There's a ship in the harbor.'

'Maybe he's got a cargo of flour.'

'We wish.'

'We can wish.'

I winced.

Krystal belted her blade in place, getting ready to leave. I hadn't seen that much of her for the last few days, as though she were not quite avoiding me, but almost.

At that point there was a rap on the door, and Krystal opened it to find both Herreld and Fregin standing there, Fregin with a staff he was using to hobble around while his leg healed.

'Master Lerris,' stammered Fregin, 'begging your pardon, but there's a tall mage, I mean, he's wearing black, and he's asking for you, and he came off the Nordlan steamer.'

'A tall mage?' I didn't know what mage might be looking for me, especially one from Recluce. So I took my staff and turned to Krystal. 'I'd like you to come.'

She looked at me for a moment. 'All right.'

I had the feeling she thought I was trying not to be condescending, but what was I supposed to do?

'Where is he?'

'In the dining hall, ser. Eating.'

We left Fregin behind as we hurried along the narrow corridor and down the twisting steps. Even that early, the corridors were not-quite-stifling. The dining hall was empty except for a single figure in black sitting near one end of a long trestle table. A half loaf of bread, some cheese, and a mug were on the wood before him.

Almost as we entered, he stopped eating and swallowed.

'Greetings, Lerris.' My father stood up from the table and bowed. He looked impressive, with the hard darkness of order laid over the twisted mix of chaos and order that Justen – and I, now – had. He also looked pale and tired.

'Greetings.' I bowed slightly and gestured to Krystal. 'This is Krystal. She's the autarch's commander. Krystal, this is my father.'

'I am pleased to meet you, Krystal, both as commander and as a person.' He bowed to her, and I wished I had his charm.

'It is my pleasure. I have heard much of you, both from Lerris and Justen.' She returned his greeting with a bow every bit as formal and deep as his.

My father frowned, then said to Krystal, 'I fear I bring ill tidings, although you may already know them.'

'We have heard that Hamor intends to attack.'

'A fleet of some twoscore ships is being assembled at Worrak, and they will sail – or steam,' he added with a bleak smile, 'within the eight-day.'

'Do you know whether there will be an attack through the Easthorns?'

He pursed his lips. 'An army is assembling, but my ability to see much beyond the waters is limited.'

Krystal nodded. 'I should notify the autarch. Perhaps you and your father would like some time together, Lerris.'

With that, and a brief smile, she was gone.

'She seems quite able,' offered my father.

'Let's sit down.' I set my staff on the floor and slipped onto the bench. 'She is more than able.'

'She seems . . . a trace . . . formal.'

'Right now, she's . . . concerned.' I didn't really want to blurt out that my consort was still more than a little angry at me, especially not right after he'd arrived.

He nodded and picked up a corner of the loaf of bread.

'Why did you come here?' I asked.

'You are my son, Lerris. Hamor is out to destroy Kyphros and you two as well.'

I swallowed. It didn't make sense. My father had sent me away without answering my simplest questions, yet he had come to Ruzor. I understood him even less than Krystal, and I still didn't understand her. 'I still don't understand.'

He drank some water from the mug and cleared his throat. 'You understand the Balance now, I trust. You also understand why Recluce has opposed the spread of knowledge or machines, even since the time of Dorrin.'

'Because more order leads to more chaos, and, I guess, the more of each, the more the chance for even greater destruction.'

'That was the idea. It was even my idea, and Justen's as well. He was one of the finest black engineers, you know, and even he thought that ordered machines couldn't be made without black iron. We were wrong. Better metalworking techniques changed that, and Hamor has created more order, and more chaos. Recluce has weeded out, over the generations, wizards drawn to chaos, and chaos has found it harder – that's not precisely correct – to create chaos foci. There never were very many wizards in the rest of the world, besides Candar, probably because most wizards come from demon or angel stock, and those few were easy enough to find through their ... modifications of order.' He sipped more water. 'It's dry here.'

'Demon or angel stock?' That was something I hadn't heard before.

'It's not widely spread for a number of obvious reasons. There's no record of flame-red hair or silver hair like Creslin's before the fall of angels and the beginning of the Legend. That's all buried in the Brotherhood archives.'

'Why are you here?'

'You'd have been hard to find in Nordla, and you wouldn't have lasted a week in Swartheld – that's where dangergelders go if they go to Hamor.'

'Wait a moment.' I was getting angry. 'You got me put into the dangergeld before I knew what was happening just so I'd be sent to Candar?' There he was, still trying to manage me, bend my life to his pattern without telling me even what was at stake.

'Not exactly. Elisabet and I knew that, once you found out what your abilities were, if you were exiled then, you'd be so angry that you'd probably lash out blindly. I'd also hoped you'd meet with Justen. He usually finds dangergelders with your abilities.' He gave a bitter laugh. 'You can be angry. I would be. I'd be very angry.'

That stopped me. I just sat there, openmouthed. Finally, I closed my mouth, although it couldn't really have been open that long.

'You had a brother – about a hundred and fifty years ago. He died in Hamor – three days after the ship landed. I tried to get the Brotherhood to stop sending black staffers there, and usually they don't now. Hamor's more for adventurers, people like ... the trader ... Leith something or other. I told Martan – he was named for someone who saved my life once – I told Martan everything you've had to find out, and he was so angry he never figured anything out.'

Finally, I looked at my father again. He did look tired, and somehow older. 'Do you want anything else to eat?'

'No.'

'You still haven't said why you came here.'

He shrugged. 'No one can save the world alone. Justen couldn't. I couldn't even save Recluce. And you can't save Kyphros – although that's just the beginning.'

Once again, I was lost, just as I thought I was beginning to understand. 'What do you mean?'

He smiled, a sad smile. 'The struggle between order and chaos never ends. The difference between Recluce and the Legend is not all that great. Recluce fights, and never wins, not for long. The druids in Naclos work to maintain the Balance in their own quiet way, but the work never ends. Nothing's ever over.'

'That's awfully fuzzy.'

'Do you think that Hamor, with more than five hundred iron-hulled warships, will sit back if we destroy this small fleet and their small armies?'

'You think we should give up?'

He shook his head. 'Then blind chance wins.'

I needed to think. It should have been clear, but clear thinking isn't easy when I'm upset, and I'd received two shocks in almost as many days. 'How is Mother?'

'She's fine. She sends her love. So do Elisabet and Sardit. He told me that you'd better mark all your pieces so that future collectors wouldn't have to argue whether something you'd done was a genuine Lerris.' He chuckled. 'Your crafting may well outlast anything else you do. That's something I tell your mother about her pottery. I don't have anything like that.'

My father, envying us for our crafts?

As I tried to gather myself together again, I heard steps. My father looked up and saw Justen walking into the dining hall with Tamra. 'Justen!'

'Well, look what the light dragged in.' Justen grinned.

'Speak for yourself.'

They hugged, as though it had not been long years since they had seen each other.

Tamra looked at them, and her eyes began to water. Then she turned away. I walked over beside her.

'It's all right.'

She kept her face averted and shook her head. 'You have a family . . .'

So I patted her shoulder. 'I'm glad you suggested I write.'

'Lerris . . . will you ever learn?'

Learn what? I sighed.

'Not all tears are sad.' She wiped her face. 'I'm glad they got back together.'

As if to confuse things, Krystal came back through the door. Everyone turned to her and waited.

'The autarch is meeting with some ministers at the moment. She would like to meet with all of us in the small dining hall after lunch.' Krystal walked over between the four of us. 'I have to meet with Subrella for a bit.'

'Gunnar looks as if he could freshen up,' said Justen. 'Then I'll show him around. You won't mind, will you, Lerris? You've seen him far more recently than I have.'

'No.' I forced a smile over my confusion. 'That's fine.' I watched as the two men left.

Krystal and Tamra watched me.

'Dazed, wouldn't you say?' asked Tamra.

'It's good for him.' Krystal nodded and said to me, 'I'll see you in the small dining hall.'

So I watched her leave as well.

'I promised Weldein I'd spar with him.' With that, Tamra was gone, and I stood alone in the empty dining hall.

Feeling somewhere between abandoned and useless, I wandered out to the courtyard and stripped off my shirt and began to exercise. After a while I sparred against Haithen, Berli, and Dercas, although Jinsa shamed him into it, by telling him that he didn't have enough nerve to face a staff with a wand.

Nerve or no, he was good, not that any but the best would have been Krystal's guards.

Then I washed up and grabbed some bread and strong yellow cheese for a midday meal.

Krystal and the autarch weren't in the small dining hall when I got there, but Justen, my father, and Tamra were. So was Dayala, and she sat between Tamra and Justen. There were also pitchers and mugs on the table, and I poured a glass of redberry and sat down.

Just as I'd thought I'd finally figured out some things, everyone was treating me as if I knew nothing at all – or that what I knew didn't matter in the slightest.

'Going to be quite a gathering,' observed Justen, lifting a mug of the dark ale that only he drank, though Krystal might when she arrived.

'You're still drinking that swill?' asked my father with a smile.

'I could ask the same of you,' pointed out Justen. 'It's good ale. It tastes good. There's no point in drinking anything else.'

The door opened, and both Krystal and the autarch entered, without guards, although I could see several station themselves outside the door before Krystal closed it. The autarch seated herself at the end of the table, and Krystal sat to her right, almost across from me.

The room, with only high windows, was getting warm, and I wiped my forehead.

'I understand you are a weather mage.' The autarch looked at my father.

'Yes.'

'You wish to help us? Why?'

'For two reasons.' He smiled. 'Lerris is my son, and this is his land. Second, by helping you, I hope to help Recluce.'

Kasee nodded. 'I said I would make a decision several days ago, and I delayed that on the advice of the druid. Dayala convinced me that any decision would be premature, and I can see that she was right.' She paused. 'A decision is still necessary.'

I tried not to fidget in my chair, hard as the wood felt under my trousers.

'How much warning can you provide us, Mage?' she asked my father.

'At least a little over two days, perhaps longer. Their steam cruisers can travel the distance between Worrak and Ruzor in a little over two days, if the seas are not rough. That does not mean they will attack immediately when they arrive.'

'We understand that.' She turned to me. 'How long will it take you to reach the mid-point in the Lower Easthorns?'

'I haven't traveled the whole route from here, but if the maps and the reports are right, between five and six days.'

'Could you move an army that fast, Commander?'

'Possibly,' answered Krystal.

'Any faster?'

'No.'

'It would appear that our decisions are made for us. We cannot risk having the bulk of our forces as much as ten days' travel from Ruzor. Tomorrow morning, the mages will begin their travel, with a small escort and some messengers, to the Lower Easthorns —'

'I beg your pardon,' interrupted my father politely, waiting.

'Yes, Mage Gunnar?'

'I have little in the way of abilities to add to those of Justen or Lerris, not in a conflict so far from the ocean. Nor does the mage Tamra, although she already has considerable skill with the weather. As weather mages, we may be able to disrupt, perhaps sink, at least a few Hamorian warships, although the iron-hulled steamships are much harder to damage than ships with sails. For those reasons, I would suggest that we might be able to add to the defenses of Ruzor. While we certainly could not stop all the Hamorian troops from landing, we could reduce their numbers.'

Kasee looked at Krystal. Krystal shrugged.

'In that case, the mages Gunnar and Tamra will remain in Ruzor. Otherwise, the plan remains the same.'

So, from what I could figure, Justen, Dayala, and I were headed north and east, while my father and Tamra were to help Krystal hold Ruzor.

Then, abruptly as they had entered, Krystal and Kasee rose and departed.

Before I could say a word, the silver-haired Dayala slid into the chair beside me. Had I not known who she was, except for the darkness behind her eyes and the sense of power within her, I would have said that she was younger than Tamra, yet she was probably older than everyone in the room. Who knew how much older?

'You are troubled because your father remains.'

'Yes. He can stay and protect Krystal, and I can't go out and do the same thing. Krystal's not angry at him because he's using his air wizardry to help protect Ruzor . . . or her.'

'I wouldn't be sure of that.' I got a smile that could only have been druidic.

Behind me, I could hear Tamra asking Justen, 'Are you sure I can help more here?'

'I have Lerris and Dayala. You're an air mage, and you need to help Gunnar, and to watch him and learn how he does what he does. There's no one else who can.'

Somehow, I was perversely gratified to hear that Tamra was getting the same treatment I was.

'You both have much to learn, and there is little time,' Dayala explained to me.

'Little time?'

'Before everything changes.' She paused. 'You must learn. I also must teach you.' She rose.

'Now?'

'One must start sometime.' She nodded to Justen, and he gave her a smile.

I followed her into the small garden behind the barracks where she knelt on the ground beside a line of plants I didn't know, but I didn't recognize most plants. Trees were one thing, plants another. She was barefoot.

'Do you always go barefooted?'

'How else can I touch the earth?'

'In snow?'

'In snow or ice, I could wear boots, but they are . . . confining.' She looked at me. 'Give me your hand.'

I had to kneel down, but I did.

She positioned my hand with my fingers just barely touching the leaves. 'Now . . . just feel . . .'

I shook my head.

'Feel . . .'

So I tried. For a moment, nothing happened. Then, I could sense the flow of order and chaos within the plant, just as I had deep beneath Candar, except the flows moved more quickly, intertwining . . .

The feeling vanished, and I looked down. Dayala had removed her hand.

'You try it.'

It took a while, and by the time I could do it each time I tried, the sweat was pouring down my face, and the sun hung low in the western sky.

'Is that all?'

'It is a great deal, young Lerris. Few indeed ever learn that, and all who do are druids.'

'But why?'

'Because there will be few druids before long.' She smiled sadly, and, while I tried to gather myself together, was gone, like the mist of a forest morning, it seemed.

I wandered in a half-stupor back to the dining hall, where I ate tough lamb silently at the end of a trestle table. I didn't see Krystal, but I wasn't sure I would have seen anyone.

Then I went back to Krystal's room where I dug out *The Basis of Order*, except I couldn't find anything, really, about the intertwining of order and chaos.

By the single lamp, I was still reading *The Basis of Order* when Krystal returned.

'You're up late.'

'I was waiting for you.'

'Are you packed?'

'Yes.' I gestured toward my pack and staff in the corner. 'Everything I'll need is there, except for food.'

'Good. It's going to be hot tomorrow.'

'It's been hot for I don't know how many eight-days.' I closed the book, trying not to yawn, and sat up with my feet over the side of the bed. The relatively cool stone felt good on my bare feet.

'Now I know why you have trouble understanding,' said Krystal, stripping off her vest and tossing it on the table.

'Why?' I gritted my teeth and left the vest where she had tossed it.

'If you'd ever admitted to understanding anything, your father would always have had you thinking his way.' She sat in the chair by the window and pulled off her boots. 'How does your mother deal with him?'

'She's a potter. I told you that. She does her pieces – they're considered the best in Recluce – and she never talks about order, chaos, the Council, or whatever he does. That's probably one reason I never really understood how powerful he was.'

'You didn't want to.'

I couldn't help but nod, since she was probably right.

'Come here. Stand by me.' She stood before the window, still in shirt and trousers, but barefoot.

I stood next to her and looked out at the blackness of the Southern Ocean beyond the few scattered lights of Ruzor. Lamp oil, like everything else, was scarce.

'I understand, Lerris, but, somehow, I'm still angry at you. It's not fair, but I am.' She held up a hand in the darkness. 'That doesn't mean I don't love you. I do, but love doesn't always take away anger, and this is one of those times.'

'I'm sorry.' There wasn't much I could say besides that.

'You are. I know, but you still don't really understand. Maybe it's better that you're going with Justen and Dayala. Talk to her.'

She squeezed my hand. 'We need to get some sleep. You'll be up early, and it won't be that long before the Hamorian ships arrive, according to your father.'

So we did sleep, after a while and after a fashion.


# C

# Worrak, Hydlen [Candar]


The man in the tan uniform crosses the wooden slats that cover the iron-plated deck, repositioning the tan field cap over his bald scalp. He pauses beside the turret and studies the gun barrel that rises from the armor. Then he turns and climbs the iron ladder to the bridge.

'Marshal Dyrsse.'

'Commander Gurtel.' Dyrsse bows. 'I came to wish you well and offer the Emperor's blessing.'

'Thank you. I received your orders, and I regret you won't be accompanying us. You won't reconsider that, ser, would you?' asks the fleet commander.

'Unfortunately not. The press of administration, you know. Force Leader Speyra and Submarshal Hi'errse are highly capable of handling their land forces, and I could certainly not improve on your knowledge of your vessels and their tactics.' Dyrsse offers a rueful smile. 'My job is to ensure that our base of operations here expands to be able to supply and support the fleet. Not glamorous, I fear, but necessary, like coal. Very necessary.'

'We all appreciate your efforts, Marshal Dyrsse, especially in dealing with such a . . .' The white-haired commander shrugs. 'You know what I mean.'

'A disrupted command structure and an unexpected amount of black magery?' Dyrsse asks with a smile.

'Yes, there has been that, too much of that, and after this effort, I hope we can turn to deal with the real problem.' The commander's eyes flick to the northeast.

'We all do the Emperor's bidding.'

'That we do.'

'I won't take more of your time. The Emperor is with you.' Dyrsse inclines his head for a moment.

'May he be with you, Marshal.'

Dyrsse receives the salute, then turns and descends the iron ladder to the main deck, where he crosses to the quarterdeck, returns the salute of the ship's guard, and walks down the plank to the stone pier.

Beyond the harbor's calm waters are thin plumes of smoke from the more than forty ships bearing the sunburst.

The marshal's eyes focus momentarily beyond the ocean and the ships, toward the unseen isle to the northeast. Then he looks back at the warships and shakes his head. 'Poor tools.'

# CI

I stood by Gairloch in the dawn, saddlebags packed, and my pack between them, my staff already in the holder. Justen and Dayala were already mounted. Although she was barefoot and rode bareback, with only a halter on her mount, she let the leads from that lie across her mount's mane, loosely knotted. The half-squad of mounted guards held Weldein and Berli and four others I didn't know, except vaguely by sight.

The day promised to be clear – and hot. Nothing had changed in that way and probably wouldn't soon.

My father stepped up and hugged me briefly. 'Let Justen pull his own weight.' He grinned and looked at his brother.

'Just so long as you pull your weight here and take care of my apprentice,' snapped Justen, but he grinned too, for a moment.

Krystal gave me a hug, and I did hold her, and she whispered in my ear. 'Let Justen do it. Stop doing it all yourself, stubborn man. I want you back, and not as a gray-beard.'

'I'll try.'

'Try harder,' she hissed.

'All right.'

She kissed me, gently, and passionately enough to tell me that she really meant it, before she stepped back, and I climbed up on Gairloch.

My father looked at me and nodded, and I nodded back.

'Just them . . . going out to stop an army?' The words reached my ear, but not the identity of those Finest who watched.

'Tough bastard, that Lerris is . . . stop an army if he has to tear himself in pieces first.' Fregin's sardonic response was slightly higher.

Krystal frowned, for a moment, before looking at me and mouthing, 'Don't do it.'

I smiled back at her, and touched Gairloch's flanks. Justen eased Rosefoot up beside me. Few indeed outside the Finest's barracks even were about when we rode out onto the old stone-paved byways and wound back and forth on the climbing streets toward the eastern road to the Gateway Gorge. Those few women out trudged slowly, most carrying bundles, some on their heads, their eyes fixed sightlessly on the future they dreaded. At least, it looked that way to me.

'Quiet, it is,' murmured Berli to Weldein.

'Too quiet, far too quiet.'

Justen looked over at me. 'Too much fear. Fear never did anyone much good.' Then he chuckled. 'I'm getting old. All people fear, but giving in to it is what causes trouble. Decisions ruled by fear aren't usually good ones.'

'Decisions forced by anything probably aren't good,' I answered, my thoughts more on Krystal, more on her words and her desire to tell me to come back. I shivered. I just hoped Tamra and my father could add something to the defense of Ruzor, but how could mere storms stop steel-hulled, heavy-gunned warships?

I could have asked the same question of us. How could an earth wizard and a druid-smith stop an army of thousands? We didn't have to guess where the Hamorians were coming from, not when the routes were limited. The more direct route from Hydlen – the one through Sunta and Arastia – was blocked by the boiling lake that had grown from the impact of chaos on the brimstone spring and by the steaming waters of the Yellow River. That left the lower pass from Faklaar.

To get there we had to make almost a huge half-circle, heading up the river road through the Gateway Gorge and then up the Sturbal to Lythga and through the pass toward Faklaar.

Riding up the river road, I could see clouds of dust rising to the east, out over the High Desert, and my throat and nose felt dry and cracked almost before we had left Ruzor and long before we reached the cliff road itself.

The section of the road through the Gorge was misty, as always, although the mist seemed not to rise as high, and the upper walls of the Gorge on both sides were red in the sunlight, and dry.

'Dry this year,' said Weldein. 'The river's down a lot, more than I've seen in a long time.'

Somehow, that figured.

'Could be hard on the crops,' added Justen.

'The orchards will be all right, the olives, anyway,' pointed out Berli.

Since I knew little about any of them, I didn't say much, though I wondered how the dry weather would affect the chickens.

We arrived in Felsa at twilight, and stayed in the near-empty barracks there. Dinner was cold mutton and colder noodles, with water. Justen had a pitcher of ale – better, he said, than anything else on the table. He was probably right, but even if I were a gray wizard, ale still didn't feel that good to me. Dayala ate only the noodles and some dried fruit that she had apparently brought. Even Gairloch's grain cakes seemed more appetizing than cold mutton, and I ate more noodles than meat, if slowly.

Dawn came too early, but we were outside Felsa's walls and on the road before the sun cleared the rounded slopes on the other side of the Sturbal that marked the edge of the High Desert.

'There are fields here,' I said, 'and over beyond the river is the High Desert. A few kays make a big difference.'

'Sometimes, sometimes.' Justen clearly wasn't in the mood for talking, and neither was Dayala, who rode bareback beside Justen. Mostly, she walked, barefoot, talking to the horse.

After that response, I patted Gairloch on the neck instead of trying to continue a conversation. I looked over again, wondering if the two were conversing, silently, and if I had interrupted them.

Justen could have been more gracious, anyway. I patted Gairloch again. At least, he *whuffed* back.

Even though the road beyond Felsa was broader than most, from the time when the mining wagons carted copper down through Felsa to Ruzor for shipping around Candar, the surface was rough. Dust and clay filled parts of the twin ruts worn in the limestone paving blocks, and the road's shoulders were uneven, and, in places, missing. After a morning of bouncing along, I was sore already. I let Gairloch pick his own way, and he did better than I would have.

'Rough road,' I finally said to Justen.

'That's what happens when order is imposed on nature and then withdrawn.'

'Another profundity.' I was getting more than a little tired of the obscurities. 'Nature has an order of its own.'

'Nature does not withdraw,' observed Dayala with a faint smile. 'Men do.'

While I wondered whether she had meant all she implied, she continued, apparently oblivious to the possible play on words. 'Nature is really more of an intertwining of order and chaos. The results look ordered, but that is why meddling by people often creates terrible results.' Dayala smiled almost apologetically.

'Because people disrupt either the chaos or the order more, and that leaves one force relatively stronger, and the Balance is thrown off?' I asked.

'Yes. It is more complex than that, but that is what happens. That is why it is often so hard for people to live in harmony with nature.'

I could see that. Some people would always do too much – too much order, too much chaos – and never understand. 'And druids can?'

'Druids can – but not all those who are born in Naclos become druids, and some who are born elsewhere do.' She grinned at Justen, and the expression made her look more like a young girl.

'What happens to them – the ones who don't understand? Do they get thrown out, as in Recluce?'

'Some leave. Some die.'

'There is a trial,' Justen added. 'No one has to undertake it, but you are effectively . . . excluded . . . from what goes on in Naclos if you don't. Some people leave, rather than face the trial. Others face it and fail to survive.'

I shook my head. How were the druids any better than Recluce?

'You are displeased,' said Dayala.

'Yes.' I was more than displeased. I was angry, though I wasn't quite sure why.

'Are all beings perfect?' she asked softly.

'No. Of course not. Not even the mythical angels.'

*Whheeeee . . . eeee . . .* Gairloch was letting me know he was thirsty.

I patted his neck. 'In a bit . . . in a bit.'

'And if a being would hurt others, or nature, then what should those others do?'

'I don't know.' And I didn't. If I imposed a forced order on someone, and I thought I might be able to, though I'd never tried, then that was violence against that person's will. If I didn't and they stole or hurt others, that was violence against those who had done no wrong. But exiling or killing someone because they *might* do violence didn't seem right. Neither did waiting until after they did. Yet exiling or killing someone to prevent wrongness wasn't right, either.

'Let me explain,' she went on. 'In Naclos, the trial is there to help someone come into understanding with the Balance. You have done this yourself, whether you know it or not. That you have done this is easily seen. Some people die because they cannot accept or understand the Balance. Others fear the trial, and we let them go live in the Empty Lands.'

'You don't send them out of Naclos?'

'No. Some go, but they are not sent. We would prefer they remain in Naclos, for their safety and the safety of others. There is some risk to them, because they must live with others like themselves, but that is either their choice or because they are flawed.' She shrugged, even as she slipped off her mount and began to walk, guiding the horse behind Rosefoot and up beside Gairloch. She walked quickly, yet effortlessly.

I knew what I didn't like about it – an individual didn't seem to matter at all. Only the community counted. Just as in Recluce, you either conformed or left.

'Someone who is different – you just throw them out?'

'No.' She gave a laugh that was half laugh, half snort. 'We have many who are different. My father was quite different. He was a smith, and you can understand that was different for druids. He still lived in the Great Forest. Justen met him.'

'He was a good smith, very good with tools,' mused Justen, as if his mind were kays away.

'So were you.'

Again, I had this feeling that I had missed something, but I plunged on. 'If you accept differences, then why . . . ?'

'Why do we exile or create death? That is only for those who will not accept differences.'

I pondered that for a time. Dayala, barefooted, kept pace with the horses without even breathing hard.

Acceptance? Was that the key? But Recluce did not accept differences. Yet clearly Naclos had accepted Justen, and he certainly wasn't a run-of-the-mill druid.

'Why do you risk your life for the autarch?'

'Because Kyphros accepted me, I suppose.'

She shrugged, as if to suggest something, and waited, but I didn't have any answers. Or all the answers I had were wrong. It was wrong, in my mind, to reject people who were different, but no group of people could accept those who would kill or disrupt a society ... I shook my head.

'Dayala, you've confused the poor man enough.' Justen's voice was affectionate.

'I confused you once, too. But not for long.'

'I'm still confused, woman, and I know it. He's going to have trouble dealing with the idea that there just aren't any answers that don't hurt people, often innocent people.'

I wanted to take my staff and bash Justen. Except ... except ... I had the horrifying feeling that he was right, and maybe that was what had bothered me all along.

Dayala handed the reins of her mount to me, and I took them, dumbly, and watched her stretch her legs and run. She was almost as frisky as a colt – a filly, I guess, really.

'She could run down any horse, you know?' Justen said.

'I didn't know, but I see it now.'

'It took me a long time to really appreciate her.' He shook his head, almost sadly, leaving something unsaid.

I swallowed. Justen wasn't exactly withdrawn. His eyes traveled every cubit of the grasslands to the west of the road, then swung back to take in the trees beside the narrow winding Sturbal. Yet he said little, less than he had said when I had traveled with him earlier.

Behind us, Weldein and Berli talked in low voices.

'... you're playing with fire ...'

'... I know ... but ...'

'Do you think she knows?'

'Probably,' said Weldein. 'How could she not?'

'I don't know, but it sometimes happens.'

So we rode through the day, along the river and toward Lythga, and each kay we covered seemed to bring me closer to the white-red mass of chaos that seemed to lurk beneath and along the Easthorns.

# CII

Four days of travel from Felsa found us nearing the high point on the pass through the Lower Easthorns. Each step eastward seemed to bring us closer to the chaos beneath, although I felt I was really the only one who sensed it. Still, I could feel the *grrrrr . . . rrring* in the deep rocks, sometimes so loudly I thought the ground would shake, but it didn't. Once, when I felt it, I looked at Justen, but his face was blank.

Dayala still walked more than half the time, and I marveled at her endurance.

'Don't you ever get tired?' I finally asked.

'Not often,' said Justen.

'The body is meant to work, and enjoy what it does – we are animals and need exercise.'

They grinned at each other, and, again, they looked young, far younger than I knew they were, and I envied them. Why couldn't Krystal and I understand each other like that?

Gairloch put one foot in front of the other, and so did Rosefoot, and, in time, the road leveled out in a long flat valley filled with a mixture of high green grass, short cedars, and boulders barely concealed by the grass. The road was clay, not quite dry enough to be dusty, and with few tracks indeed on its surface.

In places, the grass had been cropped short, but, as on my first trip, I could see no sign of sheep or goats, even when I could make out the ruined waystation where I had weathered the storm on my first trip into Hydlen.

'There's a spring behind the waystation.'

'I can recall when that roof was fresh-thatched,' said Justen quietly. 'It doesn't seem that long ago.'

'Thatch? It looks like sod.'

'It is,' said Dayala. 'How long ago was it, Justen?'

'Wrong waystation,' he groused. 'I've seen a few, you know. More than a few, in fact.'

Dayala grinned at me, and I had to grin back.

I dismounted and led Gairloch toward the spring. So did Weldein and his half-squad, and one of the younger troopers – Pentryl – led his mount up beside Gairloch.

Gairloch and the other horses drank from the lower, wider pool. I took out my water bottle.

'What are you going to do when we see the enemy, ser?'

'That depends.' I hadn't the faintest idea, really, and looked toward Justen.

He shrugged.

'Are you going to bury them in hot rock the way Berli said you did the last time?'

'That was rather costly.'

'But they're the enemy, ser. They'd kill us as soon as look at us.'

'Some would, and some wouldn't.' I looked at the youngster's face and realized he wasn't all that much younger than I had been when I had left Recluce – older even, maybe. I didn't feel just a little older than he was, though. I felt older, a lot older. Not any wiser, though, just older. I bent down and began to fill the bottle.

'If you don't kill them, then they'll just keep trying.' The youngster was insistent.

'You're right. And if we do kill them, then all their relatives and everyone in Hamor will want to kill us even more.'

'Always the problem with war,' offered Justen. 'That's why so many conquerors just didn't bother to let anyone live.'

'That was why the angels fled.' Dayala began to fill her water bottle as I was capping mine. 'They did not wish to fight a war that would destroy both sides.'

'Did it, Lady Druid?' asked Pentryl.

'That is what the Legend says.'

'One thing we also know,' added Justen as he took his turn filling his bottle. 'If you fight, you eventually lose. If you don't, you lose immediately.'

Pentryl looked from Justen to Dayala to me. 'But . . . ?'

'What the mage means, I think,' I attempted to explain, 'is that war is a necessary evil, to be avoided whenever possible, and to be won as quickly and effectively as possible when it cannot be avoided.'

'Pentryl! Move that beast. There's others of us need to water mounts.'

'Stuff it, Huber,' retorted Pentryl, but he led his mount from the spring.

Feeling guilty, I also led Gairloch away from the water and out under a low pine that offered some shade. Justen followed.

'That wasn't a bad answer, Lerris. I'm not sure I agree, though.'

'Why not?'

'Because he doesn't want you to stop asking questions,' answered Dayala. 'There are no lasting answers.'

'You keep reminding me of that,' said Justen, taking her arm for a moment.

She tilted her head and kissed him, gently, and yet, I could feel the emotion behind that single kiss, and hoped that even in ten years Krystal and I would feel that strongly.

Somewhere, deep in the iron beneath the Easthorns, chaos rumbled, and I swallowed.

After looking away for a time, I finally asked, after making sure the rest of the Finest were still at the spring or out of earshot, 'What are we going to do about the Hamorians?'

'Do you want to know?'

'Probably not, but I should.'

'We'll have to unbalance the Balance, raise order and chaos, and split them, and then let them reunite where the Hamorians are.' Justen snorted. 'That assumes we can touch the Balance, that there's enough chaos energy beneath us, that the Hamorians aren't spread all over the countryside, and that they're stupid enough to try an attack, or not retreat.'

'There's more than enough chaos beneath us, and it's stronger.'

Justen looked at me and shook his head, almost sadly. I wanted to ask why, but did not, and then Weldein rode up.

'We're watered. Shall we go on?'

Justen nodded. As I mounted Gairloch again, I looked over at the waystation where I had first found the cedar length I hadn't really carved because I was still trying to determine the face beneath the grain. Why had I thought about the carving? Was the face Justen's? Or Krystal's Or was it guilt that I hadn't finished it?

I shook my head, not having an answer, and looked beyond the half-ruined sod roof to the patches of snow higher in the low mountains. As Gairloch carried me upward, I glanced back once more at the old waystation, where the ancient door had rotted off the heavy old iron hinges. In the late summer, the part of the sod-grass roof that had not collapsed into the hut was not only green, but still dotted with sprigs of small white and blue flowers.

The sun had almost touched the rocky peaks behind us when Dayala nodded, and Justen held up his hand. I reined up, and so did Weldein, his arm upraised.

Below us, the road swung in a wide circle, and on the far side of the turn was the gorge where the road joined the Fakla River. For at least several kays, if my memory were correct, the road would run on the south side of the stream that would become a full river many kays downhill.

'. . . about time to stop. Don't want to make camp in the dark again . . .'

'. . . stop complaining, Nytri . . .'

'. . . you could be getting bashed by cannon in Ruzor . . .'

Weldein gestured again, and the troopers fell silent. I could see the young faces of Pentryl and Huber straining to see what Justen was doing.

'Lerris, where will that deep chaos be easier to touch? Here or farther downstream? Does it make any difference?' Justen frowned just slightly.

I turned with a start. 'I don't know. Let me try to check.'

All the troopers – even Justen and Dayala – seemed to hold their breath as I sent my senses out and down. How long it took, I didn't know, only that the sun was half behind the mountains when I blinked and answered. 'It's about the same, but it's a little easier to touch a kay or so downhill.'

'That's not far. We'll camp somewhere around here. The Hamorians are about a half-day away, and they've stopped for the night.'

'How . . . ?'

'Dayala – she can touch the trees and the life web better than I.' He looked at Weldein. 'Anywhere around here. I'd suggest very small fires.'

Weldein turned. 'Over there, on the higher flat above the stream.'

He'd picked ground with access to water and overlooking the road, which made sense if we were attacked, but I hoped it wouldn't come to that.

Justen, Dayala, and I shared a small fire, and I used my single pot to heat some water for an herbal tea. One pot made three small cups, and I sipped mine slowly, trying to make it last.

'Good,' admitted Justen.

'Very good,' added Dayala.

'Tomorrow,' began Justen. 'Tomorrow, just try to think about skill, Lerris. Skill is using as little force – order or chaos – as possible to do the job.' His eyes flashed at me. 'Do you understand why the minimal use of order, even in dealing with chaos, is better?'

'Would I have aged less if I'd used less force?'

'Probably. I wasn't there. I couldn't say for sure, but that's usually the case.'

'What are we going to do?' I asked.

Justen sighed. 'Kill a lot of mostly innocent soldiers. For no good reason except that they'll kill even more people if they're not killed.'

'I hate to say this,' I said slowly. 'But if we just let them take Kyphros, wouldn't fewer people die?'

'No,' said Justen bleakly. 'That isn't the point of any of this. It wouldn't make sense. If we stepped aside, Kyphros would fall, and at least the autarch and the Finest and the outliers would mostly be killed, because they defied Hamor. Then, more armies and ships would arrive, and Gallos would fall. Then Spidlar. Then Suthya and Sarronnyn. After that, Recluce, and then Naclos. But I don't think this invasion really is designed to succeed.'

'What?'

'Emperor Stesten can't lose. He's only got perhaps ten thousand troops here and thirty-odd ships. That sounds like a lot, but Hamor has a fleet of close to five hundred steel warships and almost a hundred thousand trained troops, maybe more. That sort of equipment gives some credence to his claim to be Regent of the Gates of the Oceans.'

I was lost. Ten thousand troops still sounded like a lot.

'If this Marshal Dyrsse wins for Emperor Stesten with these forces, then he's in that much stronger a position. If not, the Emperor can use the defeat to demonstrate the need to destroy Recluce – because only wizardry will have stopped Hamor.'

'I don't understand. What has Recluce done to Hamor?'

'Outside of ensuring its traders don't monopolize trade in the Eastern Ocean? Outside of exiling the Emperor's grandfather? Outside of destroying almost a score of warships? Outside of killing two regents and a fleet commander? Outside of humiliating Hamor for over a thousand years?' Justen paused to sip more tea. 'I'm sure I could think of a few more reasons, if you need them.'

'But why does he need a defeat? Isn't that throwing away troops and ships?'

Justen looked at me, and his eyes almost glowed. 'Is it? There's no one on Recluce who can match Gunnar and me, except maybe Elisabet, and we're ancient. That leaves you and Tamra. And we're all here in Candar. How many more battles like that business in the mountains can you take, Lerris?'

I swallowed. 'You mean, this whole thing is to wear us down?'

'I wouldn't say that it's the whole thing, but this has been well thought out. How much of Candar does Hamor control right now?'

'Freetown, Sligo, Montgren, Certis, Hydlen – that's the whole east – and Delapra and half of Southwind, from what I hear.'

'So . . . with less than ten percent of his forces, the Emperor already controls over a third of Candar?'

'I guess so.' I hadn't thought of it quite that way.

'Recluce has lost two of its three invisible ships, and only replaced one. Its trade has been blocked . . .' Justen went on, quietly detailing how bad things were, and I had to believe him. At the same time, I was asking how Recluce had let things get so bad. Was it just because Recluce had turned its back on machines? Or had the nature of the Balance changed? Or had Hamor changed it, and what did that show? I shivered.

'. . . most people don't understand that Recluce has a lot of people who can use order to some degree, but only a relative handful can concentrate it. There might be another ten on Recluce with your skills, but half have probably never discovered their abilities, and the Brotherhood has always been content to leave it that way because it made governing easier. Now, the Council is paying for that ease.'

'Why?' I was still asking why.

'Look at how much change you and Tamra and Krystal have created. Change isn't something that sets well with people, especially people with coins or position. Change is a threat to both, and order-mastery usually leads to change.'

I pondered his words.

'And that's been the appeal of Hamor – or Fairhaven. Everything is predictable. People like that. Hamor doesn't like change, unless it controls the change, and emperors don't liked being thwarted.' He paused. 'Do you see?' he finally asked.

I nodded.

'Good. Because I don't. All this is still stupid on Emperor Stesten's part, but that's what is happening.' He shook his head. 'Brew some more of that tea, will you?'

I got up and walked down to the stream, where I refilled the pot.

A figure stepped out of the shadows – Berli.

'Good evening, Master Lerris.'

'Good evening, Berli.'

'What will happen tomorrow?' she asked.

'A lot of sundevils will die – or we will,' I answered. 'Or both.'

She shivered. 'That's not encouraging.'

'Sorry. I'd rather not do any dying, if that helps.'

'Early?' she asked.

'I'd say not before midday, maybe not until mid-afternoon.'

'That makes for a long day, ser.'

'Yes.' And a long night, I thought to myself as I walked back up
and added the tea to the pot before swinging it over the fire.

The night wasn't that long, because I was tired, and I slept, and
I wasn't arguing with Krystal about being a hero or rehashing what
I should have said, and the deep growling of chaos only woke
me twice.

We had herbal tea and cheese and travel bread for breakfast, and
Dayala shared some dried fruits of a type I'd never had.

Then Justen, Weldein, Dayala, and I walked down the road, and
Justen stopped and studied everything. We walked down almost three
kays, and then back.

Almost every hundred cubits, Justen had me check the closeness
and strength of chaos. I wasn't sure which was more tiring – that or
the walking. When we finally got back to where we had camped, I
just sat down.

Dayala sat beside me. I still couldn't believe that she walked
everywhere barefoot and that it didn't bother her.

'Krystal thinks I should talk to you.'

She smiled, just waited, as I guess I expected a druid to do.

'She thinks I'm getting too tied up in liking to be a hero, but I don't
want to be a hero. At least, I don't think so.'

There was more silence, a lot, before she spoke.

'I do not always understand people, Lerris. That may be because I
see the web of life, and it is honest. People deceive themselves rather
than face pain, and that deception leads to violence. Violence leads to
pain, and pain to more deception and violence.' Then she rose, even
before I could say anything. 'I need to think, and so do you. Your
questions will only have meaning if we are successful.'

As I was pondering what Dayala had said, Justen called to me.
'Lerris? Can you create a small dam down at the point there?' Justen
pointed downstream to where the canyon narrowed.

'Probably. How high?'

'Only so high as you can get it without drawing on chaos – even
channeled through order.'

I frowned. That would make it harder. 'I'll see what I can do.'

That meant shifting order bonds in the rocks around the point. Still,
if I strengthened some, that would change the force of others . . .

Letting my senses roam through the rocks and pathways for a time,
I tried to get a feel of the land. I also found some underground streams
and caves. After thinking about Justen's earlier comments about skill,
I tried little nudges here and there, little shifts. It took longer, but
slowly rocks began to slide into the canyon that was really more of

an overgrown gulch. Then larger rocks followed, and some clay, and more rocks.

Finally, I withdrew my senses from the ground and sat on a stone, sweating.

'Here.' Dayala handed me my water bottle and some travel bread. 'It is almost midday.'

I didn't question how she knew. I just drank and ate.

'You were very gentle,' she said. 'Justen was pleased. The water is rising now, and there will be a small lake before they arrive.'

'There's not enough water to drown them.'

Her face turned bleak. 'We cannot afford to be that kind.' She shuddered.

So did I. Then I ate a large chunk of cheese and took a short walk into the woods.

Justen was waiting when I returned.

'See if you can get an idea of when they will reach the turn in the road down there.'

I sat back down on the boulder again. By extending my senses, I could feel out the Hamorians, from the heavy tread of massed feet echoing through the ground to the hoofs of their scouts leading the way. How many score were there? Several hundredscore, it appeared, as the line of troops seemed to stretch back over two kays on the winding road.

Justen was waiting as I looked up.

'Before mid-afternoon, or a little later, but they're stretched out for nearly two kays on the road.'

'I'd figured that.'

'Are you going to turn that lake into boiling water?'

'Something like that,' he admitted, 'except worse.' He paused. 'Lerris, just let me handle this. Watch – with your senses – but don't try to do anything unless I fail.'

'How will I know?'

'I'll be dead, and even you can figure that out.'

I let the words pass, understanding that their bitterness came from his own fears.

'Wouldn't it be easier if I helped?'

He looked at me with cold eyes. 'We'll both be needed later, and your technique is still too rough. You did all right with the dam, but you had time, and you wouldn't with the sundevils. So watch and learn. This is something you can't practice. You've already figured that out, I trust.'

I had, and I shut my open mouth. I didn't feel better about it, but

I had been the one complaining that he hadn't been around when I'd stuck out my neck. So how could I complain when he told me to stand back, especially when I felt that he was right?

Dayala touched my arm, just touched me, and I felt the warmth of reassurance – and a touch of fear.

'I could help,' I whispered to her.

'Not now. He is right, and how would he explain to Gunnar if anything happened to you? If we need you, you will be rested to help him.'

I looked at her, and her eyes were dark. She straightened and then followed Justen to a spot under one of the pines, where the needles had made a long soft cushion. They lay there, fully dressed, except Dayala was barefoot, holding each other.

*Grrrurrrr* ... Chaos rumbled beneath us, enough that small waves licked across my makeshift lake.

So I watched the road, watched the dust rise and grow ever nearer to where we waited, listened as Weldein checked to make sure his people were hidden, and that all the fires had stayed out.

And the tramp of feet neared, and chaos rumbled beneath us, and even the ground shook slightly, but enough that I saw Berli stumble.

Faint steam began to rise from the water, and dust puffs rose off the road below as the ground shook.

I extended my senses and tried to follow what Justen was doing, as he structured, more than opened, dozens of narrow passages from the mixture of chaos and molten iron beneath toward the stream and my makeshift lake.

The sound of hoofs neared, followed by heavy feet, and behind, the squealing of supply wagons. Even from more than two kays away I could hear the sundevils, making no particular effort to be still.

> ... had a girl and she was mine
> Had a girl and she was fine.
> Took a merchant through design,
> But her bouncing boy is mine ...
> ... three, four ... out the door ...

Just below the pine tree, Justen now stood on a solid wedge of rock far enough back from the lip of the canyon that he could not be seen from the road below. Beside him stood Dayala. With my senses extended, I watched.

*Grrrurrrr* ...

The narrow order passages swelled, and through them came heat, steam, and boiling water – below that were ropes of molten iron, twisting upward. Yet Justen was not close to touching that mix of chaos and order. Instead, it was almost as though he were building structures for those fiery elements to follow, letting them follow the easiest courses – those he had constructed.

Now the ground around us was shaking, and I grabbed a pine limb to steady myself. My hand got sticky from the sap, but I held on, glued by resin and muscle, even as my legs tightened to balance me against the growing tremors rumbling up from beneath us.

*Wheeee ... eeee ... eeee ...* Horses whinnied, but I couldn't tell which horses – those of the sundevils or ours.

The sundevil column slowed, still almost a kay below my makeshift dam, where small waves rolled back and forth and where steam was rising now almost like a fog.

My fingers tightened around the tree limb, but it bent as I rocked with the swaying of the ground, then began to crack. I staggered and sat down hard, partly on the rocky ground and partly on a small scrub cedar that jabbed my leg through my trousers. After scrambling off the offending cedar, I sat on a flat boulder uphill of a low pine that I could peer through at the road below.

Justen and Dayala continued to weave their order webs, and that intertwining conflict between order and chaos that I had sensed and struggled with deep beneath Candar rose closer and closer to us, and to the waters of the lake, where low waves began to form.

As I watched, trying to keep my eyes fixed through the near continuous swaying of the ground and rumbling, I could sense Dayala building a shield on the uphill side of the stream and lake, even as Justen began closing his order tubes. Closing?

*Grrrurrrrrrr ...* The ground rocked more violently.

The Hamorians had bunched up even more, and I could see a sun banner or two, and a few scouts. A heavy haze had appeared, shading the sun so that it shimmered without much heat through a layer of fog above us.

The lake steamed so much that I could not even see the water, just clouds of mist and vapor. I was sweating, and I wiped my forehead.

Just out of sight, the Hamorians continued to bunch up, for a time, until two scouts finally rode around the corner and turned uphill, moving at not much more than a walk.

They seemed to study everything. Then one pointed – right toward me, it seemed, though I was behind a low pine. But his gesture was toward the steaming water. The other pointed down at the steam rising from the stream water.

They rode up the road just to where they could see the lake. Both were wiping their foreheads, and they turned back downhill. I tried to extend my senses to pick up what was happening.

The ground rocked even more violently, and one of the sundevil scouts grabbed his horse's mane. The other mount tried to rear, but only went halfway up and staggered coming down.

*EEEEEeeeeeee!!!!!*

A thin line of steam and heat erupted up through the lake, then another, and a third, and the water began to bubble violently. I could sense an immense bowl of chaos and order beneath the water, so hot that I could almost feel my forehead blistering.

The ground heaved, then rocked, and the mists and fog had grown so much that it seemed like twilight.

*Whhheeee . . . eeee . . .* All the horses were screaming, rearing, lashing out with hoofs.

A tall pine above the road snapped, and began to fall, slowly, toward the boiling lake.

The chaos and heat beneath the lake grew greater, and then . . . Justen squeezed off his order tubes.

The ground beneath the road swelled, and great cracks ran down through the clay, and steam hissed into the air.

Dayala struggled to hold a shield between us and the lake.

With the *CCCCURRROUMMMMPHHHHhhhhh* greater than a falling mountain, steam, boiling mud, red-hot rocks, gouts of molten lava, and boiling water flared upward, some of it toward us and against Dayala's shield, and then all of it gushed downhill.

Trees were ripped out of the hillside. Boulders were thrown down through the canyon almost like massive shells from stone bombards. Loose branches and splintered trunks shredded through vegetation and troopers and animals and wagons.

So fast was the explosion of heat and steam and rocks and molten metal that almost no screams competed with the roiling, rumbling, explosion of destruction.

A wave of whiteness flared away from the destruction, whiteness filled with death.

I sat there on the boulder and squeezed my eyes closed for a time before I staggered upright. When I opened my eyes, they stabbed, and I hadn't even been the one handling order and chaos.

The ground continued to heave even after I looked at the huge hole where there had been a lake, even as molten rock continued to ooze forward. Steam rose from that hole as the stream dropped into the pit from above.

I stepped back to keep the heat from blistering my face, and tried to sense the destruction downhill. For more than two kays, there was no road, just a boiling mess of mud, rock, and vegetation. Beyond that the stream boiled, what little of it was left, and the waters would steam for a long time. Higher on the hills, leaves were boiled off limbs, and bark off trees, leaving them like bleached bones rising from mud and sodden vegetation.

The second major road to Kyphros was blocked, although, certainly in the Lower Easthorns, an alternative route was possible. What wasn't possible was the immediate re-creation of the Hamorian army.

So far as I could tell, no one had walked or run away from Justen's and Dayala's wave of destruction. And so far as I could tell, neither had even come that close to touching chaos.

I swallowed and walked toward them.

Justen looked haggard, and he swayed where he stood. Dayala, standing beside him, also swayed.

The whiteness from the mass of sliding clay and steaming water had shivered through me like a hammer on steel, and my head still rang like an anvil, and knives stabbed through my eyes, but I walked up to them. Neither really acknowledged my presence, and I turned and headed toward where I had tied Gairloch, hoping that he was still there.

Weldein looked at me and swallowed as I passed.

I only counted seven mounts, and there should have been nine, but Gairloch and Rosefoot were still there, and I patted Gairloch for a moment. 'Good fellow ...' Then I grabbed the water bottle and the provisions bag from behind the saddle and started back across the steaming hillside.

Weldein looked at me. 'Hersik and Nytri are gone.' His face was red, almost blistered.

'If they went downhill they're dead. Otherwise, they're probably all right.' I kept walking, and he walked with me for a time.

As we passed, Berli looked at Huber. 'See why you don't want to get one of them really mad at you?'

Huber gulped. Behind her, Pentryl stared at the boiling and steaming mass that seethed and oozed down the canyon that had held the stream.

I stepped up to Justen. 'Sit down and have a drink.'

'What is it?' He slumped onto the pine needles. So did Dayala.

'Just water.'

'Better than nothing,' he rasped. Deep wrinkles gouged his face, and his neck was old and wattled.

After he drank, I offered him some of the white cheese from my saddlebags in return for the water bottle.

'Better.'

He didn't look that much better. His hair stayed silver, almost all silver, even if some of the wrinkles faded from his face.

Dayala didn't look that much better, once I looked at her, and handed her the water and some cheese. She was wrinkled also, and while her hair remained silver, it seemed duller, as though some of the life had gone out of it, which it had, I supposed.

I walked uphill to Rosefoot and pawed through Justen's saddlebags and found some of the dried fruit. When I got back, I practically thrust it at her.

Then I could have kicked myself. I touched her arm and offered a touch of order. She didn't protest, and a little fire appeared in those green eyes.

I did the same for Justen. Then I sat down next to them.

For a long time, none of us spoke.

'See what I meant about technique?' asked Justen. The wattles on his face and neck had disappeared, but his face was still wrinkled and his hair silver.

'You never even got close to the chaos.'

'There's always a link. You try to keep it as far away as possible, but it's there.'

*Ggrrrurrrr* . . .

The ground shook again.

'We probably need to go. This place isn't stable, not now, not for a long time,' he muttered as he slowly stood.

I offered him a hand, and he took it.

'Chaos will be here for many years,' affirmed Dayala. She too remained wrinkled, although some of the luster had returned to her hair.

We walked back to the horses, and mounted. Even Dayala rode as we threaded our way uphill, avoiding the crevasses in the road, and the occasional jets of steam.

Pentryl kept looking backward. Huber just looked at the road. The two I didn't know rode slowly, while Weldein and Berli brought up the rear.

Weldein kept looking, I thought, for the two missing troopers, but I didn't see any new hoof prints in the road.

Justen and Dayala rode side by side, almost close enough to touch, lost in their own private world.

I looked at them, suddenly old, and felt very young, but I swallowed and kept riding.

# CIII

A light haze blurred the hills behind Ruzor, but the sky above the harbor remained a clear blue-green. Only a slight chop marred the harbor waters, and the faintest of whitecaps tipped the waves beyond the breakwater.

Gunnar and Tamra stood on the northeast corner tower of the old fort that had once been thought adequate to protect Ruzor. Thirty cubits below them, the waters lapped gently at the base of the tower.

Behind them stood only a handful of troopers. Krystal had marshaled the rest from the fort to the bluff just north of the river, from where they could be dispatched as necessary. While Gunnar could have directed his storms from the bluff, the fort offered better vantage. Should the Hamorian fleet discern from where Gunnar and Tamra directed the storms, there would be less chance of jeopardizing the troops on the bluff, mustered behind solid earthworks concealed with turf. The troops of Kyphros were few enough, indeed.

Neither mage spoke, their senses extended to the south, riding the winds and the air currents, trying to discern the numbers of steel-hulled warships that steamed toward Ruzor.

'They're still a good five kays out,' said Tamra, and her eyes unglazed. 'They haven't turned toward the harbor. How far can those guns reach?'

'Five kays, maybe farther.'

'Oh . . .'

Gunnar's eyes glazed over again. Tamra waited, then shrugged, and her eyes blanked as well, her senses following Gunnar.

After a time, Gunnar touched her shoulder. 'It looks as if they're turning toward the harbor.'

'How soon before they begin to attack?'

'When they can be sure the shells will hit something.' Gunnar displayed a crooked grin. 'It's time.'

'For what?'

'To raise the great winds, so to speak.' Gunnar squared his shoulders.

'How is that different from the regular winds?' Tamra asked, trying to catch Gunnar's eye.

'Just try to follow me. I can't explain it in words. I never really could. Not to Lerris or to Martan.'

Tamra's face wrinkled, but she nodded.

'We need to get the storm raised before the ships come too close. Don't want those cannon firing too much.' Gunnar ran a hand through his mostly blond hair, though the light wind disarranged it before his fingers left his scalp.

'Can you use a storm against them before they get close enough to use their guns?' asked Tamra.

'No. The storm would not be violent enough to do what is needful. The bay provides the confinement. Just watch and use your senses. You will have to do this one day soon.'

The air wizard leaned forward so that his crossed arms rested on the ancient stones of the parapet and sent his thoughts seaward and skyward.

Tamra settled herself against the parapet, then tried to force her thoughts after those of the older mage. Even the lower winds seemed to buffet her thoughts, to force her down toward the growing whitecaps.

She struggled to follow Gunnar toward the chill far above the harbor, far above the warm air of Kyphros. The cold of the skies shivered through her like a blade of ice, and her body swallowed twice, once as she first sensed the iron-cold power of the winds and again as she felt Gunnar's senses slip around the forces of those winds.

Her thoughts crumpled as she tried to grasp that chill power, her mind numb, as numb as an arm smashed by a staff. Again, she forced herself upward, slowly easing her powers into that frigid torrent of air.

Under Gunnar's power, the winds dipped, then bucked skyward, then dipped farther toward the ocean that seemed so far below. Tamra brought her own winds down, down with those of Gunnar.

The first cooler gusts of winds rippled across the inner harbor, lifting the chop into the slightest of whitecaps. The chop became full-cubit waves, then two-cubit waves that fell against the breakwater. The salt mist rose around the silent figures on the tower, but neither moved. Neither spoke, and the wind rose, and rose.

Beyond the breakwater, the force of the winds whipped the low whitecaps into waves nearly four cubits high. The spray fled across the breakwater toward the harbor, and the waiting troops.

The first Hamorian cruiser steamed through the heavier waves of the outer bay toward the breakwater still several kays ahead. A gun barrel lifted, and a puff of smoke followed. A second cruiser followed the example, and then a third.

*Crumpt!* The first splash landed a half kay short of the fort that stood at the shore end of the breakwater. So did the second, as did the third, and the winds pushed the spray almost to where the mages waited.

With a grim smile, Gunnar touched the winds again and whipped them out of the south toward the Hamorian ships. In the shallower waters of the outer bay, the first half dozen or so vessels nearing the breakwater pitched more and more from the six-cubit-high following waves. Their guns puffed smoke again.

The shells raised three columns of water just short of the harbor fort's gray stone walls. More spray drifted across the fort, mixing with the whitecaps of the waves in the harbor.

'... shit ...' murmured a Kyphran soldier behind Gunnar, but neither mage acknowledged the exclamation, not as they wrestled with the winds.

*Crumpt! Crumpt!*

One shell from the third volley struck the stones ten cubits above the water, and stone dust and stones cascaded down into the gray water, where the waves foamed around them.

A low moaning rose, and the skies slowly darkened, and clouds, scudding out of the south, began to cover the sun.

More stone fragments broke from the center wall of the fort, even as the sky darkened more.

Another shell sprayed water against the already gaping hole in the center wall of the old fort.

The moaning of the wind became a howl, and the waves in the harbor rose man-tall, half-white, and fell on the shore and piers with the force of hammers.

In the outer bay, sledges of water, capped with white, smashed on the anvil of the Hamorian ships, but the ships steamed northward, north toward Ruzor, and their guns loosed their own hammers.

Under the impact of the shells, the southeast tower swayed in the wind, then split. Stones, dust, and masonry arched into the spray and into the waves that broke against the gray rock slabs of the tower footings.

*Crumpt! Crumpt!* Shells fell across the entire shoreline of the bay. A gout of turf and soil erupted from the bluff, and dark dots that had been soldiers scattered and flew into the surf below, their screams lost in the howl of the wind and the thunder of the cannon. The river pushed dark brown water down toward its mouth, toward the whitecapped surf.

'It's not enough!' yelled Gunnar, his face set against the wind coming in from the south. He wiped the spray from his face.

Tamra glanced from the tall mage to the outer bay, where the darkhulled ships swarmed and fought their way through the waves toward Ruzor. The guns continued to fire, and the shells continued to fall.

The end of the long pier exploded in a hail of timbers, and the waves ripped through the sagging framework. The shipyard beyond the pier crumbled into rubble and splintered timbers.

Gunnar's eyes half glazed, indifferent to the winds that tore around him, as his senses reached even above the high winds, to the great winds, the winds that buffeted the Roof of the World, the winds that determined the rains and the droughts, even life and death, the winds that none had summoned since Creslin wrought the Great Change.

Like rivers of ice, those torrents that ruled the upper heavens, the great winds, radiated chill that slowed perceptions, slowed senses, and numbed thought. Gunnar plunged his senses into the chill torrents.

After a moment, Tamra followed, shuddering, but sending her perceptions after Gunnar, though she but observed his efforts.

As the Hamorian shells dropped across the inner bay, Gunnar tugged, then wrenched at the great winds, only to be struck back. His body shuddered, driven back from the parapet. He lunged forward, wrapped his arms around the stone, and waited for the reaction to subside.

Another handful of Hamorian ships opened fire, and more shells fell across the harbor, across the waterfront, and shattered timbers from the lumber racks of Aflac the lumber trader speared into the harborside streets like massive javelins. An orange flame flickered from where the waterfront cafe had been and began to grow, despite the rain that the winds had also brought.

*Crumpt! Crumpt!*

Gunnar again sent his senses into the high winds, and Tamra winced at the shivering power that Gunnar struggled with and against. As she reached out – the older mage slapped her hand and senses back.

'No!'

*Crumpt!*

More stones fell, and the southeast tower crashed down across the breakwater, leaving nothing except a few water-swept rocks, and a swirling of waves and foam across the stones that filled the bottom of the harbor.

The sky darkened as Gunnar bent the cold winds from the Roof of
the World down, down, downward across the outer bay. Beyond the
breakwater, twin towers of darkness loomed in the skies, both squat,
both elemental, and both swirled toward the line of steel ships.

Gunnar kept his awareness focused on the dozen ships just off the
breakwater, even as he flung wind and sea against them, as he tried to
sweep the steel hulls shoreward, toward the stone breakwater suddenly
surfpounded, toward stones that had become as hard as black iron to
the onrushing cruisers.

The guns turned toward the city, and the bluff, but fewer shells
fell, and many struck only waves and foam.

Tamra reached for the Hamorian warships, almost recoiling from
the dead steel order within the dark hulls, and from the chaos bottled
inside the steel shells stored within each vessel, but cast the high winds,
not so mighty as the great winds, but strong enough to add to the force
applied by Gunnar.

*Crumpt!*

The shrieking of metal melded with the shrieking of the winds as
steel hulls scraped onto hard stone, but from the outer bay, other
guns picked up the rhythm, and their shells arched into the harbor
and fell across the waterfront, hitting the old dry-goods warehouse,
and igniting another tower of flame, then the produce factor's sheds.

Gunnar swallowed and seized his winds more firmly, dragging their
chill power to the ocean's surface beyond the breakwater, where the
waves crested over the bridges of the ships, again and again.

But the shells continued to lash the lower city, and plumes of dust
rose against the rain, against the spray from the harbor.

*Crumpt! Crumpt!*

Gunnar slammed the high winds through the second echelon of
ships, but the guns, fewer now, continued to target the city.

*Crumpt!*

Another section of the bluff collapsed, and more soil slid into the
Phroan River. On the smaller bluff across the river, the redstone pillars
of the mansion just recently completed by the wool factor Kilert bowed
out and collapsed, and the red roof tiles cascaded over the rubble.

The bay raged white, and Tamra held tight to an ancient brace as
water, impossibly, cascaded over her, yet flowed around Gunnar. The
old mage clasped the winds to himself, and to the bay. Behind them,
the three soldiers had no chance to scream as they were swept into
the mass of foam and raging water.

*Crumpt! Crumpt!*

At the end of the short pier, the harbor-master's square structure and short flagpole vanished in an eruption of dust and smoke, and a haze of white agony and dying souls screamed behind the wind.

With a wrench, Gunnar seized the closest storm, twisted it until it swirled along the line of steel cruisers that had arched shells shoreward. Lightning flashed down from that darkness and sparked on steel, and more unheard screams and a white haze of death bathed the bay.

Tamra hung onto the brace as another huge wave pounded the tower, and swallowed as she watched a line of waves smash through the harbor piers, flattening them and the buildings behind them. Then she regained her grip on the high winds and forced them against the Hamorian cruiser nearest the inner breakwater, pressing it toward the hard stones.

Another set of lightnings flashed and flashed from the elemental storms, stalking the steel hulls out in the bay, but the guns, fewer still, fired yet.

The cobbler's thin shop swayed, then collapsed into rubble, and the surging sea swept away snapped roof timbers while the shattered roof tiles sank into the sand and mud cast inshore.

Sand and water geysered through the surf, and a blue-clad soldier's body bobbed between two barrels. Another body clad in the tan of Hamor joined the first in an unrhythmic dance.

Another volley of shells dropped amid the rubble beyond the shattered long pier.

Gunnar gripped the stone more tightly as waves poured over the tower. His jaw tightened, and another round of lightning flashed through the scattered ships just beyond the breakwater. One exploded in a roar of flame, louder than a handful of cannon shots, followed by a second.

The impossibly high waves smashed over the remnants of the Hamorian fleet, pounding them like plate upon the angels' anvil. Another cruiser split into two halves – both halves dropping beneath the waves.

The sky lightened slightly, but no more shells dropped, and the harbor waters darkened with the slit from the collapsed bluff.

Tamra watched as the handful of Hamorian ships struggled through the dying waves that still dwarfed them toward the open sea, as the dark clouds began to lift from the outer bay.

'Oohhh . . .'

The white-haired man slumped forward and started to slip onto the stones and ankle-deep water behind the crenelations of the harbor keep, behind the parapets of the sole remaining tower.

'No . . .' The redhead's mouth dropped open as she bent and saw the whiteness and the wrinkles that enfolded his face.

The winds lashed the rains against the stone so hard that the impact of the raindrops sounded like hail, so hard that each droplet raised a welt on the faces of the Kyphran troops.

The outer breakwater held a dozen broken steel hulls. Jammed into the sandbars by the river mouth were also a pair of hulls – cracked and beached.

The surf tossed dark splotches – corpses – up upon the southern sands of the bay, tossed them up and sucked them back, tossed and retrieved, tossed and retrieved.

Beneath the whitecapped waters of the outer bay were dark hulks, dark hulks of dead order containing steel-cased chaos.

Tamra and the sole remaining trooper struggled to lift Gunnar, to carry him to a healer, through the knee-deep swirls that washed over the inner breakwater, through the remnants of the storm.

Farther out upon the Southern Ocean, six ships fought the waves, fought the foam, and slowly struggled eastward.

# CIV

I didn't know what I expected, but the blue and white flowers waving in the sod roof of the waystation were still there, although they seemed mostly gray in the late twilight. The spring was unchanged, and the waystation itself looked no different with the holes in the roof and its doorless entry.

Yet, solid as the old walls were, the waystation seemed fragile.

I looked around the long valley, from the western rim, where orange from the vanished sun still glimmered, to the winding road we had traveled both east and west. Beyond the darkened eastern horizon, I could sense clouds and chaos.

Slowly, I dismounted. Gairloch didn't even whinny, and I hugged him for a moment, just for being there and being dependable.

'He likes you, too,' said Dayala from the dimness beside me.

I probably blushed, but answered, 'He's good and strong and dependable.'

'You often put his care before your own,' she continued.

'He's in my care. He doesn't have a choice.'

'But he does. He could throw you, or bolt, or refuse to eat.'

I hadn't thought horses, or ponies, considered such choices, but Dayala was a druid. 'Oh?'

'He wouldn't think that. Ponies don't think the way we do. He would just do it,' she clarified.

That made sense. I began to unsaddle him, not quickly, because I was tired.

Dayala looked at me in the gloom, probably far more tired than I was. 'Krystal's not a pony.'

'What?' I wasn't thinking too clearly. What did Krystal have to do with being a pony?

'You can't protect her from everything. If you protect her too much, then you protect her from being close to you.' She nodded and led her mount over to where Justen was grooming Rosefoot.

I groomed Gairloch mechanically, trying to understand what Dayala had said, but the words kept slipping through my mind, except I knew Krystal wasn't a pony.

# CV

## Worrak, Hydlen [Candar]

'Marshal,' says the white-haired officer, 'no fleet could have withstood that kind of storm.' The fleet commander glances around the veranda, then out toward the hills to the west. He does not look at the half-dozen battered ships in the harbor below.

'There are limits to their powers, Commander Gurtel. According to my sources, that storm was raised by the only truly powerful storm wizard Recluce has. That single small storm aged him decades.' Dyrsse smiles, though not with his eyes, and his fingers steeple for a moment before he rests his arms on the table. 'Ruzor will take years to rebuild. The storm caused as much damage to the city as to the fleets.'

'But not to the autarch's troops, ser.'

'The autarch isn't the real enemy. She never has been. The enemy is the black isle.' Dyrsse takes another sip of the wine. 'I was commanded by the Emperor Stesten himself to bring an end to the black city, beginning by destroying the black meddlers' power in Candar.'

'That may be, ser. But what about the army, ser? Not a trace of it remains. Not a trace. Three thousand troops and a good force leader lost in the Lower Easthorns, and they're all gone. So are the thousands that were on the ships. What can you say about that?' Gurtel's voice rises slightly, but only slightly. His fingers stray toward the goblet he has not touched, but stop short of the crystal stem.

'The same is true there. It took the only other strong wizards from Recluce. One was young, and he is now middle-aged. The other, like the storm wizard, has also aged decades.' Dyrsse lifts his goblet and sips again. 'Not a bad wine, though not so good as the Delapran.'

'You weren't in that storm, ser.' Gurtel looks at the wine, and his nose twitches, and he shudders ever so slightly.

'No, I wasn't. But that storm was within one bay, not in the open sea, and even so, that wizard almost destroyed himself in sinking perhaps fifteen vessels.'

'A score and a half is more like it, unless some come limping back.'

'The grand fleet has thirtyscore warships, and will put an end to this foolishness.' Dyrsse's voice remains calm, almost flat.

'There's a whole isle of wizards, ser.'

'No. Recluce has never had more than a handful of real wizards, and now they have less than that. Had they as many wizards as you say, then they would not have required their concealed warships – which we sank, you may recall.'

'We sank one, ser. Maybe two, but we couldn't find any traces of the second.'

'They only had three, and that leaves them with one ship. No matter how mighty, one invisible ship and five exhausted wizards will not stop the Empire.' Dyrsse takes another sip of wine. 'They have not even felt the real might of the Empire. The mighty Stesten has given us a charge, and our duty is to fulfill it.'

Gurtel exhales slowly, and his eyes again look to the west.

'Now is the time to destroy these vipers. This is the weakest that Recluce has ever been.'

Gurtel shudders.

'It is true, and now we have the opportunity to rid the world of this scourge, and we will. It is the Emperor's command.' Dyrsse smiles once more. 'We leave for Dellash in the morning. That is where the grand fleet will marshal.'

'Yes, ser.'

# CVI

## Nylan, Recluce

'His Mightiness Stesten, Emperor of Hamor and Regent of the Gates of the Ocean, was not pleased with the destruction of more than thirty of his ships.' Heldra fingers the edge of the map on the ancient black oak table. 'Nor the total loss of more than six thousand troops.'

'That's one way of putting it.' Maris coughs. 'He was so pleased that he's assembling a mere four hundred steel-hulled warships and over fifteen thousand troops. That doesn't count the cannon.'

'That's all an excuse,' snorts Maris. 'Those ships were ready to sail long before he found out.'

'How will he feed them?' asks Maris.

'Always the trader,' sighs Heldra.

'It's important,' counters Maris.

'Sammel took care of that,' answers Talryn. 'He told them about order-preservation, how to use chaos-steam to preserve food.'

'That traitor . . .' says Heldra.

'So . . . it's not as though he gave them a way to create wizards, thank darkness,' counters Maris. 'It's a good thing they don't have many wizards.'

'How could they?' asks Heldra. 'None of the ancients ever went to Hamor.'

'The food-preservation thing is bad enough. That's how they can get all those troops on their ships, just because Sammel told them how to do it with boiling water and metal or glass containers. He gave the method to Colaris . . .' Talryn rolls up the map and crosses the room to the cabinet, which he opens. He slides the map into its slot and closes the cabinet.

'And Colaris gave it to Hamor in return for troops and weapons, especially those cannon?'

Talryn nods slowly.

'You know, Justen already proved that too much order results in chaos.' Maris looks nervously at the depressions in the smooth stones of the floor.

'What do you mean?' asks Heldra.

'Maybe ... maybe the Council put too much order into Candar ... with Lerris, and Tamra, and Sammel ...'

'I notice you're not saying "we," Maris.'

'I wasn't a member of the Council then. Hundril represented the traders then.'

'Well, he's dead of old age, and you're the traders' representative now. What should we do?'

Maris looks back at the floor.

'Complaining won't solve our problems.'

'Do we want a solution?'

'Stop asking questions and provide some constructive thoughts,' snaps Heldra.

'My point,' returns Maris, his voice edged, 'is that solutions are sometimes worse than the problem. We forget this because big problems don't happen often. Nearly two centuries ago, Justen solved the problem of Fairhaven, all right. And back at the beginning, Creslin solved the problem of Recluce. We all know how the great Dorrin solved the problem of how to make Recluce independent and powerful. But because those were a long time ago, we forget that solutions have high prices.'

'You'd rather that we'd didn't exist?' muses Talryn. 'If any of those "solutions" had failed ... we wouldn't be here.'

'We wouldn't, but the solutions were hard on the people of those times. Justen destroyed half of Nylan and over two thousand people there alone to bring down Frven, and the rest of the deaths were never totaled. The deaths caused by Creslin's meddling with the weather have never been summed, and Dorrin changed everything – we're still paying for his discoveries. That Hamorian fleet wouldn't be possible without his discoveries.'

'That doesn't exactly help, Maris. Probably all of Nylan would have died if Justen hadn't stopped Fairhaven.'

'Fine.' Maris smiles. 'Make sure Gunnar and Lerris and Justen and Tamra and Krystal know about the Hamorian fleet.'

'How will that help?'

'I don't know, exactly.' Maris shrugs. 'But I'd bet they won't stand aside and let Recluce fall. I also bet there will be times you'll wish they had.'

'Stop being so damned cryptic! Why?'

'I don't know. But if you put Lerris's youth and audacity together with Justen's and Gunnar's knowledge, and the judgments of those two women, I wouldn't want to be in the Hamorians' boots. But, then, I wouldn't want to be in ours, either.'

Heldra and Talryn exchange glances.

'Do we have any choice?'

'Probably not. Not this late.'

'How do we let them know?'

'Write Gunnar in Ruzor, and send it by the last of the trio. That will convey some urgency. And charter a ship to get them back here.'

Heldra and Talryn exchange glances.

'Unless you want them on the *Dylyss*.' Maris raises his eyebrows. 'If you have any better ideas . . .'

Heldra looks up. 'There's more than one use for the black squads.'

'Don't be a fool, Heldra,' says Talryn slowly. 'If you try to double-cross them, there won't be enough of you to feed to the minnows. And if they don't do it to you, I will.'

'Strong words . . .' But Heldra looks down as Talryn's eyes catch hers.

Maris swallows, then says, 'Should I write the letter?'

Talryn nods, not taking his eyes off Heldra.

# CVII

When we rode around the last corner of the High Desert mountain road, and Ruzor spread out below us, no one spoke.

The harbor fort lay in ruins – a rocky heap on the north end of the breakwater with but a single tower standing out of the rocks. Only the single stone pier remained standing, and even from where we rode, the sounds of saws and axes tearing apart the wreckage of buildings and piers cast down or into other buildings echoed out to us. Dozens of homes appeared destroyed, just piles of rubble, and nothing within two hundred cubits of the water appeared to be intact.

A chunk had been gouged out of the bluff to the south of the Phroan River, and even several gaps leered from the wall of the autarch's residence.

The autarch's flag continued to fly, and with a bit more concentration, I could see at least several wrecked hulls apparently smashed across the breakwater, and others driven into the sands on the far south end of the bay. They must have been huge ships to be visible from so far, and yet they were strewn across the shores and breakwater as though they had been toys.

'I see Gunnar got over his reticence in employing force,' commented Justen wryly.

I just looked, seeing for the first time the enormous damage wrought by the Hamorian guns, and, in return, by the storm or whatever that my father had called. I had to shiver, although the road was hot, and I was sweating, thinking about the power he had wielded. In some ways, because of all his logic and reliance on words, I had considered him the last man to resort to force.

In a strange way, I supposed, that made sense. How could he resort to force, knowing what he could do? How could Justen use force if he thought any alternative were possible?

'You look thoughtful,' offered Weldein, riding up beside me.

'I am.' I gestured toward the ruined city that had been Ruzor. 'Look at that.' After a moment I added, 'I hope everyone is all right.' Then I had to laugh. How could everyone be all right with such destruction?

He was silent for several moments, then asked, 'Do you think that such destruction shows what happens when machines and magic clash?'

I hadn't even thought of it in quite that way, but as the conflict of different peoples who were all too alike in wanting things their own ways. 'I think magic and machines are only the tools people use to express their will. It is the willingness to use such tools that bothers me.'

'Both can be horrible tools,' he answered.

'Yes.' Horrible tools, indeed, but I didn't see many alternatives when someone was out to enslave or kill you and those you loved. What seemed so futile was that it seemed to go on and on. If we were successful, then that would just make Hamor madder and more determined, and as the tools got better, the destruction would get worse. We were already seeing that. But how did we stop it, short of destroying Hamor?

For all the ruin, there were smiles on the faces of the Kyphrans in the streets, as they lifted stones hurled hundreds of cubits. Smiles on many faces, at least.

I did not smile. There were some houses where black and white bows graced the doors, and where the feel of tears persisted. And there were those houses that just were no more, only piles of stone and masonry that had crushed all beneath their crumpled walls.

We rode down the winding streets from the upper gates and finally reached the barracks, detouring around a pile of rubble just outside the barracks walls.

My father was waiting in the barracks courtyard. So were Krystal and Tamra, and so was the autarch.

I looked at Krystal, and she looked back at me, with a brief and faint smile that vanished too quickly. I took a deep breath and waited, patting Gairloch on the neck.

Kasee looked at Justen, and then at me. Justen glanced to me.

'There is no Hamorian army. Nothing remains.'

'Those who would have brought destruction to us have suffered it themselves,' said the autarch slowly, her eyes resting for a time upon Justen and then Dayala.

'As it should and must be,' added the druid.

'I could feel it,' said my father. He looked older, his face wrinkled, his hair mostly silver, just like Justen and Dayala.

'And your losses, Lerris?' asked Kasee.

Tamra just nodded, and her eyes flicked to Weldein and then to me.

'We lost two. They got separated in the chaos, and I think they ran the wrong way. We couldn't find any trace of them or their tracks.'

'They were swallowed by chaos.' Dayala shivered.

'Once again, you, and we, have paid a heavy price.' The autarch's voice was almost flat. 'We thank you.'

I wiped my forehead with the back of my hand and slowly dismounted. My legs were sore. The Finest might be used to riding days on end, but I wasn't, and my body was older, unfortunately. I smelled, and I wanted to wash up and get into clean clothes.

I still had to unsaddle and groom Gairloch. Justen, Gunnar, Krystal, and Kasee gathered together, but no one asked me to join them. So I walked him into the stables and curried him and watered and fed him. Then I patted him on the neck. 'Thanks again, fellow.' Sometimes, I felt he was the only creature who really cared. Probably stupid, but that was what I felt.

When I went back to the courtyard, Krystal was waiting. The autarch and Tamra had disappeared, and my father, Justen, and Dayala slowly walked from the courtyard and into the shade, and, if they did not quite shuffle, neither was there spring in their steps, nor joy in their bearing – not exactly a joyous victory celebration.

Krystal followed me as I carried my gear to the washroom.

'How did things go here . . . for you?' I asked as I stripped off my filthy shirt and began to wash off layers of road grime and sweat.

'Not too badly. Your father insisted that we abandon the harbor fort, except for him and Tamra and a few troopers. He was right. The guns pounded most of it to rubble. They almost drowned, I think, when they left, and she had to drag him clear because he was so tired.'

'It looks as though he raised quite a storm.'

'No one who lived here has ever seen anything like it. We can salvage all that metal and some of the equipment from the hulls. It will take a while, though.' She laughed a short laugh. 'A Spidlarian metal merchant already showed up with a bid on one of the wrecked ships. Bodies are still washing up on the beaches.'

I kept washing. 'What about the Finest?'

'We lost maybe twoscore, but when they started shelling the bluff, we lost nearly a thousand outliers.'

I winced, thinking of even more Pendrils and Shervans.

'Then the waves came, and the storm, and the rain, and probably scores more will die of the flux. If we're lucky.'

I dumped my shirt into the tub and quickly scrubbed it. The water turned black, and I had to rinse it with water from the pump spout.

'How does the autarch feel?'

'She's tired. We're all tired, and she's worried. More than that, I don't know. About some things, she doesn't say.'

We walked up to her room, silently. I just wore my trousers because the shirt was wet from my impromptu laundry efforts.

Herreld held the door for us, and Krystal closed it while I stretched the shirt across the stones outside the window. Then I found my last clean shirt and struggled into it before beginning to dig things out of my pack.

'How about you?' she finally asked. 'What did you do?'

'I did some scouting, told Justen where the chaos was, and watched.'

'You did let Justen handle it?'

'I did as he suggested, watching and helping a little, but he and Dayala did it all. And it was hard for them.'

Krystal waited.

'Two of the troopers ran off in the mess, and I tried to find them, but we couldn't.'

'That's what Dayala said.'

'Sorry. I'm tired, and I'm not thinking that well.' I looked toward the window and the hot sunlight. 'What else happened here?'

'You've seen it. Their guns killed close to a thousand troops, mostly levies as it happened. Probably twice as many townspeople died. The whole waterfront except for the old stone pier is gone. We don't know how many homes and other buildings were destroyed, but I'd guess several hundred. A few Hamorian sailors managed to get ashore. By the time we could get to the shore, we couldn't save them.'

'The storm?'

'No. The townspeople.'

'Oh.' More hatred, more killing, yet, in a way, who could blame them?

Krystal sat down in the chair at the end of the table. There were deep circles under her eyes.

'You're tired.'

'Yes, Lerris, I am tired. It goes on and on. Every time we survive, we have to fight a bigger battle, and more people die. We won, I think. But the city is a mess; thousands were hurt or died; and . . . for what?'

I understood, and I wanted to say so, but it was worse than that. 'It's not over,' I finally said.

'It's not? You have to find another cause to be a hero?'

I shook my head. 'Look at Justen and my father and Dayala. Do they look like they're filled with joy, like everything's all over? Do you remember what Justen said about Hamor really being after Recluce?'

'So you will get to be a grand hero after all?' Krystal stood and walked toward the window.

'Will you stop it? That isn't what I meant at all. You said that it didn't seem like it ever would end. I feel the same way, and I don't know what to do.'

'That's just it. What *you* have to do! You, you, you! You and your father, Tamra and Justen! Why couldn't you all have left Candar alone?'

'You're from Recluce, too.'

'I don't feel like it. I pick up a blade, and it seems so useless. You destroy armies, and your father destroys fleets. My troops die and die and die, and nothing I do changes anything.'

'You held Kyphros together before I ever showed up. You also routed the Hydenlese when I was lying on a baggage cart.'

'And lately?'

I looked at her, trying to penetrate the darkness in her eyes. 'As you keep telling me, just how many times can I do these great deeds? What you do is not limited that way.'

'I don't know that I believe that.'

I sighed.

'I don't understand you,' she finally said. 'You can craft beautiful things, and worry about chickens and people who have nowhere to live. And then you can go out and help destroy thousands of people. And all you can say is it's going to get worse.'

'You've used a blade.'

'And I've killed people. I admit it. But I didn't slaughter them as though they were sheep, by the hundreds and thousands. They were still people.'

'They're still people to me. It hurts when people die. It hurts when I ride past piles of stones that used to be houses.'

'It doesn't seem to stop you.'

'Corpses haven't stopped you, either,' I snapped.

She looked at me with cold eyes and turned. 'I need to meet with Subrella and Kasee.' Then she was gone.

I walked to the window and stared out at the blue waters of the bay, at the already rusting hulks strewn there. I didn't understand. Why was Krystal ready to take off my head? Dead was dead. Why did it matter how someone died?

More important, what could I do about it?

# CVIII

I didn't seem to be able to do anything about it. Every conversation we had turned into an argument, until I was afraid to open my mouth around Krystal. I saw less and less of her, except at night, and there was a wall down the middle of the bed. I felt as if I'd been hit with an iron-tipped staff from behind.

I decided to talk to Tamra one morning after we sparred. She didn't seem any angrier at me than before, and she didn't try any harder to maim or dismember me.

As I wiped my face, Weldein stepped up. 'You've gotten better, ser.'

'Me?'

'Yes, you,' said Tamra. 'You were using your anger. I really had to work. With a little more effort, you could be dangerous.'

'I wouldn't want to be anywhere near him,' said Weldein with a laugh.

'I need to talk to you,' I told Tamra.

'All right.' She looked at Weldein, and he smiled, and faded off to the other side of the courtyard. 'What is it?'

'Krystal.'

'That's obvious. It's colder than the Roof of the World around you two.'

'Every time we talk it gets worse.'

'The problem's simple enough.' Tamra shrugged. 'I haven't any idea how to solve it, though.'

'It doesn't seem simple to me.'

We walked to a shaded corner of the yard. Behind us, Weldein and Yelena started working with wands, and the dull sound of heavy wood echoed off the walls.

'It is, though. You fell in love after Krystal grew up but before you really did.'

'Huh?'

'Oh, you were a hero, Lerris, a sort of innocent, what-did-I-do type, but you still hadn't grown up. You still haven't.' She raised a hand. 'You're trying. Very trying,' she added with a laugh. 'I have to give you that. But Krystal didn't understand you weren't grown. She is the autarch's commander, and you've probably done more for Kyphros on three occasions than she has the whole time she's been here. Not only that, but you're a mastercrafter whom everyone respects and who makes lots of golds. Now, you're becoming a pretty decent warrior, and you're still perfectionistic enough not to want to recognize it. And, like all young bucks, you want – and probably deserve – recognition.'

'But I couldn't do what Krystal can, not day in and day out.'

'I'm sure she'll be so pleased to know that she's a better drudge than you could ever be.'

'That's not what I meant,' I protested.

'That's what you said, and it is what you really meant. Besides, it's not true. Some of that crafting is dull, dull, dull drudgery, and you excel at that, too.' She smiled brightly. 'So . . . you see why I don't have an answer?'

'That's not much help.' I wanted to thrash her, really thrash her, with the staff.

'I can't help you. You need to help yourself.' She paused. 'The only one with enough patience to help you might be Dayala.' And she was gone.

For a time I just stood there.

Then I trudged out of the courtyard and to the washroom, to wash, and to try to find Dayala. I did not find her until late in the afternoon, after Justen found me and took me off to an audience with the autarch for a detailed report on the destruction of the Hamorian army. Krystal was not there, which seemed odd, until Justen explained it later.

'You often defer to Krystal, whether you know it or not. So the autarch wanted to hear a more honest and complete story.'

After he left, I had to wonder. Was I becoming less honest? How was that possible? I could still use order. or did others get the impression that I was less honest because I was seeing all sides of things, the greater complexity that Justen had alluded to?

That bothered me, and I tried to follow Justen to find Dayala, but they both disappeared. So I got something to eat, then went back and reread more of *The Basis of Order*. After that I decided to dig my tools out of the stable. Surely, I could make myself useful somewhere in helping to rebuild Ruzor.

So it was late afternoon before Dayala returned and I rapped on her door.

'Come in, Lerris.'

Her face still bore a fine tracery of wrinkles, but she no longer looked ancient.

'You look better.'

'Thank you. I'm glad that I no longer look ready for the worms.'

I blushed.

She smiled. 'How might I help you?'

'Tamra said you were the only one who could.'

'I am flattered.'

'You and Justen understand each other,' I blurted out, feeling that if I didn't get it out, I wouldn't. 'I feel like every time I turn around, Krystal and I are arguing because she can't understand what I feel and she doesn't think I understand what she feels. And it's getting worse, not better.'

'You think that I can help.'

'You understand.'

'You left Recluce because you did not wish to take the words of others on faith.' She frowned. 'Why would you take my words? Or are you hoping I will confirm what you already believe?'

I almost wished I hadn't come, but I looked at her.

She sighed. 'Go ahead and sit down.'

I sat on one of the two stools, and she sat cross-legged on the stone floor. It would have been uncomfortable for me, but she didn't seem to mind.

'You feel she does not understand you.'

'If she did, she'd know I love her.'

Dayala laughed. 'Love is not based on understanding, but on acceptance.'

I must have looked confused. She just looked up at me from where she sat on the stones. So I tried to think it out.

'Justen is better at this than I am, I think, but you would not listen to him,' she added.

Finally, I said, 'You mean Krystal does understand, but she doesn't accept what I'm doing?'

'You would have to ask her. She might. Understanding is useful only when it leads to acceptance. When it does not, it leads to chaos.'

'How can we accept each other? We can't even talk.'

She paused. 'I need to talk to Justen. Just wait here.' Still barefooted, she slipped out the door and left me sitting there.

Outside, a small bird whistled twice. I thought it was a bird, but it could have been a lizard or some trooper.

Dayala returned before long. 'I thought I might be wrong, but . . . Justen doesn't think so.'

She looked at me, and it was like looking into the depths of the demon's hell. I thought so, although I'd never done so, but I could feel so much . . . pain, suffering, ages of birth and death . . .

I tried to keep my eyes open, and I did, but I had to stand up.

'Justen was right.' She took a deep breath. 'You can sit down.'

I sat, feeling I wasn't going to like what came next.

'Lerris, Justen says this is very simple. You can die younger than you should, by all rights of your talents, and be respected and loved. Or you can be the greatest mage of all time, and leave the world a far worse place. By telling you this, we hope to save you, and the world, great agony.'

'Me?'

'If you want to be the greatest mage, all you have to do is walk away from Kyphros, from Recluce. That is all. The rest will happen naturally.'

'What if I don't want either? Why couldn't I be great and still be respected?'

'The Balance doesn't work that way, not now.'

I stood up. 'That's manure. You're no better than my father, or Justen, telling me whatever will make me do what you want.'

She stood, and blackness rose around her like a storm. So did chaos.

I walked to the door and turned back. She just stood there, but that order seemed rooted in the earth, and I realized that she was a druid, and I couldn't see a druid, or her, lying.

Still, I stood there for a long time. So did she, and it almost felt as though the room, and the world, stood teetering on the edge of a knife. Then I took a deep breath and walked back and sat down on the stool.

Outside, the bird whistled again, and I felt as if I'd stepped away from a cliff.

'You are generous at heart, and you want Krystal to say that you are generous. You want her to say it again and again. You will give, not just because you wish to give, but because you want everyone to tell you how good you are.'

I shivered.

'Goodness is not giving for praise. Goodness is giving when you are cursed, or when your children do not understand and may never understand. Goodness is being silent, when you could have praise, because you know the good you do will be destroyed by praise. The more powerful you become, the harder it will be for you to be honest with yourself, and the more you wrestle with chaos, the harder that honesty becomes. Yet you will have to wrestle with chaos, and every day may be like the times you have wrestled before.'

I shivered.

'That is the price of power, and you are powerful, and nothing can take that from you. Without honesty, you will lose. As Antonin did, as once-humble Sammel did.'

'How do I hold such honesty?'

'Are you willing to accept total honesty, and another's judgment, a judgment that you can never escape? Will you pay that price?'

I swallowed. 'Yours?'

She shook her head. 'I have lived almost all my life with such a judgment. So has Justen.'

The tie between them? 'You want to link us the way you and Justen are linked?'

'I do not want anything. You are too strong to listen to anyone you are not forced to listen to.'

'Why would that make me listen?'

She smiled, and the darkness rose again.

I waited.

'If I die, so does Justen. If he does, so do I. He can no more escape what I feel than I can what he does.'

I shuddered.

'Yes.' Dayala waited, then asked, 'Are you able to accept such honesty?'

I thought about asking how it was honest, but after a moment of reflection I understood. Were Krystal tied to me, and I to her, any false feeling would be open, any self-deception obvious. I shivered again. The question of self-deception was coming back again. Could I be honestly self-deceived? Justen had hinted that was possible.

'After you decide, if you decide, then I will talk to Krystal. She may not agree. And this should not be done unless you both agree.'

'Could it?'

'It has been. That link, between Creslin and Megaera, created the greatest good and the greatest evil Candar has ever known, and you, and I, and Justen are still paying for that. Good cannot be forced. Only evil.'

I could only answer, 'I don't know.'

'You are honest. That is a good place to start.'

I walked out of her room and down to the harbor. As the sun touched the western plains and the bluff with the center cut out, my feet carried me to the piles of stone that had been the old fort. I stood on the half of the northeast tower that remained and looked out at the flat waters of the harbor, turning from blue to black as the sun set.

None of my choices were good. I'd touched Antonin, Sephya, Gerlis, and Sammel enough to know that I didn't want to end up like them. I barely knew who I was, and Dayala was telling me that I would have to give up being me, in order to stay honest, because the kind of power I could hold would destroy me through self-deception. And Krystal, would she resent being a check on me? Would she come to hate me? Every time I tried to do something, she seemed to think that I was trying to make her seem less important. Couldn't she see that one of the things she was doing was rejecting my attempts to be honest? Why couldn't she see that, over time, I could not do much more, not if I wanted to live?

All I had to do was look at my father and Justen and see that. Did she think I was too stupid to understand?

I stood, watching, listening as the harbor waters lapped at the stones spilled into their dark shallows and depths.

# CIX

## Dellash, Delapra [Candar]

Dyrsse leans back in the wooden chair, watching the heavyset officer in the tan uniform. The younger man steps out of the full sunlight of the courtyard and looks around, studying the bay below and the rows upon rows of black ships anchored in the bay. From a host of funnels rise thin lines of smoke.

A faint smile crosses his face as the naval officer turns, his eyes barely resting on the low forested hills to the west before he crosses the covered veranda to the corner table where Dyrsse waits.

The brown-haired and brown-skinned officer stops and gives Dyrsse the faintest of nods. 'Fleet Commander Stupelltry, at your service, Marshal Dyrsse.'

'You and your fleet are most welcome, Fleet Commander.' Dyrsse smiles politely. 'Please have a seat.' His almost delicate fingers jab toward the other wooden armchair.

Stupelltry sits down gracefully. 'I am here to serve the Emperor and you, as requested by His Majesty.'

'That's true. You are here because the Emperor Stesten has decided to eliminate Recluce, and we are the tools to accomplish this. It is our duty.'

'You have worked closely with the throne, Marshal, and the Emperor is well aware of your dedication, and your accomplishments in taking over a third of Candar with a relatively small use of resources.'

'Yes, it was relatively small.' Dyrsse nods to the pitcher. 'Delapran wine. I wouldn't know, but it's supposedly not bad. Would you like some?'

'No, thank you.'

Dyrsse looks out at the bay, and the rows of ships. 'A man of decision, wanting to get on with it.' He smiles. 'What do you wish to get on with, Fleet Commander Stupelltry?'

'I would be less than candid if I were to say that I was pleased to have the bulk of the Emperor's fleet so far from Afrit. I wish to complete the subjugation of Recluce and Candar and return to Hamor.' Stupelltry's voice is level, and his eyes do not flinch as they meet Dyrsse's.

Dyrsse laughs. 'Candar is far indeed from Afrit. I share your desire to subjugate Candar and destroy the power of Recluce. Are you ready to commit all your fleet? It will take no less.'

'Surely the third of the fleet that has arrived . . .'

Dyrsse laughs again. 'Take your ships home. Send a courier boat out to tell those en route to return to Hamor.'

Stupelltry flushes.

'Forget Candar. Recluce is what has stopped the Emperor. With Recluce's power destroyed, twoscore ships would be enough to capture and hold Candar. Without Recluce's destruction, your fleet will never provide enough support to take Candar.'

'You presume —'

'Too much? I presume nothing.' Dyrsse straightens. 'It will take all of your ships to destroy the handful of black ships and the city of Nylan.' He shrugs. 'Once that is done . . .'

'And what clever tactics will accomplish such a difficult feat?' Stupelltry pauses but for a moment before pressing on. 'You are so sure of your mandate —'

Dyrsse ignores the irony placed on the word 'difficult' and leans forward. 'The Emperor is the liege lord of Afrit, Regent of the Gates of the Ocean, and Emperor of Hamor, the mightiest empire in the history of the world. Yet, for all that mightiness, twice before have we been humbled in Candar and before Recluce. Our traders continue to labor under trade rules forced by Recluce. Over the years, those unseen black warships have sunk traders for trifling violations of the trade laws laid down by one small isle. For whose benefit are those rules enforced? For the black isle, of course.

'Candar is rife with strife, with chaos wizardry, and with violence. People live in terror of most of the rulers. Compare that to Afrit, where no one fears invasion or war. And who fosters that terror? The black isle, no less.'

Dyrsse pauses and smiles. 'Are you sure you would not like some of the wine?'

'No, thank you.'

'As you wish.' The marshal leans forward again. 'You asked about clever tactics. Clever tactics won't work. What will work is thousands of iron shells falling on Nylan nearly all at once. It's that simple and that difficult. Can you do that, Fleet Commander Stupelltry? Can you bring your ships to Nylan through the heaviest storms you have ever seen and pound that city into a mass of crushed stone and black gravel?' He pauses. 'That is what the Emperor needs. That is our duty, the one laid on me personally by His Mightiness Stesten – to crush Nylan into black gravel.'

'I am a fleet commander, not a stone crusher.'

'No . . . you and I are the Emperor's stone crushers . . . and we will be crushed if we fail.'

# CX

It wasn't that long on that late afternoon before I finally went back to Dayala, and ended up sitting on the stool again, looking down at her as she sat there cross-legged and open-eyed.

'I don't have any choice.' For all the concern about honesty, I couldn't lie, and I couldn't see that there was any real choice if I wanted to live with myself.

She looked at me with those deep eyes, and my tongue seemed to swell.

'All right, even ponies have choices. But I don't want to end up like Sammel, and that's not a real choice.'

She just kept looking at me.

'What am I supposed to do? I've seen what power does. I know I have the ability to tap a lot of power. Am I supposed to beg and grovel to you and Krystal and Justen? "Please save me. Please save me from myself." I'll bet Justen didn't beg.'

I could feel a deep sadness welling up in the druid, but I waited.

'No. He and Creslin were forced. They had no choice.'

'And you? Did you force Justen? Like you're forcing me?'

'I chose. Justen would have been linked to someone. I chose to be that druid.'

'She also saved my life when I would have died,' added Justen, stepping into the room. 'More than once. And she's suffered a lot of pain because I didn't choose to understand.' He laughed. 'Like you, Lerris. It must run in the blood. Like self-serving pride.'

He looked at me, and I finally looked away.

'You want to believe that you're always doing things to be good, Lerris. And you are good at heart. But you're also doing good things to get the praise you never got from Gunnar because you weren't perfect. And Gunnar couldn't praise you because he felt he wasn't perfect, and I have trouble because I'm not. All of that's self-deception. Why can't you tell Krystal you need to be praised?'

I just looked at him. He looked back at me again.

I couldn't. I just couldn't. If I had to ask for praise, it wasn't worth anything, and I couldn't voice that, either.

Then I looked at Dayala and back at Justen. They said nothing.

'If this link is so wonderful, why doesn't it happen more?'

'Because it could kill you both,' said Justen bluntly. 'If one dies, so does the other.'

'Let me get this right. If you link us together the way you and Dayala are, it could kill us both. And I'm supposed to consider this as a solution?'

Dayala stood. 'I will be back.'

Justen nodded at her, although I knew more had passed between them than the spoken words. He slipped onto the other stool.

'Well, Uncle Justen. Give me one good reason.'

'I can't. It would be my reason. You know who you are. You know who Krystal is. You know what you are. If I give you a reason, Lerris, then you will use that reason either to reject the link or to put the responsibility on us. You know who you are. You know what the link is, and what it does. You should know that it makes two people one, and that if they cannot stand each other inside it will destroy them. You also know that such closeness makes deception impossible, and most people cannot live without self-deception. Most people cannot face themselves. We will not make those judgments for you. You have to make those judgments, or you will blame me or Dayala, as you have blamed Recluce ... and Krystal.' He sat on the stool and waited.

I walked over to the narrow window. All the barracks windows were narrow. From there, I could see the ruined walls of the harbor fort, and the sagging waterfront buildings across the narrow tip of the bay – and the long shadows.

All I wanted was to ... to what? To be close to Krystal? So why had I pushed her away? Or had she pushed me away? Could I take her honesty, or was I supposed to be honest for her?

My eyes burned for a moment, and I shook my head. It wasn't fair. It wasn't fair. I could walk away, but, even as I thought that, I knew I wouldn't have another chance, because Krystal would stay in Ruzor ... and Justen and Dayala would die if they had to save the city – I'd seen enough to know that. And that wasn't fair, either.

I didn't have to be fair. Who had been fair to me? I'd been deceived, and maneuvered, and forced to choose between risking my life and losing Krystal. Why did I have to be fair? I didn't owe it to anyone.

So easy ... just walk away and become the great Lerris. In time, who would know? Who would know? Who?

The faintest murmur slipped up the walls from the courtyard, so faint I could not make out the words.

So who would know if I left Ruzor and Kyphros?

I would. I remembered the faces in the depths, and now they all had my face – even Shervan. It wasn't fair that he died, but he had.

Fair? I would have laughed, but my mouth was dry, even when I swallowed.

The waters of the bay were flat, without the slightest hint of whitecaps, and the hulls of the wrecked ships seemed more like enormous boulders, sunken remnants of a past that would not die.

Yet, though he had Sephya with him, Antonin died alone. And so did Gerlis, and Sammel ... because no one cared.

Was that what I wanted? I'd hated it when I felt no one in Recluce had cared. But why couldn't Krystal understand? Why wouldn't she?

I recalled Dayala's word – acceptance.

A faint puff of warm air caressed my face, with an acrid scent, the scent of death, perhaps from townspeople, or more decomposing sailors' bodies.

I turned, but Justen sat there, waiting, not saying a word.

The harbor seemed flat, the waves lifeless.

Acceptance . . . of what?

I took a deep breath.

Outside the air was still, acrid, hovering between life and death, it seemed.

I turned back to Justen and nodded.

'It takes two,' he said. 'Dayala is talking to Krystal.'

He sat, and I waited, looking out beyond the breakwater, wondering how Krystal felt, wondering how it had come to this, wondering why love was so hard and took so much work and hurt so much.

# CXI

The two women sat on opposite ends of the bed, and the hot breeze wrapped around them.

'I told Lerris he was in great danger, because as he grew more powerful, he faced constant temptation to become less honest with himself.' Dayala looked toward the commander.

'I've already seen that. That's why we're having troubles.' Krystal did not look at the druid, but glanced toward the open window, toward the ruined harbor and city beyond.

'You are not honest, either, Lady,' said Dayala, 'and that is also part of your problem.'

Krystal continued to study the harbor. 'Part, perhaps, but it didn't start there.'

'You wanted love and affection from Lerris – unquestioning love and affection. He has grown, and he has questions, but he loves you.'

'Love shouldn't be given with reservations and questions.' Krystal's voice was hard.

'No. It should not,' says Dayala. 'Love flowers on acceptance of what is, not what is desired. Lerris desires praise, especially your praise, and he will do almost anything to earn it. You are afraid that as Lerris has grown, so he will see you as you are, and not as the perfect woman as he has.'

'I just want him to accept me.'

'He does, but he feels you do not accept him. Do you?'

'I love him, but he doesn't always have to save the world.' Krystal's hands twisted around each other, and her eyes fell toward the blade at her side.

'Would you love him so much if he did not wish to do well?'

'He doesn't always have to be a hero and save the world.'

'No one does, but if no one does . . .' The druid did not finish her sentence.

'That's not fair. He doesn't have to be the one.'

The two women's eyes met, and the hint of putrescence drifted into the room on a puff of hot air.

'But he does. If he does not save the world, he will destroy it.'

'You are asking me to chain myself to him to save the world? That's not a choice – it's as much force as a blade is.'

'I am saying that the man you love will destroy the world you love unless you can accept him and he can accept you. If you choose to call that force, then it is.' Dayala pauses. 'That is what is. That is what makes the choice hard, because you must put aside your resentment and your anger. They will not change the world. You must accept Lerris, and you must not hate him because of the choice, or, in the end, you will destroy not only yourselves, but the world you love.'

'I already accept him.'

Dayala looked steadily at the commander.

Finally, Krystal's eyes dropped down to the coverlet. Her fingers traced out the star pattern. 'Why does he have to save the world? Why does it have to be him?'

Dayala did not answer, but waited.

'Why does he have to be a hero?'

The druid continued to remain silent, and her deep eyes watched the woman in leathers.

'Why . . . ?' Krystal shook her head and stood. 'Why doesn't matter, does it?'

'No.' Dayala smiled sadly once more.

They walked out of the tower room.

# CXII

The door opened, and Krystal stood there with Dayala. Her eyes were bleak, like the rocks on the shore in a storm. Mine didn't look much better, I was sure.

'Hello,' I said. I could hear the unsteadiness in my voice.

'Hello.' Her voice trembled.

My commander's competent voice trembled.

After a moment, I couldn't see her because my eyes burned so much, or maybe because the ground was shaking, but I did manage to stammer out her name. I still couldn't see much beyond her blurred figure in blue, but she was shaking, too, I think, and I took a step toward her. She must have taken one, too, because we did manage to hang on to one another. That was about all we did.

'Holding on is harder than finding each other. I think you're beginning to find that out,' Justen said after a time.

By then we'd stopped shaking, but Krystal's fingers were as tightly wound around mine as mine were around hers.

'I take it that you two are willing to do this.'

I nodded. I was afraid to speak. Krystal nodded. Maybe she was, too.

'Just sit on the stools, next to each other.'

We looked at each other, and then sat down.

The physical procedure didn't seem terribly mystical or powerful – a slight cut, some mixing of blood – but Dayala put what I could only call an order-chaos lock and twist on the blood, and with my senses, I could feel immediately the thin line of order between us.

No thoughts, no feelings, just order.

'Like anything living, it takes a while to grow, for which you should both be thankful.' Justen's voice was rough, almost gruff. 'Be kind to each other.'

Be kind to each other. Just a simple statement, yet one that made all others secondary.

'Remember,' Dayala said softly, almost like the whispering of the Great Forest from which she had come and which I doubted we'd ever see, 'you have chosen each other twice.'

'Now, get out of here, and leave us ancients in peace,' added Justen.

Krystal and I walked out of the room slowly and stopped in the narrow corridor. We looked at each other. She didn't look any different – the same black eyes, the same short silver-tinged black hair. Neither did I.

'Let's take a walk,' I said.

'Where?'

'Down to the old fort on the breakwater.'

'That would be nice.'

I still hadn't let go of her hand, and I wasn't about to, not then, even if our hands were getting sticky.

'Lerris . . . ?'

'Yes?'

'Could we change hands? I won't go away.'

So I let go, crossed behind her, and took her right hand in my left. We both were sweating by the time we reached the breakwater, and we probably looked like the demons' hell, but I didn't care.

Only the corner of the one tower remained. The rest was rocks, little gray rocks, big gray stones, fragments of bricks, and gray dust.

I spied a flat chunk of stone in the shade of the tower. 'We could sit there.' My feet hurt. In fact, I ached all over. 'Do you ache all over?' I asked.

'Not all over. My hair doesn't hurt.'

We laughed for a moment, and hugged, and then sat down.

From across the bay came the sound of rebuilding – hammers, saws, and the clinking of stonemasons' tools – not to mention the voices. Nothing in Kyphros ever got done quietly, or without a lot of conversation.

A puff of warm air, still bearing a hint of death and decay, wafted past us. The harbor waters lapped the stones like a murmur from a distant corridor.

'Why did we do this?' she asked.

I squeezed her hand. 'Because we're desperate. Because we don't want to lose what we think we're losing, and we're willing to risk our lives to keep it.'

She looked out at the flat waters.

'Do you want children?'

I swallowed. I hadn't thought about it.

'I hadn't really thought about it, except that someday we would.'

'When will someday be?'

When will someday be? Just a simple question, but I held her, and we both cried . . . because . . . because someday might never come, and we both knew it.

The harbor waters murmured, and the hammers hammered, and we held on.

The next morning, we woke with a cool breeze coming in through the open window, and I reached for the coverlet.

I didn't quite make it because my arms were full.

'Don't . . . we can't lose each other . . . not again . . .' Krystal's words were in my ears. But she shivered; so I did pull up the coverlet, but only with one hand.

In time, we got up, but I kept reaching out to touch her, perhaps a few times too often.

'I'm not going anywhere,' she finally grumped, possibly because I had startled her as she was washing, and she had to blot water off her trousers. So I refrained while she dressed. Instead, I straightened up the room.

'You do good work.'

'Thank you.'

'But don't let it go to your head again.' She smiled, and it was warm, not edged, and I smiled back.

When we left the room for breakfast in the dining hall, Herreld was outside.

'Good morning,' I said.

Krystal nodded to him.

'Take care,' said Herreld. 'Both of you.' He looked down at the stones before we could answer.

Krystal squeezed my hand, and I squeezed back, but I didn't say anything until we were down one flight of stairs and around the corner. 'Herreld's getting soft.'

'He always was. He just didn't want to show it.'

Like most people, I figured, even Tamra.

# CXIII

For several days, nothing out of the ordinary happened, thank darkness, except that Krystal and I talked and spent time together, when she wasn't meeting or strategizing. I went back to working with her trainees with the staff. That way, I could at least look over at her occasionally. Sometimes, I even caught her looking at me. We tried not to laugh.

That morning, three days after our 'rediscovery,' I was looking out the window, just after sunrise. Krystal was still asleep, curled up on my side of the bed. I'd stayed in bed for a time, but I was stiff, perhaps from more exercise, or from the age I hadn't wanted, and I'd needed to get up, but I hadn't wanted to wake her. She seemed tired, and I wanted to let her sleep.

The coolness hadn't lasted, but the morning didn't seem quite so warm, a sign that fall was approaching. Out in the bay, I saw several fishing boats, but nothing large, certainly no warships or traders.

I turned and watched Krystal, and she smiled in sleep as if she could feel my gaze and my affection, and I wanted to reach out and touch her, but I didn't, instead turning back to the window.

While I could not be sure, it seemed as though the chaos that underlay Candar had swelled slightly, although it was hard to sense that with the continual rumbling and groaning that I seemed to feel all the time.

The fishing boats disappeared behind hills that marked the south-west side of the bay, and the sun lifted the shadows of the eastern hills from the waters, and Krystal slept.

How long I watched, I didn't really know.

'You should have gotten me up.' Krystal bolted upright. 'I'll be late.'

'You needed the sleep, and I was stiff.'

'That's strange. For a while, I was dreaming that my back had been hurt.'

'I wonder —'

'— if we're beginning to sense what . . .'

'Probably,' I said. 'At least, we won't have to guess.' I bent over and hugged her.

'I really do have to get dressed.'

We dressed and hurried down to the dining hall – I didn't even make the bed – and wolfed down bread and cheese with water.

After my session of sparring with the troopers, while Krystal went off to meet with Yelena and Subrella, I collected my tools, commandeered part of a keg of nails, and wandered down on the waterfront and to the chandlery, where I tied Gairloch.

The roof beams were in place, and they were nailing down stringers, or whatever the boards are called that hold the beams together that the roof tiles are laid on. The stringers had been cut down and shaped from the pile of debris that included everything from pier planks to splintered doors and other unrecognizable chunks and lengths of wood. One ship had arrived with lumber, trying to sell it at three times the normal price. The autarch had bought the cargo and resold it at normal prices.

'Could I help?'

'Got no coins,' admitted the curly-haired man who was wrestling with a roof timber.

I shook my head. 'The autarch sent me down.' I looked at the heavy timber. 'I'm more of a crafter. I could put those windows back together. You'd have to get a glazier, but I could set the frames right.'

'The autarch sent you? Right.'

I spread my hands. 'Look. I'm not asking for anything. I don't want anything. She's feeding me and paying me. My job is to help get the waterfront back together.'

'Why?' asked a balding fellow, still young.

'She told me – well, she didn't, a woman by the name of Krystal did – that the sooner the port was rebuilt, the sooner she'd get customs duties and trade. But I'm not a stone mason or a carpenter.'

The two looked at each other. The older one shrugged. 'All right. What would you do to fix that?' He pointed to the crumpled frame that was half torn from the bricks.

I studied it for a moment. 'Most of the sections are all right, except for the bottom line, and the brace. I could cut a piece from one of the short ones there, brace it with those ... it'd probably be better if I took it out and rebuilt it.'

'Where?'

'Right here.'

'Go ahead.'

So I did. The mitre cuts weren't what I could have done in my shop, but the wood was mostly pine and fir, and it cut easily. The first frame was quick. The second was trickier, because one of the side sections was splintered where I hadn't seen it at first. So when I got to replacing it, I had to chisel grooves for the glazier. I also had to use nails, but trying to dovetail everything would have taken forever.

'Neat work, fellow.' A white-bearded man wiped his forehead. He had been mortaring back the front wall of the dry-goods store. 'Don't recall you.'

'I came from Kyphrien,' I admitted.

'You help me next?'

'If I can. Can only commit to one job at a time, and I could get called away anytime.'

'Well ... if you can?'

I nodded, because I had to concentrate on the grooving.

The white-haired man wiped his forehead again. 'Awful mess. Terrible price to pay ... just terrible ... but better that than having the sundevils here.'

'Sometimes you wonder.' I finished the first groove and began the second so that when I slipped the replacement piece in place, held mostly with dovetails, the grooves for the glass would line up. The woods wouldn't match, because I was working with an aged piece of something like cedar, and the original frame had been pine, but it would be painted or whitewashed anyway.

'Don't wonder at all. My grandfather jumped ship, and you jump ship on an imperial ship, right over the side at sea. Otherwise they send guards after you and quarter you right on the pier. He pretended he couldn't swim, and they left him. Almost didn't make it, but he did, and that's why I'm here.' He shook his head.' Anyplace bad enough that people have to jump into the ocean ... don't want to live there, and don't want them telling me how to live.' He wiped his damp forehead again. 'Need to be getting back to work. Bricks don't put themselves back in place. Didn't catch your name, young fellow.'

'Lerris.' I'd started on rebuilding the third frame, since I'd need help putting the first two back in place, both with wedges, and then reframing.

'Lerris? That's not a Kyphran name.'

'No,' I admitted.

'You a carpenter?'

'Not really. I'm a crafter. I do pieces like desks, chairs, tables ... but I was here and thought I'd help while I could.'

'You said ...'

Both of the men on the roof were listening now.

I shrugged. 'I'm not good at telling partial truths. If it helps any, I'm the consort of the commander. I am a woodcrafter.'

The white-haired man stared at me. 'You wouldn't be the one who's a mage, would you?'

'I've been called that, but I am a crafter.'

'Goodsa, stop bothering him,' called the curly-haired man. 'I don't give a frig where he came from. He's put two frames back together that it would've taken me all day.'

Goodsa humphed and wandered back to his mortaring, but he kept glancing at me.

A while later, near midday, the darker-haired man climbed down from the roof for a drink from his water bottle.

'That true, about being a mage?'

'Yes. Order-mage.' I was sweating heavily, and trying to finish the last section of the front frames.

'Why couldn't you use magic to put this back together?'

I laughed. 'It wouldn't work. When something like a storm mangles this, it's like chaos. The best defense against chaos is good crafting.

Besides, I can't do that kind of magic, and if I could you wouldn't want it, because if anything happened to me, it would fall apart. Good crafting doesn't.'

He nodded.

'Light! Look at that.' The curly-headed chandler pointed toward the harbor.

I turned and looked. A low black ship had appeared, as if from nowhere, at the stone pier, a ship of black steel and a raked appearance, and one that made the big steel ships of Hamor look clumsy.

I knew that ship, had known it from my dangergeld training, but had not known what it represented.

As I watched, a flag unfurled, the black ryall on the white background fluttering in the wind. A dozen marines in black stood loosely in order on the deck as if waiting.

'The black devils . . .'

'. . . don't know as which be worse, them or the sundevils . . .'

'. . . our luck to be caught 'twixt 'em.'

I asked the dark-haired man, 'Can you help me wedge the frames in place? I can't do it alone, and I'm going to have to leave pretty soon.'

He looked from me to the ship. 'Sure . . . I guess. That ship mean more trouble?'

I nodded. 'But not for Kyphros, at least not now.'

'Not ever, I hope.'

'Me, too.' But I didn't know.

It didn't take that long to wedge the three frames in place, but I took a little while longer to shape and put the front pieces in place. The work was rougher than I would have liked, but the windows were back in place, anyway.

I wiped my forehead and began to pack up the tools.

'You're just leaving?' asked the curly-haired man.

'I'm sorry. I wish I could have done more.'

'That'd take me days.' He looked from me to the windows. 'You sure you don't want anything?'

I shook my head. 'I wish I could have done more.' That was getting to be the way I felt about everything. I closed the bags and untied Gairloch. 'Good luck.'

'Mage or not, you're all right.' He looked up at the other man. 'We still might have it back together by end day.'

'Not if you don't get back up here.'

I left them talking and rushed Gairloch back to the barracks at a fast trot. I unsaddled and brushed him quickly, then hurried to the washroom.

'Where were you?' asked Tamra as she burst into the washroom as I was splashing off grime and sweat.

'Down on the waterfront, helping some folks rebuild their chandlery.' I wiped my face.

'Your father and Krystal are looking for you.'

'I'll be right there.' I stopped. 'Where?'

'In the small dining hall. I'll tell them you'll be there.'

Dayala, Justen, Tamra, and Krystal stood around my father, who held a flat envelope in his hands.

'I'm sorry,' I apologized. 'I was out of the barracks, but I came as soon as I could after I saw the ship.'

'This letter was addressed to me here,' began my father. 'By the Black Council.' He looked around the dining hall. 'Hamor has begun to assemble a grand fleet and appears to be readying for an attack on Nylan and Recluce. The Council has indirectly requested that I enlist whatever help I can and return to Recluce.'

'We don't have many troopers to spare,' pointed out Krystal.

'I believe that the Council is hoping that Justen can repeat his feats of the past and present, and that Tamra and I will raise more storms, and that Lerris will use order to call chaos to the defense of Recluce.'

Tamra opened her mouth and then closed it. She was pale.

I looked at my father, and he handed me the letter. The gist of the request lay in a few words near the end, after all the flowery phrases.

> While we cannot request that you return to Candar and assist us in the defense of order, the Council would deeply appreciate it if you, and all those you could enlist, such as the mage Justen, and Lerris and Tamra, would consider returning to defend the last bastion of order against the onslaught of the dark ships of Hamor . . .

'You don't have to go. Nor does Tamra,' he said. 'Neither Recluce, nor I, have been kind to you.'

I looked at him, at the age and strain in his face, and wondered how I could have thought he did not care.

'It doesn't matter,' I finally said, and I realized that the past did not matter. For all of Recluce's faults, for all of my father's mistakes – and I had begun to wonder if they had really been mistakes – there was little real choice. If Recluce did not defeat Hamor, then Kyphros would fall, and all the good that Kasee and Krystal had done would be lost.

Then, too, Recluce had meddled in Candar, usually to remove truly evil rulers, and Justen had done what he could. No ... it hadn't acted perfectly, or even well, at times, and sometimes Recluce had failed to act ... but compared to what else I had seen ... there wasn't that much choice.

I turned to Krystal. 'What do you think?'

'You're right, and I'm going,' Krystal said.

'Is that a good idea?' I didn't really want her hurt, and yet I didn't want to leave her.

'I feel the same way, and,' she added softly, 'from here on, we both live, or we both die.'

It could have been my imagination, but I felt her confusion and conflict as strongly as my own, and I reached out and touched her hand – only to discover the feelings were even stronger. We just looked at each other.

The dining hall was silent.

'If we win,' Krystal said quickly, and with my hand in hers, I could feel her passion, 'then Kasee has no real problems. If we lose, nothing can stop Hamor.'

'Nothing?' asked Tamra, turning to Justen.

Krystal leaned over and whispered to me, 'I love you. The first thing you did for me almost killed you. The second aged you more than ten years. I'm not leaving you alone a third time.' She paused for a moment and then glared at me and spoke in a normal tone. 'Even your father understands. He wanted me here.' Then I got a smile, if only briefly. 'You're not the only one who gets to be a hero.'

After another short silence, Tamra spoke. 'Just how are we going to get to Recluce?'

My father cleared his throat, and the mutterings died down. 'I asked the captain if he could transport us, but he didn't seem that keen on it. He did say that the Council had already chartered a Nordlan ship to port here and take us back.'

'Still fearful, after all these years,' snorted Justen, 'as if I couldn't diagram the whole *Dylyss* from memory. None of the black ships have changed that much.'

Sometimes, it was hard to believe that Justen had been a black engineer, especially when he seemed more like a grouchy uncle than a mage or someone who had built black warships. Yet he had engineered the devices that had destroyed Fairhaven, devices that no one yet had duplicated, for which I was most grateful, and yet those were accomplishments I never would have thought of when I had met him in an inn in Howlett.

'We need to see Kasee,' said Krystal slowly.

'Oh ... of course.' Krystal was still the autarch's commander, and not even a request or an invitation from the Council of Recluce changed that.

'She'll let you go,' said Tamra. 'She —'

Justen touched Tamra's arm, and she closed her mouth.

'Is there anything else we should tell the autarch?' Krystal asked.

'I think you probably know more of that than we do,' my father answered with a faint smile.

I nodded, even if his words were better than mine would have been.

After leaving the small dining hall, we started down the corridor toward the courtyard. My stomach growled.

'Lerris ...'

'I'm sorry. I haven't eaten since this morning.'

'You really didn't?'

'I got a little tied up.'

We began to cross the courtyard.

'What were you doing? You were in Ruzor, the town, weren't you?'

'I was making myself useful, helping some folks rebuild their chandlery. How did you know I was in Ruzor?'

'I just felt it. Why ...' She let her words trail off.

'Something Dayala said about doing good things without expecting praise ... it didn't work quite that way, but I might get the hang of it someday.'

'Oh, Lerris.' But the words were affectionate, and so were the feelings behind them.

Kasee, according to her personal guard chief, was in the old study, and we made our way along the paneled corridors to the waiting room. We didn't have to wait long.

Kasee sat behind the old circular table, surrounded by the shelves of old books and older knowledge. Her hair was disarrayed, her cheek smudged, and her tunic frayed, clearly not the image of a ruler. She gestured toward the chairs on the other side of the table.

We sat down, and I waited, since in many ways the business was between Krystal and the autarch.

'I understand a ship from Recluce arrived in Ruzor,' Kasee said.

'It brought a message from the Black Council.'

'Obviously, not to me.'

'It was to Gunnar, but he was requested to enlist such aid as he could, including Justen, Lerris, and Tamra.' Krystal spoke slowly, clearly. 'The Black Council believes that Hamor will move against Recluce before it attempts any more conquests in Candar.'

'In that case, I wish them well. I assume you are going, Lerris?'

'I don't know.'

Krystal reached out and squeezed my hand. I squeezed back.

The autarch rubbed her forehead. 'I take it that somehow this concerns me?'

'Yes. Lerris needs to go, but we need to go together.'

For a long moment, the study was silent. I tried not to hold my breath, and I felt as though Krystal were doing the same.

'You are willing to give up everything to accompany Lerris to a place where you both might be killed?' asked Kasee.

'He was willing to do it for me – or for you,' responded Krystal. 'Besides, if we stop the Hamorians, you won't have to worry about them for a while longer.'

'I'm not sure I like the word "longer."' The autarch's voice was dry, and she brushed back a strand of silvered hair, revealing another smudge on her forehead.

'No solutions are permanent, no matter what wizards and rulers think,' I blurted out.

'Death is rather permanent, I believe, young Lerris.'

She had me with that one, and I bowed my head.

'Do you really think you can do anything about this Hamorian fleet?' she asked me after a moment.

'I have to try.' I had to shrug.

Kasee's lips twisted for a moment before she turned her eyes on Krystal. 'What am I supposed to do for a guard commander?'

'You could appoint Subrella.'

Kasee smiled. 'She can be acting until you and Lerris return.'

I thought Kasee demonstrated a great deal of faith, and my face must have shown that.

'If anyone can work miracles, you two can.' She frowned. 'Take your personal guard. I'll pay them. That's a cheap enough investment.' Then she gave another dry smile. 'Try to come back in one piece. I've lost too many guard commanders.'

'We'll be back,' I said.

'I believe you, Lerris, but I'll be a great deal happier when you return.' She stood, and we stood, and bowed, and left.

Outside the closed doors of the study, Krystal turned to me. 'Why did you blurt that out?' Her voice was gentle.

'I just felt it, and someone I trust a great deal told me I should trust my feelings.'

She took my arm, and we walked back through the residence and the courtyard toward the dining hall. My stomach growled, and this time, Krystal's did, too.

# CXIV

## Dellash, Delapra [Candar]

'You are aware, Marshal, that a Recluce ship was sighted returning to Nylan, presumably from Ruzor?' Stupelltry's fingers almost caress the sparkling, untouched, and empty crystal goblet on the veranda table.

'I cannot say that I am surprised,' Dyrsse admits. 'I would gather that the black devils have reclaimed their wizards.'

'So you will return to the attack on Kyphros? That would leave Kyphros in our hands.'

'Why? The Emperor has commanded us to remove the vipers of Recluce. That is our duty. That has always been our duty. If we remove them, Candar will fall. Fail to remove them, and we will never take Candar. Besides, they could return the wizards as quickly as they took them. Their ships are faster than ours.'

'Speed is not everything,' points out Stupelltry. 'They have neither the cannon nor the numbers of troops armed and trained as well as ours. While they may rely on magic, I prefer cannon, well-turned steel, and rifles that kill before a sword can respond. With a rifle, each trooper is as powerful as the average mage, and there are far more soldiers than mages.'

'True.' Dyrsse nods toward the pitcher on the table. 'Would you like some of the wine? I am assured that, as Candarian wines go, it is rather good.'

'No, thank you. It doubtless does not compare to the vintages the Emperor favors.' Stupelltry smiles.

'Doubtless, although I would not care to guess what the Emperor might favor in anything. My duty is to follow his commands as he has expressed them, not as I might guess.'

'Yes, his commands . . .' muses the fleet commander. 'They are our duty, and we will counter any speed of their ships with our numbers and cannon. Cannon reach farther than even the greatest firebolts of these western wizards.' He pauses. 'Are you convinced of the speed of the black ships?'

'They have provided rather convincing demonstrations. That is another reason why it would be better to strike now, before they can build more ships and before their wizards recuperate.'

'Would it not be easier to mount an attack holding all of Candar? That would provide an even more secure base.'

'How? You have Freetown, Pyrdya, Renklaar, and Worrak in the east, and control of Summerdock, Southport, and Biehl in the west. Is that not sufficient?' Dyrsse nods toward the empty goblet. 'Are you sure that you would not like some wine?'

'I do appreciate the kindness, but I must defer.' Stupelltry nods toward the ships arrayed in and beyond the harbor of Dellash. 'Since you and the Emperor are convinced, I will begin preparing for the stone-crushing efforts, and that will require a clear head.'

# CXV

The *Dylyss* disappeared after my father provided a letter saying that he would return with such aid as he was able. The captain had promised that a Nordlan ship would be porting within the next few days.

'A few days?' asked Tamra at breakfast. 'A few days? First, they want help, and then —'

'You don't move a large fleet that quickly,' observed my father. 'Most of the Hamorian ships are still in Dellash, according to the captain, and there are still a few more en route from Hamor. That's three days from here, and another three to Recluce, but they'd probably take on fresh water and supplies in Freetown and Renklaar.'

'Still . . .' mumbled Tamra, as she munched through hard bread.

The plain fact was that we didn't have a ship, and Recluce didn't like the idea of us on one of the secret warships.

After chewing our own way through the hard bread and harder cheese, Krystal and I walked out into the courtyard, and the sunlight, a shade less intense as the fall finally neared. The warmth felt welcome, but in a strange way, since I wasn't cold.

'You're cold?' I asked.

'The sun feels good.'

Was I feeling what she felt?

'Yes.' The words came with a smile.

I reached out and touched her fingers, and the feel of chill and the welcome of the sun's warmth were stronger.

'This is odd.'

'You feel warm enough,' she said, 'but I'm a little chilly.'

There was a silence.

'Have you talked to your guards?' I finally asked.

'I don't know that I want to take Perron,' mused Krystal. 'He has a three-month-old son.'

'Weldein would go,' I pointed out.

'You noticed that?'

'Even *I* noticed that.'

'Kasee probably wouldn't mind, but I'll have to talk to her. What are you going to do?'

I didn't know. 'Maybe help the townspeople.'

'Hmmm . . . well . . . they could use it.'

I could sense some doubt. 'You're doubtful?'

'Yes. I don't know why.'

'I'll groom Gairloch and think about it while you're talking with Kasee.' I kissed her cheek, and she smelled good.

'Lecherous man.'

I was. I couldn't deny it, but she smiled, and I hoped she always would. Then she walked toward the autarch's residence.

I had just about finished brushing Gairloch when Justen wandered into the stable, except the gray wizard never wandered anywhere. His eyes fell on the tools. 'I see you're thinking about helping more with the rebuilding of Ruzor.'

'I had thought about it.'

His skin wasn't so wrinkled, but his hair had remained gray, and he looked older, almost beyond middle age. 'Have you thought about how you intend to take on the Hamorian grand fleet?'

'No.' I'd thought I'd think about that when the time came.

He sighed, and I knew I'd said something wrong. So I put down the brush, and gave Gairloch a thump on the neck.

*Whheeee . . . eeeee . . .*

'I know. Uncle Justen has reminded his nephew that he has once more failed in his duties.' I smiled at Justen. 'Where shall we go?'

He sat down on a bale of hay. 'Here's as good as anywhere.'

I sat down on another bale.

Justen just looked at me. Finally, he asked. 'You love Krystal, don't you?'

I nodded.

'Then, if you don't want to kill her, why don't you start thinking?' He held up a hand. 'I've seen you do woodwork. You plan. You sketch. You check wood. You test finishes and all sorts of other things I wouldn't understand in years. Why is working with order and chaos any different?'

I just sat there. Why wasn't it any different? It wasn't. So I shook my head.

He stood.

'Wait. You're putting this all on me. The Council asked my father.'

'Your father nearly killed himself destroying perhaps thirty ships in a relatively small bay. I aged a lot in destroying a few thousand troops, and I had your help and Dayala's.'

'I aged —'

'That was stupidity and lack of planning.' He shrugged. 'It's your choice. I just thought I'd ask.'

He nodded and walked out. I picked up the tools and put them back into the bin where I'd stored them. Then I walked down toward the old fort on the breakwater. I knew I'd be alone there.

The pile of rubble outside the barracks was gone, but the hole in the wall remained. There weren't enough stonemasons for all the holes in Ruzor. Something glinted between the bricks, and I bent over. What looked to be a silver fragment of a necklace lay between two old bricks. Whose? How long had it been between the bricks? I studied the wall, felt its sense of age, and wondered if fragments of jewelry, or less, were all that any of us left. I swallowed and resumed walking.

The fort wasn't as quiet as I remembered. The Spidlarian iron merchant had levered aside the fallen stones to open the breakwater to his wagons and workers, and like ants, they clambered over the nearest Hamorian hull. Banging and clanging echoed across the harbor.

I kicked a fragment of shattered stone, and it splashed into the water. What could I do? I mean, what could I really do? The shattered stones piled across the breakwater showed the effectiveness of the Hamorian cannon, and hundreds of ships could rain down enough shells to turn Nylan into a pile of gravel. Out in the Easthorns, I hadn't been able to deflect a boulder or two without nearly getting pulped. I couldn't imagine stopping falling shells.

I kicked another stone chip into the harbor and looked down the breakwater at the dark hull that the Spidlarian iron merchant's crew was already chiseling apart.

If I couldn't stop falling shells, then that meant stopping the ships before the shells were fired. But how could I do that?

I kicked another stone chip, trying to let my senses touch the ship's hull through the cold water. I shivered. The days before we left seemed short, all too short for what I had to learn.

# CXVI

As the captain of the *Dylyss* had promised, a Nordlan ship did enter the bay and dock at Ruzor less than three days later. The *Feydr Queen*, like the *Eidolon* that had brought us to Candar, was an older vessel, with paddles and shining brasswork.

'Our passage is being paid by the Council,' my father said as we walked up the pier.

'So kind of them,' groused Justen, 'since they need our help.'

'They'll take us to Land's End, though, not Nylan.'

'That's five days' ride from Nylan, and they expect us . . .' Tamra went on to say how stupid it was for the Council not to have just transported us on the *Dylyss*. Somehow, I thought the Council decision perfectly understandable. Not wise, but understandable in light of their fears.

I was thinking, momentarily, of Gairloch, who remained in the stables at Ruzor, since the *Feydr Queen* had no stalls, nor equipment for handling horses. Berli had promised to take care of him, and of Rosefoot, and that was all I could ask.

As we walked up the plank, the master nodded to each of us, but the more interesting words came from the mutterings of the crew.

'. . . more damned wizards than I've ever seen . . .'

'. . . better be a bonus on this run . . .'

'. . . she's a druid . . .'

'. . . a druid? Oh, shit . . .'

'. . . three gray wizards.'

'. . . beyond shit, Murek.'

I wasn't sure that I liked being classified as beyond manure, a dubious distinction at best.

Somehow, Tamra, Krystal, and I, and Haithen, shared a cabin, while Justen and Dayala had the smallest one to themselves, and Weldein, my father, and the two other guards, Dercas and Jinsa, shared the third.

No sooner were we on board, though, than the lines were loosed and the paddle wheels engaged, and with a continuous thump, thump, thump, the *Feydr Queen* was on her way seaward.

Side by side at the polished wooden railing, Krystal and I watched Ruzor dwindle, the faintly acrid smoke from the stack swirling around us intermittently.

'Still glad you wanted to come?'

'Glad?' asked Krystal. 'No. We belong together. That's not a question of glad or sad. I wish we could stay in Ruzor, but we can't. Hamor would come and destroy it.'

So I had to find a way to destroy them, or their fleet.

'Yes.' She answered the unspoken thought, as was becoming ever more common between us.

I had an idea, only an idea, about how to do it. Of course, it would take every bit of molten iron beneath Recluce and beneath the Gulf, plus every bit of storm energy my father and Tamra could raise, plus more luck and good fortune than even seen anywhere – and it still might not work.

I shook my head.

'I'm sorry.' Krystal squeezed my hand.

'So am I, but —'

'— we have to do what we have to do,' Krystal finished.

After the *Queen* left the bay, the ship began to pitch, and Tamra hung over the rail. She had been terribly sick on the way to Candar, as well.

This time, though, Weldein stayed by her. Unlike me, the first time, he had sense enough not to talk, just to be there. The young subofficer had guts, that was certain. I still worried about his judgment, since Tamra wasn't always gentle.

Justen and Dayala stood at the railing near the stern, their hair fluffed in the slight breeze.

'I need to talk to Dayala. Would you mind?' Krystal asked.

I could sense both the concern and a need. 'No. Not too much, anyway.'

'It's for us, but I'd feel . . .' She was telling the truth about that.

I had to smile. 'Go ahead.'

She walked along the polished rail, toward the stern. As I watched, the two women leaned over the rail, enjoying the brisk breeze and the sunlight. Dayala frowned at something, and Krystal touched her arm. Finally, Dayala nodded and smiled, but the smile was a sad one.

The druid seemed to be explaining something, and I turned away. Whatever it was, Dayala could explain it far better than I could. Far better, I suspected, than Justen could.

Justen stepped away and headed forward, finally leaning on the rail beside me. 'How are you doing?'

'You mean how am I coming in developing mass destruction and disaster?'

'It might help if you didn't look at it quite that way.'

'I'm not. It's going to take a lot of iron, and a lot of order, and a storm and who knows what else.'

He waited.

'I think I can do what you did, but open a channel through the water if there are order-based storms in the skies.'

'For three hundred ships?'

'I was thinking of the water they were sailing across acting as a chaos-binding agent.'

'Steaming across,' Justen corrected automatically, before frowning. 'It might work. It would take a great deal of order.'

He was right about that, and I didn't really want to think about how much order.

'If you start preparing the channels ahead of time, you might be able to make it work.'

'How soon?'

'As soon as you set foot on Recluce.' He nodded to Krystal. 'Your consort thinks in large terms.'

'We have a large problem.' Her laugh was forced, too.

'We do, unfortunately.' Justen turned.

'What were you and Justen talking about?'

'Death, disaster, and destruction, and how to create them.' I forced a bit of a laugh. Justen slipped away.

'You don't feel that way.'

'No.' I looked at her. 'It's already getting harder, isn't it?'

'To be deceptive? Yes.'

'I don't like what I'm planning, and I don't have any better solutions. Neither does Justen.'

'That bothers him. That's what Dayala said.'

'It bothers us both, then.'

She squeezed my arm for a moment, and I could feel the warmth and the affection. I closed my eyes and enjoyed it.

'You don't do that often.'

'Not often enough.'

So Krystal and I talked and watched Tamra and Weldein and the crew until we were called to eat.

When we entered the mess, my father was sitting at the end of one of the wooden tables bolted to the floor. 'The tea's strong. You can smell that, but the biscuits are hot. The cheese will be dry and flaky.'

'Resting?' I asked.

'Thinking,' he answered with a smile.

Dry, flaky cheese or not, the biscuits and tea were good, and so was the dried fruit – if chewy.

After the plain and dry – but filling – dinner, Krystal and I went back out on deck.

The foam where the bow cut the water almost seemed to glow in the late twilight, and the pitching of the ship was less. Tamra was up near the bow, where the breeze was strongest.

'Do we ever escape our past?' I wondered, thinking about returning to Recluce.

'Not often,' interjected Justen as he and Dayala neared. 'People think they can, but' – he shrugged – 'most of us won't pay the price.'

'Why not?' asked Krystal quietly. 'Is it that high?'

'High enough,' answered Dayala. 'Who wishes to admit honestly her mistakes, and not blame them on someone else? Who can accept the understanding that we cannot change the past, only the present?'

We both shivered, and our hands reached for each other's.

# CXVII

As the *Feydr Queen* eased up to the old stone pier at Land's End, the pier that was supposed to predate the Founders, one figure waited in the late afternoon sunlight. Almost no wind crossed the harbor, unusual for Land's End. I recognized the short hair and slender frame. So did my father, but he only looked and raised his hand.

'Your mother?' asked Krystal.

I nodded as she raised her hand in greeting.

'Landers off.' One of the sailors leaped onto the pier and looped a line around one bollard and then raced down the pier to take another.

'Easy in! Easy!'

The *Feydr Queen* edged toward the pier, her sides cushioned by heavy hemp bumpers, as the sailors doubled up the lines and made the old steamer fast.

'Pleasure serving you all,' said the captain to my father as he waited for the plank to be lowered. 'Here's hoping you can do something about those Hamorians. Hate to turn the eastern trade over to them, too.'

'We'll do what we can, Captain.' My father inclined his head.

'. . . not want to get in his way . . .' came from one of the line-handlers.

'. . . avoid 'em all when you can, and be nice when you can't . . .'

Justen and his silver-haired Dayala stepped down the plank after

494 · · · L. E. MODESITT, JR.
494 · · · L. E. MODESITT, JR.

my father. Then came Tamra, and Krystal and I, then Weldein and the rest of Krystal's guard.

My father had his arms wrapped around Mother for a long time, longer than I had ever seen, or perhaps only longer than I had ever noticed. I was afraid I understood. Whatever happened, it wasn't going to be good. My mother had almost never left Wandernaught. I glanced up at Dayala, her hand and Justen's twined together. Nor did druids normally leave the Great Forest of Naclos.

I squeezed Krystal's hand and could feel her sadness, as well, as we all gathered around my mother and father.

'Donara, this is Dayala, and this is Justen.' Even as he introduced his brother to my mother, my father held her hand, almost as though he never wished to relinquish it.

'Mother,' I added, 'this is Krystal.'

'You are lovely, although that is certainly secondary to your abilities.' Her eyes took us both in. 'I do not think you would have found each other in Recluce, and that is something to rejoice in.'

The guards and Tamra stood back, but I gestured. 'This is Tamra, and Weldein, and Dercas, Jinsa, and Haithen.'

'You are all quite impressive.' Mother smiled.

Impressive? Then again, maybe we were. Impressive for the arrogance or desperation to think that we could stand up against scores of iron-hulled ships with thousands of large explosive shells.

'Cynical man,' whispered Krystal, but the words were warm, and so were the feelings behind them.

'I did prevail upon the Council for a warrant,' my mother explained to my father. 'We have two of the guest houses at the old inn, but must pay our own meals. I've arranged for mounts. I thought everyone would be happier that way, rather than in a carriage.' She glanced at me, and then at Justen. 'There weren't any mountain ponies.'

I grinned and shrugged. We walked slowly down the old pier, to the sound of the water lapping against the stones, and the shouts and rumblings as the *Feydr Queen* made ready to depart Land's End.

'Not even off-loading,' said Dercas. 'Doesn't that beat all?'

'They don't want to be anywhere near Recluce,' responded Tamra.

'Would you?' asked Haithen.

In front of us, my parents walked down the damp stones of the pier, arm in arm, as did Justen and Dayala. The town was already in shadow from the western hills, although the ancient flag – the crossed rose and blade – flying from the old keep still caught the last of the sunlight.

We passed the single-storied harbor-master's building between the old pier and the newer pier – the newer one a mere six centuries old.

From the staff above the building flew the current ensign of Recluce – the stark black ryall on a white background. The flag flapped twice in a sudden gust of wind from the hills as we walked past.

In front of us, Tamra gave her head a small shake, murmuring words to herself I could not catch. Weldein coughed slightly, and I looked back, and tried not to frown at him.

'Where's this inn?'

'To the left here and up that lane,' said Krystal. 'The bigger building is the inn, and the stable is in back of it. On the low hill to the left of the stable are the guest houses.' She definitely knew Land's End.

The gas lamps flared on at the Founders' Inn as we approached, the yellow light reflecting off the time- and foot-polished black stones of the street.

Outside the inn, a girl in clean brown leathers jumped up as we approached. 'The guest houses are to the left of the stables, and the evening meal is being served now.'

'Thank you.' My father gave a head bow.

'Is there enough space in the guest houses?' questioned Tamra.

'Each guest house has four bedrooms, and more than adequate water and showers,' my mother explained.

'. . . they believe in a lot of washing here . . .' grumbled Dercas.

'That will do you, and us, good,' said Haithen sweetly.

We stopped in front of the smaller guest house.

'If you don't mind,' said my mother with a smile, 'those of us with more history will take the smaller place.'

The rest of us walked to the second guest house, where Weldein stepped ahead and held open the door. Tamra gave him an exaggerated nod.

Krystal and I got the bedroom at the west end, which combined a sitting area holding a table and two matching armless chairs with a bedroom, and a double-width bed with a simple red oak headboard, a dressing table, and two matching wardrobes. The coverlet on the bed was a simple design of silver and blue repeating circles, without lace, and the bed had real sheets. Beyond the large bedroom and sitting room was a bathroom, with a shower, but no tub.

We unloaded some of our packs into the wardrobes and hung up our spare outfits. I leaned the staff against one of the wardrobes.

'I am going to use that shower,' Krystal said.

'You can certainly go first.' I sat down in the chair, conscious of how filthy I felt. My hair itched from salt spray, and my legs ached.

I must have been tired, because Krystal was suddenly standing there with damp hair and a towel wrapped around her saying, 'You can take your shower.'

After giving her a long and gentle kiss, I did take a shower, but the water was getting cold, probably because the sun-warmed cisterns on the roof only held so much warm water, and a lot of people were showering. Still, it felt good. Then I rinsed out my dirty clothes and hung them over the shower.

Krystal was dressed in greens, without her vest, by the time I dried off. 'What are you going to wear?'

'The grays.'

'Tamra will laugh.'

'Let her. I'm feeling perverse.'

'Good. I hope you do later.' The warm, almost-leering smile I got was worth it.

After I pulled on the grays, we walked out through the hall and down the narrow street to the inn, where the girl in brown leathers opened the door. Her eyes lingered on my grays, but only for a moment.

The public room was pleasantly cool, with some of the ancient leaded-glass windows ajar. A handful of tables were occupied, mainly by men, except for a couple in one corner and two women near the door. In the far corner, Weldein, Tamra, and the other guards sat at a large circular table. Weldein gestured. 'Commander.'

Krystal acknowledged him with a nod, and we walked across the room and joined them. Several of the men glanced from Weldein to Krystal and to the deadly blade that still seemed a part of her.

'. . . greens . . . Kyphran . . . what about the gray?'

'. . . must be a gray wizard . . . looks like trouble . . .'

'. . . another gray wizard outside.'

'. . . no good'll come of that . . .'

'. . . mercenaries, the lot of them . . . woman commander . . . colder than the Roof of the World . . .'

I gathered that the general consensus was that we looked dangerous, and I had to admit to myself that pleased me.

'You're terrible,' Krystal murmured.

'Not so much as you.'

The table was polished red oak, smoothed by care and age, with real pewter cutlery and gray tumblers. We sat down at the two chairs left, with me beside Haithen and Krystal beside Tamra.

'Redberry's in the white pitcher and ale in the gray,' offered Weldein.

'Bread's good,' mumbled Dercas, jabbing a dark crust toward the basket. 'Real good.' Another basket rested between Tamra and Krystal.

'Those will be your dying words,' laughed Jinsa.

The blond serving girl stopped beside Krystal. 'They told me to wait for you. Tonight you can have either whitefish, with baked quilla on the side, or grilled chops. They also come with the quilla, and we do have honeyed maize cakes as a sweet.' She nodded at each request and was gone.

I filled Krystal's glass with ale, then mine with redberry. 'Could I have some bread?'

'Nervous?' Krystal sipped from the gray glass, then passed the basket.

'A little.' The warm and crusty dark bread carried the scent of trilia.

'So am I.'

'Who wouldn't be?' asked Tamra.

That was the first time that Tamra ever had admitted anything.

'There's a first time for everything.' Krystal added quietly.

Tamra's brow wrinkled for a moment, but she didn't respond.

I tried not to shiver, even as I felt her concern. Each of us was definitely feeling more and more of what the other thought and felt. I chewed on a corner of the bread, then offered the basket back to Krystal.

'No, thank you.'

'You two are getting more alike,' offered Tamra.

I shrugged. If Tamra had been able to see the order tie between Justen and Dayala, she could see the one that linked us, fainter though it was.

Krystal smiled. 'Let her guess.'

Tamra raised her left eyebrow.

Weldein cleared his throat.

'Bread's really good,' said Dercas.

The serving girl returned with the fish, serving Krystal first, then Tamra, and then me. Krystal, wielding her knife as efficiently as ever, cut a slice of fish. My stomach growled – twice. How long had it been since we'd had something to eat besides bread and cheese and dried fruit – or mutton?

My parents and Justen and Dayala slipped into the public room, and sparked another round of comments.

'. . . another fellow in gray . . . and a druid . . . has to be . . . barefoot . . .'

'. . . think the big guy in black is a storm wizard . . .'

'. . . never seen so much trouble in one place . . .'

Two men left coins on the table and hastily scurried out.

'I can see why people hate Recluce,' Haithen said after swallowing a mouthful of redberry.

My mouth was so full of warm and tangy fish I didn't dare open it.

'Oh?' asked Tamra.

'It's rich, and the food is good.'

Quilla was good food? A small bite showed me it was as crunchy as I remembered, and it still reminded me of sawdust. But the whitefish was firm, and the golden sauce gave it just enough tang.

When we finished, the serving girl whisked off the big brown plates and replaced them with smaller light brown dishes, each containing a large honeyed maize cake.

'Really good stuff!' marveled Dercas.

'He travels on his gut.'

'Not a bad way to go.'

Still, for all the size of the cakes, Krystal and I did finish ours, as did everyone else. I'd forgotten how good honeyed carna nuts tasted.

As the serving girl passed, I touched her arm. 'How much?'

She shook her head. 'The black mage there is paying for your party.' She smiled as my mouth dropped open.

Tamra frowned. 'Something's not right.'

Krystal and I turned to her.

'No,' she said, 'it's not that at all. It really isn't.'

'Just a moment.' I told Krystal as I eased out of my chair and walked over to my parents and Justen and Dayala. 'You didn't have to do that.'

'After you've traveled so far?' My father grinned. 'Besides, the Institute can afford a few meals. Especially now.'

Although his expression was cheerful, like Tamra, it bothered me, but I couldn't say why. 'Thank you. It's the best dinner we've had in a long while. A long while.'

'We're glad,' my mother said. 'Enjoy the guest house. Things will be more cramped when we get to Wandernaught.'

'We need to leave right after dawn,' my father added. 'Pleasant dreams.'

While they weren't quite a dismissal, his words indicated that anything serious was going to wait, and, in a way, that was fine with me.

'He said the Institute could afford it,' I told Krystal.

'It probably can,' observed Tamra. 'Still . . .'

Weldein just looked puzzled.

'We're tired,' I explained, as Krystal rose.

Of course, we weren't that tired, but my mother had been the one to suggest we enjoy the guest house.

# CXVIII

As we climbed out of the early morning shadows and reached the top of the hill and the road broadened into the beginning of the High Road that ran from Land's End to Nylan, we passed the four black buildings surrounded by emerald grass that comprised the Black Holding of the Founders where the Council sometimes met.

'It's hard to believe that's where it all started,' I said to Krystal. The black mare skittered slightly, as if reacting to the ages of order that seeped from the structures. 'They say that Creslin built most of it with his own hands.'

A huge, nearly perfect oak dwarfed the buildings.

'Do you really believe that he planted that tree?' Tamra's voice was light.

'Of course,' I answered, just to annoy her. Besides, he probably did.

Krystal grinned and shook her head.

'Who was Creslin?' asked Weldein.

'One of the founders of Recluce,' Tamra answered. 'Supposedly, he was the greatest weather wizard ever. He changed Recluce from a desert isle into the pleasant place it is now and destroyed who knows how many fleets, including two belonging to Hamor. He was also a Westwind-trained blade who slashed his way across Candar, charming women along the way with his singing. In his later years, he was a stonemason, developed the famous green brandy, and generally served as the local equivalent of the angels.' Tamra turned in the saddle. 'Did I miss anything, Krystal?'

'Well ... you forgot Megaera. She was nearly as great a storm wizard and blade as he was, and after he went blind, she took up his blade. She almost died in childbirth, though, and they only had one child.'

A moment after Krystal finished, we looked at each other, suddenly cold inside. At that, Tamra gave us a puzzled look.

'Is that all?' mock-complained Weldein. 'You mean he didn't destroy the white wizards single-handedly?'

'No,' said Tamra. 'Justen did that – somewhat later.'

The blond guard raised his eyebrows.

'He did,' confirmed Krystal.

'Justen's around two centuries old,' I added.

'Didn't you realize what you were getting yourself into?' asked Tamra.

Weldein shifted in his saddle and tried to contain a swallow.

Ahead, I could hear my mother's clear voice. 'The cherries were early this year, but very firm, and the pearapples and apples are just coming in now . . .'

Before too long we reached the kaystone that offered an arrow to the right and the name 'Extina.'

'Do you want to stop?'

'No. There's no reason to, none at all.' Krystal's voice was remote, almost detached.

I reached out and touched her arm. 'You don't have to. The past is past, and it ought to stay there.'

'I hope so.' She looked ahead at the even paving stones of the High Road that seemed to stretch forever. 'Thank you.'

'No one on this road . . .' said Dercas.

'Not yet. This used to be the most populated end of Recluce, but people have shifted south, especially around the Feyn River. The land is better there, and more timber is grown here now. Timber and black-wooled sheep.'

Timber and black-wooled sheep . . . and legends that were hard to live up to and harder to live down.

# CXIX

Riding hard, we reached Mattra in four days, even before twilight. In between times, I read through *The Basis of Order* and thought a lot about how I could use the waters of the Gulf and the deep chaos against the iron ships of Hamor – and the cannon and troops those ships carried.

When we reached the lane leading to Uncle Sardit's, the sun hung just above the apple trees and below a few white puffy clouds. My mount's hoofs clicked on the even stones, and the muted chirping of insects whispered through the trees. The apple leaves rustled in the light breeze, and the not-quite-ripe feel of the apples seemed to fall across us.

'If you don't mind, dear, and Krystal,' my mother announced, 'I thought that you two, and Justen and Dayala, could stay with Sardit and Elisabet. Tamra and Weldein and the other guards would stay with us.' She looked at Krystal. 'That would be all right, wouldn't it? You wouldn't need personal guards that close in the middle of Recluce, would you?'

I looked at Krystal.

'That would be fine. Lerris has spoken of his uncle Sardit.' Krystal glanced at Tamra and Weldein. Both looked away from her amused glance.

When we all rode up to Uncle Sardit's and Aunt Elisabet's, they had been waiting on the side porch and came down to meet us in the side yard, in front of the shop. Sardit even wore his clean dinner clothes. The shop was not only closed, but the shutters were in place, so tightly fitted that not a crack appeared. I didn't see any sign of an apprentice.

'So . . . the crafter returns.' Sardit looked little different, short and wiry, with the salt-and-pepper hair and beard, still slightly disheveled in appearance. 'I hope you're still not putting too much pressure on your clamps.'

I did flush a little. After all, that small fault was what had led to my dangergeld.

'It is good to see you, Lerris. And this must be Krystal,' said Aunt Elisabet. I hadn't realized how much she looked like my father, and, how, in some ways, Justen and I looked more alike, although I was slightly taller than my uncle.

'Dayala.' Elisabet bowed to the druid, accompanying the gesture with a warm and real smile that I could even feel.

The druid blushed, ever so slightly, as she returned the smile. 'I have heard much of you.'

'I am sure, but please don't hold it against me after so many years.'

Justen hugged my aunt for more than a moment, and both their eyes were damp when they stepped back.

Elisabet turned to my parents, still mounted. 'Surely you'll stay for dinner.'

My father shook his head. 'We need to go . . .' His eyes were dark for a moment. 'You understand.'

'Of course. Then we'll see you in the morning.'

I watched as they rode down the stone-paved lane back toward the High Road, with Tamra and Weldein right behind them. Haithen looked back for a moment. Dercas and Jinsa didn't.

'Well ...' began my aunt. 'Lerris, you know where everything is. You show them where to wash up. You and Krystal have the rear guest room, and Justen and Dayala have the front room. By the time you're washed up, dinner will be ready.'

The spotless gray washstones and shower hadn't changed, and the towels were thick and smelled fresh. In the end, we all had showers, and mine was cold, because I let the others go first.

'Don't always be so noble.' Krystal used her towel on the fine short black and silver hair that always seemed to fall into place.

'I won't.' I let my own towel drop. 'You can warm me up.'

She started to say my name, but our lips got in the way, but only for a little because Elisabet started calling for dinner. Having an aunt who is also a mage can be disconcerting.

'You're all tired, and probably wish an early bedtime.' Aunt Elisabet's eyes twinkled for a moment as we took seats at the table. 'Dinner is simple, since I didn't know exactly when you would arrive. It's a spiced fish stew and noodles.' She set two dishes on the big circular table, and stepped back into the kitchen, returning with two baskets of bread. The cherry conserve I favored was already on the table. She turned to Dayala. 'I have some mixed greens here for you, with some new apple vinegar, and some fresh and dried fruit. The noodles, of course ...'

'That is kind.' Dayala smiled.

'We do not see druids often, and I wish I had had the chance to meet you earlier ... much earlier. Life can be so short, and ...' She shook her head as she pulled out her chair and sat.

'Let's have the noodles,' suggested Uncle Sardit.

'By all means,' said Justen.

'Where did you ride from today?' Elisabet handed the bread basket to Dayala.

'From Alaren.'

'That's a long ride, and tomorrow will be even longer.' Elisabet looked at Krystal. 'Not so much for you, I suspect. From what I understand, you're more experienced with long rides.'

'Any day on horseback is a long ride.'

'Especially when you're with those of us who aren't used to it.' She smiled at Krystal. 'Has Lerris improved any? He wasn't much for riding as a boy.'

'He rides well now.'

'So long as I have Gairloch,' I added, serving the noodles for Krystal as she held the bowl.

'Even on other mounts.' Krystal passed the noodles to Justen, and I served us the stew, trying not to choke at her suppressed amusement.

Aunt Elisabet's fish stew was good enough that it wasn't even fishy, but I still had three chunks of bread with the cherry conserve. Even Krystal had two pieces with the conserve, and for a while, no one did much besides eat. That always seemed to happen when people rode all day.

'I got a note from Perlot. He wrote something about your ordered chairs creating a stir.' Sardit broke the silence.

'Yes. That was one of my stupider accomplishments.'

'I doubt that was stupid,' said Aunt Elisabet.

Justen and Dayala nodded.

'When it's beyond good crafting it is.' I explained as quickly as possible how my putting excess order into the chairs for the subprefect had disrupted Gallos and forced me to leave precipitously. That didn't even cover leaving Deirdre and Bostric. '. . . forcing excess order where it doesn't belong leads to problems.' I smiled ruefully, before adding, 'Of course, that hasn't stopped me from doing it, just from realizing what a mess it causes.'

'Perlot said you started a new idea – children's furniture.' Sardit raised his glass and took a healthy swig of ale, and I understood another reason why my mother had thought Justen might be happier with Elisabet and Sardit.

'I was looking for something for Bostric to do, and I thought some of the gentry might pay for furniture designed for children. I was lucky. They did.'

'Perlot said that they still were.'

'I suppose I could try that in Kyphros.'

'It might be more appropriate than doing dining sets for Antona.' The mischievous feeling I got told me Krystal wasn't serious, or not totally serious.

'And this Antona is attractive?' Even Aunt Elisabet's eyes twinkled.

'She is an older woman, who runs the local . . . pleasure trade . . . rather well. She commissioned a desk, and then a dining set.'

'An ornate and excessively ornamented piece, no doubt,' laughed Sardit.

'It was tasteful, elegant, and the autarch would have been jealous,' said Krystal.

'Oh, dear,' said Elisabet. 'There is nothing so dangerous as a courtesan with intelligence and taste.'

'Maybe Kasee ought to make her Finance Minister,' I suggested, not entirely in jest.

'She might be easier to deal with than Mureas,' admitted Krystal.

'Wouldn't anyone?'

'Would you pass the bread?' asked Justen.

'And the conserve?' responded Elisabet with that glint in her eyes.

'Of course.'

The conserve pot was nearly empty, and so were the bread baskets, both for the dark bread and the white loaf.

'What else are you working on?' asked Sardit.

'I was doing some travel chests. Is there anything better than fir for lightweight things you want to be strong?'

Sardit frowned, scratching his head. 'Probably not, although they say there's a Brystan spruce that's good, but it rots too easily, especially around water, and if you're traveling a lot by water ...'

'Then you'd have an unhappy traveler after a few short years.'

He nodded. 'How are your inlays coming?'

'They're still weak. I'm cheating, in a way ...' I went on to explain about Wegel and his carving, and that led somehow to discussions of finishes, which turned into whether brasswork should be varnished.

Krystal yawned, and Aunt Elisabet stood. 'You two could talk about woodwork all night, but we all have to leave early in the morning. The Hamorian fleet won't be waiting for us to finish craft talk.'

'You're going?' I asked, realizing as I did that Krystal wasn't in the least surprised.

'I wouldn't miss it for anything. Justen and Gunnar declared I was too young for their last ... adventure, and I'm not about to miss this one.'

My eyes went to Sardit, and he smiled, not totally cheerfully. 'Someone has to keep her feet somewhere near the ground, and that's me.'

Once again, I knew I was missing something, but Krystal and I made our way to the rear guest room, immaculate, and with a double-width bed and a down mattress over a tight canvas frame, one of Sardit's innovations that I probably should have copied, if I ever had the chance. The combination made for a comfortable sleep.

The quilt coverlet was a light silvered green with a darker green star pattern, and I didn't remember it.

'It bothers you that your aunt and uncle are coming, doesn't it?' asked Krystal as she pulled off her boots, and then her shirt.

'Yes and no. Aunt Elisabet has always been more than I think most people realize, but I think my mother's coming, too, and there's nothing either my mother or Sardit can do.' I put my boots in the corner and hung my clothes on the pegs in the wardrobe, next to Krystal's.

She turned back the coverlet. 'They don't think you can win, and they don't want to be alone.'

# CXX

## The Great Forest, Naclos [Candar]

The three druids and the ancient stand before the sands, watching as darkness boils out of the sand map of Candar and rolls toward the dark isle beyond the Gulf. Yet a whiteness surrounds the darkness that creeps across the blue sand of the Gulf.

Above the four rustle the branches of the oak more ancient than any kingdom or any legend of any kingdom, save those of the angels.

'Once again, the armies of darkness and light come together,' declares the ancient.

'But the lovers . . . they wield the demons' towers for order. What a song that would be. Perhaps someone will sing it,' suggests the frail silver-haired singer.

'Dayala has left, and she knew there will be no last song, Werlynn,' says Syodra. 'What would you sing? Or do you dream that your son's heritage will prevail?'

'There are always songs. The singers change, but the songs endure.'

'I admire your faith, but this darkness is soulless and enduring, and the machines only imprison order and do not sing.'

'They will not prevail,' declares the ancient.

'Would Dayala offer chaos against them? Even she would not,' says Frysa.

'No. She cannot stand against the surges of order and chaos that time alone creates, and she knew that. Neither will we.'

'What will happen then?' asks Syodra.

'The songs will endure,' Werlynn says softly.

'So will the Balance,' adds the ancient, 'no matter how great the price, no matter who pays it.'

The branches of the ancient oak rustle in the center of the Great Forest.

# CXXI

Dawn came too early, but we struggled up and into our clothes with only a hasty washing. I couldn't believe that Aunt Elisabet had flake rolls for everyone and fruit and even egg pies – or that we were on the road not much after the sun peeked above the horizon, with the whole house closed up as tight as Uncle Sardit's shop. That was another thing that bothered me, cheerful as Aunt Elisabet was about it.

It was still early when we turned to the right off the High Road and followed the narrower way into Wandernaught. Hoofs clipped on the stone of the road as we rode into the center of the town. The door to the old post house was open, and beyond it a thin line of smoke puffed from the main chimney of the Broken Wheel, a two-story stone and timber building and still the only inn in Wandernaught, as it had been, according to my father, for centuries. The owners changed, but not the inn itself, or not much. The facade and sign had been freshly painted, but in the same cream and brown colors.

Beyond the square, a youngster sat on the step of the coppersmith's, waiting for someone. I waved, and he waved back, his eyes a bit wide at the sight of six riders so early in the day, although riders to the Institute were not that uncommon. Two heavy-looking barrels stood outside Lerack's dry and leather goods, almost as if they had been rolled the hundred cubits from the cooper's.

I shifted my weight in the saddle as we rode west and out of town. On the south side of the road rose those gentle rolling hills that held the groves – cherry, apple, and pearapple. A low stone fence separated the trees from the road.

On a low hilltop in the middle of the groves was the Institute, just a single low black stone building. 'There it is,' I told Krystal.

'Never should have told him to put it there,' said Justen.

I looked at my uncle.

'We stood right there – that was a long while ago, when I was young and about to build the fire-eye and the land engine – and I asked him if he were going to move the Council here, and he said it was a good idea. Instead, he created the Institute and put it there. Waste of a good hilltop.'

'The trees didn't enjoy the view,' Sardit said.

'Sardit.' My aunt sounded slightly exasperated.

Dayala studied the trees, then nodded. 'They are good trees.'

I thought so, but she'd certainly know better than I would have.

Both my parents and Tamra, Weldein, and the other three guards were waiting, their mounts saddled, and packs in place, when we reached my parents' house.

'You look as if you had a good rest.' Tamra's eyes flicked to Krystal.

'It was very nice,' answered Krystal, and I could sense her amusement, along with a touch of sadness, almost pity.

Weldein's face was professionally cheerful.

'Did you sleep well?' my mother asked.

'Very well.' I leaned over in the saddle, managing to hang on, and kissed her cheek. 'How about you?'

'We managed. Your father worries too much, but he always has.'

'You have gotten to be a better rider,' said Krystal as the others mounted up.

We rode back through Wandernaught, and the same boy sat on the coppersmith's step, and his eyes did widen as we passed this time, probably because of the four armed guards – or maybe it was the combination of armed troopers, and black and gray mages.

The High Road south was the same as ever, straight, wide, level, and a trace boring.

I did smile as I saw the sign for Enstronn.

'What's so amusing?' asked Krystal.

'Here's where I met Shrezsan . . .'

'Shrezsan?'

'Leithrrse's old love, the one —'

Tamra and Krystal looked at each other.

'What is so strange about Lerris's remembering that?' asked my father. 'It's an old Recluce name. There have been several Shrezsans. I think Justen was sweet on her great-grandmother or maybe several greats older than that. Anyway, this one must have been something. Leithrrse named a ship after her.'

'He did?' Krystal looked at me. 'You didn't mention that part.'

'I didn't know.'

'Well,' my father added with a chuckle, 'I didn't know it was named after her until now, but it follows. He was a trader, and he had a ship named the *Shrezsan*, one of the newer steel-hulled Hamorian merchants. I remember the name because it was after

Lerris left when I found out that they were building steel-hulled warships.'

'So you were right,' said Tamra, shifting her weight in the saddle of the roan.

'I have been known to be right, once in a while,' I teased.

'Once in a great while.'

'A little more than that,' suggested Krystal.

After Enstronn came the kaystones for Clarion, and then Sigil, and we stopped for water at the waystation where the trader had tried to force me into selling my staff. The waystation was the same – tiled roof, windowless walls, hard wooden benches.

Only a bit over three years – had it been such a short time? Less than four years before I had been walking the High Road, whistling, unsuccessfully trying to flirt with the woman named Shrezsan, using my staff on a foreign trader, not even knowing its powers, not knowing that Tamra and Krystal even existed.

I took a deep breath as I remounted.

'Memories?' asked Krystal.

'It seems like a lifetime ago.'

'It was.'

She was right about that. You can go home, but it's not home, and maybe that was why Aunt Elisabet had wanted us to stay with her.

As the faint black line that was the wall of Nylan appeared just about the time the sun touched the horizon, Weldein rode closer to Tamra. 'Where will we be staying in Nylan?'

Although I wasn't looking at her, but toward the Eastern Ocean, I could sense Krystal's smile.

'I don't know,' Tamra answered.

'There are the Council guest quarters,' my mother said, turning in her saddle.

'Wonderful,' mumbled Justen.

'It's for Council guests, and you are all certainly Council guests,' responded my mother. She smiled. 'I already made the arrangements when I got the warrant.'

'To save a few coins?' asked Justen.

'Those don't matter,' my mother responded cheerfully, 'as you of all people should know. The Council guest quarters are nicer, and besides —'

'—it reminds the Council that they did invite us,' finished my father.

Like the High Road itself, the walls of Nylan were unchanged also –

solid black stone, sixty cubits high, without embrasures, crenelations, moats, ditches – and only the single gate that, so far as anyone knew, had never been closed.

# CXXII

## Freetown Port, Freetown [Candar]

The lines of uniformed troops, each with blue-steeled rifle and cartridge belt, stand waiting on the piers that jut into the Great North Bay.

From the bridge of the *Emperor's Pride*, Marshal Dyrsse surveys the tan blocks of troops arrayed below.

'I trust you find the numbers sufficient,' says Fleet Commander Stupelltry. 'More than ten thousand just there. Recluce has less than three thousand, and they are scarcely trained to our standards. Nor are they armed with rifles.'

'The troops will be sufficient, Fleet Commander, provided your ships and guns are adequate.' Dyrsse smiles out at the hulls in the bay that seem to stretch for kays. 'I trust they are rigged for storm running and heavy seas. Very heavy seas. They will encounter those.'

'I have ensured that, Marshal. We are ready to undertake our duty, and all are aware of the ordeal ahead.'

'Good. Perhaps you would care to join me later, in a glass of true Hamorian wine, to celebrate the beginning of accomplishing our duty to the Emperor, since you have found the local vintages to be less than adequate?'

'I must ensure the loading goes according to plan.'

'And after that?'

'We steam.'

'Then you will join me?'

'Then I will join you.'

'Good.' Dyrsse nods and steps toward the rear of the bridge, his hand briefly touching the polished wooden rail, before he steps out into the sunlight and onto the iron ladder.

Stupelltry does not smile, nor does the captain, nor the ratings who have stood silently on the hard iron plates of the bridge deck.

# CXXIII

Krystal and I left the guest quarters while the others were still washing up that morning. The Council guest quarters – two stories with paneled rooms, and most amenities – were on the grounds of the Brotherhood's establishment. When I had first come to Nylan to prepare for my dangergeld, I'd never really questioned who and what belonged to whom. It had seemed rather useless since I was leaving Recluce.

While Krystal stopped to adjust her scabbard, I spent a moment letting my senses drop into the rocks beneath and to the north of the port, trying to locate the iron that supposedly lay beneath Recluce.

It wasn't hard, and the jolt ran through me like cold water.

*Grrrrrr!*

'Oh . . . I felt that.'

'Sorry. I was trying to seek out order sources.'

'That was obvious,' she said.

'I said I was sorry,' I snapped back.

'I think you need to eat,' suggested my consort, and she was right, even if she needed nourishment as much as I did.

Early as it was, dock workers and sailors were on the streets of the lower harbor. A horse-drawn wagon creaked down the center of the street toward the public pier where a single Sarronnese trader lay tied up.

'I am hungry,' I confessed. 'Something must be open early.'

'I hope so.' Krystal's stomach growled, almost as mine did. 'Why did you want to leave so early?'

I shrugged. 'My father said we had to meet the Council at noon, and after that . . . I just don't know. I wanted to spend some time here with you.'

A porter with a hand truck jumped off the wagon that had stopped in front of the dry-goods store, and we slowed for a moment, then dodged around him. A shadow fell across the street, then passed, cast by a small and fast-moving cloud. Out in the harbor small whitecaps tipped the short, choppy waves.

The strangest feeling swept over me. All the buildings, solid black stone and all, somehow seemed lopsided, as if they were tilting toward me and about to fall. I blinked several times, trying to rein in the sense of order-chaos imbalance. Krystal gripped my hand, and we looked at each other.

'Do you feel that?' I asked.

'Like everything is off balance?'

I nodded.

'Maybe we can eat there – and sit down.' Krystal pointed to the sign with a black waterspout.

The public room was empty, but a single serving girl smiled and pointed to a corner table. As I walked past the first tables, I saw an antique Capture board lying on the empty corner table. There were boards as old in the chest at my parents', but, outside of a few games with Aunt Elisabet as a child, I'd never played.

I waved to the serving girl in a red cap, and she scurried over.

'Do you have any fresh bread and heavy conserves?' asked Krystal. 'And some hot cider?'

'Might as we could manage that. And you?' the server asked me.

'I'd like the same, but with sausage.'

'That'll be five, ser.'

The serving woman returned with two steaming mugs, setting them down in turn with muted thumps on the dark wood table. Krystal took the mug, sniffing it and letting the steam surround her face before taking a sip.

A steaming loaf of orangish bread and a cherry conserve arrived before either of us had taken more than a sip of the cider.

'Be a moment more for the sausage, ser.'

'Fine.' I turned to Krystal. 'Go ahead. The bread's warm.'

'You can have some of that, too,' she pointed out.

So she did, and I did, and the sausage and another loaf of the orange bread arrived as we were finishing her loaf.

Then I dug into the sausage, a huge, dark, and spicy cylinder. 'Are you sure you wouldn't like a bite?' I mumbled.

Krystal finished a mouthful of bread and conserve. 'A bite. Just a bite.'

When we looked up at each other from the empty plates, I grinned at Krystal. 'You weren't that hungry?'

She laughed.

I left six coppers on the table, and we walked out into the sunlight.

'Where are we going?'

'Where we've been before.' I tugged her hand, and she followed me until we came to the harbor. I looked up and down until I saw the supply store, the one with its name in three scripts – Temple, Nordlan, and Hamorian. Then I started walking.

I could sense Krystal's amusement by the time we sat on the harbor wall by the fourth pier and opposite the store. The pier was empty, but the last time we had been seated there, I recalled, there had been a single small sloop tied up. Krystal's hair had been long and tied up with silver cords, and I had just bought her the blade she still wore.

'We were sitting here, and I asked, "What will you do?" And you didn't answer me. Then, right over there a boy and a girl ran, and she was carrying some model of his, but she gave it back.'

Krystal smiled. 'You said that they were like us, but you didn't know why.'

'And you didn't agree.'

'I didn't say that,' she said. 'I didn't say anything. I was afraid to agree or disagree.'

'Now?' I asked.

'I think you were right. We're still here, and we still don't know what will happen.'

'Except that we're going to meet with the Council.'

'Are you worried? You don't feel that way,' she mused.

'Not about the Council. If they had to request that we return, that's really an admission that we don't have anything to fear from them. Hamor, now that's another story.' I felt a chill, and shivered, not sure whether it was my chill or Krystal's. I looked into her black eyes.

'Mine,' she admitted, taking my hand again. 'I still worry about the Council. I don't think they're honest, at least not with themselves.'

I just waited.

'They sent out Isolde. You remember her?'

I remembered Isolde, and her blade, and the way in which she had dismembered Duke Halloric's champion – and the fact that the Duke had been assassinated shortly thereafter.

'Then they killed the Hamorian regents, and destroyed some ships with the invisible black ships. And they didn't want us on those ships, even if it meant the difference in whether we could help. How long have they been playing this hidden game?' The fingers of Krystal's right hand tightened around the corner of the wall where we sat.

'Ever since Justen destroyed Frven, I think. Before that, Recluce paraded its power.'

'I don't like sneaks.'

There was that. Somehow the straightforward honesty of people like Creslin and Dorrin and Justen had been lost. Or maybe it had always been that way, and the straightforward people had always been few. Was that why my father had founded the Institute?

I frowned. Had dealing with power made me more cautious?

Was that the inevitable road to corruption? Was I losing my own directness?

'Don't. Please don't.' Krystal squeezed my hand.

For a while, we sat on the wall and watched the people come and go, but no young dangergelders walked our way, and no children with model boats, and the light wind brought only the smells of the shops and the harbor, not of the past.

And beneath even Recluce, I could sense the unrest, the growling growth of the chaos I knew I must harness before long.

Krystal tightened her lips, and squeezed my hand.

When we finally walked back uphill away from the harbor, it almost seemed as if we had left another part of our younger selves behind.


# CXXIV
## The Great North Bay, Freetown [Candar]

From the Great North Bay steam the ships, smoke plumes rising at an angle into the morning sun, the smoke white against the blue-green of the sky above the Eastern Ocean.

On each ship, each of the three gray steel turrets is aligned fore and aft, the two forward turrets aimed along the course ahead, the rear at the wake behind. Although each turret holds but a single cannon, the diameter of each is two spans, enough to throw a five-stone shell more than five kays, or a ten-stone shell not quite half that distance.

Beneath the iron decks, the polished shells are racked and ready, and the sailors hum, or sing. Some look nervously in the direction of Recluce. Others look down, but most go about their daily routines.

Only the faintest touch of white graces the low waves as the Grand Fleet steams eastward.

In the stateroom reserved for the grand commander, Marshal Dyrsse carefully pours the pale amber wine into two goblets, then offers the tray on which they rest to the fleet commander.

'To success.' The fleet commander takes a goblet and raises it.

'To the success of the Emperor,' responds Dyrsse. 'And to duty.' Both sip.

'Ah, you would deny yourself success?' asks Stupelltry.

'I succeed when the Emperor does. And we have both waited long for this time, for the time to put the black isle in its place.' Dyrsse takes another sip of the amber vintage. 'Duty is more important than success. With luck, anyone can succeed. Not everyone can complete his duties.'

'In success, we accomplish our duty.' Stupelltry takes another sip of wine.

Dyrsse frowns ever so slightly, but drinks.

In the west, the faintest of clouds begin to gather, while beneath Candar and beneath the iron backbone of Recluce, the deeps tremble.

# CXXV

I brushed my grays a last time, and Krystal pulled on the braided vest.

'Do we look impressive enough?' I asked, glancing around the small oak-paneled room and the two single beds we had pulled together side by side. While I could not see the harbor from the window, I could sense that two of the Brotherhood's ships had pulled into the port since our breakfast and morning tour of the harbor, and that some considerable activity surrounded them.

'You look impressive. I don't know about me.'

'You're the one who looks impressive.'

'You're obviously in love.'

'I wouldn't deny it.' I hugged her gently, not wanting to dishevel her. 'I suppose I should bring my staff.'

'I suppose you should. Tamra will.'

We stepped into the corridor and walked down the hall and down the stairs to the foyer. Everyone was there, except Justen and Dayala.

'As usual,' muttered my father, 'Justen runs on his own schedule.'

'Don't get excited, dear,' my mother said. 'I think he's coming down the stairs now.'

Justen, like me and Tamra, wore grays, and a look of disgust. Dayala remained barefoot in the soft brown clothes she always wore.

'Before we're off to see the mighty Council, we need to confer,' said Justen.

'We need to agree on a rough plan,' my father concurred, looking at me as Justen did.

My thoughts were rough, indeed, but I offered what I had. 'There's a great deal of elemental, or near elemental chaos, beneath the Gulf, and the iron runs from the inland ranges in a line out under the Gulf. The water's relatively shallow there ... from what I can sense.'

'Only about fifty to seventy cubits until you get several kays offshore,' added Justen,' and then it runs around a hundred fifty and drops off gradually.'

'If you' – I looked at my father – 'and Tamra can call up the storms, and Justen can bring in as much order as possible, I think I can direct that chaos in order-tubes, as Justen did in the Easthorns, up under the Hamorian ships.'

Tamra looked puzzled for a moment, then nodded.

'But we'll need a place where we can see.'

'There's a flat space on the cliffs near the west end of the wall,' suggested Aunt Elisabet. 'You can see the Gulf and the harbor.'

'Rather rough, I'd say,' observed Justen, 'but there's not much strategy involved here. Anything else?'

I couldn't think of anything, except now that I'd spoken I just hoped I could deliver that chaos as planned.

Getting to the Council chamber involved walking perhaps three hundred cubits eastward through the emerald-green lawns and along the stone walks Krystal, Tamra, and I had left more than three years earlier.

A few about-to-be-dangergelders sat on benches or walls.

'Darkness! One of the big mages, the fellow in black ...'

'Are the ones in gray ... are they gray wizards?'

'The blade – she's some high officer ...'

I glanced at Krystal. 'You look impressive.'

'Only to the impressionable.'

I could sense she was slightly pleased, and so was I.

The waiting room outside the Council chamber was large enough for all of us, with some room to spare. A young man and woman in black stood by the closed double doors.

My father walked up to them. 'I am Gunnar, from the Institute, and we had a meeting scheduled with the Council.'

'Let me see if they're ready for you.' The man slipped inside the door, only to return almost immediately. 'The Council will see you now,' he announced with a smile, holding the door open.

The woman offered Tamra a tentative smile.

My mother, Elisabet, Sardit, and the guards remained in the waiting area, although Weldein's hand seemed to stray to the hilt of his blade. Tamra raised a single eyebrow, and he took a deep breath.

I let Justen and my father lead the way, and I lugged my staff along, as did Tamra. The room was large enough, but somehow seemed confined, despite the windows overlooking the Eastern Ocean and the high ceilings. Every item in the Council Room seemed dark – black tables, dark gray stone floors, immaculately polished, and even black frames on the pictures of the silver-haired man and red-haired woman on the wall behind the council table.

The Founders looked sad, somehow, I decided, for all of their handsome and clean features. The painter had captured a darkness behind Creslin's eyes, perhaps because the picture had been done in the long years when Creslin was blind, perhaps not.

My father gave the slightest of nods to the three behind the table, who had stood as we entered and remained standing.

My father straightened. 'You know me, and this is Justen, of whom I'm sure you have heard much. This is Dayala, representing the druids of Naclos. You may recall Tamra, Krystal, and my son Lerris.'

'The Council has invited your assistance, Masters Gunnar and Justen, and that of Tamra and Lerris. I am Heldra.' The thin-faced woman nodded to the others who sat behind the table. 'This is Maris, the Council's representative from the traders, and Talryn, who represents the Brotherhood.'

I knew Talryn, impossibly broad-shouldered and short and stocky, but he wore black instead of the gray I had last seen him wearing. Maris was thin like Heldra, but sported a squared-off beard that he fingered as he nodded.

'We appreciate the assistance of the Great Forest,' responded Heldra, her eyes on Dayala.

'Thank you,' the druid answered quietly.

'Lerris looks somewhat . . . more mature,' observed Talryn.

'The results of my efforts to slow Hamor,' I said.

Talryn frowned, and I had a sense of his order probing, but that probe seemed tentative, almost weak. I smiled politely, and Krystal's wry amusement bubbled up around me.

'You seem to have brought a few others beyond the scope of the invitation,' Heldra said.

'We did.' My father offered the words with a smile.

'They were not . . . invited . . .'

After begging for help, for the Council to quibble . . . Krystal nudged me gently, and I bit back the words.

'Sers,' said Justen easily. 'With the exception of Gunnar, I know of no one in our group who has any intention of remaining on Recluce after the situation is dealt with. Commander Krystal is on leave, with the permission of the autarch, and Dayala and I will certainly not remain long here, nor will the small guard that accompanied Lerris and Krystal, and Tamra.'

'Lerris and Krystal?' asked Maris, still fingering his beard.

'Although Krystal is the commander of the Finest, the autarch also has some regard for Lerris, for those talents that you have previously noted, and for Tamra.'

'That seems to be settled,' rumbled Talryn, 'although I doubt that it ever need have been raised.' His glance at Heldra would have removed old finish from any piece of furniture. Had I misjudged him?

'I only spoke for our heritage,' said Heldra evenly.

'We won't have any demon-damned heritage, Heldra, if they can't help,' snapped Maris.

'That is one way of putting it.' Heldra inclined her head and smiled toward Maris.

'Your time will come,' said Maris politely. 'Even the Founders' did, and they had a lot more to offer than you.'

'The business at hand is Hamor,' said Talryn, 'and what aid Gunnar and his group will be able to offer us.'

'It is not a question of help,' my father said slowly, 'as we all know. If we cannot stop Hamor, neither can the Brotherhood, and Nylan will be destroyed, and Recluce will fall.'

'What are you going to do with the Brotherhood troops and the marines?' asked Justen.

'Have them ready to repulse any invaders, of course,' snapped Heldra, straightening. 'Any threat to Recluce.'

'Where?'

Talryn's abrupt gesture cut off Heldra's response before she uttered a word. 'You have some concerns, Justen?'

'You can do as you wish. You are the Council. I might point out,' said Justen levelly, 'that the Hamorian fleet will probably attempt to drop enough of their cannon shells on Nylan to turn it into finely powdered black gravel. It might be wiser to evacuate the city and marshal the troops where they would not be so obvious a target.' He bowed his head politely for an instant.

'Evacuate Nylan? That has never been contemplated.'

'It should have been,' suggested Talryn, 'but that is our worry, and not the reason for this meeting.' His eyes blazed at Heldra for a moment, but the thin-faced woman ignored his glance. 'We have learned that the Hamorian fleet left the Great North Bay this morning.'

'They could be here as early as tomorrow,' added Maris. 'They're steaming quickly.'

'Might I ask exactly what plans you have?' asked Heldra, her voice dripping honey. 'Justen? Gunnar?'

'You could ask,' Justen said almost as politely as Heldra, 'but that must remain with us.'

'I had hoped . . .'

'I'm sure you did,' added my father. 'But you can rest assured that we would not have removed ourselves from the relative safety of Kyphros to Recluce without some thought of success.'

I wasn't so sure about that thought of success, but I just nodded, my senses still tied in a shadowy way to the order beneath Recluce.

*Grrrrruurrrrr* . . .

Loud as that disruption felt to me, no one, besides Krystal, even seemed to feel it. Were their perceptions elsewhere, or was I becoming more sensitized?

'And from where will you defend Nylan?' Heldra's voice was harsh, almost shrill.

'From where we must,' answered Justen smoothly. His eyes flickered to me.

'From the headlands before the western wall,' I added, 'where we can see the Hamorians.'

'I see,' remarked Heldra.

'If that is all,' my father said, 'then we will make our preparations, and I trust that you will make yours.' He looked at Talryn. 'I might suggest that what is left of the trio be employed to keep the Hamorian ships off shore, at least to begin with.'

'It will be considered.'

'Good.'

My father smiled, and turned, and we followed him out.

On the stone walk outside, as we headed back in the general direction of the Council guest quarters, Tamra snorted. 'Much good that was.'

'It was useful,' Justen said. 'We know that they cannot do anything, nor will they try, beyond suggesting the city be evacuated and sending two ships out.' He continued walking downhill.

'Has Recluce always been so weak?' asked Weldein politely, fingering his blade.

'Not until recently,' said Justen.

'Periodically,' said Elisabet at the same time.

They looked at each other. Then Justen bowed to his sister.

'Outside of the time from Dorrin until the fall of Fairhaven – the white wizards,' my aunt explained, 'Recluce has always relied on its great mages to save it, and they have. They will this time. The price has usually been exorbitant, but concealed from the outside. Creslin lost his sight for most of his life; he and Megaera died young and had but a single child. Dorrin also had periods of blindness, died relatively young, and in obscurity. When Fairhaven fell, most of Nylan was destroyed by storms, as were most of Recluce's warships.'

Weldein frowned. 'One does not hear this . . .'

'Do you think it would be in Recluce's interest?' asked Justen.

'There has always been a hidden corruption in Recluce,' added Tamra, 'where the whole truth has been hidden behind partial truth.'

'It goes back to the myth of the Founders,' said Justen. 'Creslin is portrayed as infallible, but he made a lot of mistakes. That's always the case. The Council he founded, over the years, has become more and more intent on portraying itself as infallible, and that always leads to corruption.'

In a way, I wondered if my own father had been corrupted in a silent bargain. The Brotherhood had said little about his use of order to extend his life, and he, in turn, had said little about the increasing use of the Brotherhood's efforts to ensure that Candar remained divided, fragmented, and chaotic.

Now, I had the feeling they both might end up paying, and so might Krystal and I.

I touched the order deep beneath Recluce and the Gulf, trying to gently coax it nearer to the surface. Justen caught my eye and nodded.

Yes, we probably would end up paying, but I kept working, even as Krystal touched my arm and guided me back toward the guest quarters, as my thoughts continued to open the order channels Justen had suggested I start early.


# CXXVI


From the old stone bench outside the guest quarters, I looked out at the clear blue waters of the Eastern Ocean, at the puffy clouds over the water, and at the single steamer puffing eastward through the afternoon toward Nordla.

My stomach growled, reminding me that it had been a long time since breakfast. 'I'm hungry. Do you want to eat in the Brotherhood halls?'

'Do you?' countered Krystal.

'Not really, but we have to eat somewhere.'

'I'm not hungry . . .'

'Like at breakfast? We haven't eaten since then.'

Eventually we walked back down toward the harbor, and I was glad I'd brought my staff. We passed a store with the name 'Brauk Trading' painted on the glass. The doors were bolted, but two men inside were carrying things to a wagon by the side door.

'Deception, again,' Krystal said. 'No one says anything, but those who are favored get the word.'

'Let's see.'

We kept walking along the waterfront, the stores on our right, the harbor to the left, past a door with just a crossed candle and a rose on the sign, but it was bolted shut, and no one was there. The next place, a coppersmith's, was open, and a small white-haired man sat in the back at a bench. No one else was in the shop.

Beyond the coppersmith's was a narrow alley. A handful of traders were loading a line of wagons.

'... can't take it all, Dergin ...'

'... take what we can ... won't be gravel left here tomorrow ...'

'... shut up and load ... want to get my ass clear ...'

Anger began to rise, both in me and in Krystal. We exchanged glances and walked on, past more shuttered stores. Then we turned around and walked back to the coppersmith's.

Inside the doorway were a pair of kettles on an old table, both with curved spouts and green porcelain handles.

We walked past the kettles toward the coppersmith, except I stopped to look at a pair of hinges on the wall shelf. Each was shaped like a beast I'd never seen, with a long neck, and the hint of scales, furled wings, four clawtipped legs, and a barbed tail.

'Fearsome creature,' said Krystal.

'That be the dragon, Lady Blade, or that is what the fellow who drew it for me claimed.' The smith barely reached Krystal's shoulder. 'Everyone looks at them, but' – he shrugged – 'no one wants them.'

'Have you heard about the battle tomorrow?' I asked gently.

'Some nonsense about a fleet from Hamor. Yes, I've heard it.' The coppersmith shook his head.

'It's true,' Krystal said. 'There may not be much left of Nylan by tomorrow night or the night after. The Hamorians have mighty cannon.'

'I've heard those sorts of tales for months, Lady Blade.' The coppersmith gave a faint smile. 'And if this time, they be true, then they be true. I am too old to cart everything off into the hills, and then back.' He shrugged. 'All gone. My son, my daughter, they never came back. Ellyna, she's been gone for years. I have the shop. And if I don't . . . then what?'

I tried not to swallow. So did Krystal.

'Please . . . be not sad, Ser Mage.' His eyes flicked to the staff.

'I'm also a woodcrafter,' I said almost in protest. For us not to be sad was easy enough for him to say. We'd both seen what a handful of Hamorian ships had done to Ruzor, and there were easily ten times that many likely to be turning their cannon on Nylan.

'Your kindness . . . that I appreciate. Many have walked past, and said nothing.' He licked his lips. 'I am not without some wit. When traders unload their stores and cart them off, they do so only in times of peril. What can I unload? Two kettles, ingots of copper and tin, and a pair of dragon hinges that have watched buyers for years?'

'You should leave.' Krystal looked at the smith with the thinning white hair.

'Had you come twenty years ago, Lady, I would.' He grinned at me, and I had to grin back. 'Now . . . I am content.'

'Hamor will destroy the city,' I said gently.

'As times have changed, it may be no great loss, ser.'

I tried not to wince, even though that thought had crossed my mind at points. Recluce was no paradise, and the Council was certainly less than impressive. But . . . for most people, it was still better than what Hamor offered. Not much, perhaps, and that bothered me, too. 'You could just take a long walk tomorrow,' I suggested.

'Perhaps I will, ser. Perhaps I will.'

But I could feel that he wouldn't. I looked back to the dragon hinges. Krystal nodded.

'How much for the hinges?'

'You may have them.'

'I couldn't do that.'

The old deep green eyes looked into mine. 'I will make you a bargain. If the ships do not destroy Nylan, as you feel they will, then you return and pay me five silvers. If they do, then you must keep the hinges and put them on a chest for all to see. You do make chests?'

'I have made a few,' I admitted.

He nodded. 'You measured them with your eyes, and you saw their use.'

I reached for my purse.

His frail hand touched my arm. 'No. I trust you, and that trust is not misplaced. It is time for the dragons to fly.' He picked up a packet of cloth and walked to the shelf, carefully winding the soft gray cloth around the dragon hinges. Then he handed the package to Krystal. 'On your blade. Lady, and both your spirits.'

Krystal took the cloth-wrapped dragons, but we just stood there.

'Now . . . you must go.'

The little smith practically pushed us out of the shop, and we let him. Then he said, 'Take care of my dragons.' And he closed the door.

We just stood there for a long moment.

I swallowed, and my stomach growled, and then I flushed.

'You're upset,' Krystal said, 'and you're embarrassed.'

'Yes. It just seems like the innocent get hurt, those and the helpless. I couldn't make him leave. If we can't protect Hamor, then he won't have anything left anyway. I don't know. The traders will be fine. So will the Brotherhood, one way or another.' I stopped and just let myself feel. 'You're angry, too.'

'Yes.'

I took her hand, and my stomach growled again.

'And you're hungry, still,' she pointed out. 'What about there?'

At the end of the crossroad was a small cafe, one dark oak door open. We walked down a hundred cubits or so, and I peered in the open door.

'You want dinner?' asked a slender young man, setting down a chair. 'All we have is whitefish, and you will have to eat quickly. We are packing up the kitchen, but Mama would not turn away someone hungry.' He grinned, revealing enormous and wide-gapped front teeth. 'Or with coins.'

'We'll eat quickly.'

'Not too quickly. You must enjoy it, and the fish – it would not keep anyway.' He led us across a half-empty floor to a corner booth. Scuffs in the oak showed where more tables had been. The booth had dark leather upholstered benches. As we sat, he added, 'I'll bring you some ale.' Then he glanced at my staff. 'Is greenberry all right? The redberry keg is sealed.'

'Fine.'

He darted off, scooping up two chairs as he went.

'I wonder how good it will be. They're certainly packing up.' Krystal stifled a yawn.

'You're tired.'

'So are you.'

'Here you go.' The young fellow had already scurried back with two mugs and two pitchers, and was gone with another pair of chairs.

I poured mugs for each of us, and we'd barely taken a full swallow when he'd returned with a huge loaf of golden bread. 'No spreads or conserves, but it's fresh.'

Off he went with the last pair of chairs, only to come back with a woman, who smiled as they picked up a table and eased it through the double doors.

I broke off a corner of the bread. He'd been right. The bread was fresh enough that it still steamed, and both Krystal and I began to eat, trying to ignore the dismantling of the cafe as we munched through about half a loaf.

'Here's the fish, and there's even some beans. I forgot about them.'

We looked at two huge platters heaped with whitefish under a cream sauce.

'Darkness . . . I . . . there's so much . . .'

'Don't worry. We would have had to throw it out. So you got it all. What you can't eat the dog will.' And he raced off again.

At that we laughed and began to eat. The fish was good, the sauce even better, better even than at the Founders' Inn.

'Makes me feel . . . I don't know . . .'

'Because it's something else good that's going to be destroyed?' asked Krystal.

'I think so.'

'Me, too.' Krystal pushed the platter back. 'I'm full, and I can't eat any more.'

I couldn't, either. We'd each eaten perhaps half of our platters. I looked around, but I didn't look long because the young fellow came hustling back in. I waved.

'How did you like it?'

'It was wonderful, maybe the best I've ever had,' I admitted. 'How much do we owe you?'

'I don't know. Usually, it's about five coppers, but you get more, and there's more of a choice . . .'

'Here.' I handed him two silvers. 'It's a meal we won't forget.'

He just looked at the coins.

'Call it a gift from the dragons,' Krystal added impishly.

'Thank you. Thank you.'

'Just get on with saving the place for others,' I said as we left, but he was already carting out some large kettles to the overflowing wagon in the back alley.

Somehow, with all my traveling, I'd only found two places where hospitality wasn't determined totally by coins – Kyphros, and I thought of Barrabra, and Recluce, where we had just gotten a wonderful meal even while the owners were trying to save their cafe. Maybe that showed that any country that fostered even some of that deserved saving. I hoped so.

The sun was touching the Gulf of Candar when we walked back up to the guest quarters. Unlike the port section below, the Brotherhood grounds were scarcely deserted, with dangergelders sitting on the walls and benches.

'. . . leave at dawn . . .'

'. . . sleep in . . . no big problem . . .'

'. . . you want to tell that to Cassius?'

'He's the real black mage – black all over.'

'There they are . . . she's the head of the forces of Kyphros . . . Trehonna says he's one of the great gray mages, built a mountain once . . .'

I tried not to pay any attention as eyes turned on us.

'. . . feeling a little modest, dear?' whispered Krystal.

'What about you?'

We both blushed and kept walking until we were inside our room. I set my staff in the corner, and Krystal unbelted her blade.

'I ate too much.'

'It was good, though.'

We sat on the edge of one of the single beds. Krystal unwrapped the dragons.

'They are beautiful, if strange.'

They were beautiful, and I could see them on a dark oak chest, one with no ornamentation except for a bronze latch.

*Thrap!*

'Come in,' I called. 'It's unbolted.'

Tamra opened the door and stepped inside. Weldein followed her and closed the door behind them.

'I thought I heard you two. What are those?' Tamra stepped up and peered at the hinges.

'Hinges. Shaped like dragons.'

'What's a dragon?' asked Weldein.

'I don't know,' I admitted. 'But the crafter who made them called them dragons.'

'Dragons?' Tamra frowned, then cleared her throat. 'One reason I came by was to tell you that your father thinks the Hamorian ships will arrive early tomorrow morning. He thinks we should all be up at the western end of the black wall just before dawn.'

'Before dawn. All right.' That was fine with me, since I wasn't sure how I would sleep anyway. Or how well. 'Where are they?'

'How would I know? He said he'd see us in the morning.' Tamra glanced back at the dragons. 'What are you going to do with those?'

'Put them on a chest.'

'Always thinking about crafting, isn't he?'

'Not always. Sometimes ...' I shook my head. I didn't want to explain anything to Tamra, about old coppersmiths or good people trying to pack up a cafe or traders ignoring their neighbor. Tamra had to make her decisions about Recluce without my explanations.

'Well ...' Tamra said gently. 'We'll leave you two. Dawn will come early.'

'Too early,' added Weldein.

The door closed, and Krystal and I turned to each other.

'She sees more than you think, Lerris. She's just afraid people will use it against her.'

I thought. Krystal was right. Once, on the ship to Freetown, Tamra had admitted to me that she was scared. Of course, she'd accused me of being scared first, and I'd reacted to that, rather than to her admission. 'You're right.' Then I put my arms around Krystal. 'That's one reason why I love you.'

'That's one reason why I love you. Beneath that stubborn outside, you do listen.'

Outside, the leaves rustled as the wind picked up in the early evening.

After a moment, Krystal added, 'We haven't seen Justen or Dayala or your parents. And Tamra said she hadn't, either.'

'That bothers me.' I could sense that it bothered Krystal, too, but I wasn't about to go around pounding on doors and asking them why I hadn't seen them that afternoon or evening.

I yawned, then grinned. Krystal was yawning also.

'I suppose we should try to sleep.'

'I suppose so.'

She slowly pulled off her boots, and so did I, and after we undressed, I turned off the lamp.

Outside, the fall winds rustled the trees, and mixed with the rustling of young voices. Had we ever been that young? I almost snorted, but Krystal elbowed me gently.

Neither one of us wanted to talk about the morning, and we didn't, but we knew what awaited us. We didn't go to sleep easily or early, just held tightly to each other.

# CXXVII

Just before dawn, and after a hurried breakfast of cold bread, cheese, and fruit, we gathered at the half-empty stables of the Brotherhood. The cheese lay like cold iron on my stomach, but I knew I'd need the strength.

For some reason, just before I mounted I looked toward Dayala. So did Krystal, then Tamra, and since she did, Weldein.

Justen nodded to her, and my father inclined his head as well.

Like an ancient oak, she stood there, slender but with a depth of blackness and harmony I envied, though I had seen briefly the price she had paid for that harmony and did not know whether I could pay such a price.

'We must undo the old wrongs, and we will prevail. Order must not be locked in cold iron.'

That was all, but, then, we already knew in our hearts what we had to do.

My mother reached out and squeezed my father's hand, and Justen's fingers brushed Dayala's. Weldein looked at Tamra when he thought she wasn't looking, and I gave Krystal a brief hug.

'How long before the ships arrive?' asked Justen.

'A while longer. We can take our time on the ride up there,' answered my father.

We rode up the road and out to the end of the cliffs of Nylan – to the western edge where the black rock face rose a hundred cubits from the narrow beach below. We tied our mounts well back from the cliffs, leaving our packs in place. If the Hamorian ships were as fearsome as we'd seen in the past, leaving our things in Nylan wasn't wise. Then, it might not be any wiser to have the horses near. Who really knew?

'Is this the right place?' Justen had asked.

My father and I nodded. So did Aunt Elisabet.

Uncle Sardit just walked out to the bluff where the wall ended at the sheer drop-off. 'Good stonework.' Then he walked back and patted my aunt on the shoulder.

Dayala sat on the grass and let her fingers touch the blades and the small round blue flowers that hugged the ground between the stems.

Weldein stood beside Tamra silently, and the three other guards watched him without speaking. Haithen paced out to the end, as Sardit had, and looked westward for a time before walking back to the other guards.

Even after the sun rose, there was no surf, nor even the sound of the waves lapping on the sand. The knee-deep grasses of the fields between the road and the strip of short-grassed sod that bordered the wall hung damp and limp in the stillness.

A single sea bird soared down over the water, but did not dive and vanished up the coast.

'The ocean's quiet,' whispered Krystal.

'You don't have to whisper,' I whispered back, my senses reaching again for the order and chaos beneath Recluce, that reservoir of power that ran along the backbone of the island. I kept working on opening the order channels closer and closer to the bottom of the ocean.

She jabbed me in the ribs with her elbow, and it hurt, because I wasn't expecting it, and because my concentration was elsewhere.

'I'm sorry,' she said softly.

I could sense her remorse, and realized that the link between us was continuing to grow. She must have felt the pain. I leaned over and kissed her.

She squeezed my arm, and I could feel the warmth behind and beyond the simple gesture. Behind us loomed the wall, that symbol that had defined Recluce for half a millennium, or longer, its stones still as crisp as when Dorrin had had them shaped, ordered, and laid to separate the engineers from the old mages who had insisted that machines would bring only chaos. Yet, in the end, as happened all too often, I suspected, both were wrong, for Recluce was threatened by the cold order of machines that created free chaos.

Justen and my father and Tamra turned to me. Dayala remained on the ground, and a pace back were my mother and Aunt Elisabet. Sardit was poking around the wall itself, as if checking the stone-work once more. There wasn't anything made of wood to check. According to legend, Dorrin had insisted that the wall be solid black-ordered stone, and it was, seemingly rooted into the land itself.

'Are you ready?' asked Justen.

'I will be.' I hoped I would be, though my senses were half on the cliffs and half deep below. I wiped my forehead with the back of my sleeve, half wondering why I was sweating when it wasn't even that warm yet.

'You will be,' Krystal echoed softly, and Dayala smiled.

The ground trembled, and my mother's face froze for a moment, before the determined smile returned.

Weldein led the guards back toward the High Road perhaps a dozen cubits, just beyond the horses. There he paced back and forth on the strip of shorter grass between the sixty-cubit height of the walls and the edge of the cliff, guarding us from anyone who might reach us from the land or the roads from Nylan. I didn't think there was that much chance of someone climbing the cliffs from below, not quickly, anyway.

I tried for another light touch of order in the depths.

As it rose to the east, the sun shimmered like a blazing ball of white-orange that quickly flared into white against the blue-green of the morning sky. Even with the light of the sun, the long grass to the east still hung limply in the still air.

Nylan was silent, still partly in shadow, almost like an abandoned town, and perhaps it was, since, after our meeting, the Brotherhood had somehow let out the word that everyone leave for higher ground – perhaps citing storms and possible shelling, perhaps giving no reason. After our meeting with the coppersmith, I doubted that anywhere near everyone had left, but many had, and many more might, should shells actually start falling on the harbor and town. By then it might be too late, but there are always those who do not feel disaster will ever strike them. I was one who couldn't count on luck to avoid it, no matter what I might wish.

I closed my eyes and tried to concentrate on the depths beneath Recluce to bring forth chaos guided by and sheathed in order. For a moment, though, the image of the brass dragons flitted into my thoughts. I took a deep breath and refocused my thoughts on chaos.

The trembling in the ground ran through my boots, and I could sense Krystal's awareness as well.

Krystal squeezed my arm. 'You can do whatever must be done.'

Maybe . . . and maybe I'd just create a colossal mess, but what choice did I have? What choice did anyone have once Hamor had embarked on its efforts to build order into cold steel?

'They're just over the horizon,' my father announced, as he and Mother slipped up beside us, so close that their shoulders brushed. She leaned her head against his cheek for a moment. Krystal started to edge away.

'No, you need to stay, dear,' my mother said. 'I hope you don't mind that I call you dear. I know you are a commander, and very important, but you are dear to Lerris, and dear to me for that reason alone —'

'Donara . . .'

'We have enough time to do this right, Gunnar, and I intend to, for once.' My mother continued speaking to Krystal. 'You are also dear to me because you are a special person yourself. It is important that you know this. Too many things aren't said until it's too late, and this is a very dangerous battle, or whatever you want to call it, that will happen here.'

I almost wanted to tell her not to act as if we were all going to die, but it occurred to me that she might be more realistic than the rest of us. After all, in the distance, I could already sense the growing cold order of steel hulls, of so many steel hulls.

Then my mother looked at me, and I could see the bleakness behind the smile. 'Lerris . . . we have not always done what we should have done, but, remember, as parents we do the best we can, and we have always loved you, even when it may have seemed we did not.' She cleared her throat. 'Now . . . get on with whatever you have to do, and I'll stay out of the way.' She bent forward, and her lips brushed my cheek, a gesture of love, but not love forced upon a grown child.

My father just looked at me for a moment, and I knew he felt the same way as my mother, but he could not move toward me. So I hugged him. For a moment, I couldn't see, but that was all right, because Krystal was there, and the touch of her hand on mine helped.

The ground trembled.

'There's some smoke out there!' called Weldein.

I let go of my father, and we separated, and I wiped my eyes with the back of my sleeve and got back to concentrating on raising order from the depths. Krystal touched her blade, but did not draw it, and instead walked over to Weldein.

'Once this starts, they'll all be concentrating on magic, and they'll need protection.'

'Yes, ser.' Weldein nodded, and Krystal walked back closer to me.

The surface of the Eastern Ocean was flat, glassy, in the way that I had seen it only a few times in my life, so flat and glassy that the harbor of Ruzor seemed, as I thought back, filled with small waves during its summer calms.

Out of the south came the ships, black dots almost marching across the Gulf, toward what seemed to be a mist that simmered on the water. My father frowned, and the mist thickened. The ships steamed on eastward, their smoke plumes proud in the morning light, white foam at their bows, and white wakes at their sterns.

I strained again to build yet more order bonds beneath the land, beneath the Gulf, and that order rippled through the iron backbone of Recluce, from Land's End back down to beneath where we stood.

*Ggurrrr . . . rrrrrr . . .*

The depth below seemed to absorb my efforts, and almost mock them. I wiped my forehead, and Krystal touched my arm, lightly, to reassure me as I struggled, and I could sense her frustration, both her feelings and the tightness in her arm as her hand gripped the hilt of her now-useless blade.

As I struggled with my order channels, and the chaos locked in the deep iron, the Hamorian fleet began to fill the southern horizon, black hull upon black hull, white smoke puffing from each stack, with order and more order concentrated mechanically within all that steel – and steel tube upon steel tube of powder and chaos lay within each hull. To the rear followed nearly fourscore transports filled with troops wearing the sunburst. I swallowed at the thought of all those thousands of troops – almost innocents in a way – and yet they would have no hesitation about killing should they land on Recluce.

Somehow . . . I wished the Emperor Stesten were on one of the ships. Rulers should have to run the same risks as their soldiers and sailors.

'Darkness . . .' Haithen stared at the Gulf.

Jinsa took out her blade and sighted along it.

'Never seen so many ships . . .' mumbled Dercas.

I hadn't, either, but I wasn't about to announce it.

'They're just ships,' snapped Tamra. She stepped out toward the point where my father was calling the storms, stopping beside him.

'There are a lot,' pointed out Jinsa.

A lot of ships meant a lot of cannon, and a lot of shells, and a lot of death. I swallowed. A lot of dead people on both sides.

Krystal tightened her grip on her blade, then forced her hand to relax as she watched the oncoming fleet.

Behind us, Sardit studied the wall.

My father closed his eyes. Lines of order, unseen but real for all their lack of apparent substance, flared from his arms toward the clear blue-green skies. For a time he stood there, immobile. Then he took a deep breath, without relaxing. 'It's begun.'

For a moment, I could sense the same lines of power radiating from Tamra, and a faint smile crossed her face.

The mist that lay before the Hamorian fleet seemed to thicken, and the sunlight seemed less intense, the sky less clear. A few high, hazy clouds began to form.

I reached farther into the depths, trying to use the iron beneath Candar as a lever to reach the deeper order beneath the Gulf itself.

*Grrrrurrrrrrr* . . . The trembling of the ground was stronger, and a small rock broke from a section of the cliffs beneath where the wall ended and bounced down and then into the waters of the Gulf with a splash.

The light around us dimmed a shade more.

'Don't think the mess in Hydlen was anything ...' said Dercas to Jinsa.

'When the time comes, you can let your blade do the talking,' she answered.

Haithen shook her head, her eyes traveling from the still-distant black splotches that were ships to the clouds that had begun to mass behind us in the northern sky.

My father turned to my mother and hugged her. The tears ran down her face, but she said nothing as they held each other for a long moment. Then he shrugged his shoulders and stepped back out to the end of the cliffs, facing into the mists that seemed to well in and enfold him. A separate, but interlinked, set of mists flowed around Tamra.

Elisabet eased forward, and darkness shrouded her, but she made no move to join either Justen or my father – yet she was joined to Justen, perfectly.

'Ready?' Justen looked from Weldein and the squad of green-clad troopers who guarded the approach to the point first to Tamra, then to my father, and then to Krystal and me. Dayala held his left hand.

I began to try to widen the order channels even more, guessing where they should be in the expanse of blue Gulf waters before me.

A *craccckkkk* like lightning split the air, though I saw no bolts.

At the end of the cliffs, where the wall and the cliff and the air and sea all seemed to meet, stood my father – and Tamra. Order bands like black iron stretched from his hands, reaching toward the high winds, the great winds that he had so often wanted me to reach. Similar bands stretched from Tamra's hands. And I . . . I had thought it mere laziness or fear when he had said there were reasons not to seek to manipulate those winds. I also remembered Tamra's statement that she wanted respect, that she had no need to parade her power.

The sky darkened, and puffy white clouds with dark centers rose higher into the sky to the north and scudded southward, drawing a gray curtain toward the sun. As they rose, their whiteness darkened into deadly gray, almost black.

The Hamorian fleet drew closer, smoke from the ships' funnels forming another kind of cloud.

The echo of a single cannon shot barked over the low howling of the winds.

I watched for a moment as a column of water geysered into the air nearly a kay seaward of the tip of the breakwater outside Nylan. A kay wasn't far, I realized, and I tried to hasten my efforts to widen and strengthen my order channels ... and to open the way for the chaos we needed, and which could destroy us all as well as the Hamorians, were it not well contained.

Could I contain so much chaos? Even with order?

Beside me, Krystal staggered as the ground rumbled and shook.

Another ranging shot barked across the Gulf, and another column of water exploded, still well short of the breakwater – but closer.

The Hamorian fleet steamed eastward, now starting to pitch as the warships struck the waves raised by the winds. Their raked bows cut through the foam-crested swells like heavy knives, and smoke billowed from their stacks and their squat gun turrets.

*Crumpt! Crumpt!* More water columns rose, within a few hundred cubits of the breakwater, raised by the Hamorian shells.

I struggled with iron and order, and order and iron.

The howling of the winds continued to rise ... and rise ... until there seemed to be no sounds except the wind, and my ears seemed to split with the screaming.

The sky was black behind and over us, and heavy gray over Nylan, and rain began to pelt down, cold drops that stung, cold drops that did little to cool the heat of my forehead.

I kept twisting and grasping at order, trying to recall Justen's efforts, trying to keep away from chaos while twisting order toward the comparatively shallower waters of the Gulf where the Hamorian fleet was headed, trying to let order lead chaos.

I staggered, and I could sense the rumbling and rocking of the earth even before it reached us.

*Grrrurrrrr ...*

Dercas sprawled on the grass, his words lost in the wind and the rain, and Haithen yanked him to his feet. More rocks separated from the cliff and were lost in the surf that now battered the beach and the base of the cliffs below.

One shell, then another, exploded on Nylan's breakwater, and the stone beacon at its tip sagged.

I squinted through the cold rain that slashed at us like quarrels. The sea was a tempest of whitecaps, with waves smashing over the Hamorian ships. Yet I could also sense that while more than a few vessels had plunged beneath that stormy surface, more still survived, and had been rigged and prepared for the possibility of storms raised by the great weather mage of Recluce. By my father, who stood like a giant blond oak amidst the rain and the lashing winds, order bands tying him to the soil and to the sky. A smaller, yet scarcely slighter oak – a red oak – stood beside him, also bound in order, yet nearly as strong.

All the ships in the Gulf pitched in the heavy seas, but their guns still fired, and most of the great fleet still steamed eastward, toward Nylan.

Shells began to fall along the harbor, with gouts of dust and water rising into the rain-filled air.

I wiped the water off my face and out of my eyes, conscious of the cold line of dampness that ran down my back from my collar.

On one side of me rose a pillar of warmth, and I glanced at Krystal, and her fingers brushed my neck. 'You can do it.'

On the other side rose a column of dark order, where my aunt Elisabet seemed to stretch from the bedrock to the skies, yet no order reached from her to either skies or ships, but gathered around her and swelled into a darkness every bit as deep as that raised by my father.

I touched the iron deep beneath me again, trying to coax, to wrench open order channels to bring forth that elemental chaos that yet resisted me.

Justen stepped up beside my father, and while the winds did not subside, nor their howling diminish, a bass groaning sound rumbled out of the ground, and the grass and stone beneath my feet shook again . . . and again. As with my father and Tamra, order bands stretched from Justen, but these sank deep into the earth, somehow intertwined with, yet separate from, those I had forged.

*Ggrrururrrrrrrr . . . rrrrrr . . .*

I stumbled, but managed to keep standing as I directed order-tubes filled with chaos to the waters the Hamorian ships were entering. Now those waters seemed to heave, and in spots warm mists seemed to rise out of the waves themselves.

The heavy explosive shells were falling faster, like ordered lightning through the rain and down upon the unprotected port. The sky was nearly all black, lit by reddish flares from each ship's gun and from each exploding shell.

The ships pitched in the heavy waves, and another few took on too much water and halted or began to capsize, but most kept steaming and throwing shells toward Nylan.

As those shells fell, a whiteness began to grow, from the deaths already occurring in Nylan and from the sailors on the few ships that had gone down. Despite that white knife edge of death, I forced myself to ignore that whiteness and to ease chaos up beneath the fleet, using my order-tubes.

*Guurrrrrr . . .*

The ground rocked, not so hard, and now the waters shivered. In places, wisps of steam vied with the storm-driven whitecaps.

But the guns kept pounding Nylan, and dust and stone fragments flared into the dark sky, and more orange and red billows dotted the streets of the black city. Dust, dirt, stone, ashes, wood fragments – pieces of everything flew into the air and came down with the rain and the incoming shells. And the whiteness of death grew.

I could sense a few more ships settling into the water, but the storm was beginning to wane, almost gasping.

The silver-haired Dayala lifted her right hand, and a whispering slipped through my thoughts, a sound like leaves rustling, like a big mountain cat padding down a forest trail, like a waterfall cascading down a mountainside, and the winds rose again, and the waves smashed against the gray-steel hulls.

For a time longer, the howl of the winds continued with the shrieking of the mightiest of gales, and the ground roared and rumbled and shook.

As I struggled to bring more than mere fragments of chaos to the Gulf, another handful of ships tilted – or were tilted – and slipped into the depths of the Eastern Ocean. One ship, jostled by a mighty shape, turned and crashed into another, and, locked together, both oozed toward the depths of the Gulf.

The ground shuddered, and I took two steps to keep my balance, quickly wiping the water out of my eyes, only to see that all the remaining Hamorian ships were now shelling Nylan. Hundreds of ships had their guns trained on the black city.

*Crumpt! Crumpt! Crumpt! Crumpt!* Like drumbeats, the shells fell on the port, and the very ground seemed to echo with the impacts.

Lines of flickering orange rose into the falling rain and shrouded Nylan, so many that it was difficult to tell where the lines of flame began, lines of flame not damped by the rain and chill wind.

The white screaming of dead sailors, dead gunners – and now, dying fishermen, townspeople – lashed back at me through the rain and the order bonds I had sunk into the earth. And the screaming was almost as loud as the wind, as deep as the groaning of the earth.

Yet fully two-thirds of that dark-hulled fleet remained, and the guns fired, and the shells fell in an uneven staccato pattern, ripping through the dark day like knives of pain, slashing at Nylan, crushing black stone buildings into gravel.

Tamra, Justen, Dayala, Aunt Elisabet, and my father – all were calling the forces of order – and it wasn't enough, and I still could not loose the full power of the elemental chaos I had encircled up through the waters of the Gulf.

Despite the storms, the steel-hulled ships of the Hamorians endured. Despite the rumblings beneath the earth, the troopships headed toward Nylan. Despite the efforts of the whales and dolphins and who knew what other creatures of the deep called by the silver-haired Dayala, the ships struggled onward. Despite the bolts of nearly pure order wielded like anger by Tamra, the warships and their cannons closed on the Black City.

The shells kept falling, and the fires rising, even as the winds began to fade, even as I could sense Dayala falling to the grass, and Justen kneeling beside her, somehow bent, gnarled. My father stood swaying on the end of the cliffs, and my mother slipped toward him in crisp, competent steps that began to falter as she reached him.

Elisabet stepped up beside Justen and Dayala, sheltering them, and darkness welled forth from her, and the winds rose again, if not quite so strongly, and once more, the waves smashed against the iron hulls, and across the waterfront of Nylan, and the Gulf shivered.

Though a handful more ships shuddered under the waters of the Gulf, the shells kept dropping on the already prostrate city, falling like death, despite the winds and the waves, and the blackness flowing now mostly from Elisabet and Tamra.

Suddenly, Tamra staggered onto her knees, and the wind gasped, as she tried to rise again. The blackness dropped away from Elisabet, and she, too, staggered and seemed to shrivel into a shadow of herself. The wind was dying, and the waves subsiding.

I swallowed, thinking about the fires of the depths, but it was my turn . . . my turn . . . my turn to bring the great fires from the earth.

The dark ships steamed more confidently toward the breakwater, and the shells fell like rain, even as the rain slackened.

I forced myself deep into order, and to the fringe of chaos, for every effort I had made had not been sufficient to loose the power of chaos necessary to stop the Hamorian fleet.

With that effort, chills shivered through me, and my stomach turned, and white needles flared through my eyes.

The earth shook; the waters heaved; and the last few cubits of the great black wall of Nylan shivered and cascaded off the cliffs and into the sands and waters of the Gulf of Candar with a dull roar lost in the massive groaning from beneath the waters before me.

Gouts of steam flared from the ocean around the dark hulls of the Hamorian ships, and the steam thickened.

Sweat poured down my face, and everyone around me seemed

frozen – Justen crouched over Dayala, my mother hanging on to my father's sagging figure, Elisabet slumped in a heap between her brothers, Krystal extending her fingers toward my arm.

Yet the shells kept falling, and the fires rose out of Nylan, as did the screams, and the whiteness of death and more death, and the orange-white-red of fires raging down rubble-filled streets, and waves smashing into buildings, and more shells falling, grinding the stone walls into black gravel.

# CXXVIII

## The Gulf of Candar

The water flares over the bow of the *Emperor's Pride*, water so hot that it blisters the gray paint off the metal of the superstructure, and the bow plunges into the waves of boiling water that still rise above the bridge.

As the cruiser slides into that boiling mass, the fleet commander looks at the marshal. Stupelltry's face is red-blotched from where the droplets of boiling water have splashed it. 'A handful of wizards? Demon-damn you and your handful of wizards!'

'I have done my duty as well as I can,' responds Dyrsse, clutching a bridge railing so hot that it blisters his fingers. Despite the burns on his face, his voice is firm and carries. 'So have you.'

'Damn duty! We're all dead!' Stupelltry holds the helm now, as the steersman cradles burned and blistered hands unable to grasp the wheel. The lookouts have been torn off the bridge by the waves, lost kays behind the flagship. The fleet commander fights the helm, trying to hold the cruiser into the lines of the waves.

'Without duty, there is nothing!' Dyrsse pulls the signal cords to order the guns to continue their bombardment, but there is no response, either from the cords or the guns.

'Then there's nothing!'

The ship ahead, the only other one that Dyrsse can see, explodes in a wall of flame, and iron fragments spray into the towering waves. Any screams are lost in the howling of the wind, the explosions of the shells within the other ship's magazines, and the hammering of the waves on iron.

The *Emperor's Pride* noses into the boilding water, and the odor of boiled meat rolls across the bridge with the spray, and more bodies are swirled by the turret and below the bridge, bodies either from the cruiser or from one of the other ships that has been destroyed.

'Aeeeeeiiiii . . .' The helmsman, unable to hang on with his burned hands, slides and loses his grip, then is swept into the boiling maelstrom.

'Light to —'

*CRUMMMPPPTTTT!*

The magazines below the front turret explode in a wave of chaos, flame and shrapnel, and boiling water swirls over the sinking, blistered fragments of steel, over the bobbing boiled corpses that dot the Eastern Ocean.

# CXXIX

Standing on the headland, knowing that the others – Tamra, Justen, Dayala, my aunt Elisabet, and my father – had given everything they had to give, and I had not, I strained again to weld order and chaos, to twist them through each other. I did, splitting order into smaller and smaller fragments and forcing it to direct chaos, mixing, linking, and tying order and chaos together, and creating heat, fire like the sun, as order and chaos merged under my hammer, under my will.

The earth groaned in protest, and the waters seemed to draw back in protest, and steam like fog swept among the gray-hulled ships, burning and searing. The Gulf waters exploded with gouts of steam, steam so hot that it peeled paint and instantly charred wooden railings and fittings.

Yet order and chaos twisted together into smaller and tighter fragments, and those order and chaos fragments exploded like small suns, and the whiteness of screams filled the Gulf, and along with the explosions of shells on shore came the explosions of shells within the ships that had held the sea.

Gouts of flame raced across the waters. The entire ocean began to steam, and the ships pitched and heaved upon the waters, as if those ships were too hot to remain upon the waters, and the paint on the hulls and their superstructures blistered and vanished in fine ashes as the forces of chaos flowed into the metal and that iron turned as red as the molten iron beneath the waters.

And the whiteness of death rose like I had never felt before, screaming, flaying me like burning knives.

Krystal's hand touched me, and I could feel her strength. 'You have to do it, Lerris, no matter what the price.' And I could feel her tears, and the pain of that whiteness of death and more death, and I knew there was no choice, that the ships would sear the land bare – even as I was searing the Gulf bare of everything.

Another line of chaos-steam eruptions flared across the waters of the Gulf, and more ships burned, and more sailors and troopers died in their molten iron coffins.

Steel ship after steel ship shuddered, then melted or exploded into hot fragments that rained down upon boiling water. And still the waters parted, and fire flowed into the night-dark sky, and even ashes rose from the waters, and steam gouted into the fired air of the Gulf.

Yet, some ships fought on, and their less frequent shells still continued to grind Nylan into sand and gravel. I staggered, trying to hold onto order and chaos, to twist them together so that none could wield them separately again. My eyes blind to the sea, I struggled and welded.

I went to one knee, sliding through the damp grass, still fighting to bring ordered chaos against the ships.

Two arms reached me, one warm, one ordered, and I struggled upright with the infusion of darkness and warmth, of order and strength. As I wrenched more chaos from the ground and somehow flung it into the Gulf, a massive groan issued forth from the iron beneath Recluce. That groan rose into a mighty grinding, and even more massive waves, topped with gouts of steam that resembled small mountains, burst from the waters of the Gulf of Candar.

Like a huge anvil struck like a gong, the sound of that iron being wrenched apart slammed at me, and my hands covered my ears, as I fell again with the wrenching of the earth beneath me, and the screaming of steam that whistled up through the Gulf waters.

Another clanging of that iron anvil of the depths shivered through the land and sea, and the violence of the ground's rolling threw me facedown into the grass.

As I finally struggled up, to the north, behind me, somewhere near the Feyn River, the earth could take no more, and the back of Recluce split and a river of molten iron flared into the sky like a second sun, building a wall on the north side of the new channel between the sundered remnants of Recluce. The gold of the harvest fields turned black, and the river boiled and flared into steam. The whole isle rocked, and roofs collapsed, and stones rained off Dorrin's wall and around us.

I staggered, but Krystal helped me stand, and I saw my aunt in a heap, almost by my feet, Uncle Sardit cradling her. Anger fueled my last effort, anger at the Hamorians, at their precise gray ships, at their arrogance in using machines to build order, and at their desire to hold all the world. Neither I nor Krystal nor Kyphros nor Candar would be held!

Masses of water surged from the shallows beneath the cliffs where I stood, gushing southward, and rising into a wall of steam that swept over the remaining dark hulls, bobbing uselessly in the boiling waters of the Gulf.

Another wall of water lashed across Nylan – quenching fires even as it scalded those few who remained. Hot steam rose from the sundered and flattened tip of Recluce.

While I had no order strength left, and stood gasping on the grass of the cliff line, the wall behind us swayed, and the waves surged back against the cliffs, and hot spray cascaded up the cliffs and over and around us.

Another few cubits of the end of the cliff and the wall swayed, and then tumbled into the Gulf below with a dull, booming crash. And more hot sea spray rained across us.

Krystal somehow held me, almost pressed herself to me, offering warmth, strength, and all I could do was stand there, gasping, panting, with hot sweat pouring down my face.

The ground kept trembling, as if the earth could not stop itself.

I took another series of deep breaths. So did Krystal.

She asked something, and I realized that I could not hear her, and I squinted at her.

'Is it over?' she repeated, and between her feelings and watching her lips I understood.

'Most of it.' I tried to peer through the fog and mist to the south. There were no cannon reports, no explosions, just soft hissing and bubbling sounds, the crashing of waves of hot water on the cliffs – and the smell of boiled seaweed, and boiled fish and other less savory odors. I would have retched, but had not even that strength.

The Gulf was a boiled desert, and the whiteness of death, thousands upon thousands of deaths, lay like a shroud over it.

Still gasping, I glanced around, then toward the clouded sky, wondering about the source of the flashes of darkness that intermittently blocked my vision.

Elisabet half sat in Sardit's lap, her face tired and wrinkled, and growing more so as I watched. Justen was old, wrinkled, and his hair was silvering and falling out as he bent to kiss Dayala, as she shriveled in his arms. My parents, out on the point of rock that had crumbled away to almost nothing around them, were motionless, slumping into something beyond death.

For a moment I just stared, then I began to run, except it was more like a stumble, as my eyes sometimes seemed to work and sometimes not.

By the time I reached the end of the point, my parents were little more than dust, little more than dull dust in trampled grass, as the last of the order that had sustained them dissipated.

Krystal held my arm, and I looked.

Beneath us, the hot sea threw steaming mist at us, and my face burned. So did my eyes.

My mother's words, somehow, came back to me – 'we do the best we can, and we have always loved you, even when it may have seemed we did not . . .' And in the end, they had given up a long and happy life together, for us, for who else could it have been for? My father had crossed the Eastern Ocean to help us in Kyphros . . . and I had not understood, not really . . .

'But you do now,' Krystal said, standing by my side, and, again, I had to look at her and try to sense her feelings, to understand.

'I never told them.' I watched her face, squinting through the blackness that came and went, seeing that her hair was mostly silver, and her face had wrinkles it had not had. When I could see, my eyes burned, as though arrows of fire slashed through them.

'They know. They have to know.'

I looked back, but there was no sign of Justen or Dayala, except where Tamra crouched, sobbing, her hair nearly snow-white, Weldein behind her, his hair also mostly white, holding his sword like some fearful relic.

My eyes fell to the vanishing dust. 'At least I hugged him. At least I did that.'

I'd never understood how much strength there had been in my father – or in Justen – and they were gone. I'd been too busy rebelling to understand, and it was too late.

And my mother, and Aunt Elisabet, and Uncle Sardit – all of them gone, gone . . . because . . . because . . . did I really know? Did it matter?

My eyes burned, and Krystal stood by me, and we wept, wept for what, again, we, or I, had learned too late.

Below us, the water swirled and smashed on the rocks, and the hot steam cascaded upward and around us.

I just kept looking, numb, I think, somehow expecting my parents, my aunt and uncle, Justen and Dayla, to reappear. But it didn't happen.

The hot surf crashed and boiled, and the ground rumbled, and the earth shook, and I wept, and they were still gone . . . dead.

I'd never thought they'd die. Not my father and Justen.

I shivered.

With the hot surf and mist came the smell of death, of boiled fish and boiled corpses.

Why didn't I realize that they weren't ancient angels, that they would die? My mother had as much as told me, and so had Dayala and Sardit – just by coming. How could I have been so blind?

I looked at the trampled grass, seeing not even dust.

'Lerris!' Krystal grabbed my arm, turning me, when I didn't respond to her warning.

I stood stunned at the more than twoscore black-clad figures that were running along the grassy strip from Nylan toward us. Some bore stubby riflelike devices, and others carried blades or staffs.

Flames from the two small rockets exploded along the black stones of Dorrin's wall.

I could see that the black-clad marines were yelling something; I thought I could make out something about 'the death of chaos!'

My mouth must have dropped open. What had we done?

Krystal whirled.

As I ducked and ran back toward the attackers, I reached for my staff, and I could see Tamra reaching for hers, but she seemed unable to find it, as though she groped for it. The four guards had formed a wedge around her, and their blades blurred in the hot rain that continued to fall.

Dercas lunged forward, his blade flashing, striking through a shoulder, and then across an arm, parrying two blades, and reaching toward the woman with the rocket gun, who loosed another rocket at him.

Even as the rocket turned Dercas into a flaming brand, he lifted the sword and flung it straight at the thin-faced woman who had led the Brotherhood squad and who had fired the rocket.

*Whhhssst!* Her last rocket veered off into the Gulf, and Heldra's mouth opened, and she looked down at the heavy blade through her chest before sinking to the turf.

Jinsa and Haithen began to hack their way toward the man with the other gun. Somehow, I tried to shield them. I could feel Tamra doing the same, and the rockets eased aside, splattering across the ordered black stones of the wall.

In the hissing silence that surrounded me, between the flashes of blackness and of stabbing pain through my eyeballs, I tried to keep the staff moving, although my arms burned, and I had to operate almost on feel. For once it didn't matter, and I didn't worry about who might be hurt. When I struck, it was hard, and some of them didn't get up. Deep inside, I was glad.

Beside me, Krystal's blade flickered, even more deadly than the staff, and more than a handful of black-clad figures lay strewn before her.

We backed up, and more ran at us.

Anger fueled my arms, and my staff, and I didn't even have to force the moves. Soon I was easing forward, keying my moves to Krystal's, following what she was doing, working together, without thought. Slash, parry, strike, slash, slash, parry, STRIKE!

The ground trembled, and we stopped because the three remaining Brotherhood members were running, screaming, toward the High Road. One stumbled and skidded through the grass and did not rise.

My arms suddenly felt like lead – or Krystal's did – or they both did.

I stepped back and leaned the staff against the wall, and my free hand reached for Krystal's. I felt old, and she did, too.

Tamra stood not half a dozen paces from us, shaking and sobbing, but Weldein had his arms around her, and she held to him, and he held to her. White streaked the once-shining red hair. Even Weldein's blond thatch was heavily streaked with silver.

Jinsa and Haithen leaned against each other, half gasping, half sobbing, streaks of gray in their short hair as well.

To the north, the earth still shook. Without looking, I knew that the steam still rose from the cleft that had been the Feyn River valley, from that cleft that was now a strait separating Recluce into two isles.

The fields there, those that did not lie beneath cubits and cubits of too-hot water, were blackened and burned, like Nylan itself.

Out in the Gulf, a wedge of black rock had appeared, hissing, steaming as the still-heavy waves crashed against it, welling upward into a larger and larger shape that would be an island, called someday, no doubt, by some name that reflected its origin in the great battle.

I blinked, trying to blink back the pain of seeing, and, for a moment, more blackness dropped across my eyes, but I struggled against that, and the pain of seeing returned.

I snorted. Great battle, indeed. The death of chaos, indeed, but not the way Heldra had wanted. So many deaths, so many thousands of deaths . . . would they all cling to that tiny black chunk of rock?

The trembling of the ground was less, but another section of the cliffs collapsed, rumbling down into a pile of black stone that formed a cairn shape on the narrow sands of the beach.

The water swept in and carried a fragment of burned and polished wood that banged in the foam against the dark stones, banged and scraped, and then swirled back into the Gulf. A white fragment of cloth, perhaps a sailor's cap, bobbed in the steaming waters.

I tried not to choke on the bile in my throat and looked toward Krystal.

She had sheathed her sword, and we looked inside each other, at the darkness in our eyes. Her hair was silver-white, and so, I knew, was mine.

'I never even got to say good-bye . . .' Not to my father, my mother, Justen, or Dayala. Not to my aunt, or to Uncle Sardit who had made me a crafter. My mother had known, and so had they all, even Tamra, and I alone had not. I alone had failed to understand.

'It's all right,' Krystal said. But it wasn't, except for her being there. She put her arms around me, and I sobbed, because there was too much I had learned too late.

I couldn't see for a long time, and neither, I think, could Krystal, but I needed her, and she was there for me.

The whole world had changed in a day. How could we deal with that? I'm not sure any of us did really, almost moving in a daze.

As I had known, Tamra was order-blind.

'Blind? I don't want to be blind. I suppose Lerris can see?' she asked.

I squinted, and winced with the pain of trying to make out her words.

Finally, Krystal answered for me.

'He can't hear, and sometimes he can't see. When he does, it hurts – a lot.'

'Oh, Krystal . . .'

That I did make out.

Finally, later, in the warm drizzle that followed the cold rain raised by Tamra and my father, by all of us, really, I picked up my staff.

Even with the remaining mounts, it would be a long trip north to Land's End, but that was where we had to go, now. Nylan was still the Black City, but black with ashes, black with death, and shelled into a black and gray mass of ashes and gravel, and all I had of Nylan were two dragon hinges.

And all I really had of Recluce were memories – and the two dragon hinges.

'You have your crafting,' Krystal said. 'Sardit and your parents gave you that, and nothing can take that gift from you.'

I could mostly understand her. That helped, and so did her thoughts. Not enough, not near enough, but they helped.

Tamra said something, and she shuddered. I looked at Krystal, and she repeated the words. 'To the death of chaos?'

I looked dumbly downhill at the remains of Nylan. Had it been worth it to raise order and chaos to strike down machined order?

'The death of chaos?' echoed Weldein as dumbly as I felt.

Krystal touched my arm.

I sighed. 'In a way. In a way. There's not much free order or chaos left.' I didn't want to talk about it.

Instead, I looked back along the narrow grassy strip, and slowly walked through the warm drizzle out toward the slumped end of the wall that over-looked the Gulf. Not a sign remained – not clothes, not ashes, not flesh, not bone. I'd looked before, but I had to look again. I didn't find anything, and I knew I wouldn't, but I had to look, and those arrows of pain slashed at my eyes. Would I be like Creslin, in a different way, with each vision filling me with pain? For how long?

I looked again, ignoring the stabbing into my skull, although I wanted to double over.

I owed them all my life, in different ways, and they were gone, giving what they had to help me . . . and Krystal, and even she had given her youth.

For what? For the death of chaos?

I stood and watched and listened – and remembered – and Krystal stood by me . . . and I realized that she, too, would feel the pain of each vision.

I closed my eyes for a time, not just for my own surcease.

# CXXX

We rode northward beyond the wall, toward Wandernaught, where we could rest before pushing on. A light rain continued to fall. My legs ached, and so did my arms, and my thighs. I could feel that Krystal's did, too, and we both knew it, and kept riding. It was better than walking. I didn't want to think about crossing the new Feyn Strait, or whatever they'd call it someday, but we'd find a way, somehow.

'When will it ever end?' said Krystal, turning in the saddle and speaking slowly so that I could see her lips.

After two repetitions I answered, 'Never.'

She winced at my efforts to read her lips, because when I had to concentrate it hurt. Darkness! Even my pain for my efforts was passed on to her. I closed my eyes for a moment. When I opened them, Weldein was talking.

'You . . . stopped the Emperor . . . won't send another fleet.' Weldein rode on Krystal's right, so that I could see them both, and I thought that was what he said. Tamra rode beside him.

I shook my head. 'Not for a few years, but unless things change in Recluce and Candar, this will happen again.'

Krystal nodded, surprisingly, while Tamra stopped her mount.

'Wait a moment. Explain that,' Tamra demanded. 'All this, and it was for nothing? All this?' Again, Krystal had to help get the question across to me, because Tamra still couldn't see and wasn't looking in my direction.

My eyes hurt, from both squinting and trying to see, and I could sense Krystal's discomfort. So I stopped and closed my eyes. It felt good not to have everything I looked at hurt, and not to have to move for a bit. The horse whuffed, and I patted his neck, and then wiped my face to clear away some of the wetness from the rain. Krystal touched my arm, and I got the sense that I should explain.

I opened my eyes and tried. 'This can't happen again. Not for a long time. I had to release all the order in the iron beneath Recluce and the Eastern Ocean, maybe even as far as Candar and Nordla – I'm not sure. There's so much order that every bit of chaos . . .' I shook my head, and that hurt, too. 'That's not quite right. What we – what I – did was break apart order and chaos into little tiny bits, tiny bits, and somehow, twisted them all together in tiny bits – that's what created all the heat. Order and chaos are linked together, in things, not by themselves, so that they can't join together. There won't ever be – not for a long, long time – much free chaos, or any chaos-masters. No order-masters, either.'

Tamra's mouth dropped open. 'Justen . . . your father . . . knew . . . the death of chaos meant the death of order . . .?' She said more, but I couldn't make out the words, even through Krystal.

I swallowed and nodded. It was getting hard to speak.

'. . . and Dayala?'

'It was easier for her, I think. She never thought they ought to be separate.' My throat was thick, and I didn't want to say any more.

Tamra looked down at the cold hard stones of the High Road.

Weldein rode up beside her and touched her shoulder. She began to sob.

At that moment, I wished I could cry or sob, or something, but I had cried all I could, and my guts were still knotted tight inside me. Krystal took my hand.

'Why?' I asked helplessly, knowing the answer, but having to say something.

She knew the answer, and knew I had to speak the words. So I did. 'Justen and my father weakened chaos enough that metalworking could improve with steel. Chaos could no longer tear apart machines. Dorrin saw that problem a long time ago, but he must have felt that the machines would be limited by chaos – and they were. When Justen and my father reduced the power of chaos, they made possible the growth of machines, not ones based on ordered black iron, the way Dorrin did it, but ones built like a crafter builds a table or a desk.'

'. . . no order magic or chaos magic . . . again?' When she touched my skin and talked, understanding was easier for me, and for her, because I didn't have to strain to see her lips so much.

I had to laugh, but it was a bitter laugh. 'Not for a long time. But chaos always has a tendency to separate out, and order has to be maintained, and the extra order in the world will slowly dissipate, and the chaos will grow and separate, and all the twists and hooks we established will fray . . .'

'. . . back where Creslin started . . .' asked Krystal.

'Not in a long time . . . maybe by the time of people's children's children's children's children – or longer.'

She reached over and squeezed my shoulder.

I shrugged. 'The Brotherhood didn't understand – and neither did the Emperor – not until later, anyway, that concentrating the free order and chaos in Candar and Recluce made it possible for Hamor to build its ships and machines. One way or another, order-mastery and chaos-mastery were on the way out – for a while – after the fall of Fairhaven.'

'. . . a big wheel . . . turning . . . sometimes magic works . . . sometimes . . . doesn't?'

I caught enough of her words to answer. 'I suppose so, in a way, except it always works on some level. Right now, Candar, and what's left of Recluce, have a chance to build their own ships and machines before Hamor regains its power.'

'That's not all.'

'No. The smaller countries in Candar will have to unite, somehow, or Hamor will still take them over.'

'More wars.' Krystal shaped her words carefully, and I understood.

'Sooner or later,' I admitted. 'Everything seems to lead that way. At least I haven't found anything that doesn't. Only strength stops war, and nothing changes that, and I hate it, but it doesn't matter.'

'Now . . . you know.' Krystal smiled faintly, and squeezed my hand.

I knew what she meant, perhaps really for the first time, knew what carrying a blade meant when you were as good as she was.

We looked at the gray sky. Before long, it would clear, at least for a while. Behind us, Tamra held Weldein's hand, their mounts linked by their closeness, but she had stopped sobbing.

Krystal held my hand, but the knots in my guts didn't feel as if they would be leaving soon, nor would the knives in my eyes, and who knew when I'd be able to hear again. Closing my eyes, I thought about the dragons in my pack. Dragons – though I had never seen one – they would hold a chest together. Maybe in the end crafting was all that held anything together.

# CXXXI

From that confusion shall the dark ships of the sun seek refuge, but neither the mountains nor the oceans shall provide succor. Mountains shall be rendered into dust, and oceans shall be burned and boiled, and ashes shall cover all, and chaos shall die.

Likewise, shall order die, and all manner of changing the way of the world, save through the tools of the hands, and the tools of the tools.

For, as a woman shall sow, so shall she reap, not as she wishes or would order that seed, but as the sun and the rain see fit, or as the water and nourishment she may bring unto her crops with her own hands.

Unto each generation shall the tales be passed, of how order and chaos once served, and how tools enhanced that service, and of how, in the end, order and chaos grew to such might as threatened the heavens, and were cast down.

And, in the fullness of time, it shall come that the children of the angels will fail to heed those words, and come to believe that as one sows, so shall one reap, forgetting that once it was not thus.

Yet neither order nor chaos shall be vanquished, but each shall sleep unto the generations, gathering powers until, near the end of time, each shall awaken.

*The Book of Ryba*
Canto DL [The Last]
Original Text

# Epilogue

Krystal held my hand as we walked toward the stable. I felt the strong, supple fingers, the warmth under the hardness and closed my eyes for a moment, letting the stabbing in my eyes subside and wondering how long everything I looked at would remind me – and Krystal – of the death of chaos, and of all the deaths that had ensured it.

When I opened my eyes, I saw the square-faced cow peering from the pen beyond the stable, and a goose arching its neck in a hiss from beyond the new, and already ramshackle, henhouse.

'A goose . . . I still don't . . .' I turned and glanced back toward the kitchen door where Rissa just shrugged. I tried not to smile.

Weldein waited, mounted as the squad leader. Beside him, Tamra rode Rosefoot, somehow fitting, and using her now-limited senses to compensate for her blindness, though they were good only near her in our greatly order-reduced world. Some of the gray had left her hair, but not all. Behind them were mounted Jinsa and Haithen.

Krystal's hair was black and silver, with more silver than black. I had done what I could, with the few shreds of order and skill I had left, but no one would ever mistake us for less than middle-aged.

'Glad to be home,' Krystal turned and spoke slowly so that I could see her words.

Although I caught them, the effort left spears stabbing through my skull, and I felt guilty as I could feel Krystal sense my pain. 'I'm glad you're glad.'

I closed my eyes to relieve the stabbing she felt, and the early winter wind slashed out of the north, out of a clear blue-green sky, and we held each other for a moment, and I left my eyes shut until we stepped away from each other.

'I'll be home tonight.' Her lips exaggerated 'home.'

'And tomorrow night?' I asked playfully.

The ground vibrated with the impact of hoofs, and the carriage, drawn by matched chestnuts, stopped in the middle of the yard. On the front seat were the driver and a guard with both a blade and one of the Hamorian rifles that were going to become all too prevalent, I feared. Their gray leathers matched, and so did their boots. A single recently painted *A* adorned the glass of the carriage door, and I had to smile, because the letter matched the inlaid one that Wegel had carved for the desk. Antona opened the carriage door herself and half stepped, half vaulted into the yard.

Krystal looked at me and shook her head. 'You will have a busy day.' She touched my wrist and spaced the words evenly.

By the barn, Weldein sat astride his mount, grinning.

'Master Lerris?' Antona marched up to me, then turned to Krystal, and, I presumed, introduced herself. That was the feeling I got from Krystal, along with some muted amusement.

I watched Krystal as she spoke, catching the key words and guessing at the rest. 'He did mention that he was undertaking a dining set for you.'

'... he has been ... involved ... in saving ... world – or something ...'

Once more, when I had to concentrate on Antona's words, the stabbing in my eyes intensified. Krystal winced inside, but her face remained calm. I tried to keep my expression undisturbed.

'He ... took ... time ... from his woodworking.' Krystal was trying not to grin – that I could sense – and ignore the discomfort I created.

Antona finally smiled at her, but erased the expression and looked at me. 'When will it be ready?'

'Less than a season.' I shrugged.

'You promised ... a season ago.' She brushed something off the sleeve of the green silk shirt.

I had to look at the ground. I had promised.

Antona turned to Krystal again. I couldn't catch too much of it, but she was clearly suggesting that Krystal use her powers to keep me in line and to ensure I delivered the goods.

Whatever Antona ended with, it had some effect. Krystal laughed beneath a solemn nod, and behind the carriage driver, Weldein rolled his eyes. So did Haithen. Jinsa just grinned.

I watched Krystal as she answered.

'I do have ... commissions, but I am certain that he will undertake the commission of your dining set at his earliest haste.'

Antona looked from her to me. 'Not too much haste.' She winked. 'In anything.' Then she inclined her head to us. 'I look ... to seeing your workmanship ... all your commissions.' Once more, I missed some of what she said, hopefully not anything important.

She turned and reentered the carriage. We watched as she and her small entourage departed.

Krystal was still smiling as she turned to me. 'All my commissions?'

I shrugged.

'You will have to expand the house.'

'You have plans.'

'I always have.'

I hugged her again, and Weldein rolled his eyes. So did Tamra, but she reached out and held Weldein's arm for a moment, as though she were not still blind most of the time. She had plans also.

I stood in the yard as the five rode down the drive toward Kyphrien, watching until I could see them no longer. The goose stretched her neck in a hiss as I walked into the shop, but geese hiss, and at least I couldn't hear her. Besides, what would I do about it anyway?

Wegel had picked up the broom and was sweeping the floor around his space, somewhat cleaner than the area around my bench.

I picked up the length of cedar from the corner of the workbench, taking comfort in the wood, a soothing that helped reduce the pain of those knives behind my eyes. I studied the cedar, realizing that I now knew the face that the wood held, and that the image I had of my father would hold, and I could only hope that he would have been pleased.

Then I picked up the knife.